TENDER LOVE AND SHINING FAITH AGAINST A SMOLDERING BACKGROUND OF EVIL...

A woman and a man, desperately searching for love against overwhelming odds:

LORRY—beautiful and talented, whose life has brought her everything but happiness . . .

JOHN—a man like no other she had ever met, his deep and intense faith unwavering in the face of all that would destroy it . . .

SUMMERFIELD—whose twisted mind creates a wall of distrust between them, and sows the seeds of unreason which set an entire community aflame with hatred and violence . . .

Books by
TAYLOR CALDWELL

This Side of Innocence
Tender Victory
Never Victorious, Never Defeated
Your Sins and Mine

Published by
WARNER BOOKS

Taylor Caldwell

TENDER VICTORY

WARNER BOOKS

A Warner Communications Company

This book is a novel, and all persons and organizations appearing in it are fictitious. Any resemblance of fictitious to actual persons and organizations is coincidental.

1

When matters, events, or people bored or exhausted or troubled Dr. Francis Stevens, he would retire mentally to a pleasant place where he could reflect on the fact that he so closely resembled Francis Cardinal Spellman that it had become an affectionate joke between him and his friend. The cardinal had bantered him about it, and they had had many a gentle laugh together not only on their personal resemblance but on the fact that they both had the same Christian name. Astonishingly, too, they had much of the same temperament: genial, realistic, strongly executive, merciful, and humorous, and both possessed a passionate spirituality.

I wonder, thought Dr. Stevens today, keeping a bland, fixed smile on his face for the benefit of the others in the rectory library, whether Father Francis has to suffer fools as much as I do, and be so at their mercy? Probably. He may have a special prayer he says to himself for the alleviation of aching jaw muscles and twitching lip corners. I must ask him. Dr. Stevens said aloud, "Yes, indeed. I am positive of it."

It was very seldom that these two phrases were received with anything else but pleased nods, heads inclined in gratification, or smiles of acknowledgment. He had polished and cultivated these phrases and this smile to the point where they covered practically everything. What situation could they not, indeed, embrace with suavity and good will, especially when uttered in a thoughtful or softly contemplative voice?

Dr. Stevens, a most intuitive and sensitive man, suddenly became aware that for the first time the amiable phrases had produced a shocked silence. He came out of the warm lethargy produced by boredom and the heat of the August day, and blinked. The ladies and gentlemen surrounding him were staring at him with horror and perplexity. With drowsy detachment he studied their expressions, still smiling gently and emptily, as if his companions were mere dreams. Then his facial muscles pained him acutely as he relaxed his smile, and he put up his fat white hand to his pouched jaw.

The library walls glimmered with so many sedate and profound books that the general effect was depressing, in Dr. Stevens's opinion. But that was probably, he sometimes ruefully reflected, because of their contents. Why could not religious books speak of happiness and joy and gaiety in the love of God, and why could they not have brighter and more attractive bindings, sparkling, here and there, with a touch of interesting orange or rose or gilt? Religion was not a doleful thing, full of somberness and ennui. It was a living and brilliant experience, exultant, sometimes ecstatic, a rainbow of light between man and God. It was revelation and sympathy. It was man's deepest rapture. To suggest that Christ may have laughed, that He may have rejoiced, that He may have partaken of the wine He produced at the marriage in Cana, was practically blasphemous to certain minds. It was very sad. The Bible spoke of God walking in the garden, His joy over what He had created, and His majestic satisfaction in His works. No doubt He had been happy over the plains of flowers He had caused to spring up in a dark and muddy wilderness redeemed from the waters. No doubt He had laughed with pleasure at the "hills skipping like young lambs." No doubt He had smiled at the children who had gathered about Him. No doubt but that when He had taken on the flesh of man He had enjoyed the simple pleasures of man, had liked the fresh and juicy fruit He had made, had relaxed in sleep, had gazed with rapture at a lovely dawn or a sunset of particular grandeur, and had blessed them all. He constantly created universes hardly visible to man with all his powerful instruments, but, when He was a Man, no doubt He thought a budding rose as important, as meaningful, and had stooped to inhale its fragrance. There had been loving admiration in His words, "The lilies of the field."

You'd never be able to tell this from the books written about Him, Dr. Stevens had been thinking, depressed.

Now he was abruptly aware that his inane remark had created much consternation. He blinked rapidly, and focused his somewhat glazed eyes on the ladies and gentlemen surrounding him in the library. He was sorry that he had even momentarily thought of them as fools; not only was this forbidden in Holy Writ, but it was very unkind. These were nice people, well-meaning if somewhat restricted in their ideas, full of natural good will, if not scintillating; disposed enthusiastically in the direction of "excellent works," if lacking some imagination. Moreover, a few of the gentlemen were quite astute businessmen, and Dr. Stevens admired them for their efficiency and for their determined public virtue.

They sat about him in the dark-red and dark-blue leather chairs of the library, and between him and them a tea table had been set up. Little shafts of August sun darted through the venetian blinds and struck upon the polished silver tray and teapots and china. The small tinklings which had accompanied the well-bred and quiet voices had had their part, however, in the lulling of his consciousness into that warm lethargy, during which he had made some disastrous error. Alarmed, he tried to remember the remark which had elicited his genial murmur. His eyes wandered during this effort. He looked for enlightenment at the big mahogany desk with the gold-tooled leather top, the conservative blue draperies at the tall narrow windows, the dark-blue rug, the red-leather sofa, the discreet reproduction (very good) of a Gothic English cathedral hanging between the windows. It was all very proper, very stiff, very heavy, and even while he tried to recall what the remark had been, he could not help a vagrant and uneasy thought: Johnny will be stifled by this. But what have I said, anyway?

The accusing eyes under the ladies' prosaic hats, the stern eyes of the bald and thin, or fat, gentlemen, the waiting consternation on their faces, made his round face even redder than usual. But as a clergyman he had learned to be adroit. His cherubic smile became very sweet and apologetic, his blue eyes shone tenderly. He took out his fine linen handkerchief and passed it over his polished head and bright cheeks. He laughed. "I'm so sorry," he said. "But you must excuse an old gentleman. After all I'm over seventy, and sometimes my mind wanders." He studied the ladies. The one with the most accusing eyes was doubtless the one who had addressed the fatal question to him. She was a short, fat, competent woman in her sixties, all three of her chins very determined; she was astonishingly brisk for her age, and Dr. Stevens respected her shrewdness and her realistic common sense. Though she had a passion for big floral prints, such as the dress she was wearing today, he forgave this aberration and its deplorable results. He looked into her somewhat hard gray eyes and added, "Dear Mrs. Grant, I do hope you will forgive my elderly forgetfulness. Would you mind repeating what you just said?"

The group exchanged compassionate glances, and Dr. Stevens smiled inwardly and with affection. Since they were all in their late fifties or early sixties, they were still his juniors. He rightly believed that they were thinking: Well, poor old gentleman! It's to be expected at his age. Now they smiled at him genially. Mrs. Grant said, "We were, as you know, discussing our new young pastor, whom we have decided to accept on your recommendation and endorsement, though he's had only one small parish before he went into the Army. You have told us today, and on previous occasions, that he was your favorite student at the Stevens Religious Institute."

She had spoken precisely and a little loudly, as one speaks to one who is either a "foreigner" or practically senile. The others nodded, and smiled at him. Well, he thought, I deserve it. I had no right to let my mind wander to the books, but after all ten of these long discussions over the past weeks, I can perhaps be forgiven for becoming bored. Poor Johnny!

Mrs. Grant smoothed the white gloves on her fat knees. "We all know how grateful we should be to our armed forces, and how gallantly they did their duty in Europe in the war. But we all know what militarism does even to the best characters. It—brutalizes them, in a way. My grandson, for instance, who has just returned, is not the boy he was before he enlisted. He was so sweet before! So kind to his mother, so considerate. I can remember when he was a little boy; he would cry if someone killed a housefly. Shy, too. He would color up if anybody dared to kiss him. Really!" She gurgled in a girlish manner which astonished Dr. Stevens, for he had thought better of her. The others gurgled with her, fondly. Then she sighed. "You'd hardly recognize him now, and it just breaks our hearts."

The boy should be congratulated, and the Army, too, thought Dr. Stevens with some lack of charity. He said, with mildness, "You must remember that young John Fletcher was not exactly a soldier. He was a chaplain."

"But still," said another lady, seriously, "he necessarily came into contact with—military characters. I don't read modern war fiction, of course, but my daughter does, and though I can hardly believe it she tells me that the language —and the things soldiers do—" At this point, the gentlemen looked embarrassed and smiled briefly at each other, remembering the first war.

Dear Mrs. Howard, thought Dr. Stevens, you'd be amazed how many brutalized characters there are in the world, and what language, and what things, go on busily about your innocent self every hour and every day! He marveled that even the Mrs. Howards could live six decades and not know that the world was not composed, in the main, of "good people." He regarded the smooth-faced, slender little lady with more than a touch of pity.

Mrs. Grant broke in. "And so my question to you, Dr. Stevens, was this: Was there any possibility that Mr. Fletcher had become even slightly depraved and rough and insensitive from his contacts with soldiers?" She smiled, and her big face became almost pretty. "And you answered, 'Yes, indeed. I am positive of it.'"

Dr. Stevens was appalled. That was what came of thinking of books when silly questions were being asked. Then he was immensely relieved, for all the ladies and gentlemen were laughing and shaking their heads, and were obviously commenting to themselves on Dr. Stevens's age.

He said, "How dreadful of me, and how inexcusable. Frankly, though, I am a bit tired, and sitting here among you, my friends, I allowed myself to relax for the first time in a long while." He spread out his plump little hands and beamed. "There are some people who say they can't relax in New York. But I never relax so well as when I'm here, and I can sleep like a baby, any time, at any hour."

If they had not completely forgiven him before, they forgave him utterly now, for they were all old New Yorkers, and loved their city. They embraced the new pastor, John Fletcher, in their expansive affection for Dr. Stevens. Mrs. Howard said happily, "In a way, it's so romantic that our new pastor has been an army chaplain. So colorful. What experiences he must have had! I think it is ever so exciting, don't you?" She turned to the others, and they agreed heartily.

"So many of our boys have been in the Army," said Mrs. Grant. "I'm sure that Mr. Fletcher will be a sound influence on them; understanding them. Besides, he's young, and he'll have more in common with them."

Dr. Stevens believed that stage properties were as necessary to a clergyman as they were to actors. The people with whom Dr. Stevens had to deal daily, whether in New York or in Illinois where he had once lived, were solid and conservative citizens, and so he always dressed very soberly, even for a clergyman, and he used an old-fashioned gold watch which had belonged to his father. He sometimes told himself that the watch had bridged many very awkward moments in his life, especially when someone had begun to suspect that Dr. Stevens was perhaps not so reliable and proper as he appeared to be. The watch was always reassuring to timid and conventional souls. He used it now, letting the eyes of the ladies and gentlemen touch the heavy gold chain looping across his firm little paunch, and then light approvingly on the big "repeater" with its thick, etched covers. Some of them sighed with nostalgia for a dead father, and Dr. Stevens sighed with them for his own father, who had been a clergyman also, and a grave, unworldly, and saintlike soul.

"Gracious!" he exclaimed, sitting up in his chair. "It is almost four o'clock! My assistant, Mr. Montrose, should be here almost any moment with Mr. Fletcher. The ship docked more than an hour ago. Of course, there are the Customs, and other dreary matters, but still—"

He gestured aside the efforts of a starched and elderly maid who wished to refill his teacup. A wave of subdued but excited movement ran over the ladies and gentlemen. Dr.

Stevens was touched to see the ladies pat their hair and preen a little. Dear, good creatures. The man who said, "I still feel young inside though I am over seventy-five," had spoken a profound truth. The soul never aged, even though the body withered. Its youth manifested itself in sudden quick lightings of weary old eyes, in sudden smiles of pure enthusiasm, in sudden childlike joys and anticipations. Let the narrow-spirited and shallow-hearted laugh contemptuously at elderly feminine preenings and at old men's bright ties and gay socks, at white curls, and sports jackets hanging on bent and tired shoulders. All these gave evidence of an immortal spirit which the drabness of the years and the heaviness of daily living could never extinguish.

Dr. Stevens returned his watch to his pocket, suffused with the glow which only those who understand men, and pity them, can experience. He was about to speak again when a furious clamor rose from behind the closed door of the library. It was an uproar of the kind one might expect to hear only among young wild animals in a disturbed and riotous jungle, and the discreet draperies at the windows appeared to sway in alarm. The ladies and gentlemen half rose in their chairs, their faces frightened and questioning, and they looked mutely at Dr. Stevens for explanation.

"Good God!" he cried, and for once did not glance at his audience for any reaction. "What was that?"

2

As abruptly as the clamor had burst out in the serene and quiet parsonage, as abruptly it stopped. Dr. Stevens and the ladies and gentlemen were dumbfounded. The minister sank back into his chair; the other gentlemen stood bewildered. "Some commotion in the street outside," said Dr. Stevens, but without conviction. The inhuman noise had definitely originated in the sunlit corridor outside the library. However, as there was no orderly and logical explanation for it, an illogical one had to be produced, no matter how incredible.

"It didn't come from the street!" exclaimed Mrs. Grant. "This is a good neighborhood! It came from just outside this room." She glared at Dr. Stevens, obviously demanding not only reassurance but explanation. "Why doesn't somebody open the door?"

The gentlemen exhibited no eagerness to follow her suggestion; they only stared at Dr. Stevens. In some way this involves you, and it's your affair, said their eyes accusingly. He moved in his chair, preparing to rise, when they all heard a muffled and gently masculine voice outside the door. It spoke as if it had been speaking during the clamor, and now it rose in strength and affection.

"Nobody's going to hurt you," said the voice. "Nobody ever has, since you were my kids. Remember? Nobody hurt you in Salzburg, or anywhere else, and not on the boat, either. Nobody's going to hurt my children. I've just brought you home, see. Now, Jean, you're the biggest, and you take Emilie's hand; that's right. She's just a little girl; she's your sister from now on. Right? Kathy, you take Pietro's hand; he's frightened. And Max, stop chewing your lip and stand up straight. That's right, that's right. Good kids! Now, then, just follow me—"

Where's Montrose? thought Dr. Stevens, with some wildness.

"What *is* this?" cried Mrs. Grant, outraged because she was perplexed. She was accustomed to a very orderly world where nothing unexpected happened. "Children? Whose children?"

Where, thought Dr. Stevens profanely, is that damned Montrose? They were all staring at the shut door again, and the ladies were exhibiting signs of fear and umbrage, and the gentlemen merely stood and stared blankly. It was worse for Dr. Stevens, for he had recognized the young masculine voice, so kind and loving and strong. He knew, now, what it meant to suffer a "sinking heart." "I think," he said feebly, "that Mr. Fletcher has arrived. But where is—?"

There was a shrill scream outside, followed by another abrupt silence, and the door flew open with a crash. And there was Mr. Montrose, tall, white-haired, marvelously tailored, with a flushed and appalled face. His usual dignity was gone; he gave the aspect of one who had been running madly before a high wind, with some horror behind. He looked at Dr. Stevens, who was standing now, and tried to speak, but only his white eyebrows jerked up and down and his opening and shutting mouth emitted no sound but a squeak. His large thin nose twitched, and he threw out his hands, dropped them to his side again, then threw them out helplessly.

Then he jumped. He jumped high and wide, to Dr. Stevens's dazed astonishment. Mr. Montrose was definitely not the type to jump at all, under any circumstances. Yet there was Horace Montrose leaping like a flea, up in the air, and then to one side of the door, and again he squeaked.

"Good kids!" said Mr. Fletcher's voice. "Now then, just

follow me. Don't be frightened. Just good kind people here, giving you a home—"

A mass burst into the room, a mass of jolting faces, arms, legs, bodies, all churned together as in a nightmare. White wild faces of children, thin flailing arms and legs of children, tangled heads of children, dilated and glaring eyes of children. They gave the impression of being a multitude in impetuous explosion; actually they were only five. And then behind them, smiling indulgently, stood young Mr. Fletcher, still in his chaplain's uniform.

The mass halted, breathing loudly, on the threshold, pressing together as if for protection, prepared to flee, to struggle, to bite, to tear, if necessary. They stood and looked at the petrified group in the library, and from them rose a hoarse and muttering sound, the sound of fear, panic, and hate.

Mr. Fletcher patted the nearest shoulders and heads. Then he removed his cap, smiled over the heads of the appalling tangle, and waved his hand affectionately at Dr. Stevens. "I've brought my children home, sir," he said. "They're all Fletchers. Fletchers. Aren't you, kids?"

"Your children?" wailed Dr. Stevens, putting a hand to the side of his head and thinking very chaotic thoughts indeed. "Johnny! What is all this? Who are these—these children?"

Mr. Fletcher stepped around the obdurate clot of small humanity on the threshold and advanced into the room. He held out his hand to Dr. Stevens, beaming. "It's good to see you, Dr. Stevens!" he exclaimed. "It's wonderful!" Dr. Stevens took the extended hand, less in greeting than for the need of physical support. And then a paternal warmth filled him; it was really Johnny: Johnny the tall and slender and strong and sure; Johnny whose heart always led him where wise heads would not follow—to their great, their very great, loss. It was really Johnny, with his dark face and shining, steadfast eyes, good firm chin, thick black lashes and hair, and short, sturdy nose. It was Johnny, after all, Johnny who believed in love as the one power of life. His eyes were wet, and he put his hand on the young minister's shoulder and he forgot the dreadful unknown children and the ladies and gentlemen. "Welcome home, Johnny," he murmured. "Welcome, welcome home!"

A compressed-air drill, setting suddenly to work tearing up the pavement outside, filled the library with a harsh, rattling sound like the clatter of machine guns. Instantly, from the children there rose a horrible scream of fright. They exploded into the room, rushed together against a wall, and huddled there, enclosing one another in their desperate arms, and hiding their heads. The ladies and gentlemen turned their eyes stiffly and surveyed them, utterly astounded, unable to move or speak.

But Mr. Fletcher was smiling at them with that incredible indulgence. He moved toward them slowly. "Oh, come on," he said. "You know that isn't a machine gun. I've told you we don't have them going off in American cities. It's a machine to dig up the streets so they can be fixed. Why don't you come to the windows and see for yourselves? Jean, stop acting up, and you too, Max. You're big boys. You've got the girls and Pietro acting silly too." His voice became peremptory. "All right, all right, now, break it up, break it up."

"For God's sake, Johnny," began Dr. Stevens in a weak stammer.

"Oh, they're just my kids," said Mr. Fletcher, as if that explained everything. "I adopted them. That is, I'm their foster father, until I can really adopt them. Come on, kids," he urged, "you know it's not a machine gun. I'll shut the windows."

Mr. Montrose had shrunk against the wall near the children, and now he broke away and leaped toward Dr. Stevens. He, who was always calm and urbane, clutched Dr. Stevens's arm. "You can't imagine, sir!" he babbled. "Getting them off the ship. It was a nightmare! I tried to call you, but—"

One of the gentlemen, recovering a little, said with indignation, "I think we deserve an explanation, Dr. Stevens. And introductions are in order—"

But Dr. Stevens was watching the children.

That was Jean, there, probably about twelve, with a cynical old man's hard and narrowly wise face. He gave an impression of intense alertness, and, in spite of the explosion of terror in which he had participated, he also gave the impression of being quite capable of meeting any situation; a kind of dogged defiance glimmered from his white cheekbones, hard white jaw line, and fierce, almost fixed eyes, which were pale and distended under stiff lashes. A shock of light-brown hair tumbled over his stony forehead. Definitely a strange and unattractive boy, thought Dr. Stevens regretfully, for he loved children. He did not love Jean, or feel any warm impulse toward him. And then Jean moved a little, and it was obvious that he was crippled, for his left shoulder sagged, and as he eased it against the wall he winced, and Dr. Stevens could see that his left leg was shorter than the other. Ah, thought Dr. Stevens with pain, something frightful has happened to that child!

Jean was tightly holding the hand of a very little girl, whom Mr. Fletcher was now addressing soothingly as Emilie. She clung to Jean, but she looked up at the young minister fearfully, blinking great blue eyes. "Dear," said Mr. Fletcher, touching her long and tangled brown hair, "aren't you my darling baby? Sure you are. There, now, don't cry. You know what I told you—everybody loves you here." He smiled down at her pointed little face, in which the pale lips quivered babyishly, for she could not have been more than five. She was so very thin, almost a skeleton, and now her body trembled in the ill-fitting clothing she wore. She began to sob like the infant she was, big heaving breaths of sobs, but as Mr. Fletcher continued to stroke her head tenderly her trembling died away, and she pressed her forehead against the minister's hand like a child seeking refuge. Oh, the poor little one, thought Dr. Stevens. And now the child was quiet, huge glistening tears on her pinched face.

Johnny Fletcher turned to Dr. Stevens. "This is my boy Max," he said, seriously. "My son, Max." He put his hand on the shoulder of a largish boy of about eleven, who did not look up at him. Lumpish, thought Dr. Stevens with pity, or perhaps merely dazed. Max gave the impression of not being present at all, but living in some awful experience he had half forgotten but the effects of which were still with him. His large bones gave him the appearance of being more solid than he actually was, for closer inspection showed that his shoulders were meagerly covered with flesh, and his hands, though big, were gaunt. His square face was all bone; he had famished brown eyes, staring yet empty, and his tan-colored hair was disordered, standing in random peaks all over his round head. Is the boy an imbecile? wondered Dr. Stevens sadly. He noticed that Max, after one brief upward glance at the minister, a glance that held no expression at all, fixed his eyes on his hands and stood in rigid silence. And then the hands moved together convulsively, and to Dr. Stevens's renewed compassion and dread, the hands began to wring themselves, over and over, in the immemorial gestures of utter despair —the despair of a broken man.

"My son, Max," repeated Johnny in a loud and loving voice. The boy started. Slowly the hands stopped their wringing; they remained together, palms pressed against each other. "Son," said Johnny, "you're a fine big boy. Don't you remember me, your father?"

Max's eyes, fastened on his hands, blinked. His lids moved as if very heavy, and then he raised his eyes and looked at Johnny. No expression filled them, but his hands dropped to his sides. Johnny ruffled the peaks of dry hair and smiled contentedly. "My good son, Max," he said. A deep sigh came from the child, as if he were falling asleep.

Next to him stood a boy about nine, who could not keep still. His extremely mobile and sensitive face twitched; his dark skin quivered constantly. His enormous black eyes glittered under trembling brows and a mass of black curls. He glanced everywhere, furtively but all-seeing; his arms, legs, and starveling's body jerked as if he were suffering from some grave nervous disorder. He had a monkey's air of aimless energy, and his fingers kept flaring out and in against his palm. The boy began to rise and fall on his toes; his knees splayed; his shoulders hunched. "My son, Pietro," said Johnny, proudly. "He gets around everywhere."

The shifting gleaming eyes halted, and then turned sidelong up to Johnny. The minister nodded. "Good boy, Pietro?"

A cunning flash touched those wild eyes, but the boy answered obediently with a foreign accent, "Good—boy." A liar, a conforming liar, speculated the astute Dr. Stevens. Where in the name of heaven has he come from?

"And now," Johnny went on in that same tone of paternal pride, "my big daughter, Kathy. Look at those rosy cheeks." He gently pinched the little girl's cheek, which, though it was not exactly "rosy," had a tinge of childish color in it. Kathy, like Max, was big, and she was probably about eleven years old too. Her clothes, obviously second- or third-hand, fitted her better than the others' clothing fitted them, for she had a firm and sturdy body. And she had a maternal look, absurdly touching in so young a child. Somewhere she had secured a bright blue ribbon, which she had attached to the

19

very long, very thick, braid of absolutely blond hair which dangled from her smooth golden scalp. Her round eyes were the color of the ribbon, surrounded by yellow lashes, and she had a round, somewhat pursed mouth, and a pudgy nose. Dutch? wondered Dr. Stevens. Her eyes flickered as she looked at the immobile group in the library. No trust for anyone there, thought Dr. Stevens. But she'll manage; she is the kind which always does, somehow.

She permitted Johnny to pat her head, rather than submitted to the caress. Dr. Stevens smiled a little. Johnny was turning to him. "It took me months to bring them over here, sir. All kinds of red tape. And then they couldn't come until the authorities were sure they'd become a little 'civilized,' as they said. Well, they were sort of savage, but then who could blame them?"

"We seem a little ahead of ourselves. Explanations can come later, Johnny," said Dr. Stevens. "Er—you haven't met the ladies and gentlemen here, part of your new congregation. And the President of the Board—"

The old man's heart sickened with foreboding, for the gentlemen to whom Johnny—brave, strong, and gentle Johnny—was being introduced, acknowledged the introductions with august coldness, tinged with wary alarm and expressions of incredulity. Johnny, in his somewhat disheveled chaplain's uniform, in the power of his unorthodox youth, was not their idea of a new pastor, or one they could accept. The President of the Board was particularly affronted, his voice particularly cold and distant. Dr. Stevens knew exactly what they were thinking: A "respectable" minister arrived with dignity and poise, and if it were absolutely necessary to appear before part of his congregation for the first time in uniform, that uniform should be well-tailored and worn with an air. (They'll never trust my judgment again, thought Dr. Stevens drearily.) Johnny spoke too loudly, and with too much emphasis. He even had a suggestion of raffishness about him, which Dr. Stevens suspected came from raw and dangerous experience, an experience none of these people present could ever comprehend. He also possessed a kind of innocence, almost blatant—poor Johnny, thought Dr. Stevens again.

All these things might have been forgiven him, however, "for the sake of the young people in the parish," had not

Johnny arrived with these "unspeakable" children. His calm assumption that the children, "his children," would be accepted with compassion and understanding is a great compliment he has paid all of us, Dr. Stevens commented to himself ruefully. But then Johnny always believed in the innate goodness of man. Apparently even what he had seen and experienced had not shaken that mighty faith. There he stood, tall and smiling and self-possessed, either not seeing, or refusing to see, with tenderness, that the gentlemen were repelled by him, aghast at him and what he had done. He shook hands warmly, and his very dark and very brilliant blue eyes sparkled even more warmly. They saw everything swiftly—or did they really see? wondered Dr. Stevens wretchedly.

The ladies, particularly Mrs. Grant and Mrs. Howard, were kinder than the gentlemen. Johnny had a special and protective affection for women, and they sensed it. The ladies even forgot to look at the children while they searchingly examined Johnny and considered him, and in spite of their reserved manner and their cool faces some tentative thoughtfulness replaced the original hardness in their eyes. But the gentlemen turned from Johnny and furtively studied the monstrous children, still huddled against the wall, and Mr. Montrose, who had taken refuge behind the big mahogany desk. I never knew before what a fool Montrose is, Dr. Stevens said to himself, with irritation. And what a—what is it they call it?—yes, a ham. He's not half as terrified or appalled by those little wretches as he pretends to be. Now that I recall it, he never did like Johnny very much, and always resented my fondness for him. Is he punishing us both now?

And yet, those children!

Dr. Stevens came to himself with a start. What was Johnny saying to the ladies clustered about him, speaking in that deep steady voice of his? "Yes, Mrs. Howard. That's what I called it, in Munich. Nightmare Road. I first saw it at night. Hitler's city, they called Munich; it was his headquarters, you know, his favorite place when he wasn't at Berchtesgaden. I stayed for a few days at the Four Seasons Hotel in Munich, before I was sent on to Salzburg. Once it had been the finest hotel in that part of Europe; now it was a shattered wreck. The owners were bravely putting it together, foot by foot. The great dining room, famous all over Europe, was gone, but I heard stories of its grandeur. The owners were using the 'tea room' as the dining room, and they had an orchestra, composed of old men, who played for dinner. Old men; broken, very tired, old men. Yet somehow, watching the workers rebuilding that hotel, and watching the orchestra, and watching the maître d'hôtel marching around, with his big mustaches, and bowing, and supervising what was left of the wines, and inspecting the dishes, I was proud, all over again, of my fellow man."

"But, they are Germans!" exclaimed the President of the Board. "Our enemies! Mr. Fletcher, are you proud of the Germans?"

His frozen eyes caught the eyes of the other gentlemen, and the bouquet of cold repudiation was presented to Johnny in one long stare.

Johnny was silent. Slowly those extraordinarily dark-blue eyes touched face after face, probing, seeking. But even the ladies were withdrawing from him, drawing together with the gentlemen in a phalanx of umbrage and rejection. Johnny saw it. His dark face became sad, then very stern. He seemed to grow in stature, to tower over everyone in the room, through which blew an utter silence. Even the children were still; the constant, low muttering had subsided. Even Mr. Montrose was transfixed by something strange that was happening, instant by instant. And Dr. Stevens felt a quickening of his heart. It was only his imagination, of course, but it appeared to him that the sunset light, streaming through the tall windows, was slowly concentrating on Johnny, like a nimbus.

"Enemies?" repeated Johnny, and his voice, though soft, penetrated clearly to every corner of the big library. He glanced at the children; they were listening. For a moment his expression softened, became even more sorrowful. "Enemies? Does a nation awaken one morning and suddenly decide, all at once, that another nation is its enemy? Where are those, now, who made the Germans our enemies, and the enemies of their neighbors? I tell you," and now his voice rose on a profound and shaking note, "that Hitler is dead, and Mussoline is dead, and many of their generals and their advisers are dead. But the men who made the Germans our enemies are not dead! They never die!"

His eyes were a flash of blue in his face. "They are the men who create Hitlers and Mussolinis, and Stalins, too. They are the men who hate all of us, and have hated mankind from the very beginning. They are the men who choose and set up despots, who plan, behind bronze doors in every capital in the world, what nation shall hate another nation, what war shall be drummed up from hell in what year."

His voice shook, but was charged even mightier with power. Everyone gazed at him, fascinated, immobilized. He trembled with anger. His eloquent hands lifted and gestured, not with despair, but with wrath.

"They never change!" he cried. "Down through the ages they've come, gathering force, gathering influence, shadow-faced men behind kings and presidents and dictators! Speaking in languages now dead, speaking today in English and French and German and Russian and Chinese and Japanese. And tomorrow they'll speak other languages not yet invented, to peoples not yet born, in cities not yet built, nations whose boundaries are not yet set! Our enemies!"

Oh, Johnny, thought Dr. Stevens, and his old eyes were wet. But the ladies and gentlemen had withdrawn even farther from the young minister, and they stared at him in mingled bewilderment and outrage, utterly uncomprehending, the little flowered walls of their lives trembling in a wind which had never assaulted them before.

The children—the frightful children—were listening. It was not possible that they could have understood all the words, all the implications, that came from Johnny Fletcher. Yet some emanation sprang from the young minister which they instinctively recognized, as the others did not. They stood huddled together, eyes and mouths open, listening, hardly breathing, while their elders merely gaped, looked affronted, and retreated coldly. But then, thought Dr. Stevens, didn't He say that unless we became as little children—?

"Really, Mr. Fletcher," said the President of the Board in his best director's voice. He glanced at the others, and faint, well-bred smiles of disdain answered him reassuringly. "And may I ask who 'they' are?"

"I have told you. You'll never recognize them, just as your ancestors never recognized them." For a moment, but only a moment, Johnny seemed very tired, and his voice was subdued. Then, all at once, he was tall and passionate again, and his voice rose.

"It isn't fashionable, any longer, to believe in Satan, or Lucifer. After all, we're civilized, aren't we? Lucifer, in the Old Testament, is only a symbol, our best theologians say. He is just something the best schools can eradicate with education. He is the bogeyman of the Dark Ages. He is the psychiatrist's subconscious and id. Just bring him out into the light of day, on a psychiatrist's couch, and what is Satan? Why, he hasn't any reality at all, and he can be abolished with a few soothing sessions or a series of shock treatments!"

Well, thought Dr. Stevens, that does it, Johnny!

Johnny sighed. "I should like to show you Europe now. I should like to show you not just five children like these, but tens of thousands. I should like to take you through the broken cities, the shattered churches, the ruins of museums, the rubble of schools and universities, the splintered streets. I should like to conduct you through the concentration camps, the gas chambers, the crematoriums where thousands of men and women and babies died. I should like to point out to you the endless acres where our young American dead lie, sleeping forever under the sun. Perhaps even one old man's face, or an old woman's, looking emptily on a smashed little house or a trampled garden, would be enough. Or the death cry of a child under a fallen wall. Or the blind, crazed eyes of a young soldier who will never recognize anyone again, not even his mother. And then I'd ask you—who else but Lucifer, who never sleeps, and knows his own and employs them?"

The ladies had slowly seated themselves, but the gentlemen stood around Johnny. They were like elderly terriers warily surveying a young mastiff. Really, Johnny, Dr. Stevens thought, you don't talk of evil to those whom Evil has convinced he does not exist.

Yet now the old minister spoke, mildly. "It has been said that Satan's greatest triumph was in convincing those he wished to destroy that he had no reality," he said. "I think Mr. Fletcher really means that evil men are born in every generation of men who hate others. The ignorant among them are called psychotics. The more intelligent, and influential, help to create wars and stimulate hatreds—either for financial profit, or personal satisfaction, or power."

He put his hand firmly on Johnny's left arm, and pressed discreetly. Johnny had become pale, and his exhaustion, which was more spiritual than physical, revealed itself in his abstracted face, his air of momentary withdrawal.

"Well, one can understand that," said the President of the Board loftily, giving Dr. Stevens a reproachful glance. "One doesn't need dramatics, and talk of a—a personal devil—to make that point."

Johnny stirred quickly. "We admit that evil exists. Since it is so widespread among so-called Christian nations, I believe we have opened ourselves to absolute chaos within the next few years."

"Chaos?" repeated one of the gentlemen with disdain. "The war is over, isn't it?"

"No," said Johnny. "It is never over."

They were silent. The young minister searched every face again, imploringly, hopefully, pleading for understanding. But now even the ladies' faces were nervously closed to him. He must know by now, Dr. Stevens said to himself, miserably. But he is one of the noble heroes who will never give up. Dr. Stevens was an old man, and he was very tired. His mind began to buzz incoherently. Somewhere, he remembered, a paint company had used a very telling slogan: "Save the surface, and you save all!" Too many people were trying to "save the surface," while it was cracking violently, thunderingly, to the farthest reaches of the world.

Johnny suddenly went to the children. They watched his approach with their wild and furtive eyes, their inscrutable faces, their air of suppressed savagery. Dr. Stevens shuddered. I'd be afraid to go within a foot of them! he thought. But Johnny was not afraid. He looked at them tenderly. The boy Pietro, the monkey-boy, let a glimmer of teeth show between his lips in a soundless snarl. Max, the vacant-faced, was wringing his hands again. Jean, the crippled, glowered at the young minister. The little girls merely stared at him, taut as forest beasts.

Johnny spoke to the adults in the room, but did not take his eyes away from the children. "Look at these little ones. I'll tell you where I found them in a moment. They're orphans; they don't know who they are. Their parents were murdered in concentration camps. Who killed their parents? Who drove the minds and the souls of these children back to the dawn age of man, the age of tooth and claw? Look at them, and I'll tell you the answer!"

25

Stiffly, reluctantly, all eyes turned to the group huddled against the wall. Johnny swung slowly on his heel, and he surveyed the ladies and gentlemen with mournful and piercing anger. "You will say the Germans did—the Germans, our enemies. You will accuse the frightened little German housewife, with her own brutalized children. You will say these infants here are the victims of the timid German clerk, the harassed German shopkeeper, the thin German schoolmaster, the German burgher who only wanted peace in which to conduct his business. You will confuse the instruments with those who used the instruments."

His voice rose more passionately, a true orator's voice. "I tell you that no nation is the enemy of another nation, no people the enemy of another people! There are no bad nations; there are only bad governments, which are taken over by the men of evil. 'The spawn of Satan,' as the Bible calls them."

The President of the Board said with a smile, "You're a very eloquent young man, Mr. Fletcher. Excellent training. All Dr. Stevens's graduates are. And now, since we are on the subject of governments, there is another old saying: 'A people deserve their government.'"

"No," said Johnny, and there was bitterness in his voice.

Frantically, Dr. Stevens tried to think of other churches where Johnny would be welcome after this.

"These children," said Johnny despairingly, "are not only the victims of German butchers. They are our victims too. Over ten years ago, long before the war, we gave our assent to the evil in the German government. By our silence—by our wicked silence. When only a word, only one powerful, Christian word, would have overthrown Hitler, would have saved the German people themselves, and would have saved countless thousands of other children like these. But we didn't give the word. What were we afraid of? War? There would never have been a war if we had spoken in 1936." He sighed. "And there would not be a Stalin, now, or a Communist government, if a generation ago we had given the saving word."

Now he was towering with wrath again. "Why didn't you—why didn't we—speak? Where were the pastors, the educated and civilized men? Where were our leaders—in 1917, in 1936?"

No one answered him. With the exception of Dr. Stevens's, every eye was cold. How hateful are those who demand confession and contrition from others! thought the old minister sorrowfully. How detestable is the man who shows us our sins of omission and commission! We much prefer to think well of ourselves.

Then the President of the Board turned portentously to his fellows. "I think we should have a meeting early next week," he said. "Monday, at half-past two? Is it convenient?"

He didn't ask me, Dr. Stevens commented to himself. Well, Johnny, that's the end.

Johnny must have known it too. He said, "Aren't you interested to know how I got these children? Don't you care?"

"That, Mr. Fletcher," said Mrs. Grant firmly, "is your own business. I'd suggest, though, that you put them in an orphan asylum. If the Immigration people will permit you." Her hard eyes narrowed speculatively. Johnny took a step toward her. He said, "They're not going to any orphan asylum. That was suggested for them in Europe, by others. They would have been separated, and that would've been frightful, for they trust only each other, with justification."

"Dear me," said Mrs. Howard, "don't they trust you, Mr. Fletcher?"

"No, they don't. Why should they? I've had them ten months. But I'm a man, an adult, and they know what they've suffered from men. Even I don't know the full extent of it. So why should they trust me? They don't know what a minister is. You see, they never met a minister before. And why didn't they? Perhaps you can tell me."

But no one answered him. The ladies were rising with a final rustle, patting hair, adjusting hats, exchanging significant glances. The gentlemen took up their hats and gloves. Johnny, standing near them now, scrutinized them, but no one looked at him, though his hand was lifted appealingly.

"Now, where is my purse?" asked Mrs. Grant, turning anxiously from her chair to the table. "I had it on that table near the door—I think—"

Johnny turned swiftly to the children with an exclamation. Yes, it had happened again. Kathy, the stout, sure, blond little girl, had not only pounced on the purse somehow, but she had opened it. She clutched it in her left hand. Her right

27

hand was clenched defiantly over something, and she was glaring at the adults. Jean, the fierce-eyed cripple, had moved protectively to her side, his pathetic fists knotted. The children were a wild and savage group, prepared for any violence, and prepared to return it.

Johnny said, in the gentlest voice, "Kathy, don't you remember? My little girl doesn't steal things. Kathy?"

The child's distended eyes, shining with a wolflike light, looked at him. Dr. Stevens was again alarmed and overcome. "Kathy?" repeated Mr. Fletcher, and he advanced to the girl and held out his hand. Jean took a step toward him, raising his fists, lowering his head. "Stop it, Jean," said the young minister sternly. "You know I'm not going to hurt Kathy. Behave yourself." He then ignored the boy, who continued to stand there like a belligerent statue.

"Thieves!" cried Mrs. Howard. "How dreadful, how—"

"Yes," said Johnny, not looking at her, but only at Kathy. "How dreadful." He held out his hand sternly, but with a smile, at Kathy. The other children crowded about her, glaring at him, and again that hoarse mutter rose from them, wordless but frightful.

"She doesn't want your money, Mrs. Grant," said Johnny. "She just wants your compact." He smiled steadily at Kathy. "You see, I told her, months ago, when I rescued her—from adults—that she was a lovable and pretty little girl. That she had blue eyes like flowers, and hair just like a daffodil. Someone—a man, probably—had told her she was too ugly to live, and that she was to be killed for that. That's the kind of torture they used on children in the concentration camps, before they murdered them. So Kathy steals mirrors now, to look at herself, to see whether she is really pretty, and so won't be killed."

"Well, why didn't you buy her a little mirror yourself?" demanded Mrs. Grant haughtily.

"I did. But she thinks, I'm afraid, that I just painted a picture on it of a pretty little girl, so that she'll be fooled."

Mrs. Grant and the other ladies gasped incredulously. The gentlemen turned aside their faces. They always do, Dr. Stevens thought.

"So," Johnny went on, "she keeps stealing mirrors in compacts, so that she can believe for herself, in other people's mirrors, that she's pretty and won't have to die."

He approached closer to Kathy, and she shrank away. "The purse, dear," he said. "Look, I'll buy you a pretty gold box tomorrow, with a mirror in it. Tomorrow, Kathy."

And then a strange thing happened. Mrs. Grant spoke. "Let her have the compact."

Johnny swung to her. Her firm lips were trembling. "I—I said, she can have the compact. I just want my purse."

A great joyful light burst out on Johnny's face. "You see, Kathy!" he exclaimed. "The lady said you can have her mirror. All for you, darling, so you can look at yourself. But you don't want the purse—"

The child glared at him, and then at Mrs. Grant. Then she flung the purse at the young minister's face with one strong thrust of her arm. He dodged, but it hit him on the side of the head, and he staggered at the impact of the heavy article. The children exploded into a roar of laughter and hoarse shouts of triumph. "Johnny!" cried Dr. Stevens, over the uproar.

But Johnny had calmly recovered his poise. He rubbed the side of his head and studied the children. "What monsters," murmured the President of the Board. "We'll have to consult with the Immigration authorities—dangerous to permit them at large—you never can tell—"

The children were jiggling together in a hysterical dance of hate and victory. And terror. They had begun to chant some jungle rhythm born out of the depths of their savagery.

"That's all you could do for them, in ten long months?" said Mrs. Howard, her voice shaking with fear and disgust. "You could do no better than that? Look at them! They're —they're nightmares!"

"Yes," said Johnny, his back to her. "Nightmares. Our nightmares."

He advanced to the children, after giving Mrs. Grant her purse. He said to Kathy, "Won't you let us see what the kind lady gave you, dear? Jean and Pietro and Max and Emilie would like to see it, too. Look, I'll put my hands behind my back."

The children became abruptly silent. They were one stare of hatred and suspicion and cunning. Then Kathy's eyes wavered. She held her elbow close to her side, her fingers so tight on the compact that they were colorless. Then slowly, moment by moment, as if under entrancement, she let the fingers open, and on her palm lay the compact. The children craned their heads to see, fascinated.

It was a beautiful thing, and Dr. Stevens was astonished at Mrs. Grant's generosity. It was a round circle of gold, encrusted with turquoises, amethysts, and topazes. It caught the sunset and a spray of many-colored light sprang from it. "Oh, oh!" groaned the children in ecstasy and they shuffled their feet again in that awful dance. But Dr. Stevens noted, with a shaking of his heart, that not one of them tried to snatch it from Kathy. They were rejoicing with her that she now possessed so lovely a treasure. Ah, thought Dr. Stevens, where is the "civilized" man or woman who would rejoice with anyone else, even with the closest brother, without secret envy or malice? The children's faces were a shimmer of radiant delight.

He wanted to thank Mrs. Grant. She was smiling reluctantly, and she was very flushed. "Shall we go?" she said, turning to the ladies.

The ladies left, and the gentlemen followed. The door closed after them. The room was darkening in the first twilight. The children still chanted their joy over Kathy's possession, bending their heads over it. Max had stopped wringing his hands. He was actually clapping them, and stamping his feet. Kathy had opened the compact and was gazing into it intently. Then she cried out in rapture to Johnny: "Pretty! Pretty! Me! Me!"

"Yes, dear," he said, and now when he touched her smooth braid she did not wince. "Pretty you. My pretty, darling little daughter."

3

"You mean, sir, that we have to cut up all the meat for them? Those big kids?" demanded Edith, the elegant maid, quivering with resentment. The cook, Mrs. Burnsdale, turned from the big white stove and glared at Mr. Fletcher, holding a spatula in her hand.

The children were sitting about the large round white table in the kitchen, heads bent, eyes peering warily from under narrowed lids. The hot electric light beat down upon them, revealing, without compassion, each wild face, each tense chin and curled hand on the linen tablecloth. Mrs. Burnsdale, a middle-aged woman who resembled Mrs. Grant remarkably, was particularly indignant at these "invaders," and disposed to look without kindness on the young man who had brought them to this proper parsonage. Edith, tall, nervous, temperamental, and very thin, was her niece, and Mrs. Burnsdale never let any occasion pass without mentioning that Edith was "only" assisting her here, because help was almost impossible to find in New York these days. Edith, she would say, looking reproachful, had had a high-school education, and had been admitted to a nursing school "in one of

New York's big hospitals, I can tell you!" Though this was definitely untrue, it was a pleasant fiction which enhanced both Edith's and Mrs. Burnsdale's position, they believed, with those who might be inclined to "take advantage" of them.

Dr. Stevens, sitting nearby in the vast warm kitchen, felt new depression. Why could not people learn that "service," whether in a kitchen, a pulpit, a factory, an office, or anywhere, as a matter of fact, carried no degradation with it except in the mind of the one who "served"? We all serve, he thought angrily, and who was the greatest Servant of all? God Himself. Had He not washed the dusty, calloused feet of His own disciples, in the supreme gesture of revealing to them the honor of service, the dignity of service?

"Edith ain't—isn't—a nursemaid, and neither am I!" said Mrs. Burnsdale in her gruff and sullen voice. "We always said—if a minister came here with kids, he'd have to have a nursemaid for 'em. Two maybe, if there was more than two kids. And kids like these! Dr. Stevens!" She whirled on the wilted old man. "You never told us Mr. Fletcher'd bring wild Indians here! We don't have to stand for it."

Dr. Stevens glanced at Johnny. But Johnny was watching the children tenderly, his youthful face full of compassion and weariness. He seemed totally unaware of anyone in the kitchen but those three boys and two little girls.

"There he goes again!" cried Edith, shrinking elaborately away from the sink with a gross imitation of terror. Mrs. Burnsdale rushed to her side, brandishing the spatula. Max, the lumpish, silent one, was washing his hands feverishly under the faucet, over and over, rubbing at the nails, the palms. They were already excoriated from long washing, the skin corroded. Max noticed neither the women nor the men. He moaned as he scrubbed, the suds foaming about his fingers, and then, to Dr. Stevens's broken-hearted pity, tears burst over his cheeks.

Johnny said in a calm, low voice, as the children avidly watched the boy, "It's all right, Max. Max, it's all right. You know there wasn't any stain at all, any time. Do you hear me, son?"

The boy shrank up against the sink and stared at Johnny, who smiled comfortingly. "Son, son," the boy stammered. Then he sobbed: "Papa! Papa!" He crouched, and he wrung his hands, and sobbed louder in anguish: "Papa! Papa!" He pushed his fingers through that dry hair of his, so that it was a bush of agony about his square and distraught face.

Oh, my God, thought Dr. Stevens. What is it? What is it?

Johnny still sat, but he held out his arms to Max. "Come to Papa, Max," he said. The children were completely silent, each tormented young face fixed as if in stone, waiting.

Max was shuddering, bent over, and the two women regarded him with indignant revulsion. This was no "nice" American boy, playful and rosy and natural, full of laughter and mischief. This was some awful "foreigner," with a guttural voice. "Crazy," muttered Mrs. Burnsdale, and put her arm protectingly about her niece. "Guess we'd better leave. They're all crazy."

"It was just a bad dream, Max," said Johnny, and his voice was full and sweet and commanding. "See, I'm your Papa. You never hurt me, son, never. Come."

Very slowly, the boy lifted his head and fastened eyes which appeared sightless on Johnny's merciful and loving face. Moment after moment passed; the boy's sobs became fewer. They subsided to a catch in his breath. He still looked at Johnny. And then, very faintly, questioningly, he said, "Papa? *Bist Du mein Papa?*"

"*Ja, das bin Ich,*" said Johnny, and he laughed affectionately.

Yes, thought Dr. Stevens, Our Father always replies: It is I. Would that shattered boy hear the universal answer? "Come," said Johnny in English. "Come, my son."

Max inched away from the sink, as if drawn by hypnotism, toward Johnny. He bumped into the table, without knowing; he pushed against Jean, without seeing. And then he was in Johnny's arms, held against Johnny's breast, and clinging. The children gave vent to a long deep sigh, and clenched hands on the tablecloth relaxed. Johnny said to Dr. Stevens, over the boy's frantic head, "He never remembers any German except when he washes his hands. Or in nightmares. I taught him English, didn't I, Max? We only speak English, don't we? Max knows a lot of English."

"Yes," said Max, from the shelter of Johnny's arms. "Only English. I—am—an—American—boy. You—are—my—Papa."

"That's right," said Johnny. "And Papa wants you to go and sit at the table and eat like an American boy."

Max clung tighter. Johnny said, with some paternal sternness, "Max, you are a big boy. You must help me with the little ones. Go, and show them how to eat, like an American boy. Remember? I showed you."

Pietro, the dark "monkey-boy," suddenly began to pound on the table with a big spoon. "Sit down, Max, sit down!" he clamored. The other children took up the cry, and Edith, muffling a scream, ran out of the kitchen. Johnny remained calm. Max heard the shout, however, and he left Johnny and slowly approached the table and sat down. So, they have a discipline among them, Dr. Stevens commented to himself. Pietro shoved Max's shoulder, and screamed laughter at him. The other children laughed with him, not the laughter of joyous young folk, but the thin, shrill laughter of anthropoids in a zoo, hysterically moved to a primordial mirth. Max was laughing, too, but it was a sheepish, human laugh, and Johnny must have heard it, for some of the tenseness left his mouth.

"Eat, eat," said Max admonishingly to the little girls and Pietro, after the laugh died away in one last howl. Jean glared at him from under the falling locks of his tan-colored hair, and then he must have decided that he, the elder, was losing some of his authority. He scowled in a masculine fashion at the girls and Pietro, and spoke loudly. "Eat, eat. Good food."

Johnny pressed the palms of his hands together, and his shoulders relaxed. "We make improvements and advances all the time," he muttered to Dr. Stevens. He rose and went to the sink and took up a knife. "I'll cut up the meat, kids," he said. "Steak. Juicy American steak. Just for you. Move your arm, Kathy. Don't grab, Pietro, girls come first. Ladies come first. There you are, Emilie, baby. Cut in little pieces for you."

Why doesn't he let them have knives? Dr. Stevens questioned himself. And then he saw the fierce expression on the faces of Jean and Pietro, a glittering and avaricious expression, as they fascinatedly watched the flashing movements of the knife. This is bad, very bad, thought Dr. Stevens, with new dismay. Really, they should not be here at all. If Johnny could bring them only this far in ten months, how long will it take before they are civilized? Those boys! They look like cutthroats, watching the knife. I'll have to lock my door tonight.

Mrs. Burnsdale must have had exactly the same thought, for she marched thunderingly across the gay yellow and red linoleum to Dr. Stevens, and planted herself heavily before him. "Edith and I are leaving tonight, Dr. Stevens," she said firmly. "No, right away. Our lives ain't—aren't—safe. No, sir."

Johnny continued to move about the table, cutting up the meat, smiling, and the eyes of Jean and Pietro watched the knife, and the gleam on their faces became sharper and more cunning. It was evident that they were thinking that if one knife was available here, there were probably others. But why should they want them? Normal boys, it was true, thought Dr. Stevens, like pocketknives. But these were not normal boys, and their desire for knives was not normal.

Was Johnny mad? Dr. Stevens half started up in his chair. For Johnny was laying the knife beside the plate of Jean. He was smiling down at him thoughtfully. Then he said, "Jean, you're too big now to have me cut up your meat. You know how to use a knife. Pick it up, son, and cut your own meat, and show the others."

The children had lifted meat on blunt forks. But now they had frozen again, watching Jean. Jean's eyes fixed themselves on the sharp steel beside his hand. The eyes narrowed, the face tightened, and an evil light shone on it. Johnny was close to him, too close to him! Jean did not touch the knife yet. He merely stared at it, and drops of saliva appeared at the corners of his mouth. His muscles tensed, and then his fingers crawled to the deadly thing, slyly. In a second he would have it, and then he would spring—!

"Pick it up, Jean," commanded Johnny. "It's for meat. Pick it up!"

The crawling fingers stopped; something in that barbarous mind must have stopped too, something too violent to contemplate. Mrs. Burnsdale, watching too, moved backward to the door, the spatula fanning back and forth in front of her, as if preparing for attack. The insane eyes of the boy halted; the squeezed lids opened more. And then the eyes were lifting to Johnny, were directed at him. It was like watching an animal changing into a human being, or a madman slowly realizing that his madness was passing.

"You want me—have the knife?" whispered Jean. He was trembling visibly. He licked dry lips.

"Yes, Papa wants you to have the knife, to cut up your meat. Look, Kathy's meat isn't all cut yet. Ladies first, Jean."

The small hand, the human, seeking hand, touched the knife, shrank away, then touched it again. Some fearful drama was taking place in the secret places of the boy's heart, the untamed places. Some fearful memories lay there, palpitating. And then Jean was shaking his head from side to side. "No—Papa. Can't cut meat yet. Don't—don't know how. Papa cut meat for Jean, and Kathy."

Johnny sighed with humorous impatience. "All right, just this once, Jean. But after this, you do it at every meal. Hear me?"

Jean was silent; the children were silent. Then Jean said, humbly, "Okay, Papa." He seemed smaller in the chair, and it was almost a normal boy's face which stared around the table.

"I want knife!" cried Pietro, bouncing up and down, his hands flying. "Give Pietro knife!"

Johnny held the knife in his hand. He looked at Jean. "Well, Jean, shall I give the knife to Pietro?"

Jean still did not speak. But his eyes turned to Pietro. And then, touchingly. his expression imitated Johnny's, thoughtful, a little stern, contemplating. He said, "No, no knife for Pietro. Too—too young. Papa cut Pietro's meat." He pointed a commanding finger at the younger boy. "Pietro shut up and eat, or Jean slap his face. See? Pietro behave himself."

"Jean cut Pietro's meat!" shouted the dark little boy, his black curls tossing about his forehead. "Pietro won't behave if Jean don't cut his meat!" He was getting out of control.

Jean, his crippled side sagging, got painfully to his feet. He was smiling at Johnny, as if embarrassed at the antics of Pietro. He held out his hand, and Johnny, not hesitating an instant, gave the boy the sharp knife. Jean looked at it in his palm. There was a loud banging, and Dr. Stevens knew that Mrs. Burnsdale had fled, and was locking a door behind her. Engrossed, Dr. Stevens saw that Jean was balancing the knife, tentatively judging it.

"For meat," he murmured in a dazed, wondering voice.

"For meat, for food," said Johnny encouragingly. "Not for killing, not ever again, Jean. My son."

Pietro was tossing himself about in his chair. But he was cunningly watching Jean, and his open mouth was wet and slavering.

Jean suddenly said loudly, "Shut up, you—you Pietro! Shut up!"

The younger boy subsided as if shot. Jean had lifted his left hand threateningly, in the immemorial gesture of an older brother about to discipline a younger. Then Jean, dragging himself slowly, moved to Pietro, stood beside him, took up his fork and, using the knife clumsily, began to cut up the little boy's meat. Again the children were watching, in that dreadful wariness of theirs. Sweat was coming out in beads on Jean's bony white cheekbones and forehead; his hands were shaking. But piece by piece the steak was being reduced to fragments. Pietro was as tight as a spring, his nostrils distended. A growl came from him, less from his mouth than from his whole body. Max was whimpering. The little girls—and how much more civilized little girls were than boys, Dr. Stevens was thinking—merely sat and scrutinized Jean eagerly.

The job was done. Jean moved backward from the table. He looked at Johnny. Johnny smiled at him, and after a moment Jean smiled. He put the knife in Johnny's hand, not reluctantly, but as if in relief. He said, "Jean is a good boy, *non?*"

"Jean is Papa's oldest son," said Johnny. "Thank you, Jean."

Now the children were eating, grossly. Even Pietro was eating. From time to time he shot Jean a marveling, baffled glance.

"Well, kids," said Johnny, "I'm going into the library to talk with Dr. Stevens. Jean, you take care of things. Max, you do as Jean says, and help Emilie. Pietro, you pass the bread and butter. Kathy, be sure the boys use their napkins, and don't slop anything on the table. Kathy?"

"Yes, Papa," replied Kathy primly. That touching, managing, maternal look had appeared on her common-sense face. "The boys won't slop. I'll hit them." She glowered at the three boys, twitched her long yellow braid.

The two men sat in the library, Johnny smoking his pipe, Dr. Stevens indulging himself in a cigar. The door stood open; they could hear what was going on in the kitchen. Kathy scolded occasionally; Jean commanded. Sometimes there was a brief shuffle, or a cry. It sounded almost normal, a household full of brothers and sisters. But sometimes the normality was gone, and there was a sharp, wolflike silence, and Johnny and Dr. Stevens listened anxiously. Then a childish voice asked a question, there was an answer, a clatter of china.

"I couldn't stand it, Johnny," Dr. Stevens confessed. "And, you know, the congregation won't stand it. Just as Edith and Mrs. Burnsdale won't. Those two are packing right now, you know."

"Yes," said Johnny, and he was very tired again. "You know, sir, I have always been, well, sort of idealistic. You told me that idealism is very fine, provided one sticks close to reality. I thought that perhaps the congregation would understand; in fact, I was sure of it. Aren't Americans the kindest people in the world, sending food everywhere, taking up collections, sheltering children—?"

"Americans," said Dr. Stevens wryly, "are very simple people. Give charity to the desperate, help the helpless, civilize the uncivilized, be merciful to those cruelly treated, give money, money, money, generously, wherever it will help. But for God's sake, don't bring victims too close! Aren't there organizations, set up by suprlus cash, to help, and let the rest of the world live pleasantly in the delusion that everything, really, is very nice for most people, and happiness, with few exceptions, is the general lot? The grand delusion of America—keep smiling, keep everything agreeable, save the surface and you save all."

He pulled quite savagely on his cigar. "Two wars only two decades apart, and we haven't grown up! Parades, bands, housing, playgrounds, speeches, politicians, birthdays, PTA, celebrations, cars, washing machines, airplanes, glittery gadgets—these are the all-important things. But perhaps we ought to understand. Perhaps Americans know, deep in the baseball-loving hearts of them, that, if given the same opportunities as a Mussolini or a Hitler or a Stalin, they'd be exactly like them! Perhaps that's the frightful truth they don't want to face."

"You didn't say that before, sir," said Johnny.

"But I knew it," replied Dr. Stevens grimly.

"Two thousand years of Christianity, and we haven't come any further?" said Johnny sadly.

Dr. Stevens shook his head. "No further. Not perceptibly further. Except for a few ministers and priests and rabbis. But they were always there, so we don't count them in."

"So, God became flesh, and died on Calvary—for nothing?" Johnny was leaning toward him, his youthful face furrowed, his pipe cupped in his hands.

Dr. Stevens was silent.

Johnny's voice was very soft. "God wastes nothing. He would not waste Himself."

Dr. Stevens said lamely, "Well, I suppose there are exceptions, among human beings."

Johnny smiled. He leaned back in his chair. "I'm going to find those exceptions, sir."

Dr. Stevens looked at his cigar. His face was less bitter, and very unsure. "A friend of mine, a priest, told me that saints aren't always in exalted positions. One can be in your kitchen, he said, or mowing your grass, or washing your windows. He can be at a machine in your factory. He can be your employer, your brother, the man who passes you on the street, who overtakes you in his car, who sells you ties or shoes. He can even be a politician!" Dr. Stevens laughed a little. "Well, I think he went too far, there!"

But Johnny was serious. "Your friend was right. Always in the most unexpected places, you can find saints. I'm going to look for them. I need their help. My children need them."

Dr. Stevens shook his head slightly. "Not in this congregation, Johnny! You're finished here, I'm afraid. I'll have to find another place for you. It's going to be very hard. News travels. You'll have to go to some obscure place, some poor church—someone, Johnny, who'll have you. And the children."

Johnny said, "I did, as you said when we first came in here, sound off a little too hard to those ladies and gentlemen. But, you see, I just couldn't believe it! I thought they'd understand. And then I saw they were just like the people in Europe, though they'd not suffered the way Europe had. I was disappointed, sir."

Johnny got to his feet, his face working, and he began to walk up and down in agitation.

"Americans would know; their kind hearts would ache for these children, who had no names, no homes, no nationality, no tongue, and who were only 'animals' and behaved like animals. And then I arrive here, today!" He paused, eloquently.

Dr. Stevens examined his cigar. "How did you find them, Johnny?"

The young minister resumed his restless pacing. "I went to Salzburg last October. I wanted a holiday; I'd heard Salzburg was a beautiful city. Place swarming with GIs, and I couldn't get a hotel room. But someone found me a place just outside the bridge, in a private home, very clean, very poor, but very pleasant. The Austrians are lively, friendly people—"

He stopped at the window and looked out at the avenue, dark, quiet, empty of crowds, with only an occasional cab flashing by with a silent scream of lights. But he was really seeing through his small window in the house "just outside the bridge" in Salzburg, in full sunshine. A narrow meadow, golden-starred with dandelions, and standing above it, a mountain shaggy with forests, streaked with gray stone outcroppings, patched with little fields of yellow wheat, sprinkled with little white houses with broad-tiled eaves. There was a house just opposite, just at the edge of the jasper meadow, its tidy little garden blowing with flowers and diapers on long strings, its grass tumbling with young children. And next to this house was another in the process of being built, not by carpenters and masons but by the whole family—father, mother, and two boys, one about twelve, the other about eight. A baby carriage stood under a tree, and sometimes it tossed vigorously. Johnny smiled, remembering, forgetting all the other things he had seen, the prankish palace of Markus Silicus, the grottos, the salt mines, the horrifying tour through the Alps in a jeep, and all the gloomy grandeur of peak after peak, fold after fold, and the massed purple of clouds in the passes.

"There was a family building a house," he said. "Papa in short leather pants, Mama with her hair tied up in a cloth, and an apron covering her black dress, the boys, serious and interested, in pants like Papa's. There had been a war only recently. The town had known Hitler; Berchtesgaden was right on the horizon. The storm troopers and the soldiers had marched over the cobbled streets. The Russians had been there—all the troops of the conquered and the conquering. Death had been there too—everywhere. And the sound of guns and bombs. And yet, there was that family building a house, of concrete blocks, the younger boy standing perched on a joist on top of the walls, and hauling up buckets of mortar which the older boy was mixing with his mother's help. There was Papa pounding vigorously with a hammer, and climbing up and down ladders, smoking a pipe all the while. Sometimes Mama would stop working to sit on a big stone and nurse the baby."

Johnny refilled his own pipe, and smiled that deep and tender smile of his. "I used to want to yell at them when they started the loud work in the morning, just about the time the sun was coming up. But I forgave them everything when the rooftree was installed. Mama brought a bouquet of field flowers, and Papa tied them solemnly among small branches, and carried the whole thing up slowly and prayerfully on the ladder, and fastened it on the rooftree. It was a very dedicated occasion. When Papa came down they knelt together, crossed themselves, and prayed, the whole family."

Johnny drew a deep breath. "I was pretty sick, up to then, sick of what I had seen. And I was bitter; I used to argue with God every night. That war had meant the end of everything—I thought. And then, there was the little family building that house, and there was that rooftree with its bouquet, and then, in spite of all that had happened, in spite of all the hatred and ruin and death and despair, there was that family praying together, starting again, sure in their faith that God had the answer and they were safe with Him. In more than one way, they were building in the shadow of a Mountain."

He stopped before Dr. Stevens, who was listening in fascination. Then his smile died away, and his face became somber and stern. "That was the good part. There is a part that isn't so good."

"I had lunch one day in an ancient fortress on a side of a mountain. You go up there on a funicular. The chef was doing his desperate best to serve a fine lunch to the 'nice people,' which now meant the Americans. I doubt he cared. It was his business to cook and make sauces and find wines for faceless but appreciative stomachs. That was his mission in life, and I drank a glass of wine to him, all alone, on the terrace."

He saw the wide green valley below the fortress, and beyond the valley the flat blue mountains against the flat blue sky. Mist flowed down between the painted peaks. He had looked at them long. Then his attention had been caught by something in the hot greenness of the valley: a tall, bleak, thatch-roofed house, stuccoed. It cast a sharp black shadow on the grass. There was nothing else there at all, but that house.

"There was only a white-walled house in the valley," he said. "I didn't know what it was. I only knew that there were no gardens around it, no signs of life. I don't know why, but it depressed me. I called a waitress, and she told me it was 'the executioner's house.' What executioner, I never did find out. I didn't want to know."

"So, Johnny?" said Dr. Stevens, for the young man's dark face had become lost and bitter.

"I couldn't stop looking at that house, sir, while I was on the terrace. There was something terrible about it for me now. It had a haunted look—monstrous. Its two rows of windows seemed full of evil faces. Ghosts of damnation. In all that sunshine, in that green, lifeless valley. An accursed place. I don't know how long I sat there, looking at it. It was almost sunset when I went away."

He impatiently relit his pipe, which had gone out, but Dr. Stevens knew that he was not really present in this lamplit library. The children were very silent in the kitchen. Were they listening?

"I went to the cathedral," Johnny was saying, "Dom Plaza. I didn't know anyone, and in my present mood I didn't want to know anyone. I walked through the streets when it was dark, with only a few lights here and there. I ate dinner at a PX which had just opened the day before. I was never so restless in my life. Something seemed to be calling me all the time, and my thoughts kept going back to the executioner's house. A moon was coming up, and the night was warm, though it was mountainous territory.

"And then I knew I had to go to the executioner's house, all alone in that big field, in the moonlight. It seemed a mad idea at first. Yet, there was such an urging—. I got into my jeep, and tore off, calling myself names. I was just tired; my mind was getting medieval, or something. What did I expect to find there? Ghosts?

"I parked the jeep near the old fortress, then went around it to the valley. And then I heard shouting and shrieking. A lot of men and women, looking like black specters in the moonlight, were racing across the valley, carrying clubs, toward the house. You never saw such an evil sight in your life! It was a nightmare.

"I began to run with them, wishing I was carrying a gun. I remember thinking that was a thought for a chaplain! But in some way I felt I had to get to that house with that mob, or before them. You never heard such damnable shrieking in all your life—like hell itself. I recognized the shrieking very well; I'd heard it before. It was the scream of blood lust. The mountains echoed it back; the very earth seemed to catch it up, and repeat it.

"I caught up with a man and grabbed his arm, and we almost fell down together as he tried to pull away from me. I held on to him, and demanded to know what it was all about. And he shouted at me, 'The wolf children! The wolf children! We're going to kill them!' He did pull away from me then, and flew off. I caught a woman hurtling by, her dress flying. 'What wolf children?' I asked her. She was panting, and I could see her teeth flashing like a fiend's in the moonlight. Then she saw my uniform, and stopped tugging away from me. She even cringed. She said, "Herr captain, the wolf children have been in Salzburg since the end of war. We don't know who they are. They hide, and only come out at night. They've even killed, for food, they say. They waylay late people on the streets. They break into houses and rob. They're not our people. And now we've heard they are hiding in the executioner's house!"

"Oh, merciful God!" murmured Dr. Stevens.

Johnny nodded. "That's what I said, sir, but I didn't say it in that tone of voice, believe me. I just threw the woman down on the ground, and ran after the others. They were already at the house. The door must have been locked, for they were beating on it with their sticks, and howling. Howling! The windows were small and high; some of the men were trying to get in them. And I kept wishing for a gun.

"I had never run so fast in all my life. The door was shaking before I got there. It was rattling on its hinges; they made good hinges in the old days. Somehow—it was now even worse than any nightmare—I got between the men and the door. And, like the women, they recognized my American uniform, my officer's uniform. And then a woman saw the cross on my lapel, and she must have thought I was a priest. She began to cry out, and pointed at it. The uniform—and the cross. Or, perhaps, only the cross. That stopped them."

"It always does, always," said Dr. Stevens.

"Well, sir, it did for a few minutes, anyway. I told them that if there were children in that house, young children, I was going after them, and I was going to protect them. I was going to take them away with me. They began to howl again, shaking their sticks in my face. They got so close to me that I could smell their sweat, and see their awful eyes, and feel their breath. If it hadn't been for the women, the older ones, they would have killed me, in spite of the cross.

"I shouted back at them. I probably even cursed them. That sobered them a little—a pastor cursing them! I asked them if there hadn't been enough of hatred and death. I asked them to remember their own children, safe in their beds. A man spat in my face, then spat on my uniform. I was a damned American. I had bombed their homes. I had killed them. The women muttered angrily. But still, there was that cross!"

"And?" asked Dr. Stevens, sitting on the edge of his chair. There was such a silence from the kitchen that he could feel it.

"Well, I listened to them. And then I said, 'Forgive me.'"

He waited, but Dr. Stevens, who was now quite pale and still, said nothing.

"So," said Johnny, "I stopped being enraged at those people, for what I said had sobered me, too. I just repeated, 'Forgive me.' The howling began to die down. Some of the women broke out crying. One even said, 'Oh, the poor children!' And I touched the cross that had saved not only the children, but these men and women."

He put down his pipe and pressed his hands convulsively over his face. When he removed them, there were marks like the tracks of tears over his cheeks.

"And do you know what those men and women, who had seen death and war and guns and bombs, said to me at last, crowding around me? They said, 'Forgive us, too.'"

He turned away, his back to Dr. Stevens. "We all went into the house together. It was as black as a pit in there. We told the children we wouldn't hurt them. They were hiding somewhere, and there was only the moonlight at the windows. The women crooned, as they crooned to their own children. I began to think that perhaps these children had been freed from, or had escaped from, concentration camps after the liberation. I tried what Italian I knew, what French I knew. And though we anxiously looked around, and talked softly, there wasn't any answer. Why should there have been? There was just silence, and that was all we deserved."

"But you found them, Johnny."

"Yes, in the cellar, crouched together against a wall, trying to protect each other. Baby Emilie, and Kathy, Pietro and Jean and Max. At bay, like the insane animals we had made them. In a heap, the boys trying to protect the little girls. You could hardly see them."

He swung about, his face working. "I can't talk much more about it, Dr. Stevens. Even now it's too terrible. But the men and the women helped me get the kids out. They scratched and bit and tore and barked like mad dogs. They were starved, almost naked, filthy. We had to carry them. They couldn't even speak a word; they fell out of our arms, tried to scuttle away on hands and knees. Somehow we got them to an army depot, and the women rushed away to get some clothing for them, clothing they couldn't spare. The men brought black bread and wine. I don't want to remember the next days! We had to tie the boys down, sometimes. The girls just tried to run away. You see, they all thought we really meant to kill them."

Johnny suddenly went out of the library, and his rapid footsteps carried him to the kitchen. Dr. Stevens sat alone, his lips moving silently. But he was saying over and over in his heart, "God have mercy upon me. Father, forgive me."

Johnny came back, smiling. "They're just eating their cake and drinking their milk. They are behaving themselves very well! If you think they're pretty bad now, you should have seen them ten months ago." He seemed to have recovered some poise. He even sat down on the edge of the table, and picked up his pipe.

There was the sound of firm and tramping feet in the corridor, and Edith and Mrs. Burnsdale marched in decidedly. "We're leaving, Dr. Stevens," said the older woman, ignoring Johnny. "We want our money."

Dr. Stevens regarded them coldly—the spindling Edith, who was sniffing pathetically, and glancing with affected fear over her shoulder, and the rocky Mrs. Burnsdale. "Your week isn't up," he said, knowing it was hopeless. "And you're needed here. In a few days Mr. Fletcher, and the children, will be leaving. He needs your help. Can't you give it to him, hard as it will be?"

Johnny slid from the table. He approached the angry Mrs. Burnsdale and looked down at her. "You know," he said, "I once thought people like you were kinder than—others. Kinder because you've had to work hard all your life. Kinder because you've suffered. But that's just one of the many lies I've been telling myself ever since I can remember."

His expression was severe, and he stared the woman down. She shifted her bag on her arm, threw up her head defiantly. "What!" she exclaimed. "Stay here and be murdered in our beds? Besides, what do you know about my kind of people anyway, Mr. Fletcher?"

He tried to smile. "Because I'm one of you. I was brought up in a small coal-mining town. I've had to earn my own living since I was thirteen years old. I suppose I should have had more sense. You're no better or worse than the ladies here this afternoon. Why should you be? You're only human."

Her eyes shifted a little. She tried to maintain her air of indignation.

"We'll be murdered in our beds!" wailed the witless Edith. "Come on, Auntie."

"Are you a coward, afraid of children, Mrs. Burnsdale?" asked Dr. Stevens, seeing a faint hope now.

But Johnny was speaking quietly. "You've heard of concentration camps, Mrs. Burnsdale? Well, those children came from there. They're orphans. Their parents have been killed. I taught them a little English, over ten months. They don't remember where they were born, or to whom. Why, the hungriest, dirtiest kid in Harlem, living in the worst tenement, has had a happy life compared with them! Are you a Christian, Mrs. Burnsdale?"

Shaken, she blinked her eyes. "I think I am, sir."

Edith was wailing. Her aunt turned on her abruptly. "Stop that, you idiot." She turned back to Johnny. He reached out and put his hand on her sturdy shoulder. She made as if to step back, then did not.

"We need you, Auntie," he said, and his face was all strong

sweetness again. "Just for a few days. I can't manage to feed these kids by myself. Just cook for them. Keep knives away from them—"

"Knives!" whimpered Edith.

"I'll be around, all the time," said Johnny, after Mrs. Burnsdale had thrown a devastating glance at her niece. "They won't bother you."

"I'm going home," said Edith. Everyone ignored her. Even when she shifted timorously toward the door, no one noticed.

"Let me tell you about Max, the second boy," said Johnny. "He speaks only English. He doesn't remember that at one time he spoke German. Only in nightmares. He doesn't remember anything, except in nightmares. Do you know what happened to Max, when he was probably about six years old? I heard the story, when he was asleep. The Nazis, who had him and his father in a concentration camp together, came to them one night and told them that tomorrow one of them would be hanged, and one of them would be forced to hang the other."

Mrs. Burnsdale put her gloved hand to her lips, and over it her eyes were aghast. "Yes," said Johnny, nodding. "And the father persuaded the little boy that he must be the one to have a chance of living. And so, the next day, with the help of a storm trooper, that little boy, young enough to be your grandson, was made to hang his father. That is why Max is dumb. That's why he washes his hands all the time—he's trying to wash them clean of killing his father. He doesn't remember the hanging; he only remembers he did something terrible, poor baby."

He half turned from the appalled woman. "So sometimes he asks me, 'Papa, is that you?' And I always say, 'Yes, my son.' And that helps. You see, Max is quite often on the point of losing what mind he has left, after the nightmares."

Mrs. Burnsdale began to cry. It was a curious sight; her big face worked, and then there were the tears, and she was fishing in her bag. "I—I can't believe—such things," she stammered.

"They're quite true," said Johnny. "Jean remembers the concentration camp quite well, in his own nightmares. He is probably a French boy, and in his dreams he speaks French. You ought to hear him some night! His parents were killed slowly before him. He tried to help his mother; a storm trooper attempted to kick him to death too. That's why he's crippled. That's why he is so wild, and hates people. That's why Jean killed, too, when he had a chance. But that was for food, and the man he killed was a lone Austrian soldier, standing on guard, after we Americans got in there. You see, the man had his lunch with him. Jean doesn't remember killing the soldier. All he remembers is that there was a time when he had to revenge his mother, and get food, with a knife. And he still has the idea, far back in his mind, that he must kill or be killed. Not now, not all the time, especially when he is awake. Just when he is off guard, and when he dreams."

"Oh, God be merciful to us!" said Mrs. Burnsdale in a muffled voice.

"I hope He will be," said Johnny with simplicity. "We need His mercy."

"I just can't stand listening to this!" shrilled Edith.

"And there is Pietro. I think he is an Italian boy. His parents were killed in a bombing raid on his little home in Italy. American bombers. He had an older brother. He told me about it, one night when he was more than half asleep. The Nazis, when they retreated from Italy, took the brother as a slave worker, and somehow he smuggled Pietro with him. Perhaps, in order to save the child from starvation, he offered to be a spy. I don't know; we'll never know. Anyway, they ended up in a concentration camp. Pietro's brother, Vittorio, evidently was too good an Italian to betray his country. The storm troopers had great fun with Vittorio one night. They killed him carefully, and without any hurry at all, with their knives, and Pietro saw it. So a knife means vendetta to Pietro; he wants knives so he can stab the men who murdered his brother. And to poor little Pietro, everyone who wears a uniform, including me, is somehow tied up with storm troopers in his child's mind, and a killer of his brother Vittorio."

Johnny paused. His voice had been very quiet, and its very quietness and lack of emotion had a fearful impact. Mrs. Burnsdale made no comment; her eyes were closed tightly and beneath her eyelids the tears streamed down.

Johnny went on, "Pietro's a very, very bright boy. He loves colors and music. He thinks. I expect he'll be a great artist someday. He's more dangerous than Jean, though he's younger. Jean hates openly; Pietro smiles, and hates in his heart. I have to watch Pietro all the time; he thinks every adult, especially any man, is his enemy, and had a part in killing his brother." Johnny rubbed his hands over his face again. "Sometimes I wonder if Pietro isn't right."

Edith had gained more courage. "If you don't come right away, Auntie, I'm going alone. You've heard what Mr. Fletcher says himself. Dangerous. Knives! There's the cab waiting."

Mrs. Burnsdale turned slowly to her niece and impaled her with her light-gray eyes. "If you dare leave this house," she began. Johnny and Dr. Stevens exchanged a quick smile. Johnny said, "Let Edith go, Mrs. Burnsdale. We don't want anyone around the children who doesn't understand and pity them. And Edith's right: if she shows the children she's afraid of them, why, like all wild things, they'll give her cause to be afraid!"

Edith fled, snatching up her suitcase. They heard the banging of the door outside. The children were making strange noises in the kitchen—unrelated words, slurred phrases, grunts, little squeals, then silence.

Johnny took Mrs. Burnsdale's short thick arm and gently seated her. She sat like a boulder, still weeping, but still indomitable. There was an air of resolution about her as she waited for Johnny to speak again. He said, "It sounds like a zoo, doesn't it? Well, the children have learned English from me, and so, just as very young children try to communicate with each other with a limited vocabulary, these five try to communicate. But it's a funny thing. I can talk quickly in English to them, and I often think they understand more than seems possible."

He wiped Mrs. Burnsdale's wet cheeks with his own handkerchief. She did not move, and only waited.

"There's Kathy," he said. "She thinks she's ugly; she was told that. She thinks she'll have to die, because she's ugly. She steals mirrors. Who knows what Kathy thinks, besides that? I don't. She must have come from a competent family, either German or Dutch or Danish. From the way she acts sometimes, I don't think she spent too long a time in a concentration camp. She's too neat and efficient, and likes to domineer and take care of the younger children. So it's my opinion she was the oldest daughter of a young family, and her mother's helper. Middle-class people. Kathy doesn't talk in her sleep, except about her 'ugliness' and mirrors. She never mentions her parents, or anyone else. But all her family must have died. Incidentally, Kathy has a long burn scar on her lower back, eight inches wide. Sometimes I wonder whether Kathy escaped, in some way, from a crematorium. You see, she's very much afraid of fire. The only time I've seen her hysterical is when she sees a flame, and there are times when I strike a match and she goes to pieces."

Mrs. Burnsdale put her gloved hands to her ears, and began to rock on the chair in the ancient movement of grief. Dr. Stevens stared at the floor, his cigar dead in his hand. He seemed ill and stricken, and Johnny went to him, concerned. "Dr. Stevens?" he asked anxiously. "Are you all right?"

The old man said, "I'm just wondering whether God will ever forgive us, any of us, anywhere in the world. I'm not too sure, Johnny."

Johnny said, "Neither am I. Well, there's just baby Emilie to talk about now. I think she spent every day of her life, until she escaped with the others, in a concentration camp, and she never learned to talk at all until I taught her. Five years old, I should judge. She has something wrong with her heart, and she may never grow up. I've had the best army doctors examine her. They think she was used for some experimentation by the German doctors. A guinea pig, as they say. Her blood was full of some obscure drug; it's almost eliminated now, but her heart's twice the size it ought to be. Dilation. She can't sleep lying down; she has to sleep propped up on pillows. She cried only in her sleep, whimpering like a puppy. There may be a chance for her life, if she finally is convinced someone really loves her and cares for her."

He walked up and down, up and down, and now he wrung his hands in the way Max wrung his. "Before I could bring the children here they had to have a series of injections. The needle was brought to Emilie. She collapsed when she saw it. We thought she had died. It took oxygen, over several days, to bring her around. Only a baby, and she almost died of fright. We had to give her an anesthetic, which almost killed her, before the injections could be given. So much for Emilie."

He lifted his hands, let them drop. "Only five children. Think of the millions of them who died, just as these children might have died, for the same reasons. I don't know how they were spared. I don't even know how they got together in Salzburg. I only know they were living together, in any abandoned, bomb-shattered building they could find. I only know that they trust each other, understanding each other. And all I know now is that they'll have to learn to trust me, and everyone else, or they'll surely die."

His face was gleaming with sweat. He passed his hands distractedly through his hair. "I can't tell them about God. Not yet. You see, it was 'Christian' people who did these things to them. I baptized them myself, but I didn't explain what it was all about. If I tell them about God they're going to have some very pertinent questions to ask, and I'm not ready to try to answer them. It's still too much for me."

Mrs. Burnsdale got to her feet. She said, in her loud voice, "It's nearly nine o'clock, and those children are still in the kitchen. You men should be ashamed of yourselves! What about their baths, and their beds?"

She pulled off her coat, gloves, and hat, and glared at the two ministers, mumbling to herself. Then she marched out of the library.

Johnny, anxious again, started after her. But Dr. Stevens said, "How in the name of all that's holy did you finally get them here?"

The young man smiled darkly. "Oh, I had some time, believe me! I had to fill out hundreds of forms. I had to sponsor them, as my foster children. I had to put up five hundred dollars apiece as bond, to the U.S. Immigration Service, that they wouldn't become public charges here. I had only half the money, myself. But the fellows in the Army helped me. They raised the rest. And there was a lot left over, about two thousand dollars, to help me along with the kids when I got them here."

Dr. Stevens said, "I'm not a rich man, Johnny. Before you leave here I'm giving you a check for the children, for one thousand dollars. And I'll help at any other time."

Arm in arm, they hurried to the kitchen, then paused on the threshold, incredulous. Mrs. Burnsdale had taken command. She had known shrewdly, at once, what to do. She was speaking slowly and firmly: "You, Kathy. Emilie will have

51

her bath first, and you'll give it to her. Then you'll take one yourself. Kathy, I'm depending on you as my helper."

Kathy stood up at attention, prim, ready, and competent. To the men's astonishment she bent her head politely at Mrs. Burnsdale and said, "Yes, Mutter." Dr. Stevens and Johnny gaped at each other for a moment. Kathy placed her hands on Emilie's little shoulder and said severely, "Come. Bath." Emilie slid from her chair, obediently, staring, and Kathy gripped the infant hand. "First of all," said Mrs. Burnsdale, "you say good night to your Papa."

Johnny could not believe it. Kathy was actually curtsying to him, as if remembering an old lesson. Then she was curtsying to Dr. Stevens. "Good night," she said, in a well-bred little girl's voice. Then she took Emilie, without any further nonsense, out of the room.

The boys were as dumfounded as the two ministers. So, thought Dr. Stevens, it is a woman they need. The boys turned their heads slowly to the ministers, baffled. Johnny laughed. "You see, fellows, when the ladies take over you don't ask questions."

Mrs. Burnsdale said, "They're only children, and they're going to mind me. You're Jean, the big boy. All right, dinner's over. You take that one—Pietro, is it? Good. You give him his bath, then take one yourself. And if you let him run around the house afterward, you'll hear from me, young man! I've got a hard hand. Raised four children of my own." She displayed a large hand under Jean's astounded nose, and then he nodded meekly. "Yes, Maman," he murmured. He dragged himself to his feet and seized Pietro's arm. The little boy resisted. "Come—on," said Jean, scowling ferociously. Pietro howled, half under his breath. But Jean dragged him from the chair, and they went out together, Pietro protesting, but not convincingly.

Now there was Max. Mrs. Burnsdale approached him, stood by his side. He stared vacantly before him, his lips moving. "Max?" said the woman. He shivered, did not answer. "Max," said Mrs. Burnsdale. "Say good night. To your Papa, Max. To your Papa. He never went away."

Max's face remained empty, stupefied. Then Mrs. Burnsdale bent her thick body over him and kissed him on the forehead, and put her arm about his neck. He started wildly. "Papa?" he screamed. "Papa!"

Johnny went to him. "Here is Papa, Max," he said. He lifted Max in his arms, and the boy wound his arms about his neck, sobbing. "Papa will give Max his bath, and put him to bed," said Johnny, and he carried the boy from the kitchen, murmuring to him.

Mrs. Burnsdale and Dr. Stevens looked at each other for a long moment. Then she said decidedly, "You'll have to find another housekeeper, Dr. Stevens. I'm sorry. But that young man needs a woman's help, and where he goes I'm going too. No matter where it is. That Edith!" she added, looking at the heaps of dishes on the sink and table. "Just when I need her. But she was never any good, honestly. Well, I'll wash the dishes when I've got the children safe in bed. Too bad," she continued, on the way to the door, "that I can't hear their prayers."

Dr. Stevens was alone in the huge hot kitchen. He pondered. Then he took off his coat and his tie. He found a large towel and tied it across his plump middle. He found the dishpan and soap. He began to hum to himself, his face brightening. He plunged his hands into suds, and his humming grew louder, as if some pain had eased in him.

4

The Reverend John Fletcher, standing on the parsonage steps in the early hot August day, surveyed his flock thoughtfully. And they surveyed him as thoughtfully, for this was the first time they had ever seen him in his clerical black. As he had hoped, the discarding of his uniform had given the children a little more confidence in him, for inevitably they had associated that uniform with the terror that had all but destroyed them.

The clothing the UNRRA had been able to produce for them had covered them adequately, but that was the best that could be said about it. His blue eyes began to sparkle. Pretty dresses for the girls, American T shirts and blue jeans for the boys, and nice Sunday clothes! Why, in the right kind of clothing these children would be indistinguishable from American children! Johnny firmly believed that while clothes did not make the man they certainly helped him to become a man.

Traffic streamed by, aroar with cabs and automobiles and crowds, the sun shattering back from a thousand wide, hot windows. Thank God for New York, thought Johnny.

Though the children were dressed in a most peculiar fashion, standing about him on the brownstone steps, no passer-by stared at them inquisitively. People minded their business in big cities. In fact, no one had peered at the children in Rome or Paris, or even London, that most proper place. He, Johnny, had thought of buying regulation clothing for "my children" in the smaller city where they would eventually live, and then he had remembered that smaller cities are more curious, more censorious, than mighty cities. When they all arrived—somewhere—they would look just like all the other children, and who cared about the expense? God would take care of His own, thought Johnny, trying to forget the concentration camps and the executioner's house.

Pietro reached out his brown prehensile hand and touched Johnny's black coat. He was very still, and he had begun to frown. "Yes, son?" asked Johnny. The boy looked up at him with those fathomless eyes of his; a spark glittered there. A spark of memory of some old priest in that forgotten village? "Padre?" murmured the little boy uncertainly. Johnny felt his heart lift. "Padre," he replied. Pietro laughed wildly, but his hand still clutched Johnny's coat. It was the first time he had ever touched the young minister voluntarily. His feet shuffled, as if dancing. Now Jean was studying him. His lips worked. Then he burst out, triumphantly, "Abbé! Abbé!" "Abbé!" answered Johnny, and to himself he said, "Thank You, Father." He glanced hopefully at Max, but Max was like a dreaming statue of a homeless boy. Little Emilie, so pale and pretty in the sunlight, with all that mass of tumbling curls down her small thin back, and her great pale-blue eyes watching the boys, clung to Kathy's hand. Emilie was all wonder. Kathy studied Johnny, pursed up her lips, meditating. Then her round face lighted up. "Fadder!" she exclaimed triumphantly. "Fadder," Johnny answered, nodding at her. She hugged Emilie. "Papa—Fadder," she explained severely. Emilie looked confused. "She's just a baby," Johnny said. "She doesn't know anything yet. We'll teach her, won't we, Kathy?"

"Baby," agreed Kathy. Her right hand was tightly closed about something, and Johnny knew it was Mrs. Grant's compact. He said, "I'll buy you a bag today, Kathy, and you'll put the mirror in it." He hesitated. "Why don't you let me put it in my pocket, honey?"

She withdrew from him, her round eyes narrowing, and she shook her head so violently that her braid swung from side to side. Some of Johnny's hopefulness left him. His eyes turned to the big brownstone church next door, its brazen cross afire in the sun. He pondered. Was it too early to start teaching the children something? He said after a few moments, "See that? It's a church. Let's go in." He knew that he would never preach there now.

"Church?" said Jean. His cheekbones were very white, like naked bone, in the sunlight. Johnny repeated, "Church. God's house." He looked for some response in Jean, in Kathy. Nothing answered him but blankness. Yet, they had said "Abbé" and "Fadder." They did not remember a church, then—any church—but only some priest who, probably a fugitive himself, had tried to give them comfort before he had died or had been dragged away. "God," repeated Johnny anxiously. The children shook their heads at him, and, as they always did when they did not understand him, they retreated and formed a small pack together. He held out his hand to them, struggling for words. He said, "Dio? Dieu? Gott?" Four of the children, Max, Emilie, Kathy and Pietro, looked confused and uncertain. But to Johnny's horror, Jean began to snarl, under his breath, and his face became a distortion of hatred. Ah, thought Johnny, so he remembers a little, and he remembers that there was no help anywhere, deep in the subconscious recesses of him. He said to the boy, "Not Dieu, not God, Jean, my son. Only men. They shut you away from Him." Jean's snarl was louder, but he blinked, and shook his head as if trying to recall something. Now the children, following Jean, their leader, began to mutter, and Johnny knew that he would never get used to that dreadful sound. He took Kathy's hand hastily. He said to Jean, who was glaring at him with those hot and hating eyes, "Remember, Jean? You take care of the boys, Max and Pietro. You're my oldest son. I'll take the girls into the church, and you bring the others. Mind, now." He gazed at Jean sternly, staring him down.

Jean stood in silence, the yellowish-brown lock falling over his forehead. He was obdurate, and Max and Pietro stood on each side of him, just as obdurate. Then Kathy spoke up in her new schoolteacher voice, and peremptorily: "Jean—big boy. Jean bring little boys. Follow Papa and Kathy and Emilie." Johnny turned to her in grateful surprise. She was eying the boys coldly. She was younger than Jean, but masterful in her maternal way. "Follow," she repeated. She tugged at Emilie, and marched toward the church with determination. Johnny laughed weakly. "What can we fellows do when a woman tells us what to do?" he asked.

Pietro giggled. Max had gained a little life. He smiled faintly. Jean glared after Kathy. "I'm oldest," he said, and the awful light went out of his eyes. He warned Pietro and Max with a glance, seized Pietro's hand and Max's arm. Then he looked at Johnny again, and his eyes wandered up and down the black coat and fixed themselves on the white clerical collar. "Papa—Abbé—first," he said.

Well, thank You again, Father, thought Johnny, humbly. He went down the parsonage steps. Would the boys really follow? There was a silence behind him. And then, in gratitude, he heard the small feet shuffling close on his heels. Johnny waited till a clot of people passed, then hurried. The boys kept together, not glancing at the men and women who rushed by them unheedingly. They never looked at people if they could avoid it.

Kathy drew Emilie aside as Johnny approached the big polished brown door of the church. The boys stood below on the steps. A notice had been fastened on the door. "Services every second and fourth Sunday during July and August, at 10 A.M. Communion on last Sunday." Johnny, his hand on the doorknob, looked at the notice for several long moments, then his face darkened. So God was available in this church, His church, only on certain designated occasions, was He? He wasn't needed except "every second and fourth Sunday during July and August—at 10 A.M." Let a man falter in despair, or an anguished woman contemplate suicide—they'd just have to wait for the second or fourth Sunday.

"Papa's church?" asked Kathy, curious as to why Johnny still stood there.

Johnny looked at the church. "Not Papa's church, I'm afraid, dear," he said. Nevertheless, he turned the doorknob. The door was locked. He stepped back and studied it. "Definitely not Papa's church," he added. He was sick at heart. He had seen so many cathedrals and churches all over Europe, and they had always been open. He had forgotten that most Protestant churches are closed except on Sundays and on special occasions. He had had only one church and congregation himself before he had become a chaplain in 1940. A little humble church—but the door had never been closed, in spite of the protests of the board and the sexton.

He did not know what to do. He had wanted to introduce the children to a church for the first time. He was frustrated. His angry eye wandered down the avenue, then halted suddenly. In the distance was another cross against the fierce blue sky of summer. "I think," he said, "we'll just go around —looking for God. We might find Him somewhere."

He went down to the street again, the children following closely.

"Dresses?" asked Kathy hopefully. "Shoes?" demanded Jean, pulling the boys with him.

"First," said Johnny, "we'll see if God is anywhere around. There's just the slightest possibility He is. I want you to meet Him, and the clothes will come later."

"Don't want to meet God," protested Pietro. He was becoming excited by the sights and the noise of the city. Johnny said, "Well, in a way, I don't blame you. But I have a feeling He wants to meet you, Pietro."

"Max afraid of God," said Max, in his low, wandering voice. He pulled away from Jean and began to cry soundlessly. "God want to kill Max?"

Johnny sighed. He had taken Emilie's other hand. The children waited fearfully for his answer. Tell me what to tell them, Lord, he prayed. He said, "You know I love you, don't you?" He looked from one small face to another. "You know I'll always love you. Sometimes you forget, and you hurt me, right in here." He put his hand over his heart. Max stopped crying. They all watched Johnny solemnly. "You know what it means to hurt in here. Well, that's the way you hurt me. Do you like to hurt me?"

Jean glanced away, embarrassed. Then he said, "The boys —don't like—to hurt Papa."

He smiled at them tenderly. "Well, you do, often. You keep forgetting. I'm your papa. But who is the Papa of all of us, me as well as you? Who loves all of us, everybody in the world, in spite of all the people's badness? Well, God! God is our Papa. The world often forgets Papa, our Father, and does wicked things, just as you do them. But I don't forget you, and I never stop loving you. That's the way it is with God—our Papa, our Father."

They listened, but they did not believe. He could see the wary flicker in their eyes. No one had helped them but this man. They doubted if anyone else ever would. So, Papa was lying to them, and if he lied to them he was not to be trusted. Fear whitened their faces.

"I tell you what," said Johnny. "I'll let you meet God, and if you don't like Him we'll go right away. How's that?"

Jean asked, "What does He look like—God?"

Here come the questions! thought Johnny. If he confessed he had never seen God the children would be utterly confused, utterly frightened. He smiled mysteriously. "Beautiful, beautiful," he said. "I'm not going to spoil it for you. You must see for yourself."

It would have to be a church with statues, and altars, and candlelight. He took Emilie's wet little hand and laughed happily. "First we'll just look in the door, and see if God's there. If He isn't we'll go away, and buy the clothes."

He marched ahead with Kathy and Emilie. The boys trotted behind. People dodged around them impatiently. The children were now extremely curious. Kathy shouted up at Johnny, remembering last night, "God like a lady, like Mrs. Burnsdale. God rock Emilie in a chair too?" Her pink face was lighting up.

"God," said Johnny, "is like Papa and Mrs. Burnsdale." He began to worry. How to explain the Imponderable, the Invisible, the Almighty, to these children so they would understand?

The roar of the city swallowed them. The boys were stumbling on Johnny's heels, the girls crowding him. Then, even above the roar Johnny could hear Pietro's shrill laughter. "Pietro know!" he screamed. "God big Papa, like my Papa!"

"Shut up," said Jean, to Johnny's thankfulness, for some people had stopped to stare, to look over their shoulders, to become aware of this strange troupe. Johnny was sweating, and his heart was hurrying. But he dared not stop; the cross was some distance away, disappearing now behind the bulk of the buildings. It's always that way, he thought. You can't see God for man and all his works.

It was a big church, of rough gray stone. Its doors were

wide open, and a few men and women were going in and out, singly or together. "See," said Johnny. "God's at home, after all. See the people. They are going in to talk to Him, just as we are. They are going to tell Him where they hurt, and He will help them. He always does."

He pointed to the fiery cross against the swimming blueness of the sky. "That's His Sign. It means He's at home, and waiting for us."

The boys halted. Jean studied Johnny closely. "He will make my leg straight, and this, my arm, if I ask Him?"

Johnny's face changed. He had had Jean carefully examined by the best Army doctors and others in Europe. One or two had suggested a series of operations, but not too hopefully. The majority had said nothing could be done at all. The boy was incurably crippled; his bones had not set right years ago. "If I ask Him?" Jean repeated, with a sly smile.

Johnny looked up at the cross, praying, his heart heavy. He could not lie to this child; he could never betray him.

Johnny's eyes were suddenly wet. Then all at once the cross seemed to expand against the sky in a burst of unbearable light; its arms quivered with radiance like the sun, through Johnny's tears. It soared in a circle of luminous flame. Johnny's heart trembled as he watched. Then the cross was just a bright cross again, on the steeple. But Johnny knew.

He put his hands on Jean's shoulders. He said, and his voice was loud and clear, "Yes, if you ask Him. Perhaps not today, or tomorrow. But very soon. You must keep asking Him all the time, though, and you must believe He will do this for you. He can't help you if you don't believe."

They believed him! For the first time these young faces were the faces of real children, not nightmares—smiling, wondering, hopeful faces. They were eager and stimulated faces. "Hurry, hurry!" cried Pietro.

An old priest, going up the steps, had paused to listen and to watch. He approached Johnny now, his mild brown eyes smiling. He held out his hand and Johnny took it, coloring. "My children, Father," he said. "I am the Reverend John Fletcher, just returned from my duties in Europe as chaplain." He stood among the children, and put his arms about them. "My children," he repeated, praying for understanding.

The priest nodded. "I'm Father McCloskey," he said in a serious voice to the children.

Kathy asked excitedly, "God?"

Jean and Pietro and Max and Emilie exclaimed, "God? God?"

The old priest became very grave. He looked at each young face, and his mouth trembled with compassion. He looked at their clothing. Then he looked at Johnny, smiled encouragingly, and turned back to the children. "No, my dears," he said, kindly, "just one who serves God. Like—like your own father here."

"They've never met—Him—yet," said Johnny. "You see, I took them to a church—it was closed." He stopped, painfully. "So I'm bringing them here—to meet Him." He added, in a lower tone, "I'm having one—well, quite a time."

"I should imagine," murmured the old priest sympathetically. He paused. Then he knew what to do. He knew whom to select—the most unstable. He took Pietro's hand. The boy did not pull away. "Let's all go in together and meet God," he said. "He's been waiting a long time. A very long time."

The old man, small, bent, and gentle, and the little mercurial boy, went up the last steps togther, hand in hand, and Johnny and the mystified children followed. The priest asked, "And what is your name, my child? Pietro? Ah, Peter. Your father will tell you about Peter." Pietro began to jabber, to Johnny's amazement. "Pietro—Peter! Peter—Pietro!" He peered up at the priest with his dark and dancing eyes. "Padre! Padre like Papa? Yes? Yes? Papa is padre, too. I am his boy, his American boy! We go to see God, yes? In the church?"

They all stopped in the cool vestibule. The priest was more grave than ever. He said to Johnny, "We see so many of these rescued children. God has blessed you, and them, Mr. Fletcher. But so many, many children who weren't rescued! Where is your parish, Mr. Fletcher?"

Johnny answered, "I haven't any—yet. But God will take care of that, of course." He added, "Will you go along with me, Father, and help me now?"

The priest hesitated. Then he smiled, and touched Johnny's black sleeve with a paternal hand. "I think Someone else will help you. I don't believe you need me." He turned to the children, who were gaping around eagerly, muttering to each other. He raised his voice and said, "God bless you and keep you, dear children," and he lifted his withered hand in blessing and went on into the church.

"Bless? Bless?" demanded Pietro, impatiently. "What is it—bless?"

"Come," said Johnny, and they entered the church.

The young minister halted with his flock, full of apprehension. What if the children got out of control, as they very often did? What if they began to scream and run wildly, or ask questions loudly? There were only half a dozen people in the church, kneeling in the pews or before the various altars, but they should not be disturbed. Johnny said quietly, "You must look, and listen. If you make a noise or act up, kids, you will hurt God, and me. All right?"

They stared at him; he could see the shine of their eyes in the dusk. Then Jean said fiercely to the younger boys, "You shut up, see, and no noise. I must ask God about my arm and leg. Papa says He will make them better. No noise!" Kathy took a strong hold on little Emilie's hand and said with determination: "Emilie, be quiet, and don't ask too many questions. God is listening."

The church lay before them, and all at once the children were utterly still, their mouths open, marveling, holding their breath. The gray Gothic arches sprang from the gray walls, which were pierced by the strong blaze of the stained-glass windows. The air, cool, haunted by incense, trembled with fragments of color, a lance of scarlet on a groin, a delicate blue on the white stone floor, a soft yellow on a far pew, a blade of purple on pale altar steps. There stood the great altar at the rear, with its tall golden crucifix, its flowering of silent candles, its vases of blossoms. There shone the everlasting light, like a ruby star, testifying to the Presence.

Along the walls marched the slow agony of the Stations of the Cross, and there were altars, with candle flames stirring gently, at the sides.

Where to begin? wondered the apprehensive young minister. Pietro was tugging feverishly at his arm, and whispering loudly, "God? God?" He pointed to the great altar at the rear. Johnny said, "Yes, God." He put his hand on the thin shoulder in restraint. "But you don't run to Him, not yet. You learn about Him first." Where was the old priest? He was nowhere to be seen.

With some desperation, Johnny looked at the nearest altar in its special niche. A tall arch enclosed the white, blue, and gold figure of the girl-Mother, with her Child in her arms, candles before her, her beautiful maiden's face half smiling, meditative, her Child lifting His little hand in blessing. Her bare feet stood on a globe circled with stars, and her eyes gazed tenderly upon the world.

Johnny took Pietro's hand and motioned for the others to follow. They imitated him, walking soundlessly on the balls of their feet. They stood before the altar of the Madonna and Child, and they looked up, sucking in their lips, their eyes unblinking.

"Look at the little boy," said Johnny. "A little boy like you, Jean and Max and Pietro. That is His Mother, who is holding Him in her arms, just as your mothers held you."

The children crowded closer to the altar, tense and silent. Jean stood a little ahead, his face sharp and clear in the candlelight. He was whispering something to himself which Johnny could not hear, and his lips were trembling. Pietro turned to Johnny and pointed upward to the Madonna. "Mother? Mother? My mother?" He was beginning to tremble with too much excitement. "Yes," said Johnny. "God's Mother—and yours. See how she looks at you; she loves you, dear. No, you mustn't go too close yet."

"Why? Why?" cried Pietro. "Why?" demanded the others. Only Jean was silent—too silent.

How explain sanctity to these children? Where were the words? And why could they not, indeed, these children, touch her feet at least? Johnny glanced hastily about him. The pews were entirely empty now, and there was no one in the church but themselves. Praying fervently that no new-comers would enter, Johnny bent, lifted Pietro in his arms, hugged him to lessen his trembling. He mounted the low altar step and whispered, "She is praying, and you mustn't disturb her. I mean, she's talking to God. Reach out your hand, Pietro, and touch her feet."

The quick little hand darted out, but not to the feet, as Johnny expected. The fingers closed on the hand of the Madonna. And then a great aura of light shone on Pietro's face. "Mama? Mama?" he questioned, in a passionate whisper. The statue beamed on him. "Mama?"

From what little hidden crypt in that lonely child's brain

had come the remembrance of maternal love and protection? From where had come the universal word of trusting hope? Johnny pressed his cheek against Pietro's head; he could feel the child's urgent waiting. "She hears you, dear," he said. "See how she smiles at you."

Pietro struggled in his arms, straining forward, and Johnny held him. Pietro kissed the Madonna's hand, then shyly gazed at the Child in her arms. "My Mama too," he said to the Child, proudly. He was still a moment, then he wriggled in Johnny's grasp, flung his arms about his neck and gave him his first kiss, warm with joy.

Johnny, holding him, closed his eyes briefly.

The children had been watching. They pressed against Johnny, demanding, "My Mama? She is my Mama too?" They were jealous of Pietro. Johnny said, "Well, yes, of course. If she is Pietro's mother she is yours." Then he became alarmed. What was the matter with Jean, standing so rigidly apart, with his hands clenched at his sides? Johnny said quickly, "Jean. Jean!" But Jean was muttering, "*Je vous aide.*"

Oh no, thought Johnny with despair. The boy never spoke French when awake. Johnny put Pietro down, caught the older boy's narrow shoulder. Jean was staring at the statue, tears running down his cheeks. He was blind to where he was, blind to everything but his menacing promise, his vow of vengeance, in behalf of a young mother kicked to death before him in some forgotten concentration camp.

Johnny swung the boy about to face him, fixed his eyes on those glaring, sightless ones. "Jean," he said slowly and emphatically, "listen to me. Can you hear me? She doesn't need your help. She is with God. God. Safe with God. Do you hear me?"

The blind eyes did not flicker. "Safe with God," repeated Johnny, sweating. "You can't help her. She is resting, in God. Try to understand. Jean?"

He put his hand under Jean's sharp chin and turned the little face of nightmare to the statue again. "Can't you see her smiling at you, telling you she's all right, and loving you, and watching you? Look at her, Jean!"

Jean's body was like iron. He did not pull away from Johnny. But slowly the iron softened, and from somewhere in the depths of the poor child came a sigh such as no child should ever have to utter. "Maman," he murmured, and then he smiled, and Johnny's heart contracted again with sorrow. "Mama," whispered Johnny.

"You only dream that she's dead," Johnny went on, putting his arm about the boy. "Only bad dreams. Can you remember that, Jean?"

"Only a dream," said Jean obediently, in a new voice Johnny had never heard before. He smiled at Johnny. "Mama is not dead," he announced, and there was peace in his eyes. The children, so abnormally sensitive to fear, to emotion, to passion, felt some communication from him. They began to laugh, very softly, even little Emilie, who clapped her small hands as if in delight. And the laugh was children's laughter, carefree and happy.

"Let's sit down, right here," said Johnny. "Where we can look at the Mother, and I'll tell you all about her Child, who is God. You see, God was so sorry for all of us that He came down here, Himself, out of heaven, to show us the way back to Him." (He decided the Trinity was too complex today.) He helped the children into a pew and sat among them. They gazed at the statue while he talked.

"Once," he said, speaking clearly and slowly, "there lived a young girl. Not very long ago, though often it seems like it. She was very beautiful." He glanced at Kathy, and the child's face, in all that sweet dusk and candlelight, had a sudden strange purity and loveliness, an innocence like marble. "As beautiful as Kathy," said Johnny, "and not very much older." The boys craned around Johnny to stare solemnly and with new interest at Kathy, whose yellow lashes blinked with happy astonishment before the scrutiny of the boys. She opened the compact, which she had never relinquished, and gave herself a brief inspection. Johnny tweaked her long braid and repeated, "As beautiful as Kathy and not very much older. And that statue there is a picture of her as some artist dreamed she looked. Who knows? Perhaps that is what the artist's mother looked like, and he loved her.

"Well, that young girl, in a country far away—even farther than where you all came from—loved God very much, and wanted to serve Him. God always hears prayers. So He sent an angel, called Gabriel, to see the girl, whose name was Mary."

"Angel?" demanded Pietro, bouncing on the hard wooden seat.

I keep running into difficulties, thought Johnny. He glanced around. Two plaster angels with halos knelt on each side of the great altar. He pointed. "Those are angels," he said. "They live with God.

"And the angel told Mary that she would have a Son, and that the Son was God, and that He would save our poor, bad world from itself, and bring peace and hope to all men," said Johnny.

A dark and cynical expression appeared on Jean's face, and Johnny went on hastily, "We don't have peace yet, or much hope, but one day it will come. God never lies. In the meantime we have to work for it, all of us, children and men and women. Well, Mary was frightened. After all, she was a very young girl."

But how can I explain the Virgin Birth? Johnny asked himself. These children don't even know much about natural birth. There are some things I'll have to skim over. Then he had an inspiration.

"Mary was going to marry a very good man, Joseph—"

He was interrupted by a sudden sharp cry from Max. "Joseph? Joseph? Papa, *bist Du?*" He was clutching the back of the pew before him, and his pale eyes were astare.

So, thought Johnny, that was his father's name. He said quickly, "Lots of men are called that name, Max." He reached across Pietro and gently loosened the taut hands on the pew. "Don't you want me to finish the story? Well, then, sit back like Jean, and be a good boy.

"The people were very poor, Mary's people, because a strong army of soldiers from a very big country had taken her people's own land and had made slaves of them, and had robbed them of all their money, and they had put Mary's people, so many of them, in prison."

Now he would see if he could really reach one or two of these children. He looked slowly from one face to another. Pietro was only regarding him with bright-eyed impatience for him to continue. But Jean had turned his tormented face to the minister and full comprehension hovered on it, as well as amazement. Kathy had lifted her head alertly, again frowning in an effort to understand that what had happened to her had happened to another girl. Then again, she gave the statue a loving and significant smile. Max showed the only violent reaction. He leaned across Pietro and grasped Johnny's knee in a desperate and sudden gesture. "Mary—and Joseph—their people in prison too? In—in—"

"We call them concentration camps today," said Johnny sadly, putting his hand over that of Max. "You see, it's a very, very old story."

Max pulled his fingers away from Johnny, and he began to wring his hands again. "Don't do that," said Johnny, with steady firmness. "Mary and Joseph didn't. They loved God. They trusted Him." Max's hands became still, then they relaxed and fell on his knees. But his head drooped on his breast.

"The strong soldiers from another country made life very miserable for Mary's people. They were all over, marching—marching—killing, too, when the people couldn't stand it any longer and tried to fight back."

Jean said suddenly, out of the clouded darkness in him, "Storm troopers!"

"Well, yes, I suppose you'd call them that," said Johnny. Jean looked at the statue and his fierce face became very tense. "So," said Johnny, "these soldiers—they were called Romans—had made a king—a leader—over Mary's people. Mary's people are called Jews." He hesitated. Max's head was slowly lifting. It was like the head of a young corpse rising out of a grave, blindly accusing, blindly asking why. So I have a clue now, thought Johnny. He could not stand that young blind face, those lost and lonely eyes full of confused anguish. The peaks of hair over the boy's head resembled a crown of thorns.

"So when it was very cold, and there was snow on the mountains, the Romans told Mary's people that they would have to go to the nearest city and pay out more money. And they were so poor. So Mary, and her husband, had to go to a place called Bethlehem, not only to pay out their little piece of money, but to be counted, too."

"Every night," murmured Jean, looking into space, "they counted—"

"Yes, yes," said Johnny. "You understand. But when Mary, who was riding a little horse, and Joseph, her husband, got to Bethlehem, they found there wasn't any place they could stay. All the hotels and houses were filled up with the rest of their people, who had been forced to go to Bethlehem, to be counted by the Romans and to give their money. It was terribly cold and it was snowing, and Mary and Joseph were very tired and hungry, and the only place they could find to stay was an old barn."

"With barbed wire around it?" asked Jean. He leaned toward Johnny, his eyelids twitching.

In a way, a symbolical way, thought Johnny. But these children were not yet ready to hear about symbols, or understand them. However—"Yes," he said. "I'm sure it had barbed wire, or a fence, around it." Kathy was leaning toward him now, keeping tight hold of little Emilie. "I know," she said. "There's always barbed wire around them. Sharp."

Johnny sighed. "They let Mary and Joseph into the barn. There were cows in the barn; the breath of the cows, and their bodies, made it a little less cold than outside. It was night and there was a moon, shining like ice, and there was nothing to sleep on except straw. So Mary and Joseph lay down in the straw to sleep."

"I remember," said Jean, almost inaudibly. "I was there."

"Yes," said Johnny, and he looked at all the children. "You were there. You always were. All down through the ages." His heart beat heavily, and with sickness.

The children regarded him gravely. How much do they understand? he wondered. He had the mystical conviction that they were comprehending even more than he was telling.

"And so," he went on, "while poor little Mary, that young girl, lay on the straw in the cold, covered with her husband's patched coat, God was born to her, a little Child, a Baby."

The children turned their heads to look at the plaster Child in Mary's arms. It was only a trick of the dusk, of course, and the sudden flare of the candlelight, which made the plaster face take on the radiance and compassion of flesh, which made it shine upon the children in the pew. "See," said Kathy, "He hears Papa telling us about Him."

"He was just a Baby," said Johnny. "Just as you were. Even younger than Emilie here. He couldn't walk or talk. He just had his little Mother. And she didn't have a bed for Him. So she tore up part of her dress to cover Him from the cold, and she found a manger—that's a box where they put straw for cattle to eat—and she laid the Baby in the manger, on the straw."

Jean lifted clenched hands, and all his face was trembling. "I know! I saw it, Papa! There was a baby, and the girls and women were afraid the soldiers would kill the baby, and the mother put the baby in a box full of straw, and hid it under some things—I saw it, Papa!"

"Of course you did," said Johnny, and pressed his hands over his eyes. "Of course you did, Jean."

"I won't let the soldiers see Emilie!" said Kathy with fierceness, clutching the little girl tightly to her. The boys growled in affirmation.

Won't you? thought Johnny. And who is going to protect all the mothers—in the future? Where are the mothers, now, holding their children, not knowing that tomorrow, perhaps, their children will die in their arms? Where are the "nice, good people," that they aren't working to prevent it? The nice, good people who are sure that "everything is really all right, it just takes a little time!" Time, time!

Johnny went on, "Only a few people knew that God had been born in that barn, in the manger. They were very poor men, Mary's people, who took care of sheep on the cold mountains. And an angel suddenly stood there among them, with a wonderful light all about him, and the shepherds were very much afraid. But the angel said, 'Do not be frightened, children, because I have wonderful things to tell you. God has been born this hour to save you, and He lies in a manger in the city of Bethlehem.' And the angel pointed to a great Star suddenly shining in the sky, which was the sign. And while the light shone on the poor shepherds' faces, and the sheep crowded around them, the angel said, 'Glory to God in the highest, and on earth, peace—' "

His voice broke, and he bent his head.

It was some long moments before he realized that the children were very still, and then he saw that their eyes were filled with a strange brightness. And they were looking at the crucifix on the great altar in the distance. Johnny went on, "Well, the bad king, and the Romans, heard what the shepherds had told the people about seeing God in His manger, and the king was afraid that the Baby had come to take away the country from him, for that had been told many years before. So he gave out an order that the Baby was to be found, and killed."

"Yes," murmured the children, but they still looked at the crucified Man, and not at the infant in His Mother's arms. Was it possible that they had understood something in one mystic moment?

"So Mary and Joseph left the barn very quickly, with the Baby, and the Mother and the Child were carried on the little horse, which is called a donkey, and they ran to another country so that the soldiers couldn't find them and kill them. And the name of the country where they lived for a long time was Egypt."

Max said in his low, dreaming voice, "I was in Egypt too."

"Yes," Johnny answered, "you were, Max."

He continued, "The little Family were very poor in Egypt, and no one wanted them, for they were strangers in a strange land. But they were happy together, and they loved each other, for, you see, where love is, God is also. Joseph worked as a carpenter, and the Boy, who was named Jesus, worked with him, and they made tables and chairs for people who would buy them. Often they went to bed hungry, and they lived in a very poor house, and Mary was often afraid because the people about them did not like them, and the other boys were cruel to her Boy."

Kathy interrupted, "But He was God! Why did God let Himself be hungry and hurt?"

Johnny put his arm about her. "Because, dear, He loved the world, terrible and bad though it is, and He wanted to show people that He understood what they suffered, and that He knew what it was to be homeless and lonely and hated. He wanted to show them that He knew what it was to be a man. He never spared Himself." Johnny waited a moment or two, and then said, "No matter what anyone has suffered, God, too, suffered it, and God understands."

He waited. The children sat in silence, each with his own wounds and his own confused remembrance. Max looked dimly at his hands; Jean bit his lip; Pietro's small face gleamed. And Kathy wept, bending her head over little Emilie, who had fallen asleep in her arms.

Johnny drew a deep breath. "If you're ever tired again, children, or hungry, or hated, or homeless, you must never forget that God suffered that, long before you did. God was there, first."

Jean looked long at the crucifix, and he sighed. Then he turned to Johnny and smiled, and it was the smile of a man and not a child. The young minister returned the smile sadly, and said, "I've told you the story of God when He was young like you, and tonight I'll tell you more about Him when He was a man, and home again in His own country."

He stood up, and the children rose with him.

He led them back up the aisle, toward the open doors through which the sunlight streamed. As they passed the pew where they had sat, Johnny started. The old priest was sitting there, smiling faintly. He said, as Johnny paused in disbelief, "You told the story well, my son."

"Thank you, Father," Johnny murmured in confusion. He bowed and went on with his flock. When he reached the door he glanced back, but the old priest had disappeared. There were only the altar, the statues, the candlelight, and the shadows in the arches, and the brilliant windows. Johnny said aloud and with firmness, "I do not believe in ghosts!"

"What?" asked Pietro.

"Besides," Johnny added, "his name was McCloskey, and who ever heard of a ghost by that name?"

They stood on the steps of the church, looking down at the roaring and dazzling street. "Look!" cried Jean, pointing downward. "People, people!"

"People!" the others chorused with delight.

Johnny put his hand in his pocket for his handkerchief. His fingers encountered something hard and round. It was Mrs. Grant's compact. The street below him melted into one wave of hot color.

Dr. Stevens was silent for a long time after Johnny had spoken. The children were in bed, sleeping soundlessly, in the new night clothes Johnny had bought them that day. They had eaten their dinner almost normally, but toward the end of it their eyelids had drooped and they had been glad to stumble after Johnny and Mrs. Burnsdale to their beds. It had been a long, hard day.

The old minister sighed. He had removed his vest, and he sat in his shirt sleeves, his collar unfastened. He smiled at the younger man. "I have a feeling they aren't going to cry or

71

dream tonight, Johnny. Do you know, if I were a Catholic, I'd say you were a saint." He sighed again. "Never mind, don't look so embarrassed. But you're going to have yourself quite a time, you know, if you carry out your ideas. You're convinced that Jean and Pietro are Catholic boys, and Max is a Jew; and Kathy, and probably the smaller girl, Protestants. So you intend to bring them up in their respective religions!" He shook his head. "Haven't they been confused enough without your adding to it? Even if they had been children with average backgrounds, American children, it would be appalling enough, in one household, in a strange city! You would have had, even under the best of circumstances, quite a time explaining tolerance to youngsters of different faiths and trying to get them to live peaceably together. Think, Johnny!"

"I've thought, sir. And I've also thought that each of those children has a right to his inheritance, and a right to understand that inheritance, a right to his roots. As the years pass they'll have a frame of reference. The past won't be formless and empty to them. There'll be continuity to it, even if they don't remember it, before the concentration camps."

He sat on the edge of his chair, and his eyes were extremely blue in his dark face. "Tolerance! Where better to learn it than in one household, among one's brothers and sisters? Why, those kids will go out into the world and when they see intolerance they'll remember what they themselves suffered from it, and they'll know what monstrous ugliness it is, and why it should be driven from their world. They'll know it's marked in red letters on the gates of hell. They'll know it's caused all the wars, the concentration camps, the massacres, the deaths of their parents, the pain and homelessness they endured, and the very wounds they carry in their bodies. And they'll understand what the Lord said when He prophesied, 'One Fold, One Shepherd.' Why, they've got a wonderful advantage over every kid in this country, every sheltered kid everywhere!"

Dr. Stevens shook his head again. "All right, Johnny. Never mind. I'm sorry I couldn't get you a better place than Barryfield, right in the midst of the coal region. But it's also in the Poconos, and you can always look up at the mountains."

"I'm not sorry, Dr. Stevens. I'm glad. You see, I couldn't

have stayed here even if this congregation had wanted me. I can't be minister to people who want their religion comfortable, a kind of dessert at the end of a week's pleasant dinner. You know, I've always been sorry for the Pharisees—they're such cowards. And I can't condone cowardice, and pretend with any congregation that religion's a soothing thing. It isn't. It's a call to the spirit to struggle against the flesh, and against all evil."

He stood up and pushed his hands deep in his pockets, and his eyes flashed. "So they want a pastor who'll lie to them, and tell them what they want to hear. I'm not their man, sir."

"No, Johnny," said Dr. Stevens, and smiled. "You're not their man."

5

The hot yellow sunset flowed through the library window and appeared to enfold Johnny in it, as he stood before Jean and Kathy. It was too important an occasion for anyone to sit. Jean and Kathy were very still as they listened to their foster father, Jean's wise and narrow face serious and intent, his pale eyes alert, his shock of light-brown hair neatly combed—for the first time—by Mrs. Burnsdale. Kathy was as serious as he. In her new "American" clothes she looked like a very mature older daughter of the family, responsible for the less responsible and younger members. Mrs. Burnsdale had persuaded her to part with the long queue braid, and her soft yellow hair lay in smooth folds on her shoulders. Her blue eyes no longer shifted; they were steady. Her mouth was set in womanly curves, oddly touching in a child her age. Her plump hands were clasped before her in an old-fashioned gesture of obedient listening.

"I need your help," said Johnny simply. He puffed at his pipe. "Mrs. Burnsdale is going with us to that town, Barryfield. But all she can do is to keep you kids clean, and feed all of us, and take care of our new house. I want to tell you about Barryfield first, though. It isn't like New York. They mine coal there. But it's in the mountains, the blue mountains, called the Poconos. I've seen them. We can always look up out of the dust and noise of the town and see the mountains. It's very important for people to see the mountains, out of the tiredness of daily work, and the worry and the dirt. Do you understand, kids?"

They nodded their heads, but did not speak.

He studied Jean and Kathy earnestly. Jean must have known what he was thinking, for he smiled his secret smile. "We understand," he said. Kathy nodded. "Papa is like mountains, too," she said. "But not like Alps." "Not," said Jean, and his jaw was determined, "like Alps."

Johnny sighed, but even in his sadness he was grateful. They understood. "Thanks, kids," he said. "I'm not much of a mountain, though. If I had been, and all the other parsons and ministers, too, what happened to you wouldn't have happened."

They became very serious again. "We're not going to have an easy time in Barryfield," said Johnny. "That's the most important thing you've got to understand right now. I won't have much money. I haven't even got much of a church, from what I've heard, and the house won't be like this one. It's small, and we're not going to have much room. I'll have a parish—lots of people to take care of. I can't be with you kids all the time, and maybe not much of the time, except at night. So you, Jean, and you, Kathy, have to know just exactly what we're getting into. See?"

Jean said, "Yes. We see. But it is America, no?"

Johnny said glumly, "Yes, it's America. And now I come to the most important part. I've told you what America means—freedom from fear, freedom from state police, freedom from concentration camps, freedom from the terror of having your door knocked on at night, freedom from violent death at any time from anybody. Freedom protected by law. Nobody can do to you what was done to you in Europe. Nobody is going to drag me from you, and kill me. Nobody is going to put barbed wire around any of us. Nobody is going to tell me, or you, what to say, or what to do—any time. We've got something we call the Constitution, and that keeps Americans from killing other Americans, or taking their property from them, or burning their homes, or injuring children."

"So?" said Jean. "Why then is Papa afraid? What else is there to fear if Americans have all that? Yes?"

"We have all that," said Kathy in her prim, rather rebuking voice. "What else needed, Papa?"

"Plenty," said Johnny. "Look, kids, I want you to know the worst. Americans aren't any different from the people in Europe." He paused. Jean's pale eyes sharpened brilliantly; Kathy stepped back in fear. "Wait a minute," said Johnny. "There's just one thing that is different. The law here. I told you that."

"But—if there comes no law?" said Jean tensely. "Like there came no law in Europe?"

You've got a good point there, thought Johnny somberly. Why do you suppose, kids, that I lie awake nights, thinking? He tried to smile reassuringly. "There will always be the law, no matter what the people are. And, you know what? The people respect the law, most of them. They've seen what happened in Europe when they got rid of law, and they don't want it to happen here. And we've got millions—millions! —of good people working all the time, explaining the law, explaining it to children in the schools, making it work in the courts. You know what courts are? Police. Wait. Not police like in Europe. No. Police who protect the people from lawbreakers. One of these days I'll read the Bill of Rights to you, and you'll learn about it in school yourselves. Then you'll know."

The children thought this over, various strong emotions flitting over their faces like shadows. It is not so simple, then, Johnny could almost hear them think. We are not so safe then. There are always people.

"God, and the law, are our protection," said Johnny. "No matter what else happens, they are our protection. And they'll be right with us every minute. That's the important thing you've got to remember. And that's why I need your help with Max and Pietro and Emilie. They won't understand as well as you do. You'll be with them all the time, taking care of them, for me. If you don't, we'll all fail. I mean, there won't be anything for any of us. See?"

The children studied Johnny's anxious and harried face for long moments. They missed nothing, in their preternatural keenness, which was their heritage from terror. Then, as if a signal had passed between them unseen by the young minister, they stepped toward him. Kathy took one hand, Jean the other. They smiled up at him with an ancient wisdom, and—to his humble astonishment—compassion.

"We know," they said. And they stood on tiptoe to give him their first kiss of trust and faith.

They were all gathered in the large bedroom where the boys and Johnny slept, Emilie half drowsing in Johnny's arms, the three boys on the floor, Kathy properly in a chair beside Mrs. Burnsdale, and Dr. Stevens on the side of the big double bed. The night was hot and still, with thunder murmuring in the baked air, and a heated wind blew the curtains at the long open windows. A lamp behind Johnny illuminated the book he held.

"And they brought young children to Him, that He should touch them: and His disciples rebuked those that brought them. But when Jesus saw it, He was much displeased, and said unto them, 'Suffer the little children to come unto me, and forbid them not: for of such is the kingdom of God. . . .' And He took them up in His arms, put His hands upon them, and blessed them."

He put down the book, and holding the sleeping child against him, he touched her forehead gently with his fingers in blessing. The boys on the floor watched acutely. Kathy's face shone. "Yes," she said. "He took us in His arms and blessed us. And He sent Papa to us."

Emilie sat up sleepily on Johnny's knee, staring about her with a baby's wondering smile and pushing aside her long locks. Johnny set her on her feet; she clung to his hand. He surveyed them all proudly, the girls in their pretty white cotton nightgowns, the boys in blue pajamas. They all smelled of soap and clean childhood. "My kids," he said.

They stood about him, waiting, Mrs. Burnsdale between the two girls. He bent his head, and they imitated him. Dr. Stevens glanced at them and saw their grave and serious faces. Johnny prayed, "Our Father." He paused, and the children murmured, "Our Father." Johnny continued, his voice pure and loud in the silence: "Our Father Who art in heaven, Hallowed be Thy Name. . . ."

The young voices followed him, and Dr. Stevens thought

that never had he heard the ancient prayer spoken so devoutly, with so much feeling. When Johnny had finished, the children still stood, folded hands pressed together, heads bent, for a long moment, as if the prayer they had learned was still echoing in grandeur in their souls, shining with eternal brilliance into dark and tortured crevices. Only a few days, thought the old man, but how much they had learned!

Dr. Stevens laid the envelope with the tickets on the desk in the library. "But a drawing room, for only four hours!" said Johnny. "Yes, it's true that I had adjoining staterooms on the ship for all of us, and we had all our meals in them, but I think the kids are well enough now to go by coach."

"I don't think so," replied Dr. Stevens. "Johnny, don't look so depressed. But my advice to you is not to give the children doses of the citizenry too fast. You've done wonders—er, with the help of God. Let's not push Him for miracles. You've considered the school situation, I suppose?"

"Yes. As soon as I can I am going to hire a retired teacher to teach them at home. That's my biggest problem. All of them now know the alphabet; I began to teach them as soon as I got them, and Jean and Kathy and Pietro can already read a few simple English words. I don't know about Max. I can never tell what he knows."

Dr. Stevens lifted his eyes to the ceiling. "Johnny, I don't envy you your problems. Let's hope you don't run into any difficulty with PTA in Barryfield, if they have one. Or ladies who go in for communal activities, and push their noses into everything. Activities—abominable word. I had an old Scots teacher who taught me a prayer: 'God preserve us from the ghosties and the ghoulies, and the long-legged beasties who go thump in the night.' No doubt the ladies with activities are worthy souls, but they always remind me of the long-legged beasties. Darting here and there, on very aggressive stilts of civic virtue, minding everybody's business, and trying to get everyone to conform to the norm. Don't laugh, Johnny. They can make things very hard for you and the children."

Johnny's haggard eyes sparkled with blue mischief. "Do you ever tell your many lady admirers that, sir?"

"No, they'd ostracize me, or think me senile. By the way,

where did this infernal business of women working side by side with men originate? What normal woman wants that?"

"It began in Russia," said Johnny. "I heard a lot about it in Europe." His face became dark and cold.

Dr. Stevens shrugged. "The American Communists have come a long way during the past ten or twelve years in our country, son. A long, long way. It was planned. They could contribute nothing but hatred and revolution to America, and envy, and distrust among the people, and confusion, and eventual slavery." His eyeglasses suddenly glittered with wrath. "And there are those in America, not Communists themselves, who want just that, for their own monstrous purposes.

"And that, son, brings me right back to Barryfield, and all the problems you are going to have, not only about these poor rescued children, and schools, and trying to build up an indifferent parish and a poor church, but with others. Barryfield is partly built on coal, though it has some factories. The mines aren't too big, or too productive. A third of the men work in them, and the town population is only about one hundred and fifty thousand, at the most. The coal-mine owners and operators hardly survived the depression; from 1938 to 1941 they just about broke even. The war brought them a little prosperity, but only a little. Now, in 1946, they are again losing money. The Communists have been very active there. The men aren't fools; the companies have laid the books on the table for their union delegates to see for themselves. The union doesn't want the men to strike; the men don't want to strike. But the Communists do. In number, the Communists are small in Barryfield, but they're accursedly busy and noisy, and they're experts in division and confusion and lies.

"Well, coal mining is a seasonal thing. The owners want to keep the mines open, though they aren't making a cent, hardly meeting expenses and wages. They want the men to be employed. But if the strike goes through, and the men get increases in pay, the mines will have to shut down. And that's what the Communists want."

He waited for comment, but Johnny gave none. The old minister continued, "The union delegate for one of the mines is on your church board, son. A good man, from what I've learned these past few days. He's pretty desperate. I talked with him on the telephone several times, though I've never met him. He needs your help, Johnny. So, you've got the Communists on your hands.

"And here's another problem. Barryfield was originally English, German, and Irish. It's an old city, and they had their troubles a half century ago with that explosive mixture of races. Wait a moment; I know you hate the word 'race' but I have to use it advisedly. Now Barryfield has a dozen or more 'races' and when time hangs heavy on the citizens' hands they go in for racism. One or two against another two or three, and vice versa. Not violently; just sullenly, at times. It manifests itself covertly, but it's there. All stimulated, lately, by the Communists."

He gazed at Johnny eloquently.

"I tried to get you a better place, son. You know that. Your parish has had four ministers in less than eight years. I leave it to you to guess the reason. They were all fine men, with a mission, and they tried. It wasn't any use. They either had the few well-to-do people against them or they had their own parishioners at their throats, or the union, or some alleged minority. So, knowing all this, I couldn't bear it for you to go there. But I could find you no other place, on such short order. You'll have to bear it until I get you something better."

Johnny looked up, quite suddenly, and his weary face was alive. "No. I'll stay, as long as the church wants me to stay. I'll try to stay. Somehow, I feel—and it came to me all at once, like a revelation—that it was meant for me to go there. I don't know just how to say it, Dr. Stevens, but that's how I feel."

Dr. Stevens glanced aside, and said nothing.

"It's an old-fashioned word, sir, but I think it is what they used to say was a call."

Dr. Stevens sucked meditatively on his pipe. "I'm old, and I'm afraid I've had a little too much of this world, Johnny. Don't listen to me. Perhaps you know better. Perhaps God is still interested in this violent ball of mud rolling in its own blood."

Johnny reached over and put his hand on the old man's knee, and he smiled. "Well," he said, "He thought enough of it, and was interested enough in it, to come down here Himself, to die for it. We sometimes forget that."

Dr. Stevens took off his glasses, for they had become moist. He rubbed them with his handkerchief. "All right, Johnny. I forget, but you never do. There's another thing you should know about your parish. The dominant man there is very rich, and old, and, from what I've heard, very detestable. Why does he go to that church? His father was its first minister; his father built it, almost literally. His uncle, however, was very fortunate. He went to New York, and after about fifty years he had gotten himself a seat on the stock exchange. I don't know the details. When this uncle died, unmarried, and with no other relatives, he left all his money—and it was several millions after very large contributions to charities—to this man, who is President of the church Board. He has had a very hard life himself, as a minister's son. He was determined to become a physician, and so he financed his own education by working in the mines during the summer months. At one time he was forced to leave his university for three years, to get the necessary money by working in the mines. He hardly knew of the existence of his 'sinful' uncle, as his father called him. He was already fifty years old, and practicing in Barryfield, when his uncle, thirty years his senior, died and left him all that money. His name is Alfred McManus, Dr. Alfred McManus, and he is in his late sixties now. He gave his promise that he would meet exactly what the parishioners could, or would, raise, for the support of the church. But no more; not a cent more."

Johnny considered this. Then he said, "I think I agree with him. If people want a church they should be willing to work for it, and support it."

Dr. Stevens was pleased. "I'm glad you said that, Johnny, because I see you'll have little difficulty about that with Dr. McManus. All the other ministers did, poor fellows. They thought he should be the support of the whole business. Dr. McManus, from what I've heard, is a rugged individualist. I gather that he loved his father a great deal. And he continues to practice medicine. He's got the only affluent practice in the city, and his fees are tremendous. Mr. Emil Schoeffel, the treasurer of the Board, hates him. It was from Mr. Schoeffel that I got the news that Dr. McManus is a rough, dirty, savage, and blasphemous old man, with 'no pity in his heart.' The quote is from Mr. Schoeffel, who has a small shoe factory, not very prosperous."

"You are sure they know all about me, and the children?"

"Yes." Dr. Stevens coughed. "Dr. McManus didn't want you, Johnny. Said you were probably a 'damned Communist.' To quote again: 'Enough foreigners in this town as it is.' I told him on the telephone that if he didn't take you he'd go hang for another minister, for a long time. His answer convinced me that he is not in the least a Christian gentleman, but just a hostile, embittered old man who doggedly helps maintain that church because of his father."

"Still," Johnny mused, "he wanted to be a physician."

"Probably ambitious; thought he could make a lot of money."

"If money was all he wanted, then he would have retired when he inherited that fortune. Some doctors have something in them which the saints have too."

This was too much for Dr. Stevens. He laughed heartily. "Well, son, I leave that saint in your hands. From what I hear he is probably already consigned to a place where saints don't generally go."

6

In another five minutes the train would reach Barryfield. John Fletcher looked about for all the luggage in the drawing room; there it was piled, in new, bright, if cheap, heaps, all filled with the children's fresh clothing. (His own suitcase was old and cracking, and he had his army duffel bag. It had never occurred to him to treat himself to better luggage, during the process of buying the articles for the children.) He was pleased with the impressiveness of all those cases, big and small. He ran a comb through his short black hair, and glanced at the children fondly. What a miracle a couple of weeks in America had accomplished! There was Kathy, firmly combing little Emilie's long tangled curls after a very brisk and uncompromising washing of the small child's face at the miraculous steel basin. There was Jean, yanking Pietro and Max into presentable shape, straightening ties, vexedly brushing lint off new blue suits. Both Jean and Kathy kept muttering admonishing words under their breath to the others. Johnny looked at Mrs. Burnsdale, sitting majestically near the window, permitting Jean and Kathy to take responsibility for the younger children. As small towns flashed by, and smaller stations, Mrs. Burnsdale favored them with haughty glances through the wide plate-glass windows. This amused Johnny.

He said, "I'm afraid, kids, and Mrs. Burnsdale, that Barryfield isn't going to be much better than what we've been passing. It may even be worse."

Mrs. Burnsdale replied, with even more hauteur, "Humph. Towns can be changed, if folks have gumption and self-respect. Soap's cheap, and so's paint. I never did have any patience with shiftless people. But something's gone wrong with this country, Mr. Fletcher. Everybody wants everything anybody else has, without working for it. Handouts? Sometimes I think what George Washington'd have said about such people."

"They probably existed then, too," said Johnny. "And they probably wanted everything for nothing. But they starved, or went to work. Human nature never changes very much, though we ministers try. How we try!"

She gave him a sympathetic glance. "I guess you've always tried. But it didn't do much good, did it?"

"Now you're getting cynical. Yes, I think it did, in a way. We don't starve mentally sick people to death, or drop them in snake pits, or beat them insensible. We don't let little orphans die for food on the streets. We don't set out our old folks to die on the highways. We don't kill idiots and imbeciles any longer."

Mrs. Burnsdale leaned across to him and patted his knee maternally. "Just keep trying. Maybe one of these days we'll get somewhere. Maybe in a couple of million years or so." She added, "If Barryfield's one of these towns, maybe we can get them to scrub it up, even if it's a coal town, and they have factories. That's going to be part of my job."

"I've told you the house isn't very good," said Johnny. "And it's small. I'll have my hands full with the church and the kids." He hesitated. "You see what I mean? The kids have caught some idea about the American dream. We've got to make Barryfield part of that dream—though I don't know how—so the kids won't be disappointed."

Mrs. Burnsdale shook her head vigorously. "These kids, just like everybody else, have got to face facts some day or other, and the sooner the better. What are you starin' at me like that for, Jean? And you too, Kathy?"

Jean colored, gave Max's tie a last reproving yank. Then he looked at Mrs. Burnsdale seriously. "Only thing is, there's the law." He winced. "Just the law." He turned to Kathy, who nodded strongly.

"Well, now," said Mrs. Burnsdale, relieved and pleased. "You're a very sensible boy, and Kathy's a sensible girl."

She reached out to assist Jean with his own coat, for he found dressing difficult because of his crippled arm and shoulder. But he stepped back. His pale eyes were stern. "Jean must learn things for himself, *non?* Mama Burnsdale and Papa think that?"

Mrs. Burnsdale's eyes moistened. She blinked. "We sure do, honey. Always do for yourself whenever you can. It helps your character."

The train was slowing down. They had been passing small, insignificant foothills for the past hour, green and shaggy hills without grandeur. But now, as the train turned, the mountains arched suddenly into view, powerful, royal in color, thrusting their strength against a golden evening sky. The shadows of them fell across green valleys like a benediction. Johnny called the children to him. He had no words now. They looked through the wide windows, solemnly. They saw the far nested villages under a gilded haze of mist and smoke; they saw the delicate toy arches of distant bridges; they saw the quicksilver rivers, touched here and there with scarlet. And always the mountains, always the shadows of the mountains.

Pietro, who had begun to get restless this last hour, and at times almost uncontrollable with excitement, was very still. His big black eyes reflected the golden light of the heavens, the shape of "the everlasting hills." Johnny watched him. The child's dark and mobile face had a thoughtful sternness on it, something Johnny had never seen before, a dreaming, backward-looking expression which brought no pain. Was some racial Italian memory stirring in him, of mountains and color and brilliance and beauty? Of thinking peasants gravely cultivating food, or gathering sheaves at sunset with the sound of the sweet Angelus in their ears, of smoking fires under spicy iron pots, and laughter and peace and song and gaiety and faith? Of wayside shrines in the shadows of olive hills, of pointed cypresses and pointed church towers with glowing crosses? Of red land, not red with blood, but with nourishment, of flung bridges over chasms, of the smell of jasmine and roses in the warm sunset, and the bells of cattle and the scampering of mischievous goats and the calls of sheep under trees heavy with fruit, and gray walls smothered under magenta bougainvillea and little houses with red roofs and the singing of fishermen on an enameled sea? Could any Italian, even this small lost child, forget the glory of his heritage?

"Well," said Mrs. Burnsdale with disapproval, "the mountains are fine. But look where we're stopping. It's as bad as I hoped it wouldn't be."

Johnny, with dismay, silently acknowledged she was quite right.

A dingy, cindery wooden station, with a crooked sign upon it: "Barryfield." A long wooden platform, broken, covered with powdery black dust. The same gritty dust darkened the windows of the small station, had settled itself on the one or two lonely elm trees struggling for life near the tracks, had insinuated itself in the crevices of poor railroad buildings surrounding the grassless enclosure, had poured itself on weeds and fences. The train clanged and hooted impatiently as it stopped, and Johnny agreed with it. He had seen no station as dismal as this anywhere in Europe. Even the cataract of golden light from the sky could not alleviate its general air of irresponsibility, dirt, and shiftlessness. Not even the mountains in their regal splendor rising beyond the station could give a small measure of dignity to this indifference to common decency.

The dismal state of the station was not, of course, the direct fault of the people of Barryfield, for the railroad owned this area. But still, had the people demanded that the company clean up and paint up, the company would have had to comply. In every way, thought Johnny, people are guilty of everything mean, malicious, and cruel which happens anywhere in the world, even five thousand miles away.

He made his voice cheerful: "All right, kids! Here's where we get out. I go first, then Mrs. Burnsdale with Emilie and Pietro, and then you older kids next. Jean, Kathy goes ahead of you, remember?" He was proud of them, but he was also apprehensive. Neat, clean, handsome, pretty—if one did not look too closely at their eyes. He threw his duffel bag over his shoulder, while a porter came in for the children's luggage. He started toward the door, then felt his arm caught. He turned to look down at Jean. "Jean carry Papa's—bag," Jean said, and he smiled. Johnny gave him the bag at once, with a grave "Thank you." His heart lifted a little.

The platform gritted under their feet as they descended. Other passengers looked at them curiously from the wide windows of the train. Two trainmen stared at them vacantly. Johnny saw two elderly men emerging from the station, side by side but with a cold and studied distance between them. Since they were regarding Johnny and his flock with a purposeful expression he decided that this was the reception committee.

One of the men spoke in a high and squeaky voice: "Mr. Fletcher? Thought so. Um. I'm Dr. McManus." He did not extend his hand. He was not a prepossessing man, being so abnormally wide of body that his average height was almost dwarfed, grotesquely. Johnny suspected that all that poundage was hard and solid flesh, under a light-gray suit that did not fit well and was so soiled that the soiling appeared ostentation, tinged with contempt for any local opinion. His broad shoes were cracked and dusty, his linen apparently unironed, his black tie a mere greasy string. Like his body, his face was all wide but fatless flesh, gray in color, the nose short and pugnacious, the mouth hard and lipless. He had tiny eyes, the color of old concrete, under low gray brows. Cynical, merciless eyes, thought Johnny, who was under their scrutiny. When last had that mound of gray-white hair been combed, or washed? Dandruff lay on the mighty shoulders, and this too appeared ostentatious.

The high, squeaky voice, like that of a disagreeable old woman, was ludicrous in so powerful a man, who possessed that vanishing virility of an older America. He ought to be smoking a cigar, or a pipe, thought Johnny. But Dr. McManus smoked cigarettes; one, with a long ash, was dangling from the corner of his mouth, not rakishly, but with an air of cold ferocity.

Dr. McManus turned his harsh scrutiny on the children. He said with heavy disdain, "This feller here is Emil Schoeffel—owns shoe factory. On the church Board; Treasurer. Don't know why he was elected; hasn't made such a success, himself."

Mr. Schoeffel blushed brightly, favored Dr. McManus with

a glance that contained both fear and dislike. Johnny was sorry for the elderly treasurer, who seemed to be made of lax string and tall thin boards, hanging loosely together in a haphazard manner. Even his face appeared made of wood, innocently and inexpertly carved, with large and myopic brown eyes, a long crooked nose, a gentle mouth, topped by a partially bald head. He gave Johnny his hand diffidently, and immediately withdrew it. He spoke, and his voice was astonishingly deep, "Welcome, Mr. Fletcher. And these, I suppose—I heard—are the—the children?"

"The foreigners," said Dr. McManus brutally. He added, "What's that crippled kid doing hauling that bag around? You aren't strong enough, parson, eh?"

Johnny controlled himself. "Dr. McManus, this is Jean. He wanted to carry the bag. Please let me introduce them to you. But first, this is Mrs. Burnsdale, our housekeeper, who is going to take care of us. Mrs. Burnsdale, Dr. McManus."

Mrs. Burnsdale returned Dr. McManus's stolid look as stolidly. Why, thought Johnny, losing some of his wrath, they resemble each other in a way! Mrs. Burnsdale lifted her nose and said, "Humph. Dr. McManus." She swung on her solid feet and gave Mr. Schoeffel a kind smile as Johnny introduced her. Mr. Schoeffel, coloring again, took her hand. He was very grateful, and said, "Welcome to Barryfield, Mrs. Burnsdale."

Johnny went on, helplessly putting Dr. McManus first, in spite of himself, "Doctor, this big girl of mine is Kathy, the little one is Emilie. And this is Max. And now, this is Pietro."

The children had been gazing at Dr. McManus with inscrutable expressions, which made Johnny dread the worst. But to his surprise they did not appear afraid of the formidable and ugly old man. They extended their hands to him. He stepped back, frowning. Kathy smiled at him serenely, and waited. "Well, then," he muttered. He took each child's hand with reluctance and distaste. "This kid looks like a monkey," he said of Pietro. Pietro grinned, and his brilliant black eyes lighted up and his white teeth shone. "Pietro monkey," he mocked, and his feet moved briefly in a gay dance.

"He wants to be an acrobat," said poor Johnny hastily, as Kathy set a heavy hand on Pietro's shoulder. "But I think he'll probably be an artist of some kind, or a singer. He's got a wonderful voice."

"Is that so?" said Dr. McManus ironically. His eyes studied Kathy again, the pure yellow hair, the sturdy face. A curious spasm touched his mouth, and he turned away from her. He went on to Jean, still defiantly holding Johnny's bag. "What happened to this young fellow? Why haven't you done something about that arm and leg?—and you a parson! Waiting for God to cure him, or something?"

Jean said, "Yes, God. Papa said God would cure."

Johnny, more distressed every moment, cut in: "I've had practically every orthopedist in Europe look Jean over."

"So?" said Dr. McManus, with contempt.

"I have the X rays, and all the reports, doctor."

"Is that so?" said Dr. McManus, with sarcasm. "I'd like to see them. Just for curiosity's sake. No fool like a specialist, who knows everything." He forgot Jean, and now he studied Emilie, who gazed at him with her big, radiant blue eyes. "Emilie?" he said, abruptly. The little child smiled, and her infant's face became luminous. "Can't she speak?" the doctor demanded, and there was a note of anger in his voice.

"Not much," said Johnny simply. "You see, she was probably born in a concentration camp, where her parents were murdered, and no one taught her except me."

"Poor little thing," said Mr. Schoeffel, who seemed afraid of the children.

"A Jew, eh?" asked Dr. McManus, and his tone was loaded with affront.

Johnny braced himself against his own anger. "I don't think so. I think Jean is French, Kathy of Dutch origin, Pietro Italian, Emilie from Belgium. These are surmises, but I think I am correct." He paused, and put his arm across Max's shoulders, and drew a deep breath. "Max is of Jewish origin, I think. Max, my next oldest son."

Dr. McManus's eyes sharpened on Max, and his broad face tightened at once. Max regarded him blindly. "Can't he see?" the doctor asked.

Johnny stepped forward with Max. "Yes, physically. But he isn't able to see much, yet, of the world. It's been too terrible for him. You and I, doctor, and everyone else in the world, made it too terrible."

"Papa?" murmured Max, seizing one of Johnny's hands.

"Yes, Max, Papa is right here with you," said Johnny, but he looked at Dr. McManus. He held Max's hand tightly as

Dr. McManus took an abrupt step toward him. Max began to tremble. The doctor seized his chin and looked deeply into the child's eyes. "Come on, son," he said, roughly. "Nobody's going to hurt you, though I don't know how you're going to eat on the parson's salary. Can't you see me, eh?"

Max turned to Johnny. Johnny nodded. "Dr. McManus," he said.

Max said slowly, "Dr. McManus." Then he smiled, and the blind brown eyes sparkled. "I—see," he said.

Mrs. Burnsdale was astounded. "First time he ever spoke without prodding," she remarked. "He's getting better!"

"Nothing wrong with him in the first place," muttered Dr. McManus. "Thought he was an imbecile, at first." Now he regarded Kathy again, and again that spasm touched his bitter mouth. "Kathy, eh? Nice, sensible-looking girl. Pretty, too."

Kathy beamed. "Very pretty," she said precisely.

"Don't go and get ideas," said Dr. McManus with severity. "I've seen girls like you grow up to be fat housewives, as bright as bushwomen." He turned away, as if in disgust, then suddenly swooped Emilie into his arms. The little girl cuddled against him eagerly, to Johnny's amazement. Mr. Schoeffel peeped timidly at the boys, and cleared his throat. "They all look healthy," he ventured hopefully, as if he felt some guilt in his heart and wanted to be eased of it.

Dr. McManus squeaked, "Hey, you, Jim, come on over here and help. Get a move on your damned carcass!"

A uniformed chauffeur emerged from the door of the station, hurrying precipitously. "Get those bags into the trunk," said the doctor. "I don't know what the hell I'm paying you sixty dollars a week for!"

They all moved toward the station. Mrs. Burnsdale whispered hastily to Johnny, "I think everything's going to be all right, Mr. Fletcher. I really do." Dr. McManus was stumping ahead, carrying Emilie, and the children followed him, even Max. Johnny and Mr. Schoeffel brought up the rear. Mr. Schoeffel murmured, "A terrible person, the doctor. I'm a Christian, but I must tell you. He's a miser, and a bad old man. Not a Christian."

Johnny looked at the immense back of the doctor. Emilie's small arms were about his neck; her long hair floated peacefully over one of his shoulders. "Not a Christian?" said Johnny, and smiled.

"Glad we got rid of that moss-mouth," said Dr. McManus of Mr. Schoeffel, who had driven off in a very elderly car. "Always has a new scheme to get me to spend money. The —— town needs another hospital, he says; it needs a new parsonage; the church needs repairing; the orphanage needs more private support."

"Well, do they?" asked Johnny.

Dr. McManus growled under his breath. The great limousine seemed to glide as if on oil through the dirty and winding streets. The children were very silent on the luxurious seats, and Mrs. Burnsdale had put on her haughty expression again. Dr. McManus said, "Probably. Do they think I'm made of money? If they won't do anything for themselves why should I help? Eh, parson?"

"You shouldn't," said Johnny.

Dr. McManus turned his massive head on his neck in order to survey the young minister. "What? What? Thought you were a parson?" He chuckled in an ugly fashion.

"I am," said Johnny. "And I also remember the parable of the grasshopper and the ant." His dark-blue eyes smiled at the old man. "There is nothing in the Bible which approves of a sluggard."

Dr. McManus contemplated him, scowling. He had lit another cigarette, and it trailed downward from his mouth. He said, "I didn't want you here. You know that. Frank Stevens put the pressure on me. Perhaps we'll get along. Perhaps. I give you about six months in this town, though."

"Why?"

"Because you're not a fool. Haven't you learned yet that only fools survive, or thieves?" He chuckled again, and glared through the window. "Filthy town, isn't it? Hate it, myself. Stupid rats. Maybe you think I shouldn't call them stupid, parson?"

Johnny replied calmly, "If they are, why shouldn't you call them that? But stupidity isn't the sole possession of Barryfield. It's the universal vice."

A gleam of evil amusement lit up the concrete of the doctor's eyes. "Isn't there something in the Bible about

91

suffering fools gladly? What? And what about that passage which says that he who calls his brother a fool is in danger of hell-fire?"

"Some of our greatest men are stupid," said Johnny. "But you couldn't call them fools. Napoleon, for instance, was a stupid man, and so was Julius Caesar for that matter, and Hitler and Stalin and Bismarck, and a long list of our own Presidents, not to mention some of our Congressmen, and a considerable portion of the philosohers, including Plato and Nietzsche, and Wagner among the musicians, and Darwin among the scientists, and Machiavelli among the sophists."

"Well, that's an amazing list," said the doctor. The long ash from his cigarette fell on his stonelike thighs. "What makes you think they were stupid?"

"Because they lacked compassion."

The doctor was silent. Johnny began to feel dejected. Barryfield, he decided, was extremely unattractive. The valley in which it lay was quite broad, broad enough to have afforded wider streets and larger lots for the houses. Yet the city had squeezed and cramped itself together meagerly, huddling slummishly as European towns huddled for want of space. There was something European too, something starved, in the narrow wooden houses leaning toward one another, something too old for a vast young land, something out of context with the lofty and expansive mountains, the width of gentle valleys, the numerous streams and rivers. Grimy children played in swarms, milling together, as if there were not, nearby, green earth and tall grass and trees, uncultivated by the farmers who owned them and who probably would have sold the acreage to the town at a reasonable price for a playground.

The city lay under a murk of smoke in the ocher sunset, and now, as the car rolled on, Johnny caught a whiff of a vile odor, a glimpse of a nearby mill from whose gaunt chimneys flags of a bright sulfurous yellow blew out, polluting the air, causing the children to cough. There were other mills, other factories too, all vomiting their corruption against a defaced sky, all black and steamy and rumbling. It was, in a way, good to see that they were busy, that they were employing men at hearths and at machines. But it was not necessary that they should destroy the pure and living oxygen; it was monstrous that children, and the old, breathe this uncleanness.

"Why all the dirt and the smoke?" asked Johnny of Dr. McManus.

The doctor moved his shoulders in a shrug of loathing. "Nobody cares, of course. I've been hounding the politicians for years, but they tell me that I'm the only one who complains. But what can you expect from a degenerate people? You've been away. Haven't you heard how degenerate Americans are now? Just about as degenerate as the Russians. Before we start, for instance, calling the Russians atheistic and barabrous, we'd better begin looking around at our own churches, towns and cities. And maybe our government, too—village, town, city, state, and Federal."

"Dr. Stevens agrees with you, and I'm afraid I do too," said Johnny. Was Barryfield nothing but slums? True, the mines were only "seasonal" work, but there were factories too, and the factory workers had been making large wages while the young boys had been dying in the war in Europe and in the Pacific. Then Johnny saw an American phenomenon which had its duplicate in no other country in the world: the houses might sift soot and dirt, unpainted, with dirty, uncurtained windows, with patches of grassless, hard-packed earth in front and in the rear, with tilted chimneys and broken porches, but almost every house had a brilliant car of impressive dimensions before it, glass shined, chrome glittering, and with curious ornaments on the hoods. The children might seem hardly less emaciated than their brothers and sisters in Europe, and, in many cases, much filthier—but still the cars glittered in the lemon-colored light from the defiled sky, as carefully tended as the household gods of the ancient Romans. Had America indeed deified the machine, as the Russians deified it openly, and without hypocrisy? Was there something to the British contention that America and Russia had too much in common?

"See those cars?" demanded the doctor.

"I see," said Johnny. Dr. McManus squinted his eyes and peered at him. "Come to the same conclusions I came to?"

"Yes. Doctor, where have our ministers been all these years?"

The doctor shook a tobacco-stained finger in the young

minister's face. "Now you tell me! We've had lots of parsons in our church, the Church of the Good Shepherd. Seems to me that my father was the last of the shepherds. Know what the ones we've had have been talking about? Amateur psychiatry, or politics. Is that what a minister's for? Ain't it his business to try to pound some honor in his congregation, some reverence, some hope, some idea of God, and duty, and charity, and—by God!—some contrition for all the damned crimes men commit against each other and God every day? Ever hear a preacher lately talk about penance? Huh!"

Johnny smiled at the doctor, and his eyes shone with affectionate comprehension. The doctor glared at him, and muttered something obscene under his breath, but he blinked hard for a moment. He knocked furiously on the glass panel which divided him from his chauffeur, and when it slid back he squealed, "Drive down Munston Street, to the corner of Kazinski." He flung himself back on his seat, glowering. Emilie had fallen asleep in his arms; his blunt and brutal fingers, with the spatulate tips of a true surgeon, roughly stroked her hair.

The car rolled down a particularly cramped, mean street, boiling with children, howling with children, and with sleazy women standing on sagging stoops and porches, shouting back and forth to each other. On the corner stood a small fieldstone church, very neat, pathetically dignified in that squalor, in a patch of lawn guarded by a rope and stakes. Its cross was polished against a sky that was turning a dull and tainted green. My church? thought Johnny, with hope and pleasure. The wooden doors stood open on a cool dusk, and then Johnny saw that it was not his church after all.

The car stopped. "That's the church with a funny name— Our Lady of the Rosary," said Dr. McManus, with an attempt at scorn. "A feller who calls himself Father John Kanty Krupszyk. Little older than you, but bigger, with a face like a football player. No wonder; got his education at Notre Dame, that big Papist college out in Indiana. The Big Irish! Krupszyk! Met him once at a dinner given for Mac Summerfield, the newspaper owner here in town. Said to him, 'How do you keep that church of yours clean, eh? And with grass around it? In that mob!' Know what he said? 'The people respect it. After all, God is in there. The children in the neighborhood take care of the grass and the trees we all planted, and the women clean the church themselves, and the men wash the windows and keep things reparied, and there's always food in my kitchen; they bring it for me, because my salary is small and I have family demands on it. The church and the rectory are neighborhood undertakings.' "

"As they should be," said Johnny.

"Wait till you see your church and parsonage! The roofs leak, by the way, and if you think I'm going to repair them without help you're mistaken. You can put pans under the leaks."

He lit another cigarette, carefully blew away the smoke from Emilie's sleeping face. "Went to that feller's church one Sunday. He speaks Polish. Has things he calls Masses. Two Masses in Polish, two in English. This one was High Mass. Ceremony. Ritual. Didn't believe a word of it, but I liked it. And know what his sermon was about? He gave the congregation hell! Shouted at them, shook his fist at them, called them names! Wonderful! Did they walk out mad? No sir! They listened, and looked ashamed, and were as meek as milk. Then he told them that if they didn't repent of their sins—imagine a parson talking of sins these days!—they'd end up with smoking hides. In these days!"

He chuckled with happy memory. "No little pennies in the collection plates, either. You could see they gave what they honestly could.—A little kid ran across the lawn, afterwards, and his mother whaled the devil out of him. You'd have thought it was holy ground. Yes sir, the women might not be better than the rest of the women here, but you can bet they take care of their church! They're got something they call a Sodality."

"Haven't we a Ladies' Aid?" asked Johnny, hopelessly.

"Ho, ho! You'll see!" He ruminated to himself with angry amusement. "Went to see that priest feller. He's got a library that would knock your eyes out. It's a poor rectory, but smells of wax and paint, and everything's scrubbed down to the bone. We decided I'd better call him Father Kanty; can't get my tongue around those infernal foreign names. Do you know what? He has a better education than you have; speaks five languages all together, and no amateur at them. He's writing a book, in French, about one of their saints, for a Canadian publisher. Good writing; I read his manuscript myself. Well, I asked him why he couldn't get his people to clean up their houses and their yards. Know what he said? 'I've just finished the job of getting their children three meals a day. Not a woman in my parish works outside the house, except if she's a widow, or deserted, or has a disabled husband. Give me time,' he says. And he says, 'It's taken me five years, but they now make regular confessions, and every Mass is crowded. The poor priest before me was lucky if he got them in for confession before Christmas and Easter, and most of the time the church was empty.'"

They could see the modest altar gleaming bravely through the dusk. "See!" cried Jean. "God!"

"Yes," said Johnny. He thought of the news he had to break to the doctor about the religious instruction of the children, and his heart sank. "How far is this church from mine?" he asked.

"Only about a quarter of a mile. I've been taking you around through the town, so you could see it."

Dr. McManus tapped on the glass panel again, and said, "Down to Sycamore Street. Stop in the middle, right side."

"Can't say I think much of what I've seen so far," said Mrs. Burnsdale.

"Ho!" cried the doctor. "Wait until you see what you and the parson here are letting yourselves in for!"

The car was moving down a very cramped and dismal street, not dismal so much in the sense of being dirty, though the eternal soot floated freely here too, and the stench of the sulfurous factories was ubiquitous. Rather it was bleak and parched, and completely treeless. Dusk was sifting down through narrow alleys, and here and there a poor shop had begun to light up feebly. The car stopped before an insignificant square building built of brick, with plain glass windows, and a stone arch over the narrow door. Johnny leaned forward, the better to see it. Inset in the arch were Hebraic figures, and Johnny spelled them out to himself: "The Righteous Can Enter Here." So this was a synagogue, and a very modest one too.

"Jew place," said the doctor, peering at it. "Met the feller who runs it, at that newspaper dinner. He and Father Kanty are good friends; probably sympathize with each other. Seem to have a lot in common, and shouldn't wonder. Congregations are hell; people are hell. If you haven't learned that yet, boy, you'd better start soon." He puffed violently on his cigarette.

"Feller name of Rabbi Chaim Chortow, and old as Abrham. Scholar, Father Kanty tells me, and shy as a mouse. Has a beard. That makes his younger congregation mad, though why a man shouldn't wear a beard if he wants to is beyond me. About three hundred fifty Jews in the whole town, and this is the only place they have. Know why? Father Kanty told me. The old Jewish families live in this community because it's home to them; been here since the Year One, when they built this synagogue. Old folks are the same everywhere; they hate to move away from places where they were young once, and thought the world was wonderful, and married, and had children. Well, having been curious about Father Kanty, went to see this rabbi. He lives behind his church, in a house about the size of a dollhouse, with his old wife, who wears something over her hair all the time. That makes the young people mad too, though why what she wears is worse than a bandanna is something I don't understand. The Jewish girls wear 'em on the street, just like all the other careless females do, too."

The doctor smoked thoughtfully. "Never did like foreigners; still don't. But it's beginning to sneak into me that people are the same the world over—in other words, they stink to high heaven in their hearts. Take this old rabbi. Voice like a soft old organ—you know, when it sounds as if it's thinking to itself. He's got an accent; came from Russia, or some other damnable place. That makes another thing the young Jews have against him. Heard they wanted to kick him out and get a bright new feller, all New York paint and smartness. But those bright new fellers know when they're better off, and they wouldn't come. Besides, the old folks had something to say about it, and there's one thing about the Jews: they respect their parents. Something we should learn too.

"Well, son, the younger Jews moved out to the suburbs, up there on the hills, loaded down with mortgages. Pride. Maybe our people ought to get some of that vanishing commodity, too. The old Jews are tailors and shopkeepers and have their own meat stores. The young Jews go in for law and medicine and 'manufacturing.' That means making some clothes, and selling them. By the way, two of the young Jew doctors are pretty damn clever, and I got them on the hospital board after fighting like hell with the directors. Don't like them, myself. Why? Don't know; haven't taken time off to know. That don't matter.

"Well, sir, the old rabbi tells me his troubles."

Johnny interrupted: "You don't like Catholics or Jews, but—they tell you their troubles. Funny."

The doctor said, "Shut up. I'm conducting this tour, and no comments, please, parson. The Jewish girls like to dress well, and live in nice houses, even if the mortgage is up to the roof. And the Jews in this town are just about as well off as the rest of us—which means they scrape for a living. And the Jewish girls read lots of books, and they make their men read lots of books, and they go all out for psychiatry. Jargon, I call it. Never saw a psychiatrist yet who knew anything really fundamental about human nature. So the young Jews think their rabbi should talk psychiatry and child psychology to them, and current events, and ethics, and social integration, whatever in the name of God that means. They don't want sermons on God, and the necessity for prayer, and dedication. No, sir. That's old-fashioned stuff, for the ghettoes and the old folks. 'There is only one God, and Freud is His prophet.' That's how it goes."

"That isn't peculiar to young Jews," said Johnny. "Dr. Stevens tells me he runs into it all the time, with younger, 'smarter' congregations."

"What's he do about it?"

"Well," said Johnny sadly, "he has to listen to them."

"Humph. Let's get back to the old rabbi, and the fast-moving young people he has to stand, though it makes him sick. Told me only faith sustains him. So, one Friday night, he asks them, 'Is God out of date?' Do they think about *that*, and do penance, as Father John Kanty calls it? You can bet they don't! They just get mad. The atom bomb sobered them a little, just as it sobered the Catholics and Protestants. But then human nature asserted itself again, and there they were, screaming about progressivism, and being up-to-date."

"Not original," said Johnny. "Dr. Stevens has the same trouble. Don't people understand that religion is based on eternal verities?"

"Of course they don't. They're too stupid." He paused. "What eternal verities? There aren't any."

"You know there are," said Johnny quietly. Dr. McManus looked at him and his eyes glittered with anger. "Don't be a fool, parson," he said. "I'm willing to stand by you, so long as you aren't a fool. Go eternal verities on me, and you'll be looking for a new congregation."

Johnny smiled comfortably to himself. His heart became peaceful. After all, there was God. And still men of God.

"The children are tired," said Johnny tentatively, as the car rolled on.

"Don't look tired to me," said Dr. McManus irascibly. "Little thin, but healthy. I'm a doctor, and I know. Besides, I'm not taking you out of the way, as you seem to think; only about one minute. Did you think you could hop from the station right into the parsonage? Anyway, look at the kids. They're listening the way no American kids do; they ain't bouncing around, empty-eyed, like some of our own brats. Hey, you, Jean there, have any idea what I've been talking about, eh?"

But it was Max who astonished them all by answering immediately, "Yes—doctor. You say, doctor, all people are the same? *Ja?*"

"Max!" exclaimed Johnny, with intense pleasure.

"Son, you've boiled it all down, and right," said the doctor.

Max smiled proudly. He smoothed the peaks on his head, made them lie flat. Jean said, "But there is the law here. Papa said it."

Dr. McManus appeared about to snort, then closed his mouth tightly on his cigarette, after giving Johnny a jeering glance. They were driving through a better section now, quiet, small houses with fairly clean streets in spite of the soot. Gardens were visible, alive with zinnias and marigolds and petunias and geraniums. "Our middle class, whatever there is of it," said Dr. McManus. "The vanishing Americans. If you're thinking of something to save, parson, here's your chance. Women who have pride in their homes, and read homemaking magazines and make their own draperies, and study cookbooks. Men who work in small offices, and come home at night with brief cases. Or who're skilled mechanics, or own a truck or two. The American dream—the middle class. They stand in the way of Communism."

He pointed to a few little red-brick houses, bristling with glossy ivy. "Ministers; silly men—believe in the brotherhood of man. And that house on the corner, with all those holly-hocks, belongs to Dan McGee; president of the local mine union. Gets about eight thousand a year. On your church board; fought his being there, myself, don't like people who make trouble."

"Does he make trouble?" asked Johnny, looking with interest at the bright white curtains across the clean win-dows.

"No," said the doctor, shortly and inconsistently. "Just don't like him on principle. But he stands with me on making your parishioners support their church; doesn't have the idea I should foot all the bill. He's worried to death about the local Commies; they hate him. We have lots of talks."

Johnny smiled to himself.

The car was rising on rising streets. The mountains were coming more fully into view, and the air was clearer. "See that great big white house almost covered with trees, far up on that hill? Cost over a hundred thousand dollars to build, ten years ago, when things were cheap. Circular drive; gardens; fountains; even a swimming pool. Know who owns it? Mac Summerfield, who owns and edits our one morning newspaper, and our evening one. Doesn't need the papers. Rich with oil. Inherited two-three millions from his dad, who struck oil in Titusville. He's our rich hidden Commie. Hate sheets on the side, anti-Semitic, anti-Catholic, anti-American. Got in some trouble couple of years ago on those sheets; he was all for Hitler then. Funny people don't catch on that Communism and fascism are one and the same thing. Stupid bastards."

"Can't you do anything about his Communist activities?" asked Johnny.

"Hell, no," said Dr. McManus gloomily. "He isn't an open Commie. Sometimes even runs an editorial or two taking Russia gently to task about something insignificant. Why would a rich man want to be a Commie? Sonny, you're naïve. He wants power; he wants to be chief commissar or some-thing. He hates humanity; wants to help beat its face in the mud. Perverted s.o.b. but they all are."

Johnny thought it over somberly. Dr. McManus leered at him. "He keeps his eye on all the churches. Let a minister step out of line, and talk common sense to his congregation, and there's an editorial calling him an enemy of the people, or tool of Wall Street, or something. Watch it, sonny boy. You're due for a couple of editorials in the future. I can feel it."

The doctor pointed to a row of small Cape Cod houses, all newly painted white in desperation against the soot. There was a sameness about them, but something charming also, for every garden was different, surrounded by little white picket fences. "There live the tools of Wall Street, and imperialistic capitalism, and the oppressors, as Mac calls them," said Dr. McManus. "In other words, foremen and superintendents of the mines. Mortgages on every one of them. I know. They belong to your parish, poor devils."

The streets were becoming dreary again, but they were at least neat. As it was suppertime now, there were no children on the streets, or women on the porches. Attempts had been made to grow wisteria vines over the posts, with only fair success. Lawns were dirty with soot, but grass was bravely struggling, as were the few young saplings. "Your parish," said Dr. McManus. "A good cross section of the whole town. Not a man lives here who makes more than five thousand a year, if that, either in the mills, or the factories, or in the offices, or in independent business—which is practically on its last gasp now, the way things are these days. And there's your church."

It was a wooden church, on the next corner. Apparently the architect had had some vague idea about the churches in New England, but only a vague idea. It had a thin steeple with a cross, and the steeple was too tall for the low building, which had originally been white but was now a dirty gray. The building huddled close to the ground, as if ashamed of itself for being so unprepossessing. The stained windows were cheap and poorly executed. Only the doors were arresting in appearance, dark carved wood polished and rich. "I gave those doors to the church," said Dr. McManus angrily. "I pay for having them polished every week, too. And for those little lawns. Think the parishioners are grateful? No sir. I should do it all, they think."

The parsonage next door looked very small and humble

and ugly to Johnny, of no particular style, with no good old-fashioned porch. Its windows were thin and tall in its squat exterior, and it had a narrow arched door. Like the church, it was built of dirty gray wood, once white, and had a roof with curling shingles. Though it was almost flush with the sidewalk, Johnny saw, with some hope, that it did have a large yard, the coarse grass and weeds recently cut. But there were no trees in it, no flowers, and it was fenced in.

"Like it?" asked the doctor, with ghoulish interest.

"No," said Johnny.

The doctor laughed so heartily that Emilie woke up. He patted her face. "Just having some fun, dearie," he said. She smiled at him timidly, yawned. "Good teeth," commented the doctor approvingly. "Nice mouth too."

"There can be a garden," said Johnny. "And trees."

The chauffeur opened the doors of the huge limousine, helped the children from the folding seats, tried to take the duffel bag from Jean. But the boy clung to it fiercely. All the children had been somewhat cramped in the car, despite its size, but they had not complained. The little girls shook out their dresses fastidiously; the boys straightened their ties. They regarded the house without expressions of disappointment or curiosity. As they all marched up to the door it opened, and a gray, wiry, and rather severe woman stood on the threshold in silence. Dr. McManus waved his hand. "Mr. Fletcher, this is Mrs. Dan McGee, wife of the president of the local mine union, and president of the Ladies' Aid. Marjie, your new minister. And his kids. And Mrs. Burnsdale, kind of their caretaker."

Mrs. McGee smiled slightly and shook hands with Johnny, saying in a rather monotonous voice, "Welcome, Mr. Fletcher and Mrs. Burnsdale." She hesitated, and looked at the children. "Well," she said. "I heard about these. They'll all be going to Sunday school; that's nice. But come in, come in."

There was the tiniest of entry halls, containing nothing but an ancient hatrack, the floor covered with clean but broken linoleum, of a dull-red color. It opened onto a parlor, filled with elderly furniture made of imitation maple, upholstered in a chintz pattern that had been washed so often that its original pattern was completely faded, giving a general effect of a dim pink-green. A big fiber mat covered the floor, in squares of blue and yellow, obviously new, and obviously more suited to a terrace than an indoor room. Johnny saw dark-chocolate walls, plastered, with a pink ceiling, old lamps with checkered porcelain shades or lamps made of wicker, tables of pseudo-maple, mahogany, and walnut, all glazed with fresh and ugly varnish. Along one wall stretched a big bookcase, but only five or six old books were there. But there was a fireplace, and it was to this that Johnny turned, after his first dejected survey of the room. There could be fires here in the winter, and rosy comfort, and intimacy and love.

"It looks very—clean," he said to Mrs. McGee, who was watching him closely for his reaction.

"That's about all you can say of it," the doctor jeered. "Everything is here that anybody wanted to throw away, then thought it good enough for the parsons."

"Now, Dr. McManus," said Mrs. McGee coldly. She had spirit; her pale nostrils flared in her nondescript face. "We do our best. Dan and I give all we can."

She led them into a dining room, so narrow, so dark that it was almost impossible to see that here the furniture was "mission," dating back to the early years of the century, dark ugly wood with imitation-leather seats, and a round table. Mrs. McGee snapped on a light, though the sunset was still glowing with gold and magenta outside. Then Johnny was touched. The table was covered with a cheap, machine-made lace cloth. Modest china and plated silver, very worn, had been laid out. In the center stood a glass bowl of garden flowers, fresh and sweet.

Mrs. McGee pressed her hands against the inexpensive print of her dress and waited. "Well," said Johnny, "this is very kind." He gave her his strong, gentle smile, and she smiled back at him, becoming as pretty as a girl. She explained that the other members of the Ladies' Aid could not be here just now; they had families, and it was suppertime. But they had filled the icebox and the pantry, and had brought their own "roll-out" beds for the children. Johnny was perplexed, but Mrs. Burnsdale said, "Roll-out beds! No bedrooms here?"

The two women's eyes clashed together in an invisible but palpable engagement. Then, just as Johnny was becoming apprehensive, Mrs. McGee smiled her pretty smile again, and she tilted her head regretfully. "There are only three bedrooms, I'm sorry to say. One a little big, for the minister, and two very small ones. We worried and worried about it. There were just three beds, a double for the minister and a single in each of the other rooms. Where would we put five children, and a housekeeper? We had a special meeting. We were terribly worried. Seven people. So we worked on it. Somebody had an extra twin bed, and it's in one of the small rooms. And then somebody else had two roll-out beds. They push away when you've folded them up in the morning; there wouldn't be room to let them stand open during the day. And then Mrs. Fichte got the men working, and they bought a day bed, and we put it in the minister's room. We shoved the beds around, and the only way we could think of was that two of the boys have the tiny bedroom, and one of the boys sleep in the minister's room, and the girls with Mrs. Burnsdale." She sighed and rubbed her thin arms, as if remembering strenuous work. "It's the best we can do."

Johnny said quickly, "After all, you hadn't expected five children. I think you've done wonderfully, and thank you."

Mrs. McGee became gloomy, and shook her head. "Maybe you won't be happy when you see the rest of the house."

"Correct," said Dr. McManus gleefully. She gave him a devastating glance, which made him chuckle.

Mrs. Burnsdale had a low opinion of the small dark kitchen. The pantry space was large enough for only a few battered pans, and a few dishes and kitchenware. The sink was iron, its glaze of cracked white porcelain. There was no refrigerator, only an icebox with a water pan beneath it. The gas stove, converted from coal, emitted a sickening smell, but its black sides and nickel front had been polished. Mrs. Burnsdale said, "I haven't seen a stove like that since I was in my twenties. I didn't think they could make it work with gas."

Mrs. McGee gazed at it despondently. "It's pretty awful," she admitted. "But we hope to get you a better one soon. Mrs. Barnes is going to buy an electric, when her husband gets his raise; he works for our night newspaper. And then she'll give the parsonage her gas stove, which isn't more than six years old."

"Something tells me, Mrs. Burnsdale, that you'll be cooking on that cave-man range to the end of time," Dr. McManus remarked. "Mac Summerfield doesn't believe in raises for his labor."

Mrs. McGee swung on him, her tired, shrewd eyes sparkling with anger. "Well, what's wrong with you giving Mrs. Burnsdale a new stove then? Instead of sneering all the time?"

Dr. McManus rubbed his chin and regarded her approvingly. "Marjie, you always did have guts. Women seem to have more of 'em these days than men. When you put it that way—Mrs. Burnsdale's stove—it makes me think. I wouldn't do a thing for the parson, but Mrs. Burnsdale's different. I'll think it over."

"I prefer electric," said Mrs. Burnsdale majestically. "With at least four cooking spaces, and two ovens. I'll need two ovens, with this family. Also a refrigerator, not this ice. The kids have to have fresh milk, and the refrigerator will have to be extra-large."

Dr. McManus was all admiration. "Anything else?" he asked.

She studied the kitchen, one stubby gloved finger against her lips. "Yes. more cupboards. At least three iron skillets, and a lot of new pans. I'll make a list."

"Good," said the doctor, while Johnny and Mrs. McGee gaped.

"And new linoleum," said Mrs. Burnsdale thoughtfully. "And a corner blocked off, and a table and six chairs for breakfast. I like yellow, and chrome."

"Make a list," said Dr. McManus.

Mrs. McGee looked with helpless eloquence at Johnny. And then, involuntarily, he winked. Mrs. McGee was obviously startled. She brooded on it. She came to herself, gazed at Johnny, and winked back, rejoicing. She turned to Mrs. Burnsdale. "You wouldn't want a nicer dining-room set, or new furniture for the parlor?" she asked innocently.

"I certainly would," replied Mrs. Burnsdale calmly. "I'll make a list."

"Don't be too niggardly about it," said Dr. McManus with heavy irony.

"Of course I won't," Mrs. Burnsdale promised, which immediately brought ire to the doctor's face. "And now," Mrs. Burnsdale continued, "I want to see the pastor's study. If we're to have a real congregation here, the study is very important."

Mrs. McGee coughed wretchedly. "There isn't any," she

confessed. She pointed to the artificial-maple desk in the corner, near one of the two dreary windows. Then she pointed to the abominably pink ceiling with its countless cracks. "Do you see that line of division up there? Well, there was a partition, breaking up the parlor into two rooms. But they were so tiny! So the Ladies' Aid got up a fund, five years ago, and we pulled down the partition and threw the two rooms together. You see, the study had only one window, and it was bad for the minister."

Mrs. Burnsdale and Johnny again gave long attention to the room, which was still dishearteningly small. Mrs. McGee sighed with sympathy, but darted Dr. McManus an accusing glance. "It does make it homey when the pastor has visitors—his study and the parlor all one," she ventured. Mrs. Burnsdale marched over to the desk, the floor shaking under her heavy step. She opened the small drawers, significantly examined its scarred and ink-stained surface. She looked at the bookcase which ran the whole length of the chocolate wall behind the desk. Then she put her hands on her hips and faced Dr. McManus across the length of the room.

"I have been in some pretty awful parsonages before," she said, "but this beats them all. Aren't you ashamed?"

"Yes," said the doctor, "I am. But the rest of the congregation isn't. If they want a church, a decent parsonage, I'm here to help them. I'll give exactly what they give, but not a penny more. Well?"

She considered this, and her frown slowly faded. "Doctor," she said more kindly, "I'm afraid you're right. Well, Mrs. McGee, I'm now a member of your Ladies' Aid, and when I get through with them—"

The furnace was old, broken, and dangerous, a coal-burner of some forgotten make. Mrs. Burnsdale examined the dirty cellar, the small heap of coal. The filthy, cobwebbed windows admitted no light. They had not brought the children down here, after Johnny had given a quick signal to Mrs. Burnsdale. She said in her loud and forthright voice, "That furnace'll never be used again in this house! I'm not taking chances on those five children dying of carbon—carbon—di—di—"

"Carbon monoxide is the word, I believe," said the doctor.

"It goes on the list," said Mrs. Burnsdale.

106

"How much," asked the doctor with outrage, "is going on my list, and how much does the congregation pay?"

Mrs. Burnsdale relented. Her broad face dimpled, and her eyes sparkled. She put her hand on the doctor's arm. "Just what I've mentioned. Nothing else. Doctor, you are a wonderful man. A wonderful man."

"Don't be an idiot," said the doctor brusquely, and put a safe distance between himself and the redoubtable woman. "I'm buying you what *you* need, but nothing for the parson. That's understood, isn't it?"

Johnny, after this inspection, was too disheartened to be amused. Mrs. Burnsdale was considering the cellar shelves, and frowning rebukingly. "I don't know if the other ministers had wives, but if they did they certainly weren't forehanded about canning and such. In my opinion, a woman who doesn't can hasn't any business being a wife."

They walked carefully up the molding wooden stairs. "You can buy frozen things, and canned goods," said the doctor.

"Yes, fine for emergencies and people who have to cook fast, and other things too. But give me a good home-canned peach any time, or real strawberry jam, or tomatoes, or jelly." Mrs. Burnsdale spoke with authority, and the doctor did not dispute her. When they reached the kitchen again, where the children were huddling in silence, Dr. McManus said, "You haven't seen the bedrooms yet." He chuckled morosely. "If what has greeted your dewy eyes already hasn't taken the heart out of you, the bedrooms will! They will!"

They did. The "minister's room" was even more drab than the parlor, and was furnished with the same imitation, scarred maple and indistinguishable print, with matching draperies, one small high window, round like a porthole in the leprous green plaster of the wall, one table by the side of the wilted four-poster with its cheap maroon counterpane, and garnished with a dim lamp and a cheap pink rayon shade, and a maple rocking chair. Johnny thought of the large gilt and mosaic crucifix he had been given in Rome, guaranteed to be blessed by His Holiness himself, and he thought that, hung over his bed, it would brighten this wretched room. "But the red day bed is nice, isn't it?" asked Mrs. McGee, with hope. She went to the object in question, and smoothed its coarse cotton cover. "It cost nearly seventy dollars, and they tell me it's very comfortable. One of the boys can sleep here. Or even two; it's wide enough." Mrs. Burnsdale murmured approvingly.

Johnny said, "I think Jean and Max should sleep on the day bed." Mrs. Burnsdale had found the meager closet which Mrs. McGee explained was the "linen shelves, and such." Six blankets, worn but clean, and very thin, lay there, and about ten sheets and a dozen pillowcases, and one cotton comforter.

"The Ladies' Aid, which I belong to, is going to find lots more blankets and sheets," said Mrs. Burnsdale emphatically. "And about four dozen towels. When's your next meeting, Mrs. McGee?"

"The terror of the Ladies' Aid," said the doctor with respect.

The bathroom was displayed with deep embarrassment by Mrs. McGee. The fixtures were incredibly ancient, the high tub set in a wooden frame. Mrs. Burnsdale began to express her indignation, but the doctor raised his hand. "No, Mrs. McGee, nothing here is going on the list. That's the parson's department."

"Seven people, and only this," said Mrs. Burnsdale, pointing ruthlessly.

Dr. McManus's eyes followed her finger. "Now I think that's a very nice article. Used it myself, when I was a kid. I've got a fondness for it. Did a lot of good, sound meditation there. If it's ever thrown out I'll take it for my own."

"And put it in your front hall. Everybody should have something he cherishes," said Mrs. Burnsdale witheringly, and Johnny smiled. Mrs. McGee had retreated delicately to the door, where she was pretending to examine the fiber matting in the tiny hall. "In fact," went on Mrs. Burnsdale, "why should we keep what's so dear to you, doctor? Let's make you a present of it!"

"Now that's very good of you, Mrs. Burnsdale," said the doctor, scowling at Johnny. "In fact, I'll take you up on it. Excellent workmanship there; nothing shoddy, like these days. Last a century. Let me see. I'll replace it with two of 'em. Would you, my dear lady, prefer pink ones, or a blue and a rose one?" Mrs. McGee, hearing his tone, went quickly down the twisted little stairway. Even she, who had spirit, winced when Dr. McManus spoke like that.

But Mrs. Burnsdale was not intimidated. She thought. "Well, I think I'd like pink. Nice for the girls, and girls should be considered first. That'll be the beginning for what they call matched sets. We can put a shower rod over that—that tub! Look at it! Doctor, did you meditate there, too, and what did you think about?"

Dr. McManus said, "My father was the first minister, and usually I thought of how hungry I was, and how boiled potatoes, even with my mother's milk gravy, wasn't enough for dinner. I thought of how I was going to get through medical school; I thought about adding some new odd jobs to the other jobs I had. I thought of how nice it would be if my mother could have a single new dress; she never got one for nearly five years after we came here. I thought of my father, trying to inspire the love of God, and faith and hope and charity, in his congregation, and how he wasn't doing very well at it, though he was the finest man on earth. I thought how his spirit was being broken, and how he looked when the sun was on his face in the back yard. I thought what courage he had, for many years, standing in his pulpit, talking like an angel, and nobody listening. Mrs. Burnsdale, my-lady-with-the-list, that's what I thought about."

Johnny put his hand on that incredibly wide and massive shoulder. It was only his imagination, of course, but he thought it was trembling. Mrs. Burnsdale's eyes had begun to blink. She sniffled. "Hope I'm not getting a cold," she said severely, as she fumbled in her purse and brought out a very white, starched handkerchief. She blew her nose. "Doctor," she said, and nothing could have been sadder than her voice, "why did your father stay?"

"Because no one else would take this parish at his salary," said the doctor roughly, but he stood very rigid under Johnny's hand and did not move away. "And he wouldn't desert what he called his 'people' and let the church and this house rot, untenanted." He grumbled under his breath. "He said shepherds had lived in worse places, and that the first Shepherd had no place to lay His head. So why should he complain? Taking it all in all, though, the people weren't any poorer than they are now. Twenty dollars a week at the best, but it bought more then. Well. Besides, the old ladies and the kids loved him, and they were his own."

Mrs. Burnsdale gazed at the tub, then she said strongly, "We can get rid of everything else, but not that! I'll tell the kids about it. Just a shower rod, though, and perhaps we can paint that splintered wood around it some nice color."

"Pink, no doubt," said the doctor wrathfully. She smiled at him, and they went downstairs again, after visiting the incredibly tiny bedrooms where Mrs. Burnsdale and the children would sleep. They were met by Mrs. McGee, who said, "It's getting real dark, and I think the children ought to have their supper, Mrs. Burnsdale, and it's all ready for all of you, hot in the oven. A good big pot of pork and beans, and macaroni with cheese—lots of cheese—and three loaves of home-made bread, and—oh, yes—some vegetable soup, and a nice potato salad, with greens from Mrs. Schoeffel's own garden, and milk for the children, and a pot of coffee. I can't stay any longer. I hope," she said politely, "that it'll be all right. And there's enough food here for a couple of days more, too. The ladies took care of that."

"Fine, fine," said Mrs. Burnsdale warmly, and took off her gloves. "I'll just get an apron." She hesitated. She wondered what her status would be here but, seeing Mrs. McGee's grateful eyes, she responded impulsively. She kissed the other woman quickly on her cheek.

"I'm staying for dinner," announced the doctor. "Haven't had anything to eat like that for years." He unfastened his grimy tie, and let it hang. "And, afterwards, you can give me your infernal list, madam."

They sat crowded about the small and ugly table in the dining room. Johnny folded his hands, and the children imitated him, and he bent his head. "Dear Lord, Our God, Our Most Beloved Father, we thank You for what You have given us this day. Let it nourish us, that we may do Your work, and grant us peace. Amen."

Dr. McManus, who had just sat like an enormous lump in his chair, did not join in the prayer, or even bend his head. And then he snorted, "Peace, amen! You'll need it, my bright young man. And now, pass the beans."

"Papa first," said Kathy in her admonishing voice, and the doctor dropped his hand and waited.

7

They had finished dinner and the children were in bed, and there was the good hearty sound of Mrs. Burnsdale washing dishes in the kitchen. Dr. McManus and Johnny sat in the study-parlor; the muggy air barely stirred in the close confines of the room.

The doctor laid down a heavy brown-paper parcel of X rays. He lit one cigarette after another, his big face moving, his eyebrows jerking, his mouth pursing. Johnny waited, his hands clenched on his knees, praying for some hope in the older man's verdict. But the doctor continued to sit there, dropping ashes on his thighs, muttering in his squeaky voice, scratching his ear. Four hospital calls had come in for him, but he had snarled into the telephone and had suggested aspirin or "a jolt of morphine, and tell him to shut up," and he still sat there, the mound of ashes increasing on his soiled light suit. There were sweat marks under his monster arms, and his shirt collar had become gray.

Then he said, "This is a hell of a thing."

"No hope, then?" said Johnny with despair. He tried to take the X rays away, but the doctor squealed at him, "Let 'em alone, confound you! I'm going to study them some more. That kid's shoulder—the upper arm. Hell, you've probably learned enough anatomy by now without my going into details. How he ever got even partial use of his shoulder and arm again, and his leg, is beyond me. The leg especially. Why, the damned leg is a mess all by itself. Talk about miracles! You've got one on your hands now, without asking for another. Show the average bone feller those X rays and he'll tell you it isn't possible for the kid to walk, or use his arm at all! And you ask for miracles!"

"Jean is in almost constant pain," said Johnny hopelessly. "He's learned to bear it without complaining. That's the worst part of—"

"Good God, we all have pain," said the doctor with contempt. "Every man jack of us—one way or another. Love to hear these psychiatrists talk about happy adjustment and healthy integration, and other tripe! What they mean is faceless and contented idiots. That's their aim for most people," he added darkly. "But take normal people. Even little kids, babies. Pain. A growl here, a colic there, imperfect eyes, imperfect hearing even in the best of 'em. Take kids in the teens. Aches. By that time they've got mental aches too. Natural. We don't lead normal lives; nature never intended us to be civilized, to walk on our hind legs. Now, don't start talking soul to me. Gibberish. Pain; we've got aspirin and codeine and morphine and everything else, but pain lurks right there in the background. A saber-toothed tiger, waiting. And when we're men and women, the pain, physical and mental, gets worse. Why do you suppose doctors' offices are crowded? Don't be a fool."

He looked sourly at the package of X rays. "Don't wonder that kid has more pain than most. I'll admit that. And it'll get worse as he grows older. Bones all shattered, originally. How they even knitted as well as they did I don't know! Against all laws, as we know 'em."

"Something must be done," said Johnny, with more despair. "You see, I practically promised that God will cure him."

The doctor grinned evilly. "Why don't you take him, then, to one of those Papist shrines? Heard they do miracles there." He shook his head. "But not in this case. Just plain, damned, broken, shattered bones that got healed in a hit-and-miss fashion, and I don't know how!"

Johnny waited. Somehow, and he did not know why, his own pain for Jean lessened. The doctor shook a dirty finger in his face. "Wheel chair for that kid, in a year or two, for the rest of his life. Then come the painkillers; work for a while. Then he'll curse the day you ever rescued him. What do you do then?"

Johnny said quietly, "You won't let that happen."

The doctor was infuriated. "You parsons! Haven't a brain in your skulls. Remember my father, face all lighted, talking about the mercy of God. What mercy? Tell me that, boy. What mercy let that kid get kicked almost to death anyway? What about those six million Jews in the crematoriums? And the slave-labor camps in Russia? Tell me where your God is, and was. Tell me that, and I'll believe in miracles too."

Johnny said, and there were white lines about his mouth, "That's one of the things I can't understand. But there must be a meaning to it all." He clasped his fingers together tightly. "I think of God's reply to Job's anguished reproaches. 'Where wast thou when I laid the foundations of the earth? Declare, if thou hast understanding.'"

"If God said that, then He is the biggest sophist of them all," said the doctor.

He roughly opened the package and looked at the X rays again. He shook his head. He muttered, as he turned the plates over and over. "Look," he said, "I'm a general surgeon. I operate on anybody, from a thyroid to gangrene of the toes. You're supposed, these days, to quarter every section of the body, and just operate on that particular quarter that belongs to you. Damned nonsense. I leave out eyes; that belongs to another field, and I've got too much respect for eyes to touch 'em. But the rest of the body—why, a man of sense can go anywhere into it, even the brain or heart. It's expensive to the public to be a specialist, especially a surgical specialist. But never saw a bright kidney feller who couldn't take out an appendix, or sew up a hole in the belly or do a rectal job."

He thrust the X rays back into the package with scorn. "Send that kid to me tomorrow and I'll take my own pictures. I'm not promising miracles, remember that. But maybe I can do something about his pain. Cut a few nerves here and there. More than that I'm not giving you any hope."

113

He blinked morosely at Johnny's sudden brilliant smile. "Damned fool," he said.

He dropped his cigarette on the fiber rug and deliberately ground it out there, to Johnny's alarm. "Don't worry; it won't catch fire." He lit another cigarette; he was addicted to one of the stronger varieties. "Rumors getting around you can get a fine case of cancer of the lungs from cigarettes. More damned nonsense. How do they explain the thousands of babies born with cancer? I can explain it, but they won't listen. Industrial gases and smoke. Pittsburgh did something about it; why can't other cities?

"I've got another thing to talk about. You're crazy. I gave you six months to stay here this afternoon. You won't last two weeks. Better write Frank Stevens to look around for a new parish for you. Wait until this congregation finds out you're going to really preach the Word of God!" His squealing laughter filled the room. He slapped his thigh. Then he stopped all at once, and squinted at Johnny. "Poor, damned young fool," he said soberly.

Dr. McManus's offices were huge and disorderly, with two nurses and a receptionist who seemed to adore the indomitable old man in spite of his curses and abuse. But his examination rooms were bright and shining. "Sol Klein and the other Jewish boy come in two afternoons a week and help," he explained to Johnny. "And two Catholic boys I've got my eyes on, and three young fellers from the Lutheran Hospital. No regular assistants, though, with good sound salaries. Makes 'em lazy. Just pay my boys so much a case; keep 'em hustling. Well, let's get those X rays now. It just happens Sol Klein is here. Want him to take a look at this kid."

Jean said coldly, "God will cure arm and leg."

"Oh, sure, sure!" said Dr. McManus, waving his hand. "But maybe we can help Him out, eh? Never heard He was graduated from a recognized school, though."

Dr. Klein was a slight, competent, blond young man who apparently took life very seriously. His blue eyes were steady and sharp, though kind, behind thick glasses. His white coat, unlike that of Dr. McManus, was severely clean and well-fitting. "Like this boy?" Dr. McManus asked of Johnny, putting his meaty hand on the younger doctor's shoulder. "He isn't afraid of anything, and that's what pleases me.

That's why I have him. He'll go in with a scalpel where the New York specialists wouldn't go with an X ray, or a barium meal. Had a woman two months ago with cancer of the uterus; spread to surrounding tissues and glands. Turned down in New York. Sol took a chance; she was almost moribund, anyway. And know what? She walks out of the hospital five weeks later; gained ten pounds, recovering. Cured? Don't know. But shouldn't wonder."

Dr. Klein surprised Johnny with a furtive wink. "He forgets to tell you she comes in three times a week for supplementary X-ray treatments." He looked down at Jean, and his narrow face tightened. "So this is the boy who was in a concentration camp. So God is going to cure you, I hear." He smiled, and his smile was sweet. "We doctors can help a little, or give medicine, but in the end, Jean, it is God who really cures. You understand?"

"Yes," said the boy. He stood still while the young doctor's slim hands moved expertly over his arm and leg. Johnny watched anxiously. Dr. Klein's face told him nothing; it had gone remote and expressionless. Jean was led into the X-ray room, and Johnny waited in the somewhat disorderly waiting room, filled to the very door with patients. They gazed at his clerical black and his collar, and he gave them shy and tentative smiles. Some returned his smile; some averted their eyes bitterly. He understood, and sighed. The nurses, coming and going, beamed at him encouragingly.

Dear Father, he prayed silently, let there be a way to cure this child, Thy child. A miracle. A miracle, Father, please.

He glanced at his wrist watch. The church board and the Ladies' Aid were giving him a "welcome" dinner tonight. He was apprehensive. He must tell them all, tonight, about Jean and Pietro and Max. It was only fair to give them an opportunity to make up their minds as to whether they would retain him as their pastor. He prayed again: Father, if it be Thy will, let them know, and understand. It is so terribly necessary that they understand.

He thought of his church, which he had seen this morning. Small, dark, drab, though very clean. There was not an inspirational feature in it, however, and the cheap stained-glass windows had admitted little light, though the morning had been vivid with sun. It had been explained to Johnny that once there had been a cross on the altar; but many of the parishioners had begun to object. A cross on the steeple, yes, but not on the altar! There had even been a quarrel about candles—their amount, size, and position. The "conservatives" had prevailed. Two candelabra on the altar, with small white candles. But nowhere else. A long chandelier, converted twenty years ago from gas to electricity, hung from the steeply pitched oaken ceiling. This was always ostentatiously turned on when the candles were lighted. Johnny thought of the early Christians, who carried lanterns in their hands through secret, smoky caves, and the cross which was always with them, even if only two rough sticks fastened together with hide or rude nails. He sighed.

The rooms reserved to him in the church were so small that he had barely space to move. His choir? Dr. McManus had chortled over this. Six persons, all mature men. No boys. Why? Popery, of course. There was not even a female singer. "But this sounds worse than any backwoods church of a century ago!" Johnny had exlaimed to the sympathizing Mrs. Burnsdale.

The automobile furnished him by the congregation was at least seven years old, but it was bravely polished, and a parishioner who owned a small garage and was a fine mechanic had put it in excellent condition. The children had admired it. It was theirs, and therefore finer than Dr. McManus's limousine. The younger four had cheered on the sidewalk when he had driven off with Jean this morning in a cloud of exhaust and with a brave explosive sound.

Johnny smiled, remembering. Then a nurse was beckoning to him and he jumped up eagerly and followed her into an examination room. Jean was painfully getting himself into shirt and coat, and the two doctors were watching him in a silence Johnny thought too clinical. "Well, well?" he cried, his voice trembling. Dr. McManus scowled at him. "Oh, it's you," he mumbled. "Sit down; you're not taking off just now." But Johnny turned to Dr. Klein, imploringly. The young doctor carefully lit a cigarette, his eyes half shut in thought. When Jean, with a dexterity he had agonizingly learned, flipped his coat quickly over his shoulder, Dr. Klein nodded, as if pleased at some confirmation of his diagnosis. Then he said to Johnny, "I say operate, as soon as possible. It'll be a long business, resetting, patching, and it won't be

116

comfortable." He sat down and faced Jean, and he took the boy's hand. Now his face had a quiet bitterness in it, though his voice was gentle. "Jean, you've told me your—father—said God will cure you. God has already performed a miracle for you; He let you live; He sent the minister, here, to you. Now you must have an operation. Hospital. Nurses. Do you know what I mean?"

Jean stared at him mutely, with pale and rebellious eyes. He answered after a moment, "God will cure."

Dr. Klein nodded. "Of course He will. Don't ever doubt it. You see, we doctors couldn't cure a single pain without God. We couldn't help anybody without God."

Johnny put his hand on Jean's stiff shoulder and turned the boy to him. "Jean," he said urgently. "Look. Do you see my hands? They move, pick up things, work, write. What makes them do these things?" Jean turned his stare to the young minister. Johnny tapped his own forehead. "My brain, in my head. Without my brain my hands couldn't move at all. Jean, God uses men as we use our hands. We are His instruments, He the Mover. When a doctor, like Dr. Klein here, works to cure people, God is with him. Sometimes God cures all at once, but more often He uses men for His miracles. See, dear?"

Jean still stared at him remotely, and the three men waited. Then the pale eyes slowly and wisely warmed, and Jean took the minister's hand, comfortingly. "Papa is miracle," he said. And for a moment he leaned his head against Johnny's black sleeve. Man and boy stood closely together, and Dr. Klein smiled again.

Dr. McManus said, "I think the kid's right, at that."

Dr. Klein walked to the outer door with Johnny and Jean. He shook Johnny's hand. "Old Al told me about the children and you," he said. He took his cigarette from his mouth and gazed at it contemplatively. "Somehow, you make me think of our old rabbi—I've come to the conclusion none of us deserve our pastors. We've got a fine police force in Barryfield, and a good chief. We pay them better than they're paid in any other city in the state, just to protect our property and our lives." His thin mouth twisted. "But we pay our pastors much less, for protecting our—shall I say spiritual welfare? Perhaps we think that's less important." He threw the cigarette from him, down the white steps of Dr. Mc-Manus's clinic. "I think your coming here wasn't just an accident, Mr. Fletcher."

"Thank you," said Johnny gravely. "I believe that too." He hesitated. "Jean, run down and get in the car, will you?" Jean obeyed at once, running down the steps sideways, to help his lame leg. Johnny's eyes smarted. "Three weeks ago he would contest everything I asked of him, and worse. Now, he's my right-hand man. Doctor, can you cure him?"

"Why not?" asked Dr. Klein carelessly. But his smile was quick, if brief. "After all, isn't—God—on your side?" He nodded, turned, and went inside rapidly. But Johnny swung about, catching up with him. "Just a minute, doctor." He swallowed hard. "I haven't much money. What I have was given by good men who had even less, for the children. By soldiers. I do have a check from Dr. Stevens—my superior—and that is also for the children, in equal parts. So I can't pay very much for the operation. Perhaps, time payments—"

Dr. Klein regarded him with cold surprise. "Was a fee mentioned?" he asked, and walked off angrily. Johnny watched him go.

On the way home Johnny explained the operation to Jean, who listened in silence. "So, say next week, Jean. It won't be very comfortable. But you're a brave boy. You want a miracle from God, and you are going to get it. God sent us to this city; God sent us to Dr. McManus, and Dr. Klein. Yes, God could cure you all at once. But think a minute. Maybe it was necessary for these doctors to know you, to bring them back to God. By curing you they will cure some sickness of the heart in themselves. Do you understand?"

Jean's mouth was tight, his eyes fixed. Then he said, "Yes. I know. Jean and Papa are miracles from God, to doctors. God makes miracles for many."

Johnny pressed the boy's thin fingers. But he said to himself, It'll be a miracle, indeed, if my congregation accepts me—after tonight.

When they reached home they found the bleak little house vibrating with excitement. Mrs. Burnsdale could hardly speak for joy; she tugged at Johnny's hand and led him like a child into the kitchen. Then she pointed, proudly. The kitchen swarmed with children, who circulated, with exclamations, about a gleaming new white stove and a refrigerator. Tall cartons of pans and dishes stood upon the counters and the table, a wonderful new table of yellow plastic and chrome, complete with matching chairs. A plumber had taken away the ancient sink; another was being installed, the color of honey, gay with chrome fixtures. The plumber glanced over his shoulder at Johnny and grinned. "It'll be all ready in about ten minutes more, sir," he said. "Got to hurry, so hope you won't mind my not getting up from my knees. By the way, I belong to your congregation. Can't wait to hear your first sermon Sunday."

The children crowded about Johnny, screaming with exclamations. "Upstairs, too!" shouted Pietro, pointing at the ceiling. "Pretty colors. Two, Papa!"

"Quiet now," said Mrs. Burnsdale firmly. "Go on. Scat. Into the dining room for your lunch. Jean, march those boys off first, to wash their hands, and Kathy, you take Emilie, and comb her hair too. Step!"

The children quieted immediately, and went off. Mrs. Burnsdale smiled fondly after them. "Wish our own kids had as much sense," she said, "and knew how to obey grownups. We're lucky, Mr. Fletcher."

"Yes," said Johnny. He regarded the new furnishings in astonishment. "Dr. McManus must have gotten busy at once. Probably last night, after he left here. He seems to think that we're not going to be sent away by this congregation. I wish I felt so sure."

"You're sure, sir, about everything but yourself," said Mrs. Burnsdale in a stern, maternal tone. "Now I want to know, is that right?"

The plumber glanced curiously over his stout shoulder. "First time old Al ever did anything for any minister, sir. Without the rest of us putting up half right away. Told my wife about it. She couldn't believe it. Sure we want you. Any parson who can get old Al to do something for him is the kind of parson we want. Yes sir."

He tightened a nut expertly. "Best fixtures in town. Old Al got the hardware fellows out of bed last night. 'Never mind the expense,' he says to them. They couldn't believe it. Bet the news is all over the town by now. My wife's chairwoman of the Ladies' Aid. When I left to come here this morning she was on the telephone telling all the other ladies about it."

Mrs. Burnsdale looked at Johnny and nodded pleasantly. "You see?" she said. "Well, let's go into the dining room. A furniture man called me and told me he's delivering a real mahogany set, real modern, to us tomorrow. Dr. McManus. And a linoleum man—he's coming tomorrow too, to put in new linoleum in the kitchen and bathroom and in the hall. By the way," she added carelessly, "a new rug arrived this morning for the parlor. I had it all on my list, which I gave to the doctor last night."

Johnny began to laugh helplessly.

After a very good, cold lunch, Johnny took the children into the garden. They walked on the stiff, coarse grass in the warm sunshine. "We'll plant trees," he said. "Fruit trees. Every child shall have a tree of his own—perhaps two. Apples, cherries, pears, peaches, plums. Then shade trees, And along the fence we'll have flower gardens. Every child shall have his own garden. There'll be birdbaths, and birdhouses in the trees." He drew a deep breath.

"Once there was a time," he went on, "when men were good and pure, and lived in a Garden which God made for them. And God blessed the flowers and the trees and the birds, and everything that lived in the Garden, including men."

Standing about him, the children listened eagerly.

"Nobody hated anything, in the Garden. There was only happiness there, and wonderful beauty, and singing and laughter. But it wasn't enough for men. Love wasn't enough. They wanted something else. So Evil came to them, and the Evil's name was Lucifer, one of the mighty archangels, the angel most loved by God, the angel most beautiful of all the angels. You see, Lucifer didn't like men; he didn't want them to be like the angels. Lucifer was proud. He really loved God, and so it seemed to him that God was shaming Himself by making men."

He paused, to let this much of the story sink into the children's fascinated minds. He put his hand on Kathy's neat head, which shone like gold in the sunlight. Emilie's big blue eyes were the color of sapphires. Pietro's mouth was open, like a red cherry, and eagerness stood on his face like light, and Max listened too, in that dazed bemusement of his. Jean stood at Johnny's right arm, a sergeant-at-arms beside his commanding officer.

Jean said, and his voice was the voice of a somber man, "Lucifer was right."

Johnny went on, "So Lucifer came to men and told them, 'If you eat of that fruit over there, which is forbidden to you, you will be like angels.' And so they ate of the fruit.

"Now it was God's custom to walk in the Garden He had made, when the sun went down, so that He could enjoy the beauty of it, and sit under the trees, and smile at the flowers, and speak to men. But after men had eaten of the fruit of that tree they hid themselves, when they heard God coming through the forest, which was singing to itself under the new moon. So God called to men, and they were afraid to answer Him. And when He commanded them to answer Him, and to tell Him why they had eaten of that tree, they blamed each other, and hated each other for their own disobedience. I think that made God more angry than anything else, for He saw that once hatred comes to men the world is no longer safe for anybody, or anything, whether gardens or trees or innocent animals or other men.

"So God, in His anger, drove men from the Garden, into a lifeless and dangerous world, where they were condemned to death, where they would have no peace, where they must work hard and hopelessly, where all things feared them and ran from them. All the innocent things ran from them, for man had eaten of hatred. Man was a terror now in the world, and the creator of wars and ruin."

He sat down on the grass, and the children, their misted eyes fixed on him, sat, in a circle close to him. Jean said, "And so, we had—had—" Johnny nodded, touched Jean's shoulder, and sighed.

"And God was angry with Lucifer, even more than He was angry with men, and He drove Lucifer out of heaven, and Lucifer fell and made a new place for himself, which he called hell, and he brought all the angels who hated men, too, down with him. I have told you about hell, children."

Pietro nodded vigorously, and bounced up and down. "Here is hell," he said.

Johnny was startled. He gazed at Pietro, and he thought, I never considered that. Perhaps the earth is, indeed, the Seven

Storey Mountain. If the kingdom of heaven is with us, in the world, so too, perhaps, is the kingdom of hell. He scratched his cheek, and regarded Pietro's bright countenance thoughtfully. He took out his pipe and let Jean light it for him. Jean performed the small act with grace, flair, and importance.

"Hell," said Johnny, "is the place where all evil is, where men live who never loved God, never wanted to know Him, who hate their fellow men, and never repent of their sins. It is a terrible place."

"Here," said Pietro proudly, and looked at the others for admiration of his perspicacity.

Johnny puffed at his pipe. The smoke became a small silver cloud in the sunshine.

"But men remembered the Garden from which God had driven them. So they made gardens for themselves, in the world. Mirrors of the Garden they never forgot in their souls. And that is why we must have a garden for ourselves, right here, so we can remember heaven and pray that God will let us return to that old Garden one day which still waits for us. You see, darlings, God is merciful to us. He lets us have flowers and grass and trees; He breathes His breath into them, and commands them to live for us.

"For there is no end to the mercy of God, and no end to His love. Even though we choose hell for ourselves."

They walked about the yard, and Johnny showed them where their gardens would be, and the trees, and the children were full of wonder and excitement. They came to a corner of the fence, and there they found a flourishing vine of wild morning-glories, tiny and pink and fresh. The children stared at it with joy.

"It is called the flower of the morning," said Johnny. And he looked at the bright sky with peace.

8

Mrs. Burnsdale, grumbling crossly, pressed Johnny's one and only clerical suit. "It's a disgrace," she muttered. "You never think of yourself, Mr. Fletcher."

"Why should I?" he asked calmly.

Mrs. Burnsdale tossed her gray head. "Well, that's a silly question!" she said impatiently. "Anyway, here are your pants and your coat on the hanger. Let them air a little. Still damp." She paused. "If you don't think of yourself, who will?"

"A lot of people are thinking of me," he answered. "Such as you, for instance."

He went upstairs, whistling between his teeth, carefully carrying his suit. He peeped in at the bathroom and grinned. Well, there they were, and pink, too. Still whistling, he dressed for the "welcome dinner" tonight. He could hear the subdued murmurs of the children in the parlor downstairs, and the clatter of plates in the dining room. He was filled with peace. There was nothing else he needed in his life—if his congregation permitted him to remain. He looked through the round little window in his bedroom. The sun was setting, all fuschia and cold green, above the crowded roofs of the city. We Protestants should have evening bells too, he thought. What is more consoling, more tender, more full of the remembrance of God than bells at sunset? Then he heard the evening bells over the city, from the Catholic churches, sweet and reassuring, ancient with love, speaking of surety with their joyful tongues.

The parish hall was the basement under the church, and it was even more drab than Johnny had feared. The wooden ceiling was low, and from it dangled a single glaring round white light, more fitting for a barbershop than a parish hall. Wainscoting, about four feet high, in cracked narrow lengths, ran around the walls, painted a nauseating dark brown, and above it was the plastered wall, painted a disagreeable buff. The floor, completely bare, creaked underfoot, but it was clean and polished. There were no signs that the hall was ever used for anything else but meetings. Apparently no one had ever thought of making it attractive for children, of setting up equipment for basketball or crafts. There was no evidence that it was ever converted into a place for youthful dancing and joy.

A long trestle table stood under the racking light, and it had been set with Mrs. McGee's best tablecloth, stiffly white and shining, and napkins the size of baby sheets. Some other lady had contributed the gleaming plated silver, another the bright red and blue "peasant" dishes, another the two sets of candlesticks. Another woman had brought a huge bowl of zinnias and other late summer flowers, all bronze and crimson and yellow, a cheerful and living splash on all that whiteness. The chairs were the folding variety, and uncomfortable. There were no stoves here, and the Ladies' Aid had brought the food in covered pans—the inevitable but delicious baked beans, thick slices of beef and ham and tongue, cold potato salad, buttered bread, huge brown pies, and coffee in thermos jugs.

Johnny was formally introduced to the members of his congregation who would decide whether he was to be driven away with anger, or permitted to remain. Graying ladies, some severe, some wistful, some wispy, some fat, some short, some rosy, some pale, some with cheerful expressions, some with sour, suspicious eyes. All badly dressed, in broad summer prints, imitation-pearl beads, and prim shoes. Their gray hair had been "set" in iron curls and waves, or, rather, thought Johnny, the hair had been cast in a mold, to come out in metallic convolutions. None of the ladies was uncertain in manner, or tentative in approach. They were very sure of themselves, and they examined Johnny critically. Circumscribed, small-city women, they reminded him with discomfort of the Park Avenue ladies.

Their men were more apt to regard him with tolerance and favor. They needed a minister. Dr. Stevens said this was the only minister he would send them. So, they would have this minister. It was a very simple syllogism to them, if not to their wives.

The incredible story of Dr. McManus's generosity today had served to dispel some of the ladies' natural animosity against Johnny because of the "foreign" children. Mrs. McGee had said, in her telephone rounds, "Anyone who can get old Al to give a penny, without us giving another penny, is a wonder-worker. So let's be kind to the young minister. I saw him, you know, and though he looks sort of boyish, he's made some sort of a dent on Al—funny, in a way. He's got the nicest blue eyes, too." At least four of the ladies had marriageable daughters, and the fact that Johnny was not a married man raised their interest and hopes. They felt, however, that in some way he had betrayed them by acquiring that "mob of foreigners." No sensible girl would want to marry him—unless, of course, he could be persuaded to get rid of the children.

The hostility was almost dispelled when they met him. Dr. McManus, wearing another crumpled light-gray suit, somewhat less stained than his earlier one, performed the sarcastic introductions. "Crazy feller Doc Stevens sent us. Johnny, this here is Mrs. Lovitt. Mrs. Wolfe. Mrs. Sherwood. Mrs. Long. All Ladies' Aid. Father John Kanty told me he has the same trouble with nuns, and the Sodality. No reasonable man can get along with women. This here is Mrs. Krantz—"

The ladies gave Dr. McManus a brutal stare. His associations with "that priest with the funny foreign name, and that queer old Jewish rabbi," were always a source of private affront to them. They firmly believed that his associations were carried on for the sole purpose of annoying the congregation of the Church of the Good Shepherd. They turned to Johnny, and they almost completely melted. Tall, thin, and magnetic in his shabby clerical black, he was young enough to arouse the maternal instinct in them. His strong face, so alive, so dark, so gentle, touched them. Here was no meek weakling, frightened of his congregation, anxious to please them and placate them. This was a man, and when they looked into his dark-blue eyes and saw the kind force and strength in them, and felt the warm strength of his handshake, at least half the ladies were won.

The husbands decided that though Johnny "wasn't our kind" he looked like a nice young fellow, and no sissy. Time the women were taken in hand, they thought approvingly. Here was no minister who would be bullied by the female members of the congregation. But too good-looking; all the girls would be after him, and everybody knew what trouble that meant. However, anyone who could "twist old Al around his finger" was a valuable addition to the church.

Johnny said grace in his moving voice: "We thank Thee, Father, for Thy bountiful gifts, and pray that we shall be worthy of them. We ask that in all things Thou may accept us as Thy servants in the name of the Lord Jesus Christ. Amen." To himself he repeated his prayer to God that he be permitted to remain in this drab and smoky city. Everything depended upon this evening, he thought, as his fork wandered through the baked beans and the voices rose genially around him like a cloud of warmth. Johnny could feel the cautious half acceptance of him, and he began to eat with more appetite. He could also feel, with some inner tension, the long sardonic glances of Dr. McManus. The old man would not help him, he knew. It was up to him.

"Nothing wrong with these beans. But why can't we have some beer, eh?" complained Dr. McManus. "Father John Kanty likes a big glass of beer himself, and their lunches have beer, and their picnics. Beer would go very good with this grub."

Mrs. McGee said smartly, "No, doctor! You know very well that we're WCTU. All the Ladies' Aid, that is. Beer! Why do you want to ruin good food?"

"Marjie," said Dr. McManus, "haven't you heard of the marriage in Cana? D'you think for a minute the Lord turned the water into grape juice? Lord or not, He'd have been thrown out of a respectable wedding for that, and no nonsense."

This sounded very blasphemous to the ladies, and they gave Dr. McManus another one of their combined brutal glares. He chortled. The husbands smiled uneasily. Johnny looked about the table, and suppressed his own smile.

"What do you think, Mr. Fletcher?" asked Mrs. Krantz, the plumber's wife.

He hesitated. Then he said, "I don't think there is anything in the Bible which explains that God suspended the natural laws of fermentation that day."

The men grinned. Dr. McManus squeaked delightedly, and slapped a heavy thigh. The ladies looked stern and accusing. "However," Johnny went on, with a very innocent expression, "there is nothing in the Bible which said He did not. I like grape juice, myself, and many others do."

The ladies smiled triumphantly at their husbands. Dr. McManus squealed again. "A diplomat!" he said. "A damned, striped-pants diplomat!" He leaned across the table, bias-fashion, toward Johnny, and shook his powerful index finger in his face. "I don't like diplomats. Almost all the trouble in this world's caused by 'em. Slipping around on greased heels, smirking, bowing, saying yes to everybody and meaning no in their oleaginous hearts, and carrying a knife up their sleeves. Pussyfoot around like this, too much, my boy, and I'll personally carry your bags to the station, and kick you up on the coach."

The ladies were angered at this, and broke into a flurry of exclamations. Dr. McManus preserved an inscrutable expression of sullenness at this attack on him. But Johnny smiled to himself. The men, fearing the doctor more than did their wives, became uncertain and silent. They began to ask themselves questions. A smooth sort of young man. His answer to Mrs. Krantz was a kind of double-dealing, thought Mr. Schoeffel. Didn't seem that way yesterday, Mr. Schoeffel commented to himself. Was he a radical? Maybe. Probably bled all over the place for labor. Never gave a thought, probably, to people who made it possible for labor to have jobs at all, and couldn't afford to work a forty-hour week, like factory and shop hands. Then, he had been in Europe, probably mixed up with all those Communists over there; got the kids from some outlandish place, too.

Mr. Dan McGee, a small and delicate man of slightly over fifty, with a high crown of pure silver curls surmounting a round pink face pierced with very black eyes, asked himself: Smooth? Yes. Probably trained that way. Smooth folks, with college educations, and his way of answering, were usually men who knew nothing about labor and its problems, and despised working people. Never took sides, or fought for the right and social justice. Reactionaries, that's what they were. The president of the local mine union reflected on the reactionaries with considerable gloom. Then he thought of Mr. Summerfield, the wealthy newspaper owner, and he became confused. He glanced furtively at Johnny's hands, and was surprised. Strong, competent, worker's hands, full of power and decision.

The foremen and mine superintendents were as equally divided about Johnny. Would he stir up the men? Would he denounce all strikes, indiscriminately? Was he socially conscious? Was he one of those pinkos? A Communist, maybe? A fascist, maybe? Perhaps he'd cuddle up to that damned Summerfield, with his noisy newspapers. Perhaps he was the kind that liked society. Look at his hands; probably once one of those stubborn workers himself. Two of the superintendents, wise in the hands of men, came to the true conclusion that here was a man who was no stranger to manual work, and like Mr. McGee, they were confused.

The ladies, the shrewd doctor saw, squinting at them from under his furious brows, were almost completely unanimous about Johnny. They liked him; they were beginning to care about him; his old and shabby clothes did not escape their maternal eyes. Tenderness began to gleam on their tired faces. But just wait, girls, thought the doctor savagely.

Mr. Krantz, the squat and solid plumber, felt the masculine questioning around him. He sucked on his fat lips. He was in business for himself, owning a small plumbing-contracting shop. But he had not always been in business. He swallowed an enormous mouthful of ham, drank an enormous gulp of coffee, wiped his lips, and said, "Parson, what do you think of this here minority problem you hear about these days?"

Johnny quietly laid down his fork. He fixed his eyes intently on the good-natured plumber. "Minority?" he asked, in a tone of wonder and perplexity. "I'm afraid I don't understand. What is a minority? Do you mean a political party?"

Dr. McManus rolled a chewed wad of meat between his lower molars and his cheek and smirked. The men exchanged baffled glances, and the ladies listened with an intensity that alarmed the minister. Mr. Krantz waved his hand helplessly. "No, I don't exactly mean a political party, though I guess you could call the losing party a minority. Don't know. You hear so much of stuffed ballot boxes these days, and monkeyshines around the voting machines. Don't know. No, I was meaning these here minority groups, like religious, and races, and—er—churches, and such, and labor and capital and big business, and professions, teachers and such, and doctors and lawyers, and small business. You know. Minorities."

Johnny's hands clenched on the table, but he spoke quietly for all the passionate blue blaze of his eyes. "I take it you mean you are a member of the majority, then, Mr. Krantz, and not a member of a minority?"

"Well, yes," replied Mr. Krantz uncertainly.

"You've named minority groups, Mr. Krantz. And now, will you tell me what group outside those you've named you belong to?"

"Well," began Mr. Krantz. Then he stopped. He searched his mind, and was silent.

Johnny's voice, though still insistent, was kinder. "Profession? Small business? A certain race? A certain church? A certain background?"

"Well," muttered Mr. Krantz.

Johnny smiled. He was breathing a little fast. "I think you are wondering now which minority group you belong to, Mr. Krantz." He turned to the other men. "And what minority group do you other gentlemen belong to?"

"None," Mr. Wolfe blurted with astonishment. "Or"—and he too was silent.

"Exactly," said Johnny, and leaned back in his chair. "No one in the world belongs to a minority group. No one belongs to a majority group, either. You are logical people. Take apart the question of minorities with the help of logic; think about the question for just one minute. And you'll see, almost at once, that it is a delusion, a lie. You'll see that the idea of minorities was thought up by the enemies of men, to divide them, to raise up unnatural and illogical hatred between them, to create nonexistent delusions about classes and other nations, in order to foment internal and external strife. These enemies have only one object: to confuse, to destroy, to seize power. They hate us all."

There was a deep silence in the hall. Every fork halted; hands lifting coffee cups paused in the very act. Every brow wrinkled; every mouth pursed; every head bent in thought. Dr. McManus sniffled loudly. No one looked at him. Johnny's eye traveled about the table.

He said with great gentleness, "In the beginning was the Word, and the Word was with God.' Logos, the Word, also means logic, reason as manifested by speech. Using logic, which is of God, we know there are no minorities. Using the Word, which is of God, we know that there are no real divisions among men, only evil delusions born of minds swirling in hell."

They looked up at him then, sharply. They saw him sitting there, tall and with a new majesty and authority, for all the blue and vigorous kindness of his eyes, for all his youth.

"Kind of theological reasoning I don't like," said Dr. McManus, watching the others closely. "Never mind. Johnny, what's this hell business? You ain't the kind of parson who's going to insult us on Sundays talking about medieval hell, are you? You, a modern minister? What is hell, anyway?" He gave the table a patronizing wink.

"Hell?" asked Johnny thoughtfully. "Of course there's a hell. What has being modern got to do with it? Does being modern reject the idea of the undiscovered universes, the invisible microscopic world, the mysterious powers of the mind, which are unseen, the uncharted ebbs and flows of human emotions, the passions of the spirit which have created civilizations and beauties and schools of thought, and philosophy, and cultures and infinite varieties? But if you come down to concrete facts, all these things don't exist, because they aren't visible. Yet we know they exist.

"Hell?" he repeated, after a long pause. "Certainly. And what is hell? The complete absence of God. A place, a state of mind or spirit, in which God is not. Think of it, if only for one minute. A place where God is not. Think of the cold anguish of such a place, of such a mind or spirit; think of the bitter, sad rage of such a state, the endless despair, the hatred, the madness. That is hell."

No one answered him. Dr. McManus regarded him in stony silence.

"Yet," said Johnny, "God descended into hell. No pastor has ever quite answered the question why. Not logically, anyway. Did He go there, after He died on the cross, to warn the realm of evil that it could no longer rule the world? Or—and I think myself this is a more reasonable answer—did He go there to bring hope to the hopeless?"

Mrs. Wolfe, a fundamentalist lady, bridled. She coughed. "Mr. Fletcher, hell, I believe, according to the Bible, is eternal."

Johnny became very somber. "Of course it is. As long as a soul permits it to be."

He let them ponder that for a few moments. Here and there a tired face suddenly brightened, as if a wisp of light had passed over it. So, he thought compassionately, there are some here tonight who have despaired of being saved.

He thought the time had come to speak of that of which he must speak. He said, and his voice startled them out of their bemusement, "Now that we've finished dinner I must tell you something. You know that I have brought five children from Europe with me. But you don't know their history. I will tell it now."

He told them, in vivid phrases, with vivid gestures. They listened, fascinated, absorbed. Horror leaped across some of the women's faces; reservation pouted some of the women's mouths. The men were incredulous, disgusted, sympathetic, or embarrassed. They twiddled their silver; they ran fingers around their necks. They avoided each other's eyes. One or two flushed. But they could not turn away from Johnny's face, and his glowing eyes, however they tried.

"And so," he concluded, "here are these children with me. I am their father. I am adopting them. I have given them my name in advance. I am the only hope they have. What I have done for them I have done, and will continue to do. But the rest is your responsibility."

Mrs. McGee, who had become crimson with emotion and whose eyes were filled with tears, said impulsively, "Mr. Fletcher, you know we'll do what we can. Ladies," and she turned to her friends, "we can promise Mr. Fletcher that, can't we? We'll sort of adopt the children ourselves. We'll clothe them. We'll put them in Sunday school. Civilize them. Be mothers to them."

The ladies nodded vigorously at their president. Mr. Krantz cleared his throat. "Maybe we can have a little fund, putting a couple dollars in the bank every month in their names, so they can get educations. Huh?" The men hesitated, then nodded reluctantly. Mr. McGee was the last to nod. He was still thinking of labor and capital, which the parson said did not really exist. He'd have to go over that in his mind tonight, when he was in bed. It was very confusing.

Mrs. Wolfe said, "I heard the children range from five to twelve, Mr. Fletcher. I'm assistant to the superintendent of the Sunday school—my husband. I'll take a personal interest in the children."

Aha, thought Dr. McManus with glee. Now comes the revolution. Johnny was coloring. He regarded them with grave sadness.

"I have just been talking to you about the artificial concept of minorities. I think you agree with me. But there are, I must admit, different schools of thought, a subjective world. None of these are dangerous unless we permit them to be, unless we give them an objective existence."

He looked at them anxiously, praying that they followed him. They were simple, insular people. Yet God had made such people understand, with His parables. They might be slow, but they came to solid understanding at last.

"When we make our subjective opinions, which are part of the infinite variety of the human soul, objective reality, we commit a profound logical error. Here is a late rose. I call it red; we all agree it is red. Yet, if we had the power this instant to look at this rose with the eyes of others, we might see a color which we do not call red. Who can tell us the subjective color we see is objective? Who shall dare to tell us that we are wrong? Suppose others might decide we were dangerous to call this color an entirely different color, and oppress us accordingly? How can a soul, which is subjective, be made to conform to objective illusions?"

They followed him intuitively, but they were also bewildered. Johnny turned to Dr. McManus, who was grinning nastily. "Doctor," he said, "you perform many operations every week. You will agree that though the structure of the human body is roughly the same, it is in its various parts, entirely unique and different from any other human body. You will agree that not a single human being reacts to any situation, either mental or physical, with exactly the same intensity or in the same way as another."

"All right. I agree," said Dr. McManus, lighting another

cigarette. He winked at Johnny. "A good lecture you just gave. Get on with it."

Johnny sighed. A feeling of gray exhaustion was beginning to pervade him. He closed his eyes for an instant, and prayed for help.

"Not a leaf, a tree, a mountain, a world, or man, is just like any other leaf, tree, mountain, world, or man. That is the beauty of God's creation. No uniformity, no conforming. Uniformity is the death of the soul. And that is why we have so many seemingly—and I say seemingly—different religions in the world. But in reality they are not different. They are only aspects, among the countless aspects, of God, whether Christian, Jewish, Mohammedan, Buddhist, or anything else. There has never been anything else but one Shepherd. It is up to us, spiritually, to be one Fold."

He stood up now, and gathered all the eyes together toward him.

"And that is why I must tell you something. That is why, in all justice to you, I must tell you something you don't know, and wait on your decision as to whether or not you'll keep me here, as your pastor."

They were astonished. They sat upright in their chairs.

"Why," stammered Mr. Long, "I thought that was all settled."

Johnny smiled sorrowfully, and shook his head. "I don't think so.

"Let me tell you. I've had these children almost a year now. I've listened to them in their nightmares. I've listened to the very few hints they've dropped, unknowingly, about their origins." He drew a deep breath. "I have an unshakable respect for the individuality of man, for his individual roots. Children, above all things, must feel their roots, for without them they have no subjective security.

"And so I have discovered that Kathy and little Emilie had Protestant roots. I have found out that Jean and Pietro had Catholic roots. And Max, the most frightfully injured of them all, is a Jew. All of these terms are subjective, but the children have a right to have their roots, to have a frame of reference, to know that though they have a variety of belief, they have only one Shepherd, only one God."

Mr. Krantz spluttered, "One's a Jew? Two are Catholics?" He was aghast.

"You mean," asked Mr. Lovitt, outraged, "that you, a Protestant minister, are actually planning to let three of those kids not be Protestants? Don't you believe in your religion?"

A buzz of indignation and affront filled the hall. Every man turned to his neighbor noisily. Exclamations rose like a swarm of gnats. Hands fluttered, gestured. Johnny waited in silence, and Dr. McManus watched his saddened face.

"Can't have it," said Mr. Krantz decidedly.

"Course not," said Mr. McGee.

"Ridiculous," said Mr. Wolfe.

"Wouldn't even think of it," said Mrs. Sherwood, with new indignation. "What would the congregation say?"

"It's insulting," said Mrs. Williams. "An insult to our church."

Suddenly they paused. They turned accusingly to Dr. Mc-Manus. "You haven't said a word!" exclaimed Mrs. Sherwood. "And you the President of the church Board."

But Dr. McManus looked at Johnny jeeringly. He spread out his hands. "Well, that's the end of your subjective lecture, boy. Better start packing."

He turned to the others, who were flushing. "I knew he wasn't for us. I told him. Imagine what he thought about us! He insulted us by thinking we were decent human beings, with decent sympathy and understanding! He actually thought we were different from all other people. Insulting, I call it."

They all became very still. Only their stiff eyes blinked. Under his breath the doctor chuckled.

"Well?" said Johnny, after the silence became too oppressive.

The men turned to one another speechlessly, and the women also.

"We don't want a parson who thinks we're better than other folks," Dr. McManus went on. "We want a parson who knows we're liars, and that we lie in our teeth when we talk about the Fatherhood of God and the Brotherhood of Man. We want somebody who won't bother us, and won't make us practice our religion of tolerance and kindness and love. Because we know we don't have such a religion."

Mrs. McGee, president of the Ladies' Aid, turned a vivid scarlet. She turned on the doctor furiously. "We are so Christians!" she cried.

134

"Are you?" asked Dr. McManus. "Who told you you were? Haven't seen any manifestations of it yet. A wise old feller once said, 'There was only one Christian, and He was crucified.' True. Read your papers; think over history. Christians? Naturally we're not, and we never were. Not a mother's son of us."

He lit still another cigarette, while they watched him with ashamed anger.

"And that's why I want to pull down this church. Got a big mortgage on it. We need a parking lot hereabouts. Good income. Can always use more income. So. I'm going to pull down this church. Den of hypocrisy. Hate hypocrisy more than anything else in the world."

"Your father's church!" said Mr. Schoeffel weakly.

Dr. McManus nodded gloomily. "That's right. Come to think of it, maybe he was a Christian. Or as near as he could come to being one. But he wouldn't want a church to stand that wasn't a Christian church, and so it comes down."

"If you think you can bully us"—said Mrs. Sherwood, with tears in her eyes.

"I'm not bullying you, madam. I'm just telling you the truth."

"Yes, you are! You're telling us that if we disageee with Mr. Fletcher about the children's religion you'll pull down the church."

He shook his finger irately at the poor woman. "I never said that at all! I don't give a damn whether he and his brats stay here or not. Frankly, I never wanted him here, don't want him now. He and his Christianity! Make everybody too damn uncomfortable. I vote against him." He looked at them slowly, thoroughly. "Well? What's your vote?"

Johnny squeezed his eyes shut, and the gray exhaustion flowed away from him. He heard rustlings about him, mutters, snorts, whispers, flutterings, the scraping of chairs. "Come on, vote," said the doctor irascibly. "I've got five hospital calls to make tonight. One vote for no. That's me."

"But what of the rest of the congregation?" demanded Mr. Wolfe.

"Well, sir, you're the Board. And the ladies are the Ladies' Aid. That's your job. You got your positions here by being a little brighter—but only a little brighter—than the rest of the dumb bas—I mean, sheep." The doctor shrugged, and pulled a mighty cloud on his cigarette. Mrs. Sherwood angrily waved it aside.

Johnny opened his eyes. He looked on each face, piercingly, but gently and compassionately. The ladies gulped. The men blew their noses.

Then Mr. McGee shouted, "Yes!" And he struck his fist so mightily on the table that the dishes plopped.

"Yes!" cried the others, men and women alike.

They beamed, they shone with joy and affection, resolution filled their eyes. They turned their full smiles upon Johnny, and they reached their hands across the table to shake his. "We'll help," said Mr. Krantz. "Hell, I'm a Christian, ain't I?"

"Yes," said Johnny. "We all are." He looked at Dr. McManus, and repeated, "We all are."

A kind of elation filled the ladies and the gentlemen. They glowed with delight and love. Each looked at the other, as if discovering a delightful stranger, deserving of tenderness and understanding. Hand touched hand, shyly. Tears ran down the ladies' cheeks, tears of joy and exaltation.

Johnny stood up, and they rose with him, in simple unanimity.

"Dear God, Our Father," he prayed, "look upon Thy children with love, for we have been delivered from darkness, from hatred, from ignorance. Bless us, Father, and give us strength and courage, and accept our contrition and our penances. Be merciful to us, Almighty God, and be our Rock in a weary land. In the name of the Lord Jesus Christ. Amen."

The people stood about him afterward, trying to get closer to him, feeling comfort in him. Hands touched his shoulders, his arms, his hands. He had never seen such a brightness in all his life, and his heart was humble. "Grant me the grace to lead Thy sheep, O God," he prayed inwardly.

He walked with them to the door. Dr. McManus was beside him. He bent to the old man to whisper hastily, and with a smile, "Who is the hypocrite now?" he asked, and laughed a little.

9

The rain had stopped, but the sun did not shine. The foreboding of autumn hung in the air like a sad fog, though the trees stood in strenuous green and the small lawn about the rectory of the Reverend John Kanty Krupszyk had the poisonous brilliance of artificial grass. Johnny could see the bleak street, gaunt in the early autumn gloom, through the long windows of the astonishingly large library. He shrewdly came to the conclusion that this room was not only library, but the study and the parlor too, and there were faint marks on the ceiling which indicated partitions had been removed. Nevertheless the library was impressive, every wall lined with books in crimson, blue, brown, and black, the almost bare floor darkly and highly polished, the chairs sparse but covered with leather cushions. Father Krupszyk's desk was undoubtedly his own personal possession, of which he was proud. Leather-topped, of almost black wood, it had gilt handles and carved sides.

Johnny sat near the desk, and the priest sat behind it. Jean and Pietro stood on each side of Johnny, and he held their hands tightly. They regarded the priest with respectful if fierce interest, on guard against a stranger. He in turn, understanding the fear and uncertainty in them, gave them only quick smiles, and did not speak to them immediately. He had been listening to the young minister, his deeply sunken gray eyes fixed on Johnny's face.

As Dr. McManus had said, the priest was in his thirties, and had the tall and heavily muscular physique of an athlete. His motions were sure, well coordinated, without nervousness. He had a large, darkish-blond head, a big flushed face, and a strong mouth. In general appearance he was only a bulky, strong priest, with broad peasant hands and extra-large feet. But when one looked into his steadfast and all-seeing eyes one saw an immense spirituality and resolution and fortitude, not too tempered by gentleness, and utterly devoid of illusions.

"So," said Johnny, "I baptized them—conditionally. But I am sure they are Catholics."

The priest smiled. "Conditionally," he repeated, and his light-blond eyebrows twitched. "That's a Catholic phrase. But, as you've told me, you were a war chaplain, and one of your friends was a priest." He paused, considering Johnny. He had listened in silence to the long story, and sometimes his eyes had narrowed on the minister with doubt, and sometimes with incredulousness. "I'm glad your board and the Ladies' Aid eventually agreed with you. But, you know, you're going to have a lot of unpleasantness, with the rest of the congregation." He coughed. "Esepcially with the women. I know. There's the Sodality, and the nuns in our school. Women have naturally good hearts with regard to children, but they can be very—difficult."

Like Johnny, he smoked a pipe. A large vase of gladioli in many brilliant colors stood on the desk. He stared at the flowers and thought.

"Very—unconventional," he said. "A minister bringing up two of his adopted children as Catholics. The nuns are going to have words to say about them living in your house; they're going to talk about our small orphanage. You see, Mr. Fletcher, it's human nature to distrust human nature. I'll have to talk with them emphatically, pointing out that you needn't have done this at all, but could have brought the children up in your own way. That'll make them more mistrustful and suspicious of you for a while. They'll wonder what your real object is."

He scrutinzied Johnny intently, but Johnny only smiled. "I know all about human nature. It's fundamentally all right, once you cut through the layers of animal suspicion and expediency."

The priest said, "I've been dealing with people for quite a long time. The first thing they think of when something is offered them in all goodness and Christian generosity is what they call an 'angle.' That's a nice commentary after two thousand years of Christianity. A Christian is practically as strange on this earth as a man from Mars. He needs getting used to. In the meantime, the reservation is that he has an angle, and that the angle will show up eventually. In fact," the priest added candidly, "I thought of that myself, when you called this morning."

"Why?" asked Johnny.

The priest shrugged. "I told you; I'm only a human being. I kept asking myself: What is really behind this? A Protestant minister who has two children states that he is bound by honor to bring those children up in another church, particularly a Catholic one! Wouldn't it be more logical to suppose that he'd want them to be Protestants? I'm sure every minister and priest would ask himself that same question, with doubt about your real intentions." Again the priest smiled, and suddenly his smile was kind, and a little wondering, as he said wryly, "You see, we meet so few Christians, in the full meaning of the word, don't we?"

Johnny smiled in return. He smoothed Pietro's quivering arm tenderly, and the staring little boy became quiet. "I don't know," he replied thoughtfully. "I've met a lot of Christians who didn't know they were Christians. Like Dr. McManus, for instance. And I've met, unfortunately, very vociferous Christians who were really pagans, without any heart or sympathy or compassion or kindness."

The priest nodded. He opened a door in his desk and brought out a bottle of wine and two small wineglasses. He filled them carefully, his brow wrinkling with thought. His forehead was sunburned and very broad, and peeling, for his highly colored skin was fair. He gave Johnny a glass of wine, then looked at him gravely. "To a Christian," he said, and sipped the wine.

"I do what I can, but it isn't always enough," said Johnny with a sudden depression. The priest flashed him a glance of pity and nodded again. He put down his glass, turned with an air of authority to the children, and swung his chair about. "Come, little ones," he said.

The boys stood stiffly beside Johnny and did not move. But he did not urge them. The priest's piercing eyes rested on them, and he held out his hands with gentle command, waiting in patience.

Then Jean glanced at Johnny, and the minister smiled. Then, with determination, Jean stepped forward and seized Pietro's vibrant hand, and pulled him slowly to the priest. But they stopped just beyond the reach of his hand.

Johnny spoke quietly. "This is Father Krupszyk, boys. I told you this morning. Abbé, Jean. Padre, Pietro."

"Padre!" cried Pietro, and gave the priest his blazing dark smile. He made a small jump. Jean looked at him sternly. "Don't," he said. Pietro continued to grin and eyed the priest with a kind of respectful mischief. Father Krupszyk laughed. He said to Jean, "In Pietro's country the priests are always happy when the children jump with pleasure at the sight of them. The priests sometimes play with them, throwing ball, or racing, or helping them pick flowers, or kneeling with them at wayside shrines."

"Like Papa," said Jean, and some of his austerity lessened.

"Like your papa," said the priest. He still held out his hands, and now the children approached him slowly. He put a hand on the shoulder of each of them, and as he studied their faces his own face deepened with compassion and love. He spoke to Pietro in Italian, "Little one, I am your friend. Never fear me." To Jean he spoke in French, "I am your curé, your confessor, your friend, my child."

The children gazed at him, puzzled, searching in the almost forgotten places of their minds to understand him. Then they smiled. The priest lifted his hand impulsively, and then—to Johnny's astonishment, for he had thought they did not remember—the children knelt immediately and bowed their heads, and the priest blessed them. To Johnny this was so moving that he swallowed hard. Jean had recalled, all at once, the sign of the cross, and he made it; Pietro, watching him, quickly lifted his hand uncertainly, and imitated him. When the children stood up the priest put his arms about them, hugged them briefly. Then he opened a drawer in his desk and brought out two rosaries with black beads and silver crucifixes, and gave them to the boys. They examined them with intense curiosity.

"Do you know what that is?" the priest asked of Jean.

The boy frowned, his pale eyes seeking into the distance. He rolled a large bead in his hand, and then in the voice of a sleepwalker he said, in French, "Our Father—"

Pietro cried out shrilly, as he touched a smaller bead, "Madre—Madre!" He jumped again, in his excitement. He clasped the rosary in both his hands and pressed it to his meager chest in glee. The priest watched him affectionately. He said to Johnny, "There is no doubt that they are baptized Catholics, with some Catholic instruction, which was interrupted by the madness of the war, and concentration camps."

Pietro ran to Johnny, showing him the rosary. "See! See!" he exclaimed. "Vittorio had. Pietro had. Got lost."

Johnny lifted him to his knee, and Pietro nestled against him, giggling with delight. Johnny smoothed his black curls. The priest said to Jean, "First Communion. Do you know what that is? The Table of the Lord—"

Jean was silent. Again, his eyes sought in the distance. Then in that strange far voice he murmured, "The Bread. The Blood."

"Yes," said the priest. He looked at Johnny. "He must have made his First Communion, then, long ago." He sighed. "But the little one, Pietro, did not, I think. He must have been too young. His brother taught him the rosary, apparently, in the concentration camp. The poor, devout, good young man, who must have been very young himself. There are times," the priest added, and his voice hardened, "when, in spite of myself, and when I think of what has happened in the world, and what will probably happen again, I become bitter."

He pushed a button on his desk and after a few moments an elderly nun, accompanied by a middle-aged, aproned woman, entered the library. Johnny stood up. "This is my sister, Mrs. Sakowski, who is also my housekeeper. She practically runs the parish—and me, too." Mrs. Sakowski, who was as big as her brother, gave Johnny a reserved smile, and the priest an admonishing one. "And this is Sister Sylvia," said the priest. "She is principal of our school. As school opens next week I thought she should know the children. Sister Sylvia, this is Jean Fletcher, and Pietro Fletcher. Perhaps you'd like to take them and show them the school, and the church, too."

The nun had a bright face and brown eyes glinting behind glasses. She was small and plump and motherly, and the children went to her at once. She took their hands and led them out, followed by Mrs. Sakowski. "Those two!" said the priest, as one man to another. "If one of them isn't giving me—a tongue-lashing, the other is. Sister Sylvia is quite a character. She resents my even entering her precious school, and I have to tread there lightly. She seems to think the school belongs to her personally. And my sister thinks I belong to her. The two don't agree on anything except that I'm a simple fool who has to be guided and directed and managed."

"I know," said Johnny sympathetically. "I have a housekeeper, Mrs. Burnsdale." The priest gave him a condoling look, and then they both laughed.

Father Krupszyk talked of the city. It was evident that he detested Mr. Summerfield. "A rascal," he said in a cold, emphatic voice. "He uses those papers of his to bring dissension and hatred and strife to this city, and to the county too. He writes his editorials in simple and emotional language, so that there'll be no misunderstanding. Aimed at the man in the street. I understand he tried to buy one or two New York and Philadelphia and Pittsburgh papers. But God was merciful, and—mysteriously—no one would sell to him, though one or two were practically bankrupt. So he concentrates on Barryfield.

"At first he was inclined to be friendly to me. He poses as an unconventional Christian, a noncomformist, as he calls himself. He invited me to visit him, and I did. Then he began to talk about 'the poor, Polish minority of your congregation.' Now my people are Americans; they know that their forebears were Poles. It never occurred to them that they were an abused minority. But Mr. Summerfield convinced them! Yes indeed. Then he convinced them that they were being exploited by the mine owners and the factory owners. The Polish character is not sullen; it has its playful and merry aspects. But now my people became sullen. I tried to undo the damage Summerfield had done. But people like, for some perverse reason, to think they are poor souls, badly put on. In some way I haven't yet fathomed, it inflates their ego. Makes them feel important."

He sipped his wine broodingly, and his eyes seemed to sink deeper into his head. "So now the children of my parish form gangs, and they fight their neighbors, and there's endless trouble. That's what the Summerfields want, of course. And now we have labor trouble, all stemming from the original evil. Polish people are hard workers; they're not rabble-rousers. Give them a fair wage, treat them decently, and they'll give a good day's work for a good day's pay. Now they're being 'oppressed' by their employers. However, I had some success with them. I know Mr. McGee, the president of the union, and he was alarmed as much as I was. We worked together to convince the people that the mines are paying them as much as they possibly can, and the men don't want to strike. Round one to us."

He moved the bottom of the wineglass gloomily on his desk, his head bent. A wan shaft of sun struck his hair, and it gleamed like dark gold for an instant.

"Summerfield hates me. He more than hints in his editorials that 'the shepherds are false shepherds,' and that our business is to keep our people poor and docile and exploited. We're in league with the rich mine owners. We want to keep our people ignorant. You see, I told him exactly what I thought of him, and exactly what his motives are, and exactly who he is. A man can stand anything except exposure. I told him I'd fight him. You know what he did? He wrote to my bishop."

Johnny said with anger, "And what did your bishop write to him?"

The priest smiled. "That's something, of course, that I'll never know. But now Summerfield is attacking my bishop in Philadelphia. He has a friend who is editor-in-chief of one of the Philadelphia newspapers, and he writes an occasional editorial for that paper. Not under his own name, of course. But I recognize the style."

Sister Sylvia returned with the children, shooing them competently before her. She gave Johnny a gracious smile. "They're very good boys," she said. "They like the school. Jean tells me, Mr. Fletcher, that you're going to get a retired

143

schoolteacher to instruct them for a few months so they'll be able to enter their proper grades." Her glasses glinted at Johnny with some reservation. "I know just the person."

Johnny said at once, "Thank you, Sister. I'd hoped you would offer that."

The caution disappeared from the glasses. "We'll be very happy to help the boys," she said. She paused. "They have nice manners," she added, with some condescension. "I must congratulate you. I don't see how you managed it."

Father Krupszyk laughed, and immediately the nun regarded him sternly, as one would a frivolous person. She gave the boys a severe pat on the head, which, to Johnny's surprise, they meekly endured. They also looked slightly subdued. The nun said in a precise voice, "They understand that they must behave, like all the other children. And no nonsense. Don't you, boys?"

"Yes, Sister," said Jean, in a tone Johnny had never heard before. Johnny was filled with admiration for the elderly nun. He began to feel like a schoolboy himself, as she gave him her attention.

"And they must come every morning for their catechism," she said. "Before the regular classes. They know nothing about it." She regarded Johnny rebukingly. Pietro shrilled excitedly, and in sudden defiance, "Papa is good, good, good!" And he glared at the nun. She, very expertly, glared back. "Manners, manners," she said coldly, and Petro subsided at once, to Johnny's renewed surprise. "You have a good papa," she went on. "You must obey him and honor him and love him. But I am your teacher. Remember that, child."

Dismay filled Pietro's bright eyes and he ran to Johnny for protection. Johnny put his arms about him. "Sister Sylvia is right, dear," he said. "She wants to help you to be a real American boy, and if you don't mind her she can't help you. See?"

Jean said with annoyance, "Pietro is fool." He looked to Sister Sylvia for approval, but the nun regarded him sternly. "That is a wicked thing to say, Jean. Remember to ask forgiveness for it when you make your confession." Jean, the wild, the fierce, did not retort loudly. He merely nodded his head and murmured, "Yes, Sister." Johnny was more amazed than ever.

The nun gave the four males in the library a long, suspicious, haughty gaze of warning, then departed, leaving behind her an air of proper contrition. "I told you—a real Tartar," said the priest. "I've heard that she sometimes refers to me disparagingly as 'the boy.' That's calculated to cut me down to size."

They were all somewhat melancholy, thinking of Sister Sylvia. When Johnny prepared to leave, the priest shook his hand warmly, all reserve gone. "I believe that God sent you here, Mr. Fletcher, for His own great purpose. We need you. But I must tell you that you're going to have your big share of trouble. You see, you are a Christian."

Johnny's spirits rose on the way home. Things were really going smoothly. He began to sing rollicking Army songs for the boys' pleasure. They joined in the gay chorus, clapping their hands delightedly in rhythm. Their faces took on the expressions of normal boys, and even Jean's flickering eyes were younger. Pietro's voice was pure and sweet and strong. Johnny listened to the beauty of that young voice with deep attention. A singer, he thought. His mind was suddenly dazzled by a vision of himself, older, grayer, and proud, sitting in the orchestra of the Metropolitan Opera at Pietro's debut in *Aida*. He heard the ovation of the audience, and his eyes misted in anticipation.

He tried not to think of Jean's operation next week.

The sun had come out, the early autumn sun. There was a smell of leaves burning somewhere, but that could only have been my imagination, thought Johnny. After all, it's just the end of August. Still, the shadows under the trees, the sunlight on the sides of houses and on the roofs, the feeling in the air, the movement of the slight wind, suggested autumn, and spoke of the winter. The houses seemed more closed, more isolated, the streets more barren.

Johnny went out of his way a little to show the boys the home of Dr. McManus. It stood in wide, iron-fenced grounds among lowlier houses. The lawns were sharply cropped, the trees standing alone. Beyond them was the house, huge, Victorian, unlovely, the graveled driveway raked and forbidding. Johnny thought that he had never seen so ugly a house, all wooden turrets and bay windows and gloomy porches. Even worse, the house had been painted a saffron yellow, with dark-brown trim. There were no flowers, only dark, glossy shrubbery hugging the porches. No one moved on the grounds, and there was no sign of life behind those narrow polished windows covered with lace curtains.

"A nice place," said Johnny charitably.

"Terrible," said Jean, with new confidence in his own opinion.

"Not nice," said Pietro.

Jean leaned his head against Johnny's shoulder. "Good house, good doctor, good man," he said.

"Yes," replied Johnny, moved. So Jean was thinking of the operation, too. Johnny pressed the boy's hand strongly.

Men were coming home from work, anxious, white-collar men with flat brief cases, or men with dinner pails, plodding. Johnny watched them as he drove slowly home. They were his people, these men with pale faces or stained ones, these men with their troubles, their hopes, their doubts, their uncertainties, their griefs, their small pleasures, their ambitions for their children, their love for their hard-working, hard-driven wives. Shabby suits or overalls, they were his people. They were one. He glanced up at the mauve mountains, cold and shining with the late sun. He saw the clusters of great homes there, proud and reserved, half hidden by trees. And they too are my people, he thought. He saw the white house of Mr. Summerfield. He drew a deep breath. And he too is one of us, he said to himself.

Tomorrow he would take Max to the rabbi. He had already made the appointment. The rabbi had sounded bewildered, though his voice had been full and kind. Not the voice of an old man, Johnny had commented to himself.

He passed the church, his own church, and it appeared even more dismal than before to him, with its starved steeple. From over the smoky city bells began to ring. The steeple of the Church of the Good Shepherd was silent. Perhaps there were no bells—. But of course, there must be. Johnny began to plot about ringing the bells at sunset. His first sermon, on Sunday, perhaps. The need for comforting bells.

"See!" exclaimed Pietro, pointing. "The doctor!"

Dr. McManus's car, the long black limousine with the chauffeur, stood before the mean little parsonage, all glisten and chrome. Johnny was pleased. He wondered what new articles from Mrs. Burnsdale's "list" were being delivered personally. He brought up his modest old car behind the limousine, and jumped out, followed by the children. Perhaps, he thought, he could persuade the doctor to have dinner with him and the children. He owed so much to the savage old man with the soiled hands and the furious eyes.

He and the children ran up the small stairs. Johnny whistled, and the boys sang an accompaniment. They burst into the small hall and Johnny shouted, "Hello! Hello! We're home!"

But only silence answered them. The dull sunset light filtered in through the windows, enhancing the shabbiness of the parlor, which could not be brightened even by the fine, expensive green rug, the gift of Dr. McManus. Mrs. Burnsdale had unpacked Johnny's books, but they sagged in the badly made long bookcase against the wall.

"Hello," said Johnny again. And now something gripped him with an awful premonition, a heavy falling of his heart. He ran into the dining room, and then the kitchen. A savory pot was bubbling contentedly on the new white stove, but the kitchen was empty. Johnny tried to control himself. There was an explanation, a very reasonable one, for the absence of Mrs. Burnsdale and Kathy, Emilie, and Max. Perhaps they had gone to a local store. But where was Dr. McManus? "Hello!" cried Johnny, and he rushed to the stairway, feeling the yielding of nightmare in his knees, hearing, loudly, the flap of his black coat on his body.

He was about to fly up the stairs when he heard a heavy step above. Dr. McManus appeared, grotesquely massive and wide, his hat on his head. He looked down at Johnny in silence, then slowly began to descend. "What is it? In the name of God, what is it? Where are the children?" Johnny cried.

Dr. McManus did not answer. Heavily, heavily, making the staircase quake under his somber tread, he came down. He reached the bottom. Then he looked up at Johnny and his face was malignant. "Sit down, and stop that damned yelling," he said in a vindictive voice. He paused, looked at the frightened faces of Jean and Pietro. His mouth twitched, jerked. Johnny seized his arm, and his voice was hoarse. "Something's wrong. Tell me. Don't let me wait like this."

"Tell these kids to go out and play in the back yard," said the doctor, snatching his arm from Johnny's grasp. "Go on, you two, out. Out, I said. Stop staring like idiots. Jean, you're a bright boy; take Pete here out in the yard. The yard, I said. Not on the street."

Not on the street! One of the children had been injured, probably by a car! Johnny groaned. The boys clung to him. But he spoke as gently and calmly as possible. "Jean, do what Dr. McManus said. I'll tell you if—anything—is the matter. Later. Please, Jean, my son."

Jean gazed at him and saw his terror. He smiled encouragingly. "Oh, okay, Papa. We'll play. Pietro will play with me." He took Pietro's hand and dragged the little boy out, in spite of his screams of mingled curiosity and fear.

But Johnny looked only at Dr. McManus. His sharpened eyes suddenly saw bloodstains on the old man's sleeves. Fresh bloodstains. "Max?" he asked faintly. "Emilie? Kathy? Mrs. Burnsdale? Car?"

"No," said Dr. McManus, and his squeaking voice was loaded with hatred. "Not a car. An older weapon. Human hate, human bestiality. Sit down, right there. You'll need it."

A cold film of sweat broke out on Johnny's face; it glistened in the dimming light. He swallowed, for salt water had rushed into his mouth in a nauseating flood. The doctor stood before him, his short, trunklike legs spread, his hands in his pocket. The old man stared at him stonily. "I told you, I warned you, Johnny. People are people; dogs are dogs. Same thing. The story got around, from the Ladies' Aid, to the neighborhood. Your parish. Mrs. Burnsdale and I can't get all the story yet. The girls are all right; that is, they're up in their room. It's Max."

"Max," repeated Johnny, in a feeble voice. Max, with the dry, peaked hair, the lost, dreaming eyes, the pale, empty face, little Max with his cries for his father in the night. "What happened to Max?"

"Mrs. Burnsdale let the girls and Max go out to look over the neighborhood. Ordinary, sensible thing to do. Get acquainted with where they're living; normal idea. Except that people aren't normal. People are swine. God damn them!" the doctor added, and the squeak in his voice broke, as if he were inwardly weeping.

"Max," prayed Johnny. "Is Max—?"

"No, he isn't dead. Not yet, anyway. We can't move him, or I'd take him to the hospital. Got to notify the police in a minute; haven't had time yet. Had to work fast. Hey, you're a grown man, son, and you aren't going to faint on me, and I ain't going to bring you any water, or smelling salts. Listen!"

But he put his powerful hands on Johnny's shoulders, and clutched them tightly. "Max's going to need you, boy, so don't go womanish on me. He needs you right now, in fact.

"I don't know rightly what happened, and neither does Mrs. Burnsdale. So the kids go out to look around, that sensible girl Kathy taking care of Max and the baby. Just kids, walking shy on the street. And then the other kids come. Oh, they'd heard all about you and the kids from their mothers! Mrs. Burnsdale looks out the window and thinks to herself, Well, that's sweet! Kids coming to play with your kids. So she walks back into the kitchen.

"That's all, until she hears the girls screaming. Five minutes or so later. So she runs to the door, and there's Kathy helping Max up the stairs, into the house, and the baby, Emilie, running and jumping and shrieking like she's gone out of her mind, poor baby. And Kathy's trying to control her. But it's Max Mrs. Burnsdale looks at. Max, with his right chin and part of his neck laid open and bleeding; Max, looking like he's already died. A knife."

"Oh, God," said Johnny, and he pressed his clenched hands to his forehead. "What happened, what happened?"

Dr. McManus said, "Don't know it all, yet. The girl, Kathy, can't talk right about it. Won't press her. Just got enough to know that some big dog of a boy started in calling Max a dirty Jew. Twice as big as Max. Maybe Kathy hit the boy; maybe Max began to cry or scream. Anyway, other boys started to punch and kick him. And then the big boy. Don't know how Mrs. Burnsdale got his name, but she did. I know his family," the doctor continued, as Johnny groaned again, over and over. "Father makes dental supplies. Bradford's the name. Live four, five streets from here."

The hands on Johnny's shoulders knotted into fists. "Don't worry. We'll get Sid Bradford. Boy about fourteen. Should've been in a reform school long ago. Mama's pet. Big brute of an ape. Feeble-minded, I always said. They always are. Caused lots of trouble before this. Max just happened to get in his way—. Look here, now, don't scrunch down in the chair like that, as if you'd been kicked in the stomach."

But the doctor pulled a chair close to Johnny's and sat beside him, very close, his hands on his fat spread knees. He shook his monolithic head. "God damn everybody," he said slowly, and repeated it, with hatred.

"Max," whispered Johnny. "Of all the children—Max. Max, who couldn't stand it. Max, who was beginning to forget." He looked at Dr. McManus. "How—badly—?"

"Twenty stitches in lower chin and neck. Knife just missed jugular vein, but got an artery. Mrs Burnsdale's a bright, intelligent woman. Calls me right away; just got me leaving the hospital. Carries the boy upstairs, and presses pads of cloth on the wound. Saved the boy's life. If that's any comfort," he concluded, grimly. "I got a nurse, and ordered a transfusion. Boy can't be moved. Not because of the wound, but—"

"But?" pleaded Johnny. The room was gliding about him in increasing darkness.

The doctor hesitated. "It wouldn't be a good thing to take him to a hospital. Away from you. He needs you. And so do the girls. Max'd go out of his mind if you weren't with him practically all the time. Got him under a sedative now. But though I gave him the limit he won't fall asleep. I think you'd better go up to him. Or can't you?"

Johnny began to get out of his chair, but the sinking anguish made him stagger. Dr. McManus caught his arm roughly. "Look, you've seen worse than this. The kid's quiet, at least, but he keeps staring at the door and talking that German gibberish of his. He wants you."

He helped Johnny up the stairs. He saw that the door to the girls' room was closed. He heard Mrs. Burnsdale singing a hoarse lullaby, and the creak of a rocker. But no child's voice spoke to her in the leaden silence of the house. The telephone began to shrill insistently, but no one heard it. Someone rang the doorbell, but no one cared. The minister's bedroom door was open, and Johnny, with the help of the wall, and the doctor, approached it. Then he heard a faint, familiar rustle, the whispering of Max in the terror of the nights. He pulled himself upright, and answered clearly and loudly, "Yes, Max! It's Papa."

He marched resolutely to the door with loud steps. The bedside lamp had been lighted. Max was lying in Johnny's bed, shrunken, small, as if hiding, no pillow under his head. His hair was peaked against the white sheet; his face, the color of death itself, was turned to the door. But his light-brown eyes were wild with despair and torment, his mouth open and whispering. So little a boy, so helpless a child, so innocent, so undone by a murderous, insane world.

Johnny stood on the threshold of the room, and all at once he knew hatred for the first time in his life, hatred so monstrous, so overwhelming, that he felt the lust to kill. He had often wondered what the desire to kill was like; he understood now. It was a surging of the blood, a blackening before the eyes, the curving of hands into claws.

"Steady," said Dr. McManus with compassion.

"Papa, Papa?" whispered Max, and one of his hands lifted. His face wrinkled, and he began to cry soundlessly. His neck was heavily bandaged. "Papa, *bist du?* "

Johnny went to him and knelt down by the bed. He took Max's wandering hand and held it tightly. He kissed the sunken cheek tenderly. He smiled encouragement. But, he thought—what now? How can he go on again after this, when he was beginning to trust people? He'll never forget what men have done to him before, and what they have done to him now. He's lost, lost forever. For the first time in Johnny's life his thoughts did not go at once, and instinctively, to God. There was a darkness, a silence, where the Light had waited, sure and shining and unshaken. An iron door had shut between him and God, and his hand had shut it in his despairful rage and hatred and sorrow.

He did not know that he had laid his head beside Max's until he felt a slight, wandering, blind touch on his cheek. Max had touched him, seeking. The cheap rosy light of the lamp filled Johnny's eyes with a swimming haze. His head felt enormously heavy, yet floating. He shook it, and for a terrible moment or two he did not know where he was, or who he was. Absolute blankness overpowered him.

Then he saw Max's face, very close to him. Max was smiling a little, a tentative, child's smile. But Max's eyes were clear as they had never been clear before, and full of pity and understanding.

Johnny looked at him, and the rapid fury of his heart slowly began to subside in wonder and amazement. "Max?" he murmured.

"Papa," said Max, and he spoke with painful clarity. "Papa must not cry. Papa must not be—mad. The boys—they did not know what they do—"

The muscles in Johnny's face tightened, flattened. Who had said that before? "Forgive them, Father, for they know not what they do." Ah, yes, but they always knew, they always knew!

Dr. McManus stood by the side of the bed, and bowed his head so that his face was hidden. He put his hand on Johnny's shoulder in silence.

Max's face was illuminated, as if some exaltation possessed him, some new knowledge. A little color came into his face. His hand warmed in Johnny's. And then he pressed Johnny's fingers, as a father presses the hand of a bitter child.

"They did not know what they do—this I know, Papa."

He sighed deeply. His eyes closed, and he slept.

"You can leave him now," said Dr. McManus, in a constricted voice. "And something tells me you won't have to worry about that kid any longer—his nightmares. He won't have any. He knows too much—now. He'll never be lost again."

Max slept in the light of the lamp, peacefully. Johnny stood up and put his hands over his face. The iron door had opened. The Light shone out, more vivid, more triumphant than ever. Forgive me, Father, he said in himself.

He went to the girls' room. Here a white bulb glared from the ceiling. Mrs. Burnsdale, that intrepid little woman, rocked alone in the chair. She hummed a lullaby steadily. In a corner of the room Kathy and Emilie were huddled together, the older girl's arms tightly and fiercely about the younger. When Johnny entered, Kathy's eyes flew to him, and they were the eyes he remembered in Salzburg—fierce, hating, terrified. She covered Emilie's face with her arms, protecting her; the fine yellow hair was disheveled. Emilie whimpered like a frightened kitten, and crept closer to Kathy and clung to her. The children's nice cotton dresses were stained with blood.

"Kathy?" said Johnny.

She did not answer. She continued to regard him with an animal's strange and wary fear, and wildness.

"Now," said Dr. McManus, "what's that sensible girl doing there on the floor, like a rabbit? Our sensible girl. Our Kathy."

"Never saw them like this before," said Mrs. Burnsdale wearily. "Not even the first day. I talk and talk to them, and

152

it's like they don't hear me and don't know me." She showed Johnny a long and angry scratch on her plump arm. "Kathy did that, poor little thing, when I tried to hug her—after she brought Max in. And little Emilie doesn't understand, except that things've gone back to where they were."

Johnny took the scratched arm, and then helped Mrs. Burnsdale to her feet. He drew her toward the children. Kathy shrank back, and clasped Emilie closer to her. Silence stood before them like a barrier. Johnny lifted Mrs. Burnsdale's arm, and showed the wound to Kathy. She looked at it, moistened her lips, returned that savage glare to Johnny.

He said, "You did this to Mrs. Burnsdale, Kathy? Mrs. Burnsdale who loves you, who combs your hair and cooks for you, who washes for you, who takes care of you? Kathy? You did this?"

Kathy uttered a single sound—an awful growl. Johnny remembered it. So, Kathy had retreated again, in her fear and distrust. She had retreated to the place where Max would never wander again. The wound was not visible in her flesh, but in her spirit.

Dr. McManus approached, squatted down on his heels, and contemplated Kathy. "Here's a girl I always thought was sensible." His voice had almost lost its squeak. "Let me tell you a story. Once a little girl, like you, Kathy, was born to me and my wife. But my wife died." He paused and coughed, and cleared his throat. "And then the little girl died. She had yellow hair like you, Kathy, and blue eyes like yours. I thought you had come to be my little girl; if she'd lived she'd have been like you. Or maybe not. She wouldn't have been so stupid."

Kathy's eyes flickered as she stared at the doctor.

"My own girl would have remembered how her Papa loved her. She wouldn't have hurt anyone, as you did, and as you're doing now. She would have trusted her father."

Kathy's round face, usually so pink, was very white and fixed.

Johnny said, "Max is all right, Kathy. He's much better. He'll never be afraid any more. For, you see, he trusts me, and knows I love him, and he knows that the—that the—boy who did that was sick. Here in his head. And that he wasn't to blame for being cruel. Something made him be that way. He needs our pity."

A queer, sly look passed over Kathy's face, narrowing her eyes.

"And in Europe, too? The people were sick? Pity for them, too?" Her voice was slow and cunning.

Johnny looked at her, full and serious. "Yes, Kathy. Yes, Kathy."

The convulsed arms loosened about little Emilie, and the child's eyes peeped out, eagerly fastening themselves upon Johnny. "Papa?" she whimpered, and struggled to free herself.

But Johnny repeated to Kathy, in a lower, deeper tone, "Yes, Kathy."

Again the silence fell on the older girl. She kept wetting her lips. She no longer gazed at Johnny; she looked at the floor, and she was looking into herself. When Emilie disentangled herself Kathy made no move to stop her. The little one stumbled to her feet and ran to Johnny, her arms outstretched. He caught her up in his arms and held her to him, and her long tangled hair floated about her.

Then Kathy uttered a faint, agonized cry, and tears welled into her eyes. She jumped to her feet in one swift motion. But she did not go to Johnny. She ran to Mrs. Burnsdale, snatched up her arm, cried out again as she examined the scratch she had inflicted, then kissed it over and over again, sobbing. Mrs. Burnsdale bent down and laid her cheek on the child's head.

"There now, there now," she said. "It doesn't matter about the arm. You didn't mean to do it. Did you?"

But Kathy sobbed, clutching the arm remorsefully. "Sick in the head! Sick in the head! Like the boy!"

She stopped abruptly, as if struck. She swung to Johnny rapidly. "Like the boy!" she exclaimed. "Like in Europe!"

"Yes, darling," said Johnny.

Kathy smiled brilliantly, her round blue eyes shining. She came to Johnny and took his hand. She stood on tiptoe to kiss him. Then she ran to Dr. McManus, and kissed him too. "I am your girl," she said. "After Papa's girl."

"Well, you'll have to do better than you did," grumbled the doctor, and roughly smoothed her rumpled hair. "Thought you had more sense. My girl."

Mrs. Burnsdale said, "Oh, for goodness' sake, and the stew

on the stove! Kathy, come down at once and help me. Look, it's dark outside. And the table not even set."

"Yes," said Kathy, and followed the woman out of the room. The others followed, Johnny carrying Emilie, who had begun to yawn. Max still slept in peace.

Jean and Pietro were waiting in the dingy parlor below. Pietro was gathered up in a knot in a chair, frightened and staring. But Jean was very calm and grave. He said to Johnny, "People been calling. Very sorry about Max, they say. They told me about Max."

Johnny stopped. He looked penetratingly at Jean, and with dread. But Jean smiled sadly. "So, Papa, it begins again, yes?"

Johnny touched his shoulder. "Jean, it never stopped. It never will. Until people know about God."

Jean considered this lengthily, his pale eyes thoughtful. Then he nodded. "Yes, I see. It is the world. Yes." Now he smiled without sadness. "But not afraid. Not with Papa." He turned to Pietro and said severely, "Come, we wash hands and comb hair, and help Kathy. Work to do."

Dr. McManus cleared his throat. "No need to worry about these kids any longer. Er—someone taught them a lesson today, and they'll never forget it."

10

It was only when he was among "the people" that Lars ("Swede") Swensen, who was not Swedish, used crude English, the kind of English he and so many others considered acceptable by "the workers." He knew very well that the workers were mostly young folk who had had a full high-school education, and even a college education in many instances, and that bad or crude English was instinctively offensive to them. However, he operated on what he called "seduction by flattery." By appearing "rough" and "homespun" to these workers he gave them the happy conviction that they were superior to him, in spite of his known wealth, and so they listened to him with affection. Too, he was in his fifties; he represented to them the "underprivileged" older generation who had not had their advantages. They became, paradoxically, irritable with their parents for their suspicions of this champion of the masses; older people, they said among themselves, were too ignorant to understand.

There was an even more sinister use by Swensen of his seduction by flattery. He was effectively convincing tens of thousands of young men and women that formal education was not needed by the masses, but that their children would be better adjusted in a technological world if they were taught trades and vocations, exclusively manual. After all, was he not a successful man himself, who had never had more than five years of grammar schooling? He was rugged; he was self-made. By endless struggle he had emerged from the welter of anonymity. "I would have made it sooner," he would say with his handsome grin, "if I'd had one of these here vocational educations. And by the way, what're you doin' for your kids in the schools? Why, right here in Barryfield (or Lexington or Philadelphia or New York or Chicago or Scranton or Pittsfield or Buffalo or Detroit, or Utica, Trenton, Portersville, or Greensburg) you ain't got a tenth of the vocational schools you need for your kids! Liberal education! Hell, that's for the teachers and professors and doctors and lawyers and such! Give your kids an education so they can use their hands, and amount to something." Once, shyly, addressing a large union meeting in Detroit, he had spoken of the dignity of labor. "Picked it up from a professor," he said. "But it's got a kind of good sound, ain't it? Sure. Labor. The reactionaries don't like labor, and its good dirty hands. That's why you don't get your vocational school."

All this was part of the master plan to stratify and freeze and immobilize the American people into classes. The work had begun years ago, before World War I. It was going very well. For the first time in their robust and vital flux of life, where a man today was a laborer and the superintendent of a huge steel mill tomorrow, or where an obscure student of physics in a small town today was a famous scientist a few years later, the American people were self-consciously beginning to think of themselves as groups, minorities, and, most dangerous of all, as classes, and to develop the illusion that as groups, minorities, or classes they must think the fallacies of this illusion.

"Swede" Swensen lived in a penthouse of extravagant luxury in New York, a matter carefully kept out of the newspapers, and away from any honest union leader and, of course, from the workers. He would say, "Well, now, sir, I live in a kind of a nice flat in New York; keep it for my headquarters. But I sleep anywhere. What does it matter, anyway? The world's my home."

Mr. Lars Swensen was too important a man to waste his time. When he appeared anywhere, to be with any of his associates, the matter was vital.

Lorry Summerfield, in the telephone booth of the small drugstore near her father's offices, wiped her damp hands and deposited the demanded coins for her call to New York. She had been afraid that her brother, Barry, would not be at home this hot Saturday afternoon, and she felt a relaxing in herself of deep gratitude that he was about to answer her call. She leaned forward and said eagerly, "Barry! Swensen's here again—with *him*. I saw him coming in—it must be important—"

Her brother's suddenly tense voice answered her. "Yes. He's been around to a number of newspaper offices all over the country. He isn't concentrating, this time, on the big national newspapers, just the grass-roots publications. I haven't been able to get a lead, as yet, for the kind of newspapers who follow his prodding aren't the kind who'll give out information." He laughed, a short hard bark of laughter very similar to his sister's. "Get what you can for me, Lorry, and let me know. I'll put it in my column. 'The Watchman' in the New York *Star* sometime next week. By the way, the *Star*'s circulation's gone up one hundred thousand, and that's good news. Good girl, Sis."

The "good girl" emerged from the telephone booth. The shop was cool and clean, and she hesitated, glancing at the soda fountain. The owner greeted her affectionately, but his eyes were curious. Now, why did Miss Lorry Summerfield often use the drugstore telephone, when she had such a fine big office next to her father's? Girls at switchboards gossiped, of course. "A soda on the house, Miss Lorry?" he asked, coming from behind his counter and snapping his fingers at the boy who presided over the cold delights.

"No thanks, Jim," said Lorelei Summerfield. "I'm in a hurry. Sunday edition tomorrow, you know. Things humming, as usual. I just remembered that I had to make a quick call, and couldn't wait."

"Sure," said the stout little man quickly. He had served this girl his special fountain joys since she had been a child. He watched her as she hurried out. Well, it was none of his business. She was a fine girl, in spite of that silly name inflicted on her by her sillier mother, with her silly "art-print" dresses and trailing chiffon scarves and queer earrings. The girl had had the sense, when only five years old, to insist that her name was Lorry, not Lorelei, and the name had remained for twenty-two years. Why hadn't so beautiful a girl ever married? She had all the advantages, hadn't she? She wasn't "stuck" in Barryfield. She was more often in Philadelphia and New York and Europe than in her home town, acting as correspondent for her father. Good photographer, too. He'd seen some of her work in *Life* and other magazines. But nothing she ever photographed was as interesting, beautiful, or exciting as herself.

Lorry Summerfield hurried down the short street to the fine modern building which housed the Barryfield *Press*. Passers-by followed her with their eyes, and some of the eyes were not too friendly. Too good for Barryfield, was she? And all those things about her in the Philadelphia and New York newspapers. Always being rumored engaged to somebody or other with a big name, and never getting married. She drank a lot, it was said. Bad disposition, too, never noticing anybody on the streets on which she stirred up chaff and dust and soot in the violent passage of her big, shiny Cadillac, her nose in the air, her expression contemptuous. Not like her "old man," who was everybody's friend. She hated him, it was said, and he so good to her, and letting her work as one of his editors. Probably as bad as her half brother, who'd taken his stepfather's name when poor Mac Summerfield's terrible divorced first wife had remarried. Barry Lowell, he called himself, and nobody knew where he was most of the time. Just like his sister. The name Summerfield wasn't good enough for him!

Lorry, her beautiful carved face pale with the heat, ran up the carpeted steps of the private entrance and silently pushed open the blond mahogany door. She glanced into the square hall, with its black and white marble floor. Two doors led off from it, one leading to her father's sumptuous offices, and one to her own. Everything was soundproofed; she could hear nothing. She pushed open the door of her private office, ran to her desk, and sat down. The turquoise silk of her summer dress clung to her long and graceful body with uncomfortable dampness, and her stockings felt like sheaths of clammy metal on her exceptionally pretty legs. She kicked off her black slippers, to allow the cool air conditioning to flow over her feet. Now she began to shiver as the heat of her flesh was whisked away from her. The drops of water on her face turned cold. She patted it with paper handkerchiefs. Opening a box of cosmetics she kept at hand in a desk drawer, she looked at herself briefly. Her oval face, just a trifle too long, was the tint and texture of ivory, completely colorless except for large tilted eyes the color of her dress, and her bitter if voluptuous mouth. She had her father's face, and she detested it, as she had detested it for years. She had his eyes too, and his long, slender nose, his pointed, smooth chin. There were stains like bruises in the delicate skin under her eyes, the marks of despairing, sleepless disgust.

She smoothed her fragile hands over her very smooth blond hair, which was drawn back from her face and rolled in a large knot near the top of her head. Then she slumped in her chair and stared somberly into space. In some way she must get into her father's office. When Swensen was there he never wished to be disturbed.

She glanced at her desk to see if anyone had laid anything there recently of sufficient importance to serve as an excuse to go into her father's office unannounced. But it was too early. Only the morning paper lay near her blotter. With growing anxiety she took it up, glanced up and down the black columns. All at once she stopped. On the second page, right hand, was a column mentioning "an attack on a child, Max Fletcher" by some obscure young criminal. The boy had been slashed by a knife, the police had reported, during a "childish quarrel." He was one of the five adopted children of the new minister of the Church of the Good Shepherd on Malone Street. The *Press* reporter had been interested by the fact that Max and his "brothers and sisters" were all refugees brought to this country by the minister, who had been a chaplain in the Army. Their parentage was unknown, but they had been prisoners in various concentration camps in Europe, "victims of the late Nazi horror." Max, it was noted, was only eleven years old. The family had arrived three days ago, and were living in the parsonage with their adopted father. The other children's names were given: Jean, Pietro, Kathy, and Emilie.

Interesting, thought Lorry Summerfield. John Fletcher. The minister. John Fletcher! Somewhere, at some time, she had heard that name. Had he been decorated for valor, perhaps? Had he distinguished himself in a certain manner? She frowned intently. In some way the name stirred her strangely; she felt an unfamiliar warmth, an urgent desire to remember. She read the story again. A man in his middle thirties. He had asked the police not to take into custody the boy who had attacked his "son" Max. But the police had turned the youth over to juvenile authorities.

The Church of the Good Shepherd—on Malone Street. A miserable neighborhood! She knew it well. Then she remembered something else. This was "Uncle Al's" church! He was the one man in Barryfield whom her father openly hated, openly courted. Excitement flooded the girl. Dear old Dr. Al, with his wicked mouth, his savage eyes, his great, tender hands, his honor and his ferocity! Now she smiled, and the bitterness went from her face and it was utterly gentle and lovely. He would have a real story to give her. And, in the meantime, she had the excuse to go into her father's offices.

She sprang up from her chair, went into the outer office, where her secretary was studiously typing, and ran into the hall, the newspaper in her hand. She pushed open the door to her father's offices, to be confronted, as usual, by his secretary, a wan young man with an intense, taut face, fanatical black eyes behind horn-rimmed glasses, and a body that seemed composed exclusively of hard and quivering wires under an excellently tailored suit. Lorry Summerfield despised him. Her father had brought Edgar Sloan from New York to be his confidential secretary, and he was being paid a salary so large that it was a matter of constant astonishment to the staff. But Lorry had not been in the least astonished. She knew.

"Mr. Summerfield's in conference, Miss Lorry," he said. He had a low voice, as intense and as piercing as his face. "I'm sorry."

"Who?" she demanded, curtly.

He shrugged. "I don't know," he murmured.

Lorry stared at him, the turquoise of her eyes vivid with dislike. "Well, it doesn't matter." She tapped the newspaper. "I've got a wonderful story for him. We've overlooked it, made it just a routine report. It can't wait."

"Well, can't we just send out another reporter on it for the Sunday edition?" He was looking at her with that furtive admiration and desire of his, which so infuriated her. "We don't have to disturb Mr. Summerfield."

His hand stole to the intercommunication box and he flipped the switch, bending down to speak. "Mr. Summerfield, Miss Lorry insists on seeing you immediately. She says it's very important."

"In half an hour," replied Mr. Summerfield impatiently, but Lorry ran to the desk, and bent down and shouted, "Not in half an hour! It won't wait, if we're to get it into the paper tomorrow! I'm coming in."

Edgar Sloan stood in her way, uncertainly. She looked at him with contempt, and, as if she had struck him, he jumped aside. She flung open the door of her father's office and stood on the threshold.

Everything here was in her father's favorite blond mahogany wood, enhanced by green and coral draperies at the windows and a dark-green rug on the floor. A few abstract paintings, carefully selected for their complementary colors, hung on the pale-emerald walls. MacDonald Summerfield sat behind the glimmering golden expanse of his neat desk, which matched the color of his thin sleek hair. He was a tall, thin, and aristocratic man, much younger in appearance than his actual age, and with an amazing resemblance to his daughter. But there were no stains of sorrow under his eyes, no sharp lines about his mouth, like hers. He was all suavity and health and sureness. Near him, with a lustier fairness than his own, sat the large and solid bulk of "Swede" Swensen.

Both men rose, Swensen smiling with pleasure, Summerfield frowning. "Really, Lorry," said Summerfield. But his face softened, changed almost pathetically, at the sight of his beloved daughter who hated him without—to him—any logical explanation. Hadn't she always been his darling? She had never told him how, or why, she had come to this open loathing of him. Once she had adored him, and this adoration had continued up to about four years ago. She had been a willful child, a willful young girl, but he had denied her nothing. At any rate, a psychiatrist had said with smug confidence, "I hate to mention it, but it's my opinion she's competing with you—perhaps for the newspapers, or something else."

As usual, she was ignoring him. She was smiling brilliantly at Swensen, and was holding his large pink hand tightly. "Now, why should Dad hide you from me?" she demanded, and tilted her head archly. "He knows I'm always so glad to see you, Lars, and we have so much in common."

"You'd have seen him at dinner tonight," said her father irritably. "Well, what is it anyway, Lorry?"

But Lorry sat down, being careful to flare her turquoise dress about her lovely legs like an unfurled fan. She beamed at Swensen and he drew his chair closer to hers, and she could smell the freshness of him. He was a handsome, brightly colored man, with light-gray eyes and waving fair hair, a broad nose and a splay mouth, which was always faintly smiling. He exuded power and determination, and was all compactness in spite of his size. "Cigarette, Lars?" she asked, after he had had his long and lustful study of her. She knew that neither her father nor Swensen smoked; nor did they often drink. Swensen always carried cigarettes for his friends, and he produced a gold cigarette case with alacrity, and a gold lighter. Lorry took her time, allowing him to touch her fingers in a delicate caress. Mr. Summerfield's frown began to tighten.

Swensen was smiling almost coyly at the girl; his pink cheeks had become pinker. He shook a finger at her and said, "Lorry, I'm hearing stories about your last visit to New York." His eyes pointed at her, and gleamed like bits of granite.

"What?" she said. Her voice was amused.

"Aha," said Swensen, and wagged his head. "Shall I name names?"

"Do," she replied indifferently.

Swensen hummed a new gay tune from the latest New York musical. "I was there only three days," added Lorry. "I had dinner at one club, danced at another, and saw a show. Each time with a different escort, all very respectable." She laughed. Her laugh was not sweet or musical, but strangely like a short bark.

"I have my spies," said Swensen archly. So you have, thought Lorry with anger.

"A very good-looking dark young feller took you out on a Tuesday night. To a place in the Village, all nice dark intimacy and good drinks. Why, Lorry, I saw you there, myself!" He grinned at her delightedly. "Who was the chap?"

"I'd have introduced you if you had come over," said Lorry carelessly.

"Who was he?" asked her father.

She shrugged. "A man I'd met at a cocktail party. He writes books on travel. We were discussing some of my photographs of Norway. His name isn't important." She added, "Robert Corde. You've heard of him."

"Your brother publishes his books, doesn't he?" asked Swensen, with idle interest.

Summerfield's face changed again, and this time to a heavier sadness. He rarely saw his son Barry, whom he loved deeply; Barry who was invariably cold and polite to him, and who had taken his stepfather's name, not as a child, but as a young man then twenty-one. Why? He had never explained adequately. Probably, Summerfield would think with hatred, because Ethel had lied to him, turned him against his father.

"Yes," said Lorry. "But you've always known that, Lars. Bob Corde was thinking of a bigger publisher, and Barry asked me to do some work on him to get him to stay with the Lowell Publishing Company. I did." She smiled charmingly.

"You couldn't fail, Lorry," said Swensen, entranced.

She changed the subject adroitly. "Staying long in Barry-field, Lars?"

The two men exchanged glances. Summerfield had insisted, for a long time, that Lorry could be trusted.

"But she drinks heavily. Sorry, Mac. You know we never trust drinkers, or have anything to do with them. They're unstable," Swensen had said.

Summerfield's face had darkened, becoming charged with grief and bewilderment. "Yes, I know Lorry drinks excessively. But I've never once seen her out of control. Frankly, I think she does her heaviest drinking at home, so I can see it. Why, I don't know. Even then she never loses control of herself. Besides, she writes some of our best editorials. I tell you, some of her things are prophetic."

"Let's keep her prophetic just in the newspapers," Swensen had replied. "We need all the liberals we can get—millions of them. But let them into the inner circle and they'll lose some of the stars in their eyes!" And he laughed. He had added, "Besides, there is her brother, your son."

"But Lorry reports she is winning him over."

Swensen was thinking of this conversation with Summerfield now. It had taken place three months ago. He said to the girl, "How's Barry doing with that latest book he published, *The Sleepless Enemy*, by Francis Connell?"

Lorry's full mouth thinned, became a sneer. "I asked Barry about it. I think he's exaggerating. He says it had sold forty thousand copies up to a month ago. Of course you can sell anything these days, especially if it's written in a sensational way. And it's all blood and thunder. *The Sleepless Enemy!* As if American Communism had any purpose at all but to alleviate racial discrimination, discrimination in employment, and to protect civil liberties and support labor!"

She looked full into Swensen's eyes and smiled deeply, a wise and subtle smile. The man was startled. He stared into the strange, blue-green eyes, which had become warm and intimate and knowing, and he was taken aback. Perhaps Summerfield was right about his daughter after all. His expression became grave. He coughed softly. "Well, has it?" he asked.

Lorry laughed her oddly harsh laugh, and did not answer.

"I myself think the American Communist Party is part and parcel of an international conspiracy," said Swensen, with more gravity. His smooth cheeks flattened, as he stared at Lorry. "I think it is an even graver menace than fascism was, for it is at once more concentrated and more universal, and has a greater appeal for the ignorant masses."

Out of the corner of her eye Lorry could see that her father had bent his head. A flash of hot sunlight turned the strands of his thin hair to gilt. He was preoccupied with listening, and, in his usual fashion, restless while outwardly composed, he was printing something on a sheet of white paper, abstractedly. She said, "I don't agree with you, Lars. I think we can fully integrate the American Communist Party into our system of government, for it is not a conspiracy at all, but an extension of liberalism. But then, you were always a conservative," and she gave him a mocking glance. "I don't see how you and Dad get along, he being such an ardent liberal."

She stood up suddenly, whisking out the back of her skirts, and put the morning newspaper down on her father's desk, leaning forward to do so. Her sharp eye, from long training, could read his words inverted on the sheet of paper. "Win—Peace—Win—Peace." She was disappointed. Then, as her father, coming to himself like a disciplined sportsman in a tense moment, crumpled the sheet swiftly in his hand and did not drop it into the wastebasket, her disappointment disappeared. "Win—Peace." Then that is what they had been discussing, this last hot August Saturday in 1946. But the words expressed what everyone was hoping, believing. Nothing sinister in them—except for that swift crushing of the paper in Mr. Summerfield's long and aristocratic hand.

"I've got to get back to my desk," she said. "Dad, read this story about the minister and his adopted European waifs. I think we have a big story here."

He pushed the crushed sheet carefully into his pocket and took up the newspaper. Swensen got up to stand behind him, to read also. Mr. Summerfield read rapidly. "Well," he murmured. "It's an unusual thing, for Barryfield. The UNRRA must have been supporting that mob—hmm. 'Victims of Nazism.' I don't know."

But Swensen said with enthusiasm, "A wonderful story! People keep forgetting about Nazism, though the war has been over only a year. We shouldn't let them forget. Now an editorial about fascism, or a featured article, with photographs if possible, embodying a story about this minister and the children will have a profound effect. Aren't we in danger of neofascism? Perhaps you could arrange an interview with him, and let him tell the story of fascism and how he rescued those children from it himself. Then it could be arranged for the United Press and the Associated Press to pick up the story." His face seemed to shimmer with his excitement. "Lorry, what do you think?"

"I think it's a splendid idea," she said. "And if Dad wants, I'll do the story myself. Fletcher delivers his first sermon tomorrow."

Mr. Summerfield looked up alertly. "Isn't that church McManus's?"

"Yes." Lorry laughed. "You've always called Uncle Al a reactionary and even hinted he was a fascist. Yet he, as President of the Board, let them come here."

166

Mr. Summerfield and Swensen exchanged a long, hard glance. Lorry saw it; she pretended to be busy with rearranging her dress. She asked, "Does the name Fletcher mean anything to you, Dad?"

Her father considered. "No, I don't think it does. It's a common name. I don't remember any Fletcher in particular. Why?"

"I don't know. It struck me in some way—Fletcher—a minister—a chaplain. Well, never mind. It'll come to me, I suppose. In the meantime, shall I attend that church tomorrow and arrange an interview with Fletcher? Maybe I can get some pictures of him. Good. I think we can do something about it. And now, back to the salt mines. See you tonight, Lars." She gave him another of her seductive smiles, to which he responded satisfactorily. He watched her leave the room, noting, as always, the incredible slenderness of her long waist, the set of her beautiful shoulders, the gleam of her legs. And Summerfield watched him watching, and drew in his lips.

An hour later Lorry ran into the drugstore again, and hurried into the telephone booth. Her brother was waiting for her call. "I don't know if it means anything, Barry—couldn't get anything from their conversation when I was there—but he wrote something on a sheet of paper while I was talking to Swensen—abstractedly. He wrote—'Win—Peace.'"

The hard, quick voice became slightly excited. "It's very important, Lorry. It fits in. It's what we've been waiting for. We've heard it from two other sources. Now we know. That's their new line, without question."

A few days later Mr. Summerfield's lead editorial was headed, "We Must Win the Peace!" The body of the editorial urged all American mothers to demand the return of "your boys" from Europe, immediately, and an end to armaments, and the restoration of "normal life in this country." A diatribe on war followed, scornful and bitter. Mr. Truman was accused of desiring, not peace, but "a prolonged, victorious war at the expense of American misery, and the suffering of American wives and mothers, for the benefit of a few who profit by the manufacturing of munitions." The world longed for peace, for security, for an end to bloodshed. America must lead the way to this glorious fulfillment of man's real destiny.

They were fine words. They were used, these days, by Generals MacArthur and Eisenhower, and by the President. They were used by good and decent men everywhere. But, more significant, they were used by evil men for evil and chaotic ends, who hated the President and the generals, and all mankind, and who loved, not peace, but revolutionary war.

———

11

"I've been reading the *Press* these last few days," said Johnny coldly. He looked at Lorry as she sat in his combination living room and study. He had seated himself behind the shabby desk, and his strong hands played with a pen. He thought, as he studied her, that she resembled a shining white butterfly momentarily pausing in a jungle of faded and decaying vegetation, so radiant did she seem in her white silk suit in that dismal parlor. He rarely disliked anyone; he had come to the conclusion, regretfully, that he disliked this bold and beautiful young woman with her aquamarine eyes and air of hard and cynical sureness. He noted the string of fine pearls about her milky throat, her expensive hat, her excellent slippers, the diamond on her right hand.

"You don't like the *Press?*" asked Lorry, with an acid sweetness.

"No," said Johnny bluntly. He fixed his eyes on her, and they hardened. "You see, I always recognize the—dangerous—line under noble, humanitarian phrases. I recognized it first in Europe. I discovered it in New York. And now, I see, it's even in places like Barryfield."

There was cold repudiation in his voice, and he looked away from her with sad disdain. He added, "They're old phrases. Tyrants have used them from the very beginning of time. I'm sorry. I can't give you a story. I don't want my children exposed either to ridicule or sensationalism; I don't want any more attention brought to them." He turned his eyes on her again, and they threatened her, denied her, rejected her, in one long understanding glance. "They can't stand it, you see. Too much has been done to them. Let them have peace."

"But the *Press* is a liberal, antifascist paper," said Lorry. "I think that in the service of American democracy you ought to let us have the story."

"Do you?" said Johnny. "I told you, I've read your newspapers, Miss Summerfield. I don't think you're interested at all in American democracy. I'm not, then, going to let these children be used for what you really have in mind."

Lorry leaned toward him. "And what is that?" she asked.

He smiled at her wearily. "You know, of course. I'm not very naïve."

Lorry lifted her voice and shouted, without looking away from Johnny, "Uncle Al! Come on in here!"

During the time she had been talking with Johnny she had been conscious of the happy murmur of children's voices in the rear of the house, a loud but tender woman's voice, and the homely clatter of dishes and silver. The miserable house was very hot and the sun lit up the grim furniture. But there was a good smell of roasting meat in the air, and the fragrance of soup.

But she had been more conscious of Johnny. His dark face, strong-boned, lighted by his unusually blue eyes, had moved her mysteriously. He sat behind his desk, in his very shabby, very worn, black clerical clothing which no amount of brushing or pressing could improve. He leaned his arms on his desk, as if utterly tired and despondent, and she saw the marks of grief and strain about his mouth. All at once, to her angry astonishment, she was flooded with a tenderness for him so intense that her eyes watered and her throat tightened. His face, the cropped black hair, the sharply marked black brows, floated before her, and she was conscious of nothing else until she saw Dr. McManus.

"Well, what's the matter, Lorry?" he demanded. "Parson

here giving you a rough time? He don't want a story about his kids. He don't want anything from you. What's the matter, Lorry?" he added, with quick and affectionate concern, and took her chin in his fingers and turned her face roughly to him.

She pulled away from him impatiently. "Oh, Uncle Al. I thought you'd help me. What harm can a good story do?"

"You know damn well. Most of the people in this town don't like your dad's papers. They read 'em because of some of the good woman's features, and local news, and the comics, and because they're the only papers, but they don't read the editorials much. And what they do read makes 'em mad. They'd be suspicious of our parson if you said anything good about him, and if you said your nice vitriolic things they'd despise him. That's human nature. Loves to read viciousness in the papers about anyone, and wants to believe it. No matter what kind of a story you'd write the parson'd be in a mess. Leave him alone, Lorry."

He looked at Johnny. "Don't worry about this girl, son. Known her all her life. Things I can't tell you, or anybody else, about her—yet. She just has a job to do on her father's papers. Not what you think, though. Never mind. Just don't give her anything."

Johnny listened with surprise and bewilderment. He looked at Lorry with some speculation and curiosity. What did the old doctor mean? Dr. McManus, with an expression of affection on his face so grotesque that it resembled a softheaded smirk, was lighting a cigarette for Lorry, and she was smiling up at him. What a really beautiful face she has, Johnny thought, with a lessening of his hostility. Yet when a shaft of sun struck it sideways it was not a gentle face. It might, thought Johnny, be called disillusioned and embittered and despairing. Then she turned her head and the swift revelation, if it was a revelation, had disappeared, and only ivory smoothness was there, and carved, full lips, and grace.

"You're a wonderful help, Uncle Al," said Lorry. She patted his arm. "Sit down there, right next to me." He sat down on the chintz sofa beside her, and the springs wailed. "All right," she said. "I won't touch your precious parson. Oh, I've seen your fatuous interest in him. He must be quite a boy to do that to you. Look, Mr. Fletcher, let's be friends. I won't even mention you and the children, if that is the way

you want it. I can see your point. Uncle Al briefed me about
the children before we went into church, and perhaps it
wouldn't be a good idea to bring them more notoriety. By
the way," she went on, gazing at the tip of her cigarette, "I
gathered that the congregation, except for a militant minority in the front pews, wasn't exactly friendly to you. The
church was crowded; that's because you're a freak. But
they'll tire of you; that's the way it is. You'll have lots of
empty pews in the immediate future. And—perhaps worse."

She raised her eyes to his silent face, and again that most
unfamiliar sensation of passionate tenderness came to her,
filled her with deep warmth, and a kind of yearning which
she could not recognize. An obscure, shabby young parson,
with a bizarre family of children from the ends of the
earth—how could such a man, poverty-stricken, unknown,
stir her so keenly, so passionately? Then, like a faint call from
her childhood, she heard in herself: "Nothing good can come
from Galilee!" Who had said that, and about Whom?

Don't be fanciful, she warned herself sharply. This fellow
here is nothing but a parson with a collection of waifs who
has come to a dreary small city to preside over a drearier
church and congregation—who don't want him. He has only
one friend, and a capricious one at that, who could turn
against him at an instant's notice or whim. Remember his
sermon today—only fifteen minutes. Whom did it stir? Who
listened to him, breathless? Nobody, not even me. Eloquent?
Yes, he was, but he was also anachronistic. Everybody
thought he would deliver brimstone after the assault on his
child. Or talk about intolerance or the underprivileged or
social conditions. But nothing like that at all! I can't even
remember any telling phrase of his, though he has an excellent voice. What, now, was the subject of his sermon?
Yes—silly idea—repentance. Repentance for what? Our sins!
No wonder even the most stupid there was baffled. If he were
one of those howling evangelists who go storming around the
country, frothing, one could understand. But he isn't. Our
sins, for God's sake!

She said briskly, "Well, I can at least give you a few lines
under our church notices. Let me see: you talked about sin."
She gave him an arrogant smile. "Americans don't sin. We're
the most idealistic nation in the world. We're preparing to

flood the whole world with our milk and honey, literally as well as figuratively. We love everybody. We're virtuous, childlike, simple, kind, generous, brimming with earnest faith."

"Are we?" asked Johnny. Now his eyes were full upon her, blue and fiery. "Who said so? Why, we did. We always do. Yet, we forget the atomic bomb dropped on two defenseless Japanese cities, two weeks after the Japanese government begged to surrender to us. Why did we do that? Because we are so kind, virtuous, et cetera? I tell you, Miss Summerfield, we are going to pay in blood for that crime against mankind, and for all the crimes we have committed against the world for half a century, just as other nations have paid in blood for their own crimes. There is only one way we, and all the rest of the world, can avert the consequences of our crimes, and that is through repentance and pennance."

"So you said this morning," commented Lorry dryly. She glanced with humor at Dr. McManus, waiting for his returning grin of acknowledgment of her derision. But Dr. McManus, to her tremendous surprise, was staring gloomily at the bright-green rug on the floor. He said, "Well, yes, of course. Don't know about God doing it, though. Don't believe in Him, myself, as an actual personal force. Foolish idea. Just the law of retribution."

"And Who is the law of retribution?" asked Johnny, with sternness.

"Oh, come," said Lorry, discomfited and annoyed. "Let's not get mystical, please. I'm a big girl now. Coming back to your sermon, Mr. Fletcher: think about the people in your congregation. Not a one who didn't contribute something to what was gaily called the war effort. Red Cross, blood donations, overseas packages, 'smokes for our boys,' air-raid wardens, relief donations, extra work in factories, and so on and so on, to the end of tedium. Many of them lost sons or husbands or brothers in the war. Do you speak to them of comfort, and praise them for their patriotism, or tell these miserable souls that they have done a good job? No, you tell them they are sinners, that they must repent, and do penance! For God's sake, Fletcher!"

He just sat and looked at her with that silent sternness of his. And all at once a hot sensation as of deep blushing pulsated through Lorry's body, a blushing of pain and nameless remorse, of profound sorrow. She could not understand it. She was shaken to the heart.

She got to her feet as if leaping for flight. Her purse fell, and the contents spilled. Dr. McManus, grunting a little, stooped to retrieve it. He held it out to Lorry, but she was staring at the young minister as if struck and immobilized. Her expression had changed almost to complete distortion. And now, all at once, her eyes distended with horror.

She said, in a fainting voice, "Does the name—Lowell, Barry Lowell, mean anything to you?"

Johnny, taken aback by her inexplicable violence of movement, by the look in her eyes and the change in her voice, stood up. He thought for a moment. "No, Miss Summerfield. Should it?"

"Barry Lowell's her brother, publisher in New York," said Dr. McManus with deep interest. "Was in that war. Ever meet him?"

Johnny, in spite of his weariness and despondency, tried to concentrate. "Lowell? Not that I remember. But I met thousands of our troops. I was all over, as chaplain. Where was your brother?"

But Lorry had turned swiftly to confront Dr. McManus and he had turned to her, and Lorry smiled at him, a wild, white smile, and nodded. "Well," said Dr. McManus, "there must have been hundreds like Barry for him, and so he can't remember them all, or possibly none of them."

Lorry's eyes filled with tears. She regarded Johnny humbly, struggled to speak. Dr. McManus took her arm gently. "No, Lorry. Let's not talk about it. It wouldn't mean anything to our parson. Just in the day's work. He's that kind. Don't get emotional."

"Take me home, Uncle Al," she said brokenly, and turned away. Johnny was mystified. He came from behind his desk, not knowing what to say. Dr. McManus grinned at him somberly, patted his shoulder, and said, "Let's go, Lorry. Time for my dinner, anyway."

"Is there something I can do?" asked Johnny, bewildered. "Miss Summerfield doesn't look well."

Dr. McManus paused, and fixed his concrete-colored eyes on the young minister. "Son," he said, "you're the parson. Remember Lazarus?" He smiled at Johnny's increasing bewilderment. "Never mind, boy. I just want to say, though, that that was a damn fine sermon, though I don't expect it'll do any good. And you might tell Mrs. Burnsdale that I'll consider that deep freezer for her."

He took Lorry out to his own limousine, and asked a young man he knew who was passing by to drive Lorry's car home. He helped the girl to seat herself. She seemed completely flaccid, as if she had received a tremendous shock. As the limousine rolled away she burst into dry sobs, her breast heaving, her hands clenched on her knees. "Relax, honey," said the doctor. "This ain't like you. Y'know, I'm getting kind of mystical myself. I kind of think that boy didn't come here by accident."

She whispered through dry lips, still staring ahead as if she had not heard him, "I knew there was something familiar about his name, and the fact that he was a chaplain. I tried to remember. And then, while I was talking to him, I did remember—Barry's letters—I must call Barry at once, and tell him."

Dr. McManus considered this, pursing his lips. Then he shook his head. "I wouldn't, Lorry. Not yet. Don't tell your dad, either. I have a sort of feeling that what we know is going to come in handy for our parson—one of these days. Keep him as our ace in the hole."

Mr. Summerfield wrote his own editorial on Monday night, and it was skillful. "We have won the war against Nazism, and now we, with our allies, must win the peace. Complete world disarmament—bring the boys home immediately—era of good will, new hope for the world—Russia's magnificent contribution to the fight for freedom—extension of democracy throughout the world—last enemies of mankind, hunger, disease, unemployment, must be eradicated just as we hope to eradicate war—great new hope for the world—win the peace, win the peace—"

Lorry read the editorial over and over, and so did many others who were well enlightened. These were all noble and heroic words; they were the craving of all mankind, the hope of all nations. There was nothing wrong with them at all, thought Lorry. Except that they were being used by the wrong people, for evil ends.

12

All the children trooped out to the ancient car with Johnny this wan, gray Monday morning. Heat pressed down over the city, filled with the nauseous gases from mill and factory trapped under the lowering skies. Little Emilie coughed, her frail face paling. Johnny lifted her anxiously in his arms. The other children coughed, but Johnny's attention was on the small girl. Was it his imagination, or was she more fragile than usual, more dwindled? Well, they would soon see. He and the children were accompanying Jean, now a very important person, to the hospital, where his operation was to take place that afternoon. At Dr. McManus's insistence, the others were to be given a thorough examination—partly, Johnny knew, to divert their anxiety from Jean, and partly for necessary reasons.

Jean had not been permitted breakfast. The children had regarded him with awe. He spoke of God and the mending of his arm and leg, and they nodded in silent agreement. Their confidence made Johnny's apprehension even worse. He knew how severe this operation would be; he knew all the hazards. What if Jean were to die during that long ordeal? What if there would be no success?

Because Jean was who he was, Dr. McManus had not insisted that the boy spend the last night in the hospital, in preparation for the operation. "Might be traumatic for him," he had told Johnny. "Bring the kids along, to give him moral support, and make it kind of a holiday for him and them."

Johnny wished the day were more cheerful, a gala day. But a gaunt light lay over the clouded city, hung starkly along the sides of the houses and made hollows of loneliness under the trees. A few leaves were already falling; they scratched the sidewalks like elfin fingers as the slight breeze moved them. The children were oppressed; Johnny could see that, as they went down the short walk to the car at the curb. He gave Max a quick glance. The boy, weakened though he was, and with his throat and chin still bandaged, had insisted on joining the troupe. He clung to Kathy's sturdy arm, and she held her arm straight and strong to support him.

"Be good!" called Mrs. Burnsdale from the doorway, her hands wrapped in her apron. The children waved to her. She smiled, though her eyes were as worried as Johnny's. She prayed in herself, and looked with compassion at Johnny's tall figure in its clerical black. He walked surely, with Emilie in his arms, but she knew his sadness, his discouragement, his sorrow. It was not that most of the congregation had been silently hostile toward him yesterday that had overcome him, though it had played a considerable part. He had been melancholy since the attack on Max; she had watched him brooding at his desk, playing emptily with his pen. Some remoteness had clothed him, which no one could penetrate. He seemed lost in thoughts so burdensome, so distant, that there was no approaching him. Even the children had sensed it. They rarely approached him voluntarily, but during these past few days they had wandered silently into the parlor, pressing briefly against his shoulder, touching him shyly, then running off.

"You'd think," Mrs. Burnsdale had told Dr. McManus with passionate indignation, "that the congregation would've been ashamed, after Max. But they wasn't. They just sat and stared at the poor minister, while he spoke to them of their sins and their repentance, and their faces just went lumpier and lumpier, in spite of the board and the board's wives, rooting for him down in the first pews. I never did think much of people; know too much about 'em. But I did think they'd be decent for once, considering."

"Why did you expect that, now?" Dr. McManus had squeaked, marveling. "They're just people."

Johnny had reached the car. He was about to open the door when he stopped suddenly. He was staring at the wheels. Something in his abrupt motionlessness alarmed Mrs. Burnsdale. She ran heavily down to the curb. Seeing her, Johnny pointed to the wheels. Every tire had been expertly and thoroughly slashed, and the wheels sagged. This was not the work of children. The rubber had been strongly cut, over and over, not only through the casings but through the inner tubes.

Mrs. Burnsdale put her hand over her mouth. The children were already climbing into the car, and Kathy was assisting Max. Jean, as the oldest, waited for the younger children to find places and seat themselves. He was about to enter the vehicle when his sharp intuition, born of old terror and agony, was struck by something in the air. He looked up, alertly, at Johnny and Mrs. Burnsdale, and his narrow eyes tightened at the corners.

"Something?" he murmured.

There was something in his voice which immediately caught Johnny's stricken attention. He put Emilie carefully on the ground. This was a serious day; Jean's life depended on what the day would bring. Johnny's first thought was to smile, to say, lightly: "It's the car. Something's happened to it. We'll have to take a cab."

And then he knew that evasions were wrong, with Jean. He put his hand on Jean's shoulder and said quietly, "Jean, I've told you there was law in this country. You found that out. The police arrested the boy who attacked Max; he's to be put away for a long time in a kind of school, because his mind is sick. That's the law. And now another thing has happened. The tires on this car have been cut by some wicked person, who hates me."

Jean stared at the minister's sad white face for a long moment. Then he stooped painfully and examined the tires. He nodded, over and over, to himself. He straightened, and again stared at Johnny. Then his wise old face broke into an understanding, wry smile. "A man, Papa? Yes, a man. There are always men, *non?*"

"Yes," said Johnny.

The children were peering inquisitively through the car windows at the group on the sidewalk. Pietro's lively face was squashed against the glass. "Come, come!" he cried. Jean thoughtfully considered his fellows; he could see the shadow of Max's shrunken face. He limped closer to the car, and said, "Out. The car, she is no good. Cannot run. We must have cab."

"No, no!" shrilled Pietro, who loved the car. Jean opened the door, seized the little boy's arm, and pulled him out. "Pietro is fool," he said severely. The other children followed Pietro in wonderment. They waited for Jean to speak again. "Cab," he repeated. "Mama Burnsdale will call a cab for us. Pietro, shut up."

"Why not the car run?" demanded Kathy, as Mrs. Burnsdale, turning to hide her tears, hurried into the house.

Jean warned Johnny with a swift glance. "Papa says it will not run. So it will not run. Cars do not always run. We wait for cab."

"Oh. Oh." The children mourned in disappointment. They gave the car rebuking looks. The condition of the tires escaped their notice. "Bad car," said Emilie.

Johnny was full of gratitude and pain. He put his arm about Jean's shoulders, speechlessly. Then his heart inexplicably lightened, and he was remorseful. He, a man, a minister, had been despondent and discouraged. His prayers had been lifeless these past few days. He had felt that something had broken in him. Yet here was a boy, a child, who had suffered unspeakable anguish and despair and hopelessness, and yet, under monstrous circumstances, could rise to ease another's suffering, selflessly, to retain his faith. He had accepted the evil of men, but had lost his terror of it at last.

"While we wait," said Johnny, and his voice rang with its old gaiety, "I'll tell you a story." The children eagerly pressed about him. "When the Mother of the Christ child, and Joseph, left their own country with Him, to hide Him from the soldiers of the wicked king who wanted to kill Him, they were very frightened. They had come a long way, on a lonely road to Egypt. But before they reached Egypt an angel warned them that the soldiers, on horseback, were close behind them. So they found a cave in which to hide."

"Cave," said Jean. Kathy and Max and Pietro nodded solemnly. They knew caves very well. They knew the darkness and dankness of them, the rubbly floors, the fear, the rapid heartbeat of fright, the silence, the crouching in the dark. And the listening, always the listening, for the pursuing feet of the soldiers.

"The soldiers, on the road, searched every bush and every cave and looked behind every big rock. And now they were very near this cave where the Mother and the Child and Joseph were hiding. Joseph had tied up the donkey behind some trees. He prayed that the donkey would make no sound when the soldiers approached. The Mother sat in the darkness at the back of the cave with her Child tight against her breast, the young Mother with her Baby. And then they heard the hoofbeats of the horses ringing down the road, and the shouts of the soldiers."

"Yes, yes," said the children, remembering.

"Poor Joseph could only think that the soldiers would search this cave too. He closed his eyes, and the tears ran down his cheeks, even while he prayed. And then when he looked up he saw that a very strange thing had happened, in only a few moments."

"What, what?" cried the children loudly. Pietro danced with uncontrollable impatience. Johnny smiled at them triumphantly. "A big spider had spun her web, in just those few moments over the door of the cave! A thick web, which would usually take a whole night to spin!"

"Oh," said the children, in a soft, awed chorus.

"And when the soldiers reached the cave they wanted to search it. But the leader pointed to the web and said it would be impossible that the Family was in the cave, for the web was not broken. So the soldiers rode on, down the hot white road, and after a long time the Family left the cave, and went on their way, on another road."

The children were silent, their faces shining. The dim light under the gray clouds seemed less drab than before. Then Jean said, "God spins many webs, yes?"

"Yes," said Johnny. A cab came rapidly around the corner. "Here we are," said Johnny cheerfully. He helped the children into the cab, while the driver watched curiously. Then a quiet black car rolled softly toward them, and stopped. Jean looked at it, alertly. He smiled at Johnny. "The police," he murmured, and for the first time he said that word with confidence and satisfaction, without his old intonation of terror. Mrs. Burnsdale came down the walk, and Johnny shook his head at her and furtively pointed to the police car, and she went to it at once, for she had called the nearest station. The cab passed the official car, and Jean acknowledged the young officers inside with a wave of his hand, to which they responded.

"Who, who?" asked Pietro, who always noticed everything.

Jean said, "Our friends."

The cab rolled through the silent streets. The children of the city were already in school. Now the light became gaunter, and the stench of the industrial gases more stifling. The cab wheels gritted on the thick cinders of the pavement. Here and there a flash of sulfurous yellow or poisonous green pierced the misty sky. Once or twice Johnny could hear a faint grumbling in the earth, and he knew, with uneasiness, that it came from the mines under the city. His oppression returned, and his fear for Jean. The boy sat so quietly beside him, thoughtfully looking at the streets, and his pale profile was the profile of a man who had suffered much, and remembered.

They reached the hospital, of which Dr. McManus was chief of staff. Johnny understood that it was comparatively new, hardly six years old, but its original light granite was stained and darkened, as if some leprous mildew had attacked it. Men washed cloudy windows, which would be dirty again tomorrow. Had it not been for the modern design of the building, its glass and aluminum doors, Johnny would have guessed its age to be at least a quarter of a century. However, complete air conditioning had been installed, and the interior was all rubber tile, black and white, aluminum, cleanliness and quiet. "A nice place," said Johnny to the children, who walked too closely to him in their familiar huddling. Little Emilie began to cry as a brisk white nurse passed her; she was remembering the needles which had thrown her into convulsions, and Johnny swept her up into his arms. She hid her face on his black shoulder, and panted.

The receptionist, an elderly nurse with a bright and friendly face, greeted them. Dr. McManus would be here directly. And there he was, waddling from some door, glowering, his short thick legs moving like pistons. "Fifteen minutes late!" he squealed. "What do you think this is anyway, parson? A Ladies' Aid tea?"

It was Jean who answered him, moving a step toward the violent old man, and facing him. He said, "The car—she did not run." The doctor scowled down at him. "Nonsense. The car is in good shape. Don't be impudent, boy." Jean said, almost inaudibly, "The wheels—they were cut—to pieces. Only Papa and I know."

"What!" cried the doctor, and his grayish face purpled. He turned to Johnny, and then his face crinkled into an expression of wrath. His breath whistled, and the children regarded him with interest. Then he put his hand on Jean's shoulder and said abruptly, "Things happen to cars. Well, kids, and parson, come to Jean's room. It's a sight." He fished in his pocket and pulled out a telegram addressed to Johnny from New York, and Johnny opened it. It was from Dr. Stevens, expressing his earnest hope that Jean would have a successful operation and begging to be informed immediately. He sent his affectionate regards to the whole family. "He also sent a big bunch of flowers," said the doctor, who had unashamedly been reading the telegram over Johnny's shoulder. "Well, come on."

The telegram warmed Johnny, and he read it to the children. They all went up in a very large smooth elevator to the surgical floor, which had broad and well-lighted corridors, wide swinging doors, and an air of peace. The children were impressed, but they still crowded close to Johnny, who had difficulty in walking. The doctor swung open a door to a large room, and said with grim humor, "Looks like a damned funeral parlor, don't it?"

The room was literally embowered with roses, red, yellow, white, pink, and scarlet. The roomy table near the white bed overflowed; the dresser was inundated; huge vases stood against the walls, in ranks two deep. The room was sunny, and the effect of all this fragrance and color was of a garden in full June. The children cried out in delight, and even little Emilie scrambled in Johnny's arms to be put down. The scent of the flowers was blown about the room by the gentle wind coming through the two large windows, and the children sniffed in ecstasy. Jean's colorless face took on a flush of proud happiness, and he could only stand and stare.

"Good heavens," said Johnny weakly. "Dr. Stevens sent all this?"

"No," replied the doctor. He regarded the flowers with his usual glower, but it was evident he was pleased. "Never mind. A friend. Not me. Not anyone in your congregation. Just a friend."

Johnny was struck by another thought, as a smiling young nurse appeared in the doorway. He colored. "Dr. McManus. This room. It's probably very expensive. I—I thought of a ward. That's about all I can afford, you know. And it's just occurred to me about nurses—"

"The boy can't be in a ward," said Dr. McManus roughly. "For several reasons. Besides, he'll need constant nursing for quite a while. Three nurses. The room's eighteen dollars a day; the best we have. And the nurses get nine dollars a day each, not including their board. Now shut up. It's all being taken care of—by a friend."

"Who?" demanded Johnny, suspiciously. "You? No. You're doing enough, as it is. Dr. Klein told me. I can't accept any more."

"Not me. Not Sol," said the doctor, with impatience. "Just a friend who owes you a debt that can't be paid in full. A debt so big that the friend is trying to pay just a little portion of it."

"No one owes me anything, not a cent," said Johnny, with more suspiciousness, and with a growing humiliation. "Except one soldier who played poker with me. Five dollars. Doctor, I can't take charity, even if I am a minister."

The doctor put his hands on his hips and glared at Johnny. "Now who in hell would give you charity, parson? Who in Barryfield, or anywhere else, I'd like to know? Don't be a damned fool. I happen to know about this debt that's owed you, and believe me, paying for all this is a fleabite in comparison."

"I don't believe you," said Johnny in a tired voice. "It's ridiculous."

"All right, all right, don't believe it," said Dr. McManus angrily. Dr. Klein appeared, blond, white-coated, his eyes smiling behind his glasses. He laughed at the flowers briefly, shook hands with Johnny and Jean. He admired a particular-

ly beautiful yellow rose and, asking Jean's permission, removed it tenderly from a vase and fastened it on his coat.
"They were shipped in from Philadelphia; a truckload, almost," he said. "Somebody kind of likes you and this boy
here. Well?" and he glanced at Dr. McManus.

"All right. There's things to be done, parson. Room's not
big enough with all these infernal flowers."

Johnny took Jean's hand firmly in his own. "Jean," he said,
"the doctors have to prepare you for the operation. We'll
wait until they're finished, and then we'll be back. Okay?"

Jean hesitated. All at once he was afraid. He looked searchingly at Johnny, then at the two doctors. Then he said,
"Okay."

"Good," remarked Dr. McManus. "Kid's got guts. By the
way, while this is going on, take the other kids down to the
examination rooms. I've made the appointment for you.
You'll meet one of my boys; a mick called Kennedy. He's
waiting for you."

The children, particularly Pietro, did not want to leave
Jean. They suddenly surrounded him in a tight circle, and
their eyes were again the wary eyes of animals. "Stay," said
Pietro. "We stay," said Max and Kathy. And they were alien
and cornered, confronted by enemies.

Then Jean spoke loudly and firmly: "You not stay. I don't
want you. Doctors take care of me. Out, Max, Kathy, Pietro.
Out!"

They stared at him in disbelief. He pushed Pietro and
Kathy firmly toward the door, and Max followed uncertainly with Emilie. "Out," he repeated. "Papa!" cried Pietro,
overcome with his bewilderment, and Johnny hurried to join
the frightened flock. "Well, kids," he said ruefully when in
the corridor, "we've been tossed out, haven't we? We're just
nuisances in there. Come on; we're going down to the examination rooms, where the doctors are going to see if you're all
right, and good and healthy."

They laughed with him and took his hands, relieved. Then
Johnny saw Father Krupszyk coming down the hall, and all
at once he felt the full impact of Jean's coming ordeal. "Padre!" said Pietro with delight, and ran to the priest, while the
others watched in wonder. The priest took Pietro's hand, but
it was Pietro who dragged him to the waiting group.
"Padre," he explained loftily to the little girls, and Max. The

children peeked at him shyly, while Johnny shook his hand. The young minister's heart quickened with greater fear and apprehension. "Jean's being made ready," he said.

Father Krupszyk nodded comfortingly. "I'll wait near the door, until they call me." He paused, and his broad Polish face became beautiful with his smile. He put his hand on Johnny's arm. "We'll be praying together, Mr. Fletcher. And we'll remember that God hears all prayers." His eyes showed his concern for Johnny's haggard face and saddened mouth. "I am sure that everything is going to be all right." Johnny squeezed his eyes tightly together to clear them of a blurring mist. Somehow he found himself going down the hall with the children. Pietro was chatting importantly, telling the others about his "Padre." He showed them his rosary again, holding it cupped in his little dark hands.

The examination rooms were large and bright, and Johnny was met by a slender young man with black eyes and hair who introduced himself as Dr. Timothy Kennedy. "So these are the children," he said, smiling down at the group, which was silent again. His keen glance touched their faces busily; it paused for a longer time than Johnny liked on Emilie's little frail face, so pale, so pinched. Then Dr. Kennedy reached out and gently lifted a long strand of the child's pretty hair. "I have a little girl just like you, dear," he said. "Her name is Mary. What's yours?"

She leaned against Johnny's leg and did not answer. She was trembling.

"Her name is Emilie," said Johnny, in as strong a voice as he could muster. "And she's my baby girl. My own Emilie." Her arms suddenly went about his leg and she hid her face against his coat.

It was Kathy who took competent hold. She pulled one of Emilie's hands away from Johnny, and held it. "I go with Emilie," she informed Dr. Kennedy in a severe and matronly voice.

"Well, of course," replied the young man. "Why not? Girls in one room. Boys in another." He tousled Pietro's curls, and the boy grinned at him impudently. He looked at Max again, and his smiling Irish mouth became tense. "We'll change those bandages," he said, and his eyes were no longer laughing, but hard as jet.

A nurse joined him, a short girl with a merry face, who

immediately knew the leader. "Kathy?" she said. "You'll take care of the little girl, your sister? Do you mind if I tell you that I never saw such pretty hair as yours? Yellow as a tulip. Wish I had it."

Kathy, who had been surveying her haughtily, smiled and beamed, and preened more than a little. "Thank you," she said primly. She flounced her plaid skirt, and the nurse said, "My name is Nancy. I like your dress, Kathy. I had one like it once, and I loved it."

The children were led off, and Johnny was assigned to a comfortable waiting room. No one noticed him, for the other occupants were concerned with their own fears and anxieties. He looked at the stout drab woman opposite him; her fleshy face was white, and pulled into desperate folds. She kept twisting a handkerchief in her black-gloved fingers, and she would blink dryly, over and over. Sometimes her mouth moved in a silent prayer. A very thin, yellow-faced man sat quietly beside his little wife; his head was like a skull, and death stood in his eyes. Cancer? thought Johnny, with compassion and pain. The knowledge was written in the face of his wife, who held his hand and stared before her in a dead, fixed way. There was a mother with her baby, a shriveled, wailing little thing. Her worn hand smoothed and patted its head, and she murmured constantly with anguish in her tender voice. There was an old man, his eyes covered by dark glasses, and a young girl who was almost visibly wasting away. And a boy with a fine body whose face was twisted with scars.

Johnny prayed for them, out of his own fear-stricken heart. But the prayer was a lost seeking, like a child calling to a silent and distant father. While he prayed for the sufferers in this room his thoughts kept turning inexorably to Jean, a weathercock whirling in a wind. He said inwardly, How can I pray for others, or help others, if there is only terror and doubt in me?

And then a voice spoke in him with deep and gentle authority: "Be still, and know that I am God."

Johnny sat, motionless. Several times—not very many, however—he had heard that paternal Voice, coming to him suddenly, without any warning, not from within himself, but as from outside, from radiant and pearl-colored spaces vivid with rapture, palpitating with peace, full of understanding and all knowledge. He held his breath in order not to disturb this mystical glory, this love, this comprehension, this pity and tenderness. And this indescribable silent joy, which was as if all his being had been flooded by a light never seen on land or sea.

And then it ebbed away from him, like a shining tide, but leaving him with courage and fortitude, with humility and calm. He could see that eternal tide joining the endless and brilliant horizon, hovering there, waiting, never out of sight.

He could pray now, not only for Jean without fear, but for these strangers whom he did not know. He could pray with confidence and peace, looking, with his inner eye, upon the tide and the horizon and a sky that was not the sky of earth.

Someone touched his arm, and he started. Dr. Kennedy was smiling down at him. He said, "Well, Dr. Fletcher, we've taken the clamps from Max's neck, and it's all healing wonderfully, and we've presented the boy with a big bottle of pills. Pietro couldn't be in better health, though he's a little nervous. And Kathy is all bounce and vitamins. She's convinced she must be a doctor."

His young voice was cheery, but when Johnny looked into his eyes they moved aside. "Emilie?" said Johnny. His heart shriveled a little, in spite of himself, and the tide and the sky and the horizon darkened. Dr. Kennedy glanced about the waiting room. It was empty now. He lowered his voice, and pressed Johnny's shoulder. "I suppose you know, anyway. It's her heart, sir. There was a congenital defect, to begin with. And then things—happened. Doc told me. I don't know how to tell you this, but we can't do anything. Not even the experimental 'blue baby' operation. Things—went too far. Mr. Fletcher, she can't live. A week, a month, a year? We can't tell. But she can't live. It—could be any time."

Johnny's hands clasped together tightly. His mouth and throat were like bleached old paper, dry and dusty. He tried several times to speak before he said huskily, "She was examined several times in Europe. Best doctors, too, heart specialists. I—I took her to Harley Street, in London. That was in July. He—the specialist—said she had about an even chance —I don't understand. How—how could her condition have deteriorated to—nothing?"

"These things happen," said the doctor compassionately. "She's just a little girl—five. But she has memories. You've done all your best, but the terror and the suffering remained, in her mind. And"—he lifted his hand eloquently, dropped it with a movement of despair. "Love can do only so much, you know. You'll have the consolation of knowing how much you did, and how much you gave to the baby."

"Not enough," whispered Johnny. He swallowed convulsively. "A hospital? Staying in a hospital? It might help?"

The doctor considered. Then he shook his head. "She'd have to remain in bed or a wheel chair all the time. Away from you, and the others. I'm afraid she'd go even quicker, under those circumstances. She—why, she'd die of fright and loneliness. Remember, she's not the ordinary child, with ordinary memories."

"No," said Johnny fiercely. He struck his knee with his fist. "No." Not little Emilie, with the large, strained blue eyes, the trusting child's smile, the timid small hand, the eager little ways, the shy affection. Why can't I give her my heart? he thought with agony. My blood, my flesh? My life?

Dr. Kennedy sighed. He thought of his own daughter, and he understood. "You could be mistaken," said Johnny, and he coughed as if strangling. "I think—a clinic. Mayo? Cleveland? Johns Hopkins?" His eyes searched the doctor's face for one smallest hope.

Dr. Kennedy said, "You'd be wasting your time and money. I—I've never seen a heart this bad. It's a miracle she breathes from one moment to another. Would you like to see the X rays? Look through the fluoroscope? I think it would make you feel worse. A miracle that she breathes at all. Or that she ever survived."

He added, "Keep her as quiet and as comfortable as possible. Don't send her to school. Restrict her play. Make her take frequent naps. And quiet. No excitement. Did you know she has a lot of pain?"

Pain! The child had never spoken of it, never complained, never cried! Johnny gazed at Dr. Kennedy, tortured. To him this was the supreme horror, that a child, hardly more than an infant, had the fortitude, the acceptance, the mature meekness to endure suffering without complaint, to take it as natural and normal, without adult philosophy to sustain her, or understanding faith. He said, stifled, "I—could accept that, if she were old enough—to believe in God."

"And how do you know that she doesn't have that faith?"

asked Dr. Kennedy. "Her age? Her ignorance, except what she's been taught by you? How do you know that faith is reserved only to those who can reason in adult ways?"

Johnny bent his head. "I shouldn't be talking to you this way, sir," said Dr. Kennedy apologetically. "After all, you're a minister."

Johnny looked up. "A minister," he said, with dim bitterness. "I keep forgetting what I know." His clenched hands ached, and now he smiled somberly. "Yes. I forget; sometimes logic gets me, too. Yes, how do I know that God doesn't comfort babies and little children?"

Dr. Kennedy smiled at him. "Well, I just gave the youngster a pill about half an hour ago. I wouldn't have known either, though I suspected that she might be having some discomfort. It wasn't until she—well, poor little thing—she kissed my hand and told me the pill 'took the rat away,' and she put her hand on her chest."

Took the rat away, the rat in the cave, in the executioner's house, in the forests and the hills where she had hidden with the others! Yes, she would associate a rat with pain. Dr. Kennedy was putting a box in Johnny's hand. He said briskly, to cover his emotion, "She must have three a day. It'll make her more comfortable. And here's a prescription for more."

Johnny put the box in his pocket; his trembling hands pleated the prescription blank. "I can't help it, but do you know something? I'm beginning to feel a lot of hatred lately. Even more than I did in Europe. I'm hating many things, many people. I'm beginning not to be able to stand mankind. And I a minister!"

Dr. Kennedy said, "Don't feel guilty. I never heard that it was bad to hate evil."

Kathy appeared, all pink shine and yellow hair, maternally leading Emilie. Johnny looked at the little one, at her pale, translucent skin, at the mauve shadows under her eyes, at her transparent flesh. The only healthy thing about her was that abundance of long bright hair, like a shawl over her shoulders and far down her back. Johnny held out his arms to her and she came to him and nestled on his knee. His heart almost broke. He put his cheek on the top of her small head, and stared dully before him, unable to pray, able only to feel his intense grief.

And then he saw the shining tide again, incandescent

against the eternal sky, and peace came to him. He said aloud, "I'd forgotten."

He carried Emilie and, followed by the other children, went up to the surgical floor again. Dr. McManus and the priest and Dr. Klein were talking together outside Jean's room. Dr. McManus's brutal eyes went instantly to Johnny's face, for he knew. He saw that the young man was very pale, but that he was smiling, and the old doctor sighed to himself. He said, "Well, thought you weren't ever coming. Had your cup of tea? Heard parsons are addicted to it; my father was. Or am I just remembering English novels about vicars?" His voice and his look were sour. "Go on in: we've given him his preliminary sedative. Don't disturb him. We won't know anything for at least two hours."

They went in softly. Jean looked very small and sunken on that white bed amidst the overwhelming bower of many-colored roses. His eyes were closed. But he opened them immediately when Johnny stood beside him. His hand fluttered. He murmured: "Papa? *C'est tu?*"

The sedative had him deeply; his pale eyes were glazed with dreams. Johnny held his hand tightly. "*Oui, c'est moi, mon petit.*" The boy's eyes closed again, and he smiled tranquilly, and slept. The children peered at him, awed. The smile remained on Jean's face; he was back in the quiet and sunlit warmth of some forgotten little villa, with the fragrance of a vineyard blowing in through a latticed window, and falling light on low green hills. His father was reading to him. His mother arranged crimson and yellow flowers on a polished old table. He turned his head and she gave him a long sweet look. He murmured in his sleep, comforted.

Johnny knelt beside the bed, and the children knelt with him, in silent prayer. When he stood up he said, "And now we must leave Jean to his good friends the doctors, and when he wakes up we'll come to see him again." He clung, in his mind, to the vision of the tide and the horizon and the pearl-colored spaces, and went out with the children. Dr. McManus and Dr. Klein were gone. But the priest was waiting. His concerned eyes searched the young minister's face. He said, "How about us going down to some diner and introducing the kids to some hamburgers and hot dogs and milk shakes?"

"Two hours, they said," Johnny muttered.

"It takes time," said the priest. "Well, kids, how about it?" He took Pietro's hand. Pietro was always ready for novelties, and he jumped, even under Kathy's reproving eye. Max smiled. There was a little color in his parched cheeks.

"I have a parish," said Johnny. "I must call the house first, and see if there've been any sick calls—or anything." The priest glanced aside and said heartily, "Good. We'll wait downstairs for you."

But no one had called at all, Mrs. Burnsdale said regretfully. Then she added, "I guess everybody knows you're in the hospital today." She did not go on with the thought in her mind that surely someone, anyone, might have called to inquire about Jean, or to express either approval or disapproval of yesterday's sermon, or to extend a friendly invitation. Johnny hung up. He remembered the welcome dinner. How kind, how enthusiastic, the board had been that night, how fervent the Ladies' Aid, and the other wives! Yet now there was only silence. I've failed, some way, thought the minister. Where? How? Nothing I touch prospers. The pain in his heart became a sick and fiery gnawing as he remembered Jean and Emilie.

"I think I'm a false or ineffective shepherd," he said to Father Krupszyk as they all walked down the gritty street to the priest's favorite diner. "Perhaps it's because I have doubts—I don't know. All at once I feel I'm a weakling, some way. Perhaps my first sermon shouldn't have been about sin and repentance and atonement. Perhaps it ought to have been a sermon of gratitude that my congregation had accepted me, and perhaps I should have given promises of the things we'd do together."

The priest turned to him; Emilie rode contentedly on Johnny's shoulder. The children walked closely about him. The priest said, "The gospel is always love, repentance, atonement, sacrifice. There is no other."

"But still"—said Johnny.

"There can be no consolation, no consciousness of God's love, until a man knows what he has done and is contrite. We cannot give the greatest of the Sacraments without an act of contrition first. How else, except through humility and knowledge of ourselves, can we approach God?" said the priest.

He added, "While it is true that God went out into the

dark and the wilderness to look for the lost lamb, He well knew that He had a stubborn and disobedient flock. The lamb would not have been lost in the first place if the flock had cared for it, if the flock had warmed it and kept it safe."

He patted Pietro's bouncing head. "Hi, lamb," he said. Pietro was delighted. He skipped forward a few steps, and now, to Johnny's pleased astonishment, Max skipped after him awkwardly, the first playful gesture he had ever made.

"Of course," said Johnny, and his voice was stronger.

13

But two hours later Jean was still in the operating room. Johnny rode home with the children in the priest's car, a lively and noisy ancient vehicle. "I'll be in touch with the hospital all the time," said Father Krupszyk, "and when the time comes I'll be at the hospital with you."

So there was only waiting, now. Johnny had told Mrs. Burnsdale about Emilie, and the woman cried a little. She put Emilie to bed, and Johnny and the three other children went to walk in the barren garden. "It takes time," Johnny had assured them. "While we're waiting, suppose we choose the places where we're going to plant our trees?"

He could see the bleak and cindery street over the small, leaning fence. Children were running home from school; housewives trundled by, arms loaded with bags, or pushing baby carriages. The light grew more murky; the pervading stench of industrial fumes was more sickening. Johnny and the children walked over the shaven grass and many cropped weeds, and seriously planned the coming garden. The fruit trees would line the back of the plot. Along this side there would be flowering shrubs; along the other side there would be climbing roses, and a clump of lilacs. The children were absorbed. They argued with Johnny and among themselves.

Would there ever really be a garden here? thought Johnny. He looked at the side of his gaunt little church, its dirty walls, its ugly steeple. Everything was so desolate. It extended the desolation of his spirit, in spite of himself. The silence of his congregation was ominous. He listened anxiously for a call from Mrs. Burnsdale. The back door remained obdurately shut. If only someone would call, just someone, he thought. I feel alone. But worse, I feel I've made some terrible mistake, and that I've been rejected. Or—and now he stopped, and his body grew cold—is it the children who have been rejected? Were they to be rejected forever, not only by murderers across the gray ocean, but here also? Were they never to have a home, to sink roots, to be one with the rest of humanity? Pariahs forever, these innocents who had done nothing to deserve torture and hatred? Was man's vengeance on innocence never to be satisfied?

No, thought Johnny, it is never satisfied.

The children had left him for a vehement discussion of exactly where their particular trees were to be placed. He stood alone in the center of the desolation of the starved plot, a tall black figure against the wan sky. He did not see the group of youths who had gathered on the opposite side of the fence. Their schoolbooks were slung over their shoulders. They were leering at the minister with malice, their eyes gleaming.

Then one of the boys shouted at him, in a scream of gleeful hatred, "Take the kikes out of here, blackbird! Get the hell out of here!"

"Get out!" shouted the others, and they leaped up and down on the sidewalk in their ecstasy of hate, their almost voluptuous urge to destroy and rend, an urge ever eager, never sleeping, always slavering and writhing under a precarious surface of civilization. "Get out!" they shouted. Crucify him, they said in their hearts. Crucify him, because we have never known him, and because he is harmless and innocent and is a reproach to us. Vilify him, for he is compassionate and has done no evil.

Johnny started. His first concern was for the children. They had stopped where they were, and were standing in frozen silence, their faces still. Then Kathy gathered the two boys to her tightly, her arms about them. They waited.

The fury of the big boys, however, was not directed now against the children, but against the visible symbol of what they feared and fled from, every moment of their lives.

Johnny started walking toward them, slowly and steadily, his face white, his blue eyes blazing. They stopped leaping and screaming, and waited for him, their twisted lips wet, their eyes glittering. "Who are you?" he asked sternly. "What are you doing here?"

The leader of the boys gave the others a sly and shining glance. His hands gripped the pickets of the low fence; he was bent as if about to spring. "This here's our church," he said in a voice like a growl. "We belong here. You don't. We want you out, see? You, and those"—and he uttered a foul word.

Johnny halted, about ten feet from the fence. He said, "Your parents told you that?"

They shouted a demented affirmative at him, and began to leap about again, as if mad with their orgiastic rage against him. They were the insane dervishes of all wickedness, whirling in circles. The leader did not move, however. He just kept his basilisk eyes fixed on Johnny with menacing glee.

Johnny was silent. There were no words on his tongue. What did one say to such as these? What would be effective? What would turn their hatred aside? His heart burned with anger. This was his flock; these were his children, in a spiritual bondage. Here were the youths who tomorrow would be men; here, in this church, they had been baptized, confirmed. Here they had been taught—Christianity?

Who had failed them, from the very moment they had been born?

He gave all his attention to the leader. His voice was less stern. "You say you belong here. So you must be a Christian. *Are* you a Christian, now?"

The boy licked his lips, and the sharp glitter in his eyes intensified. He was enjoying himself. "Yes, I sure am," he said. "Good, white American Christian. That's what I am. Don't like foreigners, dirty foreigners, see? We got enough in this town already, and we don't want yours. See? What kind of a minister are you anyways, bringing 'em here?"

Johnny took another step toward the fence. The other boys rushed to the side of their leader like bits of iron to a magnet. They clustered about him, all malignant and bobbing heads.

"You know," said Johnny gently, "that's what the people in Jerusalem said about Jesus. Do you know His name? Jesus. He was from Galilee. He was poor and homeless. He didn't—talk—the language—right. He had an accent, not like the people in Jerusalem, who had advantages. He was a stranger. Like my children here."

The youth had a vicious face, but an intelligent one. His eyes gleamed upon Johnny. He was silent, and his eyelids blinked. "Get him" muttered one of his companions. The leader ignored him.

"What's Jesus got to do with these here foreigners you brought here?" he asked contemptuously.

"Foreigners," said Johnny ponderingly. "Oh, yes. That's what the people in Rome called God's Apostles. And God Himself. When you pray, do you ask a Foreigner to help you? If you pray?"

The boy blinked again, and he frowned. No one ever told him, thought Johnny. No one ever told him the truth. Johnny said, "God chose a Jewish maiden to be the Mother of His Son. And her Son was clothed in Jewish flesh. Haven't you heard?"

"It's a lie," said the youth.

"Haven't you read the Bible?" asked Johnny. "Didn't anyone ever give you a Bible?"

"Never heard Christ was a Jew," said the boy defiantly.

"God is every man, every race, every color," said Johnny. He had reached the fence now, and put his hands on the pickets. "God is every Catholic, every Jew, every Protestant, every Mohammedan, every Buddhist. Haven't you heard? Where are your teachers? Where are your parents? Where are your pastors?"

The boy's hands fell from the pickets. "Uh?"

"Who betrayed you?" asked Johnny.

"Betrayed?" asked the boy in return. He scowled. He was about sixteen, with a cropped head, a lean, cavernous face, and he was dressed in a slovenly fashion, deliberately. "Oh, you mean who let me down, eh?"

"Yes, who let you down? Who let the world down?"

The boy stared at him shrewdly. "Maybe you did," he said. And he laughed scornfully. The boys jumped about him, not understanding, their eyes distended.

"Yes," said Johnny, "I think you're right."

The boy looked away, chewing his lips. His hands clutched the fence nervously. He glowered, and his eyebrows twitched. Another boy said restlessly, "Let's get goin'." The leader again ignored him.

"What do you mean, I'm right?" he asked sullenly.

"You said I did," replied Johnny, and his voice was full of regret. "I betrayed you. Every pastor you ever had betrayed you. And your parents, and your teachers. Forgive us, son, for we knew what we did all the time."

"He talks crazy," said one of the boys. "What's the matter with you, Lon?"

"Geez, he's a nut," said another.

"Shut up!" shouted the leader, and he turned with frenzy on the others. "What you doin' here, anyways?"

But it was too late. One of the boys lifted his big hand and hurled a stone at Johnny. The rock struck him on the temple, and he staggered.

Flame burst in a ring about his head. So, he thought, dazedly, that is what the crown of thorns felt like, individual points of fire piercing the skull. Now, how did He endure it, the innocent One, the blameless One? Sudden darkness engulfed him; far back in its abyss he could see the upheld Cross, somber against a livid light. Well, yes, he thought, there it is; I think I forgot. But what was this mass of faces around him now, faces like inflated balloons, puffed out, white, glaring, staring, with wide-open mouths that uttered screams and yells? Go away, he thought he said aloud. I'm very tired. I think I could sleep. I need to sleep, so I can stand what is happening to Jean, and Emilie. Rest, rest. "Sleep and rest, sleep and rest, Wind of the Western Sea," a woman sang, the sweet voice of a young woman, his mother. He had forgotten her. She had died when he was twelve. Sing to me, Mother, he cried in himself. I'm so very tired. A warm hand touched his face, and there was the dropping of tears on his cheek.

The darkness whirled about him. I shouldn't think of my

197

mother, he thought. I shouldn't remember love and softness and tenderness. What do they call these things today? Sentimentality? Eternal verities. Listen how they laugh.

A woman was calling desperately, somewhere far out in space. "Help me, help me!" she cried. Yes, he called back, but she did not hear. She turned her white face to him, and he saw her turquoise eyes, and they filled the whole universe.

"Sure, sure," said a man's young voice. "We're all right now. Everything's all right."

But it isn't, thought Johnny. Why do they always say that, when it is a lie?

He opened his swimming eyes. He saw a wide sea of vermilion through the swaying outlines of a round window. Sunset, he thought. He was lying on his bed, and he was astonished. He turned his head and met the concerned but smiling eyes of Dr. Timothy Kennedy, and he was more astonished. He said in a feeble voice, "Emilie?" The doctor nodded. "Yes, Emilie. Right here. The kids are right here." And Johnny saw them, at the foot of his bed—Emilie, Pietro, Kathy, Max, their young faces serious and pale. Then, as they saw he recognized them, they broke out in joyful smiles, and Pietro jumped excitedly. "Jean!" cried Johnny, and tried to sit up. But there was a monstrous pain in his head, and now all faces became double, and a horrible nausea rose in his throat.

Dr. Kennedy pressed him down, though he struggled. A needle was slipped deftly into his arm, and he discovered that he was undressed, and in pajamas. What had happened to him? Jean. Then—the boys, the stone. He groaned. Mrs. Burnsdale was coming into the bedroom, a bloated, two-headed Mrs. Burnsdale, and with her was a fearsome gargoyle, also two-headed, moving like a huge toad very close to the floor. He could hardly recognize this creature as Dr. McManus. He turned from the sight, sick, and then in a corner of the room he saw a large boy crouched on a chair, his hands clenched on his knees.

He groaned again, "Jean? Jean? What—what—?"

Dr. McManus lifted his wrist and counted his pulse. Then he squealed, "Can't leave you out of my damned sight a minute! Get in the God-damnedest trouble. Now lie still. You've got a brain concussion. Take X rays tomorrow. Maybe a fracture; don't think so, though." He touched a bandage on

Johnny's head and said in a deadly voice, "However, this pig ain't going to forget this day to the last day of his life."

The boy in the corner shouted, "I won't!" He began to cry.

"Shut up, swine," said Dr. McManus in a conversational tone.

"Jean, Jean?" murmured Johnny urgently. The pain in his head was dimming. But he could feel individual fire in it, points of fire.

"Well," said Dr. McManus, sitting on the side of the bed, "we got it just in time. He was developing osteomyelitis in one of the bones. Devilish thing to cure. Good chance, though, with this here penicillin; hopeless, almost, without it. We had to break the leg bones, and one in the arm. But, sir, we set 'em! Yes, sir, that boy's going to be all right! Can come home in three-four weeks. Good as new in the spring; keep that in your mind, firm, for he's got a rough road ahead for a while."

He wrinkled his thick gray brows at Dr. Kennedy. "Six clamps," said the young doctor. "Concussion, as I thought."

Mrs. Burnsdale had placed a jug of water and ice beside the bed. Her stony eyes were red from weeping. She patted Johnny's hand. "You see, it's all right—dear. Doctor told me Jean's awake, and—"

"I must go to him, at once," said Johnny, and struggled now with the effect of the sedative. "He needs me, and wants me."

"Quiet," said Dr. McManus, and there was strength in the short arm which pushed him back. "We told him, after Mrs. Burnsdale called the hospital about you, that one of the other kids got sick, and you can't leave him just now. He understands. That's a bright boy. He ain't alone. Sol Klein is still with him; God, what a job he did! He's going on the staff of that hospital or I pull it down, piece by piece, myself. Or better, I'll build a hospital three times as big, and put the best doctors on the staff. That'll teach 'em. Now, look here, you stop trying to sit up. You can't," added Dr. McManus flatly. "You've got concussion, and it could be serious. Under other circumstances, I would haul you off to the hospital in an ambulance. But the kids'd worry themselves sick. You behave, or we put you in a strait jacket and trundle you off to the hospital after all."

The floating and double heads were coming together again, becoming one. A dull, hot throbbing began in Johnny's temple. But the sharpness of agony was gone. He tried to smile, and the taut clamps caught his flesh. He winced.

"How—long?" asked Johnny weakly.

Dr. McManus was very casual. "Usual thing. When the hospital heard about it, sent Tim here with an ambulance; he volunteered. But you yelled about the ambulance; made a hell of a fuss. You wouldn't remember. So the boys hoisted you up here. You tried to walk. Funny thing about concussions. You even talked about the God-damn rotten young swine who attacked you. They ran away, of course. But this criminal stayed." Dr. McManus glared at the crying boy in the corner. "Why I don't know. And you said the police shouldn't be called; just his parents." Dr. McManus grated his throat hideously. "Well, they weren't at home. Both of them in a factory. I talked with the superintendent. Father making over a hundred a week. Not enough for the female, though they got only this one brute here. She's got to have every lousy appliance she sees advertised, so she works in a factory, and lets this infernal kid loose on the street making mischief. Big, shiny car, they got too. Better than the superintendent's. Old story. Nice for this country. Filthy little house full of every kind of machine you can think of, and dirty old furniture."

He went on, "All in all, you've been in and out about two hours. Nothing too serious, though you're going to have some sort of a scar on the side of your head. Keep it as a memento." The squealing voice became savage. "Maybe you'll learn what people are, finally."

A gentle warmth crept over Johnny's cold flesh. He smiled drowsily. "The boy," he pleaded. Dr. McManus turned his big, untidy head, its gray hair like a thatch. "Come over here, you," he growled. "The parson wants to look at the kind of punk who'd make a riot and get him almost killed. Yes, killed, I said. An inch difference and there'd be murder."

The thin and hulking boy, his sunken cheeks running with tears, sidled to the bed. He stood there, his eyes fixed on Johnny's hand. He gulped once or twice. Johnny said gently, through the comforting haze of the sedative, "What's your name, son?"

The boy gulped again. Then he stammered hoarsely, "I—my name's Lon Harding."

"And how old are you?" Johnny's voice gentled still more. The boy lifted his head and looked at him, white, feeble, and limp on his bed. Then the boy shut his eyes convulsively. "Sixteen," he whispered.

"And you didn't run away, Lon, with the others?"

The boy opened his eyes. "No, sir, I didn't. I couldn't. It was what you said—all at once I—I couldn't. You—fell. The little kids screamed, and started to run around in circles. The—this lady, here, came out of the house. I told her to call the hospital. You, well, you were kind of bleeding. I had a clean handkerchief, and I shoved it against the—we were taught that in first aid at school. Shoved it hard, real hard." He sobbed. He fumbled in his pocket and brought out his handkerchief. It was a reddish-brown stiff ball. "You kind of bled pretty bad. But the doctor here said I done pretty well; stopped an artery or something."

Dr. Kennedy regarded him in grave silence.

"And all the time, Mr. Fletcher, you just lay there and said it was all right." The boy's voice broke. "You said it didn't matter. I—put my coat under your head, rolled up. I said I was sorry; you said it was all right. You sounded all right, too." A wan grin touched his trembling mouth. "You sure tried to fight the ambulance people; kept shoving them off. And you let me help you up the stairs, and I helped get you undressed."

"You're a very bright boy, Lon," said Johnny, and he lifted his hand with a great effort and took the boy's soiled, clenched fist. "What year in high school, Lon?"

A note of pride crept into the boy's hoarse voice. "Well, sir, I'm a senior. Get almost all A's, too. High third of class. Teacher wants me to go to college, she told me. I want to be an engineer—mechanical. But there isn't any money."

"Sure, a bright boy," said Dr. McManus with loathing. "Bright enough to think up a riot, and bring other murderers with him, to frighten little children and attack a harmless minister. If that's brightness, then all such dogs should be in prisons."

But Johnny said, "You didn't run away. You stayed. You knew you'd get in trouble if you stayed. But you didn't run away."

"No," the boy whispered. "How could I? You needed me."

Johnny's hand tightened on the boy's rigid fingers. "Why, Lon?" he asked.

The boy colored; he did not try to draw away from Johnny's hold. "Well, you see, my parents aren't very—well, they never did have much schooling. But a fellow kind of listens to his parents, even if he knows they aren't very educated. And Pop was saying yesterday, 'Bringing all those foreigners in, to take away our jobs. That's what they're trying to do all the time. Put Americans on the street, and give the foreigners our jobs.' And Mom says, 'That's right. It's bad enough since they stopped the war on us, just when we were making big money, and buying all the things we want. Stopped the war on us, after they told us it'd go on for years and years yet, and we'd be rich. Lied to us.' That's what Mom said. And she and Pop went on about how everybody was sick, really sick, on V-E and V-J days. They were told by the superintendent not to worry, about V-E day. The government would keep the war on for a long time, with the Japs."

"For Christ's sake," said Dr. McManus, and he looked at Dr. Kennedy, who nodded. "So, these lumpen thought wars are run for their benefit, for big wages in factories!" the old doctor continued. Then he was struck; he wrinkled up his face. "Well, maybe they are; maybe they are!"

Lon added brokenly, "It's all mixed up."

"And so you picked the first helpless people you could find, to straighten out your mix-up!" said Dr. McManus with disgust.

The children, thought Johnny in his dream, as he floated away. It is always the children—betrayed, baffled, frightened, brutalized, forgotten. Somewhere in the warm darkness, he was holding a hand. He tightened his hold, and prayed: Let them come to me. Let me help them.

"Please," said the boy, "let me stay with him."

14

"That parson's in trouble again," said Mr. Summerfield. "I must talk with the chief of police. Perhaps we can force him out of Barryfield. We don't want troublemakers here. Lorry, haven't you had enough?"

"I can't see why we can't go to Philadelphia next Monday," complained Esther Summerfield, his wife. "The Ballet Russe. Everybody is mad about it. MacDonald, do look at the pictures, right here in your own newspaper. Such grace; such artistry. Lorry, why didn't you complete your ballet lessons? Oh, Lorry, please, no more cocktails."

It was wonderful to slip over the border, where it was all golden, all softness, all gaiety, all peace, all excitement, all vivid, incandescent meaning. Lorry Summerfield held out her glass for another large martini. She said to the butler, "Come on, George, don't be stingy. Never mind the olive or onion." It was almost possible to endure your parents, after the fourth drink. It was almost possible to endure living. Memories came back, when you drank. Not always ugly memories. Memories of quiet, elm-shaded streets and child-laughter and a father you loved and trusted, and flowers in a green garden, and the love of a brother who was so serious but who could be coaxed into a smile, and sometimes laughter. "I'm thinking of Barry," she said aloud, in a carefully controlled voice.

Esther Summerfield regarded her with delicate distaste. "You always talk about Barry when you've had too much to drink, dear. Lorry, you don't need that, you know."

"Now, how can you tell?" said Lorry. "Who told you how much I need, just to go on living?"

The golden haze hummed with bees. Evening bells were ringing over the silent mountains, sweetly, clashing, solemn, calling. But there aren't bells in Barryfield, thought Lorry with severity. Not many, anyway. Besides, I couldn't hear them here. The bells chimed entrancingly, and Lorry smiled with contentment. She let herself slide deeper in her chair, listening to the bells. They had a Mozart quality, high, gentle, infinitely harmonious. Like a spinet. At these times she always had a mysterious vision. She was sitting against a pale gold wall, dim and cold. To her left wide French doors opened, on a gray garden. Figures of men and women stood on the threshold of the room, in powdered wigs, in brocaded coats, in full and rustling skirts, bowing formally to each other before they went into that misty garden from which they would never return. Lorry could see the trees beyond the garden, all diffused and faintly luminous shapes, clouded in vapor. And in the room where she sat there was the tinkling of a spinet, melancholy, frail, and very thin. I am so alone, she would say to herself, as the others vanished into the mists of the garden. No one sees me. The spinet tinkled on and on, spraying the great spectral room with a perfume of dolorous harmony. Oh, God, she said. She watched the elegant figure of a man in a white wig disappear into the mist beyond the windows. Come back, my love, she cried in herself. Come back, and see me. Have you forgotten? The spinet tinkled sorrowfully.

"Really, darling, what do you mean?" asked Esther, impatiently twitching at her long "art" draperies. "Who has forgotten you? MacDonald, I've told you over and over that Lorry simply can't stand more than two or three drinks. Look at her. Her eyes are glazed. She glares like an idiot at the wall."

If I got up, thought Lorry, I could follow him out, and take his arm, and he would turn around and look at me with those dark-blue eyes, and he would smile. But his smile would be cool and reserved and wondering, as if he didn't know me. The woman beside him, a little, dainty figure, would clutch at him and say, "The grotto is so beautiful, down there near the stream. The violets are so fragrant." And then they would go, and she, Lorry, would not be remembered. She would stand there, in the mist, the swirling, choking mist, and there would be nothing at all in the world but that mournful spinet, crying out in the closing darkness. Nothing at all, but this deep and eternal misery of the heart.

She muttered, "Does anyone believe in reincarnation? I do. I wonder why we come back. No, it's impossible. The brain I could remember that with is mud and dust now."

Mr. Summerfield stood before his daughter, elegant, gilt-haired, and supple. He looked at the girl and his face thinned and saddened. "Lorry," he said. "You're getting morose again. Don't drink any more. Not tonight."

The frail clamor of the spinet died away. The room in which she sat suddenly surged at Lorry in fearful clarity, every color sharp, every light bitter and splintering. The ugliest room in the world, she thought with hatred. Her mother had "gone in" for Chinese décor a few years ago. Lorry doubted that a Chinese would have recognized it. It was all glittering red lacquer cabinets with black dragons crawling over them, intricately carved ebony chairs inlaid with ivory, many-sided tables similarly tortured, black lacquer chests and lamp stands, bamboo shades at the windows, draperies of gold satin on which tormented black trees had been painted, and yellow carpets on which embossed green leaves and apricot roses crept in a silent nightmare. The monster fireplace was of red lacquer too, and on the mantelpiece stood large porcelain Buddhas and a purplish cloisonné bowl filled with chrysanthemums of a deep bronze shade.

"I was just thinking that this is the most abominable room I've ever seen," said Lorry. She sipped at her drink and ignored her father. She could not endure looking at him. Her diaphanous gray dress outlined her lovely figure, made her white flesh luminous, her golden hair more striking. But her face was drawn, dulled, and empty.

"You've said that a thousand times, darling," her mother sighed. Esther Summerfield was an extremely tall and angular woman, and very thin, but, in a way, somewhat handsome.

She piled her coarse black hair on the top of her head, Chinese-fashion, for the evenings, and held it with tortoise-shell combs. She wore a Persian robe, which, in spite of its absurd artiness, was appropriate with her triangular, rather yellowish face, narrow black eyes, and thin mouth. She even affected a painted Chinese fan, and her long sallow hands, with their painted nails, moved it languidly. "And again, I say I'm sorry. Other people think it's fascinating."

"Frightful," said Lorry. "I want another drink." She added, "Why do we have to have a clash of cymbals announcing meals? I'm not ready. Another drink."

"Lorry," said Mr. Summerfield gently. His daughter looked at him with her glazed eyes. "Go away, Mac," she said. "You—obstruct my view."

Her father had hoped that Lorry had given up her periodical bouts of drinking, for there had been a four-week interval since the last time. But now she was off again, as bad as ever. He said, "Lorry, I was talking to you about that preacher who brought those children to this town—McManus's minister. Remember? He wouldn't give you a story. Well, he's in trouble again. Are you listening, Lorry? It isn't very important, I suppose. Some boy hit him with a stone yesterday. One of our reporters picked it up from the police blotter. What is he doing to make people attack first one of those children, and then himself? Is this worth a story now?"

Lorry sat up suddenly. The crystal glass fell from her hand, and the contents splashed over her gown. "What?" she cried. "Johnny Fletcher?" Full consciousness had come back into her eyes like a blaze. "What have they done to him now?"

Her father was much relieved. He gave her the evening newspaper. The tiny black letters jumped on the pages. She bent over them.

Lorry read the short column. Then she flung the paper from her. She looked up at her father, and her eyes became very large and distended. Her mouth worked. "He's hurt. Badly hurt. Concussion of the brain! Do you hear? Hurt!"

"What does it matter to you?" asked Mr. Summerfield.

Barry, she thought. Barry, who would have died—dear Barry, who looked so much like his father and his sister, and yet was not at all like them. Not in any way, thought Lorry, shaking her head in a slow motion of despair. Her voice thickened. "Never mind. I'm just thinking of Barry now. Remember when we got the telegram that he was seriously injured, somewhere in Normandy? Dad, why did you drive Barry away—as you drove me away?"

Esther shook her head significantly. "You know you shouldn't let her drink. Whenever she does, she always asks you those foolish questions."

Mr. Summerfield bent over Lorry, and rested his hands on the arms of her chair. "Dearest, I never drove you and Barry away. You always get that idea when you've been drinking too much. Lorry, why do you always say that? You never answer me."

Her nostrils flared. "I'll answer you this time. We found out about you."

Mr. Summerfield's arms stiffened, but he still bent over Lorry. "What did you find out, sweet?" he asked.

Even through her drunkenness a warning inside her mind reached Lorry. She said, "What does it matter?"

"It matters terribly to me," replied her father in a low voice, inaudible to his wife. "You and Barry—you're all I have. Get it right, Lorry; I love you both. You know that. But Barry almost never comes here now. Once he was my boy. Once you were my girl. Lorry, tell me. You hate me now, don't you? Lorry, tell me."

"Why?" she asked contemptuously.

"I love you. Don't you know that, Lorry?"

She regarded him in silence; through the sharp clarity of alcohol she could see every faint line in his smooth face, the iris of his eyes, the carved narrowness of his nose. "You look like us too much," she murmured restively. "Barry's not like you. But I am." It wasn't enough for her father. He repeated, "Lorry? What did you find out about me?"

"Why isn't anything ever enough for you?" she asked, moving in her chair. "Why do you live here in this town? Your newspapers? Just to write the editorials? You could write them in New York or London or Paris just as well. Why do you stay here?" Her mouth curled in an ugly way. "Is it because you couldn't be powerful enough anywhere else? Too many other millionaires in New York, for instance, where you'd sink out of sight? Too many polished gentlemen in Europe, where you wouldn't be conspicuous?"

His fine skin flushed. "Lorry, you know as well as I do that the newspapers are important to me. To us. To you. We stay to—watch—everything in Barryfield. We have a mission, you know. To tell the people the truth."

"Ah, yes," murmured Lorry. "The truth. How are you doing about buying the New York *Gazette*?"

He straightened up. "I had a telegram this evening. They're losing circulation. They hate liberalism, and so they're hanging on, like some patched anachronism."

He added, despondently, "So, that's what you mean when you say you and Barry found out about me. I can understand Barry; he's been exposed too long to his mother's and stepfather's hidebound ideas. But you are different. So—you hate Barryfield, hate the newspapers. In a way I can't blame you. The people here are below par, mentally. Lorry," and he tried to smile, "you had been hoping for the New York *Gazette*, hadn't you? You thought that you could be the editor on it. Yes, I can understand your ambition. You're very like me, as you said. You thought you could bring a liberal policy to that newspaper. And I've disappointed you. And that's why you've been drinking—?"

Lorry did not answer. Her father extended his hand and touched her timidly on the cheek. She held herself from flinching. "Lorry, I'll do anything to get that paper for you. Anything. I'll get in touch with Swensen."

Lorry was frightened. She forced herself to her feet. "I don't like the *Gazette*. There are as many liberal newspapers in New York as the population can absorb." Her mouth became compressed, and its color disappeared. "Never mind the *Gazette*. The hell with it."

"Lorry's right," said Esther. "Oh, dear, they've sounded the cymbals again. MacDonald, please. Do let's go into the dining room."

"Why won't you publish my articles about the air pollution from the factories in this damned town?" asked Lorry. "It's all right for us, up here on the hills. But the town's in a valley. One of these days there's going to be a downdraft or whatever they call it, and it'll be fatal to hundreds of people. You know that." When her father did not reply, she continued, "You are always attacking capitalism in a nice, gentlemanly way. Yet here's capitalism poisoning the air, right here in Barryfield. Or don't you want to offend your friends?" Her eyes taunted her father.

"You can't change things overnight," he said, uncomfortably. "It's a long process."

"Why don't you publish my articles? I've got ten of them, you know." Lorry's voice was charged with derision.

"Well, they're a little too strong, dear. Suppose you go over them and tone them down? Then—"

She laughed at him, and he winced at the bark of her peculiar laughter. "I haven't noticed that your articles on juvenile delinquency are toned down. No. You go after the subject with clubs in both hands. Slum conditions. Breeding places for crime. Inadequate police. No recreation areas for the young—how I hate that phrase! The system. Society. Low wages; cramped, obsolete houses; not enough public housing. Greed. Remember? You sent out a survey. And the survey found out—because the men who conducted it were honest—that most of our young criminals don't come from the working class. They come from families with an income beginning with four thousand dollars a year, and far up. So, the result of the survey wasn't to your liking, and you suppressed it. Yet you pound away at lies, lies, lies."

He gazed at her deeply. He thought, Swensen was right. She's too unstable. She doesn't grasp what we're after. She believes a newspaper should tell the truth. How naïve she is. Poor child.

"Can't we continue the discussion at dinner?" asked Esther, annoyed.

"I don't want dinner," said Lorry. "I'm going to my rooms. Tell them to leave out a sandwich, or something."

"Lorry," said Mr. Summerfield pleadingly. But Lorry suddenly turned the full electric force of her scornful eyes on him, and he stepped back. She went out of the room swiftly, her cloudy gray dress flowing about her. She stepped into the tiled hall, with its ugly crowding of Chinese furniture, and ran up the dark oak stairs. Her own rooms had been furnished by herself, cool, traditional, with aloof and formal colors, and crystal. She went at once to her desk, after shutting her door, and lifted the telephone receiver. She called Dr. McManus at his home.

"Now, what's the matter?" he asked irritably. "I told you this morning that the kid's doing as well as can be expected. And that's not much. We're worried. There's no change, though, except he gets delirious sometimes; high fever."

"Uncle Al, I'm not calling about Jean. Why didn't you tell me Johnny had been seriously injured yesterday by some young criminal?"

There was a little silence, then the doctor shrilled, "Well, you've got a newspaper, and reporters, haven't you? I thought you'd see it soon enough, damn it! Now wait a minute. He's not so seriously injured. Concussion. He's getting over it. He could have been killed, though. Just missed killing him. Why, he's sitting right up in bed this very minute. Forcing himself out of it; wants to get to the kid in the hospital. We've told Jean some lies, and he's too sick to think them through, and we're keeping the bad news from Johnny."

Lorry said, "And the boy who did it?" She began to shiver.

"Johnny won't prosecute. Funny thing. The leader of the gang practically lives in the damned parsonage. Brought Johnny some tobacco and flowers this afternoon. Maudlin. Sits and cries at Johnny. You ought to see his parents. Lumps. Lard. But the mother's better than the father. She came, and cried too. Everybody cries! God-damnedest thing you ever saw! Parsonage's awash. Can't stand it myself."

"Good-by," said Lorry abruptly. She hung up. She tore off her dress, and changed to a dark suit and a fur cape. She ran down the stairs silently, went to the garage, and got into her own car. She drove away furiously, down the winding mountain road. Barryfield had one smart street, which kept some of its shops open at night. Lorry stopped her car before a very exclusive store which sold "unusual gifts." She ran inside, and immediately threw the owner and his two clerks into a delightful whirl of excitement. She ran up and down the tables, examining everything, with the manager burbling at her heels. "That," she said, pointing to an Italian statue of the Madonna in blue and gold transparent glass. "Two hundred dollars, Miss Summerfield," said the manager reverently, taking up the statue, which was a foot tall. "Lovely thing, isn't it? Magnificently executed. The only one of its kind."

He held it to the light, which shone through it gently. The serene and beautiful young face came alive in a glow of tenderness, like pulsating flesh. The rosary, a long pale rope, fell from the exquisite hands. The manager glanced curiously at the girl. Now why would she be buying this? "Wrap it up," she said.

She began to prowl again. She came upon an oval gold box, three inches in diameter. The lid was intricately chased in a design of noble faces and doves. She opened it, and a faint rich fragrance rose from the interior, as of attar of roses. "An authentic Renaissance piece," said the manager in a hushed voice. "It was probably used for concentrated scents, recently. You can still smell them. I suggest this as a gift for a gentleman, for cuff links or personal jewelry."

Lorry smiled with dark humor. But she was fascinated by the box. "Two hundred fifty, Miss Summerfield. Originally five hundred. But who would buy such a thing in this city? I was just preparing to send it back to my shop in New York or Philadelphia."

"Wrap it up," said Lorry.

The manager beamed. "Mr. Summerfield will love this! His birthday, perhaps?"

"I'm sure he'd love it," said Lorry ironically.

She carried the treasures to her car and drove to the hospital. She was admitted to Jean's room without delay. Fresh flowers, which she had sent today, filled the room, and a young nurse was in attendance. Though it was hardly nine o'clock the hospital was silent, but no room was as silent as this. The nurse whispered, "The poor child. He has a dreadful fever, over 104. But he keeps swimming up to consciousness and asking for his mother."

"No improvement?" asked Lorry.

"No," the nurse hesitated. "He's a little worse, in fact. Dr. Klein was just here. He'll be back at midnight, with Dr. McManus. He's had five hundred thousand units of penicillin today, and Dr. McManus called a New York hospital a couple of hours ago for a new wonder drug."

Lorry went to the bed. She looked down at Jean, so gaunt, so dwindled, so ashen. His eyes were closed. His breathing was heavy and intermittent. He muttered constantly. Lorry looked at the apparatus which kept his leg, in a heavy cast, absolutely immobile. She looked at the cast on his arm. Lorry thought of her father, with a burst of hatred like an explosion in her heart. The enemy is never satisfied, she said to herself. They have done this to him. They are preparing to do it again, tomorrow.

The nurse retreated to her chair near the window, in the faint shadow of the night lamp. She stared at Lorry with immense curiosity. Lorry, forgetting her, bent over the child. "Jean?" she whispered strongly. "Jean?"

She had never seen any of the children before, but Dr. Mc-Manus had given her their full history. She looked at the small remote face, so unchildlike, so full of a mournful wisdom, so stern. She drew in her lower lip, and her throat contracted. She bent closer over Jean and pressed her mouth to his cheek, and whispered again, "Jean? Jean? Can you hear me? Jean?" The pain in her breast became tighter, more urgent. She kissed him again, murmuring lovingly against his ear.

The boy muttered, stirred restlessly, cried out feebly, then opened his eyes. They lay far back in his face, like pale and clouded glass, behind which agonizing dreams drifted. She floated into his waning consciousness, a white and beautiful face, the night light making a halo of her golden hair. He saw nothing else but Lorry, and his dulled expression quickened into joyful recognition. "Maman?" he muttered. "Maman?"

"Yes, darling," she answered. Her hand smoothed his thick hair. "Papa sent me."

His free hand fluttered, and she took it strongly. He could not look away from her; the dreams became peaceful and sweet. "Maman," he said again. He tried to smile; the slightest color appeared in his face.

"Jean must get well, very soon," said Lorry, with tender severity. "Papa needs him. You hear me, dear?"

His eyes remained fixed in joy upon her. "I hear," he murmured. "For Papa."

The nurse approached quickly. Under Lorry's perfume she could smell the rank odor of alcohol. The nurse was offended; then she recovered herself. One did not get offended at a Summerfield. She deftly felt for Jean's pulse, looking solemnly at her watch. "Why," she said, in wonderment, "it's—why, it's much stronger!"

But Lorry was smiling at Jean, and he was drowsily smiling at her. Then, all at once, he sighed deeply and fell asleep, turning his head toward the girl. His cold little hand warmed in hers, and relaxed. She kissed him again, rested her cheek against his forehead. It was not so hot now. A light sweat had broken out upon it.

Lorry unwrapped the Madonna and put it on the bedside table. It glowed like a jewel in the pale light. "Tell him, when he wakes up, that his mother brought it to him," she said to the nurse, who blinked.

"But he hasn't any mother," the nurse said.

Lorry stared at her inimically. She said, in a low, hard voice, "Don't be so damned factual! Tell him what I've told you. He'll understand. Anyway, how do you know his mother didn't send me tonight?"

The young girl was confused. She regarded Lorry with mingled respect and bewilderment. "Yes, Miss Summerfield," she said obediently. Someone was entering the room, and the nurse turned in relief. "Dr. Kennedy," she said.

The young doctor was all white clothing, and dark eyes and slight smiles. "Hello, Tim," said Lorry, and now she colored. "I came to see this poor little boy. I heard he wasn't doing so well. I thought I should come."

"Good," said Dr. Kennedy. If he was surprised, he did not show it. He saw the glowing statue on the table, and he studied it meditatively. "You can have it blessed, or something," said Lorry, with discomfort. Dr. Kennedy touched the small jewellike feet reverently. His thick black brows quirked. "I thought he might like it," went on Lorry. "I told the nurse to tell him his mother—brought it."

Dr. Kennedy was silent. He took the boy's pulse, lightly touched his forehead. He saw the new faint color. "He's much better," he said. He added, without looking at Lorry, "How do you know it hasn't already been blessed? Of course his mother brought it."

"Thanks, Tim," said Lorry, and took up her purse and cape. He went with her into the corridor. He said, seriously, "An hour ago I was very worried. I gave him less than half a chance to survive. There's some critical infection. It's subsided, I think." He contemplated the girl for a long moment. "I think you've done something for the boy, Lorry." He disliked the Summerfields intensely; he hated their newspapers. Now he was all wonder. He knew that Lorry was paying for the room and the nurses and the flowers. He had hardly believed it, when Dr. McManus had told him. But all this had not impressed him so much as this late visit, this bringing of the statue, this strange tenderness from a woman he knew to be careless and hard of heart. They had known

213

each other from childhood. He had often conjectured what had changed Lorry from a gay and eager young girl to a bitter, dangerous, and disillusioned woman, a female replica of her father.

He watched her swing down the corridor, her golden head high and stiff. He said to himself, softly, "Now, I'll be—"

Though the days were still hot, the nights were very cool, almost sharp. The air in the mountains was as clarified as brandy, but the streets of Barryfield were fetid and corrupt with industrial gases and wastes and the very breath of the circumscribed, cramped city. On many nights, particularly in the autumn and spring, when fog rose from the damp ground and mingled with the gases, the air was very hard to breathe. It stung the lungs and burned the nostrils and sickened stomachs. It thickened the fog in which it was trapped, and filthied it, and turned it to poison. Tonight was such a night.

Lorry Summerfield coughed and cursed to herself, as she drove through the dank streets. The sidewalks glimmered dimly; the street lamps were swathed in swirling and spectral ghosts, as if a plague were abroad. And so it is, thought Lorry. She remembered the articles she had written about all this. Tomorrow, she told herself grimly, she would have the first article slipped in on the second page of the *Press*, and her father be damned. Let him explain frantically, or smoothly, to his friends about the error. Let him upbraid his daughter. She would only stare at him, and say, "Well, tell them that you've fired the feature writer. I didn't put it under my by-line." As for the other articles, she would slip them in adroitly from time to time. She chuckled. She still felt light and potent and direct, the result of the drinks she had gulped tonight; her brain still felt very bright and teeming. Her despondency had lifted; it was always this way—in about an hour the despondency would return, more violent and desperate than ever. But by that time, she thought, I'll be home and have a few more drinks.

She pulled her car up hard before Johnny Fletcher's parsonage, which she considered somberly. A few of the abominable lamps in the parlor were still lighted, and there was a glow upstairs through a round window. Lorry got out of her car, careful of the slimy sidewalk and even more careful of the steep stairs of the stoop. She opened the door of the parsonage, to be greeted by the wide gaze of a number of neat, drab, and shabby men and women. They were sitting about the parlor in attitudes of limp distress and solemnity. When Lorry entered, like a figure of vital light, they started, recognizing her from photographs and from swift glimpses of her in the streets.

Lorry was alarmed. She said in a loud, quick voice, "Is something wrong? How is Mr. Fletcher?" Why were they congregated here, except for disaster, these weary and face-less creatures?

A little wiry woman spoke up. "Nothing's wrong, Miss Summerfield. I'm Mrs. McGee. Mrs. Burnsdale is making us some coffee. We've just been talking about Mr. Fletcher—and the children. Poor things. Give Miss Summerfield your seat," she added severely to a small, red-faced man with many white curls on his head.

"No," said Lorry. She paused. "Thanks." She studied the awkward group with curiosity. One by one the stooped men rose shyly, prompted by pokes from their wives and com-manding glances. So these were Johnny's parishioners. They did not seem particularly malevolent or cruel or stupid as she scrutinized their faces more acutely. They were just—people. Yet some of them were responsible for Johnny's sufferings. Some of them had corrupted their children's minds, to inspire such attacks on that little boy, Max, and on the minister himself. But they lied to their children only in all sincerity, as their parents had lied to them.

She pulled off her cape and threw it negligently at an empty chair. She threw her gloves after it. Then she turned the immense power of her eyes slowly to the parishioners. "I'd like to do a story about all this," she said. "I'd like to show the great Commonwealth of Pennsylvania that it has a city that belongs in the Dark Ages, or a jungle, or as the annex to a zoo. Perhaps the other cities could run buses here, just to look at Barryfield, just to look at the houses, and the people who live here. A good feature article that would be picked up by the national press, and made the subject of editorials all over the country. And, perhaps, we could have the National Guard called out, to patrol these streets so no more ministers or children would be attacked, and their lives threatened."

Mr. McGee's scarlet face deepened to crimson. He said,

"Now, Miss Summerfield. That wouldn't be fair. I—I'm president of the mine union. We—"

"Do you hold propaganda meetings for your men, and point out the ones who should be driven out of this damned city, or the children whose throats should be cut, or the men who should be stoned? Do you conduct your meetings in the best Communist style, and count those who should be liquidated? I've heard things about unions."

Mr. McGee straightened, and faced her openly, while the others, with shamed faces, remained silent. "Miss Summerfield," he said, "you know you're exaggerating. You know this town; you were born here. Sure we've got some Communists, I think. You can never tell about those fellers. I've been warning my men about them, and they hate the Communists as bad as I do." He stopped, and his eyes were hard and bright as he looked at the girl. "I can tell you one thing, Miss Summerfield—your papers have a bad reputation among decent people. I've studied Communism myself. There's a mighty lot of it in the *Press*, and I can tell you we don't like it, and you're losing circulation, and the mine-workers just use it to wrap their lunches in. Well, never mind. Maybe we aren't better than any other people, here in Barryfield, and all this about the minister and the children is terrible. But there's always a few everywhere, in any town or big city, who are born murderers." He regarded her shrewdly. "A few who want to believe stuff like in the *Press.*"

Lorry pressed her lips together to keep from an almost irresistible smile. Mr. McGee was becoming excited. He pointed a short finger at her. "I don't like saying things like this to a—a lady. But I've wanted to say them, and no time like the present. I was a miner, Miss Summerfield; I worked in mines around here for over thirty years. I know the men; I was one of 'em, and so was my father. Ever been in a mine, Miss Summerfield? No, you haven't. Whatever pay a miner gets isn't enough for what he does; if he got a hundred dollars a day, it wouldn't be enough for working in the mines. Sure, we got unions, and good ones. Why don't you read about the mining industry yourself?"

"Now, McGee," said his wife admonishingly.

He ignored her. "All us presidents of unions, any unions, want to keep out Communists, the kind of people who cause trouble and set one workingman against another, and against their employers. What help do we get, in most newspapers? Practically none. We throw Commies out of a union, and some of the newspapers write editorials about 'intolerance' or 'guilt by association,' or some other damn foolishness. What help do we get from the *Press*? Look, Miss Summerfield, if we've got people like those who hurt Mr. Fletcher and the little boy, it's because of people like you, in the newspapers, stirring up folks and making them hate one another."

A pleasant wave of happiness invaded Lorry. Her eyes began to twinkle vividly. The others, who had been listening with eagerness, straightened in their chairs and nodded severely at each other, no longer awed by the beautiful Miss Summerfield.

Mr. McGee still pointed at the girl, and he shook a finger, wrath turning his moist forehead to a purplish scarlet.

"Look, we've got trouble in Barryfield. The miners don't want to strike; I don't want them to strike; the independent owners don't want them to strike. Nobody wants a strike. We can't afford it, and neither can the owners. A third of the men work in the mines. Think what a strike would mean to them, and the owners, and everybody else. I've seen the owners' books, and they're hardly making expenses. They keep the mines open so the men'll have jobs. Yet out comes the *Press* a little while ago, telling the miners they're being exploited. And all at once there's strangers in town, talking to the men as they come out of the mines and giving them leaflets quoting the *Press*. And then, after you've caused all kinds of trouble here in your papers, you walk right into this room and call us a zoo or something!"

"That's right," chorused the others, nodding their heads vehemently.

"We've got a dirty town; air ain't fit to breathe," said Mr. McGee, his voice tight with emotion. "Does the *Press* write about it? Does the *Press* demand that the factories and mills have smoke control? Oh, no! Mr. Summerfield has too many friends who own those damned places. And he calls himself a liberal! Liberal for what, ma'am? Liberal for trouble?"

You couldn't be righter, friend, thought Lorry, more and more pleased. Keep on thinking and talking as you do, McGee, and all the millions of honest workers everywhere, and you'll defeat what my father is plotting for you. She said, "Well, that's a nice speech, Mr. McGee. I think you've got something there. By the way, you might read the *Press* day after tomorrow. I think you'll like it, for once."

She nodded at him gayly and went out of the room. One of the women said, with excitement, "You told her, Mr. McGee! And did you smell the alcohol on her! Phew!"

Mr. McGee sat down slowly and contemplated the floor. He frowned. "You know," he said at last, "there's something about that girl—I don't know what it is. I can't put my finger on it. But it isn't what we think."

As Lorry went up the bare stairs her exultation suddenly died, and the depression she always dreaded swept over her. She climbed more slowly. Why had she gone to the hospital? Why was she here? She always did the most irresponsible things after too many drinks. The brilliant clarity of alcohol was now receding; she could not remember what had sent her out into the night, like a maniac. Of course it was Barry, and this minister. But no doubt if Fletcher knew that alcohol had pitched her into this sentimentality, or even if Barry knew, they would have contempt for her as an unreliable, unstable fool of a woman. The dull confusion which invariably followed too much indulgence clouded her mind. She half turned to go down again.

She shook her head at herself; her skull was aching in a nasty way. I need a drink, she thought. Several drinks. There was a sick gnawing at her stomach. Then she impatiently pulled her drifting thoughts together. A fool shouldn't stop halfway, she said to herself sardonically. All the way, fool!

The door of the main bedroom was open; pinkish light gushed out. Lorry could hear the murmur of men's voices. She stood on the threshold, and was appalled by the dreary poverty of the room, its mottled walls, its ragged little rugs. Dr. McManus had told her that one or two of the boys slept in this room; she saw the closed day bed. And there was Johnny Fletcher, half sitting up on the sagging double bed, his forehead bandaged, his face drawn and pale, one side of it a hideous mass of bruises, purple, yellow, and green. But he was smiling, and listening to the two men near him, one a big, bulky priest and another an old man with a skullcap and a long beard like drifting sunlight. A hideous little pink light was the only illumination in the room.

The three men were absorbed in some very serious discussion. The priest was saying, "Well, now, we have those three interpretations of the Psalm. The rabbi has given us the original Hebraic version, with which the Church agrees in toto. But you, Johnny—"

It was Johnny who saw Lorry first, and his shadowed eyes fixed themselves on her in astonishment. The priest and the rabbi turned, and were also astonished.

"Am I intruding?" asked Lorry foolishly.

"Why no," said Johnny slowly. His voice was very tired. "Come in, Miss Summerfield. If you're looking for another story you won't find one. Father Krupszyk, Rabbi Chortow, this is Miss Summerfield."

The priest looked at Lorry keenly, the old rabbi inclined his head with an Old-World gesture. He was less inclined than the priest to study people with a touch of cynicism and mistrust, for he was a simple and gentle scholar who had some faith in the goodness of man, in spite of all the evidence to the contrary. His intellectuality was softened by mysticism, by dreams of the ancient past in which innocent men walked together in a lost green garden, and conversed with God. He had not endeared himself to his shocked and frightened congregation when, during the war, he had asked them to pray for the Nazi murderers of his people that they might be restored to light and humanity and the knowledge of "the Lord our God," and the humility of atonement. To Rabbi Chortow sin was evil, but not the sinner. Father Krupszyk had other and more realistic opinions, and agreed with Johnny that if there was the Mystical Body of God there was also the Mystical Body of Lucifer, to which quite a multitude of men belonged wholeheartedly, and with much more devotion and dedication than did those on the other side of the spiritual fence. However, the three were one in the belief that sin demanded not only repentance but penance.

Rabbi Chortow smiled sweetly at Lorry and, quite inexplicably, he thought of Rachel, the mother of many children. Johnny was merely suspicious and disturbed at her appearance. The minister and the priest caught the rankness of alcohol as the girl advanced slowly into the room, but the rabbi, paternally entranced by her extraordinary beauty, thought of incense, and the prophetesses.

Lorry stopped abruptly at the foot of the bed. Johnny, in silence, looked at her and waited. "I didn't come for a story," she said. Well, she was a fool. That priest was regarding her

with positive dislike. The old rabbi was beaming at her misti-
ly. Hurry it up, she thought. She went on: "I heard about
you, Mr. Fletcher. And about Jean. I knew you couldn't go
to him, so I went to the hospital to find out for myself. Doctors are such soothing liars."

Johnny quickened; he lifted himself on his pillows, and his
expression tensed.

"That was good of you, Miss Summerfield," he said uncertainly. "How—how was Jean?"

Only the priest, suddenly alerted by her slight, mobile
change of face, caught the careful evasion of her next words:
"When I left him—he was fine. Dr. Kennedy said he was
improving remarkably. His fever had dropped, his pulse was
almost normally strong." Father Krupszyk straightened in his
chair, and now his eyes were very keen on the girl's face.
Lorry went on: "He was sleeping wonderfully—when I left."

Johnny was baffled. Why had she gone there? What was
Jean to this hard young woman? But he was relieved and
happy. He sank back against his pillows. "Good, good," he
murmured. "I knew everything would be all right."

Again the priest saw Lorry's face change. He listened
intently when she continued, "Uncle Al said the boy was a
Catholic. I hope you don't mind, but I brought him a very
pretty statue of the Virgin, and put it on his table. I—I told
the nurse to tell him that his mother had sent it to him."

Johnny turned his head quickly on his pillow, and now it
seemed to him that he saw Lorry for the first time. His voice
shook a little. "I—can't thank you enough. But how did you
know—I mean, how did you understand?"

Rabbi Chortow spoke very gently: "Is understanding the
property of the clergy alone? Does not God move all human
hearts to understanding—if they will give just one little
minute to listening?" He had indicated a chair for Lorry
several times, but she had ignored the gesture. She remained
at the foot of Johnny's bed, her hands tight on the posts.

She said to Johnny with quiet scorn, "Aren't you a little
egotistic? Are understanding—and charity, perhaps—the
possession of public Christians only? Are the rest of us outside the pale of humanity, without any decencies, or the
impulses or virtues of humanity? Pardon me, Mr. Fletcher,
but how stupid can you get?"

She was immediately contrite, for Johnny colored painfully and his eyes darkened with distress. "I'm sorry," he said at once. "You were right to say that. I'm often stupid. I'm sorry."

Don't be! she cried in her heart. Don't be, Johnny Fletcher! You saved my brother's life; you literally brought him back from the dead. Not only physically, but spiritually!

The mysterious and humble tenderness she had felt before for him almost overwhelmed her. They all saw her change of expression, melting, passionately emotional. Johnny was touched, and ashamed. But he did not understand. He thought to himself, I've misjudged her. She's really very vulnerable, poor young woman, to accept my apology with such a reaction. He saw that her eyes were full of tears, and that her mouth was trembling. He said, "I'll never be able to thank you enough for going to Jean, Miss Summerfield. You told the nurse to tell Jean that his mother had sent the statue? You know, I feel that's true. She most likely did, through you, and that's another step toward Jean's recovery. And you came to tell me he was improving rapidly. That's the kindest thing I've ever heard of. I won't thank you. Thanks aren't very adequate, are they?"

"No," she murmured. She thought, To thank you, Johnny Fletcher, would be an insult. She wanted to go to him, to kneel beside his bed and take his hand. The impulse was almost too powerful to restrain. She wanted to tell him of the hatred for her father which was tearing the vital fabric of her spirit to tatters, and the reason for the hatred, and the tortured love for the same father which fought with the hatred. She wanted to tell him of the horror of her life, of the daily sickness of living, and her lostness. If they had been alone she would have gone to him and laid her cheek against his hand, weeping.

There was no wind outside, but all at once the house shivered perceptibly. Faint chatterings ran through it, and its worn timbers moaned dimly. Johnny exclaimed, "Was that an earthquake?"

"No," said the priest. "The town's just honeycombed by the mines. It happens all the time, especially in this section. Some of the richest deposits are under here." He turned his attention to Lorry again, and he thought that something was disturbing this young woman beyond the knowledge of anyone in the room.

Johnny closed his eyes in exhaustion. He said, "I'm glad you've not come for a story about me. We—we're getting too much notoriety as it is. It's bad for us."

"I don't think so," said the priest. "Part of your congregation is sitting downstairs in sackcloth and ashes, as you know. They're inarticulate people, and they can only sit there and be sorry."

Johnny smiled and opened his eyes. "You know—the day it happened—I was very worried. My sermon—I thought it was all up with me and the children after that. But now they tell me my congregation is thinking. Mr. McGee said tonight that it's just what they needed. Perhaps I was a little hard on them." His smile became deeper. "I was afraid, too, that we'd be told to leave. It doesn't matter to me, but I wanted the children to take roots, somewhere."

Mrs. Burnsdale came in with a wooden tray containing several cups of coffee. She stopped and blinked when she saw Lorry. Then she put the cups down on the table. "I think you'd better not drink the coffee, Mr. Fletcher," she said. "I brought you a cup of hot milk. It's time you went to sleep," she added, not too subtly. Now, what on earth was this girl doing here? Trying to get up a wild, silly story? She regarded Lorry with more than a little antagonism. But she had more important matters on her mind. She said to Johnny, "I talked to Dr. Kennedy at the hospital. I told him we had all the windows shut to keep out the fog. But Emilie's coughing, in spite of the cough syrup. She can't sleep. I've given her another pill."

Lorry swung to her quickly. "The fog and the smoke? It affects some people too much, especially young children, if they're feeble. Is there anything the matter with the little girl?"

Johnny said, in a voice suddenly weak and faint, "She has a bad heart. Dr. Kennedy told me she can't—"

Lorry was aghast. She looked at the priest and the rabbi and saw their grave faces. She cried out bitterly, "I know all about the smoke! Pittsburgh could get rid of it, but not Barryfield! It's too expensive—for my father's friends." Again her face changed, became ugly with wrath and detestation. "Well, we can do something about it."

If she went back to the offices at once she could slip in the article next day. She gathered up her purse quickly, and felt the weight of the golden box in it, which she had forgotten. She paused. A fool thing to do. But she had wanted to give him a small gift, because of Barry. It had seemed sensible then, but now it appeared absurd. Still, she hesitated. Then, finally, willing to accomplish the whole of her folly, she took out the wrapped parcel and laid it abruptly beside Johnny's hand. His face swam close to hers, and for one shaking moment they looked fully into each other's eyes. Lorry turned away, her hands clenched stiffly at her sides. "I brought you a little gift, too," she said with a sort of defiance. "At the time I bought it for you it seemed reasonable. I'm not so sure now." Her cheeks, usually so smooth and white, were vivid with embarrassment. "If you don't want it, I'll take it away."

Johnny said in wonder, "Why should you give me a gift, Miss Summerfield?"

"I don't know!" she exclaimed. "Why don't you look at it, at least?"

Johnny slowly unwrapped the box. And then it lay on his palm, glimmering with golden lights and shadows, exquisitely carved. He opened it, and immediately the air was penetrated by the faint, exotic fragrance of forgotten unguents, of attar of roses. Father Krupszyk bent forward to look at it, and for some reason the back of his neck prickled. There was something he was trying to remember; this was too familiar to be forgotten.

Lorry said recklessly, in the awed silence, "I don't know what you'll do with it, honestly. I thought I knew when I bought it, but I don't know now. To be frank, I'd had too much to drink." She added, "You could use it for cuff links, or anything, I suppose."

Johnny was dumfounded. He held the box so that the rabbi and the priest could examine it closer. And then he thought, It was terribly expensive, and I can't imagine . . . Why should she? And if she wanted to spend all that money, there's the parish hall under the church, and the money could have been used for play and craft equipment for the children of the parish, or for help for mothers, or the aged.

Then the priest murmured to him, "The poor are with you always."

Johnny turned to him at once. The priest smiled and nodded. Johnny said to Lorry, "It's beautiful. Thank you, Miss Summerfield." He spoke simply and gravely, and his bruised face was quiet. "If you wanted me to have it, then I can only accept it with gratitude."

They all started as they heard the hard pounding of feet on the bare stairs, and the heavy rush of them when they entered the room. And there was Dr. McManus in a rumpled and exultant hurry, more untidy than ever, as if he had thrown his unkempt clothing on his wide short body in wild haste. He squealed, "A miracle, you said! Well, Johnny, you've got your damned miracle! I just came from the—"

He saw Lorry for the first time, and he fell into a complete silence. He forgot the others; he gazed at the girl, and his stony eyelids fluttered and his face became tremulous. Then he went to her, slowly, and put his arm about her and held her tightly. He tried to speak, then he coughed raucously, and sniffed audibly. Still holding her, he let his eyes touch the priest, the rabbi, and then Johnny. He said, "A miracle. And who did it? This girl here. This wonderful girl of mine, the finest girl in the world. It makes a man feel—hell, it doesn't matter. Johnny, I can only say this. Five hours ago we practically gave up Jean. The infection—everything was a shock to him. It came up suddenly; he seemed to be letting go, making up his mind to go. And then this girl came."

Johnny sat up in bed, paling. "You mean, you didn't tell me about my boy? You—you lied to me?"

"What good would telling you do? You couldn't go to him, man. Don't be a fool. We were doing all we could. It was the boy—he was letting go, I tell you. All he could talk about was his mother, not you, not his father, not anybody else. Just his mother. Sol Klein's been with him most of the time, and me too. But it was getting bad. He wanted his mother." His arm tightened still more about Lorry, and he turned his massive head to her and gently kissed her cheek. "Lorry, you saved him. You brought him back. He thought you were his mother. And now he's looking at the statue all the time, and smiling, and then he was hungry about half an hour ago, and he's telling everybody his mother came to him and left the statue for him. He's going to live, Lorry, because of you."

The priest had stood up, slowly, large and big and still. His broad Slav face was very white. He came to Lorry and the doctor, and contemplated them speechlessly. Dr. McManus grinned at him wolfishly. "Well, Father John Kanty, there's your miracle for you. But you always believed in miracles anyway, didn't you? Maybe I do now." He turned to Lorry, who was trembling. "Honey, what made you go? I'm curious."

She said, "I don't know. I can't remember. I don't know."

The priest said, "You were right. His Mother sent him her image. Through you." And he crossed himself and went out of the room, his head bent in meditation.

15

Even the air conditioning of the fine office of MacDonald Summerfield could not completely exclude the poisonous effluvium of what the *Press* lightly called "a harmless downdraft of normal industrial smoke and heavy autumn air." The acrid and stinging stench of it seeped through the most minute of openings, and the air-conditioning equipment battled valiantly with unusually loud whirrings. The valley view from the broad windows had disappeared in a foggy unreality; only the highest dark ridges of the distant mountains peered through the uneasy and shifting gray vapor like island crags. But the gray sea of poisoned moisture and air was not uniform in color; here and there it gushed upward in yellowish fountains, from hidden chimneys, or a monstrously large black coil, like a serpent, raised itself through the silent waves of grayness.

Mr. Summerfield blew his nose repeatedly in one of his delicate linen handkerchiefs, as he angrily read the article his daughter had written about the new minister of that miserable Church of the Good Shepherd. It was a well-written article, with much color and vividness, which increased Mr.

Summerfield's anger, and it was prominently displayed on the second page, with certain paragraphs in bold-faced type.

"Yesterday marked Mr. Fletcher's return to his pulpit after the attack on him by some young hoodlums, still unidentified, four weeks ago. He was still pale and thin, and a long red scar ran horizontally from his right temple far back into his hair. That scar stood out flagrantly in the light of the few candles in the little bleak church, and this reporter noticed that the congregation repeatedly glanced at it. Perhaps it was only curiosity which had filled the church to the doors, with at least twenty standees after emergency seating could no longer accommodate the remarkable influx of worshipers. But those who came out of curiosity remained to listen. Though this reporter has covered many services before in many other churches, she was greatly impressed by the deep attention everyone gave to Mr. Fletcher's sermon. When the congregation rose at the conclusion it was less a mechanical gesture prefacing the responsive reading than a grave ovation.

"Mr. Fletcher is an eloquent speaker, but without histrionics or actorish inflections and gestures. Perhaps it was because he spoke less to impress or fascinate than to speak the truth. It is the conviction of this reporter that truth, in itself, has such power that it is not necessary to add flamboyance to it, or pyrotechnics."

Well, thought Mr. Summerfield, with a little sour satisfaction, at least here Lorry got out of the depth of understanding of the filthy masses.

"Mr. Fletcher is practically an anachronism among the Protestant clergy, especially of the more 'progressive' and 'enlightened' type," the article went on calmly. "He is not an evangelist, or a fundamentalist, so his sermon was, therefore, even the more remarkable. In a way, it was a scholarly sermon, worthy of some theological seminary president, and distinguished, here and there, by his deep sincerity and quiet passion and belief in what he was saying. And he convinced his congregation, and those there who were not of his congregation. None of the men and women crowding the pews could be called fashionable worshipers. They appeared to be of the smaller-income groups, skilled laborers, artisans, shopkeepers, and white-collar workers. They understood Mr. Fletcher completely."

Did they? Mr. Summerfield asked. That rabble?

"Mr. Fletcher, whose sermon was entitled 'The Ancient Tyranny,' was a chaplain in the United States armed services during the last war. During those years he had ample opportunity to gather information for this sermon, and he delivered it starkly. According to Mr. Fletcher, the era which culminated in a war that ended hardly more than a year ago was just another outbreak of a despotism which goes back to the very cloudy fringes of past history. And he believes the present 'peace' is only a strength-gathering interval for tyrants to renew their ancient assault on mankind.

" 'The new assault may break out in 1947 or 1949 or 1950 or 1957,' Mr. Fletcher said. 'This time the secret despots will stake everything they have, everything they cynically believe, and all their hatred for men and their lust for power, on the mightiest blow to come. The atomic bomb is only another weapon in their arsenal of hatred and destruction, for they know that no weapon, however terrible, can bring peace to mankind unless mankind demands peace.' "

The article continued more somberly: "However, Mr. Fletcher wasted little time on the immortal despots, whose history he outlined briefly. He said, 'The people, themselves, are responsible for despots. They *will* them. They give them what they want, eagerly in most cases, passively in others. The people are guilty of their tyrants; they furnish the environment in which tyranny can grow, by their demands, their appetites, their mass-hatreds and envies, their loathing for their fellow man, their prejudices and ignorances and lack of virtue, their atheism which invades even their churches, their obstinate determination to have what they have not earned and are not worthy of, their mad greed and their absence of charity and love. They exalt those who will promise to satisfy the evil in them, either by confiscation or revolution or murder.' "

Mr. Summerfield clenched his fists on his desk, and white lines appeared about his mouth. So she lied to me all the time, he thought. And then he was desperately frightened, thinking of Swensen and all his other friends. What had she found out in these offices? What had she heard, and overheard? There, on that page, his daughter repudiated him, dissected him, tore him apart, with bitter scorn and detestation and understanding. There she had made clear the reason she hated him, and he saw her face and her eyes, turned to him in cold accusation.

And yet, while he stiffened with his fear and his rage, there was a cry in him: Lorry! Lorry! My daughter! And then, with less—but only a little less—yearning: Barry, my son, my son!

"'This has always been the history of despotism,' Mr. Fletcher said. 'The history of despotism is the history of the godlessness, materialism, and hatred of the people. Implanted in the human soul is the ineradicable instinct for worship, sealed in it by God Himself. A man must always worship something; he cannot evade the dynamic of his soul. He cannot be an atheist, in the true sense of the word. He cannot even be an agnostic. He cannot, not even for an hour, be indifferent to the urge of his spirit. If he will not worship God, he must worship something else. There can be no vacuum of adoration in him, no empty place. If he will not worship God, he must worship Satan. He must belong to the Mystical Body of God or to the Mystical Body of Satan, which is absolute evil.'"

Why, the idiot! thought Mr. Summerfield with some relief. If anyone who heard him yesterday has any intelligence, his sermon will make him a laughingstock, even in this Godforsaken town.

"'In each bloody era of despotism the people have worshiped a different manifestation of the immortal Evil. With the Manifesto of Karl Marx in 1847 they began to adore another manifestation: materialism in its most profound, all-inclusive form.

"'All men, from the very beginning of history, have had some normal interest in materialism—which is the things of the flesh—for man, though a spirit, is clothed in animal garb, too, and it is necessary to satisfy the hungers of the animal with food, shelter, clothing. It was God Himself who multiplied the loaves and the fishes, who fed the multitude, who rebuked those who oppressed the widow and the orphan and made them homeless, who declared that a laborer was worthy of his hire, and who said that no one should muzzle the ox who treads out the corn. God Himself, who became man in His love for us, needed to eat and drink, to find shelter from the storm, to clothe Himself and to warm Himself. Render unto Caesar the things which are Caesar's, and unto

God the things which are God's, He sternly admonished the people. All that was unjust, all those who set the people to hungering miserably for actual bread, or paid them little for their labor, or forced them to shelter themselves in wretched hovels, or drove them starving upon the highways, or exploited them, received His anger. For the spirit of man must manifest itself to its neighbor through the medium of flesh, and so flesh itself has sanctity. God had made man from the dust, and had blessed that dust, and had breathed into it the fire of life.

" 'But one hundred years ago materialism suddenly emerged as a total object of worship, unleavened by the spirit. It became an absolute thing in itself, and the absolutism was the invention of Satan. And this doctrine was unique in history, and the despots, who are always being born anew in each generation, saw in it their final and most powerful opportunity.

" 'Out of this doctrine of dialectical materialism was born Hitler and Mussolini and Stalin, and many others with the mark of Satan upon them. But it was not Satan who created the power of these men. It was the people, in every nation of the world. Materialism suddenly became for them an object of adoration, and they adored the men who promised to give them what they wanted. Somewhere, in the red blaze of the industrial revolution, man lost God, or abandoned Him, for goods, for the things of the world. The factory and the mill, and not the church, contained the holy of holies. The altar was no longer surmounted by the Cross; it no longer held in itself the sacred Scrolls. Above the thunder of the anvil, which was the new altar, rose the new incense of industrial smoke, and from the acid cloud peered the brutal faces of the new gods which the people had created unto themselves.

" 'The new gods offered the people "security" from a violent and unpredictable universe, which only God can control. They promised them the knife of revenge on those they envied or hated. They promised to give them benefits they had not earned. They raised up false enemies out of nothing, for the people's rage and destruction. They offered them the rule of the world, in the name of fascism, Nazism, or Communism, or Statism in some other form. The State, they all said, was the protector of the people. They needed only to adore the State, absolutely and with the devotion they had once given the "myth" of God, and all their natural problems would be solved. The milk and honey of the Promised Land were here before them, for the taking, through their new gods, and not as a reward for living virtuous lives.

" 'In short, the new gods asked only one thing from the people—the surrender of those inalienable rights and liberties which only God could give them, but which evil men could take away if the people let them. And the people would never have let them if they had not first assented to the most unholy bargain in history. "Give us goods, and still more goods," said the people to their tyrants, "and in return we will surrender God and all things of the spirit."

" 'Yes, the people consented, everywhere in the world, with one loud voice, with one long devotion, with one mighty consent.

" 'Do not think,' Mr. Fletcher cried to the congregation, 'that fascism was different from Nazism, or Nazism from Communism! They are one and the same thing—they are the manifestations of Satan, the manifestations of materialism. If the despots appeared to attack each other, it was their individual madness. The men behind them, the all-powerful real despots, had no quarrel among themselves. If one ostensible despot was defeated tomorrow, the secret men could replace him easily, while the work of subduing and destroying liberty and the dignity of man could go on uninterrupted. For Evil was becoming more and more victorious, and never had Satan, throughout all of history, attained such a victory, in every nation in the world.

" 'Do not believe, not even for an instant, that Hitler or Mussolini or Stalin, or anyone else, caused the last war, and do not think that any other one man will cause the next holocaust. These men are only symbols—of you, the people. They are only your images. You created them! You put the guns in their iron hands; you gave them your motivations, and your hatreds, and your godlessness. You threw your sons into their fiery arms; you sacrificed your children to them on your altars of materialism. The graves that fill Europe, the concentration camps, the wrecked cities, the weeping children, the lost mothers, the agony and anguish of a whole world—these are your deeds, and yours only. Contemplate them.

" 'Yes, contemplate them. Look at your young sons beside you, your lovely little daughters. They are already forfeit to your greed, your materialism, your abandonment of God for "security" and glittering gadgets and goods. Tomorrow they will be absent from your side. Tomorrow your cities will be smoldering again. Tomorrow you will raise up new despots, in your name and in the name of Evil.

" 'For you have driven out of your schools and your lives and your homes the shining Name of God. And may God, whose Face you have covered with smoke, have mercy on your souls!' "

"Mr. Fletcher," the article continued, "did not join in the responsive reading which followed. He left the pulpit abruptly, and did not appear again. This was without precedent, but the men and women who packed the church seemed to understand. The responsive reading was very faint, as if the congregation was thinking. They left the church with very subdued faces. It is the opinion of this reporter that that sermon will be echoed in every home for a long time to come."

Mr. Summerfield sat for a long time in deep thought, the fine skin of his forehead wrinkling and furrowing. All that this fool of a Fletcher had said was true. Therefore he must be destroyed, driven out. He was more dangerous than an army. He had been stoned. Very good. He must be stoned again. Mr. Summerfield began to write rapidly in his tiny, precise hand. When he had finished his editorial he stood up and went to look for his daughter.

He paused, his hand on the doorknob of her office. Again he was assaulted by his sick yearning. He had started for her in anger; now he stopped. He would just laugh at her gently, in ridicule. And forever after, he would know that for her own reasons she had deceived and betrayed him. He would ask her why; he had to know. He, himself, was in peril because of her. His friends would know everything; copies of this article would reach them almost immediately. But more than anything else, he wanted to know why his daughter had betrayed him, and used him, and despised him.

He opened the door. Lorry was standing beside her desk. Her father did not at first notice that she had piled her desk with objects from the emptied drawers. He saw only her slender figure in the close black dress, the gleam of her smooth head, the ascetic profile of her face. "Lorry," he said.

She turned to him with that swift movement of hers, and he saw her eyes, large glittering ovals of repudiation. She said, "I'm leaving. Now."

And then he saw the objects on her desk—her purse, her cosmetics, her notebooks. There was the finality of departure about her.

"What?" he muttered, stupefied.

"I said, I am leaving. Now. Forever. I'm never coming back. I'm going away. I don't want to hear from you. If you write me, I won't answer. If you come to see me, I'll shut my door in your face." She paused, and there was a blaze in her eyes. "Don't you understand? I'm not your daughter; you're not my father. Forget I ever lived, just as I'm going to forget I ever knew you."

She stood before him, straight, tall, rigid, and looked at him, and there was no mercy in her, no love, no regret.

"Lorry, are you out of your mind?" He forgot her article. This was his daughter, the creature he loved more than anything else in the world, and she was denying him, leaving him, and she would never return.

"Why?" he asked, when she did not answer.

"Because you are what you are. Because I have found out all about you. Because I can't stand you any longer. I began to know about you five years ago. That's when I began to hate you." Her voice was loud and harsh in the room, and she threw the words at him like stones. "Don't ask me any more questions. I have an idea you know exactly what I mean."

He put his hands on her desk and leaned on them, for he was suddenly stricken and undone.

"Don't worry how I'll get along," she said scornfully. "Remember, I have three thousand a year which my grandfather left me—your father. And two thousand my mother's father left me. And I'll be working with Barry; I've already talked with him."

Mr. Summerfield's shoulders sagged. All that I've done, he said to himself, believing himself, I've done for you, my daughter. I wanted the world for you.

She started to pass him, and he caught her arm. "Lorry," he pleaded. "Listen to me a minute. No, I can't explain, I'm afraid. I am asking you to stay here because of me, because I love you, Lorry."

But her face was more like marble than ever, eternally shut to him, her mouth white and still.

"I can't let you go, Lorry," he said.

She pulled her arm from his hand, and without a word she left the office.

He stood there alone. The morning paper was in his hand. He saw her article again. And now he was an icy avalanche of hatred. In some way this detestable and stupid minister was responsible for his daughter's going. He, that minister, had enslaved Lorry with that mystical trash of his, had driven her from him, her father. He had precipitated something in Lorry which might have lain dormant all her life.

"I'll get him," said Mr. Summerfield, aloud and quietly, "if it's the last thing I ever do."

16

"You're crazy!" said Dr. McManus, in as much of a shout as his voice could produce. "Lorry, you can't go away now—just when you were beginning to stir things up. What about your smoke articles, eh?"

Lorry sat with him in his monstrously ugly Victorian parlor, which he had not changed since the death of his parents. The girl had always considered it one of the most beautiful rooms she had ever seen, in spite of its crimson and blue dusty velvets and velveteens, its twisted porcelain grotesqueries, its black ebony or black walnut furniture carved to the last expiring inch, its fireplace vases filled with stiff autumn leaves or lacquered cattails, its black and white engravings or dull and static portraits hanging on violently flowered walls, and its red Brussels rug. For here the doctor had read to her when she had been a child, or had told her odd or humorous stories, and had fed her with huge sugar cookies, which she ate while listening to him and idly watching the green light that filtered through the thick trees outside and into the twilight of the massive room.

The light was not green now, for wet yellow rags were

falling from the elms, and the scarlet tatters of the maples were drifting in the damp wind. She sat stiffly across from the doctor, who eyed her irascibly. She was dressed in a brown suit for traveling; her bags were locked in her car, which stood outside. The luminous quality of her pale face was obscured in weariness and pain, and her lips were white. She said, "Those articles will never get published. I found out, this morning, that he—he—had told the assistant editors that anything I wrote must be submitted to him first for approval." Her lips narrowed. "I've outlived my usefulness. Uncle Al, I think I have done enough. And, besides—"

Dr. McManus waited. But Lorry smoothed the gloves over and over in her hands, and bent her head. The old doctor felt a strong twinge of compassion. He said, "You'll want me to write to you, Lorry? You'll want me to tell you everything. You'll want to know about your father, eh?"

She said simply, "Yes." There was no hatred in her eyes now.

The doctor lit another cigarette from the end he had smoked down almost to a nubbin. He puffed, and stared before him with the most malignant expression. Then he said, "Lorry, you're a big girl. Part of the trouble between you and your father is your own fault. You deified him, until a few years ago. That was wrong. You weren't a kid; you were in your twenties, and you should've known better. I'm holding no brief for Mac; I think he stinks. I always thought he stank. He's an egotistic, posturing, lying, elegant sonofabitch. Yes, ma'am. He was that way as a kid. He was right there for you to see. You didn't see, so you blame him for your own blindness. When you got your eyesight back you hated him for being what he always had been.

"You know his background. His father was a schoolteacher here in Barryfield, where Mac was born. I knew your grandfather well, an ineffective kind of a fellow, meek-spoken, pedantic, full of schoolteacherish dogmas. He bowed and he scraped, and because he thought he was superior to everybody else, he hated those who were more powerful because they had more money. He poisoned Mac; that was inevitable. He loved money more than his immortal soul—if he had one, which I doubt. But because he didn't have money he pretended that it was worthless, and at the same time that those who had it were the only significant people in the world.

Mac might have been a sneering, superior kind of prig, when he was a boy, but, like you, he believed his father. That kind of weakness runs in the family, don't it?"

He leered at the girl, who had lifted her head with taut interest. "Well, Lorry, he was like you in more than one way. He adored that whining idiot of a father of his. 'Society' was 'doing something' to his dad. So society must be punished. The only way to punish society was to get as much money as possible, and then to get power over society, and make it scrape to him as his father had scraped to it. Scratch any of these wealthy pseudo-liberals or fascists or Communists and you'll find a story like that in the background somewhere. There never was any movement that didn't begin with secret human emotions of either love or hate. But, my girl, mostly it's revenge."

"I always thought our family had been rich for generations," said Lorry, with sick wonder.

"Oh," chortled the doctor, shaking a sly finger at her, "that's just Mac's grand illusion. He really believes it himself, now. Why didn't he tell you his father was just a poor schoolteacher in the beginning, and just made his fortune, by accident, in oil? I'll tell you why. He was ashamed that he once was poor! He, the great liberal, is so ashamed, the idiot, that he can't bear to remember. To him it was a disgrace. To him it was horrible that he ever lived among the blessed poor he now pretends to champion in those rags of his. He hates the poor, the underprivileged, the masses. Like all the others of his kind, he's built up something that doesn't exist—the mass man. Why? Because he wants to use the mass man not only to revenge himself upon his 'betters' for the humiliation of poverty he once suffered from them, but even more because he wants to revenge himself on the poor for once having had to live among them.

"Nobody," went on the doctor to the tense and listening girl, "ever brought out the fact that Marx was a comparatively well-off man, and all his pals with him. They came from sound middle-class city families. Being sound and middle-class wasn't enough for 'em, the insane brutes. They wanted money and money and money, and power and power and power. So up they built the 'masses,' a pure invention of theirs, so they'll have somebody to oppress. And get revenge on."

The doctor stood up, and waddled up and down the cluttered floor. "That's the history of those Communists who were never really poor, and those who are wealthy now. However, let's not simplify too much. Your dad and his kind are one part of Communism. There's another kind, and this kind will do in your dad and his friends very fast, if they ever come to power in this country, just as they liquidated your dad's kind in every other country when they came to power.

"I'm speaking of the fanatic, the zealot. They're born in every generation. An intelligent doctor can spot these fellers, male and female alike, right in the kindergarten, or in the primary grades, anyway. One of these days we'll have real psychiatrists looking for 'em, not the Freudian headshrinkers we have nowadays, who are even partial, some of 'em, to the kind of perverted minds the fanatics and zealots have. They're sort of partial to the intense, perverted innocence these crazy folks carry around with them, for there's nothing so damnably, dangerously innocent-looking as a man who believes fervently and absolutely in hatred."

The doctor said, still scowling formidably, "Well, Lorry, I've told you about your dad. Are you going to desert him now, seeing you understand?"

She was silent; her face stiffened. The doctor shook his head. "Y'know, I thought you'd be a help to Johnny and the kids. You seemed to go for the whole bunch. Jean. Johnny. First time I've seen you alive for years. And now you run out on 'em."

To his interested amazement, Lorry colored violently. She said. "I—don't want to get emotionally involved with—anybody. Too much wear and tear."

Dr. McManus came closer to her, squinting. "Oho. So that's it. It's not all your dad, then. You're running away, kid. Somethin' prick you?" he asked with malicious interest, as the girl jumped to her feet. "What is it? Johnny?"

She shouted at him, "Damn you, Uncle Al! Look at me! Remember me! Can you see me as a minister's wife? Even if he ever thought of it, which he wouldn't? Can you see me trailing him sentimentally, with big cow eyes, mooing around after him, doing 'good works' for him? Oh, shut up!"

She caught up her gloves and purse, and gave the doctor the full blue blast of her eyes. "Let's be realistic. I'm not living a romance. Johnny—and me! For God's sake! He's a fossil, I'm telling you. An anachronism."

"Pretty lively for a fossil," said the doctor, with his gloating grin. "What's an anochronism? Something out of time and place. Sure he is, in the general view. Believes in sin, for Pete's sake. You know what, honey? There sure is sin. You've got to accept and acknowledge it. And then you've got to do something about it. Johnny's the boy. We need a few more anachronisms in the world, that's certain."

Lorry slumped wearily. "Uncle Al, I'm not the sacrificing kind; I'm not morbid. I couldn't be his wife, and I'm not going to be a handmaiden to anybody. I'm not interested, in any event, in marrying anybody."

"Course not," said the doctor coolly. "You're still in love with your dad. Way back in that silly head of yours is poor old Mac dressed in white armor or something. In spite of everything. You just can't stand getting even an honest glimpse of him, and that's unfair. Once in a while you do, and then off you go to New York or Europe or wherever."

"Look who's the head-shrinker now!" Lorry screamed in a white fury. "Why don't you set up a couch?"

The doctor chuckled. "Hey, wait, honey." But Lorry had rushed out of the room, and then out of the house. The door crashed behind her. Dr. McManus could see the girl throwing herself wildly into her car. It roared off so fast that her head snapped back, and her hat fell over her eyes. Dr. McManus chewed his thumbnail dourly. He said aloud, "Funny. Lorry was never the girl to run away from truth, slamming doors behind her. Must have touched a mighty bloody incision in her psyche, or something. The poor girl. Well, she'll get to thinking—maybe."

It was his afternoon for hospital calls, but he went to the parsonage, which looked unusually bleak and dismal in the autumn's hollow light. Johnny was surprised to see him; the young minister seemed very despondent and preoccupied. The sound of busy young voices could be heard from the dining room, though the door was shut. "Sol Klein just left, doctor," said Johnny, leading the way into the wretched parlor where he had been working on his next sermon. "He thinks Jean's coming along fine."

"I didn't come to see Jean, exactly," said the old man,

groaning as he let himself down on the leprous sofa. "Frank to say, I don't know why I did come. How's the old—lady—who's teaching the kids? Getting anywheres?"

Johnny's exhausted face brightened, and now the scar on his temple was less conspicuous. "Father John Kanty's been awfully good. He sent his old retired schoolteacher here to teach Jean and Pietro, and she refuses to take a cent for it. Miss Coogan. Pietro goes early to school for his catechism, and Miss Coogan teaches it to Jean. And you know what? She offered to take on Max, Kathy, and Emilie." For a moment his eyes became more brooding and tired. "She says the kids are all unusually bright. Max and Kathy are learning like wildfire, and Jean and Pietro are really geniuses! Miss Coogan may be exaggerating but she says Jean and Pietro are already up to fourth grade in their work, and they ought to be ready for their regular grades next September, if they keep on this way. The kids seem to act as if it's all a very exciting game."

The doctor nodded with approval, but at the same time he was disturbed by the worn and anxious look on Johnny's face. Then he said, "Come on, something's bothering you. Tell Papa. It isn't Jean; he's coming along miraculously, Sol tells me. Why shouldn't he? He's got Sol, who drools over him as if he was his own kid; special for Sol."

Johnny hesitated. "It's Emilie, doctor. She's failing. Every time there's a smog she gets sicker. She grows a little weaker every day."

"Hm," said Dr. McManus thoughtfully. "I suppose the best thing would be to get her in some high hospital or sanitarium, away from here, where she'll have good air."

"Yes," said Johnny, in a sick voice. "But, you see, even Dr. Kennedy—Tim—admits she wouldn't get any benefit from that, separated from the kids and me. It might even make her worse."

The doctor said, "Look, Johnny, you've seen the world; you're realistic. You got a kind of miracle with Jean, but that was because Sol Klein gave him everything he had—and Lorry gave him something she didn't know she had. But you can't expect another miracle for Emilie. You saw her X rays; Kennedy's one of the best heart men in the country. Mayo wanted him a year ago, and still wants him. Tim don't hold out any hope for the baby. You know that. Just make her as comfortable as possible. Johnny, you ain't holding out for a second miracle, are you?"

Johnny replied simply, "No. I did, some time ago. But not now. Something tells me that Emilie is going to die; a finality came to me one night, when I was praying for her. I—I have always believed that even death had a meaning, in the lives of people. I'm afraid I don't, now. I keep thinking of what Emilie has suffered from her very birth—from beasts. Why can't she live, and grow up to be a happy, healthy woman, as Kathy will be?"

Dr. McManus shifted his bulk uneasily on the sofa. "Johnny, I don't know. But you're the parson. You ought to know."

Johnny said, his voice rising with desperation and grief, "I don't! God forgive me, I don't! I'm full of rebellion. I shout at God. I get only silence. How can I talk to my congregation about the mercy of God when He doesn't answer me Himself, when I pray about Emilie?"

The doctor squinted at him. "Johnny, I'm not the religious kind. Me, I'm a hard realist; the world made me that way. But I've listened to you. Maybe the answer's waiting, and will show up in time. Maybe you couldn't understand now. Hell, I'm talking like a parson myself." He lit a cigarette, frowned at it, and muttered, "War's over; why aren't the damned things tasting right yet? Johnny, you believe in the hereafter, don't you? I don't, of course."

Johnny did not reply. In distraction, he turned away and stared through the window.

The doctor heaved a gargantuan sigh. "Okay, Johnny. You don't need to answer. Let's look at it this way. The baby will—go—before she's even had time to know anything about death. From what Tim tells me, she'll just fade out gently; going to sleep. So—no fear, no anxiety. And look what you're giving her in the meantime. Love, protection, security. Think of the millions of even healthy kids who don't get a tenth of that!"

"Thanks," said Johnny, with sad humility. He sat down again. He began to drum on his creaking desk with both hands, and stared blankly before him.

The doctor went on: "Hell, the world ain't such a fine, attactive place. What do the Chinese say? 'Each man lives a life of quiet desperation.' That's right; he does. Life's a damned, unsatisfying thing under the best of circumstances. Things get lent to you, if you're lucky. And then they're snatched away. Johnny, I never told you much about my wife. Sweetest, finest girl in the world; died when our child was born. Aside from my father, she was the only thing I ever loved. And then she died, and I stood at the grave; stayed there while they let her down; wouldn't move away, in spite of fools tugging at me. And then I cursed God. Why'd Ann have to die, eh? And the baby too? I walked away from that grave, when the last clod was thrown on it, and not before, and everything I ever believed left me."

Johnny had lifted his bent head, and now he was gazing at the old doctor intently.

The doctor squinted at the ceiling reflectively. "Know something? I made a kind of oath to myself. I hated God. I said I'd work my fool head off to snatch people out of pain and death. I kind of thought of God as a Moloch who destroyed the finest and the best and the loveliest. So I'd defeat Him. I'd keep His victims out of His burning hands. I'd make Him sorry He ever tangled with me! Yes sir. He'd be sorry." The doctor chuckled grimly. "So—I didn't have much money then—I got Ann's insurance money, and I went to Europe. I studied in Heidelberg; I studied in London. When the money ran out I still studied. My father sent me some. I starved. But I was on the track of the Enemy! I worked in Edinburgh hospitals for nothing. I worked everywhere for nothing. Never told anybody but you before. Tired of the saga, eh?"

"Tell me," said Johnny.

"Thanks. You know what? I pulled scores out, when they were *in extremis!* Especially young women, and kids. Got them when they were rattling. Yes sir. I invented operating techniques never heard of before; used widely now. Know something? I even operated on the heart! One of the first doctors to do so. Men on the verge of the grave; relatives howling; doctors shaking their fool heads. And then I rolled up my sleeves and went to work. Took out cancerous stomachs, while doctors held their breath and muttered about murder." Dr. McManus sat up, and shook his finger at Johnny. "Know what? In ten years I had only two deaths, from any cause at all! A record, I tell you! I got citations, dozens of 'em! Fool things. Some say, 'In the cause of humanity.' Rot. I was just fighting God." He smirked. "You see, I still believed in God then, in a perverted way. Now I don't. Well, not much, anyway. Got hundreds of pounds of letters from grateful patients and their families. You know, I'm thinking of something. Maybe if Ann and the baby hadn't died, I'd just have been a family doctor, dozing away comfortably in this wretched town, and then inheriting the money from my uncle, and then retiring. And all the people I'd saved, thousands of them over the years, would've been dead."

He grumbled, "Don't know if I did them a favor, after all, keeping 'em alive. In this goddam world."

"But you keep on, just the same, though you don't think of God as the Eenemy any more," said Johnny gently.

"Well, yes. Crazy thing, isn't it? But can't stand pain and death and suffering. Something drives me on." The doctor grinned, his stained teeth showing between his livid lips. "Can't figure it out."

Johnny looked down at his clasped hands. "I can," he said. And in his heart he prayed, "Father, forgive me. Just give me strength. Just let me understand."

Dr. McManus waited, knowing he was praying, and then in the gentlest voice Johnny had ever heard him use, he said, "You parsons are always saying nobody's born in vain, but for a purpose. So was Emilie."

He paused, then said, "How'd you like Lorry's reporting of your sermon? Stirred up the town, I hear. Sol Klein, and the other bright, shiny boys, discuss it very seriously, in the doctors' dining room. You and Jean've done a lot for Sol. Told me he goes almost every Friday night to temple. 'Have to set a good example for the children,' he tells me, looking me hard in the eye as though he thought I was going to laugh. 'Well,' says I, 'why do you boys and girls pick on your poor old rabbi, eh?' And he says, 'I've been having some talks with him. I'm president of the men's club. And I was an usher at the holidays. We can give our rabbi some new ideas, perhaps, if we cooperate a little more with him.' And then I had to laugh, and he laughed too."

Johnny smiled slightly. But his strong brown hands unconsciously twisted together in his hidden despair. "I thought it very kind of—Lorry." He opened a drawer in his desk and brought out the golden box, carefully wrapped in tissue. He lifted the lid and sniffed. "I'm sure it's attar of roses."

The doctor was watching him keenly. The young man's face had unexpectedly lightened. "Well," said the doctor, "I told you she was a fine girl. Often wish I were young enough to marry her. She's got a reputation of being—well—wild. Drinking." He coughed. "It's her dad. She is an idealist, and he let her believe he was too. Not deliberately; it's just the way he is. I think she dreamed up an idea of him which doesn't exist. Anyway, she's gone again, and this time she isn't coming back."

Johnny's fingers tightened suddenly on the box, and his eyes darkened with dismay. "Not coming back? Why?"

The doctor shrugged, and he smiled with satisfaction in himself. "Filled right up to here with old Mac. What's the matter, Johnny? You don't look very well yourself, all of a sudden."

"Nothing," said Johnny abruptly. He looked at the box; his knuckles were white as he held it. Then he added, "I hope she comes back. I—we—though we haven't met her often, she made a deep—impression—on all of us. She came a couple of times to see Jean. He took to her right away. Showed her his statue, which he keeps in his room. Told her his mother brought it to him. And Kathy is standing up straight, the way Lorry does, and keeps talking all the time of how their hair is almost the same color, and she's practically brushing it off her skull. Pietro adores her, and even Max talked to her without prompting, and Emilie sat in her lap. Why, Max is making a statue of her; Miss Coogan brought him modeling clay." Again he got to his feet, rapidly. "Write to her. She can't leave her friends like this. She didn't even come to say goodby!"

The doctor nodded over and over. "She'll write to me, I think. And then you can write to her and tell her you need her. Eh?"

Johnny colored. He folded the tissue paper tenderly about the box and put it away, reluctantly. He said, almost inaudibly, "What can I say to her? What can I—offer—her?" He closed the drawer loudly. "Do you want to see the children? It's just about their lunchtime."

They went into the small, dark dining room. The new

244

table had been spread with newspapers, and on it were scattered piles of books. All the children were gathered about it, bending over notebooks, and writing solemnly with firmly gripped pencils. Jean was there, in his wheel chair, his encased leg elevated, his wise face full of earnest concentration. Pietro was more restless; he was writing very fast on his paper, and biting the tongue he had thrust between his teeth. Kathy was precisely putting down words, every letter neat and rounded. Max, wearing a small black skullcap, was soberly intent on reading, a pencil waiting in his hand. Even little Emilie was there, playing with blocks. Her tiny face was very translucent, like alabaster, and her blue eyes were enormous in it. She seemed much smaller; but when she looked up her expression was one of brilliant joy at the sight of Johnny and the doctor. At the head of the table sat a very little, fat old woman with white stringy hair in a coil on the back of her head, and with the bright, gay eyes of a young child.

The children all stood up at once, as Miss Coogan had taught them to do, and waited for their elders to speak. Emilie quivered; she wanted to run to Johnny, but Miss Coogan had taught her an old-fashioned respect. Dr. McManus greeted them in his usual truculent way, while they smiled at him. "What's the skullcap for?" he asked Max, growling.

The boy, whose once vacant eyes were now filled with serenity, answered, "Rabbi Chortow wears one. He gave me this. He said I could wear it." He pointed at Jean. "See. Jean. He wears one too."

"Well!" said the doctor, with a scowl.

Jean regarded him sternly. "Father John Kanty says it is—good. The bishops wear one. If I want to wear one, it is good. His Holiness wears one, too. White."

The doctor laughed derisively. "So, you're a Pope at your early age, are you?" He turned to Johnny. "I never asked you, but I've been wondering how you've explained the religious hodgepodge to these kids. Be interestin' to know."

Johnny put his hand on Jean's shoulder. "Dear, tell the doctor what I have told you about God, and religion."

Jean settled deeper into his wheel chair with importance, while the other children still stood. "Papa told us of a great King, who was good and—chari—chari—table. And he had many boys—saints. And one day he called them and told them to go out into the poor world and tell everybody about him. The King. And the saints did. They were all—different. They all had"—he floundered, and looked at Johnny pleadingly.

"They all saw the King in a different way," Johnny prompted.

Jean nodded. "That's right. They loved him, but they all saw him in a different way. But he was still the one King. And they went to many—nations—peoples and places, and they told everybody about their Father, and how much they loved Him, and they gave—messages—to the whole world, from their Father to the people. How the King loved them, too, more than anything, and wanted them to know Him, and be happy, and then come to His Kingdom to be with Him forever. And most of the people believed the saints. Almost everybody, I think, and they couldn't forget the King."

"Neat," squeaked Dr. McManus with a wry grin. "Got around to religious wars yet, Johnny, and everybody butchering everybody else in the name of the King?"

"Go on, Jean," said Johnny gravely to the listening boy.

"Well, there's Satan," said Jean. "Father John Kanty told me about him too. And Satan hates people. He—stirs—them up, to hate each other and kill each other. And tries to make them forget God. So they make wars on each other, and Satan thinks that is very good. He—made the people kill the saints. He doesn't want people to go to the Kingdom, and be with God. He wants them to go into the—the—hell, I think it is—to be with him, without God."

"Neat," repeated the doctor. "Congratulations, Johnny. Nice and simple. I bet, though, all of 'em will be savagely arguing theology with each other when they're a little older. Hope you enjoy it."

He looked at Kathy, his special pet. "Well, fat-face, how are the lessons coming?"

She gave him her prim smile, and her periwinkle eyes sparkled. "I do long division now," she said.

"You do, eh?" he asked, genuinely surprised. "Well, good for you. You'll be a help to your papa, helping him divide his little salary among all you brats. That'll be one of his miracles."

The young eyes twinkled still more. "Mama Burnsdale thinks doctor should pay Papa more."

"Is that so?" he said irascibly. "Papa probably thinks so too. Well, excuse me, scholars. I want a word with the lady-with-all-those-infernal-lists."

He stamped off, frowning, toward the kitchen. Pietro could restrain himself no longer. He cried shrilly, "Suckers all gone! Need more suckers!"

The doctor glared at him over his immense shoulder, and then glared at Johnny. "Boy," he said, "you've already got one!"

Mrs. Burnsdale was busily ladling soup into an immense, cracked old tureen. Her solid and rocky face broke into a smile when she saw the doctor, and she pushed a gray curl off her forehead. She was a pleasant, plump sight in her flowered housedress and white apron. "Well, doctor," she said, "I'm glad to see you. We're clean out of flour and sugar and a dozen other things. I've got the list ready. I was going to mail it to you this afternoon. I'm thinking of a good big ham for Sunday."

"Oh, you are!" He picked up a couple of thick sugar cookies waiting on a plate, and began to chew them. "Know what hams cost these days? And how do you explain to the parson where all the goodies come from?"

She laughed. "He doesn't even ask, poor dear. He thinks they come from the food allowance. Why, he even said yesterday that he doesn't know why people complain so about the high cost of living! Everything's so cheap, he says."

"That's nice," said the doctor. "How about stopping raiding my wallet and letting him find out some of the facts of life? Do him good."

Mrs. Burnsdale put her hands on her hips. "No, doctor. Hasn't he got enough troubles?" Her flushed face clouded uneasily. "Maybe you think I'm superstitious, or something. Maybe I am," she added defiantly. "But when things go kind of good I cross my fingers, because usually something bad's on the way. And things are going too good for all of us just now."

The doctor picked up another couple of cookies, and Mrs. Burnsdale deftly removed the plate to a safer place. The doctor leaned against the fine new refrigerator. "Don't think you're superstitious at all. Found out that a long time ago. Anything in the air you can put your finger on?"

She shook her head mournfully. "Well, there's little Emilie, of course. Mr. Fletcher can't stop brooding about her. That's one thing. But I feel it's something else, just about ready to break." She shivered. "If I was a Catholic I'd cross myself."

"Go ahead," said the doctor. "Mighty good cookies, by the way. Well, go ahead and cross yourself. Aren't you a Christian too?"

He walked over to a counter and snatched another cooky. "You've got enough of 'em. Bake me a batch, when you send the next list. I'll take the one you have now."

She found the envelope, already stamped, and gave it to him. He pushed it into his pocket. The door opened, and Johnny put his head into the room. He was very pale and unsmiling. "Doctor, may I see you a moment? There's someone here."

The doctor and Mrs. Burnsdale stared at his drawn face. Then the doctor said to Mrs. Burnsdale, "Something tells me you'd better start crossing yourself right now."

"What?" asked Johnny in a dull and troubled voice. But Dr. McManus pushed him into the dining room where a strange quiet had fallen upon the children, for their abnormal prescience scented danger. Miss Coogan sat with her withered hands clasped on the table, and her equally withered face was working. She glanced at the closed door leading to the parlor. "That—that woman, Mr. Fletcher," she faltered, "I'm afraid. She—forced me out of teaching in the schools—before I had a pension due. No—no certificate." She swallowed. "Father John Kanty made them give me—a pension"; her frail voice broke, and her gentle eyes filled with tears. "She saw me here."

Johnny stopped beside her; the children's suddenly enormous eyes fixed themselves upon him keenly, and he sensed the animal alertness in them for the first time in weeks—the impulse to flee, the flexing of their legs to spring, the clenching of their small hands to fight and tear. This terribly alarmed him. He put his hand on Miss Coogan's shoulder and pressed it hard. He smiled. "Don't worry, Miss Coogan. Everything will be all right."

"Famous last words," muttered the doctor, alive with curiosity. "Who the hell's out there? Medusa?"

Miss Coogan, now sensing the mysterious if rigid agitation of the children, smiled and blew her nose. "Well, yes, doctor. Medusa it is."

"I think you'd better tell Mrs. Burnsdale to serve you and the children lunch," said Johnny, forcing himself to relax. He patted Max's head. "I won't be here for a little while, so Max, you with the skullcap, you say grace."

"I have skullcap too," said Jean offended.

The doctor threw up his hands. "Both of you say grace, damn it!" he said. "And thank God for that thumping good soup out there." He winked at Kathy, and the bright blueness of her eyes returned, and her cheek dimpled. He looked at Pietro, whose teeth were showing between a tight slit of lips. "Hey, you Pete," said the doctor. "You eat too many suckers. I'm going to send you a bag today, with suckers as big as a plate." He scowled at the little boy ferociously, and shook his fist. Petro immediately bounced up and down in his chair with delight. "Red ones!" he cried.

"Hah," said the doctor ominously. "Red, he says."

He and Johnny went into the parlor, and closed the door tightly behind them. A small, stiff woman in a mannish gray suit and a very mannish hat sat on the edge of one of the deplorable chairs, and was distastefully surveying the room. She turned herself swiftly on her buttocks at the entrance of the two men, and Dr. McManus saw her taut, sucked-in cheeks, her sharp, jutting nose, her fanatical black eyes. Her black hair, streaked with gray, was drawn into a large lump like wood at the nape of her winkled neck. When she saw Dr. McManus her lips parted in consternation.

"Well, well," he squealed genially. "If it isn't Gussie Guston, our famous do-gooder and amateur psychiatrist and social-consciousness club girl! Hiya, Gus?" He surreptitiously pinched Johnny's arm, and then planted himself affably before the woman.

Mrs. Guston had recovered herself. Hate stood in her eyes like frozen lightning. But her voice was amazingly conciliatory, and she even smiled. "Now, Al," she said, in a voice like tearing tin. "How you exaggerate."

The doctor nudged Johnny openly, and winked. "Gussie likes me; she really does. She knows that I hold her husband's notes for forty-five thousand dollars. He runs a lumber mill. Can call in the notes any time. Always be nice to a creditor, Gussie believes."

The woman attempted friendly coyness. "Now, Al, you know my name is Augusta, not Gussie. You're the only one who ever calls me that disgusting name." Two deep lines appeared between her eyes. "I suppose you're here to see one of those unfortunate children who live in this house?"

"Unfortunate?" asked Johnny, with slow wrath. But the doctor pinched him furtively again, and sat down. "Well, Gussie, as a matter of fact, I am. Concerned about the boy who had the operation a few weeks ago. After all, he was my patient."

Johnny sat down, and his wrath quieted. "Too bad about the boy," said the doctor. "We just got him in time." He looked at the woman sympathetically. "Never mind my gibes, Gussie. I know you've got a heart of gold; just like to kid you. Where'd you hear about Jean? Guess you're here to see what you can do, eh? She's the president of the League for Social Betterment, Johnny. Well, I'm right with you, Gussie. Shame about the kids," and he shook his head dolorously.

Johnny turned to him again, and saw only the blank and bristling profile of the old man.

The doctor waved his hand. "Well, go on, Gussie. What's it all about?"

She shot Johnny a glance of the purest malignance. "It's come to the attention of the Board of Education, through us, about these five children. They haven't been registered at school, where they can be made into good Americans. They are all of school age—three boys, two girls. They should be in their classes."

Johnny said in a pent voice, "I told you that they aren't ready for school. It will be months before Jean can walk. And Max and Pietro and Kathy, if they went to regular school, would be in classes with children much younger than themselves. I gave you an idea of their background, Mrs. Guston. They've had it hard enough, without having to stand the jeers of younger children in classes. They have to—orient themselves."

She tossed her head, and eyed him with cold triumph. "I don't agree with you, Mr. Fletcher. They must learn to adjust. But that is beside the point. Much worse is really happening here. Five children, yourself, and a housekeeper. An elderly woman."

"That's right," interrupted the doctor happily. "She can't be less than eight years younger than you, Gussie."

Her nostrils flared. She made her voice patient. "Al, I don't suppose you know all the circumstances. After all, you are just a kind, good doctor, doing what you can. Such an imposition, too!" She smirked at him. "You see, Al, we've been doing some investigating these last few days. Mr. Fletcher was a chaplain, and he picked up these—these little ones—in some awful fascist place in Europe, and somehow brought them here. A call to Washington established the method. Bonds were put up for them so that they wouldn't become public charges. But"—and she paused dramatically—"they've already become public charges! The boy Jean was operated on without charge, and there was no charge to the minister for his hospital accommodations. Who paid the nurses I don't know."

Johnny exclaimed with deep and passionate anger, "I don't know what this is all about! Dr. McManus here told me that some friend owed me a great deal, and undertook to pay the expenses incurred by me!" He turned to Dr. McManus and said with rising rage, "Well, why don't you speak up, doctor?"

Dr. McManus sighed. "Go on, Gussie," he murmured.

She was gaining more and more confidence. She leaned toward the doctor eagerly, and her unpleasant voice was quick: "And there's been all that notoriety. The boy Max was attacked by some other boy; he probably provoked the attack. These Germans are so savage. But where was someone to protect him? Mr. Fletcher is a minister, but he was very remiss. We all agree on that. Where was the housekeeper? After all, a woman her—"

"Age," supplied Dr. McManus, understandingly.

Mrs. Guston bit her lip. "I'm sure she is very competent. I hear no complaints. But, after all, five children! Practically unprotected. Mr. Fletcher isn't married; he can't expect hired help to care for these children. So they will be neglected, their health and welfare ignored, their education abandoned. I saw that he"—and again she looked at Johnny with malevolence—"has a really dreadful person teaching them, as he says. Teaching! Why, the woman's senile! She's over seventy! We had to force her out of the"—and her face twisted as if she tasted something nasty—"the public school, though a priest made a fuss about getting her a pension. Really! She isn't fit to be in charge of a kindergarten. We discovered she hasn't a modern teaching certificate; she attended some nuns' school a thousand years ago, which wasn't even accredited then! Just imagine!"

"Frightful," said the doctor.

"Miss Coogan speaks, reads, and writes three languages," said Johnny, and he stood up. His heart was hammering. He continued in a lower voice, "Besides English. She is a fine mathematician. She knows more history and English literature than the average college professor. Father John Kanty assured me of that himself."

She bridled, lifted up her beetle eyes to him so that the glaring white below them shone. "Really, Mr. Fletcher! Do you take the word of an ignorant Polish priest?"

Johnny wanted to hit her. His face must have betrayed his desire, for she shrank back. But he kept his voice even: "You lie when you say that, Mrs. Guston. An ignorant Polish priest? I thought you were one of the lovers of humanity, as your kind calls itself. Father John Kanty was graduated from Notre Dame. Did you ever hear of Notre Dame, Mrs. Guston?"

"Are you calling me a liar, sir?" she exclaimed, outraged.

"I am, madam. When you say that priest, my friend, is ignorant, then you are either a fool or a liar. Take your choice."

She clenched her hands on her hard leather bag. She was one force of concentrated malice. "I refuse to argue with you about the priest. Here are these children, about to become public charges, with a bachelor foster father, who has shown some undesirable traits of character by provoking some innocent young boy into attacking him!" She flicked an eye at Johnny's scar. "We know the details. You're not sending the children to school. You can't take care of them. May I ask, Mr. Fletcher, what your salary is?"

Johnny replied bitterly, a sick lump of hatred in his throat: "I believe it is two thousand five hundred dollars a year."

She laughed disagreeably. "Well, what a lot of money to support seven people on! Even though your house is free, and your fuel and telephone. How do you expect to feed, educate, clothe, and supply medical attention for five children?"

She preened. "Al, you know I'm not the kind just to think. I act. So I appealed to the Children's Aid Society. And they agree with me that Mr. Fletcher must be subpoenaed to appear in Children's Court—dear old Judge Bridges, you know, who always has children's welfare at heart—and made to show why these children should not be placed in individual foster homes where they'll get proper attention, or, if the court rules that this would make them public charges in fact, they must be deported to the countries of their origin."

"It's already in the hands of the Children's Aid Society, and Judge Bridges knows about all this?" asked the doctor in a silky voice.

Johnny, dumfounded, began to tremble violently. Despair made his eyes flicker. He approached the triumphant woman and said in a low voice, "Are you an animal? You say you know all about these children. Do you know they'll die if they are separated?" But he could not go on. He was overwhelmed with horror. This was some nightmare; it was not really happening. The room fled from his sight, and he was running, again, across the moonlit field toward the executioner's house, with the wolf pack before him. He could actually feel the flailing of his legs, the loud and aching thunder of his heart, the sound of his own prayers in his ears. His children—they were threatened with the executioner's house again, threatened with death, with things worse than death —loneliness, hatred, abandonment. He could not believe it. His eyes looked at Mrs. Guston like the eyes of a dying man.

"You are condemning my children to death," he said, and the sickness of death was in his own mouth.

"I don't think so," said the woman, almost caroling. "After all, we are sending so much money to Europe, and there are places. The children will be happier among their own kind."

"Gussie, you said that it's already in the hands of the Children's Aid Society, and will soon be brought up in Children's Court?" asked the doctor.

"Yes, Al. We thought we ought to move fast, for the children's sake."

Now Dr. McManus stood up. His face was still genial. "Who do you mean by 'we,' Gussie?"

She hesitated, moistened the vicious, painted scarlet of her thin lips. "Well, Al, there are people, even in Barryfield —which you hate—who have the interest of children at heart. My league, for instance. And—others."

"But, it's out of your hands now, Gussie?"

"I'm afraid so, Al." She picked up her bag and gloves, smiling with satisfaction.

"I'm wondering, Gussie," said the doctor in a gentle voice, "if one of the others isn't Mac Summerfield. You're good friends with Mac, aren't you?" The doctor sighed. "Often wondered why Ben married you. But you did have some cash, didn't you? Often look at Ben, with his miserable face, and pity him."

She could not look away from the doctor. For his face was dark with loathing.

"Gussie, you were never interested in people in all your life, except when they could advance you or give you social position. Gussie, you know something? You hate children; you hate everybody. Have you ever tried to find out anything about anybody, except how to do them harm? You've known me a long time, Gussie. You never found out, in all that time, anything about me, except that I'm a reactionary, as your kind says. If you'd given me any real interest you'd have known that this is my church, and this is my parson, Johnny Fletcher, here."

"Your—your church?" she whispered, almost inaudibly.

"Why sure, Gussie. It was my dad's church too. But you're not interested in churches, are you? Bet you never went in one since you were baptized. Bet if you ever look at one you just think of the day when you hope they'll be torn down."

Johnny, looking at her, remembered the faces of the women who had leaped in the moonlight toward the executioner's house to do death to children. He had said to them then, "Forgive me." He closed his eyes. He could not endure looking at this woman. He could not say in his heart, "Forgive her."

Dr. McManus's voice could not have been more friendly and amiable. "Gussie, you've gone too far this time. Had you just waited, and come here first, without setting the Children's Aid Society and the Children's Court after the parson, we could have settled things between us in a nice and friendly way. And so I'm telling you something. If the parson loses the children, that day I call in poor Ben's notes, all of them. And his banker's my friend." He scratched his cheek reflectively. "Poor Ben. Well, let's see. Judge Bridges's boy is general manager at the mill. He knows all about lumber.

Think I'll back him with the money I loaned Ben. The judge'll listen to reason, perhaps. He's not a bad old coot. And his boy's the apple of his eye."

The woman sat up, her face bluish.

"You can't, you can't, you don't dare, you don't dare! Why, I'll—I'll tell Mr. Summerfield. Why, you don't dare!"

The doctor said in that silky tone, "Gussie, I'm surprised at you. Mac Summerfield? Why, Gussie, when he knows something I am thinking of telling him, he'll drum you out of town, Gussie. A lying scandal you spread about his daughter, Lorry, who's the heart of his life. I traced it back to you."

Johnny put his hand on the doctor's arm, and said, "The children! The children will hear!"

"I hope so," said the doctor. "They'll know, once and for all, that people like this female can't hurt them in this country."

Dr. McManus took Mrs. Guston's lean shoulders in his powerful hands and wrenched her to her feet. He shook her as if she were a wooden doll. "Sue me for striking you, Gussie. I know lots about you. It'll make a good story. And now, get out!"

Still holding her by the shoulders, he pushed her to the door. Johnny opened it for him. The doctor shoved her outside on the stoop. And there she stood, shaking with impotent rage and fear and menace.

"Go and tell poor old Ben what is going to happen to him, Gussie," he said. "That is, if you go through with your plan."

The doctor slammed the door hard. He dusted off his hands. "Well, what's the matter with you, son? If you're going to puke, better run upstairs fast. You're green."

"Why," said Johnny in a trembling voice, "I don't think that woman's human. What have I done to her that brought her here, that made her—?"

Dr. McManus grinned. He puffed a little. "Remember your sermon last Sunday, son? It was in the papers. That set her off. You're dangerous to her, Rollo."

He waddled to the door of the dining room while Johnny followed. The children were eating in silence. Miss Coogan was reading to them, her kind old face still very pale and strained. She looked at the doctor steadily. "I kept on reading."

"Good," said the doctor. He studied the children's quiet faces. It was evident that they had overheard too much. He put his hand on Johnny's shoulder. "Nobody's got anything to worry about," he said. "Nobody. I've got the best lawyers in the state. Remember what your Pa said, kids? We've got the law here."

17

Saturday was a dull, dank day. The fading trees which had scintillated the day before like golden sequins now stood clad in colorless tatters. The mountains loomed through the industrial smoke in faint purple over the city. And the air had the all-pervading stench of a choking foundry, acrid and sickening.

Johnny walked slowly around the edges of the back yard, accompanied by young Lon Harding, who carried a staggering bundle of very young trees, the fragile roots wrapped in wet burlap. The children trailed behind, intent and eager. Even Jean was there, pushed by Mrs. Burnsdale, the wheel chair rocking and wobbling. Nothing could keep him away. He winced with pain, but his pale eyes shone. Little Emilie, much weaker now, held tightly to Kathy's hand. Pietro leaped about the yard like an impatient but happily capering faun, while Max walked sedately beside the wheel chair and helped Mrs. Burnsdale.

"Jean, being the oldest, has first choice of the trees, and where they should be set," said Johnny, who carried a big spade. The miserable late-afternoon light cast no shadows; it seemed to Johnny that they all moved in a soundless, smothering world of silence and unreality. At the mention of his name, Jean indicated to the puffing Mrs. Burnsdale and straining Max that they should hurry. They triumphantly brought the wheel chair to the front. "Apples," said Jean. "Two apples."

"All right, kid," said Lon Harding, in his hoarse young voice. "Show me where." He removed his leather jacket and took the spade from Johnny. Seriously, he began to dig where Jean had excitedly indicated. The burlap was removed from the tender roots, and they were inserted in the ground. Jean leaned forward in his chair and watched the wet earth being thrown into the hole and then tamped around the tree. When the two saplings stood upright, Jean sighed deeply and contentedly.

Max was next. "Pears," he said, in a religiously solemn voice. He came closer as Lon dug. Max shyly pulled his skullcap out of his pocket, put it on his head, and intoned in Hebrew very softly, "Praise be to God, King of the Universe, who hath sanctified us through His Commandments, and hath ordained us participants in creation in the planting of trees."

Johnny listened intently, his halting knowledge of the ancient language barely translating for him. "What's he saying?" asked Lon, wiping away his sweat.

"He's calling attention to the fact that there is only God, and all things are in God, even these little trees," said Johnny.

Lon blushed brightly, in embarrassment. "Yeah," he said, as he took up the spade again. "Guess he's right. Never thought of that before. Y'know, sir, after all you've been telling me, I kind of forgot there were differences—in people and things."

He leaned on the spade a moment. "If it's so, what the kid is saying, why don't we get together? I keep telling the other kids. Know what? They look at me as if I'm nuts or something." He grinned, straightened up, and flexed his muscles. "The only thing is, I'm stronger than they are. I keep my knife in my pocket, and they know I can get it out faster than they can get out theirs. And so I'm still head of the gang." He peered at Johnny. "Perhaps it ain't right, carrying my knife around and watching the kids for dirty work?"

Johnny smiled. "I've heard that the old prophets were

258

pretty good with their fists, and some of them carried swords, too. After all, you've got to protect yourself. People don't like weaklings, you know. A prophet, a leader, should be a doughty man, as the English used to say."

"That's Chaucer," said Lon, starting another hole. Johnny was surprised. "Oh, sure, I read Chaucer," Lon continued nonchalantly. "If you read the footnotes, you kind of get what he's digging. I write poems, too, sometimes." He rubbed his hand over his round and bristling head, sheepishly. His lean, tough face colored again. He hitched his tight blue jeans about his waist and tightened the absurd, broad belt with its enormous buckle. He looked about him, scowling, as if confronting lesser punks. He said darkly, to no one in particular, "Just let anyone get ideas! Man!"

He frowned formidably. "The kid with the yellow hair next?"

"I'm a girl," said Kathy, with rebuke. "And you're just a boy."

"Okay, okay!" said Lon throwing out his arms. "I don't fight with ladies. Just tell me what you want, and this cube will plant 'em."

Pietro, who was bouncing about eagerly, shouted, "Cube! Cube! That is square! Four corners!" His bright black eyes gleamed in the sulfurous light. "See, I know!"

"That's right," said Johnny, hugging his shoulder briefly, but looking at Lon Harding. "Foursquare." The older boy blushed again, scowled at Kathy. "Well, what do you want?"

"Peaches," said Kathy, emphasizing her maternal air of authority. "And here is the place." She indicated with the tip of her new shoe, black patent leather with a strap across her sturdy arch. "Okay, peaches," said Lon respectfully. She supervised the planting of the tiny trees. When Lon bent down to insert the delicate roots in the hole she wiped his forehead with her own neat handkerchief, as calmly and as abstractedly as a mother. He glanced up at her with his sly, knowing glance. "Right, Mom?" he asked. "You kind of look like a peach yourself," he added.

As it was now Pietro's turn he was almost beside himself with excitement. He jumped up and down, grinning, clapping his hands. He suddenly sang, and his brilliant young voice, filled with exultation, startled even Johnny. It was not a song anyone knew; it came from some long-lost memory.

"That kid's real nervous," commented Lon, after the final trill fell to earth like shining rain.

"Well, yes, he is nervous," said Johnny in a low voice. "After all, he's had some terrible experiences."

Lon eyed him tolerantly. "That ain't what I mean, sir. I mean he's got something with that voice. I got some old records home; one of them's Martinelli's."

Johnny, confronted with the slang of the new generation, laughed. But he made a note in his mind to call Father John Kanty's attention to Pietro's voice; such a voice should be in a choir. He thought of his own choir and sighed.

"Cherries!" Pietro finally announced, and bounced wildly. He had tasted cherries in Paris, when Johnny had bought them for him. Lon sank his spade in the rich black soil. "Say," he said to Pietro, "stop getting in my way. This kid can dance, too," he remarked to Johnny with admiration. The cherry trees were planted.

Now it was Emilie's turn. The little girl looked translucent and exhausted. All at once she began that awful, familiar coughing again, her dwindled face turning red. Johnny lifted her into his arms, and she pressed her convulsed features into his neck. Lon listened to the strangled, gasping sounds, and he turned his head aside, looking into the distance.

Johnny said softly, "It's her heart. And this smog is bad for her."

"Yeah," muttered Lon, who knew Emilie's story. His hard thin lips parted and he drew in a whistling breath. He waited until Emilie could breathe quietly again, and then he studied the child, his eyes narrowed and bitter. He put his hand on the tiny arm, which was encased in a bright-blue sweater Mrs. Burnsdale had made for her. He could feel the fragile bones trembling under the skin. He said, and his voice was low and loving, "All right, baby. You have the plums."

Emilie's cheeks were running with her involuntary tears, but she gave Lon a radiant smile and he turned away quickly. Kathy fastened the buttons of the warm sweater with deft fingers; Max gazed at the child, Jean's face tightened, and even Pietro was sobered. Emilie leaned from Johnny's arms to watch the planting of her trees. When it was finished she crowed with delight, and insisted upon kissing Lon, to his immense but touching embarrassment. "Better watch that little skirt when she grows up," he said to Johnny. But he knew.

There were two trees or shrubs left. Lon looked at them, lying waiting at his feet. Then, without a glance at Johnny, he said in an offhand voice, "The fruit trees won't be much for several years. The big kids can wait. But I got something for the baby. Lilacs. Real white French lilacs. Planted a couple last year in our back yard, and you oughtta smell them. Man! They'll come out next spring."

That piercing pain which was becoming familiar to Johnny ran through his chest again. He pressed Emilie to him. He said to the child, "Emilie has plums, but she has flowers too. Beautiful flowers, just for Emilie."

No one spoke, not even the jealous Pietro. The little boy's eyes looked at Emilie and shone with tears. So, thought Johnny, even the children know. They knew out of the torturous wisdom they had acquired in their own agony.

Now they all solemnly contemplated the infant plants. There was not a trunk which even Emilie could not have encompassed with her hand. But small as they were, they stood gallantly in a rising wind, bending and swaying like wands. In a few years, thought Johnny, these heroic little things will be thick, tall, and strong, blossoming in the spring, alive with bees, and heavy with fruit in the fall. They're like the children. In a way they *are* the children. He looked at the lilac bushes, and again his heart contracted. They will remember Emilie every spring, he thought, when the flowers are out. He tried to send out a prayer from his anguish, but there was no answer to his silent cry of sorrow.

The children were fascinated by their trees. Their faces glowed. They walked about them, touching them with gentle fingers. Emilie watched from her nest in Johnny's arms; Mrs. Burnsdale uncomplainingly trundled Jean to his own trees. It was hard to take the children into the house again, where there was hot chocolate waiting in the warm kitchen, and large sugar cookies and a dish of red apples.

"I wish," said Johnny, "that you'd let me pay for the trees, Lon."

The boy's expression became cold. "They were cheap," he said. "Almost nothing. Besides, after you found me those car-washing jobs, and jobs washing windows and putting up storm windows, I got enough cash. I wanted to give something to the kids. I'll be watching the trees too. First I ever planted, except the lilacs at home."

He gazed at Johnny with the unreadable eyes of the street-fashioned young. "Mom's home now, all the time. And I got myself a job delivering groceries in a truck on Saturdays; almost enough, with Pop's new Saturday job, to pay off the installments. The man who sold us the stove's willing to wait until we can get around to him. Not a bad joe. And mom's looking better every day, and we got new curtains. Kind of nice to see her when I come home from school." He picked up another cooky, and chewed it casually. "Dr. McManus gave me a job, too, for the winter. Shoveling snow."

"But when will you do your homework?" asked Johnny anxiously.

The boy let out a rude snort of laughter. "Man! I don't do it! Don't need to. What there is, when I do it, I do at our life-adjustment class. Under the desk, on my knees. Mrs. Guston got that one in—life adjustment."

Johnny was puzzled. He said, "Well, life adjustment doesn't sound too bad. Tell me about it, Lon."

"Guess things have changed since you were a kid," Lon said, staring at him cunningly. Johnny immediately felt a twinge of senility. The boy went on, "Pop doesn't have much education, himself, but after you talked to him couple weeks ago he decided he ought to be interested in what I was doing. So first thing he asks me about was my school. You could see he was being conscientious, as you told him, but he wasn't really interested. Not till he looked through my books." Lon picked up another cooky, and chewed thoughtfully. "Funny, I never thought the old man was very bright. But he began to read my schoolbooks, and then he blew his top. He jumps up, and yells, and keeps stabbing pages with his fingers. Mom had her palpitation, as she calls it. And Pop says, 'What the hell they teaching you kids nowadays? Where's history? Where's arithmetic? Where's English? Where's George Washington and geography? And what's this crap'—excuse me, but that's what Pop says—'consumer economics, and how to have a successful date, emotional health, and how to keep your teeth white, and the dynamics of group dancing?' And I says to Pop, 'that's what they call dynamic, functional learning.' Then he blew his top again."

Johnny's face darkened. "Is that what they're teaching you in school, actually, Lon?"

"That's right, mister." The boy grinned at him. "Well, Pop goes off up in the attic and he brings down his old schoolbooks. Don't know why he kept them. After all, he's an old so-and-so, nearly forty. And he yells, and throws the books at me, and says, 'Ninth-grade books—1918! Look at them!'" Lon's tough face sharpened. "Well, mister, I look. And you know what? Why, we kids in senior high couldn't do the algebra problems in those books, and we don't know anything about the ancient history they taught way back there, and there was a French textbook, first year high, and American history in one whole book, not what we have now, social sciences, and an English grammar book that even the bright joes in our class wouldn't know anything about. Diagrams and things. And civics. Who knows about civics in the schools? And commercial geography, with big maps. I look through the civics, and first time I ever heard about how cases get to the Supreme Court, and the functions of the Supreme Court."

Lon was speaking again. "We got a good handball team at our school. Oh, they teach us lots of sports! Pop loves sports himself, but he says all that sports in school do is to take up our time so we can't learn anything or want to learn anything. Well, we play the other public high schools. And then there's a private school in town, just one. The Beaverbrook School for Boys. And that private school challenges us to a game. The principal didn't want that. He refuses. So the Beaverbrook joes needle us. So the principal agrees, when we threatened to stage a strike. We wanted to show those high-class joes with their convertibles and their girls with pink cashmere sweaters and their golf clubs. Then the principal gets us together and talks about us beating the pants off those joes. Well, we won the game, and we didn't even work up a sweat. But it's funny; a couple of us got to know a couple of their guys, and one of them's a friend of mine now. His old man is what our teachers calls an absentee landlord or something; he owns stock in the New York Central and other railroads, and just lives here because he was born here. And, yeah, something else I didn't think about until now. Bob's old man was a miner, right here in Barryfield, and he invented an automatic coal-mining machine, and an automatic warning

263

device when the coal gas begins to get thick. Bob's proud of his old man. Wish my dad would invent a machine or something, so I could have a convertible myself, and one of those dolls too." His young voice was wistful. He sighed. "Guess I'll never have a chance to get anywhere. Just for the fun of it I applied for admission to a university where they got a wonderful engineering school, and they sent me an old entrance exam, and, damn it, I couldn't answer half the questions! Maybe Pop's right."

He forgot Johnny and brooded, and his face was no longer young but filled with a mature anger and frustration, and his eyes glittered with furious resentment. Johnny saw this, and said to himself, There must be tens of thousands, perhaps millions, of boys like this one.

Lon's hands began to play with that huge belt buckle which Johnny had thought was touchingly absurd. And then he saw that it was a weapon, a lethal weapon attached to a thick, wide belt of leather.

Lon's sharp voice, so devoid of proper diction and so slurring of consonants, broke in again, "Well, Bob and I got to talking about school. He's a senior too. He showed me his books. You know what? I've been getting books from the library and studying all kinds of things, by myself, but Jesus! Bob's books were Greek to me! They had all the things Pop says he learned in school, and I didn't. Nothing about 'group and social adjustments,' 'life adjustments,' and machines, and other crap. Mister, I say crap, and this time I don't apologize. Nothing about what to do on a date, or insulting things about brushing your teeth to make them white. Jesus, we know about toothbrushes, don't we, and girls are just girls, aren't they?"

"Yes," said Johnny.

Lon stood up, tall and lithe, and he hooked his hands in his belt, and his lean, intelligent head was held high. "Well, Bob got me a midyear sophomore exam. Here I am, a senior in the Lenox Street High School, and I answered seven out of every ten sophomore questions right! The other three? Never heard anything about them. And Bob says it wasn't an accident; it was planned that way. So he gets me sophomore textbooks, and here I am in high school, a senior, and I study up on them, and finally, I pass them—the sophomore exams.

Bob sneaked me out a copy. And this year he got me junior textbooks, and I'm studying them."

He stared before him, lost in grim and furious thought. "You know what they say in our school? There shouldn't be competitve exams! No 'child,' they say, should be made to feel inferior; it might hurt his life adjustment. Just knowledge isn't enough. But then we're just due to drive trucks and work machines, anyway."

He caught Kathy gazing at him intently, her blue eyes very serious. "Hello, yellow hair," he said.

She said precisely, "You are a fine boy. I think I shall marry you when I grow up."

He waved a grubby, calloused hand largely. "Oh sure. Just give me a ring when you're eghteen. I'll take you out on my truck route, and we'll eat hamburgers." He turned back to Johnny, whose pallor and strain stood out on his face. "Bob takes me to his school one day. A small, dark-brick school on a nice street. Old school. Old steps. Kind of high, pointed windows. Nothing like our school, yellow brick and big hunks of glass making walls all around. Old beat-up desks, fastened down; ours can be shoved around to make things cozy, when the dumb kids want to sound off. The rooms in Bob's school are dinky; floors polished, but dark and uneven. We have bright, fresh linoleum, with designs, and our rooms are big as hell. But, you know something, mister? There was kind of a smell in Bob's school—"

"I know," said Johnny, trying to smile through his dread. "It's called the odor of learning."

Johnny moved a spoon on the plastic table top. What can I do for this boy? He thought of the money he had placed in the bank for the children, the money given him by Dr. Stevens and the soldiers. "For the kids," they had said. And here was another of the lost and the betrayed. Johnny came to a quick decision. "Lon, you told me you wanted to be an engineer. How'd you like to go to Bob's school for your last year? It isn't too late to enroll."

Lon eyed him, astounded. He said slowly, "Look, mister, are you nuts?"

"No, Lon. Never mind about your clothes. I'm sure you have something else besides those jeans, and the belt—and things. And I'll help some way. Listen, Lon. I'll call the principal of Bob's school. You'll get in! And—I have a friend, Dr. McManus. And then, Lon, when you graduate, with the honors you'll get, there'll be a good university. You can work your way through. I did."

Lon could not speak. He looked into Johnny's dark-blue eyes, which were full of fervor and resolution. "If I can just save one of you," said Johnny, "it will be something. Just one of you. And you'll remember, and later you'll help."

"Papa knows best," said Kathy, from out of some forgotten memory of discipline.

The others echoed her, soberly. Pietro screamed impatiently, "Lon must do as Papa says!" The volatile little boy could not understand the older boy's absolute stillness, his fixed expresion, his fallen, limp hands.

"You mean it, sir?" Lon said huskily.

Johnny stood up. "Yes, Lon." He put his hand on the lean shoulder and shook it affectionately. "Think about it. Call me tomorrow. Talk to your parents. It's getting dark, and you ought to be on your way home."

18

The children could talk of nothing else but their trees. They sat about the table with Johnny, eating heartily, except for little Emilie. There was color in Jean's sunken cheeks, and even in Max's. Max was really the wonder, thought Johnny, with a satisfaction that almost overcame his despondency. The shut and empty look had gone from his brown eyes; he did not speak often, but he looked about him with interest and attention, and when he caught Johnny's eye he would smile shyly. Kathy said, as she urged Emilie to eat, "Isn't it wonderful about Emilie's flowers? We didn't get any flowers. Lon must like Emilie the best of all."

Immediately there was a little silence, and every youthful pair of eyes was turned sorrowfully upon the child, who was smiling with proud radiance. How much they know! thought Johnny. "Emilie give flowers," said Emilie. Yes, thought Johnny, with the sorrow wizening his heart again, you will give flowers, my darling, for many years. Now his fierce rebellion tore him once more, and with this rose his old hatred for those who had almost shattered these children's lives, not only in Europe, but in America. There is no end to man's evil, he said to himself, and he remembered how only a short time before he had had compassion upon mankind for the evil it embraced every hour of every day.

"Lord," he prayed silently, "why didst Thou come? Why didst Thou climb Calvary, and hang upon the Cross? Two thousand years—and man is no kinder or more merciful. Out of love, Thou tookest on his flesh, yet he gives Thee no love in return. How lonely it must be for Thee, out in those spaces, remembering!"

He thought of that loneliness, and he was pierced by a fresh and more powerful sorrow, and this time for God.

"Well, well, eating again, stuffing yourselves at the expense of those who work!" a familiar voice squeaked. The children raised a cry of pleasure, but there was no pleasure on Johnny's face when he turned to see Dr. McManus, more uncouth and untidy than every, more formidable of expression. "Any apple pie left?" asked the doctor, after a swift glance at Johnny.

Johnny stood up. "I don't think so," he said. "Besides, I want to talk to you, doctor."

The old man raised one of his craggy brows. "Talk to, not with, eh?" he said. "Remember, I'm your senior, parson. Don't be disrespectful. All right, come on." He waved his hand at the children and went with Johnny into the parlor and sat down.

Johnny told him everything about Lon. When Johnny had finished, the doctor was silent for some time, twisting his cigarette reflectively in his mouth. Then he exclaimed, "Thought what little cash you had was for your kids! Your idea is the damnedest one I ever heard! Of course you aren't serious."

"I am," said Johnny firmly. "And that's where you come in. You know Mr. Beaverbrook. I wish you would speak to him and try to get Lon into his school. I'm not worrying about the money."

"God will provide," said the doctor sardonically.

Johnny looked at him straightly. "He always has," he replied. "He provided what little money I have; He sent me here; and He gave all of us you, and Sol Klein, and Dr. Kennedy, and Father John Kanty, and Rabbi Chortow, and Lorry. I'm not sure why I'm here yet, but perhaps I'll find out eventually."

The doctor looked at his newspaper. "Perhaps sooner than you think, Rover boy. All right. I'll see Roger Beaverbrook; you commit me to the most hellish and ridiculous things. I don't know why I stand for you. You've upset my whole life." He looked slowly about the parlor. "What a foul room. By the way, has the roof been leaking?"

"Of course," said Johnny, smiling. "But I took your advice, and we use pans."

But the doctor was serious again. "This was my father's home. I always thought it was miserable. No one would do anything about it, though. Anyway, I don't want to pull it down. Perhaps"—The doorbell rang, and Johnny got up and went to the door. He said over his shoulder, "But we'll still have to do something about the deliberate mediocrity of the school curriculum, and about the bright kids." He opened the door, turning on the raw bulb over the stoop as he did so. Three men stood on the threshold, the ruddy-faced little Dan McGee with his pile of white waves over his round head, a tall, robust blond man with very pale blue eyes, and a slender medium-sized man of about fifty-five with an anxious face which was singularly ghostlike.

Dan said, "Hello, Mr. Fletcher." He indicated the last man. "This here is Mr. Glen Dowdy, one of the mine owners around here. And this," indicating the smiling blond stranger with his remarkably well-tailored clothes and air of sophisticated assurance, "is Mr. Lars Swensen, who's got credentials. Can we come in and talk to you?"

Johnny looked at Mr. Swensen, puzzled. If this was a union man, he was an entirely new kind. He glanced at Mr. Swensen's smooth, big white hands, and thought, This man's never been a miner. A "city" man. And in what they call "Brooks Brothers" clothing.

The minister admitted the three into the house, still frowning in some bewilderment. Dr. McManus raised his formidable eyebrows, focused for a hard moment on Mr. Swensen, and thought, So this is the Swensen Lorry's told me about. Mac Summerfield's friend. How come he's interested in our piddling little mines around here?

Johnny introduced Mr. Swensen to the doctor, and Mr. Swensen murmured courteously. Dr. McManus grunted, shifted on his huge buttocks. "Heard about you, Mr. Swensen," he said. "Friend of Mac Summerfield's, ain't you?"

Mr. Swensen smiled his happy smile. "As a matter of fact, I do know Mr. Summerfield slightly. I think we've met once or twice, but I can't remember where."

The doctor was silent as he lit his cigarette. Swensen was lying. Why? A man usually had an urgent reason for lying. What was Swensen's reason now? Suddenly McManus became aware that Swensen was giving Johnny a long, appraising look, a thoughtful look, a weighing look, and the doctor sat upright in his chair. A sharp sense of uneasiness caused a tingling in his hands and feet.

"What're you doing here, Mr. Swensen?" asked the doctor, suddenly and bluntly.

Mr. Swensen smiled again. "You might say, doctor, that I'm interested in justice."

"Um," said Dr. McManus. He looked at Johnny, who was utterly baffled, and then at Mr. McGee and Mr. Dowdy, who slumped dejectedly in their chairs. "Justice," said the doctor. "Seems I heard somewhere that justice has got a thousand names. Depends, too, on your politics, your religion, your employer or your employees, and even your wife. Loosest word in the English language, which sure is a very loose language. Means anything at all, to anybody." He grunted as if amused. "Studied semantics, myself. We ought to have a more precise language, like the French. So we'd each know what we mean. Now what would you mean by justice, Mr. Swensen?"

Mr. Swensen appeared to be enjoying himself. He gave all his attention to the doctor. "In this case," he said gently, "justice means the right thing for the miners of Barryfield."

Mr. Dowdy coughed miserably. Dr. McManus looked amazed and said, "So you're interested in getting justice for our miners, are you? That sure is damn nice of you, Mr. Swensen! But how come? What's it to you? What's this all about?"

Then he turned quickly to Johnny, before anyone could answer him. "Hey!" he exclaimed. "Think I'm getting an idea about Mr. Swensen here, who knows Mac Summerfield, he says, 'slightly.' Johnny, you got tonight's paper here? Get it. Always did think I could qualify as a private eye."

Johnny hesitated, blinking with his bafflement, looking at the other three men for enlightenment. Then, as no one spoke, he went to his desk and lifted the current issue of the

Press and gave it mutely to Dr. McManus. The doctor stood up, balancing himself on his broad, short legs, the newspaper concealing the upper part of his body. "Johnny, here's your last sermon. Mac's commented on it tonight. That's why I came over. I'll read the editorial, and then we'll begin to understand things, I think. All right, listen. Mac speaking:

"A certain breed of so-called liberals are the real despots,' Mr. Fletcher said last Sunday, in the ranting voice of the demagogue.

"'Because the peoples everywhere in the world have demanded decent housing at the expense of the wealthy, a fair share of the profits of capitalism, social security, socialized medicine, and some of the fruits and pleasures of the earth, Mr. Fletcher has denounced them as materialistic parasites.'"

"Why, the damned liar!" cried Johnny with rage. "I spoke of liberty, of the right of a man to choose."

The doctor said mournfully, "Son, you're losing your Christian temper. I heard your sermon. You said that a man has the right to be a real liberal; that is, a man who don't want any government interfering in his affairs so long as he is behaving himself like a decent human being, and don't want any government brooding over him like a cannibal hen, waiting to peck out his eyes if he resents being a helpless chick all his life. You said a real liberal stands for liberty, for the dignity of man, and let the government keep its damn sticky hands off. I remember. But Mac didn't like your sermon. Shut up, and let me go on.

"'The peoples'—get that, Johnny? We're not people in the world any longer, we're 'peoples!'—aren't interested in some mystical reward for their planned suffering on this earth, so, according to Mr. Fletcher, they deserve the wrath of whatever gods have been invented by their oppressors. Is it liberty for a man to starve, to be homeless, to die in absolute poverty, to see his children hungry? Mr. Fletcher implies that is so. If that is free enterprise, we want none of it, and let Mr. Fletcher take notice of that fact. The function of government in the modern world is to care for the welfare of its peoples, to provide food and shelter, free medical attention from physicians who have been taught to serve rather than to earn, and security from the cradle to the grave. Mr. Fletcher, as one of the hired men of the forces of reactionary wealth, denies that this is the function of government. By implication, too, he denounces all unions, for unions are among those modern organizations set up to protect the peoples from starvation and misery.' "

Johnny said, trying to control himself, "The man's not only a liar, but he sounds like a Communist. I wonder how many of his millions he's willing to turn over to the government for all those things?"

"Why," said the doctor calmly, putting down the paper, "none at all. He just wants to be a rich commissar, with thousands of meek slaves. The giving up is going to be done by people who are obstinate enough to believe in liberty, and the right to order their own lives. People like you. You're on the liquidation list, son. And so am I. Too bad. We're just Americans, like most people in this country."

Mr. Swensen was silently amused. His eyes sparkled on Dr. McManus. Now why would this rich old fool of a doctor care what happened to the stinking masses in America? It wasn't in character.

"Nobody," said Dan McGee, "with half a brain listens to what Mac Summerfield says."

"Well, who said the populace ever had more than half a brain, anyway?" asked the doctor.

Mr. Dowdy sighed. "Mac Summerfield's caused more trouble in this town than almost anyone else. He wants to set every man against his neighbor." He smiled faintly at Johnny. "He never had much opposition until you came."

"Damn right!" said the doctor. "Let Mac hire goons to stir up strikes, and cuddle up with the Communists, and no one dares to whimper. Except Johnny. He says it's because he's got God. And maybe he has, Mr. Swensen. And that brings us back to you. What have you got to do with all this? With Mac Summerfield and this stinking editorial? Why are you here?"

Mr. Swensen smiled. He had excellent teeth, the doctor noted. And that smile had long practice behind it. "I came to bring peace to Barryfield," he said. "But nobody's asked me to show what Mr. McGee calls my credentials. Would you like to see them?"

He opened a gold-tooled leather wallet and handed the doctor a card. The doctor frowned at it a moment, then read aloud, "Industrial Relations Foundation, New York, N.Y. Director, Lars Swensen." He rumpled the card in his hand and looked at Mr. Swensen. "I've heard of your organization. Nonprofit. Supported by the fortunes of dead old tycoons they used to call robber barons. Yes, I've heard. Supposed to be a mediation and conciliation outfit between capital and labor during disputes. Funny." The doctor's small stony eyes smiled grimly into space. "Foundation created by tough old rascals who never asked for quarter, or gave any, and were responsible for massacres whenever the poor workingmen tried to organize, or rebelled, or dared to ask for a living wage! Fine old days of exploitation and suffering! I remember something of them myself. Now the old devils leave foundations! Is it conscience? Trying to buy themselves out of hell?"

Mr. Swensen seemed a little surprised. He studied the doctor more closely. The doctor continued, "Well, there's retribution. Seen it work myself. Here's a foundation set up by robbers and murderers to help the sons and grandsons of their own victims. That's irony for you. Like foundations myself, though, when they go in for subsidizing research in medicine and science, and giving scholarships, and advancing money for decent housing, and promoting tolerance and such. Wonderful."

Mr. Swensen was all superior urbanity. "Glad you approve of us, doctor," he said, smiling.

"Don't put words in my mouth!" exclaimed McManus sharply. "I didn't say I approved of you. I was talking about legitimate foundations. All right, so you call yourself a foundation, but all I know about your outfit is what I've just said. So who are you, anyhow? And what are you up to here in Barryfield? Just tell us that. I got a pretty shrewd notion, but I ain't tipping my hand. So come on now, Swensen. Tell us."

Mr. Swensen retained his air of general affability, but there was a distinct hardening of his eyes as he looked at the doctor. "Well, doctor," he said amiably, "if that's what you want I'll gladly tell you. We're what we call trouble shooters. That's why I'm here. We've heard there is a pending strike. We've considered all the facts, and we feel that the miners in this city need help. I'm here to help them."

The doctor stood up, and like a fat and massive old terrier he walked slowly around Mr. Swensen, elaborately considering him. Mr. Swensen preserved an expression of gentle amusement. Now the doctor stood before him. "Swensen, you're a liar. You're not interested in the miners of Barryfield. Who's your real target?"

Mr. Swensen was patient. "Doctor, our motives are purely humanitarian."

"All right. Lie, if you want to," said the doctor, and sat down again. "We'll never get the truth out of you. Dowdy, let's get down to business."

Mr. Dowdy spoke with sick apprehension. "We need to shoal up some of the mine walls. We don't have the money. And now Mac Summerfield's trying to stir up the miners to strike for higher pay. We don't have the money for that either. As things stand, we're lucky if we break even." The mine owner shook his head dismally. "Maybe I'm not very smart; I just don't understand what's happening. Mine Seven's in a bad way, and so is Mine Five, and we got to make them safer if we're to let the men work in there. They're our richest veins. But if we haven't got the money to exploit our best assets, how in the world are we going to pay higher wages? Summerfield knows this, so I just can't figure out what he's up to."

"I can," said Dr. McManus heartily.

"But it doesn't make sense," said Johnny. "If Summerfield knows all this, why in God's name would he choose this time to incite the miners to strike for higher wages?"

The doctor sighed patiently. "That's just the point," he said. "His timing is perfect. Get one thing in your head once and for all. Summerfield ain't interested in the welfare of the miners. That's camouflage. All he wants is trouble."

At last Johnny began to understand, and he turned all his attention to Mr. Swensen. His face became grim and alert. Mr. Swensen returned his scruitny with calm indifference. Johnny was not deceived. He said to himself, with alarm, Why, his eyes look like the eyes of some of the Nazis I saw in Europe! Glass—no emotion, nothing, nothing behind them. Nothing except hate.

"I've gone over Glenn's books, and the books of the other mine owners too," said Mr. McGee in an anxious voice. He pulled his plump torso to the edge of his chair. "They're just barely breaking even. They need more money to make the mines safer, and they don't have it. They can't pay our men more, and that's what I've been telling Mr. Swensen here.

And then, tonight, I thought about Mr. Fletcher. I thought we'd all come here, and maybe Mr. Fletcher could sort of take a hand in this, and show Mr. Swensen there wasn't really any trouble between the miners and the mine owners, except that some of the miners get leaflets from strangers near the shafts."

Mr. Swensen seemed interested. His expression was most friendly.

Mr. McGee went on. "But Mr. Swensen says the men've got to have uniform union wages, like in the big mines, and bigger and better benefits, and a big medical plan, and a big pension plan. Believe me, I'd sure like to see them have all that! Mining's hell. If a man got a hundred dollars a day it wouldn't be enough. I know; I was a miner. Well, anyway, what Mr. Swensen says the miners should have in Barryfield just ain't possible. If Glen and the other mine owners had just made enough money these past twenty years, well, they could've opened new mines, or shored up the best veins they've already got. But they didn't have the money, and these mines they have are pretty well worked out, and now they've begun to operate at a loss. But they keep going, hoping for the best, and things just get worse. And they've always got lawsuits from people who get cracks in their houses when blasting goes on, and so there's another drain on their funds."

"Of course," said Mr. Swensen pleasantly. "The owners must be responsible for the damage they do. But that has no bearing on their other responsibility—to give their miners a decent wage."

Johnny, who could not forget Swensen's eyes, said angrily, "Don't be an idiot. The mine owners invested all they had in the mines; they take the risks, they opened the mines. The miners get their wages; they don't suffer losses like the owners. Do they work for nothing, as Mr. Dowdy seems to be doing? Mr. Dowdy and his friends don't have pension plans for themselves, or sick plans, or unemployment insurance. They just have the anxiety, the straining to keep up with all those plans, the taxes, the worry. And people like you come in here just to make trouble."

He regarded Swensen with open and fiery disgust. "Equal rights do not mean equal rewards. Yet you seem to believe that if Mr. Dowdy practically works for nothing just to keep the mines running, his employees are entitled to a raise. That isn't even Communism. In Russia the miners work as slave labor, with a whip at their backs, and the bureaucrats take all the profits. Is that what you want, under all your philanthropy?"

"Sure," said Dr. McManus, cackling.

"Let's not be childish," said Mr. Swensen. "We are here to discuss matters, not to make foolish accusations. I'm not a Communist, Mr. Fletcher."

The very ill Mr. Dowdy turned to Mr. Swensen. He said imploringly, "You know the truth. You've seen my books yourself. Look, we want to keep the men employed. Haven't you any heart at all? Don't you care about our poor miners? Don't you know what it'll mean to them if they go out on strike? They can't get blood out of a stone, and most of them know it; and Dan here knows it, and he's told them. They're good fellows, our miners, and decent. But a strike'll just mean they'll be out of work, maybe permanent. I don't want to shut down the mines. But if you push me I'll have to, and so will the other owners. What will the miners do then?"

"Oh, they have unemployment insurance," said Mr. Swensen with a slight smile. "They can wait." He gave them all the bright sunshine of his happy smile.

"John L. didn't send you, that's for sure," said Dr. McManus thoughtfully. "He wouldn't. He knows about the mines in Barryfield. There's something or somebody you're after, Swensen."

Mr. Swensen ignored him. He waited for Mr. Dowdy to continue.

"Well," said Mr. Dowdy, "if the men wait—and how long does the insurance last?—they'll just have to wait forever, or get themselves other jobs. I wouldn't blame them if they did. I wouldn't be a miner again for ten thousand a year, something I never made in all my life. I'm going to die soon. Al here has told me. I've got a little insurance for my wife to live on, if she's careful, and I've got a boy in college who'll be a doctor soon. So I'm not worrying much about anything, except the miners. It's getting awful hard for me, now, to work and try to keep things straight and even."

Mr. Swensen remained remote and amused. "Nevertheless, I can't accept all this. The miners in Barryfield must have justice, must receive the same wages as others get in the general mining field. I had hoped," he added regretfully, "that Mr. Fletcher would agree with me, and persuade you to raise the men's wages. It seems that this informal discussion has been just a waste of time."

Johnny moved to him quickly, but Mr. Swensen merely gazed at him reflectively, and with his automatically friendly smile. He said, "I'm wondering about you, Mr. Fletcher. You aren't very important, are you? A small city minister, with a very low salary, probably. Yet, you've acted as a dangerous catalyst here. The question I ask myself is: Why are you here? Who sent you? How have you managed to bring disparate elements together?"

Before Johnny could reply, Dr. McManus put his hand on his shoulder. He grinned. "Who sent him? Why, God, he says. Johnny's what the Bible calls a just man, and that's why you don't understand him. Just men can sure play hob with the world. They always have. That's why they're always getting crucified, or murdered, or assassinated, or hounded into economic excommunication by politicians or their own people. Uncomfortable kind of life."

Mr. Swensen lifted his folded hand to his face, and concealed the lower part of it while he still contemplated Johnny.

"I'm what you see, a minister," said Johnny. "That's all. Never mind me. Do you mean you're going to incite the miners to strike? Then I'll fight you. I'll go to them myself. They'll listen to me. I was a miner once. I know their language."

Mr. Swensen suddenly laughed. "You think they'll listen, Mr. Fletcher? When did what you'd call reason ever win over a prospect of more money?"

Mrs. Burnsdale knocked on the door, then opened it a trifle. "The children want to say good night, Mr. Fletcher," she said. Her gray hair was damp and curling from the heat and moisture of the kitchen. Her small eyes were tense, and she glanced quickly at Dr. McManus and jerked her head in a signal to him.

"All right, in a minute," said Johnny.

Mrs. Burnsdale's face disappeared, but Dr. McManus got up and casually walked out after her. "I'll help with Jean's chair," he said.

He found the children standing very still in the kitchen,

close together, in a semicircle around Jean, and the doctor saw, with a curious knotting of his heart, that old look on their young faces, the look of frozen terror, hatred, and distrust. They were alien again, lost and stricken, and prepared for flight and struggle. Even Kathy's smooth yellow hair had risen over her round head like a mane. Worst of all, to the doctor, was the fact that Jean's left hand was grasping a long sharp knife, and Pietro held a hammer, and Max's eyes were vacant. Little Emilie had hidden her face against Kathy's shoulder, and she was trembling violently.

Dr. McManus stopped. "Well," he said in a low voice, "now what in the name of God?"

Mrs. Burnsdale, near the kitchen window, beckoned to him imperatively. Dr. McManus started toward her, then stopped, inches away from Jean, who gazed upward at him with his pale eyes, filled now with primitive ferocity. "Jean," said the doctor sharply, "put down that knife. Reach over to the table, and put it down. Now."

Jean clutched the knife tighter; the children moved in closer to him. Dr. McManus could hardly recognize them. He was terribly dismayed, and he thought, It's no use, all the work Johnny has done, all the prayers, all the suffering, all the faith. But I knew that, from the beginning. When'll he learn, himself? His heart, so old, embittered, calloused, suddenly ached for Johnny, and tears came into his eyes. "I don't know what's wrong with you kids," he said, and his voice actually faltered. "But when you look like this, act like this, you aren't human. You aren't your father's children any more." Jean still held the knife strongly, but someone, one of the girls, suddenly whimpered. "All we've done for you is nothing, I see," said the doctor.

The wild ferocity subsided in Jean's eyes, but he held the knife like a bayonet. "The doctor doesn't understand," he said. "It's Papa who is in danger."

He pointed the knife at the window. "The doctor will please look?"

Dr. McManus regarded him in astonishment, then went to the window. The knife brushed against his sleeve, and he heard the hiss of it. Mrs. Burnsdale had drawn the cracked shade; she was crying silently, and now she pulled the shade away from the black glass. The doctor peered out, and could not believe what he saw. The window looked out upon the yard, and the fence that surrounded it, and beyond the fence stood a soundless wall of people, men and women, in motionless and ominous ranks. They passed out of sight, the wall of them, and around the corner, and in front of the house, where scores more must have been staring speechlessly at the front door.

"What?" whispered the doctor incredulously. "What—what do they want?"

"I don't know," said Mrs. Burnsdale, her voice broken. "I heard a noise out there a few minutes ago; thought it was thunder, or something falling, and I thought about Mr. Fletcher's car, and I was worried about it, and I peeked out to see. And then I saw all those people! Kathy saw how frightened I was, and she looked and told the boys, and then Jean wheeled right to the drawer and got the knife, and Pietro got the hammer—and everything began again." She sobbed, and the children looked at her soberly, and Emilie wailed. "I never *saw* such a thing!" cried Mrs. Burnsdale. "I'm scared, doctor. It takes a lot to scare me, but this time I am. This is a mob, doctor, and I can't think why, except that maybe someone's trying to hurt Mr. Fletcher again."

"They want to kill Papa," said Jean. Pietro jumped and waved the hammer dangerously in the air. "Kill, kill!" he shrieked thinly. "We kill them!"

"Don't be stupid," said the doctor, leaving the window and planting himself before the children. "Think this is Europe? This country ain't a land of sweetness and light; it's just like every other country. Except we got the law, and it works, and I'm going to call the law right this minute. Jean, the knife, please." He held out his hand, and Jean, after a moment, gave it to him. Pietro threw the hammer on the floor. Kathy suddenly smiled, and Emilie's sobs faded away. Max said, "The law."

Dr. McManus went into the parlor. None of the four men was speaking now. Johnny was sitting on his desk and regarding Mr. Swensen with a black face of frozen hatred, of which the doctor heartily approved. Mr. Swensen had an air of bored waiting, and his head was half turned toward the outside door. The doctor's old flesh prickled and tingled as he looked at him. But it was necessary to be calm. Dan McGee and Mr. Dowdy sat side by side in an attitude of complete dejection. "Where are the children?" Johnny asked in surprise, taking his attention away from Mr. Swensen.

Dr. McManus said heavily, "I've sent them upstairs. And now I want to use the telephone." He passed Mr. Swensen on the way to Johnny's desk, and said, slowly and deliberately, "You murdering sonofabitch." He picked up the telephone and said, "Police, and make it fast. Here's the number of the house—name of street—"

He scrutinized the faces in the room. Three of them had turned utterly blank. One had not. The doctor said to that face, "You knew. You planned it all. If—anything happens—you won't leave here alive. If I have to do something myself."

"What?" cried Johnny. "What is this? Are you crazy, doctor?"

"You were his target all the time, Johnny," said the doctor. "I suspected it. Now I know."

A heavy stone banged against the door, and a huge shout arose from outside, a savage and primeval cry. Johnny instinctively started for the door, and the doctor squeaked, "Stay away from there, you half-wit. There's a mob outside. Swensen arranged it."

Dan McGee, his plump face as ghostly as Mr. Dowdy's, slowly rose from the sofa. Mr. Dowdy got up also. Then Johnny, halfway to the door, suddenly swung on his heel, ran to Swensen, and caught him by the throat. Johnny's face was terrible. "You," he said. "You brought them here to frighten my children, to stone my house. Listen, you. If one of my children is hurt, I think I'm going to kill you. Do you understand? I'm going to kill you."

Mr. Swensen was no longer smiling. He stood very still in Johnny's grip, but his affable face had become a marble effigy of contempt. "Take your hands off me," he said in a quiet voice. "You've brought all this on yourself, parson."

Johnny drew back his big right arm like the flash of a piston, and his fist crashed onto Swensen's jaw. Swensen staggered, and while he did so Johnny hit him again, and then again, until he fell to the floor. Johnny's leg retracted for a kick into the man's side. And then it dropped. His panting filled the room, stridently. He looked down at the half-conscious man on the floor and he said, "When you get up I'll hit you again, and this time you'll stay down." His eyes flashed about the room like blue lightning. "I'm a minister," he said. "And I'm also a man."

Dr. McManus was recovering from his amazement. "Good," he said. "You're growing up, Johnny." The other men looked at Swensen, and then at Johnny, incredulously, and they rubbed their dazed faces with their shaking hands. They watched Johnny as he tore open the door and stood on the threshold. The night air poured with its sickly stench into the house, and there was only a pent silence outside as he appeared.

He stood with his long, muscular legs apart, his hands clutching at the doorframe, and he said with great quietness, "What do you people want?"

Only the silence answered him for a few moments, and then an immense roar went up, confused, rageful, hating, and full of blood lust. "Get out! Get out, you dirty Nazi! Get out of town, you dirty fascist! You union buster! You scab!"

Why, thought Johnny, of course. These shouters are one and the same people, no matter what the epithets! They always were, from the beginning of time.

Dr. McManus, his mighty old legs trembling, went to the door and peered over Johnny's shoulder. The misty lamplight outside glimmered on at least one hundred wild and inhuman faces, on women's tangled hair, on men's bare heads, on open, wet lips and glinting eyes. Shadows hid their bodies; the faces and the heads floated in a slight yellowish fog, like disembodied nightmares. Now women began to laugh, high demented laughter of hatred, and foul words and obscenities rang in the damp autumn night.

Johnny stood there and did not move. A woman screamed, "Get those goddam foreign kids out of here, right now, or we'll take 'em apart with our hands!" A pair of clutching, tearing hands rose above the bobbing heads and made rending motions. "We don't want no foreign kids here in our town, you lousy bastard!" A roar of approval echoed her.

Johnny started to take a step forward, the terribleness brighter on his face, but the doctor seized hs arm. "Let me pass," he said, and he sidled around Johnny and stepped down on the stoop below. There he stood, steadfast and as immovable as a boulder, his hands in his pockets, his shock of ashen hair blowing stiffly in the wind. He surveyed the mob with an evil smile. They had fallen silent at the sight of him, except for a low muttering.

"Hello, pigs," he said. "I see a lot of faces I know here. I operated on some of your stinking bodies. I see you in clumps on my free-clinic days. Remember? Don't come to me again. Take your whimperings and your whinings to doctors who'll charge you, like sensible men."

Something hissed through the air, and twanged, just missing the old man. It was a knife, and the blade buried itself in the doorframe hardly two inches below Johnny's hand. Deftly and swiftly the doctor pulled it from the rotting wood and held it. A few alarmed cries rose. "Who threw that at the Doc? Hey—you!"

"Well," said the doctor, "I've got a knife now. I'm picking one of your faces, and the next move you make, that particular face is going to get this knife right between the eyes. Just don't move."

A ripple of fear ran over the mass of restless faces; tongues licked lips; a growl rose from many throats. Someone yelled, "We ain't got nothing against you, Doc! We don't know who threw that knife! Just get out of the way, Doc! We don't mean no trouble, if that minister just gets out of town with his foreigners tonight! Ain't we got a right to say who lives in this town?"

"You," said the doctor calmly, balancing the knife in his hand, "ain't got a right to live." He did not look away from them. He held the mob with his malignant eyes. "In a couple of minutes the police'll be here, and I've got influence, and I'm going to tell the boys to shoot to kill, and use their clubs, too."

He could hear them listening uneasily. But only the night wind sounded through the thinning trees, and over the houses opposite the yellow crescent moon hung in silence.

Then Johnny said, loudly and clearly, "I'm not going away. Nothing, nobody, is going to drive me away from the place where God has brought me. You're just people, my people, and I don't hate you, but you're frightened, and you've been driven crazy by lies. Who made you come here tonight?"

A howl answered him, rising almost palpably from the glistening faces below, but it came from scattered places, and the men and women looked fearfully to find the howlers. Then there was silence again, and a shuffling of feet. Suddenly a man raised a newspaper in the air and shook it. "It's right here in the paper!" he shrieked. "The big interests sent you here to break our union!"

"Who're you?" a man demanded. "What mine you work?"

Someone else pushed around Johnny and ducked under his arm and stepped down, and it was Dan McGee. At the appearance of the little plump man they knew and loved, there was a clamor of dismay and astonishment from the faces. Dan raised his arms, and the men shouted at him in acknowledgment. "It's Dan! Dan. Let Dan speak! What're you doin' here, Dan?"

"He's sold us out!" a man bellowed.

Faces swung angrily to the speaker somewhere in the crowd. "Dan wouldn't sell us out! Hey, never saw you before! Who sent you?"

"Yes," said Dan gently. "Who sent him, and the others?"

The mob swayed and twisted. "Fellows. Guys. Said they was union men from Scranton," someone answered, uncertainly.

Dan smiled at them, his round red face beaming in the lamplight. Windows in the houses across the street had been thrown open, and the apertures bobbed with curious and alarmed heads, the light behind them a dull yellow.

Dan was considering. There would be blood shed tonight unless the agitators realized their danger and got away. And blood that was shed inevitably brought guilt and misery to those responsible for the shedding. So Dan waited, and he was relieved to see that here and there slight agitations appeared in the mob, movements as of men escaping as swiftly and as neatly as possible. The people were so intent upon Dan that they were hardly aware of these agitations and movements, serpentine and quick. The breath of the mob rose like steam above their heads in the dampness. Now earnest, shamed, and sheepish eyes regarded Dan.

Then Dr. McManus shouted, "How'd you like to get your hands on the man who's responsible for bringing you out here to hurt our good friend here, and his children, eh? And Dan too—he wanted you to tear Dan apart."

The mob's voice rose on an insane and jubilant and eager note. "Where is he, Doc? Give him to us, Doc! We'll get him, Doc!"

Johnny's heart suddenly swelled in him with an enormous

sickness. A mob was always a mob—it only wanted a victim, no matter who. He clutched Dan's shoulder, leaning down from the door. "Talk, talk," he said urgently. "And shut up the doctor! For God's sake." Dan glanced up at him, and his kind face changed.

"Now," said Dan, "let's wait a minute, and talk this over, see? I want to tell you boys something important. There isn't going to be any strike, or any raises either."

"Shall I—?" began Dr. McManus gleefully; but Dan raised his voice commandingly to drown him out. No one noticed that Johnny had disappeared.

Dan continued: "The owners can't afford it. I got to talk fast, for the police are about here now. Hear that siren?" The crowd listened anxiously. "I got some sad news for you boys. You always liked Mr. Dowdy. Well, sir, he's a dying man, worn out and sick. But he's left you his mines—they'll all be yours, too soon."

A deep, profound murmur of wonder and shame rose from the wall of men and women.

Dan went on rapidly. "Mr. Dowdy knows you're here. He doesn't know why. We won't tell him, huh? Make him feel much worse, you see."

The sirens were approaching with loud, primitive wailing. The crowd drew near the house as the three police cars pulled up.

"We didn't mean anything," a confusion of voices said in honest bewilderment, forgetting. "Don't even know why we came."

I got to hold them a little longer, thought Dan desperately, still clutching the doctor's arm. The doors of the police cars opened, and the people jostled. They did not drift away. Most of them knew all the members of the police force of Barryfield, and as the burly young men began to get out of the cars there were shouts of relieved greetings. "We didn't do nothing, Jim! It was just those guys kind of stirred us up—lies. We don't even know who they are!"

"They ought to be shot!" some women screamed. Now the whole mob was clamoring angrily, and with righteous indignation. They surrounded the police, incoherently pleading innocence and outrage, and looking about them for the strangers.

I don't know what Mr. Fletcher's doing, thought Dan, but I hope I'm giving him time.

Johnny had run into the parlor. He had found Swensen sitting weakly on a chair, mopping at the blood that ran from his mouth and nose. He kept shaking his head as if to restore his faculties. Johnny dragged him rapidly from the chair, and said in a fierce, repressed voice, "The mob wants you. They want to tear you apart, kill you. The police will soon be here, but the police won't be able to hold them. Come with me! Stand on your own feet!"

He dragged the dazed and bleeding Swensen, who was no longer elegant and urbane, to the foot of the stairs and listened. Mrs. Burnsdale had sensibly taken the children to their rooms, and a soft murmur floated down the stairs. "Come!" cried Johnny softly, and he pushed the man ahead of him into the kitchen, supporting his staggering body, holding him with all his strength. "The police won't help you," muttered Johnny, and he panted with his efforts. "Make an effort to help—come, on your feet—they'll kill you."

Swensen was breathing raggedly with confused fear. His clothing was spotted with blood. As he struggled to support himself, with Johnny's hands on his back and arms, he could hear the howling of the mob, and then, faintly in the distance, the wailing of sirens. "Hurry, hurry," pleaded Johnny, distracted. "We've got two, three, four seconds—no more. Here, put your arm around my neck. That's better."

Together they stumbled into the deserted kitchen and toward the back door. Johnny peered out into the darkness. No one was there. The mob was howling out front and the sirens were closer now. Johnny opened the back door, and the fresh air suddenly hit the dazed Swensen and began to restore him to his senses.

"Why?" asked Swensen, taking great gulps of the cool air into his lungs. "Why are you doing this? You have every reason to hate me."

"Why?" Johnny repeated the question. "Because I'm a Christian. And because I know that mobs are never impelled by a true anger or a true sense of justice. They just want to kill. Anyone will serve. A few minutes ago they wanted to kill me. Now they want to kill you." He looked at Swensen's nose, with the blood still dripping from it. He sighed, and then his face tightened. He could hear the police out front now, and the furious, demanding voice of the mob, still seeking a victim, again justifying itself. "Are you all right now? Can you navigate?" He helped Swensen down the back steps into the yard. "There. Stand on your own legs, man. I've helped you all I can. From now on it's up to you." Johnny removed his hands from the shambling form and for a moment it stood there weaving, like a drunk about to collapse.

"But why?" asked Swensen, coming out of his daze and turning to Johnny. "I don't get it. Why are you helping me to get away?"

"The answer," said Johnny softly, "is in the difference between us—the difference in what we believe. I know why you came here. You came with hate in your heart, and the hatred in your heart made me all hate you a little while ago. You represented to me all the evil I saw in Europe—the concentration camps, the crematoriums, things I can't even mention. And then, suddenly, you became not the hunter, but the hunted. So now it doesn't matter to me any more that you believe in one thing and I in another. You are the hunted, now, and a mob is always a mob, and a mob is monstrous. I have to protect you from it."

For a long moment Swensen stood there, bleeding and motionless, his light eyes fixed upon Johnny, and those eyes reflected incredulous expressions of sharp derision, contempt, and bafflement.

"Yes, yes," said Johnny sternly, taking his arm. "I know. I'm a weakling, you think. Your kind is strong, and so you'll inherit the earth—you think. But you won't, you won't! Because all the time you are the cowards, not we, for we aren't afraid of anything, not even you. We don't think it's necessary for us to kill, just to survive."

"Why?" asked Swensen, wiping his oozing mouth with his handkerchief. "Why are you saving me from that mob?"

"You wouldn't understand," said Johnny with bitter anger, pulling him toward the fence.

"Wait," said Swensen, resisting, and now his eyes were strange and intent. "Yes, I hear that pack of curs howling—"

They could now see the mob beyond the fence swathed in sickening and coiling copper drifts of smog under the street light. "There's the fence," said Johnny. "Get over it, someway, into the next yard, and then to the next street. What are you waiting for?" he cried, in fear and exasperation. "Dan Mc-Gee can't hold them much longer!"

"I'm waiting for the answer to my question. An hour ago I wouldn't have understood your answer. But I think I do now." He smiled at Johnny, and shook his head as if in wonder, and not with derision. "Yes, I think I do."

He shouldered past Johnny, and then touched his forehead quickly in a humorous salute, and was gone. Johnny stood there a moment, then closed the door. He leaned against it, exhausted and frowning. We're all guilty of his kind, he thought distractedly. We "good" people let them into our lives, because we lacked the positive force of the moral law to keep them out. Yes, we are guilty. Guilty of the betrayal of a whole world. *Mea culpa. Mea maxima culpa.*

The doctor was in the living room when he came in, and suddenly Johnny remembered the children. With a new strength he rushed to the stairs and, followed by the doctor, he ran up to the floor above. The children were gathered together in a white-faced cluster around Mrs. Burnsdale in Johnny's bedroom. When they saw Johnny they rushed to him, even Jean, pushing his wheel chair furiously.

"It's all right, kids," said Johnny, gathering them to him. He wanted to soothe them with evasions, but when he saw Jean's wise eyes and Pietro's sharp smile, he knew he had to tell the truth. "People can be very stupid," he said. "You already know that. Sometimes you're stupid yourselves. But we had the law tonight, and the police came, and the people were sorry, very sorry. We must forgive them."

He looked at Kathy's round pink face which was now very obdurate. He said, "Don't I forgive you, all of you, no matter how impossible you get sometimes?" He turned to Max, who said in his uncertain voice, "Yes, you always have to forgive."

Jean said, mortified, "I am thinking about the knife. I am no better than those men, Papa. I am not a Christian. How can you forgive me?"

Johnny bent down and put his arms about Jean. "It was St. Peter, dear, who cut off the ear of a soldier with his sword, when the Romans came to arrest Our Lord. It was St. Peter who denied Our Lord three times. God forgave him, for God understands the hearts of men. When you accuse yourself of

287

your own guilt, as you did just now, you don't need to ask my forgiveness. God has already forgiven you."

Pietro jumped up like a spring, laughing. "Oh, what I must tell the Father! He will make eyes, so," and the gay little boy made his black eyes gigantic and rolled them to heaven, and clasped his hands together in a parody of holy horror. He was delighted when everyone in the room burst into uncontrolled laughter.

It was Dr. McManus who, without comment, brought Johnny a copy of *The New York Times* a few days later and showed him an item. "Mr. Lars Swensen, director of the Industrial Relations Foundation, has resigned from his post with that organization. . . ."

19

Sunday was another day.

It began about dawn, dolorously, with Johnny's dream.

First he was aware, in his dream, of a great sorrow in himself, which had no source he could discover, and a great yearning. All this was part of a gray and dark chaos in which he was standing. Then the chaos swirled away, and he discovered himself standing in a lonely wasteland, bleached and parched and empty, and utterly silent under a sunless sky. There was not a tree or a blade of grass or a flower. The wasteland cracked, here and there, in an intricate and meaningless pattern, running to the horizon. Johnny walked, and his steps were soundless. He looked for hills, and there were none. He looked for water, and there was none. All that I thought I had was only a dream, he said to himself in his dream. He bent and picked up a piece of earth; it was the color of whitish clay; it dissolved to dust in his hand, and it blew off in a wind he did not feel.

He remarked on his extraordinary exhaustion, as if he had worked himself to the point of death. Finally he stopped walking and stood looking at the endless desolation to which there was no end. He had no memories; he did not think of any future.

Then, all at once, a patch of brilliant and shining blue appeared on the horizon, a tiny patch no bigger than his hand. It is the sky, he thought, with joy. But it was not the sky. It was moving toward him, a strange and luminous color, and suddenly his heart pounded with eager happiness. He began to walk rapidly in the direction of the color, and then he saw that it was in reality a little figure, and it was waving to him, and he lifted his hand in a returning salute. He hurried. Then he noticed a most extraordinary thing. The wasteland, as if given a mysterious signal, was breaking out into herbage of a bright green tint. It reached his ankles, began to climb, rustling, toward his knees. In an instant or two more it was filled with flowers of every hue, red, yellow, white, lavender, pink and gold, and perfume rose in clouds from it. Johnny was filled with strength; he could actually feel the quickened flow of his rejuvenated blood.

He could not take his eyes from the figure in the distance. Birds were singing now, and the sun came out in a burst of light. It shone on the figure, and it was a young woman with pale and luminous hair, and Johnny knew her, and he shouted, "Lorry! Lorry!" He broke into a run.

She was suddenly in his arms, and all the flowers, the songs of the birds, the sun, were emanations of her. He had never felt such delight, such fulfillment, such rapture. He held her face in his hands, and looked into her eyes, and they were not the hard and ruthless eyes he now remembered, but eyes of misty sweetness and tender beauty, and they regarded him with love.

"I thought you had gone away," he said. "I thought I'd never see you again."

Lorry laughed and laid her cheek against his. "I never went away," she said. "How could you imagine such a thing?"

"I sent you away in my thoughts," he replied, humbly. "There were the children—"

She laughed at him, lovingly. "The children? Johnny, they are mine too. So many children, so many thousands of them. Listen to their voices!"

He listened, holding her hand. Now the air was clamorous with the voices of a multitude of children, seeking voices, lost voices, infant voices, calling voices. Johnny looked about him in bewilderment, but there was no one else there but himself and Lorry.

"Because of you, they are my children, all of them," said Lorry, and leaned against him. "Because of you—"

He awoke then, in his dreary bedroom. He could hear Jean breathing in the semidarkness. The autumnal rains, gray and unrelenting, poured heavily from dejected skies; he could hear them pounding in the streets, washing his one small window. Johnny lay still, trying to hold to his dream, but it slipped away from him, and he was left with an enormous sense of loss and grief. A dream, he said to himself, a dream that could never happen, because she could never want me or care about me.

He did not sleep again. When he got up the house was just beginning to stir. In a state of mournfulness and sadness he dressed, went to the church, and glanced in. It was, at least, clean, in the leaden light from the sky.

He ate his breakfast in an exhausted state of mind, and hardly spoke to the children, who looked at him soberly with large eyes. Kathy was dressed in a new plaid skirt and white blouse, ready for Sunday school later. She was already a power among the little girls of her class, and was not above correcting the rather pale young teacher in a precise voice when Miss Fair misquoted a word or two from the Scriptures. The other children regarded Kathy with awe, for she was so brisk and efficient, and handed the prayer books around with an air of no-nonsense-and-let's-do-this-properly. Pietro had returned from early Mass, and was slightly subdued. Mrs. Burnsdale had caught a cold and was inclined to be brusque. Jean's arm and leg were paining him this dank morning, and Max was too quiet, and little Emilie was in bed with a fever. Moreover, Johnny's sermon did not please him. He also had a premonition of more anxiety to come.

This was a Communion Sunday, and Johnny was not certain how many glasses stood in the dusty cupboard, and whether they would be sufficient. The sacramental wine, he had discovered, was of a very cheap variety, and had a bad color. It also had dregs. He sat at the breakfast table and gloomily contemplated the rain. "There were many people at Mass," Pietro said. Johnny answered with rare sarcasm, "I won't have to worry about that in my church, I suppose."

Mrs. Burnsdale said sourly, "You don't have enough candles. And those piddly little candlesticks! I suppose if you turn the lights on there'll be complaints about the electricity bill."

"Our church," said Pietro, with some condescension, "has many candles. On all the altars. Pretty statues, too. Our Lord has a new gold halo."

Johnny uneasily reflected on what Dr. McManus had told him. He said carefully, "Well, God hears us without candles, or with candles, provided we really pray to Him."

The telephone rang, and Johnny went to answer it. The caller was Dan McGee. "Say, Mr. Fletcher, terrible weather, isn't it? Don't suppose there'll be many people in church this morning." He coughed. "Wonderful, though, how everything went last night, wasn't it? Lots of the miners called me to tell me how wonderful you were. Sorry they aren't your parishioners, though."

Johnny waited. His premonition was very lively now.

Dan went on, after another cough. "Guess, though, our own parishioners don't like it. They called me too. They think the miners are pretty trashy folks, and never have anything to do with them. They wondered why the miners should march to your house and raise hell—I mean, the devil. They don't think it was dignified." He tried for a laugh. "Some of 'em have their noses in the air about it. I told them off."

Johnny still waited.

"You can't tell about people, Mr. Fletcher. They were all excited, and mad, about the miners. They—kind of think in some way it was your fault. I tried to explain. They said it never happened before, to any of their other ministers. Mobs, and things."

"In other words," said Johnny, "I'm in the doghouse."

"Oh, I wouldn't say that, Mr. Fletcher."

"Well, what would you say, Dan?"

The union president hesitated. "Just take it easy, and don't worry, sir. If the church isn't filled this morning, just let them get over it. Most of the board members will be there, with our wives, to give you moral support."

"So I need moral support?"

"Say, Mr. Fletcher, you don't sound very cheerful. You mustn't take it that way."

"It's Communion Sunday," said Johnny.

"Well, so it is! Maybe lots of people forgot."

Johnny went back to the kitchen in less than a happy state of mind. He picked up his coat and trousers which Mrs. Burnsdale had carefully pressed. "They're pretty green," she said reproachfully.

"Mildew," said Johnny, and went to dress. It was almost time for the service. The little room behind the altar smelled of mice and dust and old wood, and the raw bulb in the ceiling seemed particularly dreary. Johnny counted the glasses. There would be quite enough. The organ had begun to whine dismally, faltering stiffly over a few notes, for it was second-hand and had been cheap originally. Johnny winced, waiting for the reedy-voiced choir of elderly folk to begin. They did. And then, to his surprise, he thought he detected a happy note in the hymn. He put the glasses on an old japanned tray and carried them into the church.

Then he stopped in astonishment. On each side of the altar had been placed huge baskets of golden chrysanthemums, shining like ragged golden balls in an amazing display of candlelight. The little candlesticks had been replaced by two giant seven-branched candelabra, each of the many sockets blazing with stately white candles, the carved silver glittering, the bases gleaming with reflected light. The altar seemed to be a focus of incredible shifting brilliance in the dark church, casting bright shadows on the close old walls, and stretching up long fingers of radiance to the groins of the wooden ceiling. There was no need for the mean chandelier, and only a few small electric lights burned in the rear. It was magnificent.

Johnny's eyes filled with tears. The grace of light had been given him. He had seen those enormous candelabra in the doctor's Victorian mansion, standing on an immense bureau. He put the glasses on the altar with trembling hands. He looked at the flowers; they exhaled a scent of the living earth. The fourteen beeswax candles, each fully two feet tall at least, sent out their clean odor as their golden tips illumined the cold air. Johnny slowly turned to his congregation. Dr. McManus was sitting lumpily in his first pew, staring at nothing, refusing to meet Johnny's eyes. "Bless you," said Johnny to himself, in a mist that almost blinded him. All at once it did not matter that there were only forty people in the church, the nearest pews filled with resolute middle-aged ladies and their upright board husbands, and behind them a straggling of uncertain folk. And Lon Harding, with his parents.

Johnny stood in all that vast aureole of light and did not know that he had a youthful majesty and that his face glowed and that his eyes were filled with an intense blue. Now the voices of the choir, for all the chronic laryngitis which usually afflicted it, rose in exaltation and the nearly empty church enhanced the music until it shook with power, for all the banality of the hymn. The rain could pound against the windows, and the autumnal winds howl dolorously. The hymn took on some of the grandeur of a Gregorian chant.

His sermon, finished yesterday under appalling circumstances, was not in keeping now, he knew. So he lifted his hands a little and said in a voice of loud and triumphant passion, "And God said, Let there be light; and there was light."

The choir murmured softly into silence, and there were only the rain and the wind and the great candelabra with their fourteen slender columns of resplendent flame behind the minister. And now the women's cheeks were touched by tears, and the men's mouths moved in a trembling. Dr. McManus raised his eyes and regarded Johnny fixedly.

"There is always the light of God," said Johnny, and his voice broke. "The eternal light which, when created, was commanded never to darken again, not anywhere in the universe. The interstices of space are illuminated with it; the stars roll in it, in their mysterious passage; the galaxies drift in it. The soul is bathed in it, shut though it is in the darkness of the flesh. The light which is the love of God for all He has made can never be extinguished, nor can the grave hide it, nor the hatred of man dim it, nor sorrow, nor war, nor blood, nor death, nor pain diminish it. It is the boundless ocean which flows through all things, and blends the suns and the hearts of men into one body and one being, with God."

He paused, and the mighty candles rose on a wave of effulgence.

"In all the terrible centuries which have passed, and in this terrible day in which we stand now, and in all the terrible days to come, the light remains. The works of man and his confusions and his fears, his ambitions and his dreary hopes, his disappointments and his agonies, his griefs and his bitternesses and his lostness, are like a dark city, windowless and walled in black stone, closed against the sky and the love of God. We dwell in that dark city, and think of it as the only reality, and we look at the somber shadows and call them life.

"And yet we need only leave that city, for the gates are not locked, though we believe they are. We need only walk a step, and open one door. And there is the light, and the dazzling thunder of its reality, and the endless realms of peace filled with its radiance.

"No one halts us on that step; no jailer bars the door; no evil can challenge us. It is we, and we alone, who have set the chains on our hands and about our ankles; it is we, and we alone, who have said, 'There is no light behind these walls, beyond these gates, beyond this door.' We have bound ourselves with our gloomy imaginings, our faithlessness, our dejections, our terrors, our envies, and our greeds. The streets of the sunless city we have made are ghostly with our lightless forms, and echo with our lamentations. We cry for light, and yet we do not open that door."

The church stood in absolute silence. Dr. McManus bent his head and half covered his face with his hand.

Johnny moved closer to the step that led to the altar. He held out his hands. "I too have done that, though I know the light is waiting for my asking, for my one step." He smiled. "Only a short time ago I stood in the little room behind this altar, and I said to myself that nothing is waiting for me here, in this church, that I was abandoned, that I had failed, that I was utterly useless, and the work I have tried to do had collapsed about me. Like Job, I questioned the reason for my existence, and I had no answer, for the walls had closed shut around me, by my own faltering will, my own failing faith.

"And yet—and yet I opened the door of that little room, and I stepped in here among you, and there was the light, the visible, shining light, and your trust, and the flowers; and my soul, imprisoned in its despondency and hopelessness, turned again to the Eternal Light of God, and knew it was there, changeless, smiling, filled with everlasting love and consolation."

He could not speak for several moments. As if it had a life of its own, and was not stirred by human hands, the organ spoke in soft joyfulness, and the music lingered in the cold shadows of the church.

Johnny said unsteadily, "I can say no more. There is nothing else for me to say, except to give you my benediction, and ask you for yours."

He turned to the altar and knelt before it, and the little congregation slipped to its knees. A woman sobbed, and a man or two cleared his throat. The candlelight soared, and the organ spoke again.

Johnny was not at the door, later, to shake hands with those who had come courageously to be with him, and uphold him, nor would they have wanted him to be there. They walked outside into the rain, entranced, without speaking. For the first time in many years the communion service had not been a mere ritual to them; it had been a sacred rite, full of divine meaning, and happiness.

The minister stood in the little room behind the altar, himself dazed and greatly moved, forgetting to take off his vestments. He stood with his hands clasped before him, his head bent. He started when he heard Dan's subdued voice: "Well, sir, that was a real sermon. No, not a sermon. It was like someone talking, saying something we'd forgotten. Something we hadn't remembered, away back, maybe when we were kids."

Mr. Schoeffel was with him, his gentle face blurred with emotion. He held out his hand to Johnny, and Johnny took it. Dan McGee passed his broad miner's hands over his white drift of hair, and shook his head wonderingly. He and Mr. Schoeffel had brought in the two collection plates which had been used that day. "Look," he said. "A sprinkling of big silver, and twenty one-dollar bills! But look what's on top! Two one-hundred-dollar bills! Old Al just threw them in like they were nothing at all. And those candlesticks! He told us this morning, before services, to tell you he was loaning them to you, as long as you stay here. They don't belong to the church, he says. Just to you, long as you're here. You know, it was funny, Mr. Fletcher. At eight o'clock this morning my wife says, 'Dan, I have a feeling the Ladies' Aid should dress up the altar real nice this morning, with extra-wonderful flowers, in honor of Mr. Fletcher,' and she calls up a couple of ladies, and the flowers got here just ten minutes before service, just when Al's man Joe was bringing in the candles and the sticks!"

"It was kind of like a message to you," said Mr. Schoeffel,

awed. "You know, Mr. Fletcher, I never saw a hundred-dollar bill before."

"I think," said Johnny, "that in gratitude to my congregation I should buy myself a new coat." And he began to laugh softly, and the others joined him. All the children must see the candelabra blazing, he thought, and the flowers. It will be a message for them too.

That afternoon, in spite of the rain, Father Krupszyk and Rabbi Chortow visited Johnny in the parsonage, to comfort him because of his ordeal of the night before. There had been something on the radio about it. They found him romping with Pietro and Kathy and Max in the drab living room, full of laughter. They had never seen him so gay and so boyish. He shook their hands enthusiastically, to their astonishment. "You must come into my church at once!" he said. "I want to show you something." He smoothed down his hair, released himself from Pietro's gleeful grip. "No, you can't come again, Pietro," he said. "You saw everything once. That's enough."

The three clergymen went out into the rain, and Johnny led them to the front door, which was unlocked. The priest commented to himself again that never had he seen so dreary a church, no, not even when he had been a very young man with a country parish. He said, "The door isn't locked in the afternoon?"

"It's never locked," said Johnny gaily. "Except at night, of course. I gave orders the church was to be open not only all day Sunday, but every day. You see, I've seen too many locked churches, and I always wondered why God had to be under lock and key all the time."

"Well, well," said Father John Kanty, pleased. The rabbi nodded his head sagely. "In the old country," he said, his delicate beard gleaming with little drops of rain, "the doors were open for the prayers of the weary. There is no special time when men should pray; they need to pray when the need comes. And who should deny them their temple?"

Johnny threw open the doors with a flourish. The dark little church was full of golden light, for the candelabra still stood on the altar, and the flowers shone like suns in the illumination. If the other two clergymen were astonished, Johnny was more so, for the church was half filled with seated or kneeling worshipers for the first time in its history on a Sunday afternoon loud with rain and wind, or on any

Sunday afternoon for that matter. "What do you know?" Johnny whispered, as he led the way down the aisle toward the altar. So absorbed were the men and the women in the pews that they hardly noticed the passing clergymen. News spreads, thought Johnny with joy. He saw strange profiles he had never seen before, and children, and young boys and girls. A lump rose in his throat.

"Beautiful," said Father Krupszyk, looking at the great candles, which had hardly dwindled. He stepped closer and smiled broadly. "Why, those candles came from our religious supply store! They're imported. I shouldn't wonder if they had been blessed!" The old rabbi went very close to the candelabra, and his tired eyes widened. "Those are Jewish candlesticks!" he whispered, agitated with amazement. "At least three hundred years old, or more! See, I recognize them by this, and this," and he pointed to the carving on them. "There is a history about them."

Their faces, above their somber clothing, floated in the broad and soaring light, like the heads in a Rembrandt painting, vivid and moved and full of expression against a dark background. They stood there a long time. The priest noted that there was no cross in the church. Johnny said in a low voice, "I hope to have a large cross, very soon, above the altar."

They returned to the house, where Mrs. Burnsdale had sent the children upstairs, had put an extra shovel of coal on the furnace, and was now preparing tea in the kitchen. "I'd never have believed it of Al McManus," said the priest choosing his seat cautiously in the parlor with due regard for broken springs. "And I'm not gong to give him, even now, any credit for symbolism. I've seen those candlesticks in his house many a time, and he told me he bought them in Europe, and I know he doesn't have the slightest idea what they are. And he sent out for those candles to our store, because we're the only ones who carry them. I think this is all a mysterious message to us from God."

Mrs. Burnsdale proudly brought in the tea and a plate of cake. The china was very delicate and pretty, and Dr. McManus had sent it to her from the limitless supply in his house. Father Krupszyk was a man of taste, and he examined one of the fragile yellow cups. "Antiques, and very beautiful," he said. Mrs. Burnsdale said to the old rabbi,

"There's only good fresh sweet butter in that cake, sir, and no lard." He smiled at her gently, and took a piece of the cake. He tasted it. "My wife can bake no better," he assured her.

The two clergymen decided that they would not mention the riot of the night before to Johnny, for they saw that it no longer meant anything to him. It was obvious that he believed everything was now very splendid. The priest and the rabbi, who had had more experience with men, were not so sanguine. A lion may lick your hand today, thought the priest, but tomorrow he will bite your head from your shoulders. He sipped his tea, and one of his blond eyebrows rose speculatively. He only hoped that Johnny would have some respite for a while, before coming face to face again with the world of men.

Johnny spoke of Lon Harding, and an idea he had evolved. "Lots of churches go in for athletics and dancing and juke boxes in the parish halls," he said. "But the kids get all that in their new schools. What they don't get, in some of our public schools, is a full education. They get group integration and life-adjustment stuff instead, and a smattering of mechanical trades in the vocational schools. Not in yours, though, Father," he said to the priest.

"No," replied the priest thoughtfully. "We still believe in education, in the liberal arts, in religion, in languages, and Latin, in the humanities. 'The whole child,' the educationists say. But the brain, and disciplined learning, are part of 'the whole child' too. They forget that. Or," he added sternly, "maybe they know only too well, and they don't really want 'a whole child' at all. Just robots.'"

The rabbi nodded. He took another piece of cake and eyed it approvingly. "Have I not been telling my people, the young people? Have they listened? No." He looked at Johnny with his luminous eyes. "Not until recently. There is Sol Klein. He led the young people in their modernism. President of the men's club. They have discussion groups about 'modern education.' It is all very foolish; they know nothing at all. Johnny, you have changed Sol. Our Sunday school is flourishing as never before. Sol led the way, with his own children. We must build a larger Sunday school, Sol has said." The rabbi chewed his cake, and the luminous quality of his eyes deepened with tenderness as he looked at Johnny. "You

299

have done so much good, my son. You have not heard? The young men and women have gravely decided, after a discussion group led by Sol Klein, that their rabbi is not really so stupid and old-fashioned after all, and that eternal ideas have not been destroyed by modern advancement. They have decided their rabbi must have a bigger and finer synagogue, and a nice new house." He shook his head. "I was told, not consulted," he added with a loving smile. "They sat about me, like children around a beloved, wise old father, who had too many greater things to concern him than the mere building of a new temple, and they asked my opinion of many things, and they seemed a little ashamed, the dear young ones." He laughed gently. " 'I must play my part,' I said to myself. I am the old wise man in the gates; there must be no worry about money for me. I am above such things. They informed me that my sermons are very inspirational!" He sighed, smiling.

"I wonder how long all this will last," said Father Krupszyk.

"Don't be cynical," said Johnny.

The priest was silent a moment, then he began to smile. "Young Dr. Tim Kennedy's parents once belonged to my parish. Now they live on The Heights, where the young priest is very brisk and modern, as far as what he thinks is due to his particular church and school. No nonsense about Father Frederickson. Well, he'll get older in time."

He grinned at Johnny, and his broad face brightened. "I wanted to tell you about Tim Kennedy. He collected money from the boys who were once in my parish, before they all got to The Heights. Eight hundred dollars. They sent it to me for the church. And last Sunday they came in a body to High Mass. The sermon was in Polish. They sat there as if they understood every word of it, and looked very righteous and pleased with themselves. And afterward they said they'd never forget me again. So you see, Johnny, you've helped me, too."

Johnny blushed. He pretended to be very busy pouring fresh tea as his friends smiled at him. "Let's get back to what I was talking about," he said. "I want to turn the parish hall into a library, with tables and good lights. And with teachers, after their classes, coming in to help the boys and girls, using advanced textbooks. It's an idea I discussed with the doctor, and the board. The children would learn things they never learn in school. A couple of teachers could teach French or German in the parish hall. Others could drill the kids in English, and in English literature, and decent penmanship. The kids wouldn't come, the doctor said. I don't believe that. I'm sure lots will."

His voice rose a little vehemently. "We're going to disprove the old European idea that a laboring man breeds stupid children, and that these children should be taught only trades, because they aren't intelligent enough for anything else! Who says they're not?"

Father Krupszyk stood up. "Johnny, your troubles have just begun."

The priest looked at the whitening scar on Johnny's temple. Johnny said, "Father, would you withdraw from any battle in which you had engaged in the name of freedom, God, and justice?"

Father Krupszyk thought of the years he had spent in one unending struggle in his parish. As he was, above all, an honest man, he pondered Johnny's question. His wide Slavic face became very grave. He began to speak, slowly, "I am a Pole. My people have always been freedom-loving, and religious. They were betrayed to Russia by those who had sworn to protect them. The struggle, Johnny, is mighty. And now, answering your question, I can truly say that I would never withdraw, and I'll never withdraw, either. I'll fight with you, Johnny, no matter what it costs me."

Rabbi Chortow echoed his sigh. "I am an old man," he said. "Long ago, my years made me a peaceful man. This is no time for peace, for peace has become a betrayal. The Jews, who are an ancient people, prize peace above all things, and cooperation in the name of peace. My dear son, I will fight with you, too." He gently smoothed his floating beard, and sighed again. He thought of his quiet library, and his old wife who was always so anxious about his health, and who was very timid and avoided all arguments. She must understand that even old people must forget their age and their love of peace, for these were terrible days. The old had much to offer in wisdom. If, in the name of God, they were called again, even to die, then they must die, and offer an example. For what else was a man born?

"I'll need some books," said Johnny, "for my library."

The rabbi gazed at his strong and confident face, and again

he sighed, this time in aged sympathy. The priest said, "I have a whole storage of advanced textbooks in my cellar. I'll send them to you tomorrow. And others—about Our Lord. And His love for the world.'"

"But love," said the rabbi, "is all there is, and ever will be."

The priest was more practical. "Perhaps you can persuade your Lon Harding and his pals to protect you. You'll need it, Johnny."

Johnny waved away this eminently sensible remark as puerile. "So, I can get all the books I want, thank you, Father, and I am sure that Sol Klein will be able to get me scores; all his group, and his club, subscribe to the book clubs, and read many other books, and the rabbi probably has dozens too. And I'll talk to the Ladies' Aid about having their teacher friends help us in the parish-hall library. The only thing," he added, as if it were a matter of no consequence, "is having those bookshelves put up, and the reading tables and good lights and chairs, and a desk or two for the teachers."

He was very enthusiastic. He looked suddenly much younger. The priest and the rabbi regarded him with compassion. The priest said, "You've got powerful enemies. They're not going to let up on you. Last night's affair wasn't spontaneous, as you know; it was planned. Worse things can happen, too."

"The only really bad thing would be for me to be kicked out of my parish," said Johnny. "And that won't happen. I've got lots of friends here. Why, the Ladies' Aid is going to have a special Thanksgiving dinner for me and the children; that is, they are going to give us a big turkey, already stuffed, ready for roasting, and everything that goes with it. To save Mrs. Burnsdale work, they said; like Kathy, she's become very outstanding in the church." Johnny smiled, thinking of Mrs. Burnsdale's rather brisk remarks about the lackadaisical Ladies' Aid. "But about the affair last night. Well, it turned out for the best, after all. Our Lord usually manages that."

The priest and the rabbi went out to Father Krupszyk's battered car, and drove off in a spume of smoke. Johnny's mood of elation sustained him. Not even the thundering rain could drench his spirits. The priest was telling the rabbi, as they rattled through the streaming streets, about a priest of whom his grandfather had told him. "He was young, like Johnny, Rabbi. And he believed in people, that is, most of the time.

He lived in a wretched little mud village—I've seen some of the Polish villages myself. He decided that the people not only lived like pigs, they thought like pigs. It was not their fault, he said. No one had tried to inspire them, to lift them up, and to teach them that the landowners were only men and could be brought to reason and justice, and to cease their oppression of the people. So the priest set up a little school, to teach not only children, but men and women, how to read and write. The landowners didn't like that. But the people were so devoted to the new young priest that the landowners were afraid to bother him—much.

"His father had been a poor peasant. But the old priest of the village had detected a vocation in the young boy, and so he was educated for the priesthood. He would devote his life to his people, he said. And so he began."

"It's an old story," said the rabbi with apprehension.

Father Krupszyk nodded, deftly swung his car away from the flooded gutter. It lurched. "Mustn't get the points wet," he said. "Sorry. One of these days I'll try to find out how you get money enough from a parish to buy yourself a car that doesn't break down and get its points wet all the time. A good thing for me that I'm a mechanic too. Well, about that young Polish priest. When the adults could read and write, the priest got books for them, though how he managed that is still a mystery. So they began to read, and when they began to read they began to think. My grandfather was a descriptive old party. I could see those poor peasants, huddling together, men and women alike, in the priest's icy parlor, with the stove in the corner and sunflower seeds drying on the top of it, and not giving out much heat either, for priests were supposed to keep warm in the ecstasy of God—and the young priest in his worn cassock reading to them, and talking to them, and discussing things with them, and, later, giving them hot tea in thick glasses and perhaps some black bread smeared with pork or mutton fat, and the kerosene lamp fluttering and smelling, and, at the bare narrow windows, the snow coming down and down and down, mixing with the mud until it was all one flux, and the sky about the same color—well, I could see the big peasant faces turned to the young thin priest, the women's hair under handkerchiefs, and all of them, men and women alike, in high felt boots, stamping their feet to warm them."

The rabbi was half dreaming. He remembered those villages very well.

"The priest," said Father Krupszyk, "had a wonderful voice, my grandfather told me. He could sing like an angel. And he had a flute. After the lessons were over he'd sing for his 'children,' though they were old enough, most of them, to be his parents, and he'd play his flute. It was a fine silver flute. He never mentioned who gave it to him. The peasants began to believe the priest was a saint. They were more and more devoted to him. They held up their heads a little. Then some of the peasants who worked on the land, encouraged by the priest, began to demand that the landowners treat them a little better, and mend their thatched huts, and give them some money. Ah," said the priest, shaking his head, "that was a bad day for our young priest."

"Naturally," said the rabbi sadly.

"On more than one occasion," his friend went on, "the young priest would lead delegations to the grand houses, and would talk temperately and gently to the owners, who let him come as far as the door. You see, they had their own church, about five miles away, and a very able priest, who had expressed his serious doubts of the young priest on more than one occasion. In fact, he'd written their bishop about Father Ignatius very strongly. The bishop would reply soothingly; he was a very just old man and not very popular with the landowners himself. He too had been a peasant's son, and he was a little skeptical of the other priest who had been a landowner's son, and who had ambitions to replace the bishop in the not too distant future. It wasn't until much later that it was found out that the bishop had given Father Ignatius his beautiful silver flute. It's in a church in Poland now," said Father John Kanty thoughtfully, "unless the Nazis or the Russians stole it.

"The landowners decided that Father Ignatius was a menace. How to get rid of him? A delegation, in fine carriages with black horses and silver harnesses, went to see the bishop. The bishop knew they were coming. He deliberately received them in his kitchen, to their disgust, and as they talked to him he reflectively cracked sunflower seeds and threw the shells on the tiled floor. Then he said to them, 'Go home, treat your people as fellow Christians in the sight of Our

Divine Lord, and honor Father Ignatius as a devoted priest.' You can imagine what they thought of the bishop then!"

"I haven't any difficulty imagining," said the rabbi.

"So they decided they'd have to take things into their own hands. Nothing as crude as the hired police, of course. That would make the people suspicious, and they'd resist. Moreover, the people said, the priest was performing miracles. Children brought to him *in extremis* suddenly revived. Men coughing their lungs out in consumption got up from their beds and went directly to the fields. Women lying in childbirth suddenly delivered, sat up, and demanded hot tea. That was during, or just after, the time Father Ignatius had visited them. This alarmed the landowners more than anything else. A saint would be much harder to discredit than just a poor young priest."

"But saints die oftener," said the rabbi. "And more terribly."

Father Krupszyk nodded grimly. "At this point my grandfather would become a little obscure, and brief. He didn't know just what happened. But all at once smooth men appeared to harangue the peasants in the fields. The priest was in league with the devil. They had been born, the peasants, to a humble station ordained by God; they would suffer hellfire if they rebelled, and if they asked that their rumbling stomachs be filled a couple of times a week. The priest was leading them right down into the pit, teaching them rebellion against their ordained masters. It was anarchy."

"A very old story," said the rabbi again.

Father Krupszyk deftly brought his complaining car in front of the rabbi's house. "There," he said, "we got here, though I had my doubts that we'd make it."

"What happened to Father Ignatius?" asked Rabbi Chortow.

"Oh, he was canonized quite a few years ago," said the priest. "After all, he was a saint. They built a shrine to him, and the miracles went on. At least, that's the last I heard, before the Nazis, or the Russians, got there."

The rabbi looked at the priest's strong, blunt profile, and he saw the brooding anger on it. He said, "Of course, Father Ignatius overcame his enemies, and lived to a fine old age, in honor."

"No," said the priest. "You see, the peasants burned down his house one night, and killed him." He tentatively raced the ancient motor of the car. "They found the flute in the ruins. It wasn't even smeared with soot."

20

"I can find nothing in the record to show that Mr. Fletcher has neglected either the health or the education of his foster children," said old Judge Bridges, pulling at his long, thin white nose with its red tip. "Except for a few anonymous and obviously malicious letters. The officers of the Children's Aid S o c i e t y have conducted a proper and thorough investigation."

He glanced at the United States Immigration and Naturalization officer from Philadelphia, who said, "We find no real substance for any report that any of these children have become public charges, or that they were likely to become public charges at the time of their entry into this country."

An officer of the Children's Aid Society agreed to all this, after an inimical glance from Dr. McManus. "Mr. Fletcher has promised that when his foster children have reached their age-group level in the public schools, he will send them to these schools. We agree with him that to send them now would be harmful, psychologically, to these children, for they would have to attend classes with children much younger than themselves."

The courtroom was bare, dreary, and filled with the shadows of the driving rain outside. A news photographer from the *Press* snapped Johnny's photograph.

"I find," said the judge, "that Mr. Fletcher has taken out fifteen thousand dollars insurance on his life, to provide for these children in the event of his death, and Dr. Francis Stevens of New York, a very prominent minister, has sent me an affidavit to the effect that he has established a trust fund for the benefit of these children. Moreover," and the judge coughed, "Dr. Alfred McManus of this city has assured me that he has made a new will leaving these children a very considerable sum. They are very fortunate indeed."

Johnny looked with amazement at Dr. McManus, who ignored him. The lawyer representing him and the children then rose and thanked the judge, gathered up his brief case, shook hands with Johnny and the doctor, and ran out. "There goes three thousand dollars," muttered the doctor crossly. "Don't bother me, son. I've got to get to the hospital. Shut up. I'm not going to talk to anyone as stupid as you about wills. How's Jean getting along on the crutches?"

Johnny smiled at him, still amazed and confused. "You know how he's getting along. You were with us last night. I still can't get over how fast you medical fellows can heal bones these days, with pins and things."

The clerk was calling another case, and they left. "Well, that's over," said Johnny, pulling on his raincoat. "I couldn't help worrying. But after all—"

"God provides," said the doctor gloomily. "It's a good thing He has people like me around. I'd like to see how He'd get along if there weren't so many suckers in this world—like me, for instance. Well, I have my price too. You know I'm coming on Thursday for Thanksgiving dinner? I haven't had a Thanksgiving dinner in that house since I was a boy."

Johnny, later in the day, appeared in County Court where he was given preliminary adoption papers. Here he encountered a small difficulty. A little brown woman he had never seen before rose up with a flash of eyeglasses and remarked that Mr. Fletcher was not married. The judge sarcastically called her attention to the fact that the unmarried state was not detrimental to adoptions, and that the court had investigated. He looked at Johnny and his eyes twinkled. "And there's no guarantee that Mr. Fletcher will escape matrimony in the long run. He looks sound in wind and limb."

Johnny went out into the dark wind and dark cold. As he was about to cross the street a young woman passed him with a long stride, her raincoat glistening, her blond head held high and proudly. Johnny's heart jumped with unaccountable hope. But she could not be Lorry Summerfield! Now he was namelessly despondent, remembering his dream. A sense of profound loneliness and aching came to him. He found his ancient car, but did not start it immediately, looking through the streaming windshield at the mournful street. Why had he hoped, with that bounding of his heart, that the girl he had seen was Lorry? Why did the very thought of her make him tremble, and his face become hot? She was in New York; she was working with her brother. This Dr. McManus had told him.

"She wouldn't even look at me," said Johnny aloud, as he turned the ignition key. "There isn't any place in her life for me. The idea's ridiculous. And coming down to it, there isn't any place in my life for her either."

He arrived home much depressed, to find only a few calls for him, none of them sick calls, to his relief. All matters referring to meetings and church affairs. He sighed, sat at his desk, and listened to the sound of the children's voices in the dining room as they discussed lessons with Miss Coogan. He opened his desk drawer and took out Lorry's golden box and held it tightly in his hand. It seemed to give out a tender warmth against his flesh. Mrs. Burnsdale, glancing in at him maternally, thought to herself that he needed a wife. He gave so much to everybody, but no one, she reflected, gave him anything. Except, of course, affection. But one of these days—and she knew how time passed—the children would be grown and gone, and he would be alone, and the children would have their own lives. She could see him, gray and lonely and old, in this very wretched room. He was still young, but tomorrow he would be middle-aged, then elderly, then aged, watching for the children's letters, listening to the wind and the rain, getting up to visit the sick, returning to an empty dining room, reading alone, then going to a cold bed. And then, finally, a lonely grave in a forgotten cemetery, like too many ministers.

Driven by these emotions, she went as fast as possible into

the parlor. The lamps had been turned on; Johnny was writing his sermon for Thanksgiving Day. The golden box was near his hand. He looked up and smiled at Mrs. Burnsdale as she came in so precipitously. "Anything wrong?" he asked. "Am I needed?"

She stood before him, her hands on her hips. "You know, sir, that's what you always ask! Nobody asks that of you. Nobody!"

He put down his Army-issue fountain pen and looked at her, puzzled.

"How's your cold?" she demanded, in an unusually loud voice. "After being out in the rain?"

"My cold?" he said. He coughed tentatively. "Why, it's practically gone." He smiled again. She came closer to the desk, and her blunt features worked. "Mr. Fletcher, I'm awfully worried about you. All the things that've happened here in this town. Mr. Fletcher, don't you think you should get another parish, in another city?"

"Why, that's what Dr. Stevens asked me in his letter the other day." Johnny was amused. "He's worried about me."

"Well, I am too!" Mrs. Burnsdale suddenly gulped. "I'm afraid of this town, Mr. Fletcher."

Johnny studied her contemplatively. "Well, I'm not. People are the same everywhere. And the children are putting down roots here. Pietro's got friends from his church, and Kathy's got friends from the Sunday school, and even Max has brought a kid or two home. He models them in his clay. You know, he's going to be a sculptor! He's always working in clay. He made a head of Rabbi Chortow, and it's wonderful. And Father John Kanty sends over children to visit Jean. And Pietro's in the choir of the church. They like the town. So do I."

Mrs. Burnsdale was silent, but the terror did not leave her. "What's wrong?" asked Johnny gently. "Are you afraid that there'll be more trouble?"

She shook her head dumbly. Her small eyes implored him. Then she said, "I don't know, Mr. Fletcher. I was thinking about you, in the kitchen, and I—well, I sort of saw you in this room, old, you know, and the kids gone and grown up, and you not having any wife, or anybody."

To his distress, one or two tears ran down her cheeks. "Mr. Fletcher, we couldn't get along without you. You've got to take care of yourself. It isn't that I don't trust God." She pushed out her lower lip, then tossed her head defiantly. "Well, maybe I don't, in a way. You trust God, and something awful happens, and you can't see why. You're supposed to trust Him, but trusting can sure be pretty hard on you."

He patted her fat shoulder. Oddly, his loneliness had lifted. He walked with Mrs. Burnsdale into the kitchen, and sniffed appreciatively at the pots. "Ah! Spareribs and sauerkraut! And lemon pie."

At this point Pietro marched into the kitchen, fixed his merry eyes with as much sternness as possible on the minister, and announced, "My name is Peter."

"Why, so it is, Pietro," said Johnny.

"I mean, Papa, I am not Pietro now, I am Peter. Pietro—poof!" He made a wide circle of contempt with his arms. "It is not American."

"Who said so?" asked Johnny, approvingly inspecting another pot.

"Keep out of that pie!" shouted Mrs. Burnsdale, slapping Pietro's wandering hand. He sucked the meringue from his fingers and said, "I say so, Papa."

"A man called Petrus, or Pierre or Pietro, is still Peter," said Johnny. "Besides, I like your name. Why should you have a name that's no different from anyone else's? Don't you want to be different?"

Pietro looked longingly at the pie, then at Mrs. Burnsdale's threatening face, then with bright interest at the stove. Like Johnny, he inspected the savory pots. "No," he said.

"Why not?"

Pietro was uncertain, now. Then, after a long contemplation, he said, "Okay. Pietro. I am going to be a priest, Papa. Do you believe it?"

"No," said Johnny.

Pietro laughed. "No. I shall be the great singer. I shall make a lot of money."

"No doubt," said Johnny.

"And the ladies will love me," said Pietro with satisfaction.

"Now where does that kid get his awful ideas?" asked Mrs. Burnsdale disapprovingly.

"He comes by them naturally," said Johnny. "The Italians are the one race who really appreciate the opposite sex."

"I have thought of marrying Miss Summerfield," said Pietro seriously. "But then she is too old. Kathy has hair like hers. I think," he said, giving the matter thought, "that I shall marry Kathy. I like yellow hair."

"If you don't get away from those cookies," said Mrs. Burnsdale, lifting a ladle menacingly, "you'll have a different color on your behind, young man."

"What is a cooky?" said Pietro, disdainfully, as he chewed it with appreciation. "Yes. I shall marry Kathy. For her hair."

Kathy, who had heard her name mentioned, came briskly into the kitchen. "What's the matter with my hair?" she demanded.

Pietro studied her admiringly. "I have just seen you are pretty," he said.

Kathy gave him a formidable stare. "A kid like you," she said, scornfully. "By the way, Papa, I have another name."

"You too?" said Johnny.

Kathy, seeing that Mrs. Burnsdale was washing some dishes, automatically took up a dishcloth, and Mrs. Burnsdale gave her a loving glance. "I have met a girl, in Sunday school," she said. "Her name is Charmenz. We all call her Charm. So, I am now Charm. At home, of course. There is no use having two people with the same name in Sunday school; it's confusing."

"It's stupid," said Mrs. Burnsdale severely. "I don't know what's got into you kids. Pietro wants to change his name, and then you do."

Kathy was startled. She looked at Pietro, who was reaching slyly into the cooky jar again. She screamed, "Stay away from those cookies! You eat everything, you pig!"

Mrs. Burnsdale, who was an expert in these matters, swiftly folded a towel into a deadly length and slapped Pietro heartily about the legs. This delighted him. He made high short leaps around the kitchen, stuffing cookies into his mouth, while Mrs. Burnsdale pursued him. Johnny laughed at the sight of this dark faun skipping ahead of the not very agile Mrs. Burnsdale, while he ate with measured enjoyment. Finally he gave a very long leap, and in the very midst of it he pushed open the dining-room door and disappeared.

"I think," said Kathy coldly, "that I'll still be Kathy. Anything Pietro wants to do is wrong. Of course."

"You are such a sensible girl," said Mrs. Burnsdale. There was a small mirror over the sink. Kathy studied her reflection, preened a little, saw with pleasure that in the steam of the kitchen a curl or two had developed around her temples, and that her round cheeks were satisfactorily pink. "I hope not," she said.

Johnny, unaccountably lighthearted now, went out into the rain. There was nothing like children! Nothing! Especially his. And how they had changed these many weeks. It was rare, now, to see the old gleaming hatred in their eyes, the old fear. Sometimes they reacted a little too strongly to situations, but even these occasions were becoming fewer. They were devoted to their lessons; they learned with a kind of consuming avarice. The head-shrinkers, thought Johnny, would say they are becoming adjusted. They are only becoming aware that love will never fail them.

He went through the church, where the great candelabra stood on the altar, the candlelight dissipating the dark and surging against every wooden pillar. Fresh flowers stood beside them. Above the altar gleamed the faded gold of a large cross. No one had protested, to Johnny's knowledge. He had paid twenty-five dollars for the cross, secondhand. "Lord," he said, "I know it doesn't matter where a man prays, but I'm glad Thy House is bright."

Humming to himself, he went down into the basement, the parish hall, where a great deal of hammering was going on. Bookshelves lined the old plastered walls; the wood was a soft and lustrous pale tint, faultless and exquisite. Johnny vaguely assumed it was pine, but it was, in fact, the best mahogany, unstained. Several men, and boys, were in the process of making tables. The basement smelled of sawdust. Among the men was George Harding, Lon's father, and among the cropped-headed, thin-faced boys, was Lon himself. They greeted Johnny with friendly reserve, and went on with their work. Johnny said to Lon, "How's the new school these days?"

"They sure work hell out of you," said Lon earnestly. "Hey, I'm sorry, sir. I mean, there's no fooling around. I really have to work." He grinned. "I'm learning a lot." Now his opaque eyes looked at the minister with intense affection; he picked up his hammer and began to pound on a table. Johnny smoothed his hand over it. It was darker wood than the bookshelves, so sleek, so blond, so well made. It was oak. Well, oak was even better than pine for tables; it didn't splinter. Again Johnny looked proudly at the bookcases. "Best pine I've ever seen," he said.

One of the boys made a choking sound, then coughed abruptly, and with convulsive movements of his shoulders. Johnny gave him a cough drop, absently. He hoped to have his "school" ready after Christmas. Huge cartons of books stood in the corners of the hall, under the raw bulbs, and there were other cartons, containing student lamps which Johnny had bought secondhand. He could see the shelves filled, the lamps glowing, the heads of young boys and girls bent seriously over the books, the teachers sitting among them, piles of neat white paper and many pencils close at hand. He went to a bookshelf and smoothed his hand over the satin finish. The wood had been donated by three friends of George Harding's, who worked in Ben Guston's lumber mills. He turned to them, smiling, and caught sudden and anxious expressions, before they bent their faces over their work again. "I hope it didn't cost you fellows too much," he said. "And I don't have to tell you how grateful I am."

Miss Coogan was going to help in the evenings, though Johnny had protested. The Ladies' Aid had, with grim determination of which Johnny knew nothing, literally impressed three elderly retired women teachers into service.

Dr. McManus was again thinking of Johnny as he sipped his after-dinner brandy in the living room of MacDonald Summerfield's home. He was also unusually irascible. "That confounded head-shrinker," Dr. Somer Granger, the psychiatrist, was present, and he was indiscreetly, and with amused and superior laughter, relating tales of his patients, who were all known to his host and hostess. Dr. Granger called a spade a spade, but his frank mention of delicate places of the human anatomy did not offend Mrs. Summerfield, who smiled. Everything in a man or a woman's life, Dr. Granger always insisted, was directly connected with these delicate areas, and he proved it in his stories.

"Well, there's been a short circuit, then, in your own life," Dr. McManus often remarked sourly. Dr. Granger was a bachelor. Esther Summerfield, at this, would look casually amused. Though her husband and daughter, and most of her friends, considered her a harmless and not very bright faddist, Dr. McManus knew better. She's the only one in the house who isn't a fool, he would remark to himself. There was only one thing that he could not understand about Esther, and that was her affection for her husband.

Dr. McManus, tonight, tried to get his mind off Johnny. He said, as he had said many times before, "Somer, one of these days I'm going to remember my medical ethics and report you to the AMA for revealing your patients' names, and that'll be one idiot less in the medical profession." Dr. Granger laughed heartily at this; he was a close friend of Mr. Summerfield. "Can't doctors talk about patients with each other?" he had asked. "Besides, we're all friends here, and not gossips."

"Well, you are, you damned old maid," said Dr. McManus, and shifted in his chair. It was not a Chinese chair. The Chinese motif had vanished suddenly from this large room. Now it was all Hindustani, which the doctor considered even worse. Esther Summerfield was swathed in a sari of a light pink, bordered with gold, with a headpiece, "like an infernal swami," the doctor commented to himself. She had talked of yoga that night, with considerable animation. She was taking lessons, by mail, from some organization in Los Angeles. Her tilted dark eyes danced on Dr. McManus. "Imagine, Al. Later on I'll be able to sit in absolute and motionless silence for hours, hardly breathing, if even that."

"Why don't you teach it to Somer?" asked the doctor. The psychiatrist was jeeringly announcing that he expected one of his more distressed patients to commit suicide at any time. Dr. McManus said, "Maybe he'll stop breathing forever."

Dr. Granger, hearing his name, said impatiently, "What? What?"

"I'm wondering when I'll have the pleasure of signing your death certificate," said Dr. McManus. "We were talking about yoga, Esther and I. From what I hear, I think you should take it up, yourself."

Dr. Granger knew all about yoga. He was an authority on it, he said. He was an authority on everything. Pompously, he gave a brief lecture which embraced the mysteries of Hinduism. Mrs. Summerfield listened idly. Dr. McManus suddenly remembered, as Dr. Granger's voice droned on, that someone had told him Granger "had something" on Summerfield. He stared at Mr. Summerfield intently. He had always thought of Mr. Summerfield as a wealthy man, who, perhaps for reasons of ennui or something slightly more sinister, was trying to play Machiavelli in Barryfield. But all at once the doctor thought that he discerned a change in his old acquaintance's face and manner, a dimly distraught, confused, and faintly agonized change. Nonsense, he said to himself. He's just the same as ever. Then he stared harder at Mr. Summerfield, and told himself, with wonder, that this was no change at all, but something which had always been there. Now I'm fanciful, said the old doctor irritably in his mind. Just gossip.

"Now," said Dr. Granger, "there is the Gita."

"Oh, shut up!" said Dr. McManus. "You don't really know a damned thing about the whole subject. I do. I spent two years in India, trying to find out why in hell the poor devils who bathe in the filthy Ganges not only don't pollute the water with their disease, but actually get cured of it. Never did find out; medical mystery to this day."

"Psychosomatic," said Dr. Granger, unoffended. "They aren't really ill, they—"

"Never heard of a psychosomatic germ yet," said Dr. Mc-Manus. "By the way, not to change this fascinating subject, what happened to Sloan Meredith, who went to you when I told him he ought to have his gall bladder out?"

Dr. Granger waved a large and meaty hand in derision. "He stopped treatments, against my advice, about six weeks go. I was just getting deep into his subconscious, and his wife was reporting that he was having fewer of his alleged attacks at night. It seems that he and his mother—"

The doctor's eyes sparkled like hoarfrost. "Never mind about Sloan's mother. I'm asking you about Sloan."

"I told you, Al. He suddenly stopped coming. His wife said that he was beginning to feel worse. That was because I was probing too deep for him."

"With what? A scalpel?"

Dr. Granger paused. "What do you mean?"

Dr. McManus moved in his uncomfortable teakwood chair, which was inlaid with ivory. "Well, it turned out that one big gallstone he couldn't pass perforated last night. He died on the operating table this morning. I couldn't save him." With satisfaction, he watched the younger doctor pale. "It was gallstones all the time, not his subconscious."

Dr. Granger's authoritative voice faltered. "But—but—he was very disturbed—"

"Sure he was! Ever have a gallstone attack, Somer? No? Well, I'll remember to ask for a few for you in my prayers. Nothing like a gallstone attack to make even a psychiatrist crawl all over his bed, whimpering and screaming like a wounded puppy. Give you an idea of what a psychosomatic stone can do to your nerves, and your subconscious!

"Somer," said the old doctor as he pulled his massive body upright, and shook his finger at the psychiatrist. "You knew damned well that I'm a conservative surgeon; never advise an operation unless it's a matter of saving a man's life. I don't usually operate even to cure moderate discomfort; a man can get along with that, with a few aspirins now and then. And what's discomfort? I'm not one of those money-hungry fellows who rush a patient to the hospital with an appendix which is acting up a little for the first time. So, when I heard Sloan'd gone to you, I called up and told you the whole story, and I sent you his X rays. A thing I never did, without being asked, any time before in my life. You're a medical man, as well as a damned head-shrinker. You can read X rays. Yet, just because Sloan was making a lot of money in his foundry, you took him on, though you could see with half an eye what was really the matter with him."

The others listened avidly. Dr. Somer Granger swallowed visibly a few times. He was a big man in his early forties, athletic and swift of movement, with a long, rectangular face, narrow blue eyes, a bald head, and an absurd pug nose. Always fluent in speech, he could not speak now.

"You killed him, Somer. Oh, you can't be hanged for it. I know. They used to hang medical men in the healthier times of the Middle Ages when they were guilty of malpractice. Not now, unfortunately. Look, I'm not saying that psychiatry doesn't have its place. It does, emphatically, but it should always be under the close jurisdiction of the family physician; it should only supplement general medicine, not replace it. And I'm dead sure, from my experience, that a priest or a minister or a rabbi could work better in that direction than you fellows. You've become the high priests of esotericism; you've got a yoga jargon of your own, and it's dangerous—for fools. You should be forced to wear the peaked hat and the yellow zodiacal robes of the wizards of the Dark Ages. Just so people could recognize you for what you are."

In spite of his preoccupation, Mr. Summerfield suddenly looked amused. Esther laughed.

Dr. Granger had not recovered his color, but only his bumptious aplomb, which rarely failed him. He said, "Now, Al, that's going too far. You surgeons are all for surgery. Yes, I looked over Sloan's X rays, and your report, very carefully. But I've known dozens of cases where gall-bladder trouble was psychosomatic in origin; in fact, I'm sure that practically all cases are such. Aggressive, hostile personalities, most of them, suspicious and usually obese, for they try to alleviate their tensions by overindulgence in rich foods. In many cases psychiatric treatment has completely cured their trouble. How was I to know that Sloan's wouldn't too? He was getting along all right; reduction in weight, less insomnia, general well-being. It wasn't until I started probing about his mother—well, I'm sorry. I'll go to see Molly first thing in the morning."

"I wouldn't," said Dr. McManus. "She was against you from the start. And she's got three big brothers, who kind of liked Sloan. No sir, I wouldn't go, if I was you." He regarded the psychiatrist somberly.

He said abruptly, "Do you believe in God, Somer?"

"What? What?" Then the psychiatrist smirked indulgently. "I see you don't. You know what I'd do if I had the power? I wouldn't let a psychiatrist practice his art, if you can call it that, unless he was convinced of the existence of a God. Too many of you have contempt for your patients; you wouldn't have, if you believed in the existence of God. You're dangerous."

Mr. Summerfield said smoothly, with no expression on his face, "Al has gotten religion since he installed that troublemaking minister of his in his church. He's gotten soft in the head, our old reactionary Al." He gave Dr. McManus a long, pale-blue glance.

"Keep away from my minister, Mac," said the doctor, with cold anger.

Mr. Summerfield laughed. "I told you that Al's gotten religion! If it weren't for him, that rabble-rousing minister would have been thrown out of this town by now."

"When did he ever rabble-rouse?" asked Dr. McManus with rage. "You helped send that mob to the parsonage!"

No one answered him.

"You stay away from my boy!" shouted Dr. McManus, turning purple.

"Curious case," said Dr. Granger. "Here's a young man, not married, and apparently not showing any interest in getting married. In some way he acquires five children, from different backgrounds. He brings them to this country, sponsors them, gets ready to adopt them. I never met him, but he interests me, as a psychiatrist. I've talked with a lot of people who've met him. Very strange. I talked with old Judge Bridges and the head of the Children's Aid Society, adoption division. They were uneasy about him."

"That's a lie," said Dr. McManus.

Dr. Granger shook his head soberly. "No it isn't, Al. Somebody, though, put pressure on them. Maybe we don't have to look far to find out who it is. From what I've heard, the man isn't quite normal. Normal men don't get stoned, don't incite mobs against them, don't stir up people."

"Christ did," said Dr. McManus.

Dr. Granger waved his large hand indulgently. "Well, we psychiatrists have a theory about that too. Normal men are adjusted, well-balanced, integrated. This man isn't, or he wouldn't have aroused such controversy in Barryfield. He would have settled down here comfortably, set about the business of raising those children under average and peaceful circumstances, and no one would have heard about him at all. The children, I understand, are completely abnormal."

Dr. McManus sat utterly still, his eyes stiff and unwinking.

"You see, Al," said the psychiatrist smugly, "I've investigated. It comes from my training in normal and abnormal behavior. There was one of the children who got his throat cut by another child. Normal children don't arouse that kind of hostility. I talked with some of the nurses in the hospital where one of the boys had had an operation—you operated, Al? They said he was completely out of his mind. Talked about his dead mother coming to see him every night, and jabbered in French when under sedatives, and sometimes screamed about soldiers coming to kill him. Delusions. He definitely had a persecution complex; I'd say he was suffering from schizophrenia. He sometimes blabbered to the nurses about his mother having been kicked to death, or something equally absurd. Definitely suffering from delusions."

Dr. McManus stood up, his squat and powerful body shaking. "Who told you to investigate an obscure and poverty-stricken minister and his children, Somer?"

Dr. Granger paused. His eyes flickered.

"What made you, a rich-as-hell Philadelphia psychiatrist, take an interest in him?"

"Now, Al. Everybody's talking about him. So I took on the investigation, naturally."

"You're a liar," said Dr. McManus brutally.

He drew a long and trembling breath. He turned to Mr. Summerfield. He said in his low and squealing voice, and he spoke with slow emphasis, "Mac, I warn you. Keep your hands off Johnny. You hear? Keep your hands off Johnny from this time henceforth. For, Mac," and he took a step closer to the other man, "if you don't, you're going to suffer for it."

"Al, are you threatening me?" asked Mr. Summerfield, with genuine concern. "Come now. We're old friends, though we don't see eye to eye about some things."

"I'm not threatening you, Mac. I'm just telling you. One of these days you'll know something about Johnny. I'm not ready to use it against you, just yet. But when you do know, it's going to break your heart, Mac. It's going to make you grovel, Mac."

Mr. Summerfield regarded him with narrowed eyes. "Look, Al, I don't like your protégé. But I sympathize with him. You think I'll sympathize with him more, when I know about him?"

"No," said Dr. McManus, and now his tiny eyes warmed with pity. "You'll sympathize with yourself, I think. Or others will feel sorry for you."

He turned and stumped out of the room. They were accustomed to his abrupt departures, and only Esther Summerfield followed him and took his arm. "Let's go down to the breakfast room, Al," she said, and her usually idle voice was urgent. He went with her, and they sat down together in the only normal room in the house, in the doctor's opinion, for it was all warm chintz and golden plain furniture. Esther, swathed in her diaphanous draperies, was incongruous there. She looked at her old friend gravely.

"You don't know what it means to me, dear, to be able to meet Lorry at your house when she runs into town for a weekend now and then. I think I never really knew Lorry before. No, Mac doesn't suspect that she is ever here. He writes to her in care of Barry, in New York, but she replies only to me." Esther turned her head aside sadly. "You know how I've tried to talk to Lorry about her father, but each editorial he publishes, sneering about Mr. Fletcher, or even some small quip, hardens her even more against him. A stony emotionalism, I suppose you'd call it. In a way," and now Esther smiled fondly, thinking of her daughter, "I can see her point, considering how much Mr. Fletcher has done for her. Who'd ever have believed it of Lorry, who only a few months ago jeered at pity and mercy and concern for others as weak sentimentality?"

The doctor chuckled. "Well, she wouldn't be showing it now if she hadn't had it in her to begin with. She was always one of those idealists; that's how the trouble started between her and her father years ago. Y'know, I begin to think about her and my boy, the parson, and then I wonder if there isn't what he'd call a pattern in human affairs after all. He's stood this town on its ear, right out of his own innocence, and partly because he honestly believes most people are decent, and will go the decent way, if they're shown. I don't agree to that, but I'm watching!"

Esther looked thoughtfully at her long dark hands. "Al, about Lorry and Mr. Fletcher. I know she comes here to get personal reports about him from you. Do you think—?"

"Romance?" The doctor grinned. "It's already there, but they're both too stupid to realize it. Oh, you're thinking of Mac. And Mac and Lorry, and the way they're wound up together. I don't know, Esther." He paused. "Is it my imagination, or something, or is Mac changing? He was always kind of remote and aloof, all his life, and never swooped down to reality even once that I can remember. Lorry's too much like him—all seething emotion under smooth white—what did you call it?—stone. But she's got common sense, too. Now, Mac—he's farther away from reality now then he ever was, seems to me. Abstracted. Looking at you, sometimes, as if he was both blind and deaf, and confused. Jumps, if you call him by name. Am I imagining things?"

Esther looked at the wall, and her face became taut with distress. "It isn't your imagination. Do you remember the first time MacDonald met Somer Granger? He met him, you know, in Philadelphia, and three years later induced him to open an office in Barryfield for one day a week. I—I never did think the association healthy. There's morbidity in such men as Somer, and he brought out morbidity in MacDonald, a thing I didn't realize he had. It was then that the trouble started between Lorry and her father; I hold Somer responsible for that. It's something that doesn't quite come out in the open; I can't put a finger on it, but it's there."

The doctor frowned, then nodded. "You know, most doctors who've been practicing long enough to get an insight into human nature, and how it works through the body, mistrust psychiatrists. Doctors have known all about psychosomatic medicine since Hippocrates, and even before him, and have taken it into all their calculations. Then along come the head-shrinkers, thinking they have a bright new idea, and only the young medical graduates or doctors who don't have confidence in themselves go for it. I often listen to the jargon. Worst of all, it's getting into the vocabulary of fools, and doing all kinds of mischief. When it reaches into politics, then God help us all!

"I never knew a psychiatrist who didn't have something mentally or emotionally wrong with him. It could be one or two of a million things; healthy people have quirks too, but they take 'em in stride. Psychiatrists can't handle them; they get patients, and they 'project,' as they call it, their own secret terrors and guilts and suffering on their patients. Or, even worse, they find themselves most congenial with patients who are enduring their own horrors. Then it's just an exchange between them, like ping-pong, or each one burrowing into the other's psyche for relief. Of course, occasionally one or both of them go mad."

Esther looked at him with sharp fear. "Yes, I'm sure you're right! MacDonald is getting worse all the time. It's—quickening—now. You know he never went in for all that radical business until he met Somer. Somer brought him to that; Somer directs what he does with his papers! How do

I know? I don't have any real proof, but there is always something vicious and inciting in his editorials after he's had a session with Somer. No, neither one of them is a Communist. Somer's an opportunist, and MacDonald thinks he's God."

She stood up, in her fear. "Al, MacDonald never speaks of his mother. Did you know her?"

"Why, yes, I did. A real nice girl, Esther. A healthy, witty girl. She used to think Mac's father a pompous, pretentious fool, in a nice affectionate way. She died when Mac was about thirteen, I think. They'd already left here." The doctor scowled, concentrating. "It was an accident. They'd just bought a big house in Philadelphia, and Evelyn was helping the servants get the house ready. It was a long time ago. She fell from the third floor, right down to the marble first floor. It was in the newspapers. They said she had been leaning over the balustrade, dusting off the big bright chandelier they'd just imported, and lost her balance."

The old doctor stood up suddenly, and took Esther by the arm. She stared at him with a kind of still terror. "What is it?" he demanded, in a hushed voice. She replied faintly, "I don't know. It's just—well, for a long time MacDonald's been muttering about his mother in his sleep. I think he hated her."

The doctor shook her. "Esther! Don't you get ideas now! Stop it, you hear? Stop it!"

She whispered, "Al, once I overheard MacDonald and Somer talking about Mrs. Summerfield. They were in Mac-Donald's study. I just caught one word: 'guilt.' Al, I'm afraid."

The doctor tried to laugh. "I know what Granger was up to. He was trying to convince Mac that he felt guilty for hating his mother, and maybe wishing she would die, or something, and then the accident happened, and he kept it in his mind, which hasn't really grown up yet, that his wish about his mother had something to do with her death. I wonder," he added, "how much Somer hated his own mother?"

Esther sighed. "Frankly, I think the whole world's losing its collective mind. Either the war caused that, or it caused the war. Sometimes I have nightmares, wondering what the world will be like when governments go insane—like the Russian government. What will happen to the rest of us?"

"Oh, they'll think up a whole series of wars then. And

when they find clumps of sane people huddling together, they'll murder them. They always have. But, somehow, a few sane people manage to survive."

They moved together toward the shut door. Esther said, "Al, your minister's in danger, and his children, too. MacDonald will never let up on him. He looks and acts demented whenever his name is mentioned. MacDonald's ruined other men before, you know. Who will protect your minister?"

"Why," said the doctor with a saturnine smile, "God will. That's what the parson says. Hope he's right."

21

The children listened with the deepest interest to Johnny's story about Thanksgiving. But after he had finished they sat in silence, puzzled. This was not exactly the reaction Johnny had expected. He had bought the children a large book on the subject, filled with colored pictures of Indians and Pilgrims and snow and turkeys and wigwams and log cabins. Jean held it on his knee now and thoughtfully pulled at his pale lip. The other children craned around his chair to watch the pictures go by slowly. "Well," said Johnny, nonplused, "isn't it a wonderful story?"

"I think the Indians were stupid," said Jean.

"Stupid?"

"Or, Papa, perhaps not stupid." Jean gave him that wise old smile of his. "They were like you, perhaps? They forgave men who injured them, yes? The white men came to this country, the country of the Indians, and cut down the forests to build their houses, on the land of the Indians, and made the Indians help them whether they wanted to or not, and though you did not say, I believe they thought the Indians not so good as they. Yes? I have been reading books Miss Coogan brings me, about Indian wars, and I have been thinking, and I do not find the white man—heroic—is that the word? I find him very wicked, and always very wicked, and very much more wicked in the way he stole the country of the Indians from the Indians. And that was not enough for the white man, all the land and the mountains and the lakes and the fish and the game. He must make slaves of the Indians, and kill them, when they try to keep the land which Our Lord gave to them."

"You have a point there," said Johnny, thinking of India and China and all the lands of the exploited, oppressed East, where the white man had set up his colonies and had treated the natives as less than men. There was something brewing in Asia now, something explosive and terrible, and very ominous.

Jean sighed. He ran a thin finger gently over the noble picture of an Indian chief depicted as humbly offering a basket of fruit to a very haughty Pilgrim and his purse-lipped wife. "See," said Jean. "The chief gives the fruit of his land to a man who should be on his knees to receive it, for he is a thief, and should beg for forgiveness. The chief has permitted him to keep the land he has stolen or taken in blood, and has forgiven him."

"He is very beautiful," said Kathy. "His skin is prettier than the Pilgrim's. He is like a bird. The Pilgrim is very ugly."

"Why didn't the Indians drive off the white man who stole their country?" asked Pietro.

Johnny said grimly, "The white man had guns. He always has. And now he has the atomic bomb. That makes him even more superior."

Max was very grave. "Who told him the white man is better?" he asked in his low, uncertain voice.

"He did," said Johnny. He had almost decided that his Thanksgiving story was a failure, or that, at the very least, it had holes of some dimensions in it. "You can't go too deep into things," he added, without much conviction.

Pietro flashed him one of his sharp white smiles. "Why not?" he demanded. Why not, indeed? Johnny asked himself. "Well, anyway," he said, "I suppose we should thank God that He permitted us to stay here, in the country we stole from the Indians. It's a beautiful country."

Kathy looked smug. "Miss Coogan says the Pilgrims didn't

like people who didn't believe what they believed. They made others leave the colonies—and other places too—when these men wanted to love God like Jean and Pietro do. Out into the cold and the forests, the Pilgrims sent them. The Pilgrims," added Kathy, "were very bad men, and I don't love them at all, and I don't think I care about their Thanksgiving."

Pietro had picked up considerable American slang from the children in his catechism classes. "It is a fake," he said.

Johnny was holding Emilie in his arms, and smoothing her long curls as she half dozed, in content. He looked at the triumphant children; their eyes were a little accusing, as if he had offered them something bogus. He was not quite sure that he hadn't. He said, "Well, it's become a different story now in our country. We thank God that He's had mercy on us, and kept us—well, safe, shall I say?—and that we have friends and families to love us, and food to eat. It's a general Thanksgiving, to God."

"Just once a year?" asked Pietro with false demureness. "We should thank God just once a year? He should be pleased with that?"

"Now look, kids," said Johnny, with some sternness. "You know that isn't what I mean. Don't we thank God for every meal we eat, at this very table? And as often as possible, in church, and before we go to bed? Can't we make a special day of thanksgiving too? Any law against it? Look at us. Here we sit in a warm dining room, after a good dinner, and we love each other, and you know how much I love you, and there's Mrs. Burnsdale in the kitchen, and beds upstairs, and heat, and you've got good clothes, and hundreds of other things. Can't we make a real special occasion of thanking Our Lord, on a very special day, without all these arguments? You kids argue about every infernal thing. I don't know where you pick it up."

"Okay," said Pietro, coming around to Johnny's chair and giving him a warm kiss. "We make a special time to thank God. If that pleases Papa."

"Pleasing me has nothing to do with it," said Johnny helplessly. He continued with some reproach, "I'm not so sure that Father John Kanty is doing the right thing, Pietro, in making you one of his altar boys. You don't have the proper attitude."

The dramatic Pietro folded his hands together, rolled up his eyes, and said meekly, "Okay, okay. I have the proper attitude."

Kathy came to Johnny's rescue in her efficient way. "It is your turn, Pietro, to wipe the dishes, so go into the kitchen. Max, you must take the pie plates away, and all the silver. Come, come, you lazy boys."

Max and Pietro obeyed Kathy as they did not always obey Mrs. Burnsdale. They were often mutinous and impatient, and raucous in their demands and protests. For this Johnny was deeply grateful. He would especially rejoice in himself when Max complained of being given too large a share of the household chores; sometimes Max would even slam a door, and stamp off. No day passed but the children became increasingly more normal, and more like children. Jean, older, wiser, and with a longer memory, kept too much of his reserve, and thought too much.

Only Jean, Johnny, and the sleeping child remained in the dining room. Johnny said gently, "Jean, son, sometimes it isn't the best thing to ask too many questions in front of the younger children. Besides, a lot of them are questions for which there aren't any answers. Do you understand?"

Jean considered this. He looked at Johnny with his light eyes, always so inscrutable, yet sometimes tender, as they were now. "It's best, sometimes, to get busy, like Kathy?"

"Well, yes," said Johnny. He thought of Martha, who was "busy with many things." He often believed that poor Martha had not been sufficiently appreciated by the clergy.

Jean folded his hands with that strange quietness of his, and rested them on the book. He studied Johnny for a long moment or two, and again his face was the face of a man who had known too much pain and too much sorrow. Yet it was a still face, grave and thoughtful. It was not the face of the wild and savage "wolf child" of a year ago.

Johnny waited. Jean said softly, "I often dream of my statue which my mother sent me. I often dream of the Lady whose image it is. The word is image, isn't it? You see how well I know my English now." He smiled.

"It's really remarkable. You kids study all the time," said Johnny.

"I love the Lady very much," said Jean. "Miss Coogan brings me books about her. God knew He was God, but

Mary knew He was her baby, her child, her son. Perhaps she thought more of Him that way than she thought of Him as God. It is like a mother?"

"Yes," said Johnny. "It's like all mothers, I think."

Jean repeated, "I love her very much. I think of her when Dr. McManus sends his car for me and Pietro, on Sundays, to go to Mass. And so at Mass I think of the Lady." He paused. "I want to be a priest. I have spoken to Father John Kanty. He thinks I am older than twelve, though I don't know, and I don't have a birthday, except the one you gave me when I came home from the hospital."

Johnny had given all the children birthdays, to give each a day of his own, and to add to the festivities. He said, "I don't think you're much older than twelve, Jean. But you were talking about becoming a priest. What does Father John Kanty say about it?"

"He thinks I have a vocation. Papa, you think so too?"

Johnny said silent. He looked into Jean's eyes, at his still hands. Then he said, "Yes, I think so."

"You aren't sorry?"

"No," said Johnny, greatly moved. "I'm very happy. If you're sure, Jean."

"I'm sure," said the boy. And now he was indeed a boy again, and his thin face lighted up mischievously. "And so," he said, "we'll have our Thanksgiving tomorrow, and we won't ask you too many questions, Papa."

Johnny carried Emilie up to bed. It seemed to him that she was gaining a little weight, and that there was some color in the small, translucent face.

Thanksgiving Day, after all the rain, was a day forged out of gold and distilled from light. The golden mountains leaned against the brilliant pale-amethyst sky, and the valley in which Barryfield lay, not smudged now with "smog," cradled the light in pure clarity. There was a radiant, ringing sound in the streets, created by children's voices, footsteps, horns, and the murmur of automobiles; there had been a heavy frost early in the morning. Its sequin glitter rebounded from the edges of windows, from the gray boughs of the trees, from every blade of grass, from the sides of buildings. It was indeed a day to give thanks for.

Johnny had not expected many to attend the service in the morning, for there were too many turkeys to be stuffed, too many last pies to be baked, too many houses to be given a last polish and dusting. But he found to his pleasure that every pew was filled, tightly. He walked to the altar buoyantly, in the shimmer and waves of candlelight. He smiled at his people, and they smiled back at him, not decorously, but with friendship.

"A man who observes Thanksgiving, or pays it lip service on just one day of the year, does not give thanks at all," he said. The church was cold, but the people listened to Johnny's deep and sonorous voice with unaffected attention. Dr. McManus was there. He sat huddled in the most bulky and most untidy brown overcoat Johnny had ever seen; it was impossible not to avoid the unreadable stare of his eyes, as he sat in his usual place in the first pew. Sometimes that stare disconcerted Johnny, and it did today, as he delivered his sermon. He looked beyond Dr. McManus.

"The Jewish people, at Passover," he said, "declare that if God had just rescued them from Egypt, that would be enough, that would be enough for thanksgiving. If He had only rescued them from Egypt and brought them safely through the Red Sea, that would have been more than enough for their reverent gratitude. If He had rescued them from Egypt and brought them through the Red Sea and had fed them with manna in the desert, that would have been boundlessly enough for them to give Him praise and worship. To all these He had added much more, without request, and only from His hand, which is never emptied of His love.

"And I say to you," continued Johnny, his voice rising in jubilation, "that if God had permitted us to live only one day, to know that He is, that would have been enough for us. If He had permitted us to live only one day and to know that He is, and had allowed us to see one sunrise or one sunset, that would have been more than enough. If, in addition, He has granted us one hour of loving, and being loved, how greatly has He blessed us!

"But, out of His endless bounty, He has given us thousands of days to know that He is, and to see the sunrises and the sunsets, and to love, and be loved. So now, indeed, we should say, 'It is enough, it is more than enough, it is bounty overflowing and running over! There is no need for more.'

"But He gave us still more. He gave us an eternity of beauty and love and knowledge of Him, not for an hour, a day, a year, or a thousand years. But forever. By no merit of our own, but only by His merit. Still, this was not enough love for God to give us. He must give us the ultimate. He must walk among us as a man, in order to show us the way through our self-willed darkness and agony and terror—the way to Him. He must die for us, and lift up His cross like a blazing light on the black hills of our sins.

"Not by our merit," said Johnny, his voice dropping into profound meditation, "but only by His most blessed merit, only by His love, which we do not deserve and can never deserve. For that love of God for us let us give thanksgiving. All else is as nothing compared with that, for it contains all we have, and all the gifts heaped about us. It is not possible, for these stupendous joys, to thank God adequately. But we can try."

The doors of the church were opened wide after the service, and it seemed to many that they were seeing the sunlight for the first time in years. They looked at the sky, lifting up their tired, earth-bound eyes, their weary hearts, their faltering faith, their faded hopes. It is enough, they said to themselves, many of the exhausted middle-aged, that I can see the mountains today, the mountains that were always there but which I hadn't seen for a long time. The younger folk hurried home, saying in their hearts, it is enough that I have a little warm house, and the children are waiting, and there is a turkey in the oven. And they all said to themselves, it is more than enough to know that God loves me and cares for me.

"Well," said Johnny later, going into the kitchen, "how was the sermon?"

Mrs. Burnsdale's eyes were slightly red. "Wonderful," she answered. "So short, too."

Johnny burst out laughing. "Is that your measure of a sermon?" he asked.

"Now you know that isn't so," she replied crossly. "You know, Mr. Fletcher, you're too good for this town and this church. You should have one of them cathedrals they've got in New York, on Riverside Drive, with bells that play hymns, right over the Hudson."

"Near Grant's Tomb," said Johnny. He looked at the oven. "How's the turkey coming along?" The kitchen was filled with celestial perfumes. Mrs. Burnsdale, with quiet ostentation, opened the oven door and gave Johnny a delightful glimpse of a turkey sizzling richly in a wet patina of golden butter. "Ah," said the young minister, "you know, even this would be enough."

He looked with pleasure at the rack of pumpkin and mince pies, at the peeled and waiting potatoes, the cranberry sauce. "To think I'm having a Thanksgiving in my own home," he said. "And with my own family. It's something to think about."

He and the children were permitted a small sandwich and milk in the dining room. Pietro had served as altar boy for the first time that morning. He was full of fascinating news, and explanations. He spoke with authority. Johnny said, "To listen to you, a person would come to believe that you instructed Father John Kanty yourself. Did you really tell him what to say, and where to stand?"

Pietro laughed. Kathy said, "He tells so many stories."

Jean was about to deflate Pietro thoroughly, for he had been at Mass too, then reflected this was no kindness for a coming priest. He said instead, "Pietro did very well. Not perfectly, of course, but well. He stumbled only once or twice, and was a little late, but only once or twice. But after all, he's new." He laughed at Pietro. "When I am a priest, you can be my altar boy."

"When I am the great singer, I shall send you a ticket," replied Pietro, condescendingly. "I have seen pictures of the Metropolitan Opera. There is a high balcony. You will like it up there."

Max told of the Thanksgiving service in the synagogue. "So many people," he said. "The rabbi was pleased. They put out iron chairs to sit on, in the back, and the upstairs was filled too. So soon we shall have a very big synagogue. The rabbi spoke of it, and said we should give thanks. Dr. Klein sent all of us his love."

"No one," said Kathy, "can speak like Papa. People wiped their eyes." She beamed at him lovingly.

"I love Papa," said little Emilie, nestling her head against Johnny's arm. Her big blue eyes shone on him, and his heart felt the familiar ache. But, surely, she was looking much better. There was a little bright color on her cheekbones. He was afraid to pray. He was afraid to touch her face, for fear that the color was fever.

They all went out to look at their trees. They looked, too, at the great purple mountains and the effulgent sky. Johnny was filled with rich content. He could not remember when he had been so happy. Now, if only Lorry were in town, everything would have been perfect. Her eyes were very vivid, all at once, in his inner sight. He sighed, and deliberately tried to forget.

At quarter to three Dr. McManus arrived, growling as usual. The children swarmed about him, while he pretended to fight them off. He had brought a large box of candy in the shape of pumpkins and turkeys for them. They were entranced. He went out into the kitchen, holding the box high over his head, while their hands reached for it. He gave it to Mrs. Burnsdale to put on an upper shelf. "None until after dinner," he said. He too looked at the turkey and the pies with satisfaction. The children, disappointed, left the kitchen. The doctor leaned against the refrigerator and smirked tolerantly at Mrs. Burnsdale.

Mrs. Burnsdale said, "Don't you touch those tarts!"

The doctor chewed one happily. "Homemade," he said. He stared at Mrs. Burnsdale, who wore a very neat black dress with a round white collar and cuffs. Johnny had given her that modest opal pin on the dress for her birthday in October. It was set in silver. She was wearing her very best "foundation" and her stocky figure had full and pleasant curves. Her gray hair was freshly waved, and had silver highlights, and her face glowed with natural color. "You know," said the doctor, "you're a very good-looking woman, Mrs. Burnsdale. How old are you? Fifty-seven? I'd say you're five years younger since you came here. Climate must agree with you." He looked at the dish of tarts, then put his hands in his pockets. "Best cook I ever saw. You wouldn't consider marrying me, would you?"

Mrs. Burnsdale laughed heartily. "Well, you ask me when Mr. Fletcher gets married and the kids are grown up! Doctor, you're a card."

"You're not up on modern slang," said the doctor. " 'Card' dates you. I've been learning slang from Pietro and that Lon Harding and his bunch of young delinquents. It's interesting. I think they'd call those tarts real frantic, or something. So, I have to wait until Johnny's married, eh? And then I'll be a doddering old—well, something, and you'd be marrying me only for my money. Whereas if you marry me right away I'll have my whole youth to give you."

Mrs. Burnsdale's eyes danced; a bloom of youthfulness covered her moist face. She said, "That reminds me. I've got another list."

"Not today you haven't," said the doctor, and bolted.

The dinner was a mighty success. Johnny looked at the young faces about him, at Mrs. Burnsdale, and at the doctor, and he marveled that God had been so exceedingly good to him, and had brought him to this city which had needed him and which he now loved, and in which his children were tentatively sinking their frail and injured roots.

"I had a call from Dr. Stevens this morning," he said as he demolished a drumstick, "from Florida. He had had something he calls a virus, and he is down there recovering. He's an old man now, and I think he's tired."

"Who wouldn't be, in this world?" asked Dr. McManus, thoughtfully eying the chestnut dressing. "Thanks, think I will," he said to Mrs. Burnsdale as she scooped out more of the crumbling, hot fragrance. "What do you mean, 'old man'? He isn't much older than I am, and I don't think I'm old."

"You've never been a minister," said Johnny. Dr. McManus gave him a sudden keen glance. Was it imagination, or were there really deeper lines in Johnny's face, older lines? Johnny continued, "It's a terrible responsibility, I know, to be a doctor, and have to care for the bodies of patients, and to wonder if you're doing the right thing. But to be a clergyman is an even more terrible responsibility. For you have to heal and minister to men's immortal souls. You know how eternally you can hurt, if you make a mistake, or you're careless, or in doubt yourself, or become mechanical in your ministrations. Father John Kanty told me that familiarity is the pit into which any clergyman can fall, to his awful harm and the harm to his people. The message, though never changing, fixed in eternity, is yet ever new, ever living, ever born in every instant, can never be slighted by hastiness, by taking for granted."

"You fellers remind me of Sisyphus," said the hardhearted doctor. "Every day you try to roll the big stone of your message to the top of the hill, sweating and bleeding in your tender consciences, and every morning it's down at the bottom again, and the people going along unconcerned at the top of the hill. At least when I take out a gall bladder it's out, and when I fix a leg it's fixed, and that's the end of it. If I had to repeat the same performance on the same people every day—well, I'd think I'd gotten into hell or a perpetual nightmare." He looked at the dressing on the platter again, but Mrs. Burnsdale shook her head sternly. He grumbled.

"One of these days," said Johnny, "we'll get the stone to the top. One fold, one Shepherd. Pietro, you know we don't suck our fingers."

"No?" said the mischievous little boy. "It's—appreciate."

"Appreciation," said Johnny absently. He paused, looked at his plate. "Is Miss Summerfield home for Thanksgiving, doctor?"

"No. Haven't heard from her lately," the doctor lied airily. "Why the interest?"

Johnny colored slightly. "Well, after all, I know her, she was good—she did such a wonderful thing—the children adored her."

"Ah," said the doctor, deftly slipping some dressing onto his plate when Mrs. Burnsdale's attention was on Pietro. "Just the children. By the way, Pietro's right. In Italy, where the people are civilized, it is considered a compliment to the cook to lick a finger or two delicately. That doesn't mean the whole hand," he said to Pietro.

"What is this football?" asked Max, who had become a devotee of the large and handsome radio the doctor had given the family a few weeks ago. "It is all exciting, and running and kicking."

"It's a game," said Johnny enthusiastically. "I was a quarterback." Kathy looked aloof and superior, but the three boys listened with sparkling attention. Max, however, had one small doubt. "But the people who watch, and the men who play—is it a waste of time?"

"Not at all," replied Johnny, with some irritation. "Remember, there is much room in life for joy and laughter and gaiety, Max, as well as for study and prayer. Besides, God wants us to enjoy His world." He was immediately contrite, for Max's face had become confused and a little lost again. "Enjoy it, son," said Johnny, more gently. "You are learning to play, but you must learn a little more. I'll buy you a football and teach you three boys to play. By the way, Kathy," he said, noting the girl's smug expression, "I hear you're doing pretty well, yourself, on your Sunday school softball team. I also hear that you've thought up some very funny ideas about new rules, not in the book. You're a tyrant, Kathy."

"I improve things," said Kathy loftily, as she reached for another tart.

"You're not improving your figure with all that overeating," said Mrs. Burnsdale. "Besides, you abide by the rules of a game. Remember that, miss."

Even little Emilie was eating well. When anyone's eyes met hers she gave them her radiant, blue-eyed smile. But the doctor studied her closely, and relapsed into melancholy thought.

Mrs. Burnsdale stood up briskly. "If anyone thinks I'm going to wash these dishes all by myself he and she are mistaken, I can tell you that. All you kids do is talk. Well?"

"The direct type," said Dr. McManus.

Kathy jumped up, heaving a happy sigh of repletion. Pietro and Max rose with less alacrity. "It is woman's work, dishes," said Pietro.

"Who told you that?" demanded Kathy. "You get the funniest ideas. You ate off the plates, didn't you?"

"It's a man's duty to pray, a woman's duty to work," said Max, not too hopefully.

"Get," said Kathy to him. She said to Jean, "Are you going to try to play the grown-up man again? You can sit in a chair in the kitchen and scrape and wipe, too." She handed Jean his two canes with an uncompromising air, and helped him out to the kitchen.

The doctor said, "I pity the man who will marry that girl. She never heard of equal rights, but she's already inventing them."

Emilie was taken upstairs for her afternoon nap. Johnny stood by her bed. She held his hand tightly, and looked up at him eloquently, for she had no words to tell her love. Johnny bent over her and kissed her gently, and he prayed, and again there was that mysterious lack of answer. He went downstairs to join the doctor in the parlor, and the lines in his face had grown deeper.

"Never mind your pipe," said Dr. McManus. "Try a cigar.

336

Dollar apiece." He looked about him, satisfied. "Things have taken on a pleasant air around here. By the way, I've been trying to get you a new furnace. But all I hear is shortages. Maybe some people are hoping for another war. Anyway, I've been promised a new furnace by February."

The sky had darkened, a wind had risen, and now the atmosphere was cold and ashen. A few flakes of snow drifted by the windows. The two men smoked in silence.

Then the doctor said, feeling suddenly oppressed, "This is the best Thanksgiving Day I ever spent. Thanks, Johnny."

But Johnny did not hear. He was filled with an intense and imminent foreboding and despondency. He looked at the snow, which he had always loved, and now he felt that all the world had emptied for him, and he was utterly desolate, as he had been in his dream. In his mind he looked for that patch of radiant blue, but it did not appear.

22

December was a month of drizzle and smog. Little Emilie's improvement ceased, and she began a rapid decline. "The fellers who make the smog don't care," said Dr. McManus wrathfully. "They live up there in the foothills and mountains, and their offices are air-conditioned, so what does it matter to them? I talked to the mayor and others a couple of months ago, but they're not of my political party, and they hinted I was a busybody. Well, one of these days we're going to have a real inversion, and a few dozen old folks and children and invalids are going to die, and then we're going to get action. Not until then, though. Just like they put up traffic lights after people get killed, one after another, at an intersection. Proof, they want. Well, they'll get it. In the meantime, let's see what we can do for this baby."

The *Press* did not complain, nor the *Press*-owned morning newspaper. They did publish a few mild complaints in the "People's Column." There were no editorials. In the meantime, the people coughed miserably on the streets, in their factories and offices and shops, and children developed bronchitis and asthma. The wet streets of Barryfield gritted underfoot with the fine drifting of soot, which could not escape under the stifling clouds of moisture. The mountains disappeared, until people almost forgot they existed. If the sun occasionally appeared, it was a diffused ball of cloudy saffron, which threw a sickly yellow on the clouds at sunset, and smeared the dirtied houses and other buildings with sulfurous shadows.

Air conditioners were still in short supply. "When's that goddam war going to end?" asked Dr. McManus. "It's been over for a year. I'll manage to get an air conditioner somehow!"

He did. He brought it to the parsonage, and it was installed in the girls' room for Emilie, who lay gasping and blue on her small bed. "It'll help a little," said the doctor. "We'd better have the filters changed regular, though. The smog fouls them up fast." He gave the little girl an injection of adrenalin. She had peered frantically at the needle until the doctor had said with rough affection, "Come on now. You know this is going to prick, and that's all." He made a gargoyle face at her, and while she coughingly laughed he deftly slipped the needle into her tiny and emaciated arm. Then, before she could cry, he stuffed a lollipop into her mouth. "Keep her in bed," said the doctor. "That adrenalin wasn't the best thing for her heart, but it was a toss-up between her lungs and her heart, and what could I do? Give her five of those pills of Tim's every day, instead of three." He patted the pallid little cheek. "There's my girl," he said gruffly, lifting her higher on her pillow. He smoothed the long curls with a tender hand, wiped away the tears still on her cheeks. She began to breathe more easily, and sucked noisily.

This was the eighteenth day of the smog. All the children, and Johnny too, coughed wretchedly, and blew their noses and wiped their eyes. But Christmas was coming, and even smog could be forgotten in view of the excitement of the children's first Christmas. Emilie, relieved by the air conditioner and the attentions of both Dr. McManus and Dr. Kennedy, became excited. Johnny entered into a conspiracy with the children which gave them much giggling delight. He encouraged them to make out lists, and optimistically considered that one hundred dollars would be more than enough for gifts, for everybody. On Saturdays, the four older children went with Mrs. Burnsdale on mysterious errands of their own, for they had their own small allowances now. They came back with wildly excited stories of the shops. Pietro pranced dramatically to describe the wonderful rocking horse, costing only fifty dollars, which he had decided would be his main present.

"Fifty dollars!" said Johnny, with dismay.

"What is fifty dollars?" asked Pietro, with a high, fine flourish of his arms. Only about a week's pay, thought Johnny.

"A doll like an angel, almost as big as Emilie," said Kathy. "Only twenty-five dollars. I shall have the heart broken if I don't get it."

Max was more modest, for his important present. He wished a complete modeling set; price, ten dollars. There went eighty dollars at one clip, Johnny reflected. Jean was set on a bicycle, which he could use in the spring. The cheapest was thirty dollars. Emilie, listening rapturously to the other children, wanted everything, and Kathy wrote a list for her.

"Christmas," said Johnny, "is Our Lord's Birthday. It doesn't consist mainly of presents."

"But He gave us the best of presents—salvation—didn't He?" asked Pietro with his sly and gleaming smile. "Can Papa not be like Our Lord, and give what he can?"

"There's the matter of cash," Johnny suggested.

"Pouf," said Pietro. "What is cash?"

"Only a matter of life and death for most people," said Johnny, annoyed.

He was more annoyed with Mrs. Burnsdale, who calmly collected the lists and turned a bland ear to Johnny's protests. "Let the children have their fun," she said serenely. "And a rude awakening on Christmas morning," said Johnny. He was desperately worried. In all conscience he could not withdraw any of the children's money for gifts. Besides, there were future Christmases, too.

Pietro said one day, "Sister Maria Bernadine said when we think only of gifts, and not the meaning of Christmas, we do wrong. She forgets," said the little one with a wise smile, "that the Magi brought gifts to the Christ child. Gold!" He rolled his eyes and rubbed his hands very tellingly.

"And myrrh and spices," Johnny reminded him.

"Hah!" said Pietro. "What could they buy? The Holy

Family couldn't have gone to Egypt without that gold, could they? That donkey cost money, and so did their dinners. Could they have eaten the myrrh and spices?"

"I never gave it a thought," said Johnny, amused in spite of himself.

"I think many things," said Pietro mysteriously. "And all wrong, too," Kathy added. She was beginning to give Johnny worried glances.

Mrs. Burnsdale gave the lists to Dr. McManus. He squealed when he read them. "No!" he said. "It's ridiculous."

"You never had any children before," she said. "Think what fun you're going to have buying all those things."

"I definitely withdraw my offer of marriage, madam. You're too loose with my money." She gave him a box of cookies made especially for him. "I suppose," he said, "the parson'll think that the trash dropped from heaven, the way he thinks his dinners do. It's time he knew the facts of life."

The doctor wrote to Lorry Summerfield, his usual weekly report, "I don't think I'll write to you any more. You ought to be here for Christmas. Never mind Mac."

One evening he said to Johnny, "I haven't seen your noble 'project,' confound the word!—but I'd like to inspect the parish hall for the first time and see what you've done."

He was dumfounded. The work was all complete, the tables and the chairs in place. The faintly golden shelves had not an empty space. He shouted, "Where did you get that fine mahogany for the shelves? Must have cost a fortune! Best I ever saw."

"Mahogany?" asked Johnny. "Isn't mahogany red? This is a kind of blond color." He was incredulous.

"Blond mahogany!" shrieked the doctor, rubbing his arm along one length. "Guston's best! Don't tell me he donated it? I wouldn't believe it! Where did you get it, anyway? It's priceless."

Johnny sat down suddenly and turned pale. "Why, three of the men who work at Guston's brought it, over a period of several weeks, piece by piece," he said. "They told me it cost practically nothing. It was waste, they said. Lumber thrown away."

The doctor was gleeful. "Well, I'll be damned. If that lumber was thrown away it was first stacked nicely, out of sight, before it was thrown away. Son, you're a receiver of stolen goods!" He slapped a massive thigh in its crumpled suiting. He cackled. "The parson's a fence!"

Johnny said, aghast, "Could they be arrested for it?"

"Of course they could! Look at that finish. Finished mahogany. Furniture mahogany. I happen to know that Guston prepares this for the best New York furniture makers." The doctor cavorted delightedly.

Johnny stood up, grim and white. "I'm going to write Mr. Guston and tell him, and ask him what the wood is worth, and then I'll try, someway, to pay him."

The doctor suddenly became very sober. "No you won't," he said. "In the first place, Guston's just looking for a chance to get back at you, because of his wife. First thing he'd do is to notify Mac, and there'd be the funniest spread in the papers about it. Mac's got a real comedian on his staff. Could make you laugh at your dying mother. And then Guston would have your pals arrested. By the way, how did they get it past the foreman, and how come the foreman didn't notice the disappearance?"

"One of the men is the foreman," said Johnny weakly. He shook his head. "I've got to pay Guston, someway."

"And put your pals in prison? That'd be a nice return, wouldn't it, for all their work, and sinning up their souls for you?"

Johnny was silent. Then he said angrily, "Well, what'll I do?"

"Nothing, of course. Just keep your mouth shut. And don't mention it to the men. They thought you deserved mahogany, and that's a compliment I wouldn't pay you myself. Don't disillusion them."

"You're a criminal anyway, doctor."

"Well, sure. Who ain't, by God? Besides, didn't God Himself forgive the thief on the cross who repented?"

"I don't think my boys are doing any repenting," said Johnny. He had to smile. "I think they feel they're terribly clever, getting out that mahogany. They brought it at night. In a truck."

"Look," said the doctor. "Guston don't have much heart for his men. He gets the last drop of sweat out of them, and they hate his guts."

"You're making me feel better," said Johnny. "But still it isn't my wood."

"Coming down to it, nothing is anybody's anyway, if you want to get real metaphysical. Didn't you once say everything was only lent to us? Okay. This is being lent to you. And stop talking so much."

"I don't think I like the shelves very much," said Johnny—"now."

"Of course you do. Don't be a hypocrite. Those men worked for weeks on those infernal shelves for you."

"I know!" said Johnny, becoming inspired. "I'll just invite them over here, the three of them, for a beer with me, and then I'll look them in the eye and suggest that they each give a pint of blood regularly to the Red Cross, for a year."

He did. First he admired the shelves extravagantly, walking about the hall, and rubbing his hands over the wood. He thanked the three happy men. Then he stopped before them, fixed them with his dark-blue eyes, and said slowly, "Boys, the Red Cross needs blood. Now you're all husky specimens. Don't you think you should offer a pint as often as you can? Say for a year? Yes, I think a year will do it."

They understood at once. They regarded him with admiration, studiously avoiding looking at the shelves. They brought him their Red Cross cards later, and nothing more was said.

"Talk about Shylock," said the doctor, with even more admiration.

"We won't," said Johnny. "Besides, the boys are staining the mahogany red."

"Appropriate, and discreet," said the doctor approvingly. "And I hope every time you look at the shelves you'll have a qualm, or something."

Lorry wired the doctor, briefly: "Expect me day after Christmas, darling."

The party for the children, held in the parish hall two days before Christmas, was a great success. All of Johnny's children attended. They could not get over the giant tree, wonderful decorations, and lights and all. Kathy efficiently introduced Jean, Pietro, and Max to her Sunday-school friends, and Emilie, considerably recovered, sat in a chair and gazed radiantly at the star on the top of the tree. At times she clasped her small hands tightly together in a convulsion of joy. She sat and sucked a peppermint cane. Mrs. Burnsdale had made her a blue velvet dress with a lace collar and Johnny thought the baby looked like an angel. As he moved among all the small guests he frequently stopped to kiss the child, and roll one of her long curls over his fingers.

The parish hall was noisy with excited children, who sang Christmas songs while Mrs. McGee played the ancient piano. The adults admired the shelves and the books. The gleaming tables, covered, were now being used for punch and cake and ice cream. Kathy had a few complaints about the amount of food being consumed by Pietro, and she had dire predictions about the state of his stomach tomorrow. She patrolled not only her family, but the other children who were celebrating, until Johnny told her severely, "Look here, dear, you're not a warden. You're not even a schoolmistress. Let them enjoy themselves. And if Max wants to wear his skull-cap, to show off or something, even though the rabbi says he doesn't need to wear it all the time, let him alone. It gives him an air, and he likes to explain what it is. Why don't you relax and just have a good time?"

Kathy said, "Is it a good time when people do things wrong?"

"Sometimes," Johnny assured her cynically. She frowned at him. "I mean," he added hastily, "people can often enjoy things which are bad for them, such as the wrong food, or too much candy, or coffee. It's just one night; let them be sick if they want to. Part of the price of liberty is paying for it, one way or another, disagreeably. By the way, what is that you've got in your hand behind your back? Fudge? You know chocolate gives you hives."

"It's just one night," Kathy said, her eyes twinkling. "All right, Papa. I will relax."

Johnny moved about among the milling and excited children and adults. Mrs. McGee pounded away determinedly at the Christmas hymns, and was joined by loudly singing groups. She murmured to Johnny when he approached, "I don't know about your Christmas services, Mr. Fletcher, the midnight one. The board is behind you, but some of the people have said it's Roman Catholic, and they don't look so pleased. I tell them some Protestant churches here have the midnight services, and some are sensible enough to nod their heads, and some of them look huffy and talk about John Knox. Who is he?"

"A man with his own ideas, like me," said Johnny.

Max, he found, was staring with delight at the star on the top of the tree, and demanded an explanation. "It is the guiding light," Johnny told him. He was finding it a little difficult, these days, to keep his eyes on that light himself. He wondered if parishioners ever knew that clergymen sometimes had their own confusions.

On the day before Christmas, in the morning, Johnny received a call from a parishioner to say that her old mother was dying and wished to see him. The name, Baxter, was not familiar to him. The woman, speaking in a dull and sullen voice, answered his question. "Oh, we kind of come in to hear you sometimes. You ain't like a lot of ministers. But I don't believe anything you say."

"No?" said Johnny, picturing her as a short and stubby middle-aged woman with a coarse pale face, untidy light hair, two chins, and a general air of dishevelment and slovenliness. "Why do you come then?"

Her voice rose roughly. "How do I know? My man and I just think we should go to church sometimes, but we didn't until you came, and then we didn't go anyways for a while. Until there was a lot of talk in town about you and people against you, or maybe for you, and we went, and my man says, 'I like him. He says something sometimes that makes me feel funny inside!'"

Johnny contemplated this dubious compliment a moment. "Well, do I make you—er—feel funny inside, sometimes?"

There was a silence. Then she said resentfully, "How do I know? For a while I feel different, sort of as if the world wasn't the damn place it really is. Well, are you coming or not?"

Johnny got into his elderly car and drove off in the wan and smoky light of the December morning. The streets were crowded with shopping women and their excited children. He looked at the tired, cross, hopeless, pleased, or worried faces, and he thought to himself that no matter how often he looked at his fellow man he was always new, always deserving of love and tenderness, always to be regarded with compassion. A light snow was falling, very fine, but mingled with it were huge white flakes like random butterflies, fluttering lightly in the air. Here and there tinkling bells sounded.

He turned into a very shabby street of old attached houses, grimy windows, splintered doors, and broken steps. He found the number he was looking for, and the door was opened for him by a woman so exactly like the one he had pictured in his mind that he could only gape for a moment in astonishment. Her shapeless body was swathed in a wrapper of some indeterminate color, mostly dull orange, fastened with a huge safety pin, and a rank odor emanated from her. "The minister?" she asked, scowling at him as if he were an intruder. "All right. Come in."

He followed her into a tiny parlor, dark, dirty, strewn with newspapers, beer bottles, and saucers full of cigarettes from the night before. He was angry. Poverty was one thing, and a thing one could respect. Filthiness was quite another. The woman saw his rebuking eyes looking about the room, and she said defiantly, "Well, we had some friends in last night, and I didn't have time to clean up."

Dust was everywhere, gray on the maroon mohair furniture, which was of the poorest quality, on the cheap end tables, and on the green rug and drunken lamps. Johnny said nothing. Again he followed Mrs. Baxter into a black hole of a hall; she opened a door with the gesture of a contemptuous jailer. Again he was astonished, for the room resembled a nun's cell, full of light from a tall, clean, and undraped window which looked out on a miserably filthy yard. The floor was scrubbed almost white, with no rug upon it, and the old brass bed had a patched white coverlet and snowy pillows. Nothing else stood in that small and narrow cell but a single kitchen chair and a yellow pine chest of drawers on which were neatly arranged a comb, a brush, a Bible, and a drinking glass. The air of austerity was almost stringent; never had Johnny seen a room with such dignity.

"Well, here's the minister, Ma," said Mrs. Baxter. "Mr. Fletcher, this's my ma, Mrs. Woodley."

An old woman was half sitting against the clean pillow, and she looked like an old and dying nun, for her gaunt face had a steadfast and haughty quality, the faded blue eyes sunken above wide cheekbones, the nose jutting out like a finely carved piece of fleshless wood, the mouth cold and remote. Her white hair, sparse but brushed, had been drawn back tightly from her face and fastened in a knob on the back of her head.

She did not reply to Johnny's greeting. She regarded him with the far indifference of the dying, yet he felt that she saw him fully and completely. He sat down beside her. Mrs. Baxter closed the door and left him alone with her mother.

There were things a minister said to the dying, consoling, reassuring, courageous, and pious things. But all at once Johnny had nothing to say. He and the old woman looked at each other in a long silence. He could hear Mrs. Baxter cursing and grumbling in the front of the house, rattling bottles together, pushing furniture into place, snarling at someone who had knocked on the door, then slamming the door until the whole tiny flat shook, then grumbling again. Mrs. Woodley seemed not to hear anything; her waxy hands, worn and with knobby joints, lay folded on the white coverlet, which was no more colorless than they.

Then she said in a thin, bleak voice, "I'm dying. Maybe I won't be alive tomorrow."

She had spoken with that far indifference. She added, "Takes a sight of time to die—right from when you're born. Too long."

"For a lot of us, yes," said Johnny.

She sighed. "From what I've heard, you've set this town on its ear." Now she smiled, mournfully yet indifferently. "Thought you'd look different. You look like a stevedore. My husband was one, on the docks."

"I was one too, once," said Johnny. "While I was going through school."

"Always did like a man that looked like a man," said Mrs. Woodley. "Why you could go right on the docks, this minute, or maybe in the mines."

"I've been in the mines too," said Johnny.

Her voice was not panting, nor did she speak with difficulty. She nodded her head. "Thought so." The pallid light streaming through the polished window showed too clearly the gray shadow of death that hovered over her ascetic face.

"I've got the cancer," she said, without emphasis.

Johnny wondered whether she were suffering. His big strong face expressed his compassion. She saw it, waved it away wearily with one of her hands. "What does it matter? I know what you're thinking. Does it hurt? Mister, it hurts worse than hell." The word, as she spoke it, was simple and factual, and he accepted it as such. He nodded. "Of course," he said.

"And that's why I asked you to come," she said. "To tell me why."

Johnny leaned his elbow on the chest of drawers, and supported his chin on his palm.

"If you looked like I kind of was afraid you'd look, I wouldn't ask you. I wouldn't even have talked to you," said Mrs. Woodley. "But you're my kind of folks. I sort of thought so, from what Millie and Jack told me, and from the papers. A man like my man."

She paused, closed her eyes briefly, and rested. Johnny sat in silence. He saw a spasm running like water over her flesh-less face, the stern twitching of her lips. He could not turn away from the sight of that noble agony.

When she opened her eyes again they were filmed with the moisture of torment. "Do they give you anything?" he asked gently.

She smiled for the first time, a dry and papery smile. "Yes, the doctor left something. Dope. Not for me. My ma brought me into the world without it and I'll go out without it. The pain ain't nothing to me. Not after what my life was. So, you've got to tell me why, so I'll know." She regarded him keenly. "I don't believe in no God. Thought I'd be honest with you, right from the start."

Johnny said, "You couldn't ever be less than honest, Mrs. Woodley. And I'll be honest with you. Tell me."

She sighed; she seemed to sink deeper into her pillows. With an effort, she raised her hands and regarded them as if she could draw her story from them. She said, "I wasn't born here. Born in a little town in New York State. Out in the country. Ten kids of us. Remember the house well, four rooms. It was a farm, and we all worked it and I said to my-self it was too much work, and no farmer's life for Sally. That's me. I was the middle girl, and was kind of pretty." She looked at him. "You wouldn't think so. I'm seventy-two. But I was." She smiled, not bleakly now, but suddenly, and all at once she had an old beauty like a faded portrait. "I was going to be an actress.

"A long time ago. It all comes back to me though. So one

day I packed a suitcase, it was made of wicker—funny I can just see it, all yeller, and the top fitted right on it, like a market basket. The only one we had. Ma's. Put my best two dresses in it, and wrote a note and said I was going to be one of them actresses, you know, like Lillian Russell, with champagne and diamonds. I had yeller hair, and it sure was a pretty sight when I brushed it out."

She stared straight before her. "Well, suppose you've heard the story before. A country girl goin' to the city, on the steam cars. Took all day. I can just see it now, with kerosene lamps, and mattin' on the floors. That was for poor folks. I had eight dollars. Been savin' it for a long time; I had some of the egg money. You should have seen New York in them days. Mister, it sure was different from what I see in the magazines about it, and smelled of coal gas and manure, and was full of carriages and wagons and carts." She smiled at the long-dead picture. "I was scared to death of all them people. I was fifteen years old."

"Yes," said Johnny.

"Well, sir," said Mrs. Woodley, "I didn't know where to go. So I asked a policeman, and he told me about a rooming house, and put me on a horsecar, and I sat and held my suitcase on my lap, and I just couldn't believe there was all them people in the world! Lordy, I was a greenhorn."

Now she was no longer amused. Her sunken face became stern and still. "My pa was always readin' the Bible. And I sat on the seat and I prayed. God would take care of me. He sure would!"

Johnny was silent.

Now Mrs. Woodley's voice sank. "Just an old story. The policeman'd given me the address of a house. A whorehouse. Know what that is, mister?"

"Yes," said Johnny.

She turned her head and gazed at him keenly. "It don't make you sick?"

"Only for you," said Johnny.

Again she nodded. "Oh, they didn't give me any of them drugs they talk about, or anything. The woman, Madame Le Fleur they called her, was kind of nice, and sensible. Asked me if I didn't want to go home, and she'd give me the money. I couldn't go home. And I didn't have nowheres else to go. You know, mister, Madame Le Fleur was a lot better than some of the 'good' women you hear about. And I thought of the farm, and none of us eatin' too much, and Ma and Pa working like the horses, only harder, and the kids, Mary had the consumption, and there was something else wrong with the others, and I thought maybe I could send them some money. Oh, I knew it was wrong. No use sayin' I didn't know. Know what despair is, mister? Well, that's what I had."

"And you were fifteen," said Johnny.

"The house was full of girls from the country, who'd run away like me to be actresses; and we talked about how we used to work from sunup to sundown, and how there wasn't no hope for any of us. And so I stayed."

She looked at her hands again, as if seeking an answer. "It wasn't no fancy house. Just sailors and soldiers comin' in, and workin' men and stevedores and fellers who drove beer wagons, and maybe sometimes a bookkeeper with a cough. They wanted to talk, too. They didn't know why they was born. Neither did us girls. One feller kept talkin' about it all the time, and one night he killed hisself, right in the house. You wouldn't think people like us would wonder why we was born, would you?"

"We have more reason to ask that than anyone else," said Johnny.

Mrs. Woodley lifted herself higher on her pillows and gazed at him with such penetration that he was taken aback.

"Well, yes," she said slowly. "I guess you do too, and you a minister."

She lay back on her pillows. "I was there for ten years. Hardly never went out. Afraid of all them people. And sick, real sick. Couldn't make any money for a long time. And when I was twenty-five the sickness did something to my leg, this one here, and I never could walk straight again. I met my man in the house, a stevedore, like I said. He was a good man, forty years old, and we got so we loved each other, and he took me out. I wasn't so pretty no more, either."

She twisted her hands together in a pathetic gesture. "Well, sir, I still believed in God, and I had my man, and we was married by a minister, and we moved right into Larry's room near the docks. I can just hear them steamboats whistlin' even now, and see the fog comin' in, and there was the smell of the water and the fish. But I was awful glad I was with Larry.

We'd work together and we'd get somewheres, and be real folks. I was real sorry about the house, and I asked God to forgive me."

"He did," said Johnny.

Her mouth opened in an agony of flesh and spirit, and she could not speak for a while. Then she shook her head slowly. "No sir. He didn't. But that don't matter, because I don't believe in Him no more. I stopped believin' when Larry got hurt. He was unloadin' a ship, and a big crate fell on him. And after that he didn't work no more; his legs got useless. He couldn't walk, and him a great big feller like you, and eyes like you got too, and nice, kind hands. We had just that one room, with a stove for cookin' and heatin', and Larry lay on the bed and kept cryin' because of his legs, and because of me."

Again she wrung her hands. "I was goin' to have a baby. So I went back to the house. I told Larry I was workin' in some sweatshop at nights. I'd tried the sweatshop. They gave me three dollars a week, just enough for the rent; nothing for food, or for medicine for Larry when the pain got too bad, or the doctor. So, it was the house. Madame Le Fleur looked at me; I told you she was good, and she said I couldn't do what I did before. She let me do the scrubbin' and such, and makin' beds, and washin', and she paid me twelve dollars a week. So Larry and I could eat, and Madame would give me a basket of pies and bread and some meat when there was leftovers, and just for a while, when Larry wasn't too bad, it was real good again, and we loved each other."

The old, dying face took on an aura of joyful remembrance. Johnny said nothing, and he waited until the aura faded. Mrs. Woodley spoke listlessly. "Funny, I can think of what happened and not feel it much. Like it was a palsied place in me. I came home one morning—it was just the day before Christmas, and I had a present for Larry—and the house where we lived was burned. Yes, sir, right down to the ground. Nobody'd thought about Larry, helpless in the bed. There wasn't even a bone of him left."

Her head rolled weakly on the pillows. "Not even a bone. I fainted on the sidewalk, and somebody got an ambulance. They took me to the poor hospital, and Millie was born that night. A long time ago, a long time ago. It was a terrible hospital; beds pushed up against each other, and dirty. Mister, it was sure dirty, and it smelled, and you didn't ask for nothing, they'd just shove you and tell you to shut up. I got up from my bed in three days and I left, with Millie. It was snowin', real hard."

"And where did you go?" asked Johnny.

"Why, back to Madame Le Fleur's. The girls were crazy about Millie, though she wasn't no beauty. I had one of their beds, and they called a doctor, and paid for him, too. The girls always paid for everything. They weren't no cheap girls, not there. They bought clothes for Millie, too. Didn't have nothin' but an old blanket for her when I brought her there; she was mother-naked. And when I was able, I worked again in the house. Millie and me was there for five years."

"Yes?" said Johnny, after she had rested again.

"Well, sir, the girls and me didn't think it was good for Millie to be there. So I put her in the orphan asylum, and I paid five dollars a week for her, and I worked in the house. But times got different. There was bad times; that was around 1907, I think. The men stopped comin' and the policemen got mad because there wasn't no money, and they shut us up. And I got a job scrubbin' and cleanin' in one of them big brownstone houses, and Millie got bigger, and then when she was fourteen she got herself a job like mine. I saw her 'bout once a month. She never knew anythin' about the house."

"And?" asked Johnny gently.

She looked at him in surprise. "Why, there isn't no more. Millie got acquainted with the milkman at the house where she was workin'. A small-town boy, right here from Barryfield. Jack. Millie never did really like me. But Jack did. Kind of like Larry; laughed a lot, and we had jokes. Millie didn't like jokes; doesn't now, either. Nothin' wrong with Millie, except she kind of hates everythin' and I never did, and she fights with Jack because he's still a milkman. He gets good money too, though you wouldn't think it. Likes his beer, and the only time he ever fights with Millie is because she don't keep things clean. He's like me; he wants things clean. And Millie drinks too much beer. That makes him mad."

Mrs. Woodley looked at him expectantly. "You see, don't you! I was wonderin' if you could tell me why I was ever born, that's all. Just why was I born?"

Johnny said, speaking gently and thoughtfully, "That is the question every man and woman asks sometime in life. It's a question I've often asked myself, too. And it was because I knew there was some answer that I became a minister."

He paused. The grayish-mauve shadows rippled over the old woman's face as she listened. He said, "You've said you don't believe in God. Now people who really don't believe in Him think they're just accidents, being born in this world, and so there isn't any answer, because there wasn't any reason to begin with. But when you asked me for an answer I knew at once that in your heart you believed in God, and that there is an answer—for you—and that you felt God has it.

"Let me say this. There aren't any accidents anywhere in this world and in the universe. Scientists have proved there is cause and effect in everything. Nobody like you was ever born before, and nobody like you will ever be born again. Nobody will ever live exactly the life you've lived. So, because you're so—different—from anyone else, you had a place to fill in life that nobody else but you could fill."

He looked at Mrs. Woodley. Her face was so quiet that she might have been in a trance. Her dim eyes stared straight before her, and her hands lay quiescent on her breast.

"When I worked in a mine," said Johnny, and he moved closer to the dying woman, "there was an explosion. I got out, and they got out Bill, my best friend. He'd had a terrible life. His father had died in a mine blast, and he'd starved and slept on the streets and eaten garbage until he was old enough to work in the mines, because his mother had died when he was little, and there wasn't anyone to take him in, and nobody cared, anyway. I was only seventeen when the blast happened.

"Bill was nearly fifty. He'd married a waitress when he was along in years and they loved each other very much. And now they had a boy in school, about my age. They'd been saving all they could to send him to college. I remember him a little." Johnny smiled reminiscently. "I was a lively, active kind of boy, but Joe wasn't. Bill wanted him to be an engineer; somewhere Bill had gotten the idea that being an engineer of something or other was the very finest thing to be. Maybe Joe didn't want to tell his parents that being an engineer wasn't his idea at all; he was afraid to disappoint them.

"Well, anyway, when they got Bill out of the mine he was

dying. He lay right there on the ground and he began to cry. He knew I wanted to be a minister, and he asked me to tell him why he was ever born. He swore and cursed and cried, and said everything he and his wife had done had come to nothing. Joe had left home two days before and said he wasn't coming back, and couldn't stand the school anyway. So Bill wanted to know what all his hunger and misery had amounted to, and he hated God, if there was a God, because there wasn't any answer. Even his boy was gone."

Johnny reached out and took one of Mrs. Woodley's hands. It was as cold and dead as wax. But she turned her head to him, and there was a strange listening look in her eyes.

"I told Bill," said Johnny, "that God had sent us here to know Him and love Him and serve Him on earth, so that we could join Him in heaven. It comforted him, I think. It was all I could do."

Mrs. Woodley spoke. "Yes sir, it was all you could do. But it wasn't no real answer. Why was your friend Bill born? The real reason besides what ministers tell folks?"

Johnny smiled. He looked before him, and his blue eyes were filled with light. "You know, I was thinking myself, and asking questions too, before Bill died, and I'd almost decided not to be a minister. But I did. I knew there was an answer, someplace, and God had it, and you just had to wait and then you'd know the answer."

"But nobody ever heard of Joe any more," said Mrs. Woodley with frail bitterness.

"Oh yes," said Johnny. "The whole world knows about him, now. He just received the Nobel Prize. That was two months ago. For his medical research. Millions of people may not die of cancer, now, because of Joe. He always wanted to be a doctor. When he went away he worked and put himself through medical school. He's only thirty-eight now. He's just beginning. If there hadn't been his father, Bill, there wouldn't have been Joe. And, do you know something? When he got the prize he said, 'My father always taught me that the greatest thing in the world for a man to do is to try to help his brother, his fellow man.' There's quite a monument to Bill in the cemetery."

Johnny held the old hand tightly. "Now, Mrs. Woodley, can you tell me why Bill was born? Or was it just an accident, and isn't there any answer?"

She gazed at him with enormous intensity, and did not speak.

"Let us take Larry, your husband. I gather he didn't have anyone to love him but you. Is that so?"

She nodded dumbly.

"You gave him love. Maybe you don't think that's important, but it's the most important thing in the world. Tell me. Before he lost the use of his legs, did you and he love each other as much as you did later?"

Mrs. Woodley regarded him quietly. "No. We didn't. Things were even sort of beautiful for us, after that, in spite of everythin'. Yes sir. I didn't tell you. Larry was all alone while I was workin'. He wasn't much of a scholar, but he could read. I used to buy old books for him, and he'd tell me stories I'd never heard of from the books. And he liked the Bible best of all. Why, he was kind of peaceful all the time! I'd wash or sew and cook, and he'd read the Bible to me, and the other books, and I thought I was in heaven."

She looked at Johnny, and something came alive in her sunken face. "Larry said he'd never been converted. He didn't know anythin' about God, until his legs went. Why, people'd come in from the rooming house just to hear him talk about the Bible, and Jesus, and tell them Bible stories! Poor, miserable people just like us, not havin' enough to eat, and no hope, and they'd go out like they was in a dream. And somehow, because of Larry, they'd think up things to do to help themselves. Why, there was a fellow who was a thief. Everybody knew about him. And then he wasn't a thief any more. He got in the Salvation Army."

Johnny held her hand more tightly. She half rose from the pillows in excitement, and her face became beautiful again.

"And," said Johnny, "if you hadn't been there to work and take care of him he wouldn't have had the books you bought, and the Bible, and so many people would have been lost."

She sank back against the pillows, and her shallow breath quickened.

"Nobody but you could have helped Larry. You are responsible for Larry, and everyone he saved."

"Me!" she whispered. She closed her eyes, and suddenly slept.

Johnny walked out of the bedroom and sought Mrs. Baxter. She was sitting slackly in the still dirty parlor. He sat beside her and began to talk. After a while she was weeping. He took her hand and led her back into her mother's bedroom. Mrs. Woodley was groaning softly. She opened her filmed eyes and looked at them.

Mrs. Baxter, dirty and disheveled, sat down on the edge of the bed, crying. "Ma," she said, "I didn't have no words to tell you. Honest. But the minister told me to tell them to you." She faltered, and the tears ran down her soiled coarse face. "You was always so smart, Ma. And so pretty, and nobody even thought about your leg. And you told me always to be a good girl, and I knew I couldn't let you down." She gulped. "Ma, I never told you, but when I was eighteen, and working in a kitchen in somebody's house, I got to hating my life. There was other ways of making a better living, people told me. In a house." She paused, fearfully, and shrank. "Ma, you don't know what a 'house' is?"

A spectral smile hovered over Mrs. Woodley's mouth. "I've heard about 'em," she said.

Mrs. Baxter was blushing. She hung her bedraggled head like a child. "Well, Ma, I thought about it. But there was you, so smart and so good, and not afraid of anything. You know, Ma, you never knew I loved you. But I did, I did! And I knew I couldn't let you down and be bad. So I was a good girl."

Mrs. Woodley looked at Johnny, and her ravaged face lighted with joy. She put her hand on her daughter's head and drew it to her breast. "You loved me, Millie? You loved me?"

Mrs. Baxter sobbed. "Oh, Ma, you wouldn't believe how much I love you! But I didn't know you loved me too. You so smart and pretty and moving fast and doing everything, and taking care of me."

"My baby," said Mrs. Woodley, and her voice was rich with happiness. "Why, I lived for you, baby. You was all I had."

Mrs. Baxter wept. "I'm just no good. Letting things go and breaking Jack's heart with the dirty house. Ma, I'm going to be better. I'm going to be the kind of wife Jack wants. I've been mean, because I never thought I could be like you, so smart, so wonderful."

"Yes you can," said Johnny, and he lifted Mrs. Baxter's head and smiled at her tear-soaked face. "You can be the woman your mother wants you to be, and knows you can be. For your sake, and your husband's."

"I will, I will!" cried Mrs. Baxter fervently. Then she pulled his hand to her lips and kissed it. "You're so wonderful, Mr. Fletcher. You don't know what you did for Ma and me. We're going to be in the church all the time, Mr. Fletcher. We sure are. Jack and me."

Johnny looked at Mrs. Woodley, who smiled with the fullness of knowledge.

23

When Johnny reached the street again he saw that the murky December light had changed suddenly to a thick yellowish fog, so sickening, so choking that he began to cough violently. His eyes stung; his throat closed; his lungs rebelled. He groped to his car, feeling the heavy warmish moisture of mingled fog and smoke pressing against his face. The snow was vanishing in this new and sudden change. He tried to see the sky through his dripping eyes; it was the color of sulfur. Was this the inversion Dr. McManus had told him of, this impenetrable and deadly effluvium which was smothering the city?

He had to drive carefully. Cloudy and hurrying forms, shapeless and without sex, were looming up before him. His fear rose for Emilie, and he tried to comfort himself with the memory of the air conditioner. Cars moved with a ghostly sound, shrilling their horns in warning. Children called, and their voices were hollow.

It took him a long time to get home. He abandoned the car thankfully and ran into the house. Dr. McManus was there, his stained hat stuck on the back of his head, his overcoat hanging on his wide body, helping the excited children to decorate their own small tree. The children milled about him, exclaiming, handing up glittering balls of gold and blue and silver and scarlet; yards of tinsel draped a chair, and thin strips of tin foil. Emilie was not present; she had been rushed back into the safety of her room.

"Hello!" cried Johnny happily. The children were too bemused with happiness and absorption to give him more than an absent answer. Dr. McManus said, "Just dropped in from the hospital. You know something? They're bringing in loads of sick kids and old people; we've got a first-class inversion. If we don't have an epidemic of deaths over this, then I miss my guess."

"I'm going to do something about it immediately after Christmas," said Johnny.

"Oh no you're not!" said the doctor. "Remember what I told you before about rendering to Caesar." He glared at Johnny, who was silent. Then he softened. "Never mind. Want to tell you something." He drew Johnny to a little distance and whispered, "I've got all those things the children wanted, down in the parish hall under the big tree. And some small things for them for this tree here. You can take 'em to the hall after they've examined what's here." He raised his voice. "I almost forgot. I've something for the kids right now!"

The children, screaming with anticipation, surrounded him. He fished in one big pocket and produced a tiny cocker spaniel. Now the children were dumb with delight. Pietro held out his dark little hands, clutching with frantic speechlessness; Jean touched the miniature head with one finger; Max could only stand and gaze, longingly. It was Kathy to whom the doctor gave the dog, and she hugged it convulsively.

"A dog," said Johnny, itching to take the dog himself.

"What did you think it was? A flea? He's got a damn-fool registered name, with papers, but I call him Coffee, because that's his color."

"We'll lose Mrs. Burnsdale when she sees it," said Johnny.

"She won't say a word. After all the lists she's given me she'd better hold her tongue," said the doctor, gratified by the pleasure and excitement he had created. "Kids ought to have dogs. Hey, you, fat-face," he said to his favorite, Kathy, "let the other kids hold him too. Careful there, Pietro. That's a baby, not a stuffed animal. Come on, now let Jean hold it, and Max too."

The children, absorbed in the tiny creature, moved apart, and the doctor said to Johnny, "I've got a fine surprise for you, son, on Christmas Day. Can't tell you yet. What's the matter?" he asked, seeing Johnny was grave again.

"It's what I told you. I've got to do something about this smog. It's killing people. I am going to do what I can."

"Oh you are, are you?" said the doctor. "The next time you get in trouble the mayor'll personally escort you out of town. Let me know in time so we can get a new minister."

Dr. McManus had arranged for his chauffeur to take Pietro and Jean to Midnight Mass. But before that time Johnny read to the children the old poem, " 'Twas the Night before Christmas." The children listened, crowded around Emilie's bed, their mouths open, their eyes shining. It was their first Christmas; they could not get enough of the delight and wonder of it. Their stockings already hung at the fireplace in the parlor. The fragrance of mincemeat and pine hovered over all the house. Holly wreaths hung at the windows and on the door. The little tree was brave and twinkling with lights, glittering with tinsel. The ugliness of the parsonage had been alleviated by strings and festoons of red and green twined paper in every room.

Johnny thought that the joy and anticipation of the children made up to him for all the long years of his own deprived childhood. Those years were now compressed in an essence that threw out an incomparable scent, soothing and healing something in him.

Johnny, for the children's pleasure, was fully dressed in his new black vestments, which gave him added dignity and even a touch of majesty. His white collar shimmered over the moderately priced broadcloth. He was not only a foster father but a priest, and even Pietro, growing more pert and mischievous every day, looked at him with respect.

The poem was hardly finished, and the children were just beginning their demands to hear it again, when Mrs Burnsdale came upstairs with a special-delivery letter for Johnny. "Another card for us," said Johnny, pleased. He opened the envelope. A green slip of paper fell out. "Five hundred dollars!" exclaimed Johnny faintly. "From Dr. Stevens!" On his card Dr. Stevens had written somewhat cryptically, "God bless you and the children, dear Johnny, and protect you all in the coming year and forever, and forever give you courage and peace."

Without warning, a frightful sense of foreboding clutched at Johnny's throat. He read the card to himself now. Why should those simple words from one minister to another, ordinary words, and customary ones at this time of the year, sound so ominous? Courage and peace. A man always possessed them, with God. The foreboding grew stronger in him, a kind of amorphous terror struck at his heart. He looked at Emilie, basking contentedly on her pillows, immune to the deadly fog outside, her large blue eyes half closed in drowsiness. Even Dr. Kennedy had admitted that she was better, and his manner had intimated some hope.

He stood up abruptly. His dark face paled. Mrs. Burnsdale got up also. "What is it, Mr. Fletcher?" she asked fearfully.

"I don't know," he admitted slowly. "Something just came to me—. Things have been a strain lately, I guess." He looked at the card in his hand, and the words "courage and peace" leaped at him as if wreathed in light. He blinked his eyes. The words fell back on the card and the light was gone. He was a mystic, like all true priests, and again the foreboding struck at him savagely. He could not accept those innocent words as a promise; they seemed to him a warning of some coming terror, and an exhortation to have faith in the ultimate outcome.

He went to each of the children and gave them a tender and paternal kiss. "Pietro and Jean, you'd better get ready, for you're going early because of Pietro's place in the choir tonight. Kathy and Max, you'll be in bed in half an hour. See, it's almost ten." He lifted Emilie in his arms, and she cuddled against him, soft and fragile as a doll. "My darling, my darling," he whispered in her ear. She wound her little arms about his neck and sighed blissfully. Her breathing was normal and quiet. The fragrance of her small body was, to him, the most wonderful scent in the world.

He put the child back into her bed, and almost immediately she fell asleep, holding his hand. He stood bent over her, and forgot everything else except his nameless fear. He prayed silently for the little one, and for the first time his full urgency had an answer. He could feel that old familiar wave of tenderness reaching out to him from the farthest space, almost too sweet and too powerful to be endured. His eyes filled with tears. All would be well for Emilie, and for all of them.

Mrs. Burnsdale remained behind to help Pietro and Jean, and to see that Kathy and Max went to bed. She often thought that the most improvement had come to Max. The dry peaks of his hair had been trained by her, with oil and brushes, to a smooth pompadour. The square face had color, and when he smiled he was an average boy. He chattered to her confidently as he put on his pajamas. "I'm going to have Christmas presents too," he said with happy anticipation.

"Is that right?" asked Mrs. Burnsdale with mock severity. "Who said so? Didn't we all give you Hanukkah presents, and didn't you have a—a Menorah, candles and things, and didn't you say prayers with your skullcap on? This is a racket, young man."

Max, to her pleasure, gave her a sly and brimming smile. "No. I am lucky. I get Christmas presents too. I know."

"It's a good thing Catholics and Protestants celebrate the same holiday at the same time," said Mrs. Burnsdale, "or there'd be three gift rackets in this house instead of two. There now, go and brush your teeth, and don't forget the back ones, either."

Johnny sat at his desk and considered his sermon. He looked at the middle drawer of his desk and was very still. He opened it finally, and took out the gold box. It lay in his palm, and it seemed to grow warm and heavy in his hand. After a time he wrapped it in paper, and put it far back in his desk. A slow, weak pain flooded him.

The yellow fog thickened outside. Johnny went to a window and looked at it. He could see nothing of anything but the fog, swirling like hordes of malignant ghosts in the light from the window. Dr. McManus said the hospitals were filling with young children and old people. Johnny's jaw became stiff and hard. His next job would be the smog. It could wait no longer. Inversion. The warm ceiling of moist air hanging over the city, through which industrial smoke could not escape—but there should be no industrial smoke. There were ways of eliminating it, if greed did not interfere.

He looked at his watch. He was surprised to see that it was a quarter to twelve. Now he thought only of his sermon, and put everything else out of mind. If only a handful of people came it would be enough. Next year there would be more.

Now the bells of the churches began to sound, coming in ghostly echoes over the city. They joined together, retreating like the waves of the sea, then advancing, clearer and loud, and then fading. Johnny listened anxiously for the sound of the miserable little bells in his own steeple. They were supposed to answer now, in the joyous chorus. No bells answered. He started across the room when he heard, loud and clear and majestic, the most marvelous carillon of them all, triumphant, victorious.

He stood, agape, disbelieving. The carillon was playing the ancient hymn, "Adeste Fidelis," in long and beautiful harmony, so close that it shook the parsonage. The walls vibrated; the lamps flickered in the waves of sound. The very floors trembled. "Come and behold Him!" the bells commanded, in powerful and lovely accents. "Born the King of Angels!"

"Oh God," murmured Johnny. "Oh God, Oh Father!"

He felt someone beside him, and starting violently, he turned. Mrs. Burnsdale was there, smiling and crying. She said, "Oh, Mr. Fletcher! It was a surprise for you. The doctor did it. From Italy, he said."

He put his arm about her, and there were tears on his own face. They listened as the bells announced the everlasting tidings of joy and hope and the Word made Flesh. They soared against the evil sky, defying it. They soared against all the walls of hatred and lust and anger and terror in the world. They called to the heavens and to the earth.

24

Johnny moved to the altar, dazed and shaken. The enormous and stately candlelight rose high over the pews. For a moment Johnny could not see. And then he saw that the church was not only full, but overflowing.

The pews had never been so tightly packed. People sat crowded together, and there were scores of strange faces there. The ushers were frantic. They had borrowed and begged every available folding seat, and it was not enough. The people had been coming since quarter after eleven. Now they stood at the sides of the church, and there was a thick formation in the rear. And still the open doors showed bobbing heads and faces, forcing themselves in, sidling into every available few inches of space. Beyond them, the steps were mobbed.

And, over all, the bells shouted their exultation so that the church shook. "Come, all ye faithful!" they urged, with ever-mounting rejoicing. And the faithful came, and looked up at Johnny, and smiled. It was like a sea smiling. The bells were the surging on an eternal shore. The candlelight rose higher, as if in response.

The choir answered in harmony, and, without a gesture or a word, the congregation in the pews spontaneously rose and their voices joined the choir and the bells. The walls shuddered and echoed. Ecstasy touched all faces. Johnny stood, and could not believe, and could only repeat in himself, "Oh God, Oh Father!" His tall, black-robed figure was like a statue in the light, against the cross.

Then, trembling, murmuring, the bells receded, and there was only the candlelight and the flowers and the people, and Johnny before the altar, and deep silence.

He said, "Now God so loved the world—"

The ancient, timeless, and eternal Gospel was spoken again, and, as always, it was new, a new message to man, shining like the sun, full of promise and glory and forgiveness and love, not old, not worn, not heavy with age, not dogged with weary and mechanical voices uttering a meaningless ritual dusty with bygone ages, but the triumphant call of the immediate hour, freshly born, freshly enunciated, announced like the blaze of trumpets from a hilltop, resounding from kingly palaces, and in the market places, the bazaars, the crowded, sweating streets of men.

"Unto you, all you tired and heavy-laden, unto you who are hopeless and sad and dwell in the darkness of sorrow, unto you who are caught in the web of your sins and your crimes and your agonies and your hells, unto you who weep and find no joy in your lives and no faith, unto you who are victims of injustice and despair, unto you who have been injured, and who injure, unto you whose lives are as stone and steel and you who are tormented with pain and the fear of death and whose children have abandoned you, and who weep in the night and find no peace therein, unto you who labor and find no sustenance in labor, and no meaning, unto you who may die tomorrow or the day after tomorrow and who cry in the darkness without an answering voice from man, unto you, the friendless and the homeless and the lost, unto you who hate in your grief and you who hate without reason but only through blind and ignorant envy, unto you without love and who have never been loved—

"Unto you, this night, a King has been born. A King of love and mercy and salvation and understanding, a King who will bind up your wounds and touch your blind eyes and take away your hatreds and your sorrows and comfort you, and who asks only of you, in accents of eternal love and compassion: Follow Me.

"Unto you, the Word has been made Flesh, out of love for you, out of mercy. Rejoice, therefore, that God has been born in your flesh, and waits for you in His Manger.

"Unto you, unto all men, God has come, to fulfill His promise of the ages. Follow Me. Sound, you bells, to the night! A King has been born, saying: 'I am among you, even to the end of the world. Follow Me.'"

25

It was seldom that Johnny could not fall asleep at once, and quietly, after his prayers. But tonight, Christmas Eve, he could not sleep. He was oppressed with a feeling of profound dread, which had come upon him again the moment he had returned to the parsonage. He tried to analyze it; he remembered the joy and excitement of the children, the arrival of Dr. Stevens's check, the bells, the incredible crowd in the church, the happy voices. Nothing but good had been his this day. Everywhere he had been offered love. He had comforted a dying woman, and brought her and her daughter together. He had thanked God for all these miracles which had come in a few hours to him. The dread remained.

He rolled on his bed. Jean was sleeping on the day bed near him; his breathing was regular in the darkness. Johnny decided a pipe might soothe him, so he got up carefully, threw on his old brown woolen bathrobe, and crept from the room. He felt his way downstairs, and cautiously clicked on the light in the parlor. Immediately the little tree sprang into brilliance, shimmering as if drenched in silver. He smiled. The children's stockings bulged; as many smaller presents as possible lay under the tree. The children knew that larger and more exciting gifts were waiting for them under and around the big tree in the parish hall, for the house could not accommodate them.

He heard a faint whining, and went into the warm, clean kitchen. The puppy, Coffee, lay in a carton carefully lined with an old blanket, and newspaper was spread prudently about. He lifted his tawny head as Johnny entered, and the infant eyes brightened with eagerness. He whined again. Johnny picked him up, and the minute tail wagged frantically. The little head pressed against the palm of Johnny's hand. He held the dog against his cheek, then set him down, found a saucepan, and opened the refrigerator. For a moment his nameless despair lifted when he saw the contents: the goose already stuffed, the pies, and the ice cream, all waiting for the festivities tomorrow. He took out milk, heated it, put in a little sugar, and poured the milk into a saucer. "There," he murmured to the puppy, putting the saucer under the frenzied nose. The puppy drank rapidly, and Johnny stood and watched, smoking.

The old radiators hissed and gurgled comfortingly. But the house felt a trifle too warm. Johnny went downstairs and checked the furnace. It ate contentedly; the firebox was cherry-colored. On the stairs, going up, Johnny suddenly stopped. He had the sensation that he was not alone. His heart beat quickly, he went down again and searched the cellar, a long piece of kindling wood heavy and reassuring in his hand. But the cellar contained only the usual things. Now, he thought, I'm surely getting neurotic. He looked into the dark dining room, the little pantry, cold as ice, where the vegetables were kept. The puppy whined anxiously in the kitchen. Johnny went to soothe him, and the stealthy sensation followed, like a shadow. "Nonsense," said Johnny aloud.

He turned off all the lights, a slight drowsiness came to him, very welcome. Yet when he was again in bed the premonition of disaster lay down on the pillow with him. He firmly tried to control it. Finally, out of pure weariness, he began to doze, but very lightly, part of his mind still awake. Once he thought he heard the faint closing of a door, decided a child was visiting the bathroom. Now a wind began to complain dully against the windows. Jean slept.

Johnny rose out of his drowse to hear the wild beating of

his heart. It was then that he smelled smoke. He sat up, sniffing. It was definitely smoke.

He jumped out of the bed and ran to the door. The hallway was hot, and it was filled with billows of smoke. He felt rather than saw them. He coughed violently, and shut the door. He ran to the lamp, turned it on, panting. Jean sat up in bed, blinking. "Look, Jean," said Johnny, trying to control his voice, "let me help you up, and then dress. Fast! Fast, Jean! The house is on fire!"

Jean said nothing; he only turned very white. Johnny pulled him to the edge of the bed. Then he saw that the smoke was gushing under the door. It was too late for dressing. He threw Jean his own blankets. "Wait!" he cried. He held a pillow against his face, rushed out into the hall, closing the door behind him. Now he shouted, as the very floorboards sent waves of heat against the soles of his thin slippers, "Fire! Fire!" He pounded on the door of Kathy's and Mrs. Burnsdale's room. There was a confused muttering inside, then Mrs. Burnsdale, suddenly realizing what she had heard, stumbled out of bed. "Don't open the door yet!" cried Johnny. "Just put coats on you and Kathy." He thought wildly of Max and Pietro, then remembered that because Jean had a slight sore throat they were sleeping on a couch in the room with Kathy and Mrs. Burnsdale. "Hurry," he begged. "Hurry, for God's sake." His eyes were burning with heat and smoke. "And put blankets over your heads, and hold them tight against your faces. And shoes, shoes! Oh, God in heaven, Emilie!"

"Oh God," said Mrs. Burnsdale simply. "Oh God!" The children were awake; Max had begun to scream in a terrible tone. Kathy was consoling him in a stern voice, and pushing him. Pietro shrieked once, then was silent.

Johnny ran into Emilie's room. The air conditioner was whirring steadily. The little girl slept, and did not awaken when Johnny turned on the light. Even then he could pause for an instant, looking at her small face; she was smiling in her sleep. He caught her up, rolled blankets around her, and before she was fully awake, he had covered her face. "It's all right, darling," he said. His heart pounded almost too frightfully for him to speak. "It's only Papa." He glanced at the air conditioner in despair. He ran to the door with the whimpering child, and shouted, "All right, everybody! Downstairs, outside, as fast as you can! Don't stop for anything; run like hell!"

He heard a crackling and snapping. The walls groaned. The fire was rushing up through them. But Johnny waited until he heard Mrs. Burnsdale run, crying, sobbing, coughing, with the other children. Then he flung open the door, rushed into the hall where the gray billows of smoke were now tinged with the faintest crimson. Emilie struggled in his arms, trying to breathe. He pressed her face against his chest as he flew down the stairs. Somehow, Mrs. Burnsdale had remembered to turn on the parlor light. She stood outside now, on the stoop, with the other four shivering children. He could see their faces, wild, ghastly, their bodies huddled in blankets and coats, their naked feet in any shoes they had found. From behind them, like another fire, the smog poured in, to join the smoke. The whole house was snapping now. And Emilie was curling in convulsions in Johnny's arms, coughing stridently.

In this nightmare, which Johnny told himself was not happening, he ran to Mrs. Burnsdale and thrust Emilie into her arms. Mrs. Burnsdale saw his face, and she said, "Oh, Mr. Fletcher! Mr. Fletcher!" He said, "Get off the stoop. I'll be with you in a minute!" He pushed her, shouted at the children, "Down on the sidewalk, all of you! Take Emilie next door; they'll let you in. Take all the children."

He ran to his desk. The nightmare was enhanced by the calm glitter of the little tree. He dialed the operator and croaked, "Fire! Church of the Good Shepherd parsonage. Fire! Hurry, hurry, for God's sake!"

He hung up and called Dr. McManus. He heard the ringing of the bell. Now the parlor surged with smoke. Johnny held part of his bathrobe against his face. The edges of the new green rug were curling in blackness, filled with sparks. Johnny coughed and choked, and prayed. Then he heard the doctor's angry voice, "I'm not coming out for a bellyache at this time of night! Who the hell is it?"

"Doctor!" groaned Johnny. "The parsonage. It's on fire." He looked up at the ceiling. A vicious red crack was opening in it. Then the lights went out. Johnny threw down the telephone and raced to the door. He had just reached it when the ceiling, screaming and tearing, fell in blazing fragments to the floor.

It was nearly three o'clock in the morning, but disaster had brought hastily dressed people into the streets. Johnny, his lungs almost bursting, ran down the steps of the stoop. Lights were on in the house next door, and he hurried toward it. The smog made it unreal, shifting and blurring. His legs felt as heavy and lumbering as iron. Someone opened a door as he mounted the porch steps, and without glancing at his host or hostess, he darted inside. In a small neat parlor, under a glaring overhead light, Mrs. Burnsdale, with Emilie on her lap, sat with the children on golden-oak modern furniture. Her face was streaming with tears. But the children sat in a white and dreadful silence, staring emptily before them.

"Emilie?" said Johnny, through a smarting throat. He went to Mrs. Burnsdale, lifted away the blanket from the child's face. The child looked at him, and her eyes were distended and blank in a taut face. She did not recognize him; her gray lips sucked in and out. And then she coughed, over and over, cringing, cowering. "Baby, baby," said Johnny, in a voice like a prayer, as she paused to catch her laboring breath. "Emilie, dear."

Someone had taken hold of his arm, and he turned feebly. An elderly man in pajamas, quite bald, was looking at him in concern. "Gee, Mr. Fletcher," he said, "it's awful. My wife's in the kitchen, making some coffee." He added anxiously, "Hope the engines get here fast. We're awful close to your house at the back. Sit down, man."

"The church?" said Johnny, and pulled away from him. He rushed to the door. There was a ripping anguish in his chest. Not conscious of the people outside, not conscious of his blazing house, not conscious of the smog or the deepening cold, he ran down the slippery sidewalk to the church. But though the very roof of his house was vomiting sparks and shafts of flame, and the walls were curving and buckling, the church was in no danger as yet.

The fire lit up the thronging faces, the excited eyes, with scarlet. The air was acrid, and intensified the stench of the smog. People were gabbling and pointing. "There's the minister!" someone cried. "Hey, it's the minister!"

Johnny looked at his house. And then he remembered the puppy in the kitchen. He started automatically for the parsonage. Suddenly one of the walls fell inward, and the whole street was lighted by the red flood. Johnny pressed his hands to his face, and a long shuddering went through him.

Now the street clanged with bells, the roaring of fire trucks. Standing there, feeling nothing at all now, Johnny watched the helmeted men leap from the trucks, watched them unroll the anacondas of their hose. Police had arrived, bustling and efficient. They forced back the mobs of people. Then they saw Johnny, in his bathrobe, standing blindly on the sidewalk. He had lost his slippers somewhere. His naked feet stood in gritty slime.

A policeman ran up to him, took his arm, and pulled him away. "You're standing in the way, Buster," he said. The whole street clanged and screamed. "Hey, you're the minister, aren't you? Better go in a house somewhere."

Johnny looked at him dumbly. He said, "It's Christmas Day." He swallowed, his throat in spasm. "It's Christmas Day," he said again.

Johnny sat with Emilie in the crepuscular dawn. She lay in a wide warm bed in Dr. McManus's best bedroom, under an oxygen tent. A nurse sat alertly near her head, watching, her fingers never leaving the child's pulse. Dr. McManus stood in the shadows cast by the lamps; now and then his face worked, crinkled, squeezed. For Emilie was dying.

The shock, the smog, the terror had been too much for her heart. Dr. Kennedy was downstairs, drinking coffee with Mrs. Burnsdale. He could not speak. His youthful face was bitter. Mrs. Burnsdale wept silently. The children were all in safe beds, but they were not sleeping. They cried for the puppy, their tree, their presents, for their own bewildered fear, their first, lost Christmas. "Look," Dr. McManus had told them, "most of your stuff's in the parish hall. And we'll have our own Christmas right here, damn it. Got a house full of servants. Stop that yammering. You, Pietro, if you don't stop squealing like a punctured rat I'm going to slam you, hard. Max, you shut up too. Kathy, help them get to bed. Jean," and he looked at the silent, stiff-faced boy, with his canes beside him, "help Kathy, if you can't do anything to stop these kids."

It was Mrs. Burnsdale who had looked at him with stark eyes and who had said, "It's your fault. It was that old furnace, falling apart. I was always afraid of it." He had not answered her, but had turned away to go upstairs again.

Dr. Kennedy came up very shortly. There was no sound in the bedroom except the slight hissing of the oxygen. The sullen yellow dawn moved closer to the windows, and the lights became dimmer. Johnny sat like a statue, not moving, bent forward, looking at Emilie's dwindling face, at her closed eyes, at her little, heaving breast. Her color was already bluish-gray; her lips stood open, and her nostrils struggled, pinching in, flaring out. Dr. Kennedy glanced at the nurse, who shook her head sorrowfully. She stood up to give Dr. Kennedy her place. The young doctor had dressed hastily, and his hair was rumpled. He took Emilie's tiny wrist in gentle fingers, carefully closing the folds of the oxygen tent around his hand. Then he put his stethoscope to his head, leaned in under the tent, and listened to the child's heart. Very slowly, he withdrew. He looked at Johnny and his own heart clenched with compassion. Dr. McManus came fearfully out of the shadows, and Dr. Kennedy lifted his shoulders in wordless despair.

Now they could hear the unendurable panting of the dying child; her body stiffened, shivered. Johnny leaned closer. He could see the ripples of the water of death flowing over her fragile flesh. His face was expressionless. Emilie moaned, and it was as if the dolorous sound came from some depth in her, and not from her throat. Then she opened her eyes and looked directly at Johnny. They were filmed and dulled.

"Darling," said Johnny. "Baby. Darling."

The weighted eyes gazed at him, mutely. The long tangled curls lay on the pillows like bright floss, enhancing the deathly appearance of the little head from which they fanned. Then the most exhausted expression, hopeless, blind, and seeking, stood on the child's face. She moaned again.

"It's Papa, darling," said Johnny. "See, it's Papa. I'm here."

The child panted and moaned. Then, suddenly, her face flooded with light and joyful recognition, and very clearly, in that silent room, she said one word. "Mama."

The smile remained, though the child died in that instant, and the eyes still gazed off in an entrancement of recognition and delight.

Johnny threw aside the oxygen tent. He lifted the little body in his arms. He sat down with it, and held it to his breast. He smoothed the long, pretty hair. He closed the blue and filmy eyes. He rocked back and forth, soundlessly.

He did not see Father John Kanty Krupszyk and Rabbi Chortow enter the room. He did not hear them when they spoke to him. The priest knelt down, crossed himself, and prayed, the tears streaming down his cheeks. And Johnny rocked and rocked, and held Emilie to him.

Dr. McManus came to him speechlessly and put out his arms. Johnny shook his head, and then could not seem to stop shaking it, as he rocked. It was the priest, after a long time, who gently took the child from him, laid her down on the bed, and covered her face with the sheet.

Johnny stood up. He looked at them all, and suddenly his face was terrible.

"Father," he said, "do not forgive them, for they knew what they did."

"Johnny," said the priest, pleadingly.

Dr. McManus stood in a trance, and his face was no less deathly than Emilie's. Once or twice he sobbed, dryly. The rabbi sat in a chair and murmured the prayers for the dead.

Johnny repeated, in a louder voice, "Father, do not forgive them!"

He did not feel the sting of the needle in his arm, or the rubbing of the alcohol. He did not feel anyone leading him from the room and into the yellowish morning light of another bedroom. Someone pushed him down on the bed; someone put his flaccid arms into the sleeves of Dr. McManus's pajamas. Now he was swimming in gray and black shadows. When his legs were lifted to the bed, and his head fell on the pillow, he still did not know.

The nurse stayed with him. The doctors and the clergymen went downstairs. The scared servants were already in the kitchen. Mrs. Burnsdale was gone. Coffee steamed, and bacon fried on the big stove. The men sat in the ugly Victorian parlor and stared between their knees at the floor.

An hour later two police detectives came to the house. They had a brief message. The old furnace had not set the fire. Johnny had known, from the deeps of his agony. There was evidence of arson, evidence enough for anyone. Only Johnny and the criminal had known.

It was Christmas Day. In ten thousand homes in Barryfield children were singing and laughing and playing, and in the churches the choirs sang, "Joy to the world!"

26

Lorry drew up before Dr. McManus's monstrous house and then sat in her car, looking at the distant doorway with utter numbness. She had felt nothing for the past ten minutes, when, stopping for gasoline, a station attendant had told her of the tragedy that had fallen on Johnny. She sat and stared, tearless and without emotion, at the cluster of pure white lilies and white ribbon which hung on the door, a lovely and sorrowful declaration that in that house a dead child lay in her coffin.

Children ran joyously up and down the street, playing with their Christmas toys, still elated over the holiday of yesterday. Their voices rang and shrilled and laughed on the otherwise quiet street. Lorry began to watch them, automatically, as detached as if she were paralyzed in a nightmare. She saw that many automobiles were lined up and down the streets; a cluster of people were quietly coming from the house now, and another cluster was making its way up the circular driveway to the door. She averted her head; she did not want to be recognized. She lit a cigarette and blew a large cloud of smoke before her face and pretended, as the group leaving neared the sidewalk, to be idly waiting for a passenger. But the group, absorbed in genuine sadness, did not notice her. She rested her head for a moment or two on the steering wheel, overcome with the exhaustion of shock and grief. Finally she left the car and walked up the gravel walk to the house, her high heels slipping on icy patches.

It was Mrs. Burnsdale, and not the doctor's "man," who opened the door for her. Mrs. Burnsdale's face was swollen and blanched, her eyes reddened with weeping. "Miss Summerfield," she murmured in vague surprise. The doctor had forgotten that Lorry was to arrive today, Thursday, the day after Christmas, and had told no one.

Lorry said faintly, "I just heard, ten minutes ago. I didn't know anything. The doctor expected me. I—I wonder if someone will drive the car in and get the luggage out? I"—she stopped, and closed her eyes tightly for a moment. She whispered emptily, "Oh, God."

Mrs. Burnsdale took her arm and gently drew her into the huge dim hall with its polished floor and Oriental rugs. A murmur of voices, so low that it seemed but the slightest rustling of trees, pervaded the house. The reception room at Lorry's right was filled with sitting and standing men and women, Johnny's parishioners and friends. She could see the blurred shadows of them in the early dusk, the gleam of dark mahogany here and there, and the wan rectangles of windows. To her left the wide sliding doors of the huge Victorian parlor were shut, shut with a palpable finality.

Mrs. Burnsdale was crying again, helplessly. She said, "The minister's in there just now. He just comes in once in a while, and he won't let anybody in there with him, except Father Krupszyk and Rabbi Chortow. But he doesn't even talk to them. He doesn't talk to anybody, not even the children, poor little things, and he won't let them go into the parlor. He hasn't had a thing to eat since last night, and here it is after five. Miss Summerfield, I've seen grief before, but this is worse than grief. The only people he talks to are the police. He keeps going to the telephone every half hour or so asking them if they got the man."

She led Lorry upstairs to a back bedroom, chill and dark. "I'm terribly sorry," she faltered. "The doctor didn't say anything. So we've got the children in some of the rooms, and I'm here, and here's Mr. Fletcher, and this is the only room left. I'll put Kathy in here tomorrow, and you can—"

"No, no," Lorry murmured. "No, no, no." But she was not saying this to the room. She sat on the edge of the narrow tester bed and her blue-green eyes were clouded and expressionless.

"I have to chase the people out, when I hear him coming downstairs," said Mrs. Burnsdale. She pressed a wet crumple of handkerchief to her eyes. "That's the way he wants it. He doesn't want anyone to console him or comfort him. He doesn't even speak about—that poor little baby. Mis Summerfield, maybe if you just slip in quietly he wouldn't notice. I think the priest's with him now."

She helped Lorry take off her heavy mink coat, and Lorry removed her hat and gloves. Then she stood in the center of the room, forgetting where she was. Her dark-blue woolen dress appeared too large for her, for she had lost weight. Her beautiful face had a gaunt look and there were sunken places under her wide cheekbones, and her mouth was without color. Only the pale gilt of her hair lightened her weary appearance. Poor thing, she's awfully tired, thought Mrs. Burnsdale, and worn out.

She pulled the bell rope that would arouse attention in the kitchen. "Will you have some tea?" she asked. "You look so tired, Miss Summerfield. Or," she added awkwardly, remembering the rumors of Lorry's drinking, "perhaps you would like some—some—"

"A Scotch and soda," said Lorry absently. Then she started. "No, tea will be fine. Anything. I don't care."

She sat down on the edge of the bed again and covered her face with her hands. She said behind them, "Yes, I am tired. You see, my brother, who is a publisher, is in Europe, and won't be back until March, and I have to help with the business in New York for three days a week, and I work in— Philadelphia—for four days." Her voice was abstracted and indifferent from behind the thin white wall of her hands. Mrs. Burnsdale could see the hollows in the long slender neck, the weight of exhaustion on the broad shoulders.

"Won't you lie down?" asked Mrs. Burnsdale compassionately.

"No. Please, no," said Lorry. "It doesn't matter. Nothing

matters." She dropped her hands and again stared emptily before her. Oh, Johnny, she said in herself. Oh, God. Oh, Johnny. Johnny, Johnny, Johnny.

She jumped violently at the clatter of the tea things. When she saw them she became suddenly nauseated, and stood up. "I'm sorry. I couldn't—could I just go down now? I—want to see him."

Her dry eyes implored Mrs. Burnsdale, who took her arm again and led her downstairs, as if she were blind. They halted a moment on the shadowed stairs until a group left the house, closing the doors silently behind them. Then Mrs. Burnsdale rolled back enough of the parlor door to admit Lorry, and she left her.

The crimson velvet draperies had been drawn over the immense windows, and the parlor was lighted only by the two great candelabra which had been brought in from the church. In the aura of one stood a small white casket on a bier covered with white velvet. Every available space spilled with white, pale yellow, and pale pink flowers, delicately scented, in baskets, in pots, and in bouquets.

Lorry leaned against the closed door, weak and undone. This was like some dark and formless dream to her, illuminated only by the shifting candlelight hovering over the casket like angel wings. Lorry could see Emilie's little head on the white satin pillow, the fan of bright curls, the sleeping eyes, the ecstatic smile of knowledge and joy. Her small body was clad in the blue velvet and lace dress Mrs. Burnsdale had made for her for Christmas. She isn't dead, thought Lorry, and her throat contracted. She is only asleep, the darling baby. But Lorry thought of the laughing and playing children on the street, and there was a darkness before her eyes. Emilie's first Christmas had been her last. She would never play again.

Someone was touching her arm gently, and her vision cleared and she saw the tall black figure of Father Krupszyk near her. The big priest was very pale, his mouth strained and taut, but he was trying to smile, pityingly. He spoke in a low voice, and not a whisper, "Miss Summerfield, I'm glad you came."

"I didn't know—" she answered, through her white lips, "until about half an hour ago. I was expected—by Uncle Al." She could not say anything further.

She looked beyond the priest and then, for the first time, she saw Johnny sitting in the shadows behind the candles and behind the head of the casket. He was staring sightlessly at the floor; one of his hands rested near Emilie's head, clutched tightly over the silked side of the thing which contained the body of the child. Lorry put her hands to her throat. "No, no, no," she said, over and over.

Johnny had not seen her enter; he did not hear her. He was hearing nothing now. The candlelight moved as if in a draft, and Lorry saw his face, strained, lifeless, yet grim, as if he had died himself, in one long last agony. She said, "He is dying. Where is Uncle Al? Why did he leave him?"

"Unfortunately, people need sudden operations, even when there is death," said the priest. "And this was an emergency, and the man is an old friend and wouldn't have anyone else."

"Johnny's taking this so hard—I mean—he is a minister."

"And he should rise with sure faith and confident peace to the situation?" The priest's face darkened. "Too many people think the clergy are not men at all, and have no hearts of flesh, and no sorrows and no private anguishes. They forget that even the saints suffered, perhaps more than any average man could ever imagine."

"Sorry, sorry," whispered Lorry, with piteous humility. "It's just—he looks as if he would hate you if you offered him any comfort."

"You mustn't forget the circumstances," said the priest. "This isn't an ordinary death. This strikes at his very soul; he remembers what the child suffered all her life. He can't be reconciled—yet. I talk to him, and he won't look at me or listen to me. We must give him time."

"But—his God," stammered Lorry, and now she wrung her hands a little.

"He's closed all the doors of his spirit to God," said the priest. "He's barred the windows. He doesn't hear anything just now, but what he heard when he first got the children. If this child had died quietly, as expected, it wouldn't have been too bad. But you know how and why she died, and he can't forget that. He can't forgive either God or man." The priest sighed. "I must go now. Don't talk to him; he won't answer."

They had talked near the door, but Johnny, far to the front of the long room, had not seen or heard them. He was lost in some frightful dream of his own. The priest went to him and put his hand on his shoulder, and he did not respond in the slightest. Then Father Krupszyk knelt beside the casket, and prayed for the soul of the innocent child, who, to the last, could not escape the evil of men.

Lorry was alone in a moment or two with Johnny and the flowers and the dead child. She walked unsteadily to the casket and looked down, and then, for the first time, her eyes flooded with desperate tears. She fell to her knees and leaned her head against the bier, and cried soundlessly. Her tears ran down her cheeks unimpeded, and splashed on her hands. They seemed to rise from some bottomless well in her spirit which had never flowed before.

Emilie slept and smiled, far removed from all grief and pain, under her blanket of white roses and lilies which Father Krupszyk had sent. There was no shadow of death on her face; her long lashes lay gently on her cheek. She had nothing to say to the stricken man at her head, or the weeping woman beside her. She had been delivered finally from anything the world of men could inflict upon her.

Lorry, sobbing silently, heard a slight movement near her, and she lifted her tear-disfigured face. Johnny was standing very close to her, and she began to tremble, for his eyes were not the eyes she remembered, and this was not his face. He was a man of vengeance now, a man of hatred, and she could not help seeing it.

"What are you doing here?" he said in a loud, abrupt voice.

At first she was afraid that he had not recognized her, and then she knew that he had. She tried to speak through the flood of her tears. "Johnny, Johnny. I just heard. I—was expected." She lifted up her hands to him in an eloquent gesture of pleading, as two thousand years ago a woman like herself had lifted her hands to God.

But Johnny did not remember God now, nor think of Him except with cold and passionate anger. He looked down at the woman at his feet and stepped back, and his pallid mouth contracted. "I can't talk," he said. "I don't want to see anybody. Will you please go?"

She lifted herself upright on her knees, dropping her hands, her golden hair disheveled around her face. They gazed at each other, Lorry with mourning and mute appeal, and Johnny with the silent rejection of all who wished to console him and grieve with him. This, to Lorry, was more awful than anything else, and she pushed herself to her feet. He took another step backward, and his face became whiter.

By the time she had reached the door, and had looked back, he was again in his chair, in his terrible vigil, wrapped in his terrible thoughts.

Lorry went upstairs to the gigantic master bedroom where Mrs. Burnsdale had told her the children usually gathered. She found them there, sitting in unchildlike silence, in the light of the scattered lamps. The house was almost emptied of visitors now, and empty of that rustling of voices.

The huge and ancient furniture almost engulfed their small bodies. Rosaries hung from Jean's and Pietro's hands, limply. Max sat very close to Kathy, and she was clutching his hand tightly, like a mother, for he had that blind and seeking look again, that shattered look. Oh, thought Lorry, the poor children. They understand so much more than Johnny does. They stared at Lorry in silence, for their suffering was too great for speech. The one in whom all their faith and trust and love had been poured had deserted them, no longer knew them, and they were totally abandoned.

They noticed, with their reddened eyes that never missed anything, that Lorry had been crying, and as she stood there among them, her arms dropping to her sides, Kathy gave a dry, gulping sob and dropped her head on her breast. Max wailed feebly; Pietro called out once; but Jean did not move or speak.

"Hello, darlings," said Lorry, her voice shaking with tenderness. She sat down on the floor in the circle of looming furniture. At a distance stood the enormous white bed with its black ebony posts. She longed to throw herself on it and give herself up to sorrow. Instead, she smoothed her hair with the palms of her hands, and then raised her head with its old gallant gesture. Her eyes slowly studied the faces of the children. All were extremely pale, and unnaturally drawn, even Kathy's. These were not bewildered children who grieved, but souls who had known incredible pain and despair, and had half forgotten, and then had known again.

"Emilie," said Lorry, trying to speak with quite surety, "is asleep. When I was a child I heard that God has said that the guardian angels of little ones like Emilie look upon the face of God Himself. And now her guardian angel has carried Emilie to the presence of God, and she's safe there, and so happy, and she's thinking of you and praying for you, and hoping that you'll remember her, and not be too sad."

Max's blind eyes turned to her, regaining conscious sight. He said, "It is not for Emilie we are so sad. We knew Emilie would go to God soon, even before the fire, just as Papa knew. It is that we are sad for Papa. Papa remembers—nothing, not even what he taught us. It was not a lie he said, but he forgot the truth."

Pietro spoke in a high and wavering voice, tinged with hysteria. "If Papa forgets, then perhaps it is not the truth at all? It is a lie we hear?"

Jean spoke sternly. "Pietro, you are being the fool again. Papa does not say things that are not true. Father Krupszyk does not lie. God does not lie."

Kathy lifted her fallen head and gazed at Pietro severely. "If you believe today, and not tomorrow, then you do not believe at all. Things must be happy for Pietro, or Pietro gets mad, and everything is bad."

Pietro began to cry, and his mouth pouted mutinously. "That is not so!" he said. "But what shall we do with Papa? Why is it Papa will not see us, touch us, or pray? Why does Papa lock himself in his room, and never answers, and such a face? He is a stranger. We would love to put our arms around him and kiss him, and we tried, but he wasn't there, Miss—"

Lorry stretched out her slim arm and took Pietro's warm, wet little hand. He cried, jumped from his chair, and flung himself down beside her and buried his face in her breast. She held him to her and said, "I'm Lorry to you, dears, your Aunt Lorry, if you want to call me that."

Kathy slipped down to join Pietro, and then Max did, and finally Jean, pushing himself painfully from his chair and dropping near her knees. They clung to her and cried bitterly in their misery and longing. She put her arms about them and kissed their lips and their cheeks. There were so many children she had held this way over the past months, so many children who had come to her instinctively. She consoled those lost ones again, as she consoled these. Pietro, moved, ran his hands over her hair, feeling for comfort. Kathy leaned her head on Lorry's shoulder. Max was at her knees, and Jean clasped her arm in both his hands. She stroked them, drew them to her, comforted them. Her head rose from among them like a gleam of light.

"If you were just ordinary American children I couldn't tell you about your father," she said steadily. "But you aren't. All of you have known sorrow and homelessness and fear and anger and hatred. They were things you knew for a long time. And now your father knows them, perhaps for the first time in his life. He's been—struck down. Like you, he asked questions, but he won't listen for the answer. He gave you time, and loved you while you were trying to find your way home. You must be good, and give him time to find his way."

"But Papa is a man, and he was always strong," said Kathy fearfully. "If men don't look at God, and they aren't strong any longer, what is it for us?"

"It's experience that makes people strong and faithful," said Lorry with aching compassion. "You've had your experience. Now he has his. You must treat him as he treated you, and you must wait for him to come to you, as he waited for your love."

"Papa is angry, real angry," said Pietro, the intuitive one.

"Just as you were angry," said Lorry. "You wouldn't trust him in the beginning, and he was your loving father, who had patience, and now he doesn't trust God, who is his loving Father and has patience."

She added, "Sometime he will need you, and call for you. Be sure of that."

They thought of it with their old prescience, and then a spontaneous chorus rose from them, muted and trembling, "Papa, poor Papa. We'll wait for Papa. We love him."

They cried again, clinging to her, weeping not for themselves but for Johnny, and Lorry thought this so touching that her eyes swam with tears again.

"We have seen Emilie. She is so beautiful," said Pietro. "She was never so beautiful. She played with us a little, but she always was so tired. Awful tired. She knew she was going away. But Papa held on to her, when it was God's will that she go home to heaven. The Father told us so. Why, then, is Papa so angry?"

"Because she had suffered so much, and he hoped to make her happy, so she would grow tall and strong like you, but God had willed it otherwise. So Papa won't accept God's will. Besides, she died when she didn't have to die, just then. There were all the toys, and it was Christmas, and—"

"And bad men killed her," said Kathy. "That is why Papa

is angry. He hates God because God let the men kill her. We heard the police."

"The Father said Emilie was pure, and just a baby, and we mustn't worry about Purgatory," said Pietro with hope. "I have a song for Emilie. It is the Ave Maria, Our Lady, who loves little children. Why doesn't Papa know that the Blessed Mother holds Emilie in her arms? Why doesn't he—believe?"

Lorry sighed. "He will. One of these days. He is sick; he can't forgive. He hates. Those things blind us to God. They shut Him out. But God is waiting, too."

She had learned to pray only recently, to ask, to see her prayers answered. "Suppose we all now pray, not for Emilie, but for your father?"

They knelt together, all except Max, who stood up and prayed for the dead child's peace, and for Johnny. He said thoughtfully, "But Emilie has peace. It is just Papa. And I can't say Kaddish for Papa."

The short and pathetic prayer concluded. Pietro kissed Lorry fully on the lips and said, "Aunt Lorry will be our mother, and she will not leave us."

Two servants brought in trays of hot food for the children and Lorry. "Now," said one of the maids affectionately, "this time we'll eat, won't we, and not be bad and make things worse?"

"Of course we will," said Lorry confidently. "We'll sit right here around the big table. And—well, Kathy, you will dish out the soup, won't you? You are the mother of the family."

"No," said Pietro, looking at Lorry with liquid eyes floating in love. "It is Aunt Lorry who is our mother."

The maids went down to the kitchen and informed Mrs. Burnsdale, with relief, that the children were eating at last, and that they'd heard Pietro laugh, and the others had smiled.

"We'd like to see Emilie often," said Kathy. "But Papa won't let us. When he found out we'd seen her he gave orders that we mustn't go in there again. But all the people come, who never loved or saw Emilie, and never knew about Emilie."

"You see," said Lorry triumphantly. "He loves you and remembers you, at all times. If he didn't, he wouldn't care how many times you went to see Emilie. He wants to spare you suffering."

"But we know all about pain, and death," said Jean. "We could teach Papa."

Max added, in his low, uncertain voice, "We saw death long ago, and we know now it is nothing."

"We cannot go to the grave with Emilie," said Kathy, with the sadness of maturity. "We can't say good-by to Emilie."

"What does that matter?" asked Lorry. "I will not go either. And I'm sure your papa won't be allowed to go. It would be a bad thing for him to look at her grave, with all his sorrow and hatred and forgetfulness."

Jean remembered something. "But it is terrible to me that the image my mother sent me, when I was dying, was lost in the fire."

"Ah," said Lorry, making a mental note, "your mother will send you another image. Just you wait and see."

She helped put the children to bed, assisted by Mrs. Burnsdale. And beside each bed Lorry Summerfield, the once harsh and ruthless and bitter, said a simple prayer, and left the children to immediate sleep and comfort.

27

"My girl," said Dr. McManus quaveringly, holding and kissing Lorry, "you don't know how I've missed you." But Lorry, with alarm, saw how old he had become, and how shrunken. Even his voice had lost its rough squeak of angry power. "I suppose you've been told everything?"

They sat together in the old back room which had once been called the breakfast-conservatory room. Ancient racks, shelves, and flowerpot holders lined the walls, but nothing grew there now. The doctor, who was not allergic to flowers "growing right in the damned garden where they belong, and not having their torsos chopped off with a knife," was allergic to flowers in the house, possibly, Lorry would think, because he loved them and unconsciously believed that flowers had a right to remain where they lived, and that they too were conscious of pain. They drank coffee, though it was long after midnight.

"Yes, Uncle Al," said Lorry, trying to keep her anxiety for him out of her voice. She wiped her damp palms with her handkerchief, and her new gauntness made her appear ill. "Is—he—still in there with Emilie?"

"Yes. That's the only time he is sure people won't come in and stare at him. People, even the best, are curious. You'd be surprised, damn 'em, to see mobs strolling by at night, after work, just to rubber-neck at the house." The doctor savagely bit through a new cigarette, discarded it with a curse. "And, I hate to tell you this, it's because of Mac—he's always printing little insinuations. Here's one tonight." He spread out the newspaper and showed it to Lorry, whose lips took on a livid color.

"There are still a number of unanswered questions about the unfortunate death of Emilie (last name unknown) who was the ward of the Reverend Mr. John Fletcher of this city. Why hadn't the child been removed to a hospital a long time ago, when her condition was known? Services for the child will be conducted on Saturday by the Reverend Mr. Gordon Hemsmith of the Barryfield Community Church, as it is rumored Mr. Fletcher is still in a state of collapse."

Lorry put down the paper in silence. The doctor said, "There was another question just this morning, under a photograph of the burning wreck of the parsonage. 'Mystery surrounds death of child, Emilie, an alleged orphan, who died in this fire. Who is Emilie?'

"I've watched the faces of the brutes passing here—not our parishioners—and I tell you they look like the lynching kind. But why? Why should they bother about that poor baby? Well, Lorry, I'll tell you, knowing all about people. The lynching kind is a big minority in every country, and they don't care who they kill, or why, just so they can kill. When a war blows up, they're the hero-boys who get medals, lots of 'em, for running right at the enemy with hand grenades. Think most of 'em really think about fighting for their country? Nope. Most of 'em born killers, and this is their chance. I've studied lynching, just out of curiosity. And when the police catch lynchers, guess what? Lots of 'em are heroes of one war or another!"

Lorry, thinking with horror of what her father was writing about Johnny, who had been stricken almost to his own death, hardly heard the old doctor. "Now," he said, "if I was a head-shrinker, and employed by the Army, know what I'd do? I wouldn't kick out the psychopaths and the bloodthirsty neurotics. They'd be the first I'd pick; I'd even look for 'em hopefully. They'd do the best job in the world, on the double, too."

The girl knew he was trying, mercifully, to distract her

attention from the black grief in this house, and she tried to smile at him. "Uncle Al, they should make you a five-star general," she said. But she was thinking with loathing of her father, whom she loved. She added, "I called Mother tonight, poor dear. She's coming in to see me tomorrow, and she's asked me—she begged me—not to let people know I'm here. For—for his sake. How she can love him I don't know. I promised, though, I'd keep out of sight and wouldn't go to the funeral, where there'll probably be his photographers."

"That's why we're going to give Johnny a shot of something a couple of hours before, so he can't go either. Well, poor Esther." He heaved a deep sigh, and reached out to take Lorry's hand. His swollen eyes blinked movingly. "My girl, my sweet, wonderful girl. Lorry, I didn't want you to know; I even forgot all about you. But you're a comfort to me now."

She had told him of the children, and he blinked damply again. "Poor kids. They'd be the best thing in the world for Johnny, and maybe he knows that, and maybe he thinks if he talked to them he'd break down, and perhaps forget how he wants to kill the man or men who burned down his house. Oh yes, there's evidence of arson."

"I know. Mrs. Burnsdale told me." Lorry lifted her head sharply, and her voice rose. "These insinuations in that paper! Are they insinuations— Oh, no, God, no! He—couldn't be thinking of that! He can't be as bad as that!"

"Your dad would think of anything, do anything, to get rid of Johnny, one way or another. Wait, honey. Sit down. He won't dare say anything really libelous; there's the laws. He's going as far as he can. We're watching."

The actual funeral was private. The dcotor had arranged that, and so it was that only a few friends were there. Johnny was not there while the services went on in the museumlike parlor; he had been drugged, not by assent, but because the doctor had given him several capsules in the morning and had said in a loud voice, "Johnny, if you want to hold up today, you'd better take these." Johnny, who had not eaten since Christmas Eve—and today was Saturday—took the capsules just to be relieved of the doctor's insistence, and then clumsily climbed to his room and fell face-down on the bed. He did not wake until ten o'clock that night.

The children were permitted to attend the services in the

house, and they sat close to Emilie's casket and did not cry. The doctor pitifully wondered what they were thinking. They were so very grave, even Pietro. He and Jean knelt by the casket before the services, beads slipping through their hands. The minister was a shy young man who was painfully disturbed about the whole matter. He had a child Emilie's age, and each time he glanced down at the little face on the white pillow he thought of his Toby, and his eyes filled with tears.

A mob gathered on the sidewalk outside, a sullen mob of men. The doctor said to Father Krupszyk and the rabbi, "What the hell are they doing here?"

The rabbi said sadly, "It is an old mob. I know them well."

The children were not permitted to go to the cemetery. "I know, I know!" the doctor told them irascibly when they pleaded. "But look. We let you attend the services at home, and your father wouldn't have wanted that, either. Don't ask for more. This is what they call a compromise."

Boys of the Sunday-school class were the pallbearers, and among them was the tall and lanky figure of Lon Harding, whose face was so swollen with tears that it was almost unrecognizable. "I don't care if it'll look funny, having me stand head and shoulders over those kids," he had obstinately told the funeral directors. "I loved that kid. She was my pet. I planted lilac bushes for her." The doctor upheld him.

The photographers were already waiting in the lonely, desolately white cemetery when the funeral party arrived, the white hearse leading. They snapped many pictures. Later, under the picture that was printed there were about three lines. "Very few attended the funeral of Emilie (last name unknown) yesterday morning, who died in the mysterious fire on Christmas Eve and who was buried today. The police are still searching for alleged arsonists, and known arsonists have been brought in for questioning."

Emilie went down into the grave, and the doctor thought, Well, honey lamb, no one can hurt you now, never again. God bless you, bless you, bless you.

His face, and the faces of the clergymen and Doctors Sol Klein and Tim Kennedy, filled the photograph.

Lorry remained in town. She stayed upstairs with the children, when visitors arrived, for her mother's sake. No one outside the house knew she was there. She told her mother, "I've got to stay. I've got to wait until I know he's better. Uncle Al says if he doesn't begin to eat properly in a day or two he's going to take him to the hospital and start forcible feeding. He will, too," Lorry added with a faint smile. "Uncle Al says nothing gets people to eating heartily so quickly as a tube in the stomach or a long needle in the arm."

"I don't know what I'd do with the kids if it weren't for you, Miss Lorry," Mrs. Burnsdale would say. She herself was at loose ends, until Lorry and the doctor suggested that she might like to do all the cooking. "But the other help; they'd be offended," said the poor woman eagerly. This, however, was arranged tactfully, and Mrs. Burnsdale was occupied so completely that she found her grief for Emilie and Johnny almost endurable.

New Year's Eve came in with purified skies. Now deep snows lay in the valley and on the mountains. New Year's Day was not a celebration, but Mrs. Burnsdale had cooked a huge roast and everyone pretended to enjoy it, except Johnny, who rarely left his room, and would eat nothing. Lorry entertained the children, sang to them softly in the back parlor, told them stories. She forced them to go out in the air, to try the new sleds and other outdoor gifts the doctor and friends had given them for Christmas, and which had been safely stored in the parish hall. Lon Harding, who felt himself responsible for the whole family, would take them to the zoo or to a show, or even to his own gym at school to let them admire his talents at basketball and other sports. For now it was January 5, and school had begun again.

Johnny was eating a very little, in his room. The doctor had told him bluntly, "I'll have you declared incompetent, so help me God, man, unless you cooperate with us. I'm not telling you to go out, or anything, or resume normal life, becuase I know what you're going through, but if you don't eat I'll take you to the hospital and you'll have something else to think about, believe me."

Johnny did not answer, but dimly he understood that the doctor was not speaking mere threats. He did not want to see the children, yet he felt he could not leave the house where they were. He would catch glimpses of them at a distance; they did not run to him, because they had been told not to by the doctor. But he never stopped or looked at them, never went into the back parlor where Miss Coogan was again teaching them. He had not gone into his church since Christmas Eve. At times he wandered in white speechlessness about the doctor's house, as if searching for something, and hardly aware that he was searching. Every hour or so he came to life long enough to call the police and ask them if they had any news for him. His eyes retained their terrible, fixed look of preoccupation. He no longer wore his clerical clothing; he wore one of the old civilian suits, bought long before the war. It hung shapelessly on his thin body.

Sometimes he gazed about him, blinking, as if wondering where he was. If Mrs. Burnsdale spoke to him he did not seem to hear her. When he slept, it was only after a sedative. He would say only one thing, when pressed by the doctor: "I must find them. I've got to find them." And his face would become even more terrible. He never spoke of Emilie. He never asked about her funeral.

His friends, the priest and the rabbi, came almost every day. Fellow ministers, almost strangers, also came. He would listen politely to their expressions of condolence, but his steadily shrinking face told them that he did not hear them at all. He seemed to be able to endure the ministers more comfortably than the priest and the rabbi, for he knew that the latter loved him and he could not stand love now. It was a fear to him. He felt that if he even acknowledged it he would crack asunder and be devastated, and he would have to begin the long road back from hatred and grief, and this he did not want to do. He wanted to retain his rage, his turning away from God.

Another minister was temporarily taking his place. Dr. McManus, in a pathetic but useless attempt to stir Johnny, removed the great candelabra from the church and pointedly placed them in the parlor where he could not help seeing them when he went into the room. He went into the parlor more frequently than into any other room. But he never looked at the candelabra. He had one small and unchanging world like the grave, with but one desire.

If he saw Lorry he gave no sign of recognition. She would put herself in his way, and he would pass her without a glance. She would speak to him, in a broken voice, and he would not answer. "Doesn't he know I'm here?" she asked

Dr. McManus. "Yes, he does, honey," replied the old doctor. "But he won't have you, just as he won't have John Kanty and the rabbi. Because he knows you love him, and he doesn't want love. He wants hate. If you went into him, in his room, right now and said, 'They've got the man who did it,' he'd jump out of his chair and be out of the house in five minutes, racing for the police station."

Lorry said, in tears, "Well, I don't blame him. And I understand."

The doctor, worn out with worry, worn out with work, for there were so many operations these days, ran his fingers wearily through his hair, which he never seemed to comb. "He talks to me, sometimes, in a dull kind of way, because he's afraid of me, afraid of what I might do to him, and so I keep scaring him about hospitals, and he feels he has to appease me some way. God, Lorry. I'm at my wit's end."

She became stern. "Uncle Al, he had so much faith. Faith was as much a part of him as his eyes, his hands. He had so much love—for God. In the name of God he forgave so many things. Why doesn't he turn to God now? Doesn't he believe any longer?"

"Maybe, but just a little. I've talked to John Kanty about it. He says it sometimes happens, especially with men like Johnny. If someone had blinded or crippled him, out of hate or craziness, there Johnny would have been, comforting him, forgiving him, protecting him, and talking about God. He would have hung on his own cross, consoling his enemy, forgetting his own agony. But he goes crazy when someone or something hurts one of his kids. Why, I remember the time Max's neck was cut. He was almost out of his mind, for a while. I don't know what would've happened if Max'd died. Something like this, I suppose.

"In some distorted way, too, he's holding God accountable for Emilie. If Emilie had just faded away, peaceful, the way she was supposed to, he'd have had his faith back in a couple of days. But the way things happened"—the doctor shook his head. "Even if they'd all had a happy life until now—the kids—it mightn't have been too bad, either. If they ever do find the man who did it, they'd better watch him. Johnny will tear him apart." He added, "I think he's hating God, deep inside him."

But it was Lorry who obtained the first response from

Johnny. She found him sitting in the dark parlor at twilight, where he had sat at the head of Emilie's casket. His head was bent, his arms dangling between his knees. She approached him, and said, "Johnny? Speak to me, Johnny." And she held out her arms to him imploringly.

He lifted his head slowly, and his sunken eyes regarded her dazedly. Then he said, "Lorry?" His voice was very faint. "Lorry, Lorry. Don't bother me, Lorry. Go away, please." She stepped back, and then agony rushed over his face. "The box, the box, you gave me—it's gone too."

She reported this to Dr. McManus, who became excited. "He's coming out of it, maybe!" He called Father Krupszyk and asked him to come in that evening. He called the old rabbi, who was ill, partly from influenza and partly from grief for his friend. He had been forbidden to leave his bed.

"We'll jump him all at once, the three of us," Dr. McManus said to the priest and Lorry that night. "We'll give him hell; we'll catch him off balance."

Father Krupszyk was dubious. "Suppose we just get his full attention first, doctor? You don't whip a dying horse, you know. But perhaps you could give him something to arouse him for a little while, just so we can reach him."

28

The children were in bed, and Lorry was in her room, praying with all her heart, her tears running over her clasped hands. "It was because of him that I came to know You, and to work for You, Father," she pleaded. "We all need him so much. We love him so much. And we need him and love him because You made him necessary to us. Help us, help us, tonight!"

She changed her dress to one of light-blue wool, her hair loosely coiled at the nape of her neck. She could do nothing with her emaciated face, in which her turquoise eyes seemed far too large and distended. Then she went downstairs. Johnny was sitting, as usual, in his old place, silent as ever, as engrossed as ever in his own thoughts. But the doctor had given him a stimulant, and this had made him dully restless. He wrung his hands, he clasped his hands tightly over his knees, he moved his head as if in pain, and sometimes he glanced up unseeingly. Father Krupszyk was already there, and the doctor. Johnny had not spoken to them.

When Lorry came in quietly, Johnny's head jerked up and she knew he saw her clearly before he averted his head again. She sat down near the doctor and waited. She did not know what anyone would do. They would have to await some signal, either from Johnny or from some mysterious force. Father Krupszyk's lips were moving silently, and he held a small prayer book in his hand. Dr. McManus, almost as restless as Johnny, moved incessantly in his chair.

The candelabra had been brought into the dark parlor, and they stood at each end, filling the big room with soft and shifting radiance. Sometimes Johnny glanced at them with dim surprise, as if wondering what they were. Sometimes he looked at the three people, now, and his brow wrinkled like a man suffering from amnesia, who is trying to remember. Somewhere a clock ticked remorselessly, and the winter wind tried the windows angrily.

Then Father Krupszyk stood up and approached Johnny. He waited until Johnny looked at him, and then he tried to hold that feverishly bright eye. He began to speak with force and quiet surety.

"Johnny, I feel that Our Lord has sent us to you tonight, and that He has given you a solemn command to listen. For we are not here for your sake, but for those who love you, and those you have utterly abandoned in your preoccupation with your own grief.

"Men who are called to serve God must serve Him with all their hearts and all their souls. They must be all-understanding. They must know mankind, yet forgive it and love it. They must not think of themselves, and their own ideas of hatred or—vengeance."

Johnny's eyes flickered, but there was no other movement in his face. He started to drop his head, then, as if someone had seized it, he lifted it.

"You have failed, Johnny," said the priest sternly. "You have failed God and man. We don't need any explanations, or any pleas. We know, and we suffer with you. But you, a minister, have failed. Have you asked forgiveness for that?" He looked at Johnny's worn civilian suit. He pointed at it. "You've taken off the vestments of your faith, in hate and defiance and rage. You have offended God, and that pleases you. You can't stop believing in Him, so you offend Him. You've driven Him from your presence. Johnny, you are in hell."

Johnny's expression remained motionless, but his eyes were flickering faster, not with shame or sorrow or sadness, but

with unspeakable anger. Once they blazed out at the priest,
and once he seemed about to speak. He watched, like a wild
and wary animal, the closer approach of the priest, and he sat
upright, pressing his back against the chair as if he were
trying for escape.

The priest continued in a louder, clearer voice. "Our Lord
knew what He would have to endure in this world. You, as
His minister, know only too well that the Way of the Cross is
the way of those dedicated to His service. As willingly as He
came, as willingly you took on the duties of His service—to
bring men unto God.

"Torture was the gift Our Lord offered to God, for He
loved men and He lifted up His agony in their behalf. He
hung upon His Cross, bleeding from the wounds of the flesh,
and the wounds of His Spirit. Humbly, He raised all His
Passion to the throne of God, in atonement for men's sins, for
the saving of men's souls.

"Johnny, what have you offered God, in your extremity?
Your grief, your loss, your torment—as a gift, for the salvation of souls? Have you shown humility and have you said, as
Our Lord said, 'Thy will be done'? And have you then
opened your soul, waiting for the answer which is ready for
you, but which you will not have?"

Johnny's anger shot from his eyes, and his mouth opened.
"Why, thank God," said Dr. McManus.

"No, listen to me," said the priest, even more sternly, and
pointed a restraining finger at Johnny. "Perhaps you'll never
listen to me again. Perhaps, if you reject what I say to you
now, I'll never come to this house again."

He paused. Johnny's hands had clenched into fists. He
could not look away from the priest, whom he now hated
almost as much as he hated God.

"What do you know of God, Johnny? You've been a good
minister, a good man. You've comforted the sick and the
dying. You've rescued the helpless. You have prayed, and
believed in your prayers. Is that as far as you can go? A limited man? A man who cannot accept his own agony, cannot
offer it to God as a supreme gift, but who feels that he, above
all other ministers, all other priests, has a special protection
from the torments that afflict all of us, sometime or other?
Johnny, you are a man of pride, of vainglory. You have committed a deadly sin. Johnny, you are not a minister. You have

offended the all-loving, all-merciful God, with your pride, your self-pity, your unwillingness to find, through prayer and hope, the reason for your pain. Johnny, I am leaving you now. I don't think I can ever come back. It's too painful for me to see a minister fall away from God."

Lorry, watching Johnny, saw the ultimate agony on his face, for all the fury in his eyes. Oh, please, please, she said in herself to the priest, you are hurting him too much, too much.

Johnny's hands gripped the arms of his chair. His face became convulsed, like the face of a dying man. Lorry could endure it no longer. She stood up and ran to him, and fell on her knees before him. She broke into a great burst of tears, and put her head on his knee.

Johnny's hands slowly relaxed. He looked down at Lorry, and the torture left his face and was replaced by a wondering expression of pain and mystic revelation. The priest stepped back, and Dr. McManus leaned forward in his chair, trembling with the certainty that something strange and mysterious was now occurring. He could not believe it when he saw Johnny's hand lift slowly and feebly and rest itself on Lorry's head. She had pinned the long lengths of her hair too loosely, in her haste, and at Johnny's touch, at the pressure of his hand, her hair spilled down over her shoulders and covered her neck and back, glimmering like fire in the candlelight. Her face was hidden on Johnny's knee, and her sobs filled the room, and echoed back to all of them.

The priest moved backward into the shadows, and he closed his eyes briefly. His heart began to beat fast.

Then Johnny, with infinite tenderness and understanding, put his hands on Lorry's cheeks and raised her head and looked into her eyes. He smiled at her, with profound sorrow. She leaned against him, weeping uncontrollably.

"Johnny," she said brokenly, "listen to me. Do you know what you've done for me? You've saved my soul. Do you know what I was before I knew you? I hated everybody, I hated myself, I believed in nothing; I wanted—revenge—for what I believed someone had done to me. He had done it, yes, but out of his own viciousness and ignorance. You made me forgive him, Johnny, almost forgive him. With your help, I can really forgive him.

"I was a bitter and ruthless woman, Johnny, and you sent

me on my way to do the things you would want me to do. For four days a week, since I left here, I've been working very hard with the American Friends Committee, the Quakers, rescuing children from Europe, just as you rescued your own children. I've given money, but more than all the money I've given, I've given my hands, the faith you gave me, and the love and understanding you gave me."

Johnny's hands held her face tightly. He bent over her, as if in protection and comfort. His fingers were buried in her hair and he drew her closer to him, and his face was full of light and love.

Lorry raised herself a little and put her head on his breast, and his arms closed about her.

"Because of you, Johnny," she said almost inaudibly, "I did this. When I became too tired, I thought of you. When I looked at the poor terrified children, I remembered you, and I said to them what you said to your own, and they were comforted and not frightened any more. Because of you, Johnny, because of you."

Dr. McManus, whose eyes ached, dimly, looked at the priest. But the priest was still praying.

Johnny was rising in his chair now, holding Lorry in his arms. He pressed her against him, and then gently kissed her forehead. "The children," he said, "the poor children. God bless you, Lorry, my dear, my dear."

The priest turned abruptly and left the room. Dr. McManus sat and watched as Johnny comforted Lorry. Johnny was actually saying, "I was wrong. I've sinned too, Lorry. I don't know where I've been all these days. I wonder if God will ever forgive me! I wonder if He'll accept me again? I don't know. He may never listen to me again."

Now he was full of a new sorrow, and a terrible remorse and humility. He saw Dr. McManus for the first time, and smiled slightly at him over Lorry's head.

Now there was a rapid drumming of many feet on the stairway and the priest entered again, and with him were the children in their night clothes, crying, holding out their arms. "Papa, Papa!" they called in tears, and they ran to Johnny.

He put Lorry gently aside, and the children swarmed about him, and he hugged them to him, comforting them. "I've come home," he said. "I was away for a while, but I've come home."

Now he was alive, awake, still torn with grief, but accepting it humbly. He held out his hand to the priest without speaking, and Father Krupszyk took his hand and pressed it in silence.

The next Sunday Johnny delivered his first sermon since Christmas Eve. His regret was that Lorry had had to return to New York.

29

Pietro and Jean went to early Mass so they could see Johnny before he went into his church. Max, too, returned early from Sunday school. They were happy and excited, though more subdued than usual, remembering Emilie. However, there was their father again, smiling, though abnormally thin and pale, waiting to greet them, to ask about church and Sunday school. His arms ached for the lost little body of Emilie in his arms, and Pietro, with the fine sensitivity of the Italian, knew this, and pretended to be pettish, and climbed upon Johnny's knee. Johnny felt the pressure of the slight and wiry body and was speechlessly grateful. The other children understood too, and did not give Pietro their usually scornful glances for his emotionalism.

They were now told of the love between their father and Lorry, and of a future marriage. "But not too far in the future, though," Johnny had added hastily, at the look of disappointment on their faces. "You see, Aunt Lorry made a promise to God, a few months ago, that she would help Him with His orphan children from Europe, children like you. And who breaks a promise to God?" He thought of his own broken promise, but he knew he had been forgiven. However, his face had taken on a shadow, for all his smile.

"Sometimes," said Pietro thoughtfully, as he brushed a little lint from Johnny's shoulder with his restless hand, "it is not well to make a promise to God that you can't keep. Or that it's silly to keep."

"This isn't silly," said Johnny. "Aunt Lorry's promise doesn't end until late in the summer, and you've got to be patient. Yes, Kathy, of course you can be the flower girl. And now, pests, I've got to leave you and go into the church." They kissed him and watched him go, and each, in his small way, realized that some mournful change had come to him. They were too young to know it to be spiritual growth.

The congregation could not fail to notice how deathly pale their minister had become, how emaciated. The church was crowded, to give him comfort and sympathy. They saw the gray streaks at his temples and sighed, yet he stood with dignity, his hands clasped loosely before him. There was something remote about him, yet paradoxically, something charged and imminent. His voice, when it came, was not faint or weak, but forceful and strong.

"Our Divine Lord," he said, "has spoken of the punishment which those who offend the little ones who love him shall inherit.

"In my house there was such a little one, almost an infant, who used to listen to me with rapture when I told her of Our Lord's love for her. You see, until I found her she had never known the meaning of love, or what love was, or the joy and the wonder of it."

He paused, his throat tightening. The eyes of many women became wet, and men bowed their heads.

"I loved her, and so did the other children I rescued from death. She couldn't get over it. When I kissed her, even on the night that she died, when I tucked her in her bed as you tuck your own children, she would smile at me wonderingly—and blissfully. I taught her to love God. She couldn't wait, that night, for the morning when she would celebrate His birthday. But—she never had the chance. She had said her child's last innocent prayer to Him, in confidence that He had heard her and had blessed her. And no doubt He did." His mouth twitched with bitter agony, and he could not speak for several moments.

"Shall this child have died in vain? I have heard that ninety-six old people and little people like my Emilie died

401

during what the scientists nonchalantly said was an 'inversion.' They were killed by it. I see that several fathers and mothers are not in church today. They are home, still mourning their dead, the little ones like Emilie who had done no harm, and who had loved their parents and God, and who had waited, like her, for Christmas."

He took a step or two closer to his congregation, who listened in deep silence.

"I have read the papers, as you've read them. The doctors say, very cautiously, that the smog with which this city is afflicted was only a contributory cause of these ninety-six deaths. 'Only,' they say. These weak and ill old men and women and children were barely holding on to life anyway. They would probably have died a day later, two weeks later, two months or perhaps a year later."

Johnny's voice rose passionately. "And who are those who have deprived these ninety-six victims of those days, those weeks, months, or even years? Who shall say to any of us that it is no matter that we have lost a few more smiles, voices, laughter, and love on this earth? Who shall have the arrogance to dare say that what we have lost, and what our loved ones have lost, is nothing at all, because the victims were doomed in any event? Who has given them the right so to poison the living air that they can be the sole judges and tell us how long our children and our parents may live, and how long we may see their beloved faces and hear their voices? Those precious days, hours, week, months—they belonged to us, and not to those who, out of their monstrous greed, have spread corruption and death over our city."

The congregation sat upright in the pews, and the candlelight revealed the flash of scores of furious eyes.

"Who has given these men the power of life and death over us? Who has said it is their right to inflict suffering upon us? I know them. You know them. They live far up in the hills, where their own children do not gasp to death, and their old fathers and mothers do not stifle. Many times these things have been brought to their attention, but they have only smiled, and done nothing. One, I heard, even said that it was a good way to keep down the population!"

A deep murmur of anger ran through the church. Johnny leaned forward, his hands clenched together.

"They have assumed the prerogative which belongs only to

God—the right over life and death. They have offended the little ones. They say it will cost too much money for smoke elimination. What money? The money which was earned for them by those who have had to watch their children and their parents die, and could do nothing!

"I have the figures here which tell exactly how much it would cost these men to eliminate the smoke from this city, the grit and filth from its streets, the stinging sickness in our lungs and the stench in our nostrils, the staining of our homes and the killing of our gardens and our lawns. I have the figures which are a matter of life and death for the helpless. They are not small. But neither are they so large that one child is not worth more. The cost would not deprive the men who pollute our city of their fortunes. Yet they refuse to do what they must do, to prevent their poisoning of us, their killing of us. Why? Is money so precious, so sacred, that in comparison our lives are nothing?"

The congregation stirred.

Johnny lifted his hands. "If murderers were caught poisoning our water system, justice would be swift and sure. Yet these men who have made our air a source of death are not punished. They are not even reprimanded! And why? Because they hold the marvelous power of profit over our politicians, because our politicians are their creatures, and because of the bounty of the masters the creatures, too, can escape the yellow death that swirls through our streets."

Johnny advanced almost to the wooden edge of the three steps that led from the altar. His face was blazing. "The people's patience is long and mild. But the time has come when patience is no longer a virtue but a cowardly vice. If you, the people, do not do something now about this death in our streets, then you too sin by your silence and cowardice, and you are as guilty as they."

His voice dropped exhaustedly. "I have never believed that the pulpit is the place for discussions of worldly matters, but a place where ministers should speak of God. But I am now impelled to speak to you to have mercy on the sick, the dying, the children—some of whom may be in your homes at this very moment. On your way out at the doors, you will find mimeographed petitions I have had prepared for you. Take them, fill them with names. Send them to the mayor of this city. Urge immediate action; demand it. Let you men who work in the foundries, the mills, and the factories declare, through your officers, that if the smoke is not eliminated you will remain away from your open hearths, your benches, your machines. The source of the yellow death will then be eliminated.

"You can be sure," he added, "that these men who have killed those we love can never withstand the wrath of a whole populace. Pittsburgh and other cities have eliminated the sulfurous evil that had been poisoning them. They did this because their people demanded it with one loud, sure, and determined voice. You can do this also.

"You can begin tomorrow. Perhaps the next inversion may not come for a year, or two years. But it may come in a week, or a day. Who, sitting here now, can say with truth that in so short a time your houses may not become houses of mourning?

"Has my child died in vain? Some of you women have seen her. Some of you will remember her, on Christmas Eve, sitting in the pretty dress in which she was buried three days later. You will remember her child's face, her smiles, her ecstasy of anticipation, which was never fulfilled. I beg you, I implore you, not to let her death be in vain."

He could speak no more. He looked at them imploringly, his hands held out. And they looked back at him with hard resolution or weeping silence.

When he joined Dr. McManus, he had the satisfaction of seeing that the petitions had been taken, to the last one. He leaned back in the limousine and shut his burning eyes. The doctor glanced at him, hunched forward, and drew his eyebrows down almost to his very eyelids. They were nearing the Victorian mansion when the old doctor said, "They'll fill 'em out! They'll be piling up in masses on that damned mayor's desk in a couple of days. You'll see."

"I hope so," Johnny answered. His heart was palpitating, and he was breathless.

The doctor chewed his lip. "No time like the present," he said. "I'd like to tell you about some people I know. Good people. The father was a clerk in one of the men's shops here. He died, two months ago. And a week ago the wife died, in childbirth. The baby died too. Just young, nice, kindly people. Respectable, independent, patriotic, brave, and hopeful. I want you to see what's left."

"Not now, for God's sake," Johnny murmured, out of the depths of his sorrow and weariness and his lonely yearning for Lorry.

"Yes, now. Tomorrow may be too late. Somebody needs you more than *you* need you."

Johnny thought of Emilie's chair, forever empty. He thought of the small, translucent face and the large blue eyes and the eager little hands. She had a special call for him when he came home from church, or from his sick calls or other duties, a rapturous call as if she had not believed that he would ever return. He kept his eyes shut, and he heard Emilie's voice calling him anxiously.

He did not know that the limousine had stopped until the doctor rudely poked him. "Come on," said the doctor. "You aren't dying. Stop stewing in your misery. You're needed. What's a minister for?"

They were standing before a small gray house, neat and clean, with a red roof, and a little lawn heaped with snow. Using all his last strength, Johnny dragged himself from the limousine and went with the doctor up to the steps. He made one final effort. "I'm not in a mood to comfort anybody just yet," he said. "There's still not much comfort in me."

"One sometimes finds comfort in strange places," said the doctor, ringing the bell.

The door was opened by a minute old woman in a gray gingham dress with a shawl over her shoulders. It was evident that she was not in the least surprised to see them. She smiled wanly. "Come in, please," she said. She looked at Johnny with an expectation he could not interpret. "I hope it'll turn out all right, Mr. Fletcher," she said. "I sure hope you'll like Debby."

"Debby?" repeated Johnny. "Your daughter, your granddaughter? Is she ill?"

"You ask too many questions," said the doctor.

They entered the tiniest of neat parlors, with braided rugs and old furniture. A canary sang somewhere in a cage, and a kitten slipped down from a chair. The doctor whipped up the kitten expertly in his hands. "Always hated cats," he said, nestling the little animal on his shoulder and stroking it fondly.

"So I see," said Johnny, smiling in spite of himself.

"That's Debby's kitten," said the old woman, who had been introduced to Johnny as Mrs. Dietrich.

"Well, get her," said the doctor. "We've got a dinner waiting."

Mrs. Dietrich left the little parlor, which had an odor of potpourri and wax. Johnny looked about him with interest, saw the bric-a-brac in a corner closet. "Is Mrs. Dietrich a German?" he asked. "She's got an accent."

"Yes," said the doctor. "And those two young people I told you of were Germans. They got into this country in 1939, eight years ago. Something to do with politics. They weren't Nazis. Young kids then."

Mrs. Dietrich was entering the room again, holding the hand of a little girl about five years old, carrying a rag doll clutched to her breast. Johnny's heart contracted in a spasm of pain. The child was a bit small for her age, but she had a chubby infant body, a round and rosy face with gay blue eyes, and a mass of auburn ringlets. She had the prettiest of pink mouths, and she was smiling unsteadily under a plump, upturned nose. Her dress was of white and black checks, with a big red sash around the protruding middle. Now, as she saw Johnny, she wet her lips with a tremulous little red tongue and clung closer to Mrs. Dietrich. But the doctor held out his arms and she squealed and ran to him, still clutching the doll. He lifted her in his arms and looked at Johnny. "This is Deborah Woltz," he said. "What do you think of this charmer, eh? She winds me around her little finger. Here, stop looking in my pockets, you gold-digger."

"Where's my candy?" asked the child, reproachfully. She peeped at Johnny slyly.

"Never mind the candy," said the doctor. He put the child down, and patted her head. "Mind your manners, now. This is Mr. Fletcher, a minister."

The child eyed Johnny with great but bashful interest. "He's my new Papa?" she demanded.

"Now, how can he tell?" demanded the doctor crossly. "You haven't even shaken his hand. Go on, now, and be polite."

The little girl wobbled toward Johnny, almost reached him, then gave him a touching curtsy. "They bring them up well in the old countries," said the doctor with pride. "She was born right here in Barryfield, but her parents taught her how to behave."

Johnny held out his hand gravely, bending toward the little one. She gave him her small fat hand, and the touch of it brought back the pain that never left him on a higher and more poignant wave. She said, "I'm in kindergarten. I can read some words, too. And I know the alphabet," she added, hopefully.

"That's wonderful," said Johnny. "I have five—I mean—I have four children. They'd like to know you, Debby. Such a smart little girl."

"As old as me? Five?" asked Debby, with more interest.

Johnny was silent. He looked down at the child, and the gray hollows under his cheekbones deepened. The doctor said, "Debby's got no one in this country, and no one in Germany, either. Everybody's dead. When her mother died Mrs. Dietrich took her in, but the Children's Shelter is after her." He stared at Johnny significantly. "You know the Children's Shelter. Place like a jail. No money. And then they'll put her in a boarding home, and then in another foster home, and more foster homes, or maybe she'll end up in an orphanage. You've seen it, son. Nice prospect for a nice little girl, isn't it? And nobody wants, very much, to adopt a child this age."

He waved his hand. "Some foster homes are good, some bad. But bad in any event for a little kid. Some people take them in for the money they get from the welfare. I can tell you of some kids I've seen in the hospital who were brought in from boarding homes. But not a good idea at best for any kid, who's got to have roots and a feeling she belongs. Especially girls. Girls are insane about families. Can't stand them myself."

Debby was gazing at Johnny eagerly. "I take my bath, myself," she said. "And I hang up my clothes. Mama taught me. I'm a real nice girl." She lifted up her dress and showed Johnny, proudly, her starched petticoat and little white panties. "I keep clean," she added. "I never bother anybody. I'm real good."

The doctor sighed elaborately, not looking at Johnny. "Well, hope you'll be real good in a foster home," he said. "Hope I don't see you next time in a hospital, with a cracked skull. Such pretty curls, too."

"You're not very subtle," said Johnny. He sat down and

held out his arms to Debby, and she bounced at once to him and jumped up on his lap. He shut his eyes and closed his arms about her, and it was like closing his arms about Emilie. He kissed her, and she hugged him vehemently. "You're a real nice Papa," she said.

"No doubt this was all stage-managed beforehand," said Johnny to the doctor.

"Well," said the doctor airily, "not to the last gesture, anyway. But I've been telling Debby that I'd bring her a new father. If not you, then somebody else. She was to take her choice. She's apparently chosen you. And, by the way, she's not a pauper. Her father left five thousand dollars in insurance." He shook a finger at Johnny admonishingly. "If Debby hadn't like you, son, that would have been all. She had her choice."

Debby perched a very wet and enthusiastic kiss on Johnny's cheek. "I like my new Papa," she announced graciously. "And my suitcase is all packed, too."

Johnny's heart was faltering. He smoothed the pretty auburn ringlets tenderly. "I—I don't know what Mrs. Burnsdale will say," he said. "It's only fair to tell her first."

The doctor thought this a big joke. "Why, Mrs. Burnsdale's been around three times! She and Debby get along fine. In fact, she said if you didn't take Debby she would, and when you went into the new parsonage she'd stay with me, and maybe marry me, and we'd adopt Debby ourselves."

Johnny gave him an eloquent look which made the doctor and Mrs. Dietrich burst out laughing. "I'm being blackmailed," said Johnny. "What else can I do but surrender?" He wound one of the bright ringlets about his finger, and it clung to him as Emilie's curls always did, and for a moment he thought he would groan.

The doctor jammed his hat on. "Well, that's settled. I'll take care of the formalities in Children's Court. All right, miss, put on your hat and coat. We're going home."

"Yes," said Johnny, with the pain lifting a little in his heart. "We're going home."

Dr. McManus offered a reward of $10,000 for the apprehension and conviction of the arsonist who had burned down the parsonage, and the whole city eagerly began to search.

30

The boys were enchanted with Debby, who, after studying
them closely, apparently decided she would be able to manage them without much difficulty. Kathy was another matter.
She had not succumbed to Debby's charms and her bouncing
ways and her assured prattle. She pulled Debby from the
bewitched circle of the boys, in which Debby had been enter-
taining them with stories about her kindergarten, all lively
and a little elaborated for effect. Debby fell immediately into
a respectful silence, looking up at the taller girl meekly. But
her blue eyes danced.

"After Papa, and Mrs. Burnsdale, I take care of things
around here," said Kathy severely. "You'll be our sister if you
mind. I'll teach you to wipe dishes, and dust. And I don't like
stories, either, 'specially if they are not true. Hear me?"

"They were so true," said Debby, looking as if about to cry
with embarrassment. ("I want my Mama," she murmured,
but no one heard her.)

"We have enough story tellers around here without another one," said Kathy, with a quelling glance at Pietro. She
scrutinized Debby. "I think you will be all right," she added.

"After you are trained well. And we can plant some trees for you—if you mind." Then she relented, bent and kissed the younger girl. "I think we'll love you."

"And I," said Pietro grandly, "will marry you, Debby, when you are old enough."

"I thought you were going to marry Kathy," said Jean.

Pietro tossed this absurd thought away. "Gentlemen like the young girls," he said. "Kathy is too old for me."

Mrs. Burnsdale and Johnny listened to this with high amusement. Then Mrs. Burnsdale said, "It's those comics he's always reading. And the movie magazines I get."

"If you think I'd marry a boy who doesn't always tell the truth, and makes funny faces all the time, you are wrong," said Kathy with disdain.

Pietro eyed Debby critically. "I like her hair best," he said.

Debby had her own ideas. She shook the brilliant ringlets decidedly. "I will marry my new Papa," she announced. She gave Kathy a sly glance. "My curls are real," she said. Kathy colored. She was putting up her hair at night, now, on Mrs. Burnsdale's curlers. "My," said Mrs. Burnsdale with admiration. "Imagine a baby five years old knowing anything about curls being real or not."

"I'm real smart," said Debby smugly.

"Show me how smart you are with a dish towel," said Kathy, pushing one into Debby's fat little hand.

Johnny had feared that when Debby would take her place at the table he would suffer renewed sorrow. But, to his surprise, she filled the chair without giving him a single thrust of pain. It was as if Emilie were there, an Emilie grown strong, cautiously impertinent, respectful, interested, healthy, and full of laughter. It was as if Emilie had sent him this buxom child, eager for his love, this parentless child he had rescued. No more would his nights be haunted by dread, tormented by anguished and unanswered prayers. He had his five children again, and all of them bursting with vitality. Even Jean was gaining weight very fast. Johnny would think, If Emilie had lived, I'd never have known Debby, and she would be in some foster home or orphanage, and utterly abandoned. Emilie is safe; now Debby is safe.

She was accepted by the other children and she had accepted them. She abounded with curiosity, with affection, with stories that surpassed even Pietro's. She had a fairy godmother, she announced, who kissed her every night and made her hair nicer and her eyes brighter. Johnny checked Kathy, who was about to introduce a note of dull realism into this gay fantasy. "I'm sure you have, darling," he said. "But we call those 'godmothers' guardian angels." He bought a lithograph to hang over Debby's little bed, a picture of a benign angel with loving eyes and outstretched hands. This moved Debby, and mollified Kathy, who was such a stickler for facts. "Papa's and Mama's angels called them home," said Debby, and her lip trembled. Johnny took her up in his arms, and saw her efforts to control herself, and smile. The baby is so valiant, he thought with a thrust of pain.

He entered her name for adoption. He did not know that Dr. McManus had had a hard time arranging things, for again the Children's Aid Society had tried to cause trouble. There was a waiting vengefulness about those people, the doctor would think. But, hell, I've got a lot of money, and a golden sword holds buzzards away.

Debby, on seeing the school arrangements at home, decided that she preferred them to kindergarten. But on this Johnny was firm, despite her tears. He drove her to the school every day. She would return to the impatiently waiting children to give the most appalling account of her experiences. The teacher had pushed her; the children had tried to fight her, but she had kicked them right away, she had; she had poured water down another child's neck; she had torn a dress; the teacher had cried; she had stamped on the crayons. Debby was a devil. Only Kathy listened with a frown. One day Johnny visited the young teacher himself, who affectionately assured him that Debby was a model child, a leader, full of bounce and vim and adored by the others. Still, Debby's stories enlivened dinner, so he did not as yet interfere. She had a wonderful imagination, and half believed her stories, and there was no malice in them, only a desire to entertain.

The wound was healing rapidly.

The petitions were piling up on the mayor's desk, much to his wrath. He cursed Johnny, the instigator. His friends upbraided him; he showed them the petitions, and the threats implicit in them.

Mr. Summerfield's assistant editor was unable to ignore the petitions. He had his "comedian" write light and ridiculing editorials about them. Circulation suddenly dropped off alarmingly. The "comedian" was replaced by a more sober editorial writer. He introduced the "pro" and "con" method, inviting the people to write in about the petitions. He wrote several of them on the "con" side of the petitions and put them in the "The People Write." Unfortunately for him, his were the only contrary letters. The "people" responded with violent invective and angry replies to the fictitious initials in the column and to the editorials.

"All the people in Barryfield are with the minister," Lon Harding reported contentedly. "Except the ones whose old men own the factories and the mills. But they keep their mouths shut."

In the meantime, Johnny's parish-hall school was booming with young boys and girls eager to learn what they could not learn in school. The old teachers, including Miss Coogan, were exhilarated with joy. It was now the end of February, and unusually warm, and people reported that when they passed the parish hall four nights a week they could hear the excited voices of the young people who were discovering the world of poetry, glory, patriotism, and literature which had been denied them, "In the interest of society, and in the cause of realistic life-adjustment."

The murderer of little Emilie had still not been found. Johnny did not give up hope.

One afternoon the chief of police called Dr. McManus. "I don't think we have something here, Al, but I thought I'd tell you about it. A woman's here, name of Sheila Gandy, from Wilkes-Barre. She says her husband set that fire in your minister's parsonage. He's dying, she says. And she wants the reward, because he wants her to have the reward so she'll have something when he's dead. Kind of a stupid woman. Probably just another false alarm. But there was something. She told how he'd told her he'd stuffed the hot-air pipes of the furnace with gasoline rags, put strings to 'em, and then set 'em on fire and got out of the house. Got in through the cellar and hid behind the furnace when the minister was searching. That checks. And you know we did find some evidence like that. Did any of that stuff get in the newspapers?"

"No!" squealed the doctor. "What a hell of a memory you

have! Nobody let it out, except that maybe one of your boys did, but I don't see why. Your department kept it quiet. Did she say that Communists told him to do it?"

The chief paused. "No, she didn't. Why don't you come down and bring the minister, right now?"

The doctor had just come from the operating room. Tired though he was, he told a nurse to call Johnny and tell him to appear at the office of the chief of police.

Johnny came, as white as death, trembling and speechless. "Don't get your hopes up, son," said Dr. McManus. "The chief thinks this is just a false alarm. He's told me about a lot of others and we decided not to bother you, for they were fakes. This has something that sounds a little like it, but not much. Try to control youself."

"I think this is it," said Johnny in a stifled voice.

"Well, don't fly off half cocked, as usual. I know women. They get hysterical, and I hate hysterical women."

They went into the chief's dusty and gritty office, which was crowded with files and ancient furniture. Beside his desk sat a big, fat woman with a face like dough, thin black hair floating about her face, clumsy limbs, worn clothing, and a cautious, belligerent expression on her shapeless features. Her large hands, in black cotton gloves, were tightly clasped together. She stared at Johnny and the doctor with no pleasure. "Why the minister?" she demanded sullenly. "You just said two friends, chief." Then her expression changed, became charged with alarm. "Is this the minister, huh?"

"Yes, Mrs. Gandy," said the chief of police. He nodded to the young policeman who sat at the end of the battered desk, and who held his pencil poised over a notebook. "Mr. Fletcher, this is Sergeant Batson. He's been taking notes. Sergeant, read them off, will you?"

Mrs. Gandy said in a faltering voice to Johnny, "Gee, parson, I'm terrible sorry—about that little girl. But my man—"

Johnny looked at her without speaking, and she flinched and turned away from him. Dr. McManus sat down. "All right," he said, "go right along, sergeant."

Mrs. Gandy listened, and now her round black eyes became defiant, and she set her head at an arrogant angle and listened as intently as did the others.

413

Merrill Gandy, her husband, was now thirty-nine years old; she was forty-two. They resided in the city of Wilkes-Barre. Her husband had been drafted in 1944. They had no children, and Merrill had been a machinist. They had been married in 1939, and at the time of the draft they had had but two hundred dollars saved. "What could you expect, with the depression?" Mrs. Gandy had asked. They lived on a mean street, and had no friends. They had never had time to make them. Mrs. Gandy worked in a bakery and, during the war, in a war plant. They still had a little money by the end of the war. "Well, we got a new radio set, some furniture, and a used car, and went out bowling a lot, and made some friends, and the money went," Mrs. Gandy had said resentfully. "Beer and clothes and things cost a lot."

Merrill was discharged from the Army in the spring of 1946. He went back to work in his factory. In August, 1946, several months later, he complained of his back. He thought at first that it was due to "heavy liftin'." But the plant physician said it was an old injury, four ruptured discs in his spine. Then Merrill, frustrated at not collecting workmen's compensation, suddenly remembered that he had sustained the injury in the Army. He had never gone overseas. He had remained in the same camp where his talents as a machinist were appreciated—Air Force. "Lots of men comin' and goin'," Mrs. Gandy had said. One day he was standing behind an open engine he was working on, and "some smart aleck" got in the seat, and started it up, and the two right wheels ran right over Mr. Merrill's body, "hurtin' his spine."

The chief of police had asked why he had not reported it immediately. The reply was that he had done this, and had been treated in the infirmary. But Merrill could remember nothing of the doctor's name, or the names of any of the nurses, or the "smart aleck." "Whole place too crowded, and everybody comin' and goin'." Merrill had remained in the camp, after apparently recovering. "Trouble didn't show up until he got to workin' on heavy stuff in the factories," said Mrs. Gandy. Then he could not work. He applied to the Veterans Administration for compensation, but they could find 'no records. The bureau acknowledged that during the confusion of the war years such things very often happened. He had been hospitalized in a veterans' hospital. While the administration again searched records, and investigated, they took X rays. They told Merrill that they could do nothing about compensation until his case was approved to be service-connected.

Merrill, after several weeks, told his wife that he "wasn't goin' to stay in this damn hospital no longer," and he went home and to bed. Oh, sometimes he'd get up and go and play cards with the boys, and have a beer, but he couldn't work. Back too bad. So he went to a doctor and had X rays, and here they was, right there on the chief's desk, and the doctor's report.

Dr. McManus held out his hand for the X rays. He studied them intently. He looked at Mrs. Gandy, then muttered, "Well, they're the discs all right, but not too bad. Seen worse in men working every day. Couldn't give him too much trouble, except every once in a while, and then he could sleep on the floor a few nights, and take some aspirin, and get right up again. But that's not the trouble. Look here at these big shadows." He held out the X rays to Johnny. He whispered, "Cancer. Of long standing. The man's dying, and it's not near the spine at all, and had nothing to do with it."

Mrs. Gandy demanded loudly, "What you whisperin' about? Can't you read X rays? Tryin' to cook up something against Merrill?"

Dr. McManus said gravely, "Madam, I agree with you that your husband is desperately sick, and I agree with you that he hasn't long to live."

Her face changed, then she began to cry. "I don't care for nothin' but Merrill. And they did that to him and they won't give him a cent compensation, and they won't give me nothin' either, when Merrill's dead."

"Does your husband cough much and complain of pains in his chest?" asked the doctor, with real concern. The woman nodded her head so vigorously that the cheap velvet hat wobbled. "He sure does. All the time. Coughs up blood, sometimes. It's those discs."

The doctor said, "I'd advise you to send your husband back to the veterans' hospital immediately. He hasn't very long to live, I'm afraid."

The dreary story continued. Merrill began to hate the Veterans Administration "for bein' so mean to him, and not giving him no compensation after the Army hurt him, and me havin' to work all the time in the bakery, and gettin' only fifty-five dollars a week. If Merrill'd been a rich guy with a lot of pull, he'd have got compensation fast enough! Why, there was fellers holdin' down big jobs and gettin' big compensation, right there in Merrill's plant!" Johnny looked at the blubbery and shaking face, and the tears, and his heart softened in pity. But he hardened it almost at once. "It was all sassiety's fault," said Mrs. Gandy. "The rich guys with their big, shiny new cars—they don't want the little feller to have anythin'. No, nothin'." And so Merrill, who had not been injured in the Army at all, and who was dying of cancer, began to hate some amorphous and nonexistent thing as "society." He wouldn't stay in bed at home, but went out for beer and cards while his wife worked—and hated. The boys talked, and the hate grew. Somebody gave Merrill a copy of a Communist newspaper. Merrill devoured it, believed it. It was a conspiracy against him, on the part of sassiety, a conspiracy directed against all the drab and hopeless people in the world, especially Merrill.

"He got so he couldn't talk about nothin' else," said Mrs. Gandy, wiping her eyes with a trembling hand. "And it sure is true. And Merrill got to goin' to meetings and listening to people tellin' him how people like us ain't got a right to live, the rich guys say. And how someday there'll be a change, and the rich guys'll get what they got comin' and we'll have somethin' and Merrill will have a chanceta—"

The sergeant read on. He read the sordid story of ignorant and guided hatred. Merrill met "a man." Never did find out his name. Met him in a beer joint. But he was a good man. He gave Merrill twenty-five dollars, "just because Merrill's a little guy and a victim of sassiety," said Mrs. Gandy. Merrill kept going back to the veterans' hospital to see if they'd found anything, and the doctors begged him to stay. But he wouldn't. He'd read in the Communist paper that sometimes poor little guys like him was kept in them hospitals just for the doctors to try things on 'em. Like rats, was it? Or maybe the mice. Merrill wasn't going to do any such thing, no sir.

And then one day the kind man who was sorry for Merrill told Merrill about a minister, who was a tool of the big interests, a fascist, a rich man, in Barryfield.

Johnny, who had been listening mournfully, sat up, and his eyes flashed with an intense blue. Dr. McManus said, "Easy now; just sit and listen."

Well, the kind man told Merrill a lot about Johnny, "the fascist." He'd busted a union here in this town; he was down on the workers; he'd broken a strike. He was all for "sassiety." Big interests, big rich guys. Why, he'd given a sermon, and he'd cursed the poor little feller, and did all kinds of terrible things, keeping the workers down. It was all in the Barryfield newspapers. He ought to have a lesson. He was a real dangerous man.

As this part was read, Mrs. Gandy sat up in her chair and flashed Johnny a look of the purest hatred. "Sure I'm sorry about the little kid, but I sure wish you'd burned up!" she exclaimed. "That was the idea, anyway."

Sergeant Batson read on calmly. So the kind man had offered Merrill five hundred dollars "to do the job." To teach the minister a lesson. The rich minister, the tool of the interests. Two hundred fifty down, two hundred fifty after the job. And then the kind man would "force" the Veterans Administration to give Merrill compensation. There was ways.

No. Merrill never did rightly get the man's name. Never asked, maybe. Merrill sure hated the big guys now. And people like the minister, who help them, rich fascist ministers, who get paid off with big money. Shouldn't be allowed to live. No, Mrs. Gandy had known nothing of the plan. Merrill just told her, day before Christmas, that he had to go out of town, but would be back at night. He had bus tickets. Maybe a job, he said, coughin' his poor lungs out. So he went away.

And a couple of days later there was all that news in the paper. Mrs. Gandy did not connect this news with her husband, who was now "terrible sick," and couldn't get out of bed. He'd got a cold somewhere. No, he wouldn't have a doctor. All caught up on doctors, who ain't got no use for the little feller.

And then, yesterday, Merrill had told his wife that he was dying. He loved her. He did not want her to work in the bakery any more. He had no money. But there was that big reward in the newspapers. He had told her the story. She was to go to Barryfield, to the police, tell his story, and get the reward. That would "set her up." No use worrying about him any longer. He was dying. They couldn't do much to him.

The story continued. The whole idea, Merrill explained,

was to get the rich fascist minister out of town, by burning his house, and showing him little guys wouldn't stand for him. Merrill was a little surprised to see how small and mean the parsonage was, but then, people like "him" are misers, anyway. He got in through the cellar window, and waited for the family to go to bed. The minister came down in the cellar, and began to look around. He didn't look behind the furnace, though, in the dark. Merrill sure was scared. He'd put on coal to make the furnace real hot, and then when the minister went upstairs again he stuffed the wool waste in the pipes, right near the furnace, and they were soaked with gasoline. Merrill was scared; afraid he'd burn up too. Then he thought that it would take a little while, and he'd just go upstairs himself, and look for some of the money the minister had. He didn't find anything downstairs, and he couldn't go up to the bedrooms. So he left the house, and he went through back yards and got away.

That was all. The kind man met him a couple of days later and gave him the rest of his pay.

The chief said, "I called Wilkes-Barre, and they talked to Gandy, but he's incoherent. They took him to a hospital, and now he's in a coma. Frankly, I think he read about the whole thing in the newspapers. There must have been a leak. The poor devil had a lot of time to think. He cooked it all up, knowing he couldn't be tried, and that he was dying, and he wanted to leave his wife a lot of money—the reward."

"That's a lie!" shouted Mrs. Gandy. "Merrill ain't no liar!"

The doctor shook his head. "It could be true, of course."

He looked at Johnny. The minister said unsteadily, "I think it's true."

The chief sighed. "Sorry. I don't."

"Oh, you don't!" exclaimed Mrs. Gandy. "Well, sir, here's your proof." She opened her imitation leather purse, lifted something out, and banged it triumphantly on the desk.

It was Lorry's golden box, and it glimmered, and a sweet scent rose from it. They all looked at it, in a desperate silence. "That's all he could find in your house, parson," said Mrs. Gandy. "No money. Just this in your desk, and he took it."

Johnny reached for the box and held it tightly in his fingers. Now, for an instant he forgot what he had heard. He saw Lorry's face, and he smiled inwardly with an overpowering joy. Then he put the box down and looked at Mrs.

Gandy, who glared at him murderously. He studied her for a long moment or two.

He said finally, "Yes, this is my box, and it was taken from my house, and the story is true. But there is something you should know. Your husband had no service-connected injury. He is dying of cancer, and no one knows why or how it comes."

"I don't believe it," said Mrs. Gandy weakly.

"Yes, it is true," said Johnny. "And it isn't the fault of 'society.' No one has injured you, or your husband. The veterans' hospital wanted Merrill to stay. They had mercy on you and on him; they didn't tell you what they'd really found. But they were trying to help you some way."

He was torn with compassion for this weeping woman, and all the ignorant millions who had been deceived by the Communist murderers, and all their agony exploited.

He went on. "I'm a poor man. I have a very small salary. I'm not the 'tool of the interests.' I'm nobody's tool. I just try to serve God the best way I can. You see, I am trying to rid my town of hatred, to bring people together so they'll love each other, and God. For that I was to be destroyed. Your husband couldn't have known anything about me but what he was told, and what was given him to read in that Communist newspaper. He believed it, because he was suffering, and didn't know why."

She looked at the compassionate blue eyes, the pain-filled face, and was silent.

"Your husband was used, and others like him are being used, by the Communists. To enslave or kill all of us—you, me, the doctor here, and the chief of police. Everybody who stands in their wicked way. You see, we are 'society.' Yes, you are part of 'society.' Society means the people, and we are the people."

She stared at him, and blinked her wet eyes. He spoke with gentle authority and truth, and she believed him, though she tried to resist.

"We are the workers, all of us, whether rich or poor," said Johnny. "Anyone who works with his hands or his brain is a worker, whether or not he makes one thousand dollars a year or one hundred thousand dollars. The few who don't work don't count; they're so very few. Do you understand?"

She nodded, dazedly.

"Tell me," said Johnny, "was your husband—sorry—when he read that my little girl died because of the fire?"

She gulped, and wiped her eyes. "Well, I remember he was terrible excited, and he said it was awful, and he got worse right away, and went down and down. He couldn't stop talking about that little girl. We never had none of our own. He—well, he said—the man who'd done that should die, killing a baby. He couldn't seem to rest." She sobbed bitterly. "I think that's really killing him now."

Johnny stood up. He put his hand on her shoulder. He said gently, "Forgive me for hating him. For he was ignorant and deceived by evil men. Go to him right away. And if he can hear you, tell him it's all right, and that I've forgiven him too."

But they never found the shadowy Communist. Like his brothers, he moved in silent darkness, and watched and waited, and never slept.

31

It was not until the first of February that Johnny received a stunned and grieving letter from Dr. Stevens. "News from Barryfield does not seep down here to Florida," he said in his letter, "so, dear Johnny, I did not know anything about your great sorrow until our mutual friend, and would-be elderly Mephisto, Dr. McManus, condescended to let me know a few days ago. His explanation was that he wished you to become 'thoroughly stabilized' before informing me, the implication being that I would rush to your assistance and comfort, if I had known earlier. That is quite true. But I consider him very highhanded in this matter, for you are like a son to me. Please convey my rebuke to him. And now, write me at once and tell me everything." Johnny showed the letter to Dr. Mc-Manus, who said hardily, "My God, there were too many hot little hands dabbling in—everything—anyway. Why add another? As it is, I've had to get a dehumidifier for the house."

He was avidly curious to see Lorry's twice-weekly letters, but Johnny hardheartedly locked them away with a smug air. "Do you let me see what she writes you?" he asked. "Or are you interested in romance, at your age?"

March came in extremely mild, but not sweetly, for the smog was always present. Johnny took the children to the parsonage garden, and the trees. Because the earth was not too hard, Lon Harding had been able to plant two cherry trees for Debby. Debby was so pleased that she announced her engagement to him, to Kathy's severe reproach. Behind the sodden garden the parsonage was rising; bricklayers were working very fast, and so were the carpenters. In June the family would move in. But the children were less interested in the house than in the trees. Johnny showed them how the buds were swelling, some pink, some still brown. "You see," he said, "life never dies, for it comes from God." They looked in silence at Emilie's lilac bushes. The buds were larger here, the little branches tense. Johnny touched the shrubs with a tender hand, and Pietro, the dramatic, kissed them. No one ridiculed him; it seemed a lovely gesture.

Debby's kitten had become the family pet. And now two others were added, the brother of Coffee, also called Coffee, and a canary in a fine cage, both gifts of the doctor. "Place like a zoo," he grumbled, monopolizing the pets when he came home.

As he had never been happy before in all his life he did not recognize that he was happy now. He ascribed his anxiety to get home "early" each day as "my encroaching old age. Don't seem to have the interest I used to have in my work. Have to leave more and more of the load to the boys." He would scowl at Johnny. "I sure wish they'd hurry up with the parsonage so you and the kids and all those damned pets would be out of here, and a man could have some peace." Johnny, knowing, would pat his shoulder.

But when the doctor thought of the exodus he became heavy and weary and lonely, and he did not recognize that he dreaded the day when his house would be quiet again. He grumbled to Mrs. Burnsdale, complained that the builders were delaying too long. She smiled at him, watched his diet, and occasionally made a special dish for him to eat at night, before bedtime. "No calories to amount to anything," she would say.

One night Johnny said to the doctor casually, "This is a big house, and you don't need it, and it's outdated, and you could sell the whole thing at a profit. So why not sell it, and move in with us?" "Good God!" cried the doctor, with what he hoped was an expression of horror. "With all that menagerie? Do you think I'm out of my mind?" But Johnny saw him consulting the blueprints later, and later heard him talking to the architect, very casually, about "three or four good rooms on the third floor."

He became bad-tempered about the meeting Johnny had scheduled in the Town Hall. "Go, and have 'em mob you," he growled. "I won't be there. Hate the sight of blood." He arrived fifteen minutes after Johnny had arrived. He was amazed to see such a gigantic crowd, filling the halls, the sides, and every available spot. Policemen watched, intently. But the crowd was almost silent. On the platform sat the mayor, Johnny, Father Krupszyk and Rabbi Chortow, and "a select delegation of citizens." A miserable muddy light filtered through the tall old-fashioned windows, and outside a drizzle had begun to fall. The overhead lights had been turned on, adding to the air of intense gloom. In the first rows sat the local manufacturers and their attorneys and their industrial engineers, a solid phalanx of alert and quietly resistive men, each with a brief case. The mayor was wretched. His own political county chairman had told him that his future was finished if he did not accede to the demands of the people.

His friends had informed him that he was "done" if he did accede to the demands of the people. Money, they had told him cynically, was more important than mere votes, for, without money for the campaign next year he would lose his bid for the state Senate. Let his chairman endorse him; they, with their money, would put up a real "candidate of the people," and this candidate would win. Voters have short memories and quick passions. They would forget, next year, that he had been instrumental in stopping the smoke nuisance. Votes? Money bought votes, through propaganda.

They had overlooked one thing, however. The mayor was a Catholic, and there, at his right hand, sat Father John Kanty Krupszyk, whose eye was very stern. The mayor was a devout man, and of Polish descent. His wealthy backers had told him this would be a matter they would use against him for the first time.

Dr. McManus found a spot in the rear in which to stand, and looked at the platform. Johnny seemed abstracted; the mayor rubbed his big, workman's hands over and over; the priest was calm; the rabbi, who believed utterly in the intrinsic goodness of man, was even calmer. All of them were praying silently, even the mayor. The priest had told him earlier, when they were alone, and when the desperate mayor had wailed his fears, "You trust too much in vain, Walter, though I see you at Mass every Sunday, and you confess regularly—what confessions; you should be ashamed!—and you regularly appear for Holy Communion. What are you, a ritual, cradle Catholic? It looks like it. Why don't you, just for once, abandon everything to God, and do your duty to Him and His children?"

"Yeah," said the mayor somberly. "But what about the money for my campaign? I suppose, Father, you've got a lot of money hidden away somewhere, and so has that minister and that rabbi? Well, none of you look it. That old car you've got—"

"You can present me with a new one, next year, when you're state Senator," said the priest. The mayor had shaken his head, more sorrowfully and dejectedly than ever. "I think," said the priest, with a look of deep pleasure, "that I'd like a Buick. I'll wait until you're Governor for a Cadillac. And, by the way, there is the matter of the statues of the Holy Family. They're falling apart. A contribution campaign, through the Holy Name Society, begun very soon, would be very helpful. I'll remember you particularly," said the priest, "in my prayers."

"Aren't priests supposed to keep out of these matters?" the mayor had demanded. "Like the smog?"

The priest had answered virtuously, "Am I interfering in worldly matters? Walter, eight old people and three children of my parish died in that smog. It is a priest's duty to keep silent when his people are afflicted? Anyway, I'm not influencing you at all in your political affairs. Prove it."

The mayor was no man for a discussion of the niceties of dialectic. But as he prayed today he felt resentment about the Buick. And the campaign he had begun through the Holy Name Society for new statues. Then he said inwardly, "Holy Mother, if you'll just intercede for me, and not get my name made mud, and if you'll help me be state Senator, I'll get that priest his Buick and a fine new statue of you."

He was a big man, in his early forties, with a broad face, almost whitish hair, and pale-blue eyes. He smiled, and his smile was charming. The crowd, staring at him, smiled back with sudden warmth, and the warmth went all through him, giving him a sense of surety. Maybe "that priest" was right. Maybe the people wouldn't forget.

A school band struck up "The Star-Spangled Banner," and everyone rose in one rumbling mass, looking at the flag on the platform. Now everyone joined in fervently, and so did the mayor. What did the "big guys" say? Patriotism went as far as a man's purse, and no further. The mayor, all at once, did not believe it. He almost, in spite of his political knowledge, believed in the virtue of the people.

Everyone sat down, except the mayor. On the table before him were heaped the thousands of petitions. He put his calloused hand on them. He had never been able to rid himself of the calluses, after all these years, for they were now part of his flesh. All at once, he was proud of them, for the first time.

"My dear friends and fellow citizens," he said, in his strong, accented voice. "You've asked for this meeting today, and I am here to serve you." He kept his glance away from the first two rows, from which he felt strong animosity and cool disdain. "I'm a workingman myself, though you made me your mayor. I've still got the calluses on my hands," and he lifted them up and showed them. One of the men in the first row whispered something to his attorney, and they both smiled with derision.

"Well, anyway," said the mayor, with simplicity, for this time no one had prepared a ringing speech for him, and he was lost. "Here you are, and here I am too, and we're just people and we've got a—a grievance. A terrible grievance. I don't live up in the hills; I live right down here in the valley, and my wife's got asthma and the smog didn't help her at all. And it killed a lot of poor old folks and children, and maybe the next time it'll kill more. A real massacre. We don't want to wait for that."

There was mad applause, except for the front rows. Men shouted hoarsely; women cried out incoherently. The mayor listened, with swelling joy. He waited until the applause died away, and resumed bluntly. "Well, ladies and gentlemen, I've been told that if I stand with you, and enforce—things— about the smog, I'm finished, done, out. No more Walter Slavak for mayor. No more Walter Slavak running for the state Senate. Just back to the mills for Walter—if I can get a job. They tell me you're not very bright, you voters. They tell me they'll put up another man, and smear me so you won't vote for me. All right. I'm going to chance it. If you forget, maybe I'll be bitter, tossing away my future to help all of us. But maybe you won't forget."

He hoped for applause, but he had never expected the thunderous volume of it, the shouts of support, the screamed vows, the stamping of feet. The walls trembled; the lights trembled. The men in the front rows listened in consternation. "We won't forget!" shouted a man. Then, spontaneously, the crowd took up a chorus, "We want Walter! We want Walter!" The demonstration lasted for more than five minutes. The clergy on the platform glanced at each other and smiled.

The mayor held up his hand, bashfully. "All right, folks, I believe you. But let's get down to business. I hope," he said, blandly ignoring the first two rows, "that there's some people here who heard you just now. I sure hope so. I've tried to be a good mayor; sometimes it wasn't possible. I leave it to you people to guess why. Now, let's get down to business." His good-natured face became hard. "It won't take long. I've looked at all these petitions. Lots of you men say you won't go back to the mills and the factories if the smog doesn't go. I think you mean it. I'm sure you do. So," and now his eyes kindled with fire, "it's up to those responsible, who aren't here today, I see, to take on the responsibility of making our town safe for our mothers and fathers and babies. It's their responsibility. Maybe it'll cost a lot of money, a lot more than ninety-six funerals and ninety-six graves still raw down in the cemeteries. I've talked with representatives of your employers before I came here. They say it would take almost too much money, and at least six months, to eliminate the smog. Well, I always figured people's lives and happiness are more than money."

Again the hall erupted in a volcano of enthusiastic cries and shouts and applause. The mayor listened, not smiling now. He leaned his arms on the table, now letting the demonstration take its course. He waited for a long time.

"All right, folks," said the mayor eventually. "Just go home and do a lot of thinking."

He looked only at the men in the first two rows. "This is

all I've got to say now. I give the owners of the factories and the mills just six months to clear up this smog. If the smog isn't gone by then, I'll order the closing of any mill still polluting our air, and I don't care if they carry it to the Supreme Court! That smog's got to go—in six months. I've got the health authorities on my side."

Again the hall erupted. Men tried to push their way to the platform, holding out their hands. The police restrained them. The mayor held up his hand. He looked at Johnny and beckoned to him, and Johnny joined him.

"Here's a minister who lost a little girl," said the mayor. "And he's responsible for this drive against the smog. He's the one you should applaud, not me. Here's Mr. John Fletcher, minister of the Church of the Good Shepherd."

Now the police could not restrain the people. They surged in swirling masses toward the platform. Hundreds of hands were held up to Johnny, hundreds of smiling faces confronted him. He bent down and shook as many hands as possible, and he could not speak for emotion.

The *Press* did not mention the meeting at all, except for two lines on a back page in the morning newspaper, near the classified advertisements. But it did have a feature article about Johnny in the Saturday paper.

"A few months ago Mr. Fletcher was forced to appear before the Children's Court to answer to alleged accusations that the children were being neglected. The U.S. Immigration and Naturalization Service and the Children's Aid Society had become interested because of several complaints lodged with them. Mr. Fletcher was "cleared" of charges by Judge Foster Bridges.

"Mr. Fletcher arrived last August with the children, to take up pastoral duties at the church. Almost from the beginning he was the center of controversy and curious events, which included the assault of an unnamed juvenile on one of the children, an assault on himself by another unnamed juvenile, and the mobbing of himself and the parsonage by an indignant gathering of citizens who had been aroused by a certain sermon he had given during which he defended the rights of property and intimated that progressivism, materialism, and Communism were one and the same things. Apparently Mr. Fletcher believes that public housing and other social advances, and the campaign to spread the wealth of the country over all citizens, is Communism, instead of progressive democracy.

"It is believed that his parish upholds him in all his public controversies, with the assistance, it is alleged, of unknown persons. It is alleged that he induced the mayor of this city, Mr. Walter Slavak, who was elected on a progressive platform, to attack our institutions, and to attempt to inflict undue hardship on certain members of this community who employ large numbers of men, and who are known for their patriotic contributions to various national and local organizations."

Dr. McManus, beside himself, immediately sent a copy of this article to Lorry in New York, with no comment.

32

There is nothing so depressing as a last snowfall, Johnny thought one morning, seeing the gray March blizzard at his windows. One expects spring, the yellow explosion of forsythia, the deep blush of the crab apples, the red and golden cups of tulips, the frail and unearthly beauty of the narcissus. The unseen sap of the trees was running like eager blood to the last tip and pale bud, and the blood of men was quickening too, in anticipation. But men saw the snow, and their hopes diminished. Only the trees had faith in spring, which neither spectral cloud nor blizzard could cause to languish.

Johnny had taken the children out into Dr. McManus's wide grounds to show them the crocuses a few days ago, and the green little daggers of tulips thrusting themselves through the dark breast of the earth. "Soon," he said, "it will be spring, and the sun will be warm, and one morning you'll get up and see all these shrubs bursting in color against the blue sky." The silent hosanna of the earth to God, thought Johnny. He pointed out a few adventurous robins pecking in the gardens. It was as if these children had never known spring before, they were so excited at the prospect. Yet, in truth, they had never known a spring before. They waited for it, as men wait for a miracle. Then—today there was a blizzard.

"It will never be spring," said Pietro, the eternal skeptic. He spoke in the calm voice of authority.

Johnny was irritable this morning. He was afraid he was coming down with a cold, and as an exuberantly healthy man, he detested illness in himself. Besides, he had too much to do. Spring inevitably brought heart attacks and pneumonia to the old, and his calls were heavy. He said, looking at the children's gloomy faces and at Pietro's serene bland eye fixed on him, "You know better, Pietro. Of course there will be spring. Never mind pointing at the snow! I can see it too. What do you want me to do? Go out and ask God to stop it from falling?"

Pietro said, his eyes dancing now with mischief, "There was the saint who prayed to God for rain on the fields—there was no wheat—and God sent the rain."

Johnny almost shouted, "I'm not a saint, dammit! Never claimed to be one! Debby, stop fooling around with that syrup; pour it on your pancakes, but don't make designs on them with the syrup. No, not pretty at all. I used to lecture parents on getting impatient with kids, and clobbering them, God forgive me! Now I know what they were up against. Kathy, I'm not going to apologize for swearing; I wasn't really swearing, so stop looking cold and superior. Jean, you are positively not going to get more eggs; those on your plate are not too soft! Max, stop skimming off your hot cocoa; that skin is congealed cream and is good for you. Debby, you're spilling your milk!"

Dr. McManus, in hat and rough coat, came into the great, dusky dining room. "What's the uproar, now?" he asked. "Could hear you out in the hall."

Johnny said, "Sometimes these kids get in my hair. Look at Kathy now, moving off with dignity with an extra-heavy load of plates. That's to show me that she's offended. What a prig. No, go away," he said to Debby, who was now trying to climb onto his lap. "I think I'm getting a cold." He pushed her down, turned her about, lifted her bright curls, and kissed her on the nape of her neck. She giggled joyously, and ran after Kathy. "She's like a fresh breeze in this house," said

Dr. McManus. "A real hardy American brat, full of brass and fun."

Kathy returned and surveyed Dr. McManus critically. "You are not going out without your rubbers, Uncle Al," she said in a formidable voice.

"You're not my mother, fat-face!" he exclaimed. "And I'm not"—but Kathy, moving with determination, went into the hall closet, and returned with the rubbers and laid them at the doctor's feet. Grumbling, he got into them. "I see what you mean," he said to Johnny, and winked. "By the way, you don't have a cold. It's an allergy."

"Everything's an allergy," said Johnny. "What are you doctors trying to do? Get rid of the germ theory?"

Miss Coogan arrived, the children joined her in the library, and Johnny prepared to take Debby to kindergarten. She stood beside him, rosy and gay, like a small brown bear in her snowsuit. She had decided not to make a fuss this morning about the suit and the rubber boots. Femininely perceptive, she knew this might be dangerous. Dr. McManus pinched the firm pink cheek, and her blue eyes twinkled at him. "I think Uncle Al will take me to school," she said, and dropped Johnny's hand and snuggled against the doctor's coat. "There, you see," said Johnny, smiling; "she's punishing me for not appreciating her artistic efforts with the syrup."

"You just don't know anything about women," said the doctor. "Me, I'm an expert. I don't fall for their flattery." He took Debby's mittened hand and said, "All right, I'll take you to school. And don't you kids forget I'm taking all of you to the zoo this afternoon. Unless somebody decides to have an operation or something. Hell of a life, a doctor's life. Snatch an hour when you can."

He went off with Debby, muttering. Johnny went up to his large bedroom, which he also used for a study these days, stamped into the bathroom adjoining and grimly gargled. Then he sat at his desk, to prepare his Sunday sermon. The snow came down, and now a gale accompanied it, shouting at the windows. Johnny put down his pen and picked up the large, silver-framed photograph of Lorry which she had given him. He smiled at the slender, faintly smiling face, the gently cynical eyes, and then was filled with longing. If only he could spare a day or two to go to see her in Philadelphia; if only he could forget, as in a breathing space, for only a few hours, that he was a minister! He thought of Pietro's teasing about the saint, and smiled again. As this was supposed to be a special saint's day—which Johnny doubted very much—Pietro and Jean had not gone to catechism this morning. It was a holiday, Pietro had informed Johnny loftily. Johnny suspected it was the promised treat of the zoo. Jean had looked too solemn for verity.

At eleven a maid came in to inform him that "some lady, who is crying" was on the telephone, and wanted to talk to "the minister." Johnny picked up his extension, with a sigh. "Mr. Fletcher!" cried a young woman's voice hysterically, "we're in your parish, though we don't go to church much—Mr. Fletcher! My husband's going to kill himself! He's locked in his room. Please, Mr. Fletcher, come right away!"

Johnny knew too much about human nature to try falsely to soothe her. "I'll be there at once," he said quickly. "But don't tell him I'm coming; just talk to him through the door, as quietly as you can. Never mind about frightening the children; kids don't frighten easy. And you can't spare them from living, you know, Mrs. Thorne. Let them talk to their father through the door, too. Anything."

He ran out into the blizzard to the garage and started his old car. The smooth tires skidded and churned in the snow, then finally the roaring and spitting car was out in the street, and Johnny was off on one of those emergenices known only too well to doctors and priests.

He could not place the Thornes. They were probably young "floaters" who occasionally attended a church in their immediate neighborhood, dropped a few silver coins, even less occasionally, in the collection plate, and sent their children intermittently to Sunday school. That entitled them, in their opinion, to say "we're in your parish." Then Johnny was ashamed of himself; it was just that sore throat of his, he thought, in excuse. No, he added, it's just that I'm normally peevish this morning, and human, and I've forgotten that all men are in a Parish, and all priests are their shepherds.

The snow clung to his windshield, and the wipers groaned in protest. Fortunately, Boone Street was not too far away. It was a small, quiet little street, filled with crowded and quiet little houses, most of them single, clapboarded one-family homes, with short lawns and long rear yards. A respectable, lower-middle-class street, with white curtains at the windows and miniature verandas. He found number ninety-eight, stopped his car abruptly, and ran up the snow-covered steps of the house. He shook off his hat and brushed off his shoulders while waiting for the old-fashioned bellpull to be answered. The door opened on a gush of clean warmth, and there stood a weeping, neat young woman with smooth black hair, wearing a print dress and clean, fluted apron. She had a pretty, undistinguished face, now blotched with tears. Mutely she stood aside and let Johnny into the smallest, most crowded, but most cosy of parlors. Nice people, he commented automatically, nice, self-respecting young people. Hard-working people, too. Now, what would make a man of this kind want to kill himself?

He threw his coat and hat on a chair, but Mrs. Thorne, for all her tears and incoherent murmurings, picked them up, straightened them out, and hung them in a tiny closet. Johnny's good opinion of her increased. "Quick, tell me, Mrs. Thorne," he said, rubbing his cold hands together.

She pointed miserably to the ceiling. "Howard's up there, in our bedroom. With the Luger he brought home from the war. He locked the door after I got up and when I went up to call him to breakfast because he didn't come down, he said, real peaceful through the door, 'Trudie, don't be afraid. But I've got to die, and you'll have the insurance for yourself and the kids.'"

She put her young and work-worn hands over her face and sobbed desperately. The house was utterly silent. "We've got two children, Joe and Elsie," she stammered. "Joe's seven; Elsie's five. They're sitting on the floor near the door, upstairs, but Howard won't listen to them. But he won't shoot himself, either, long's they're there." She wiped her face as simply as a child with the palms of her hands, and looked at Johnny with her wet eyes. "Is that why you wanted them to talk to him?"

"Yes, of course," said Johnny gently. "He's a good father, and doesn't want to frighten them. Tell me about him. How old is he? What does he do? Why does he want to kill himself?"

Howard Thorne was thirty-four. He and his wife had been born in a very small country town in West Virginia; they had been "sweethearts" all their lives, and so they had married when Howard was twenty-three and Elsie was twenty. They had come to Barryfield shortly after that. They had no "folks" back in West Virginia, none that mattered, anyway.

Mrs. Thorne kept her trembling head cocked in terror toward the ceiling as she talked, sitting on the edge of a chair and wringing her hands. They were Methodists, she said, but they were broad-minded, and went to Mr. Fletcher's church. She appealed to Johnny for understanding of her broad-mindedness, with a pleading look in her really pretty black eyes. Johnny nodded without comment. "Well, anyway," said Mrs. Thorne, her voice shaking, "Howard always worked hard in that big service station out on Union Road, and we saved our money, because Howard wanted a service station of his own. He is real handy with tools; he can take apart a car and put it together again like nobody's business. Then Howard was drafted, and he and the government sent money, but I had to get a job part time in a store to make out. I didn't really have to work; we'd've got along, but I wanted to save Howard's money so he could get that service station when he got out of the Army."

A childish voice floated down the stairway. "Daddy, Daddy, we want to come in and talk to you. Daddy, this is Joe. Please, Daddy." A little girl's voice cried out once, piteously, and Mrs. Howard jumped to her feet.

"Leave the children alone with their father," said Johnny. He was sitting on the arm of an old but polished rocker. "Go on, Mrs. Thorne."

Howard Thorne had returned from the wars—the everlasting, accursed wars, thought Johnny with bitterness—eager, happy, ambitious, and without a scratch. He and his young wife had figured out it would take about four more years of careful saving, or maybe only three, to have that coveted service station. "We didn't want to be left broke," said Trudie Thorne, "so we wanted an edge, for a down payment on a house. Howard don't hold with government loans. He always said a man's got to stand on his own feet, or what'd become of the country? Anyway, Howard got his old job back in the big service station, with a big raise, Mr. Judd was so glad to have him back. And then Howard's legs got weak. He didn't pay too much attention. That was almost two years ago. But the legs got weaker, and he'd come

434

home, and he'd have to sit down right away, couldn't play with the kids like he used to do, and then he'd get real tired and go to bed early, not even staying up for the radio, even his favorite stories."

And then, four months ago, Howard's weak legs got very much worse, and he went to a doctor. It was multiple sclerosis, a particularly rapid and relentless kind. In the past two months he had not been able to take more than two or three steps at a time, and then only a few times a day. He had had to give up his job. He had had to give up his ambition for his own service station. The doctors had said that the disease was temporarily arrested, and that his arms were not affected, and might not be for years. But what could a man do without his legs, asked Mrs. Thorne, with a fresh burst of agonized tears. "Especially a big, upstanding man like Howard, who liked sports, and couldn't hardly stay still a minute, even after working hard all day."

So for two months Howard had sat in this little snug house, brooding desperately, sitting alone in silence for hours, not answering his wife or children, not laughing. "And he's got such a big fine voice," said his wife tearfully. "The best and nicest voice in the world. It's like he died, two months ago. It's like having a stranger in the house. And I do try, I do! I thought about my old job, they wanted me back full time, and I said to Howard I'd go back, and he could watch the kids from a chair, a wheel chair. That made it awful bad for Howard when I said that, but I was just trying to cheer him up and showing him it wasn't the end of the world, or something. But after I'd said that he wouldn't even take his medicine, and wouldn't let the doctor examine him or do anything for him. He was like he wanted to die."

Johnny nodded compassionately. Yes, Howard Thorne had wanted to die. He felt he was a burden, and for such a man the idea was intolerable.

"He just sits with the bankbook," said Mrs. Thorne, gulping painfully. "And then I go every week and draw some money out, and he looks at the balance again. Sure, it's going down, but it kind of hurts him terribly. Once in a while he'll say, 'Well, Trudie, there goes a little more of our service station. And one of these days, maybe in a couple of years, it'll all be gone. And what then? Welfare? Our kind of folks don't ask for that; we'd rather die!' " Mrs. Thorne lifted her head proudly. "And we sure would, and that's why I know how Howard feels."

There was five thousand dollars in GI insurance, Mrs. Thorne said, and Howard also had fifteen thousand dollars in other insurance. Today he'd told his wife that would help her, with their five thousand dollars savings, for a number of years, "until the kids can take care of themselves." Worst of all, sobbed Mrs. Thorne, he'd told his wife that she was still young, and still pretty, and she could marry again, "and have a real man. Mr. Fletcher, that's what he said. A real man! As if my Howard isn't! Why, I never looked at another man in my life, and I wouldn't look at another, that's for sure!"

Johnny stood up. He said gently, "The situation for Howard isn't as desperate as he thinks it is, Mrs. Thorne. In fact, no situation is quite as terrible as we all think. He's been hit pretty bad, I know. I'll go up and talk to him, and you come too."

The little hall upstairs was hardly more than a box with three doors leading off from it. But the floor, though bare, was brilliantly polished, even in this dim light. Crouched on it, in a miserable small heap, were two very blond children, their faces stained with tears. Their heads were pressed against one of the doors, and they were whimpering dolefully, face to face for the first time with absolute tragedy. They did not even look up at their mother and Johnny. As Johnny stood over them, aching, the boy lifted his fist and beat mournfully on the door, and cried, "Daddy, Daddy, come out!" The girl cried, rubbing her hands into her eyes.

A man answered in a muffled voice, "Go away, Joe, boy. Go away, Elsie, honey. Go away to your Ma. Don't cry, don't cry. Daddy can't stand it. He's got to do something for you, and you're stopping him."

"Howard, Howard, darling!" sobbed Mrs. Thorne, and leaned across her children and put her lips to the door. "Don't do this to us, sweetheart. Don't!"

Howard's voice came subdued, mourning: "Trudie, Trudie. I've got to. You'll have the money. If I don't, how're you and the kids going to live? I'm no good, God damn it; I'll never be any good from here on, don't you know that? Take the kids away. I've got to do a little praying, first."

Johnny spoke up, firmly, "Don't pray, Howard. It won't do you any good. God won't forgive you."

"It's the minister, Mr. Fletcher," Mrs. Thorne said with haste. "The minister, who's in the papers, Howard, you know, the one you like. I called him, honey."

There was a little silence, and then, heartbreakingly, Howard began to sob, the heavy, dry sobs of a man in total anguish. "You shouldn't've called him, Trudie. You shouldn't've troubled the Reverend. What can he do for any of us? A man's got to face God all by himself."

"That's right, Howard," said Johnny. "All by himself. But you're not facing God. You're not telling Him your troubles, and asking for His help. You're hating God, Howard. You're trying to revenge yourself on Him, because of your illness. You'll show God, won't you, that He can't do this to you?"

"That's a goddam lie!" Howard shouted, and there was a squeak of wheels, and Johnny knew that the poor young man had come closer to the door. "I just want to do something for Trudie and the kids! I can't do nothing for them no more! You ministers, why, you—!"

Johnny waited until the raucous panting close to the door stopped. Then he said, "All right, Howard. You want to make your family feel wretched and guilty all their lives, because of you. You aren't a brave man; you're a coward. You haven't any self-respect, because you think that a few thousand dollars are more valuable to your family than you are! How much? Twenty-five thousand dollars altogether! Why, in the old slave days a man could buy a couple of slaves for that! Is that all the pride you have in yourself? Howard Thorne, sold for twenty-five thousand dollars!"

"Minister or no minister, them's fighting words, mister!" Howard's voice rose to a yell. "If I had my legs I'd make you eat 'em, so help me God!" He beat frenziedly on the door with his fists, and they sounded like the roll of drums. The children raised their voices in a wail of fear.

Johnny smiled at the furious passion in that Southern voice, and he said cheerfully, "All right, let me in, and make me eat my words. You're not convincing me that you're worth even twenty-five thousand dollars. You convince me, and I'll"—he paused, for he had been about to relapse into lusty Army language. He coughed. Howard was listening, then he grunted. "It's a trick, a lousy trick," he said. "You probably got some cops with you."

"No cops," said Johnny. "But I warn you, I'm a big man and I can take on ten like you, Howard. Ten like you even with good legs."

He smiled again at the angry and contemptuous snort. Make a would-be suicide enraged, and half the work was done. Howard said, "I can lick you even now, with these damn legs of mine, and I can prove it!"

"What're you doing in a wheel chair?" asked Johnny.

Mrs. Thorne said eagerly, "Howard made it for himself, Mr. Fletcher! He sure did! When his legs got real bad. He can walk downstairs, but then he goes up and gets around in his chair. It's got rubber wheels."

"To match a rubber head," said Johnny. The children were staring up at him, their tears drying on their cheeks. This was a refreshing note to them, a normal, happy note, in the incomprehensible horror that had come upon them this morning. Joe actually giggled weakly, and his sister, not understanding, giggled with him. Johnny bent and tousled their heads, and they laughed with shy pleasure. "Nice kids," he said. "Bright kids, too. Wonder where they got their intelligence. From their mother, I guess. Nobody else."

"Leave my kids alone!" roared the poor young man behind the door.

"I'm just looking them over," said Johnny soothingly, and he winked at Mrs. Thorne. "Their mother won't be able to take care of them after you've shot your fool head off. She'll want to save the money for their education, so I'll arrange for them to go to an orphan asylum. We've got a fairly good one here."

"Daddy don't have a rubber head," said Joe, and laughed happily. "He's got red hair."

Mrs. Thorne was blinking, over and over, trying to comprehend. The minister should be talking about God and sin, and sympathizing with poor Howard instead of tormenting him. But there the Reverend stood, grinning down at the children, while Howard bellowed and cursed behind the door. It wasn't good for the kids to hear such language. "Howard," she pleaded, when her husband paused for breath—and effect—after a particularly lurid passage. "The kids never heard you talk like that before. Joe's listening, and

438

laughing fit to kill. Let the minister in to talk to you, please, Howard."

"Making fun of me, my own kids," Howard groaned.

"Well, you *are* funny," said Johnny. "By the way, you've made me homesick for the Army. Where'd you steal the Luger?"

"I paid ten dollars for it!" shouted Howard. "Listen to the ——!"

"You're wrong," said Johnny. "My parents were married. Were yours? Decent people don't go around scaring the wits out of their wives, trying to drum up sympathy. Well? Let me in, and I'll weep on your shoulder."

"I'll let you in!" said Howard between his teeth. "And I'll knock your head off! Trudie, get the kids away from the door; take 'em into their bedroom. I've got something to talk about with that fella out there!"

Trudie pulled the intensely interested children to their feet and hustled them off, looking backward at Johnny over her shoulder, her eyes wide and fearful in the dusky light of the hall. He nodded at her reassuringly. "All right, Howard. They've gone. By the way, are you going to shoot me when you open the door?"

A key grated in the lock, the door flew open, and there Howard sat in his wheel chair, panting, gritting his teeth, his big hands on his knees. One of the hands clenched the evil gun. Johnny could see his tousled mass of stiff rusty hair, the broad white face, the enraged hazel eyes, the short strong nose and the big snarling mouth. Howard Thorne was a massive young man, and the legs that hung from the chair looked quite adequate, which Johnny suspected they were. "Well!" cried Howard, swinging his chair away from the door, "come in, come in, damn you, parson!" He rapidly propelled the chair into the center of the room, breathing heavily, glaring with hatred at Johnny.

Johnny stood with his hands in his pockets. He looked about the shining little bedroom with pleasure. Something in a niche in a corner attracted his wandering eye, and he was surprised. Still looking at it, he said, "I've got to congratulate you and Trudie. Fine, upstanding people. We need a few more million like you. Wonderful kids. Too bad they had to be hurt this way. They'll remember it all their lives. Maybe Elsie might be unhappy, sometime, when she's older, and then she'll think she'll tell you, and then she'll remember this morning and know that you have no real help for her. And Joe. Big, handsome boy. He won't have a father to be proud of. Perhaps you should have blown your head off, after all. Of course that would give the kids a nervous shock they'd never get over. And they'd blame their mother, though she's blameless, of course. But people are that way."

Howard did not answer, though his hard breathing filled the room. Johnny sat down on the edge of the neat double bed with its homemade quilt. He smoothed the quilt admiringly. "My mother made one just like this for me," he said. "I had it for years. Then somebody stole it. I never forgot. Star pattern, like this. It was called, I believe, the Star of Bethlehem."

He looked at Howard serenely. "When you kill yourself, your children will remember this quilt forever. That's the way the human mind works. They'll think of its pattern, the Star of Bethlehem, every Christmas, as long as they live. You won't just be murdering yourself. You'll be smearing every Christmas of their lives with your blood. And you'll have murdered faith in their souls."

Howard had become quiet, and very still. He looked at the Luger in his hand, and his big chest, under the clean white shirt, heaved in a soundless sob of anguish. Then he flung the Luger from him, and it hit the rag rug on the floor. Both men looked at it in silence. After a long minute Howard raised his head, and said furiously, "I can still lick you, big as you are! I'm bigger."

The dull light from the small curtained window struck his reddish hair, and it was a halo of pathetic wrath. Johnny shook his head, smiling to hide the pity in his heart. "Maybe. Bet you can't throw horseshoes as far as I can, though. I was the champion back home."

He looked at Howard seriously. "Why the wheel chair? I know something about multiple sclerosis. It didn't make you a sudden cripple, in spite of two years of muscular weakness. Why, I know half a dozen people who've had it for years and they've had treatment, and it can be arrested, sometimes for a whole lifetime. But you have to make yourself a wheel chair immediately! Trying to torture Trudie, eh?"

"Shut up! That's a lie! I just wanted her to see what'd

happen to me later, so she wouldn't be crying for me long. The doc told me I'd probably be this way in maybe eight-ten-twelve years, that's all!"

He pushed himself out of the wheel chair and, with a slight swaying, stood up. He took several slow steps, and Johnny watched keenly. Yes, the legs were definitely weak, but inertia was weakening them beyond their time. "Look at 'em!" said Howard with loathing. "I can't stand on my feet for hours, as I should! How can I run my own station, or anybody else's? The doc said I couldn't."

He looked at the wheel chair and shivered, took a step toward it, glanced at Johnny, hesitated, then stood stiffly, his hands clenched defiantly at his sides. There were marks of suffering about his mouth, his eyes. Johnny nodded.

"I think I can agree with you that you can't stand all day, any longer. But I have a friend, the famous Dr. McManus. I'd like him to look you over, but I warn you his fee is large."

"Hell," said Howard, contemptuously. "I can pay. I got some money. Doc McManus, eh? Well, let him come."

"I'll call him in a little while. But let's talk about you. Want to sit down?"

"No!" shouted Howard, and began to walk up and down the room, at first with obvious difficulty and pain, and then with more strength.

Johnny crossed his long legs and said thoughtfully, "When a man wants to commit suicide it isn't because of the immediate cause, as he thinks. He feels his back is against a wall. But millions of people go through that every day, and they don't shoot their blamed heads off. They come out fighting, away from the wall. The man who kills himself, though, hasn't any fight; he can't face the thing he has to face. It's just another of a hundred things he's been up against, probably all his life. Not just that one thing. Howard, when did you first feel your back was against the wall? When you were a kid in your teens in the Army?"

Howard stopped his pacing, his head bent. Then he swung to Johnny rapidly, and his face was bitter and alive. "When I was fourteen years old! Look at that thing over there! I whittled it when I was a kid. I been whittling all my life. But my pa said I got to stop it and get to work, and so I did, and nobody's going to tell me I didn't make a good living for my

441

wife and kids. Maybe Pa had good sense, but I never did get around to forgiving him. Maybe he didn't know any better, and he was right all the time."

Johnny got up and went to the small wooden pedestal hanging in the corner. He lifted down the magnificent statue of dark wood and held it reverently in his hands. Howard watched him. He laughed shortly. "Trudie liked it. She got it from me on her birthday, when we was both kids. I keep wanting to throw it away, but Trudie kind of likes it, and so do the kids. Fool thing."

The statue, fourteen inches tall, was incredibly beautiful and awesome. It represented Christ as a young and virile man, in a simple robe so exquisitely carved that it seemed stirred and blown backward by an invisible and eternal wind. Strength and power were here, and exultation. This was no meek and gentle Christ, but a man of force whose hands had hurled suns and worlds and galaxies and universes, blazing with light, into a black and voiceless abyss where they would burn forever, conflagrations of life and glory. Here was the God who stepped from constellation to constellation, leaving His radiant trail behind Him in time and space.

The face was vital and strong, calm and smiling with deathless youth, lifted to listen to the music He had created everywhere. The small hands, powerfully carved, were half raised in a gesture of imminent creation. Here was the simple Man of Galilee, but here also was the triumphant and mighty God.

"You did this?" asked Johnny in a hushed voice, charged with amazement. "When you were a child?"

Howard swaggered a little. He came close to Johnny and looked over his shoulder at the statuette. "Fool thing," he said proudly. "I was real religious in those days. A fella back home offered me ten dollars for it when I was a kid, but I gave it to Trudie."

"You did this?" repeated Johnny. He had to sit down. He held the statuette and shook his head incredulously. Then he looked at Howard's hands for the first time, and saw the lean brownness of them, the sensitive length of the calloused fingers, the nervous tenseness of them. He sighed, and closed his eyes.

Still keeping his eyes closed, as if in protection against a light too intense to be borne, he began to speak softly.

"I am a minister, yet every hour of my life is a revelation to me. Of God and His strange and mysterious wonders, and commands. He gave you genius and the ability to create marvelous things. You were stopped, partly by your father, partly by yourself, because you have the spirit of an artist, and that isn't always strong enough to defy the world of men. For every artist who survives and lives and creates, fully ten thousand of him have gone down into the dust of obscurity, and have died like half-men, not having ever lived. Why? Because they lacked faith in themselves, and in God? Because they had feeble bodies, or because they were too sensitive? I don't know."

He opened his eyes now and looked suddenly at Howard, who was standing near him, listening painfully.

"I know a writer who is famous now," said Johnny. "But he never had a book published until he was forty. He was always a writer; life and petty things just got in his way, and it took him a long time to climb over them to freedom. That is what happened to you. But God didn't want to wait until you were middle-aged, and had completely forgotten. He didn't want you to work at small things any longer. So He took away the strength of your legs, and commanded you to use your hands again, to do the work He had ordained you to do."

"Now look," said Howard sheepishly. "You mean that thing there means anything? Hell, I showed it to a couple of ministers, right here in town, and they said it was—what did they call it?—blasphemy. One said it wasn't any good, anyway. Another said I should make another, kneeling and just praying. I told Trudie it wasn't any good, but she made me show it to them ministers, and did I laugh at her afterward!"

He reached out and took the statuette from Johnny and held it in his hands, and all at once the broad pale face changed, became tender and brooding and full of sorrow. "But I sure like it," he whispered. "That's what He still looks like to me."

"And to me," said Johnny.

Howard turned to him abruptly, and he was no longer a workman, but a spirit of eager life and hope. "You mean I could make a living, whittling things like this?" he asked, and his voice shook.

"You could not only make a fortune, but you could become famous, all over the world," said Johnny. "I am not lying to you. I know. I've never seen work like this, not even in the museums in Europe. If I didn't know what miracles God performs constantly, I could not believe you had done it." He laughed shakily. "You and your service station! You, and gasoline! In the Name of God!"

Howard looked at him mutely, his hazel eyes blazing with an almost uncontrollable excitement. Then he stammered, "You—you aren't kidding me—are you?"

Johnny put his hand on his shoulder. But he could only stand and shake his head, in wonder, in joy. At last he said, "I'd like to get down on my knees and pray. Howard, when Dr. McManus comes, I want you to show him this. How much cash have you? Five thousand dollars, eh? That'll last you long enough to get started. You've got to carve more statuettes, of anything you wish, religious, your children, your wife—anything. About half a dozen. And then you'll take them to New York. Dr. McManus will find an outlet for you; he knows everybody. You may need some lessons, a very few, for you're probably rusty. But not too many lessons, given by people with less genius!"

Howard ran, not walked, to his chest of drawers, and pulled open the top drawer. He snatched out a long box and tumbled the contents on the bed. They were a collection of half a dozen tiny statuettes, of children and birds and animals and angels, each wonderfully perfect and sternly delicate. Johnny examined them speechlessly.

"I never did give up whittling," said Howard. "Have to do something with my hands all the time. Kind of like being hungry, and you got to eat. Trudie wanted to put them on tables, but I keep hearing my pa say, 'Stop that damn foolishness and get to work like a man!' So, I was shamed."

Johnny was examining a five-inch statuette of a mournful child, ragged and despondent. It breathed desertion and misery. Yet the half-turned head had a look of listening, of fragile hope. "You like that?" asked Howard. "I saw a kid like that in Europe. A refugee kid. Say, do you want it? You can have it, if you do." His voice was assured, modestly proud, the voice of a creator.

"Thank you," said Johnny. He touched the tiny face, and thought of Emilie.

Howard took the statuette from him in gentle fingers, as if

444

it were alive, and lovingly wrapped it in a piece of tissue paper. He put it in Johnny's palm. He said, looking into the minister's eyes, "You've made me live again. Why, hell, I feel life coming back all over me! Like I've been born again!"

"And so you have," said Johnny.

But Howard was shouting at the top of his lungs. "Trudie! Joey! Elsie! Come on in here and listen to the Reverend! Come on in! And hey, Trudie, better start frying that chicken. He's staying for dinner!"

33

At two o'clock, in that house of rejoicing and laughter and young faces and gratitude, Johnny called home. Yes, Mrs. Burnsdale said, there were three sick calls for him, one at the hospital. The doctor had just taken the four older children to the zoo, but Debby had been sent home from kindergarten. She had a slight fever, the school nurse had said. "Measles coming on, maybe," added Mrs. Burnsdale with nonchalance. "Measles!" cried Johnny, dismayed. "And all those other kids!"

He added gloomily, "I'll probably get them too. Never had them."

Half an hour later a maid came into the kitchen where Mrs. Burnsdale was happily making the doctor's favorite dessert for dinner. "Miss Summerfield's here," said the girl. Mrs. Burnsdale ran out of the kitchen, followed by Debby, who resolutely refused to go to bed and preferred the excitement attendant on the preparing of meals in a fragrant and steaming warmth. Lorry was already taking off her gloves and hat and coat when Mrs. Burnsdale reached her and took her cold hands, and beamed at her with delight. "I decided to come home for the week end instead of going to New York," she said, and bent to kiss Mrs. Burnsdale on the cheek. "Well, well," she added, putting her hands on her knees and bending down. "So, this is Debby. What a pretty—"

"You're Aunt Lorry," said Debby. She skipped gayly, and flung her arms about Lorry's neck. "I saw your picture," the child said, after a hearty kiss, nestling close to the girl. "Papa's got it. I can be flower girl, Papa said."

Lorry picked up the child in her arms and hugged her. Mrs. Burnsdale's welcoming smile became somewhat fixed. She saw that Lorry looked too worn, too thin, and her mouth was very pale. "Debby's too heavy for you, Miss Lorry," she said. "A great big girl acting like a baby!"

But Lorry clung to the child hungrily. Debby leaned back in her arms and said importantly, "I'm getting the measles."

"Oh, for heaven's sake," said Lorry, and put her down with haste. "And I'm with kids three days a week, or more." She stroked the gleaming auburn curls, sighed, and smiled. There was something troubling her, thought Mrs. Burnsdale, who suggested hot tea and sandwiches, which Lorry gratefully accepted in front of the great living-room fire. Debby sat near her, bouncing with pleasure. "We're going to have a new home," she informed Lorry. "And a big room for Kathy and me." She bounced again, her brilliant blue eyes lit with anticipation.

Lorry looked about this old, ugly room, and at the fire, and sighed again. She and Debby were alone. She listened to the child's prattle with a kind of contentment. It was wonderful to be with a little girl who bore no spiritual or physical wounds. An American child, who had known nothing but love! How marvelous, how satisfying, how hopeful. "Never mind the measles, if you're really getting them," said Lorry, holding out her arms. "Come sit on my lap and tell me all about yourself." It was blessed that the other children could have this child for a sister, so vibrant, so healthy and so fresh.

Debby happily accepted the invitation. Her sweet infant voice went on and on, and Lorry nodded her head soberly at intervals, merely listening to that voice and drawing courage from it. She thought of the other children of this house, and her courage became steadier. If they could be saved, only by love, then the others could be saved too. In fact, she added to herself, look what it did for me. And think what it could do for the whole wretched world.

Then she noticed that Debby was no longer chattering. The child's face was still and withdrawn, and she was looking at the fire. "What is it, dear?" asked Lorry.

Debby leaned against her breast. "Papa told me about my own Daddy and Mama with the angels," she said in a small, lost voice. "I wish they could live with us in our new house."

Lorry stroked her curls tenderly. "You don't see them, darling, but they see you and love you. Always. Besides, what would Papa do without you now? God sent you to him. Didn't you know?"

Debby's rosy face changed, and she looked at Lorry, enchanted. "He did? Was it because He took Emilie? Kathy told me about Emilie. Was she nicer than me?"

Lorry rested her cheek on the warm round head. "Every child is nice," she said. And her weary eyes stared at the fire, seeing the frightened and lonely and injured children whom she classified, consoled, and comforted these sad and bitter days. What if there was ever another war, with more shattered cities, more horrors, more death, more broken children, more wasted homes? Never, never must it happen again, God, she prayed, and she was full of fear. There were too many men like her father in the world now, the hating men, the men who wanted vengeance—for nothing. Or, worse still, men who wanted profits. She squeezed her eyelids together, thinking of her father, not detesting him as she had once detested him, but fearing him.

Debby was drowsing in her arms and Lorry leaned her head back against the deep wing chair, and suddenly she was asleep, sprawled in an attitude of complete exhaustion. When she awoke it was dark, and Johnny was standing beside her, his hand against her cheek, and Debby was gone. Wordlessly he bent and kissed her lips, then sat on the arm of the chair, holding her head to his chest. A sensation of rest and bliss came to her, and a desire to weep, not from pain but from peace.

The fire chattered softly on the hearth, and rosy shadows curtsied and swayed on the dusky walls. Then Lorry began to speak.

"Johnny, I've come here because I'm so tired, and I need you. And to give you a chance to see things—right. Johnny, I don't think I'll be good for you. In fact, I'll be very bad for you. I've been doing a lot of thinking."

"And all foolish," he said. "What do you mean, bad?"

"Can you see me as a minister's wife? Honestly, Johnny? Lorry Summerfield, president of the Ladies' Aid! It's—incongruous. For you. This town, and everything. I'm not the type, Johnny, and you know it."

He came around before her, sat on his heels, and held her hands.

"Don't you want to marry me, Lorry?" he asked.

She looked down into the deep and shining blue of his eyes, and began to cry, the tears sliding down her haggard cheeks. "Oh, Johnny," she murmured, and leaned her head against his. "But my father, Johnny. He never lets you alone. Never. Uncle Al sends me all his squibs and jeers about you, until I feel like coming home and killing him." She tried to laugh, and only sobbed. "Think of marrying a woman who has murder in her heart! Because of you."

"I don't mind what your father writes about me, darling," said Johnny. "What does it matter? Let him imply what he wants to, whenever he wants to. Nobody believes it, anyway. Why, he now lets Father John Kanty alone, since he has me. Some men seem to need someone to hate, and I'm the joker just now. Tomorrow it'll be someone else, probably."

"That's what I'm afraid of," said Lorry. Johnny smiled up at her in surprise. "Never mind," she went on. "Let's get back to us. Johnny, do you need me, just as I am, unsuitable for you as I am? Johnny, I'll never be able to be a sweet-faced minister's wife, full of tact when fools speak, smoothing things over in the parish hall, arranging children's parties and luncheons for missionaries. Can you see me doing that, in all honesty?"

"No," said Johnny. He stood up, his hands clasped behind his back. "You have special talents. You can't confine them in a narrow range. That is why, even when we are married, you'll have to keep up your work with the Quakers. There are all those children, and, I am afraid, there will be others, now peaceful in their homes somewhere in the world—and tomorrow lost and orphaned. I feel it with every instinct I have. *I've* been thinking too."

She rose and stood beside him, and put her hand through his arm. "Johnny, I knew you'd understand. I ought to have known," she said, remorsefully. "I ought to have known what you are." She dropped her head to his shoulder, and they

449

clung together in the warm darkness of the room. Now she was completely at peace, though with knowledge that the years ahead would be hard and interrupted. There was so much to do. But she and Johnny would do it together.

They could hear the voices of the children in the upper rooms of the house, laughing, quarreling, teasing children. And Dr. McManus's growls. Lorry smiled. "I feel I've come home," she said.

Mrs. Burnsdale had put Debby to bed, in spite of protests and tears. Then when Debby saw the awed curiosity of the other children she acquired importance again. She was definitely developing a rash. Kathy, Jean, Max, and Pietro were banished to the threshold, peering over each other's shoulders and jostling each other for long examination of this distinguished child. Dr. McManus was sitting on the edge of Debby's bed, holding her hand. "Yes," he said, testily, "you can have strawberry ice cream at every damn meal, and between times, if that's what you want. But one bounce out of bed and you go on toast and milk. Hear me?"

Debby nodded so vigorously that her curls flew. The others gazed at her enviously, and she saw it. "Not everybody can have the measles," said the doctor, with gloom. "I hope." He glared at the other children, and said, "Scat! All of you. And stay away from Debby. She's my special child just now, see?"

He piled Debby's favorite toys on the bed, patted her hot cheek, and went downstairs. The living room was still redly lit by the fire. He could see Johnny and Lorry standing together, not speaking. He was pleased. He found Mrs. Burnsdale with the cook in the kitchen, and beckoned to her. She followed him into the dining room, which was already beaming with candlelight, the best silver and dishes, in honor of the visitor. "Well?" she demanded. "If you want a decent soufflé you'd better speak fast, for it's very ticklish."

He studied her in silence. Her plump figure was modishly encased in black silk, and a lace collar circled her flushed throat. Then the doctor said, "You know, madam, you get handsomer all the time, damned if you don't. It's the climate. Or, perhaps, could it be me by any chance?"

She laughed and blushed. "Now, doctor."

He jerked his thumb over his shoulder in the direction of the living room. "All this infernal love," he grumbled. "It's giving me a second childhood. Senility, that's what. By the way, when do we get married?"

Now she was serious, and her gray eyes misted. "Why, any time—Al," she murmured. "After the minister and Miss Lorry. Did you think I'd leave you?"

He held out his clever hand to her and she took it. He hesitated, then he pulled her to him roughly and gave her a hard kiss, and then another.

"I've got another reason, among many, why I want to marry you," he said, pushing her away from him. "We'll all be together in the parsonage, and we'll have to console Johnny a lot. Lorry won't give up her work; she's been writing me to prepare Johnny for what she called her 'decision.' I didn't. That's her business, and his. And I think they've solved it. What did she think Johnny was, anyway? Besides, you're going to be president of the Ladies' Aid soon; I've heard hints. What would Lorry do to fill up her time?

"And another thing," he said irately, "I'm tired of those lists. Consider yourself engaged to me, madam, and stop the lists, and buy what you need for the accursed new parsonage. Just charge it. I'm tired of having them tucked under my bedroom door at night, like billet-doux. It ain't moral. At my age!"

The children had their dinner in the breakfast room that night. Lorry, at the darkly gleaming dining-room table, sat in the old doctor's chair at the head. Her shining hair, her sparkling green-blue eyes, her long white neck and white hands, were the loveliest picture in the world to Dr. Mc-Manus, Johnny, and Mrs. Burnsdale. Her voice had lost its old harshness; when she laughed now, it was the laugh of a girl.

Johnny brought out the statuette he had acquired that day. "A friend of mine carves these things," he said, with studied carelessness. "What do you think of it, Lorry? Just a child, carved out of a fragment of mahogany, I think."

Lorry took it in her hands and examined it, then raised her eyes slowly to Johnny's. "Why, it's miraculous," she said. Her eyes moistened. "I see them every day, these children," she murmured. "Every day. What is the name of the genius who caught the very expression of a lost child, and all its misery and pain?"

The doctor peered to see. "Well," he said, "I'll be damned. I know about such things. Swipe it, parson, out of some rich man's home when he wasn't looking?"

Then Johnny told them of Howard Thorne, and they listened in wonder and incredulity. "I can't believe it!" exclaimed Lorry, holding the statuette in her hands and marveling. She stood the little object on the table and as the candlelight lit it, it caught life and full expression, and seemed to move. "A man like that!"

"Yes," said Johnny, "a man like that. And who knows what our neighbor is, after all? A saint, an angel unawares, a genius, an artist, a devil, a dreamer of great dreams, or an abscess in the form of a man? Who knows? We never really see each other, and that is at once the mystery and the terror of living."

Lorry listened, and then studied the statue again, awed. After a moment she said, "Johnny, may I take this to New York with me? I know just the right people who would be more than interested. How many does he have on hand now?"

"A few. But he won't give up the Christ. However, you must come with me and see it."

"A man like that," said the doctor, "needs all the backing he can get to start with. And I'm just the sentimental, stupid, profligate, money-tossing old bas—I mean fool, to do it!" He touched the statuette with a very gentle finger. He thought of Jean, he thought of all the other children. This was the essence of them. He added, "And he'd better come down to my clinic for a complete examination. There's things we can do about all this, not too much, but we've got some clues. And maybe if we can jolt the citizenry a little more we'll get enough money to lick this thing. Maybe. I've been doing some work on it myself."

Lorry got up and went to him and kissed him, and he blinked and put his arm tightly around her waist. "The way you all work me," he said angrily. "One of these days I'll be bankrupt."

"Too bad about you," said Mrs. Burnsdale with a fond smile. He turned his fierce eyes upon her and shook a finger almost in her face. "That's no way for my fiancée to talk!" he admonished her. "A nice beginning you're making."

"What?" cried Lorry with delight, glancing for more

delight at Johnny. But he was leaning back in his chair, ostentatiously bored.

"It's no secret," he said. "I guessed it months ago. I'm surprised at you, Lorry. Doctor and Mrs. Burnsdale have been kissing behind doors for weeks."

"That's a damned lie!" shouted the doctor. "I resent the implication. Look at that woman's blushing face and you'll know you're fabricating. I sprung it on her tonight."

Mrs. Burnsdale said, as she critically examined the dessert, "And that's a fib too. He's been running after me ever since I came here. I had to give up, finally."

It seemed to Lorry that this was the very happiest time of her life, this weekend. There was nothing to mar it, no anxious undertone anywhere, in spite of Debby's measles, in spite of the other children importantly showing signs of the same disease. The blizzard might continue, intermittently, mingling with the lessened smog, and the last ferocious gale of the winter shake the very walls of the old house. Inside there was only peace, only contentment, and all warmth and laughter and love.

She slipped into a side pew, inconspicuously, to hear Johnny's sermon on Sunday. Today she would tell him of Barry. And then she would call Barry and ask him to come. She smiled up at Johnny, and listened to his sincere and sonorous voice.

Perhaps the statue of the child had stirred him too deeply. Perhaps some awful foreboding had fastened on his heart. He spoke of the Soldiers of the Lord, "who must be forever militant against evil, and evil men, who are, even now, plotting the death of all our hopes, the shattering of our cities, the dying cries of our children, the ruin of our capitals, the murder of our youth. They are plotting a desolate wasteland of the earth, soundless to the desolate seas. We dare not be too complacent. The men of good will are delinquent. The men of evil are full of passionate intensity. The very air clamors with the conversation of devils."

His sermon was reported in the *Press*, on Monday. Lorry, helping with the children, who were now definitely in the full flush of measles, did not read the paper until the afternoon. There was her father's editorial, and never had such a denunciation been so malignant, so distorted, so full of hatred and contempt.

"For a man who speaks so constantly of peace," Mr. Summerfield had written, "it is strange that he has now become a warmonger, a rouser of ignorant and inflamed emotions. What would he have us do? Drop the atomic bomb indiscriminately on any nation that might even be suspected, though without definite reason, of 'plots' against this country? These are the days when men must use reason, and be calm and judicious and tolerant. Yet this minister would lead a mob against anyone, anywhere. This paper has long been suspicious of his real motives. It is time for him to go."

Lorry slipped from the house, and her face was harsh and white.

34

"Why, no, Mr. Fletcher, I didn't see Miss Lorry go out," said Mrs. Burnsdale anxiously. "Is her car gone? I thought I heard a car drive out of the garage about forty-five minutes ago. Maybe she's gone to visit friends, or somebody."

"She hasn't any close friends in Barryfield," said Johnny, disappointed. He had just returned from some sick calls. He felt somewhat hurt; tomorrow, Lorry would be leaving. He glanced in at the children at their studies; their heads were bent studiously over their books, so he merely smiled and nodded at Miss Coogan. The house was warm and dim in the winter afternoon, and very quiet. This was the hour when the servants were resting in their rooms on the third floor. He decided that he might as well work on next week's sermon and do something on his Easter sermon. The latter was giving him some trouble. He reflected that probably everything had been said about the Resurrection. Besides, the Bible said it much better. How could one dare compete with such grandeur?

He went upstairs to his big bedroom and looked with distaste at his neat desk. He glanced surreptitiously at the bed, then sternly walked to the desk and sat down. Happiness, he thought, was almost as exhausting as unhappiness; a man needed solitude to digest joy just as he needed it to restore himself in grief. He looked at the heading of his sermon: "Be still, and know that I am God." He mused on that, staring, unseeingly, through one of the big windows. "Be still." But no one seemed to be still, these days. "Be still!" reminded him of the large, full motion of an evening sea, its tide unhurried, its ancient way undisturbed, unchangeable even in storm, even under the moon. It spoke of eternal verities, of eternal movement yet eternal rest. "Be still." Where could stillness be found in these days of fragmentation, of tiny little frantic pieces which could never seem to fit in a pattern that was meaningful? The more activities, he thought, the less accomplished, the less serenity, the less significance. Movement in itself, frenzied movement, louder and faster voices, more clicking heels moving rapidly but without a real purpose or real goal, more clatter, more pounding, more, more, more, always more, always "new"—these had become the frenetic cacophony of the feverish way of modern mankind. Where, in this mechanical confusion, could man be still, and "know that I am God"?

Even when men were alone at night with themselves, escaped from the endless exhortation to "do something," they could not rest. Nameless anxiety filled them; they wondered, with a book idle on their knees, or in their beds, if they had left something important undone that day.

And they certainly had left something undone: prayer, communication with God. The bright shadow of His wing hovered on their uneasy spiritual horizon, but they did not see it.

Or perhaps they did see it, and were afraid. To contemplate God would negate that howling insistence from press and pulpit and books and magazines and radios to be up and doing, no matter how useless. Just to be doing. "Keep busy!" exclaimed the psychiatrists, looking disapprovingly and with suspicion on the reflective man, who sat alone in blessed silence, and thought. More, more, more. No longer were men's consciences perturbed about evildoing or neglect of God. Conscience, too, had been perverted. Now it demanded how many "contacts" a man had had that day, how much money he had been able to make, how "adjusted" he had been, how "social-minded," how "warm in human relationships." To be deliberately idle, to be deliberately alone and contemplative, was to be considered antisocial, a mark of emotional disturbance. Johnny said aloud, "Yes, the world is definitely going mad. The 'new values' are the new dementia." Was there a sinister pattern in this, too, so to fill a man's life with enormous trivialities and stupidities that in the house of his mind there was no room for God?

He was writing rapidly now. The afternoon began to darken. He did not hear the children, released, chattering in the living room below. He did not hear a bell ring. A maid knocked softly on the door, opened it, and told him that Mr. Barry Lowell, Miss Summerfield's brother, had unexpectedly arrived for a few days. Dr. McManus and Miss Summerfield were not at home. Would Mr. Fletcher see him?

"Why, of course!" said Johnny with excitement. So Barry was here as a surprise for his sister! He put on his coat, smoothed his hands over his hair, and ran eagerly downstairs. Barry was in the library, standing near his suitcase. He was smoking rapidly and glancing over the bookshelves. He turned as Johnny entered.

Johnny was smiling, his hand outstretched. He began, "I'm John Fletcher." Then he stopped. He was astounded at Barry's resemblance to his half-sister, for all the young man's greater height and broad shoulders. The same oddly colored eyes, the same shape of face, the same pale gilt hair, the same nose! It was remarkable. And then Johnny's mind shifted, and his expression became bewildered. Somewhere, at some time, he had seen this man before. Something prodded insistently at his memory, something that frequently prodded him, without a name or a clue, when he looked at Lorry in a certain light. He said uncertainly, "Haven't I met you before, Mr. Lowell?" He came farther into the room, puzzled.

Barry stood as still as a tree, looking at Johnny, the cigarette smoking unheeded in the corner of his mouth. The wan winter light outside made him appear extremely pale. His eyes fixed themselves with a strange intensity on Johnny. He put up his hand and removed his cigarette, put it back. He took a step toward Johnny, and Johnny could feel the fierce concentration of his look. "Johnny, Johnny Fletcher?" said Barry huskily.

"Why, yes. Didn't Lorry tell you about me?" asked Johnny, mystified.

"Lorry," said Barry. "She knew all the time! Lorry! What did you say? Yes, she said she was going to marry a minister, but she didn't give me your name. Why?" His voice broke. "Why didn't anyone tell me, old Al, Lorry—?"

"I don't know," said Johnny. He felt even more puzzled. "Anyway, it isn't important. Lorry told me about you, about your changing your name. But still, I know I've met you somewhere before. Haven't I?"

With extreme slowness and care Barry snuffed out his cigarette in an ash tray. Then he merely stood and looked at it, his head bent. Johnny studied him. He asked Barry's own question of himself: Why hadn't Lorry told her brother his name? She had let him believe that Barry had been told. Johnny's face flushed with mortification. He said, "Perhaps Lorry had her own reasons. Names don't matter much anyway, do they? I do remember that at one time she asked me if your name meant anything to me and I said I didn't recall it."

Barry still looked down at the ash tray. He said very quietly, "No, why should you? I was probably just one of dozens, to you. It was an everyday thing—for you, then. But not to me." He lifted his head swiftly, and turned to Johnny. "But I looked for you for years; it meant everything in the world! They told me you had been killed."

Johnny, more bewildered than ever, thought confusedly to himself, It's only my imagination. Why should he have tears in his eyes?

"I was killed?" he asked. He tried to laugh a little. "No, I was wounded very badly in the Battle of the Bulge, but I'm a husky customer, and I recovered. I was in an out-of-the-way makeshift hospital for a while. Is that where we met?" "No," said Barry. He stood and looked at Johnny, as one looks at a miracle, stupified.

In a few moments Johnny became increasingly uneasy at that intense regard, that pale face turned to him in a silent and inexplicable passion of remembrance. "I'm afraid my memory isn't as good as I thought it was," he said apologetically. "But I do seem to find you familiar, in a way. Perhaps it's your resemblance to Lorry." Somehow, he felt that Barry had put Lorry on an unpardonable plane, that Barry was actually hating his sister for an incomprehensible reason.

Then Barry came to him and put his hands hard on his

shoulders and looked into his eyes, and smiled. "Johnny, Johnny Fletcher!" he said, and his voice shook. "Old Parson Johnny! Old Holy Joe! Why should you remember me? You only saved my life, you only dragged me out of a hole on the Normandy beachhead, and carried me on your back under fire! You only stuck by my bed when I was dying, and you only prayed me alive! That's all, Johnny Fletcher!"

"No!" cried Johnny incredulously. He grasped Barry by the arms. "No!" he repeated, with an almost wild delight. "Why, sure, I remember now! I'd have remembered at once if you'd have been wearing a uniform. Barry! I can't believe it. It's impossible."

"You're alive!" shouted Barry. "God damn it, you're alive! After all these years, you're alive! Let me look at you. Same old Johnny! I'll murder Lorry, I'll kill old Al for not telling me! I looked all over Europe for you. They said you were dead." His voice broke again, and now there was no mistaking the tears in his eyes.

Johnny was both embarrassed and touched by the young man's emotion, which appeared to him to be getting somewhat out of control. "Well," he said, "I'm definitely alive. So you are Lorry's brother! She'll be back soon; she'll explain why she kept my name from you."

"Any explanation she has will be idiotic. How could Lorry do this to me? She knew I looked for you; she knew how wretched I was when I couldn't find you. She knew how I felt when I heard you were dead. Yet she could do this to me." Johnny flushed again with mortification, and Barry, always perceptive, understood. His hands pressed harder on Johnny's shoulders. "It's nothing against you, Johnny. It's some kind of coy trick she's been playing on me, though it isn't like her to be coy. Maybe she does have a reason, and I'm going to know it!"

"Let's sit down," suggested Johnny. "I see you still limp a little; that leg. I remember it. They wanted to amputate it, and you raved that they might as well amputate your head." He tried to smile, though his face had become dark with humiliation. "I remember that I stood with you, and they did save your leg. Does it bother you much—Barry?"

"The hell with the leg," said Barry impatiently. He sat near Johnny. Then he took out his wallet and carefully removed an old snapshot perpetually sealed between two layers of plastic. "Look at this," he said. "Remember old Nie Nichols and his little camera? He took this of several of us in Exeter, before D Day. There you are," and Barry smiled through his emotion, "looking more of a GI bum than any of us!"

Johnny looked at the snapshot, tried to smile again, and then was grave. Eight young American soldiers stood there with their chaplain. Only he and Barry had survived Normandy beach. Nie Nichols, from Tennessee, with his four little children. And his bag bulky with the photographs he had taken of them—towheaded youngsters whose wide grins split their thin faces. And that young Negro with the majestic face cast in bronze who had assisted Johnny at services; he had been in his second year at medical school, and he had also been a poet. "I could have begged out of the draft," he had told Johnny, "but I've studied enough, on my own, to know that we've come into the age of tyrants again. Hitler may be the first, but he isn't the last!"

"Surely not," Johnny had protested, for Charles Hartwick had been too somber. "Surely this will be the last war, the war for freedom." The young Negro had laughed bitterly. "But all the wars men have ever fought have been for 'freedom,'" he had said. "And they were only wars for a change of tyrannies. I hate war; I hate the people who make wars; I hate this war too. Wars are liars. You know why I enlisted? To help get rid of this tyrant. Tomorrow we'll fight to get rid of another, and then another, and then another. Oh, like you, parson, I felt in the beginning that Hitler would be the last of the tyrants, but now I know better. It's just the beginning, the beginning of all the reactionary tyrants. Have you taken a long look, lately, at Stalin, the greatest reactionary despot of them all? Take a look, sir, take a look."

Johnny, then, had indeed "taken a look." And had begun to see many other things he had never suspected before.

He said now, "When Charlie Hartwick died we lost a fighter for freedom. All the rest of us were merely patriots, and that's not enough. Not any longer. It's not enough for us to march in our Legion parades and show the flag and repeat the Oath of Allegiance. That's only national. The fight is now intimately in our schools, our churches, in our homes, in our arguments with others. Men's spirits are now engaged, not only their bodies and their arms." He smiled tenderly at the snapshot, sighed, gave it back to Barry.

"Lorry has given me several of the books you've been publishing. Brave men who write them. Courageous men. Isn't it a frightful commentary on our times that when men write and speak the truth they are persecuted in the press, and even by politicians? It used to be taken for granted that men had the freedom of the press and that it wasn't particularly courageous of them to tackle liars. It was only their duty as Americans."

Abstractedly, he accepted one of Barry's cigarettes. He was thinking of his young friends who had died, and he shook his head in grief.

"You're doing what you can," said Barry. "Lorry quoted some of your sermons, and," he paused, "my father's reactions to them. But she never gave me your name. I asked a few times, and she managed to change the subject. I'm not going to forgive Lorry."

"Did she tell you about my children?" asked Johnny hastily, for he did not like the look on the young man's face.

"Yes, everything," said Barry shortly. He looked intently at the minister. "That was a damned fine thing to do. You've influenced Lorry more than you know. What a—well, what a wretched girl she used to be, and now she's helping the kind of children you helped. You've saved her life, in a way, and that's why I came down now to see you personally, to see what sort of man could transform my sister like this. And I find you, Johnny Fletcher!" He smiled at Johnny, and his mouth twitched. "Look, perhaps I'm wrong about Lorry. Perhaps she wanted to keep you under wraps as a grand surprise for me."

A voice squealed from the doorway, "What's all this?" Dr. McManus stood there, in his deplorable old brown overcoat and battered hat. He tried to peer around Johnny to see the other man. Barry stood up and confronted the doctor.

"You old, lying, plotting bastard," he said softly. "You old fraud."

"Barry!" howled the doctor. He waddled rapidly into the room and threw his bulky arms about the young man and hugged him. "Well, damn it, it's Barry! God, boy, I'm glad to see you. When did you get back? Let me look at you, curse it!"

He pushed Barry away from him, blinking moistly. Then he saw the expression in Barry's eyes, and he dropped his

arms. He scratched his cheek, and his color took on a purplish tint. "Um, yes," he muttered. Then he exclaimed wrathfully, and with obvious embarrassment, "Where's everybody?
Where's Lorry? Hey, Barry, don't glare at me like that.
Remember me? I delivered your ma of you, and you were a
mean kid. Oh, you're thinking why we didn't tell you. It's a
long story." He peeped at Johnny, who was again withdrawn. "Don't you go glaring at me too, parson. Nothing
against you. Sit down, sit down! You both look like you're
going to punch me in the jaw, and me an old man. As I say,
it's a long story."

"It'd better be a good one," said Barry.

The doctor sat bunched on a chair, while the young men
stood over him menacingly. "Why don't you sit down?" he
demanded with acerbity. "And I need a drink. Several.
Johnny, pull that rope over there. This calls for a celebration.
None of your wine or sherry or brandy. Whisky and soda.
You too, Rover boy," he added to Johnny, with an attempt at
a jeer.

"You hide your whisky," said Johnny, trying to smile, for
he felt Barry's renewed anger. "I know. I've looked for it. Do
you think everybody's a thief?" He pulled the bell rope.

"If you've been looking for the whisky, then you *are* a
thief," said Dr. McManus, avoiding Barry's eyes. He threw
his old hat on the floor, dragged off his coat, then sat on it.
"I'm not what I used to be," he muttered. "Almost lost this
last ulcer case. Think I'll retire. Getting too old and nervous
and worn out."

"Too bad," said Barry. "If you're looking for sympathy
from me you won't get it. How about a little sympathy for
me?"

"I told you it's a long story," said the doctor testily; and
now he took the offensive. "You're too stupid to be tolerant,
or you'd know that Lorry and I had a reason. Oh, there you
are, May. Bring in a bottle of my Scotch—here's my key, and
bring it back—and three glasses and ice, and soda."

They waited; the doctor blinked sullenly at Barry, like an
owl. "God didn't give you any knees, eh, so you could bend
them and sit down? Look, I'm not going to say a single damn
word until I've had a drink. I think I'm going to have a heart
attack."

"Good," said Barry. But his deep affection for Dr. Mc-

Manus was beginning to smother his angry resentment. He sat down. Johnny looked from one to the other, and then he saw that the doctor was staring at him sheepishly. There was something here he did not understand, and he was not sure he was going to like it. "Perhaps I'd better leave you two old friends alone," he said stiffly.

The doctor cackled at Barry. "Parson's always very touchy. Delicate, like a flower. All his emotions are pragmatic; kid stuff. No imagination. Maybe you'd better stop that wedding, Barry, or you'll have him peering at every book you publish and screaming at some things. He's all brotherly love; he doesn't believe in hatchet men."

"Then he's considerably changed," said Barry, seeing Johnny's uneasiness. "Sit down, Johnny. I have an idea old Al's story is going to be quite a revelation to you, too. Then we'll all have a good laugh."

The maid entered with a silver tray and bottles and glasses. She poured the drinks with a sparing hand. "I'm not broke yet, May," said the doctor with sarcasm, "so let's have enough. A little more, a little more. Here today, gone tomorrow. With this household you never can tell. I'm almost bankrupt, but not yet."

He passed out the glasses; Johnny hesitated, then was annoyed at his annoyance, and took a glass. He concentrated on the adding of soda. He could hear the children's happy, released voices in another section of the big house. Barry, hearing them too, smiled. Johnny had a proud and reserved expression, and Barry was now sorry for his tactless anger which had precipitated this misunderstanding. "All right, Uncle Al," he said, "let's get down to business."

"Damned good Scotch," said the doctor, smacking his lips. "Must be a revelation to the beer-drinking parson here, and you, Barry, with your New York martinis. Never could stand mixed drinks. Bad for your kidneys."

"Never mind my kidneys," said Barry. He winked at the doctor, who, glancing at Johnny again, nodded slightly.

"Where's Lorry?" demanded the doctor.

"She went out some time ago," replied Johnny, in a cold, abstracted voice.

"I'm going to break her neck," said Barry easily. "Unless your story is a good one."

"I don't know about any story," said Johnny, exasperated.

"Well, now, it's this way," said the doctor, tinkling the ice in his glass. "Here comes the parson in August, hell for leather. Innocent and enthusiastic as some goddam Adam fresh out of Eden. All people need, thinks he, is to be told the truth. So he carries the explosive around with him. Who told him, dammit, that people want to hear the truth anyway? So, first off, the kids get into trouble—young punks and hoods attack 'em. Long story; Lorry told you? All right. So then your dad moves in, the parson's a menace, the parson's a fascist, the parson's a union buster, and enemy of the people. Oh, Lorry told you that too, did she? Don't interrupt! The parson's got to go. Where's this morning's newspaper; it was right here; you can't keep an infernal thing in this house. Your dad's editorial this morning accuses the parson of being a warmonger. Funny thing. Your father was all in favor of our getting into the war against Hitler, but now everybody who fights Communism is a warmonger."

He said to Johnny with bitterness, "Well, fill up my glass, will you? If I conk off, where'll you and those kids be? In the poorhouse, that's where."

Johnny, a little mollified now, filled up the doctor's glass. Dr. McManus peered up at him, and Johnny smiled slightly at the fierce, affectionate eyes.

"One thing you can't be in this world, boys, is consistent. You've got to keep changing your line to meet the howling demands of the maniacs. One war's good, the other's bad, depending on who in power wants war, or who'll profit from it, or what minority yells for it. You know what I'd do? I'd denaturalize every bastard in this country who screams he's a minority. I'd send him off to where he'd be a majority, and then who'd he blame? A man's an American, or he ain't. Simple. . . .

"Well, anyway. What do we do in here, sit in the dark? Turn on a lamp, somebody. So, the parson gives a rousing sermon first off, and Lorry comes out, all powder and lipstick and cynicism and jauntiness, to get a story from the parson, and he won't give it, because God did give him a little sense—but not much, mind you. And then, all at once, something comes to Lorry, and to me too, while we're in the parsonage, that the parson's your Johnny Fletcher, and Lorry gets hysterical. Yes she did, Barry, and stop that damned interrupting! She wants to tell the parson. But I've got an idea. We'll save you to clobber your dad with, when the time comes."

"What!" cried Johnny, outraged.

"So," said Barry, "I'm the club to knock my father's teeth in. What melodrama. It would've been much more sensible if you or Lorry had told him, and then perhaps some of the things that have happened wouldn't have happened. I suppose you never thought of that."

He looked up at Johnny, who was standing with his fists clenched.

Barry added, "Look, Johnny, it's obvious that both the doc here and Lorry are imbeciles. The doc's senile, and Lorry listened to him, and she was always a romantic, anyway. Can you forgive them? I already have. You don't get furious at retarded children, do you?"

"It was because of your father's attacks on me that my parsonage was burned, and my child murdered," said Johnny, and his voice was weak. Barry was silent.

The doctor reached hurriedly for the whisky bottle. He said, "Of course you always were an idiot. You started the whole thing with your infernal truth. If it hadn't been Mac, it would have been word of mouth through the Communists. Besides, the poor baby was dying, anyway. And haven't you got Debby, who needs you? Two months, three months, a year later, and it would've been too late for Debby. And you're getting a mansion for a parsonage, and you've got Lorry. But you're one of those who're never satisfied."

Johnny bent his head and looked at his feet. After a moment he said, "I sound ungrateful. Perhaps I am. But everything else aside, I don't like the idea of my being made an instrument to hit any man, even Mr. Summerfield." But he was becoming calm again, and the sick tension in him was relaxing. So Lorry had not been ashamed of him after all, as he had secretly feared. She had kept his name from her brother for her own purposes, at the doctor's insistence. He smiled in spite of his efforts to remain stern. The doctor chuckled, and pointed at him.

"He thought, because he's so stupid, that Lorry didn't tell you because she believed you'd think a parson wasn't good enough for her. How can a grown man be so dense?"

Mrs. Burnsdale came to the door of the library, hesitantly. "Miss Lorry hasn't come back yet," she said, "and it's getting dark. I'm a little worried."

The doctor pushed himself out of his chair, went to Mrs. Burnsdale, and took her hand. "Barry," he said grandly, "I want you to meet my fiancée. A damn fine woman. We'd all have fallen apart without her, and that includes the parson."

Mrs. Burnsdale blushed as Barry shook her hand. "You know how the doctor exaggerates," she said. She looked at Barry with interest. "Aren't you Miss Lorry's brother? One of the maids said you were. I'm Mrs. Burnsdale."

"Lorry's told me all about you," he said kindly. "I'm Barry Lowell." She studied him and said, "You look like Miss Lorry's twin brother."

The doctor put his hand on her shoulder, proudly. "She's going to marry me," he said. "I had to propose out of self-defense, or she'd have bankrupted me for the parson. Now the money'll all be in the family. Hell what a man has to do to protect himself, isn't it?"

Mrs. Burnsdale touched his cheek shyly. "I never knew that such wonderful people lived in this world," she said. "I never knew any before I met Mr. Fletcher and the doctor." She looked at Johnny, and was concerned. He seemed restless and anxious. At that moment the telephone rang and the doctor, cursing, took up the receiver and squawked, "Take some aspirin!" Then he was silent, listening, and his grayish face went deathly white. He kept glancing at Barry, then at Johnny, and was speechless.

After a little he said gently, "All right, Lorry. Keep calm. I'll come right away. Lorry? Your brother's here. Yes, I mean Barry, who else? Yes. Now look, honey, calm down. I'm on my way now."

He put down the receiver and snatched up his coat and hat. Barry had moved to his side. The doctor shook his head. "Come on, boys, we've got work to do. All three of us. And we don't have a minute to waste."

"Lorry!" exclaimed Johnny, with the familiar sinking of terror.

"Nothing's wrong with Lorry," said the doctor ferociously. "Don't worry about her. It's something she's done, the half-wit."

35

Esther Summerfield sauntered, swaying, into her husband's study, her Hindustani sari floating about her. It was pale blue, with silver tracings. Her dark face and tilted eyes had a musing, casual expression. She was carrying a tray holding a cocktail shaker and two glasses. "Time for our martinis, Mac-Donald," she said, and sank into a fine antique chair. She looked about the study, furnished in the most exquisite period furniture, and wrinkled her long nose. She saw the white shoulder of a mountain through a window draped in rose velvet, and thought to herself, it must be my imagination that he isn't well, even though he now stays home so much.

The early evening sky was a medieval blue after the snow. Mr. Summerfield continued to write. His wife said, "That article for the New York *Gazette-Express*? Is it so important? You're writing furiously, dear." (Why was he so pale these days, and his eyes so exhausted?)

"It's very important," he replied impatiently. "They're going to feature it for the Sunday edition. Don't interrupt, Esther."

She got up languidly, and poured him a cocktail. "You look so pleased, dear, that I want you to be more pleased. I made these cocktails myself. Very dry." She looked down at the desk, and her smiling mouth tightened. She recognized the heap of pages there, in Dr. Somer Granger's rounded, almost unformed hand, the hand of an extroverted, malicious child, thought Esther, who had recently taken up the science of graphology. A mean child, she commented; a child who is cruel because of the exaltation and power cruelty gives him. She saw that, as usual, her husband was using these notes as a basis for his article. Her swift eye caught a few lines: "The reactionary believes he is acting on 'American principles' when he denounces a progressive man for his democratic ideology. But his 'patriotism,' as the reactionary calls his aberration, is purely a paranoid fear of anything which threatens his security in the *status quo*. In many instances the reactionary's violent rejection of progressive ideas is based on subconscious hostility to a parent during childhood. The very young child is ritualistic; any departure from comfortable ritualism, even though departure is necessary for growth, arouses his fear and hatred for the unknown. . . . The reactionary, then, is in fact an emotionally and mentally disturbed person, and in need of psychiatric treatment to relieve his tensions and hostilities and to restore him to a happy adjustment."

Esther stood at her husband's elbow and reread that paragraph aloud, in a musing voice, much to her husband's annoyance. She laughed with contempt. "Granger means calm and accepting attitudes toward Communism. He has never fooled me. But now he's beginning to frighten me. He is the kind of psychiatrist who thinks of himself as a progressive. But he's not, really. He is one of the real reactionaries. He wants power, the power to create a mindless helot state, with himself among the elite. I told Granger that. That's why he hates me, and tries to persuade our friends and acquaintances, and you too, that I'm a fool of a woman, faddish and superficial. He's succeeding, too. He knows I know all about him."

Esther sat down, and her dark face was drawn with anger and anxiety. Her husband looked at her with sudden interest, as if seeing her after a long absence. "I look into the pit of his mind and I see all hell," she went on. "No wonder the Russians use psychiatrists like Granger all the time. What is happening in the world now is the supreme sacrilege, the assault on men's souls by men who are trying to play God. It never happened before in all the world's history. Antichrist at last."

Mr. Summerfield smiled indulgently. But he did not answer. Esther picked up a floating fold of the sari and looked at it. "I love you, MacDonald, and that is why I stay here with you, and play the fool. I'm bored to death, sick and bored to death. I take up fads simply to relieve my boredom. Worst of all, I'm beginning to be bored with you." She lifted her eyes and they were full of dark fire. "Smile, MacDonald, but it's true. And I know something else: you aren't a Somer Granger. You don't believe a word of what he guides you to write. You aren't a Communist; you aren't even a leftist. What has Granger to do with you, MacDonald? What kind of blackmail is he holding over your head to force you to do the things you do, the things you write?"

His face changed, hardened, and then she saw the sudden gray flashing of terror across his features. He said, in a loud and coldly furious voice, "Granger's right. You're a fool, Esther. You've said only one sensible thing, that I'm not a Communist. I never was. I am only a democratic, progressive man who is trying to right—"

"Right what?" asked Esther quietly. "The insult to your father, when he was poor and unimportant? Is that how you try to rationalize things? MacDonald, you need help, but Dr. Granger's not the man to give it to you."

The gray terror again flashed across his face. Esther shook her head. "I don't think it's all your father, after all. It's something else, something even more terrible. I don't think you have what Granger calls a guilt complex because you inherited wealth. Some other kind, perhaps. After all, what is wrong with inherited wealth, so long as a man doesn't use the money to degrade himself and do stupid things? Very few sons of rich men do that, anyway. They usually carry on their fathers' work and expand opportunities for everybody. MacDonald, Dr. Granger has made your mind sick, though he calls it 'adjustment.' He has terrorized you in some way, and made you accept his lies, and made his lies yours, so that you have come to believe them yourself. I can't stand it! I can't stand by and watch your disintegration!"

She strode back and forth, all her customary composure gone, and wrung her hands desperately. "What has he done to you? What lies about yourself has he told you? MacDonald, answer me! Each day you seem more ill, more irrational. Let me help you!"

He set down his glass with violence, but she saw that his lips were bluish. "Esther, stop raving."

She bent toward him, in naked anguish. "Darling, listen to me. I've been reading about men like Granger. They practice spiritual blackmail. Don't you remember the time he told us about some troubled college boys who came to him and confessed they had been Communists, and that they were now ashamed and sickened and full of guilt? Don't you remember how he laughed about it, and how he told us that he'd comforted those poor children and assured them they had no reason to feel guilty, and that they were really 'lovers of mankind'? He had such fun telling us. He sent those boys on their way, forever spiritually diseased and insane, to carry their infection with them to corrupt others. Just as he corrupts you."

Summerfield stood up. "Esther, stop it. You're out of your mind." He paused. For the first time in many years he saw tears in his wife's eyes, and his heart pounded with inexplicable pain. He lowered his voice. "You're giving Granger too much importance. I'm using *him*, not the other way around. Believe me."

She shook her head. "I can't, I don't believe you. I believe you've passed beyond the stage where you can recognize truth any longer." She reached to the desk swiftly, caught up Dr. Granger's notes, and tore them across and across, again and again.

He gasped, caught her ripping hands, and stopped them. She opened her fingers and let the fragments drift to the floor. She was crying openly now, and Summerfield pushed her from him, less in rage than in despair. "Stop lying, darling!" she begged him. "Stop it now, and perhaps you'll be well again. You aren't a bad man; you're not an evil man, as your son and our daughter believe you are. How can they be so blind? You are really what you were as they remember you years ago, an honest man. They love you, MacDonald, but they'll never come back, they'll never speak to you again, because you won't let them. Because, perhaps, you can't let them."

He cried out now, and she had never heard that sound

before in his voice. "Why don't you let me alone? Go away, for God's sake!"

She stood in absolute silence then, looking at him. He sat down at his desk and stared at it blankly, the muscles about his mouth twitching.

"All right, MacDonald," she said, very softly. "I'm glad you want that. I'll go away. Tonight. And I'm never coming back, never, until you've put that wicked man out of your life, until you stop pouring out his own poison in your newspapers."

His head jerked up. "Esther. Don't be a fool." His voice was dwindled and weak. "You know I can't and won't let you go away from me. You—you just irritated me for a moment. You've worked yourself up into hysterics."

"Oh, darling," she said wearily. "You can't even say a word of your own. 'Hysterics, hysterical.' Two of Granger's favorite words, to explain away things dangerous to him and to what he wants. But he is one of the real hysterics, the real uncontrollables." She put her trembling hand on his shoulder. "MacDonald, you've known me a long time. I'm the mother of your daughter. Try to answer me honestly for once. Have you ever seen me really hysterical?"

He looked again at his desk. He started to speak, then was silent. Still crying, she bent her head and kissed his cold cheek. "Darling, I'm so glad. You still haven't completely lost the faculty of recognizing the truth."

She picked up his limp hand and pressed it to her lips. He did not look at her. She thought with terror, He's ill, he's frightfully ill. Barry, Lorry! Come back and help me! How can you be so cruel to your father? Come back!

She still held his left hand, and then, to her incredulity, she saw his right hand, moving as if under an automatic impulse, take up what he had already written and crush it in his fingers. Then he sat and gazed at it emptily. She let herself drop into a chair beside him, and her heart was pounding in her ears. Her mouth moved in silent, grateful prayer, and she closed her eyes.

Dimly she heard the door open, and then shut. She turned her head to see who had come into this room unannounced, and then she cried out joyfully, "Lorry! Lorry! I knew you'd come!" She got to her feet, and her husband stood with her, disbelieving.

Lorry remained at a distance, rigid and white, and she looked only at her father, with cold and terrible denunciation.

"Lorry!" he exclaimed, and he was young again, and there was a flush of life on his cheeks. He went toward her, his hands extended, and she stepped back. "Don't touch me," she said. "Don't ever touch me again."

They stood and stared at her, speechless. And then, all at once, she felt that something had changed, shifted. She was sick with her anger and her hatred, but still she knew that something had changed. Her parents seemed mysteriously altered, greatly and emotionally moved. But it was only her imagination, she told herself, almost frightened, and very confused. That was her father there, Johnny's enemy, her enemy, the enemy of all men of good will and honor. She must hate him; she did, indeed, hate him. Her mouth shook; for a moment she felt giddy and ill. She clenched her gloved hands together, and repeated over and over, in herself, Hate him. Hate him.

"Lorry, when did you come home? Lorry, what is wrong?" asked her father, feebly. "What is the matter? Lorry, speak to me. What have I done?" He turned to Esther, who was watching Lorry with wide, still eyes. "Talk to her, Esther."

"What shall I say?" asked Esther. "Our daughter walks into our home, her home, and she's our enemy. Aren't you, Lorry? I never saw it until now; I never really knew it until today. She's our enemy, MacDonald, because she doesn't understand, and never tried to understand. She's really a very stupid girl."

Lorry removed her fixed gaze from her father and turned it to her mother with an expression of shock. She said, "How can you say that? You know all about him."

Esther did not answer for a moment. For suddenly she saw how vulnerable her daughter was, how young, how bitterly hurt and suffering, how relentless, how blindly passionate. Esther's heart stirred with pity. She put her hand on her husband's arm and answered gently, "Yes, dear, I do know a lot about your father—now. A great deal more than I ever did. And you—you know nothing."

It seemed to Lorry that the carpeted floor moved under her feet, so intense was her amazement, and then came her renewed anger. "So he's corrupted you now, too, Mother, has he? He's convinced you. You, of all people!"

"What does the girl mean?" cried Mr. Summerfield. "Lorry! I'm your father!"

"No!" Lorry's voice was almost a scream. "Not any more! Not again, as long as you live, and I live!" Her nameless fright rose, and her confusion, and the old tearing pain. For an instant she was a young child, and she wanted to burst into tears of terror and loneliness, and to run to her father and let him hold her to him, comforting her. An awful sense of deprivation clenched at her throat, an awful sense of grief, of mourning. But he had betrayed her; he had driven her, and Barry, away. He hates us, and so we hate him, her darkening thoughts rushed on. Oh, God, give me the strength to say what I want to say, and then help me out of this house forever.

She looked from her father to her mother, and there was a mute agony in her green-blue eyes, an enraged but helpless expression on her face. Esther had not come to her as she had expected; Esther stood beside her husband and her face was strangely sad, strangely waiting, and very gentle. I'm imagining things, Lorry told herself again. I don't understand—what is wrong here? What has changed? Mother, Mother. Don't you remember me? Why do you stand there with him, so close to him? And then tears smarted Lorry's eyelids, and she thought, involuntarily—just as I want to stand with him, as I used to, so long ago.

She could not take her eyes from her father now. He is old, she thought vaguely. He's suddenly an old man. I've made him old, right this minute. He isn't formidable; I just thought he was. She swallowed the huge swelling in her throat, and forced her thoughts to Johnny, and her rage started up in her again, whipped both by her grief and her consternation.

"I came to say something," she said. "It won't take long. Barry will soon know; he should be back any day." She gave all her attention to her father; she could not understand her mother's silence, her remoteness, her mysterious air of waiting. Lorry's flesh felt cold and rigid; she could not control the constant trembling that ran in waves over her body, and the feeling of abandonment, of unbearable desolation.

"Yes?" said her father. "Barry? Yes, dear. What about Barry?"

It was a nightmare, of course. Her father was speaking to her as he had spoken when she was very young, and had just awakened from a fearful dream. But he was old—old—I've made him old, thought Lorry, and shut her eyes to protect herself from her giddiness. I'm glad he's old; I hate him.

She said in a faint voice, "I've seen your last editorial about Johnny Fletcher." Now her eyes flashed at the sound of that beloved name. "Your lies about him. Always your lies, from the very beginning. And now you want to destroy him entirely, don't you, because he's done something good for this city?"

Johnny Fletcher. Mr. Summerfield, bewildered, contemplated that name. It seemed to be a name gone far off, in some shadowy distance. He leaned against his desk and tried to consider. If only his head would stop aching; he had so many bad headaches these days. They always numbed his thoughts, and took the strength from his body.

"What does it matter about that man?" he murmured dully. Esther turned to him in alarm, and took his elbow strongly. He did not feel her touch. "You haven't been here for months, Lorry. He's caused many disturbances. I can't seem to remember just what they were at this minute, but they disorganized the life of this town. There's something else I seem to remember. He influenced you against me. You left your home and your parents, because of him." He rubbed his forehead with the knuckles of his right hand. "What does it matter about that man?" he repeated.

His words, which appeared to Lorry as contemptuously indifferent and dismissing, excited her to fresh rage. "There's something you don't know! Barry doesn't know yet! Do you want to hear it?"

"What has anything about that man got to do with my son and my daughter?" Mr. Summerfield's voice faded. It was not his own strength that was upholding him. There was a strong arm about him, and he was grateful. "All I know is that he is a busybody and a rabble-rouser." He gazed at Lorry desperately, and now he could hear the rising panic of his own heart. He was almost convinced that he was dreaming this; worse still, he told himself, it did not matter whether he was dreaming or not. Lorry, in her turquoise suit and her furs, had taken on a flat, cardboard quality, like a poster. The room had narrowed, darkened, foreshortened. He was very tired; he knew these manifestations of his weariness well; he had first known them a few months ago. What did Granger call them? "Flights from reality."

"I'm not trying to escape reality," muttered Mr. Summerfield. "It's only that I'm very tired, I suppose."

"MacDonald!" cried Esther. She forced him back against his desk, for his weight had become increasingly heavy against her supporting arm. She glanced at her daughter almost with hatred. "What are you trying to do to your father?"

Frantically convinced that her mother had completely deserted her, Lorry lost control of herself. "What am I trying to do to him? How can you—? What has he done to all of us? Tired? He says he's tired! How tired we are of him!"

Her terror had returned, more frenzied, more tearing, than before. Something was wrong! This was not as she had expected it to be. She did not know where to turn, what words to choose. She could feel a terror in the room, beyond herself. "Listen to me. I won't bother either of you any longer, if you'll just listen now. I'll go away, and you'll never see me again." Her voice broke. "What has Johnny Fletcher got to do with us? Don't you remember what Barry told us about the chaplain who rescued him on the Normandy beachhead? Barry was wounded, almost fatally—you remember—and was in some rocky hole, and nobody was permitted to go after him, because the bombardment was too heavy. But one man did, though they tried to stop him. He went to Barry and crouched in the hole with him, and gave him first aid, and comforted him. Remember? And then he carried Barry to safety on his back. Remember?"

"Oh, no!" said Esther. "Oh, it wasn't Mr. Fletcher! Oh, Lorry!" This was too frightful to be true.

But Lorry was smiling fiercely, and nodding, and her tears ran down her cheeks. "Yes! It was Johnny Fletcher."

"It's not possible!" cried Esther wildly. "Things—couldn't be as cruel as that! Barry told us that the chaplain was killed in the Battle of the Bulge."

Mr. Summerfield staggered away from his desk and his wife, though she threw out distracted arms to hold him. He crept to a chair and fell in it, and his hands dropped between his slack knees. "It's a nightmare," he said in a curiously thin voice. "It's only a nightmare." He tried to moisten his dry lips, which tasted of metal, and then his mouth fell open soundlessly.

"Remember?" Lorry's relentless voice of hating accusation went on. "Where Barry went, the chaplain followed. He knew Barry didn't have much of a chance to live. You've seen Barry's scars, which make him limp sometimes. There was a night, Barry said, when he knew he was dying, and so did the doctors and the nurses in the field hospital. But the chaplain spent that night on his knees beside Barry's cot, because he knew Barry wanted to live. Barry had never heard anyone pray before; you never taught either of us to pray—"

"Lorry!" said Esther. "Lorry, look at your father."

"I'm looking," said Lorry, with a bitter green flash of her eyes at her mother. But she shrank a little when she turned her regard on her father again. She went on, "This chaplain, the man who saved your son's life, is the man you've been hounding, libeling, stirring up mobs against, trying to deprive him of his very life and the poor children he rescued. You did that to him, in payment. Paid in full, for saving Barry!"

Esther went to Lorry and stood before her and said, "You knew it all the time, Lorry, didn't you? You could have stopped it. You could have told your father from the very first. You didn't learn about it just now, did you?"

Lorry tried to stare her mother down, but she was trembling again, and the sickness was rising in her, and her fear of the unknown in this room. "Yes," she said, "I did know. But I wanted to see how far he'd go."

Esther gestured toward her husband, collapsed in his chair. "Very well, Lorry. That is as far as he did go. Look at him. Did you ever try to help him, to understand him? Never, not once. Neither you nor Barry. Did you once ever think that there might be something in his life that was torturing him, something that a wicked man used for his own purposes?"

"I don't know what you mean," stammered Lorry. She went to her father's desk and, as he had done, she leaned against it for support. There was a sharp blow of shock in her heart. "I—I shouldn't have come alone." She looked at her father, and shivered, and now she wept, putting her hands over her face. "It was all wrong from the beginning; I should have brought Uncle Al, Johnny."

"You should have told your father, from the very first. You could have saved him, then. How much you must have hated him, Lorry." Esther turned from her daughter and ran to her husband, for his face was parched and as wrinkled as a mummy's and he had the appearance of a dying man. She knelt beside him, for his head had begun to nod uncontrollably. Esther put her arms about him and pulled his head to her breast. She cried to her daughter, "I'll never forgive you, Lorry, never!"

Lorry started toward her parents, but Esther, kneeling, repudiated her with a passionate gesture. "Go away," she exclaimed. "Go away and never come back, Lorry. I can't forgive you; I never want to see you again."

Mr. Summerfield lifted his stricken head from his wife's breast and turned his anguished eyes to his daughter. He began to speak in a faraway, laboring voice. "So—much—talk—about forgiving. So many lies. There was never anything else but lies. It's very hard to explain—if you've killed somebody—I don't really think I did, now. I should have told. But it was all a lie. That's when it began, when I was told lies." His voice suddenly failed, and he slumped in his wife's arms, and she could no longer hold him. She screamed as he slipped to the floor and lay face down, without a sound.

"You've killed him, Lorry! You've killed your father! No, don't touch him! Don't dare to touch him!" And Esther, in her despair and grief, struck her daughter's shoulder with her clenched fist as Lorry bent over her father.

"I'll get help," said Lorry, distraught, rising. "Someone will help. I didn't know. I must get help!"

6

Dr. McManus came wearily down the long curve of the marble stairs and went into the Hindustani room where Lorry, Barry, and Esther were waiting for him. He looked at them from under his cliff-like brows and said, "Well, he's all right now. The nurse knows what to do, and the parson's with him. Lorry, Lorry," he said sadly, "it could have been done with more mercy. Why didn't you ask me to go with you?"

Lorry said through a tight throat, "I wanted to tell him from the very first, but you made me promise not to."

"Yes, yes, I know," said the doctor, carefully avoiding Barry's coldly condemning eyes. He turned to Esther compassionately; she sat in her chair, white and immobilized, her braids in disorder, her hands limp. "I don't know how you'll do it, but I guess you'll have to forgive us, Esther. Especially me. Lorry was all for telling Mac about it in the beginning."

"I know," said Esther. "You're not terribly smart, Al, about some things. MacDonald's been ill for a long time. I could see it. You have to love someone to see the changes. I tried to get him to go to a doctor, but he laughed at me, and there he was, changing every day, sickening. I knew there was something on his mind, something that was growing too heavy for him to bear any longer, but he refused to acknowledge it to me, or let me help him. Al, if you'd been at all intelligent you'd have known that something was wrong with Mac-Donald all these past years, and you'd have tried to help."

"Never claimed to be intelligent," said the doctor. "And I get more stupid every day."

Esther tried to smile. Her hand was clasped in Lorry's, and she pressed the girl's chilly fingers encouragingly. But Barry said, "I wish there were some law I could use against you and Lorry for your stupidity. Look what happened to Johnny and my father because of you both. I'm not going to get over this."

"And I'm not going to argue with you," said the doctor, "for there isn't any argument. You should see the parson with Mac! By the way, the parson's not speaking to me, either. I think I'll go home. What am I, a criminal?"

"Yes," said Barry. The young man was extremely shaken; he lit one cigarette after another, and prowled miserably up and down the room, which was saffron now, with all its brazen lamps. Esther gazed at him anxiously. "Barry, don't take it so hard. I don't care, as long as it isn't a heart attack, or apoplexy. You see, dear, I love your father. I'm so glad it's nothing worse than a nervous breakdown."

Hum, thought Dr. McManus. It'd be better if he'd broken both his legs. Nervous breakdown! They think it's nothing. All it is is that a man's soul gets sick to death and he can't stand living any more! Just a nervous breakdown! He coughed. "The parson and I listened to Mac before I gave him the shot of sedative. Enough to make your hair rise and go off your head forever. God damn it," said the doctor, simply. "There's devils in the world, real devils. Never believed it before, but I do now. Barry, I got to talk about this to you, so sit down. You make me jittery. All right, all right! Shut up and listen. Lorry, if you cry any more you'll be wearing spectacles the rest of your life. Your face looks like a suet dumpling now. Here, take my handkerchief. God, women! And I'm marrying one of them myself! Should be shut up in an insane asylum for even thinking of it. Well, anyway, she's a good cook, so maybe it won't be too bad. Barry, while you're walking around, how about getting somebody to give us some drinks? We all need it. And no martinis!"

"Just cyanide for you," said Barry, but he rang for a maid.

"You said something earlier, Al, about Dr. Granger's part in MacDonald's illness," said Esther, and her eyes sparkled with cold wrath. "I knew it all the time, but I never learned what influence that man had over my husband."

"Well, I'll tell you," said the doctor. He waited until all were served with drinks by the maid. The girl was extremely curious, so the doctor made certain she had gone before he began to speak.

"When I first examined Mac I thought it was his heart; it was going a mile a minute, and his blood pressure was dropping, and he had that breathing, and the pain. Looked like angina; it's usually brought on by mental stress. Well, anyway, he began to talk to the parson and me; he wouldn't talk even after the sedative until Barry went out, at my request. Kind of ashamed of what he had to tell, or maybe he thought Barry might do something violent to Granger and get himself in trouble. I told Mac," added the doctor, eying Barry severely, "that his son's got more sense. I hope." Barry made no reply, but gazed somberly into his glass.

"Well," Dr. McManus continued, "I shouldn't wonder if it was a familiar story, especially with men like Granger, who have other irons in the fire as well as their profession. By the way, we're going to send Mac to a sanitarium for a while; get him away from his emotional family where he can have peace and quiet, and though they've got head-shrinkers there they don't meddle with a man's soul and pervert it. John Kanty told me about the place: it's religious, and they heal a man's spirit the right way, through spiritual means.

"Granger's got an office here in Barryfield, though his real office is in Philadelphia; he only comes here once a week, to treat local patients. His important object was Mac, Mac the rich man who could be depended upon to donate, and Mac, who had newspapers, and who wrote for other newspapers. You know," continued the doctor, "I've been wondering a long time what makes so many rich men Communists, or fellow travelers like Mac. They got everything to lose under Communism—sort of committing suicide by just being rich. So I talked to people who know about them in New York and other places. Know what? Lots of 'em actually think the American people are so stupid that they're going to let the Communists go on infiltrating government and all our means of public communication and our schools indefinitely! But there's one thing about the American people: they got good hard horse sense, and they let criminals go so far and then they crack their heads open, kind of getting tired of tolerance. So, many of the rich fellers, believing Communism is taking over, are trying to make their peace with it, and toadying to it, or giving money to it. And then there are the boys with inherited wealth, who made fools of themselves with it, not working or carrying on their dads' work, and so they feel guilty. And then there're the haters, the born haters, and people with grudges against society, and incompetents and irresponsibles who want the goods of the earth without working for 'em, and who hate men who accept life on its own terms and get successful.

"Not to mention the insane. And the perverts. And the misfits. They go for Communism like birds for worms."

Barry stopped wrathfully before the doctor. "And in what category does my father fit?"

Dr. McManus smiled. "In none that I just mentioned. He's a special case, but not too rare." His smile stopped suddenly. "Not too unknown. But the worst kind. Barry, your dad was a victim of Granger, and if the law weren't so damn persnickety about murder I'd be out gunning for Granger. Not that you're going to be that kind of fool," he added hastily.

"You mean," cried Lorry in the shrill voice of utter anguish, "that our father was blackmailed by Somer Granger?"

"Now look, honey," said the doctor with concern, "this isn't unusual. Don't get your bowels upset too much. Yes, he was. You got to be calm in these emergencies, and Mac's in the worst kind of emergency. Now shut up and let me talk.

"You both know how Mac got to be rich; he inherited all that money from his father, the schoolmaster, who got it from an oil strike when Mac was a kid. So they went away to Philadelphia to live and built that great big mansion of theirs. Mac loved his father; he didn't think his mother appreciated the precious so-and-so. Mac was jealous; wanted all his father's pompous attention. Evelyn interfered, according to Mac's kid way of thinking.

"Evelyn and the new servants were getting the new house ready to live in, and Evelyn was on the top landing, dusting off the new chandelier. Mac was about fourteen then. Poor Evelyn, losing her balance, fell three stories and was killed."

"I know," said Esther. "He'd talk about it in his sleep, poor dear."

"But there's something you don't know. Mac was in the house; his new room was right off the landing. He was a dreamy, foolish kind of boy, had fantasies, and delusions of grandeur, and all the other disagreeable traits of an egotist. Like his son," said the doctor, scowling at Barry. "Sure you're an egotist, son. If you hadn't been, you'd have been thinking of your dad and trying to find out what made him the way he was, and trying to help him. Shut up. And stop soaking up all that whisky; remember your kidneys. And don't glare at me; I didn't make your dad.

"Mac had no business being in the new house just then. He was playing hooky, so he could sneak back in and gloat. Remember, he'd been poor until then. He came out of his room, not knowing anyone was there, for he got there before his mother and the servants, and he was on the landing just as his mother reached over the railing to dust off the new chandelier."

Esther said in a penetratingly quiet voice, "MacDonald didn't push his mother over that railing to her death. Even though he used to rave about it in his nightmares."

"Lorry, if you don't stop jumping up and down and wringing your hands and whimpering, I'm going to spank you," said the doctor menacingly. "And stop beating your feet up and down the room all the time, Barry. This's a madhouse.

"Do I get to finish, or do I go home? All right, then, be quiet. Now we come to a serious point. Mac had often wished his mother would die and leave him alone with his father. Not uncommon. Lots of offspring think this about one or the other of their parents. Kind of natural, in a twisted sort of way. A fantasy. But Mac's an intense feller. He dreamed about it, and thought of it, and how wonderful it would be, if his mother just wasn't there. He and his dad would travel, fish, walk together, go boating together, and have soul-communion. Mac was a lonely and insufferable kid. I remember. He never had a beating in his life; spare the rod and you make your kid a misfit or a criminal, or even worse.

"Well, he comes padding out of his room, the sneak, and saw his mother leaning too far over that railing. She was a little thing, but heavy, and she began to teeter. Mac's impulse, in spite of his jealousy, was to run and catch her. But he couldn't; he froze. People like Mac panic easy. Now the head-shrinkers would say that he didn't want to save his mother at all. Fool idea; a feller comes right at me one night on the wrong side of the road, with lots of room to turn in on the right side, but he froze. Never saw me in his life before; he panicked; he didn't want to kill me. He was just a hysteric. Lucky thing for me there was room to run off the road, and I did. He just panicked, the goddam idiot. Got his license taken away and probably saved a dozen lives, though he hates me to this day.

"Well," and the doctor, remembering, wiped his damp forehead. "That's what happened to Mac. He wanted to save his mother, and he couldn't move. She went over the railing, and he got enough strength back to bolt into his room before she hit bottom."

"Oh, my God," murmured Esther, and for the first time she began to cry. "Poor MacDonald. Poor child."

The doctor nodded grimly. "I repeat again, you're a sensible female, Esther. Mac stole out of the house, shaking like mad, and went back to the hotel where they'd all been staying. The news had got to his father; Mac saw his father crying, and he knew then, without any fantasy or anything, that he'd wanted to save his mother. It's as simple as that. So his mind was quieted, and he could console his father normally, and be sorrowful for his mother. Simple as that. Until Granger got hold of him a few years ago."

"When does Granger come next to Barryfield?" asked Barry, casually.

"Now look, Barry, no fool stuff," said the doctor with alarm. "I'm taking care of Granger, through the AMA. No heroics, see?

"Well, everything was all right with Mac until he met Granger. He sees, now, that the meeting wasn't accidental, and that it was arranged by others. Granger built up quite a story to give Mac, who was always a shaky and doubting, if arrogant, character, the kind of feller who'll distrust even himself yet is wide open to liars and charlatans who have plans, such as Granger had—for Mac's newspapers and his money. He had to get a hold on Mac, and as Mac, at that particular time, was more than usually unstable, Granger 'treated' him. During the treatment, out comes the story about Evelyn and her death; Mac just talked of it because his dad had never gotten over his wife's death and had only lived a few years after that. Well, that's when the terror started, and the spiritual blackmail.

"In some way Granger persuaded Mac that he hadn't frozen when his mother had begun to fall to her death, but that he had run at his mother, blindly, instinctively, and had pushed her over the railing! He just hadn't remembered that part, said Granger, but it had all come out under sodium pentathol! Mac, according to Granger, was in 'conflict' because his subconscious mind recalled the whole thing but his conscious mind was cutting off the memory, and telling him lies so he could live with himself. So now Mac had a brand-new, full-blown guilt complex, and that's when he became really sick. How could he expiate the involuntary murder of his mother? Why, by helping the 'downtrodden, the unprivileged,' of course, in class warfare, Granger said. Added to this was the old resentment against those who had snubbed his dad when he was poor, and the fact that all his money couldn't make Mac as important as he thought he should be. He had always hated, and envied, 'aristocrats' who had inherited money and had never been poor."

"I'll kill Granger," said Barry.

"No you won't, so stop talking like a fool. I told you I'd take care of Granger. We've got sensible men in the AMA. So, Granger got Mac. Granger never met Johnny, but people like Johnny are a danger to the Grangers. They've got to be eliminated. So, the editorials, Granger-inspired, against Johnny."

"But Johnny's just a clergyman, an obscure clergyman, in an obscure town," said Lorry, appalled. "Why should a man like Somer Granger, so influential, so prosperous, bother about poor Johnny?"

"Honey," said the doctor in a low voice, "nobody who fights Communism is humble or obscure, according to the Communists. And nobody's too big to attack."

He stood up. "Mac's crack-up, under Granger, would've come at any time, for it was against Mac's nature to be a murderer. I've been watching him. Don't feel too guilty, Lorry, honey. You just precipitated something which would have come at any moment or hour. He'll be all right. He understands things now. By the way, the parson's been up there a long time. Think I'll look in on them."

The lights were sheltered and dimmed in Mr. Summerfield's large French Provincial-style bedroom. The sick man lay immobile on his pillows, breathing audibly and uneasily, his bluish face as colorless as the linen sheets. His eyes were closed and sunken. His pale fine hair, so like Lorry's, glimmered in the shaded lamplight, and his features had a far look of closed austerity, an expression similar to that of his children under certain conditions. Johnny, seated near the foot of the bed, facing his old enemy, could feel no anger against him, but only compassion. This was Lorry's and Barry's father; this man would be the grandfather of his, Johnny's, children. This was a man who suffered, and had suffered, cursed by his own imaginative and unstable character, his own secret griefs and bewilderments, a man incapable of accepting love simply and giving it as simply. Everything must be complicated and torturous for him, must have its "rational reasons," its explanations. But, so God had made him. Had he ever had faith he would have been reconciled in himself, and all the disparate elements—the hidden vehemence, the lostness, the simultaneous desire for love and the subconscious rejection of it—would have flowed together and have been lost in a mature serenity and confidence. God, thought Johnny, brings order to chaos, light to darkness, and the way to the lost traveler. But if men cannot accept Him as the compass, then they are always wanderers.

The nurse sat in a distant corner, reading, but alert for any movement or sigh from her patient. She had a dark and merry face, and glanced frequently at Johnny, as if waiting for a signal. She was one of Johnny's parishioners, and she told herself that if anyone could help Mr. Summerfield, Mr. Fletcher was the man. Hadn't he helped her when she had been about to give up nursing, in despair, because of ungrateful patients, long hard work which was not appreciated, and poor recompense? "We can't all make a lot of money," he had gently reminded her. "If you had wanted that in the beginning you'd never have become a nurse. You knew what it meant. You've just forgotten. I knew I'd never be a fashionable minister, and that I'd never have any money to amount to anything, but still I became a minister. Not that I haven't wondered why, too, very often!" She had seen, then, that he and she were in almost the same service, and had gone back to her work with renewed dedication and courage. And, best of all, with renewed and youthful inspiration.

Is he sleeping? Johnny asked himself, watching the sick man. He did not believe it. Mr. Summerfield was thinking behind those parched eyelids that wrinkled nervously. Does he want me to go away? Johnny thought. He knows I'm here.

Mr. Summerfield opened his eyes, and any last vestige of coldness Johnny might have been reserving against him vanished, for the eyes were Lorry's eyes, intent and aware. "Are you still here, Mr. Fletcher?" the older man asked in a weak voice. "Why?"

Johnny smiled. "Oh, I thought you and I would have something to say about Lorry," he said. "Unless that sedative is acting vigorously on you."

Mr. Summerfield smiled faintly in answer. "I've been taking barbiturates for years," he said. "Old Al didn't know that, so his fine sedatives have just made me a little drowsy." He paused. "I'm glad you stayed. You must have an instinct for such things."

"I have. I suppose every priest has. The doctor wanted me to leave and let you rest, but I knew you'd want to talk to me a little. So I stayed. After all, I'm going to marry Lorry."

"And it wouldn't make any difference to either of you if I objected?"

"No," said Johnny frankly, "not at all. But I'd like you to be pleased."

Mr. Summerfield glanced at the nurse, and Johnny said at once, "Nancy, would you mind leaving us alone for about ten minutes?" The girl rose immediately, came to her patient, smiled at him, and felt his pulse. "Why, everything's fine now," she said. "I'll have to ask the doctor for a stronger sedative, though, seeing this isn't working very well. Ten minutes." She left the room, and the two men were alone together.

Mr. Summerfield gazed at Johnny for several long moments. "I never believed in supernatural events," he said at last, in a stronger voice. "Everything inexplicable that happens is only coincidental, or can be explained in reasonable terms after investigation. So, you can tell me how it was, out of thousands of ministers, why you of all people—the chaplain who saved my son's life, saved my daughter for me, and finally saved my sanity—happened to come here to Barryfield?"

"It's very simple," said Johnny. "I was supposed to have a fine big parish in New York, with a salary about five times what I am getting here. And then the parish didn't want me. Usually there are about half a dozen other vacancies at any time for ministers. But Dr. Stevens, to his surprise, could find only one. Barryfield. A week later, he wrote me, others opened up all at once. By that time I felt that I should stay in Barryfield, that I had a mission here. Coincidental, no doubt."

Mr. Summerfield looked away from him. Then he said, "No, not coincidental. I don't think so." He turned his head to Johnny and scrutinized him steadily. "I don't think so," he repeated. "And that's unreasonable. Yet if you hadn't come I'd probably be dead now; Lorry would still be a desperate and hating girl and my son would still be despising me; and my wife would no doubt have left me. Moreover, people here would still be dying from the smog, and you'd never have rescued that little girl, Debby, and old Al would still be the violent and vicious old man he was. A train of events—with a purpose. And that's ridiculous. Isn't it?"

"No," said Johnny.

Mr. Summerfield moved uneasily on his pillows and Johnny got up at once and helped him with sure and tender hands. Lorry's father said, "This is a long thing for a man to think about, and I'll have time." He added, "I never really hated you. You never met me before, but I've seen you on the streets many times, in your car, or walking on your rounds. I had a reporter for almost all your sermons, and I read them all. And I wanted to know you. It was like a compulsion. I thought I hated you, and I thought if you came here, on my invitation, that I'd demolish you. But I wanted you to come."

"I'd have come," said Johnny. "I thought of coming, myself, several times, and—God forgive me—I stayed away. You weren't the only one with a compulsion."

"You haunted me, from the day of your first sermon," said Mr. Summerfield restlessly. "I couldn't understand it. All my life, any strong impulse I had was attended by a more violent reaction. And always negative. Denials. My first wife stood it so long, then she left me. I married Esther shortly after the divorce. I loved her, and love her, yet I could never tell her. I've wanted to, desperately, and at those times I made fun of her, and rejected her. That's the way it's always been, since I could remember."

"You were always terribly afraid," said Johnny. "Not only you, all of us. We are born afraid of everything. Only God can deliver us from our fear. Through love. When I was a boy I found a young robin, fallen from its nest, and abandoned by its mother. I adopted it and made a wooden cage for it. I fed it and talked to it and even sang to it." Johnny smiled, remembering. "But it was afraid, even after two months, when it could fly around our kitchen. It knew the name I'd given it, but it wouldn't come to me, wouldn't eat out of my hand. If I went near it, it would rush back, huddling in its cage. And then I thought, why, that's just like us, and God. God's hand held out and we scuttling away from it and screaming in our blind terror, even while we accept the food and shelter and love God gave us. I asked myself whether we were as stupid as that little bird, and I came to the conclusion we were even more stupid, for we could reason. That's when I knew I had to be a minister."

"What happened to the robin?" asked Mr. Summerfield. His eyes were interested and clear now.

"Oh, I was eating breakfast one morning, before going on my paper route, and all at once I heard the bird flying around, and then it was on my shoulder and rubbing its head against my cheek. It wasn't afraid any more."

Mr. Summerfield was silent. He lay and looked at Johnny, who was still smiling at the memory of the bird. Then Mr. Summerfield said, "I can't thank you about Barry. I couldn't insult you by thanking you."

But Johnny said, as if he had not heard, "The robin knew, finally, that there never had been anything to be afraid of at all. It was all in its distrustful and ignorant mind."

Dr. McManus, accompanied by Esther, the nurse, Barry and Lorry, came into the room. "Oho!" said the doctor, "so you've been taking barbiturates, have you, Mac? Kind of a desperate feller, weren't you? But now we'll really put you to sleep for about twelve hours." He scowled ferociously at Johnny. "And we'll run this gabby parson out, who's been annoying you. Don't know why I left him here in the first place." The old man felt deftly for Mr. Summerfield's pulse, nodded in satisfaction. "Parson's a simple feller, but you'd be surprised at the things he can say. Mostly fairy stories; never did believe a word of 'em."

But Mr. Summerfield was looking at his daughter and his son, and they stood beside him. Barry took his father's hand and Lorry knelt down by the bed and laid her wet cheek mutely against her father's. Esther stood at the foot of the bed, her eyes full of vivid tears.

Mr. Summerfield smiled at Johnny. "I'll be well, and back again, for the wedding." He laughed feebly. "Lorry a minister's wife! I'm going to enjoy myself, watching."

But he gave Johnny his hand and the gesture was a pleading for forgiveness, and a surrendering.

37

April came in like the light on the wings of a dove, and it was almost Easter. Emilie's lilacs were in full and delicate bloom in the parsonage garden, and Johnny and the children visited them often. The little fruit trees had shed their petals like fragrant snow, and the grass was greening rapidly. Lon Harding and his friends had spaded up sections for flower beds, and had let the children assist them in the planting of perennials. Father Krupszyk brought clumps of iris and lily bulbs, and planted them himself.

Lorry was dividing her time between Philadelphia and Barryfield. "It's too exhausting for you, dear," Johnny would say anxiously. But she was blooming now, and full of a rich, soft contentment. When in Barryfield she stayed with her lonely mother, and read her father's letters to Esther. They were short, but loving and kind and full of an intangible sadness. They were the letters of a man who had once been mortally ill, and was only slowly returning to life. He invariably asked about Johnny.

Another time he wrote, "Barry visited me yesterday. He is my son again."

Whenever Lorry came to Barryfield, with her brother, Johnny felt that his life was complete, and that all the years ahead would be one deep happiness. His children were flourishing. Jean, restored to normal, was talking of joining the basketball team of the Church of the Holy Rosary. Pietro's voice was taking on more luster. Max was doing mysterious odd jobs for Rabbi Chortow, who found him a consolation for the children he had never had. Kathy struggled with Mrs. Burnsdale for authority, which entertained Johnny and Dr. McManus, though Kathy found no reason for amusement. "After all," she would say coldly, "I took care of the kids before we ever saw Mrs. Burnsdale. I am closer to them."

Debby, of the bright auburn hair and impudent eyes, was Kathy's particular cross, for the boys adored her. She could even flout Mrs. Burnsdale. It was then that Kathy became Mrs. Burnsdale's supporter. "That child," Kathy would say severely, "needs discipline. But who around here will give her that?" It was Kathy's opinion that the household was managed very laxly indeed. She took out her frustration on the little girls in her Sunday school class, who feared and respected her.

Pietro had tried to persuade Lorry to marry Johnny before September. "Why wait, when there is love?" he would ask her slyly. She would look at him reproachfully, and reply, half smiling, "But duty comes first, doesn't it?" Pietro was not quite sure about this. Duty seemed a very drab thing to him, particularly when it interfered with festivities.

"Peace, it's wonderful," Dr. McManus would say. Then he would turn to Johnny with a threatening look. "Just so long as you keep out of things."

Barry had promised Johnny that he would be in Barryfield for Easter. The devotion between the two young men was so profound that it touched even Dr. McManus. "I keep remembering the day he rushed to this town," said the doctor. "You two fell into each other's arms like fools. Blubbering."

It was Barry who insisted on furnishing the parsonage, which would be ready in June. Johnny had protested at the expense, but his friend had said, "You haven't seen the Madison Avenue shops. They're full of treasures. And after all, Lorry is my sister."

"Peace, it's wonderful," the doctor said. It was very peaceful until Holy Thursday, the day Barry arrived and went to his stepmother's house. He was fond of Esther, and pitied her courageous loneliness.

Barry Summerfield came in late on Holy Thursday afternoon, with his sister, Lorry. "In a way," said Esther, kissing them, "this is going to be one of the happiest Easters of my life." She had forgotten the pleasant Easters of her youth, before she had married MacDonald Summerfield, but Lorry had heard her speak of them, and she was remorseful. We certainly made her life miserable, she thought.

"Your father always thought it debasing for me to cook," said Esther. "But I am going to prepare the Easter dinner myself! We always had a lot of money, but Mother thought any girl who could not cook and make her own clothing was a useless sort of female."

She still looked exotic, for she was an exotic woman, though she now wore quiet and conventional clothing, and was considering another redecorating of the house in an acceptable style. Her daughter and her stepson regarded her with affection, as she talked with wit and penetration at dinner. No one looked at Mr. Summerfield's chair, but he was in their thoughts. Someday he would sit there again, full of health, his soul healed and quieted, and they all knew that but for John Fletcher he might have been dead now—for they had found tentative suicide notes in his desk. Johnny leaves his imprint everywhere, thought Lorry with love, whether he knows it or not.

The windows were open to the green and lavender mountains and the scent of mountain shrubs and trees. The edge of a moon shook like silver fire over the top of the nearest hill. Esther suddenly yawned, and laughingly apologized. "I work in the garden now," she said. "Your father would never let me do it. I get up at six; it's best then, clear and cool, and the earth is fresh. So in about an hour you children will have to excuse me." She smiled at them with content.

She left them at half-past nine. Lorry and Barry sat alone in the Hindustani living room, and pretended the furniture was not there. "The new editors I hired are very good," Lorry said to her brother. "The people in Barryfield are respecting our papers again. And our circulation has jumped a third! Imagine that."

She regarded her brother affectionately. He might have been her father in his early thirties, because of his great resemblance. "Your editorials for our papers, when you can spare time for a few, are very tactful," she went on, and she sighed a little. "Oh, yes, I know we can't suddenly reverse the usual line; it has to be done gradually. But you're doing it, and that's why we're gaining circulation. Of course everybody knows about Dad, and there's some cynicism over our new policy. And—Dad's last remarks about Johnny didn't do Johnny any good. At least, though, he isn't mentioned in the papers, except just an occasional quote from his sermons. We don't publish the few ugly letters that still come in about him." She did not mention that those letters were sometimes violent and incoherent, testifying to the mad hatred a considerable segment of Barryfield held for Johnny because of her father's malignant attacks on him in the past. Many people, she thought dismally, must hate something, or someone, in order to make their lives significant to themselves. Invariably they hated the wrong things and the wrong men, with a singular perversity. Perhaps, in their hearts, they knew this and attacked out of pure evil.

Barry said, "Johnny's told me that a number of his members have left the church since Dad's last little gem. He's tried to talk to them, but it's no use. We'll just have to go on being tactful, I suppose." He then spoke of a new author he had "snared" in England, for he saw that his sister was looking depressed. "I persuaded him we could do better for him than his old publisher." He laughed. "Higher royalties were never even mentioned, though it was tacitly understood. We talked only of wider distribution and bringing the man's message to a larger audience. Nothing so gross as money, naturally. We Americans are direct about it; it offends Europeans, especially artists. But they certainly go over our royalty reports with a microsocope!"

Lorry began to laugh. Then they heard the most sinister sound that can be heard in an area where coal mining is important. Sirens were suddenly clamoring in short quick blasts of panic, pausing a moment, then blasting again, calling for help. Lorry and Barry had heard it only once or twice before in their lives, and they looked at each other in consternation. The mechanical cries rose thinly and clearly to them, even up on the mountainside. "An explosion!" cried

Lorry. "They must be working at night again! Those calls are for help of any kind. I wonder how many men—"

"I'm going down," said Barry, standing up determinedly. "I don't know what help I can give, but I'm a newspaperman at heart and I'll get a story, anyway. Listen to those sirens scream! All hell must have broken loose. Poor devils. Some of those mines should have been closed down long ago, or the walls shored up. Don't wait up for me, Lorry."

Johnny was working on his Easter sermon with dissatisfaction a few minutes before the mine explosion. Everything he wrote seemed inadequate, banal. He paused, tapping his pen against his teeth. The God of all the endless constellations, galaxies, and universes had looked down on one small grain of dust fluttering in the timeless trail of dazzling suns and millions of swinging worlds vaster far than it could ever dream of, and He had descended upon it with His radiant feet and had died upon it in His human flesh. Why? Oh, the Bible explained, but the mystery was still, to Johnny, unsolved. And then, after His death, He had risen from the dead, to bring life to the little crawling creatures known as men—why? "Not a sparrow falls"—but we are less innocent, less harmless, even less beautiful, than sparrows, thought Johnny. And less useful. And we are murderers. The mark of Cain is on our faces.

The big old house was very quiet. The old doctor had been tired, and had gone to bed. The children were asleep, Johnny hoped. The floors and the walls creaked faintly in the warm and pleasant night. Then, all at once, they shuddered.

The mines again, thought Johnny uneasily. He stood up, without aim, and went to a window and looked out. He did not expect to see anything; he just wanted the reassurance of the calm street lamps. No one walked nearby; only an occasional automobile rolled past the house. Then he started. The sirens were beginning, suddenly, violently, in a clamor of desperate pleading for help.

He knew those sirens. He began to tremble with the dread only a miner can feel. He could, he believed, actually smell the gas, the acrid odor of coal beginning to burn, and could hear the beating of terrified hearts stricken with dread far underground. He knew it all well; he had experienced it himself. Now he was no longer a priest but a miner. The women, the children. The hammering of anguished feet running to the mines, the calls of terror, the screaming for mercy, the cries to God. And the ambulances, the lights, the rescuers. . . . He was halfway to the door when he saw Dr. McManus coming pounding down the staircase, struggling into his clothing.

Dr. McManus saw Johnny and stopped, fastening a last button. "What—look here, they won't let you near the shaft. Only doctors. Hear those damn sirens! I know all the calls; this must be bad. Look, there's wire fences around the shafts, to keep away busybodies and the women and children, and they lock the gates; rescuers can't be hampered. They want every doctor they can reach tonight. You'll just be in the way, you're a—"

"You forget," said Johnny, pale and distracted. "I'm also a miner. I know how to rescue miners; I was rescued once myself. You don't know what it's like down there—I do. I felt the blast; there're more coming. You've got to work fast in times like these."

He unbolted the door. "You'll stay away from the mine!" shouted the doctor, aghast. "You'll stay on the outside of the gates, with the other parsons. That's your job, not diving down into holes. I'm not going to let—"

But Johnny was outside, running to the garage. The doctor groaned, and followed as fast as his waddling legs would go. He squeaked to the bright, moonlit night. "Oh, the fool, the fool! He never stops to think. A miner, says he! He'll be scrambling down into the pit—he never thinks. I've got to keep him away." He yelled to Johnny, "Not your old heap, idiot! I've got a siren on my car, and we'll use that to clear the way! Look at all the fools already pouring out into the street in their hacks, getting in the way of ambulances and fire equipment and doctors! Get in, get in. And turn that siren on, and the extra light. You're not going near that mine, damn you! Careful of my bag; keep your big feet off it. You took that corner too fast—all right, straightaway. Down that next street, turn left at the corner—you're not going near that mine!"

The night air vibrated with the blasts of the frantic sirens calling for help. Houses were lit up; people were on doorsteps and stoops, scenting disaster. Voices shouted back and forth; cars backed from driveways. Women began to scream, children were crying with excitement. "Faster, faster," said the doctor, "but don't get us killed. Turn that siren on louder. Watch out! That damned fool nearly ran into you. My God! You're going to stay outside the gates—"

But Johnny was praying. His mouth moved in supplication. "Father, I know all about it," he prayed silently. "The smoke, the roaring in the earth, the shaking walls, the stench of gas, the terror, the panic of the spirit. But I remember something else, too. I was only a boy, but I remembered to stop to pray, while the men were running and screaming in the darkness, and I remembered what we had been taught, to fall on our hands and knees, to cover our faces—I had to have Thy help to calm me, before I could remember those simple things. And Thou gavest me the power so that I could shout to the men, to encourage them to follow me out, and Thou madest them listen to me, and they followed me, each man crawling with his hand on the back of the man ahead of him. We got out, with Thy help, Father, and we lost only one man who was too terrified to hear and keep his wits. Father, those men down in the mine now—calm them, reassure them, send them help. Preserve their souls; speak to their families." Johnny drew a deep breath, and while the car careened through the crowded streets and the siren screamed with the deeper and louder voices of the other sirens, he prayed the prayer for the dead.

"Down there, now," squawked the doctor, pointing. "Watch out for those ambulances! Hell, why don't the police keep the mobs back? God damn the nosy bastards! That's right, Jack!" he shouted to a policeman who was using his club to restrain the curious throngs and drive them back. "Crack their heads open!"

Now the air was full of the scent of the first explosion. "Swing around, man!" cried Dr. McManus, "there, behind that wire fence. We've got to stop there. Why don't those women and kids stop yelling?"

"Their husbands and fathers are down there," said Johnny grimly. He pulled up the car behind a swarm of other cars, flung open the door, and ran to the fence and its locked and guarded gates. This was a scene out of hell, he thought. Floodlights were trained brilliantly down the shaft. Puffs of smoke belched from the shaft, but Johnny, sniffing strongly, could smell no more gas. So there was still time to get out the men—if luck held. All around him was the confused roaring of human sound, the shrieks of praying and weeping women, the howling of the sirens, the hoarse rushing and retreating of men's voices, the ringing of bells, the threats of the police, and some hissing sound. Ambulances were drawn up near the gates; only hospital attendants were permitted inside near the shaft. The side glare of the floodlights showed the jostling and jumbled faces of men and women peering through the strong chain-wire fence, the tearful, open-mouthed faces, the smeared, wet faces of children. "Here comes the elevator again!" a man cried. "Look, they got two more!"

Johnny struggled to the fence. The elevator had risen from the shaft and rescuers, in masks, were dragging two unconscious miners out. Young interns, doctors, including Dr. McManus, were bending over the men. Now the white stretchers were out, the men lifted upon them, carried to the police-guarded ambulances, and the ambulances bellowed away in the darkness to a hospital. Johnny looked about him desperately for a calm face. Men, women, and children were pushing about him; he was pressed almost immovably against the fence. He saw the glittering eyes, the gaping mouths emitting prayers and cries. He shouted, "You're not doing any good! You're just making things worse by screaming! For God's sake, move back, let me out!"

But he had to fight his way out of the mass of hysterical humanity. He found a cleared place, ringed about by the curious. In that one small circle he saw Father Krupszyk kneeling beside a stretcher, and he knew that this poor miner, at least, was beyond help.

The priest's broad face was running with sweat, and his eyes with tears. Yet his voice was very quiet; his head was bent over the miner's bloody and almost featureless face. And from that ragged and bleeding hole, smeared with soot, came a faint whispering. Johnny came closer to his friend and put his hand on his shoulder, bending, but the priest did not remove his confessional ear from the miner's dying face. "And now," murmured the priest, "make a good Act of Contrition."

It was darker here, and quieter, and a woman was quietly sobbing; she had come to kneel beside her dying husband,

and her two little children knelt with her. Johnny could hear that bubbling whisper; he saw, now, that the miner's torn clothing was one tattered mass of red rags.

"I am very sorry that I have offended Thee," whispered the miner, struggling to live for a few moments longer for the sake of his soul. "Thou art so good—do Thou have mercy on me—I have sinned against heaven and before Thee—unworthy to be called Thy child—have mercy, Lord have mercy—sorry—"

His battered chest heaved, the priest made the sign of the cross, and the man's head rolled aside, and his dead eyes stared sightlessly at his wife and children. The priest murmured, crossed himself, murmured again, and the miner's family broke into the sad and wordless dirge for the dead. The woman laid her head against her husband's shoulder, and the priest turned to her comfortingly. Johnny moved back, weeping. Act of Contrition. The miner had made his confession, had been contrite, had not gone alone into the darkness, without comfort, without a sustaining hand. It was true that at the very end a man was alone with his God, but it was good that he could be led into the Presence by a loving hand, and with the words of sincere contrition on his lips.

He felt someone touch him, and it was Father Krupszyk. Johnny stammered incoherently, through a thick throat, "I'm a miner; I've got to go down there. I know what to do, I'm helpless this way, it's wonderful if you know how to be contrite at the last minute, but no one teaches—I wish, I wish—I've got to go down there!"

The priest pressed his shoulder. Johnny turned aside desperately. Now, through the fence, he could see Mr. Dowdy's ghastly face, and he called to him, and Mr. Dowdy turned and came to the fence. "How many?" asked Johnny. Mr. Dowdy wiped his gritty face, and Johnny remembered that he too was dying. The other man said simply, "There were sixty down there. Just one explosion so far. There'll be others. They've got out all but twelve. There's the elevator going down again, Mr. Fletcher. There's going to be another explosion soon; you can feel it coming under your feet."

Johnny could feel it; he clung to the gate. The elevator was rising again. Someone shouted, "Four!" Women screamed with joy; the press against the fence almost bent it. The rescuers, grotesque in their masks, were pulling the men from the elevator; an ambulance howled up, the doctors were quickly examining the men, then came the stretchers, the wheeling ambulance, and then another.

"Only two have died so far, Mr. Fletcher," said a shy voice near Johnny, and he turned to see the old face of a minister he knew slightly. "This is terrible, isn't it, but they've gotten nearly everybody out, and there goes the elevator again, so there's a chance for the rest."

"I'm a miner," said Johnny dazedly. "They don't understand. I'm a miner. I've got to go down there with them!"

The minister stared at him, coughed, moved back a step. Johnny saw Father Krupszyk looking at him strangely, with an even stranger smile. Johnny caught the locked gate in his hands and shook it savagely. Mr. Dowdy came closer to him. "We'll get them out, Mr. Fletcher," he said uncertainly, staring at Johnny's distracted face.

"You don't understand!" said Johnny. "There's still eight down there! I'm a miner. Open the gate," he implored. "I can help. There'll be another explosion almost any minute, and there won't be time—"

"Yes, yes," said Mr. Dowdy in a feeble voice. "I understand. Look, Mr. Fletcher, the elevator's coming up again. Look! They've got five men piled on it! Only three left now, only three—" He turned from Johnny and went to the elevator, where the doctors were thronged. He talked to the masked rescuers, then suddenly flung out his hands in despair.

"What is it?" cried Johnny. "What is it?" The rescuers looked only at Mr. Dowdy, and shook their heads. Mr. Dowdy wiped his face with a stained handkerchief and turned away, bent and staggering. "What is it?" cried Johnny again.

Mr. Dowdy started. "Mr. Fletcher," he said dully, "there're three down there, just three. Far back. We can't send down these men again; there's another explosion coming almost immediately—if they go down they'll just be killed themselves."

If he had bellowed the words the wives of the three miners could not have heard them clearer. They burst into loud and anguished wailing. They beat on the fence with their clenched fists. Their children wailed with them. Their cries rose higher, above the sirens, when they saw the rescuers remove their masks.

Johnny, distraught, looked from the women and the children, at the mobs and masses of humanity surging against the fences, at the unbearable brilliance of the searchlights, at the gleaming ambulances, police, and then at the shaft beyond the fence. The rescuers themselves were receiving ministrations from the doctors, for they were exhausted. Mr. Dowdy, like a blind man, was stumbling about, shaking his head over and over, wringing his hands, a lost and forgotten soul. Interns rushed in through a briefly opened gate to take up the last five men rescued, who had been laid upon the ground; their stretchers were blobs of whiteness under the searchlights. They moved so fast that they almost tumbled the unconscious miners on the stretchers, for the word had been given for everyone to leave the aperture of the shaft. Johnny, groaning between his teeth, shook the strong fence impotently. Someone took his arm, spoke in concern, and he turned almost furiously on the speaker.

"John Kanty, I can save those men!" he exclaimed. "I'm a miner! Why won't anyone believe me? I spent years, every summer and three straight years—God help me. John Kanty, try to help me!"

A stretcher was coming out. Johnny flung off the priest's restraining hand, seized intervening shoulders and arms and thrust them aside, and forced a passage to the gate. Before anyone could stop him he was inside the enclosure, jostling against the doctors who were leaving precipitately. All at once it seemed to him, in the press, that every man in the vicinity stood between him and the shaft. Someone tore at his clerical coat, and Dr. McManus's aghast face, enlarged in that moment before Johnny to the dimensions and expression of a gargoyle's face, bobbed up before him. "Where're you going, damn you?" the doctor squealed as he clutched again at Johnny. "Out of your mind? It's going to explode—"

Johnny swept him out of his way. He bounded to the shaft and the waiting elevator. The puffs of smoke from below were coming in billows now. One of the rescuers, gaping, stood nearby, his mask and his flashlight in his hand. "Give me!" said Johnny, and seized the mask. But he did not know how to put it on; it fumbled out of his hands and fell to the ground. He snatched the flashlight from the stunned miner and jumped into the elevator.

"Now, God," he said aloud, "show me how to operate this. It's been years."

A great roaring cry, followed by a greater silence, fell over the people as the cones of light focused on Johnny as he climbed into the elevator. He tugged at ropes frantically. The elevator swayed, began to drop in a sluggish manner. Then out of the awful silence he heard a voice calling to him. "Johnny! Johnny! Come back, come back!" And like an echo voices took up the cry: "It's the minister! It's the minister! It's Mr. Fletcher!"

His head was hardly above ground now, but he turned it and looked full into Barry Lowell's face, straining against the fence. And there was the priest, his hands clasped in prayer, and Dr. McManus. Johnny waved. "I'll be back!" he shouted triumphantly. "Just stand by!"

The ropes slipped through Johnny's hands, burning them, for they dropped him down the black shaft too swiftly for his control. The elevators he had known had not been as large as this; the floor dipped from side to side and bumped against the sides of the shaft, and he was thrown from side to side. He looked up, and the top of the shaft was a rough rectangle of blazing light which followed him. He saw a few bobbing heads, the heads of dolls. The flashlight, which he had thrust into his pocket, fell, and he bent and caught it just in time. The smoke, streaming upward, began to choke him. He remembered what to do; he tore off his coat, leaving the ropes for a moment, and wrapped it about his head and crouched down on the floor of the elevator. All at once the floor hit the bottom of the shaft, tilted, righted itself, and in so doing knocked his head against the wall so that his ears rang.

He climbed dizzily out of the elevator. "Let me remember just what to do, Father," he murmured in the depths of his coat. "Let me remember nothing except that I'm a miner."

He had left only a slit for his eyes, but they began to smart fiercely, and he was coughing in paroxysms. Then, as if by instinct, his feet felt for the narrow rails and found them; they were hot through the leather. Someone had turned a searchlight far down into the shaft, and it dazzled him. He held the flashlight and, holding to the rails with his feet, ran into the mine, going down a rough slope.

He was surrounded by blackly-gleaming and faceted walls of sifting coal. His flashlight danced on the facets, and they glimmered duskily. Johnny, the miner, was remembering. He moved faster and faster, going down and down; sometimes at intervals he pulled a fold of his coat away from his face and shouted. Only echoes answered him. He stumbled, fell sideways, returned to the rails. The heat was becoming intolerable, and the stench of the first explosion stung his lungs. He crouched almost on his heels and shuffled along rapidly, breathing as little as possible. This he remembered. Then he was on his knees, crawling, the stones and little bits of coal tearing through the cloth of his trousers to his flesh.

He could feel the earth trembling under him, sharper and sharper. Soon, there would be another explosion. Soon the whole mine would collapse. Prayer was a bright centric of flame in his mind. He would rescue those men; he would not die. God would preserve him. He could hear coal falling all about him; once a heavy chunk struck his shoulders. Somewhere in this poisonous black pit three men were about to perish. He did not count himself.

Two of the miners, apparently awakening out of consciousness of the imminence of their awful plight, had reached the rails after the last rescuers had left the mine. Johnny was upon them before he realized it. He cried aloud in his joy. Their black hands seized him; their black faces gibbered at him. His voice came in a muffled blur from the depths of his coat. "Put your coats over your faces! Keep your heads down! Crawl along the rails; keep close together, your hands on each other. Don't let go. Hurry, hurry!"

They were paralyzed with terror, and could not move. He struck one on the shoulder with his flashlight. "Go on, go on!" he shouted. "There, turn around! Go on! That way! Don't leave the rails! Hold your breath as much as possible!" He pushed and shoved them into position. One miner whimpered, "We're going to be killed." "No!" said Johnny savagely, "not if you keep your heads. Move, move! There, that's right, go on ahead, stay with the rails. You'll find the shaft. I've got to get the other man."

They were shapeless, coughing, black-shrouded animals in the feeble flare of his flashlight; docilely, still almost semiconscious, they obeyed him. They began to crawl between the rails, one man clutching the coat of the man ahead of him.

Johnny sent the beam of his light with them as long as he dared. Then he called encouragingly, "Just keep on; the elevator's there, they'll pull you up. Now I'll get the last man."

The tremors in the earth made the whole mine rumble. Johnny got to his feet, not feeling the protest of his own bleeding flesh. This was no longer a time for crawling, so he bent double and began to run deeper into the mine. Smoke was thickening; the rumbling became ominous, the rails swayed under Johnny's stumbling feet. He turned the sword of his light into every smoking crevice; a beam cracked, and Johnny instinctively jumped aside as the heavy wood fell, barely missing him. The floor was full of ruts and cracks, and once he turned his ankle so that he cried out. Now there was a sickening smell of fire and gas.

"Dear Father," he prayed aloud, behind the shelter of his coat, "let me find him. Lead me to him. He's got a wife and children up there."

His ear, remembering, warned him just before a ponderous slide of coal fell to the rails. He watched it with his light; it smoldered. Then, standing upright, holding his breath, he leaped upon the pile lightly, jumped to the other side. He wound his coat closer about his face.

Smoking, crackling silence. He called again and again. His light appeared to be growing more feeble, and for the first time he was conscious of the straining of his lungs, the laboring of his heart, the exhaustion of his muscles, the cramping of his injured legs. "Please," he pleaded, "let me find him." A horrible nausea was rising in him, and his flashlight seemed to dance insanely before his eyes. He was streaming with sweat.

He had to stop, and leaned against the wall for a rest, for the passageway was becoming narrower and narrower. Then he started. Was that just the echo of his own voice, or was it a groan, near or far? He shouted again, and the groan answered. Now in the distant blackness he saw a tiny point of light, the light on a miner's cap, on the sloping floor of the mine. There was no time for loping, for crawling. He began to run. The walls of the mine shuddered, but he did not hear. The little firefly of light came nearer, and he ran faster. And then, on the floor, he saw a semiconscious man lying, trying to struggle from under a huge beam of wood, which seemed to be steaming.

Two whitish eyes glared up at Johnny in the narrow rapier of the flashlight, and two black lips grimaced in the black face.

"Hold it," said Johnny, and he put the flashlight down carefully. Blasts of heat struck his face, his hands, fired his lungs. He bent his powerful legs as he had been taught to bend them, and he took hold of the beam in the middle, slowly, surely, with his miner's hands, and he began to lift. The beam moved in his grasp, but only a little. The miner had fainted; he lay outstretched, unknowing, uncaring.

"Now, dear God," said Johnny, "just give me the strength I need."

A deep and shaking rumble answered him, like the voice of an enraged and awakening giant. He heard it, and he knew that in a matter of minutes, probably he and the miner would be trapped, buried, lost forever. "God!" he shouted, desperately. "God!" He thought of his children, and he saw their faces, and heard their voices. He turned away from his vision of them, half sobbing, and renewed his efforts. He could feel his back and legs cracking, his muscles giving way, but he clung to the beam.

Now he heard a faint, pattering sound. Stones, he thought, struggling with the beam. There's going to be a real cave-in. The beam was coming up in his hands; one of the miner's legs was suddenly freed. Johnny kicked it aside; he rolled with the beam, and freed the other leg. But he found himself impotently rolling as the beam continued to roll, for he had lost his balance. Then somewhere there was a crash and a scarlet flash of agony, and a stunning sensation, as the beam turned on him, and pinned him down.

He lay still, shocked; one of his ankles had been caught. He was utterly trapped. He had freed the miner, but now there was no help for him himself. He tried to sit up, but the pain in his ankle sickened him and he suddenly vomited, and drew in breaths of smoking air which seared his lungs. "Help!" he called hopelessly. He said, groaning, "My children! My poor children! Father, take care of my children!"

The pattering was louder, closer, and now, to Johnny's swimming eyes, came the glare of a distant flashlight. "Help," he whispered. And then, incredulous, he heard a shout: "Johnny! Johnny!"

He pulled up his final strength and called back, "Here! Hurry, hurry, for God's sake!"

The flashlight jumped up and down and bobbed rapidly in the hands of a still unseen rescuer. The pattering became louder, and the long mine echoed. Johnny cried again, "Here, right along here." He could see a figure dimly, now, behind the flashlight, a tall figure wearing a mask. He closed his eyes, weakly, in a fresh onslaught of agony.

Someone was pushing at the beam that held him; suddenly it lifted, rolled, fell with a mutter of echoes. The miner was becoming conscious; he struggled to a sitting position, moaning. A voice was bellowing at him, "If you can do something, help me!"

"My legs is broken," whimpered the miner.

"All right," said the voice from far away, "start crawling or something, but move, damn you, move!"

Johnny, disbelieving, recognized the voice. "Barry, Barry!" he whispered at the masked face.

"Come on, Johnny, crawl up against me. That's right; hold on. Lean against my arm; hold on to my shoulder. Go on there," he said to the miner, who was dragging himself with remarkable alacrity on the floor of the mine. "Johnny, hold my flashlight; if you can use that ankle at all, use it, but don't let yourself drop."

"Barry," said Johnny, as they crept along the floor of the mine. He wanted to weep; he forgot his pain and his terror in this wonder. He pressed his coat closer about his face.

"Never mind, keep your strength. Damn air's getting worse every second. Your pal's gone quite a way ahead. All right, Johnny, keep moving."

Now they heard a thundering behind them, as the mine caved in at their rear. The thundering followed them, and dust and thicker and more blinding smoke. The pain in Johnny's ankle became a nauseating numbness; he could use it a little better now. The two men moved foot by foot along the mine floor, keeping to the rails.

Now they could see a blaze of light in the distance, and in its light the figure of the miner, moving on all fours like a bear. "Broken legs, hell," muttered Barry. His old war scars were stretching in pure torture; sometimes he had to lean Johnny against a wall and stop a moment from sheer exhaustion. The thundering was closer behind them, the lowering charge of a mighty bull, a Minotaur raging to destroy them.

"We'll make it," said Barry through the mask. "Look, there's the elevator; he's getting into it. Just like him if he gives the signal to pull up!"

"He won't," said Johnny. "No, he won't. He'll wait for us."

There was a loud and deafening singing in his ears, and a sensation of sliding, sliding down forever. Barry's voice was miles away in space, calling. And then he felt himself being pulled over a body, over something that struggled under him, and he was being carried away. He could not see now, or even hear. He felt only a tremendous straining in his arms, as if someone had pulled them about a neck. He thought vaguely, I carried Barry like this—somewhere—I don't remember. . . . There was a tearing sensation in his wrists.

He was rising. There were shouts and calls and blinding floods of light; something was creaking and swaying under him. He could see and hear again. The shaft of the mine was all about him, and above, a brilliance like the sun. He was lying on the floor of the elevator, the miner hunched beside him, and above them both stood Barry, grinning through his black lips, his mask discarded. "Well, Johnny," he said, "I guess that makes us even. You carried me out of hell on your back, and I did the same for you!"

The elevator reached the top, and eager hands seized the three men and pulled them away. Now the thousands gathered in the vicinity lifted their voices in a roaring ovation. An instant later the mine collapsed, and the earth trembled, and vomited smoke and fire which belched up the empty shaft.

38

On Easter morning Johnny stood before the altar, leaning on his crutches.

There had never been such an Easter morning since the first, thought Johnny, full of joy and gratitude and awe. The altar bloomed with avalanches of flowers which spilled down to the floor in a blaze of color and in clouds of perfume. The soft and shifting light of the mighty candelabra had never been so all-embracing. But to Johnny the most beautiful and inspiring vision was the crowded faces upturned to him in love and deepest attention. The doors stood open to the sweet spring air, and crowds jostled on the steps to listen. Sunshine poured into the church from behind them, accompanied by an unpolluted wind.

He said, and his strong and sonorous voice reached the farthest listener in full power: "There is not a day or an hour that God does not rise from the dead, when the stone of the Holy Sepulcher is not again rolled back from the tomb by unseen hands, when the Resurrection, like the sun, does not shake the soul with adoration, and blind the eyes with glory.

"Each deadened heart, each lost heart, each forgetting and hating and disbelieving heart, is the tomb in which God lies, waiting for His Resurrection. And then, at some midnight hour, at some turning in a lost lane, in some cold and colorless dawn in which there is no hope, in the shadow of a solitary tree where a lonely man rests, or perhaps in the very welter of a city or on the silence of a hill, or in the empty places of grief and sorrowing and bitterness and desolation, or in the clanging heart of a prison or in a narrow room in a tenement, the deadened heart feels the awful silence of the sacrificed God, and remembers what it has forgotten, and is contrite, and cries out, 'Father, forgive me, for I have sinned!'

"It is then that God stirs on the stony couch on which the grieving man had abandoned Him, and the grave wrappings of man's sins fall from Him, and the stone of the sepulcher is rolled aside in the passionate hands of contrition, and God steps forth in His light before the dazed and penitential heart—the Resurrection ever new, ever eternal.

"As at Christmas God is born again to man, so at Easter He rises again from the dead for man. Blessed be His Name! Blessed be His most merciful Name, forever and forever!"

Johnny looked down at the first pews, as the notes of the new organ which Dr. McManus had presented to the church in Johnny's name thundered against the walls of the little church and soared against the narrow wooden ceiling. There sat the old doctor, gazing at Johnny with the deep and welling fullness of love that a man gives to a son born to him in his aged years just when he had abandoned hope. And there was Lorry, seeming, to Johnny, to resemble an angel in her white wool suit and white hat, with the turquoise blue of her tender eyes shining with pure and serene love. And there, as he moved his glance, sat his old friend, Dr. Francis Stevens, beaming with pride and unashamed of the tears on his plump cheeks. And there was Barry, whose life he had saved and who had saved his life, most moved and attentive, and beside him his stepmother, Mrs. Summerfield, and beside her Mrs. Burnsdale.

How greatly God has blessed me, and for nothing, thought Johnny. He smiled at the McGees, at all his friends, at the massed worshipers, and he raised his hands. This was a church where the congregation stood for the benediction, but now all dropped to their knees and bowed their heads in one spontaneous motion to receive his blessing.

The bells rang triumphantly to the bright air.

"He is risen! The Lord God has risen!"

39

Johnny could limp carefully with his cane now, for his broken ankle had healed. It was June, and the parsonage was complete. The family had moved in only a few days ago, for the carpenters, the bricklayers, the plumbers, and the plasterers had worked with a frenzied zeal to complete the home of this most beloved man, in order that he might enter it as soon as possible.

Union hours had not hampered them; they had worked from sunrise to the last twilight willingly, and with sweat. In fact, their union delegates, like the masters who had stood over the slaves with whips at the building of the Pyramids, were constantly hovering around, threatening, though threats were not needed. And now it was complete, with fine new furniture, with gleaming porcelain and burnished floors and beautiful fabrics and thick rugs. The unions had contributed the imported brass knocker on the door, which had once hung on an English baronial door, and the plate-glass windows. It was the miners' union which had replaced the wooden pickets with the intricate black tracery of an iron fence.

"It is really a mansion, on the inside," Johnny would say. From the street it appeared as a snug yellowish-brick house, three stories tall, with wide windows. "I don't know why everybody does all these things for me. Everybody's planted my garden, everybody's built my parsonage, everybody's furnished all the rooms, everybody has given me everything, and I don't know why. I haven't yet been here a year, and I've stirred up a lot of controversy, and made myself obnoxious now and then with my zeal, though it's true that I've learned a lot from Barryfield. In fact, I owe Barryfield my whole life."

When Lorry had suggested to Dr. McManus that he re-build the church to match the parsonage, it was Johnny who said, "No. It was his father's church, and because it was his father's church it is beautiful and right to me. And it belongs to me, too. Though," he added, smiling at the doctor, "a new carpet wouldn't be too much out of the way."

"These parsons," said the doctor. "They've got bottomless bellies. Tim Kennedy and his friends gave John Kanty a whole new setup inside his church—everything, imported statues, lace and linen cloths from Ireland, new bells, new altar—everything. They clean up the outside of the church, and put up new carved doors. And then what does he ask? The mayor gave him a Buick, and he says, 'Well, a priest with such a fine church and such a car should not be asked to drive that car all by himself. It's demeaning.' He wants a chauffeur, he says, and means it, by God!"

"I bet he gets one, too," Johnny said.

"And there's that old rabbi," said the doctor wrathfully. "Sol Klein and his smart-as-paint pals get their rabbi big silver goblets for Passover, lined with gold, and he's pleased. For about five minutes. And then he says that his father, who had been a rabbi, had had a fur-lined broadcloth coat, and he says to Sol that he's an old man now, and doesn't feel so well in the winters any more, and he'd certainly appreciate a fur-lined broadcloth coat like his father's, to keep him warm!"

"I know," said Johnny. "He's in New York now with Sol, getting fitted. Mink, no less."

"It's all your fault," said the doctor gloomily. "You've given your friends ideas."

"A laborer is worthy of his hire," Johnny said solemnly, with a wink at Lorry.

"You cost too much. I suppose you fellers have a union, too," the doctor replied darkly. "For the first time in its history Barryfield believes the clergy are sacred and indispensable. What are you, Johnny? The clergy's walking delegate?"

It was another Sunday now, a June Sunday, and Johnny moved slowly with Lorry about his garden and looked at it with happiness. He was certain that no roses had ever bloomed as these roses were blooming, in fragrant clusters of yellow, white, pink, scarlet, and crimson. The birds, as they flew overhead, cast fragile shadows over the thick grass. And over all the untainted sun threw a cataract of light over the valley city. The mountains were visible, mantled in green and mauve and lavender, standing against a sky of the palest blue. Bees hurried among the blossoms of the garden on their ancient business of pollination, and all the business of life. Johnny and Lorry stopped before the children's trees, and Johnny touched Emilie's green lilacs with a slow hand. "I can never leave here," said Johnny. "This is my children's home; these are my children's trees; and Barryfield is my children's life."

He looked at Lorry and his dark-blue eyes softened. "Dear Lorry," he said. Her own eyes shone on him, and it seemed to him that he looked into her heart, cleansed of all ugliness and dread and loneliness and fear. "I think, Lorry, that I've always loved you, from the very first time I saw you. Only your box came safely out of the fire. If I were superstitious, I'd think that was a sign."

She put her hand over his. "Wasn't it?" she asked.

Johnny bent his head and kissed her full on the mouth, and they clung together with a sense of joy and fulfillment in the yellow radiance of the garden. Then they walked on, with Johnny's arm about the girl's slender waist. "How wonderful it is to be at peace," murmured Lorry.

He held her tighter. He looked at the sky, and then a chill wind ran along his nerves, senselessly, he thought. "Peace," he said. Peace, he prayed. Please, God, let our hearts turn to each other, everywhere in the world, and let there be understanding, and freedom again for the oppressed and the enslaved, the multitude of the suffering, and let those who do not know Thee be released from the darkness and return to Thee. Let no man's hand again be lifted against his brother, nor the scarlet thunder of guns destroy the patient land, nor death mushroom again in the eternal sky.

For what else does a man live? Johnny asked himself. He lives only to know God and serve Him in this world, and to be joyful with Him forever, after death. A man must live for God, or die in his heart and his soul, for there is nothing but God.

The children exploded from the rear door of the parsonage into the garden, their faces gleeful with mirth. Debby danced in the rear as the others rushed upon Johnny and Lorry. Pietro could not control his exuberance. "Aha!" he exclaimed, throwing out his arms. "Listen to us! We have romance!"

"So we have," said Johnny.

"It's not romance," said Kathy, the precise. "It is love."

"And marriage," said Jean. "They will be married," Max added solemnly.

"I'm going to be the flower girl!" Debby shrilled, tugging commandingly at Johnny's arm.

"Kathy too. I promised," said Lorry. "Besides, it won't be until September." She stroked Kathy's golden hair.

"No, no, you don't understand!" screamed Pietro excitedly. "You will marry them, Papa, but not in September. Soon! It is too bad they are old, isn't it?" His voice fell to a tragic note.

Then he bounced up and down like a ball with impatience. "It is the doctor and Mrs. Burnsdale! Who else? We saw them kissing, in the big room, and they told us, and Uncle Al will live here with us forever!"

Debby and Kathy, whose faces were glowing with joy, looked like flowers, thought Johnny, in their white dresses and blue ribbons, and the boys were grave young men now, as they regarded him seriously, waiting for his comment.

"The family," said Johnny, smiling at Lorry. The children watched them with shy pleasure when Lorry turned her beautiful head and kissed Johnny on the mouth.

Pietro said with a dramatic sigh of satisfaction, "It is our family."

The children raced off in a swirl of color and energy. There was Jean, running now, Jean who would be a priest, and there was Pietro, the great singer, and Max, the sculptor, and Debby, the beloved woman, and Kathy, the mother of many children. Johnny could see them all in the future, with a sudden clarity of light and knowledge. He held Lorry's hand tightly. Perhaps there would be other children too, to fill the house before these left, one by one, in the ways God had planned for them.

"They have brought me all I have, and all I will have," Johnny said. Lorry leaned against him. He touched her cheek, and added, "My cup runneth over."